C

Descending the Spiral Staircase

Descending the Spiral Staircase

HF Beaumont

Library of Congress Control Number: 2019918209
ISBN: Hardcover   978-1-7960-4772-1
                 Softcover   978-1-7960-4771-4
                 eBook   978-1-7960-4770-7

Print information available on the last page.

Rev. date: 11/07/2019

To order additional copies of this book, contact:
Xlibris
1-888-795-4274
www.Xlibris.com
Orders@Xlibris.com
800178

CONTENTS

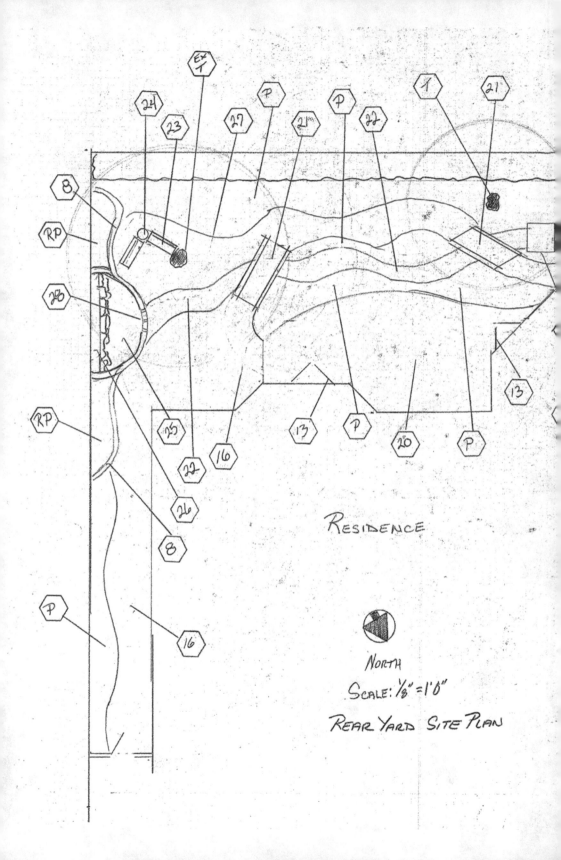

RESIDENCE

NORTH
SCALE: ⅛" = 1'0"
REAR YARD SITE PLAN

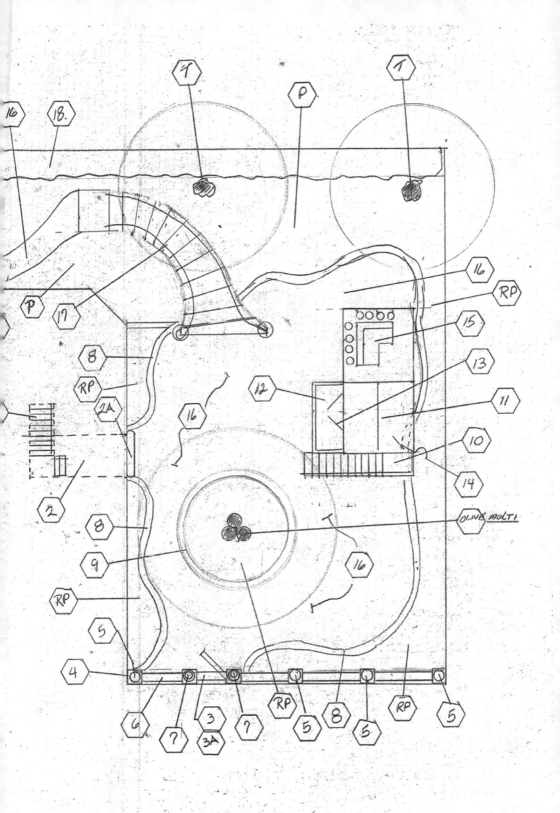

OLIVE MULTI

Albright Residence Construction Legend

Symbol	Description
1	Existing tunnel stairs, kitchen entrance
2	Existing Tunnel with new wood floor and wall sconces
3	Arched gateway with brick fascia, Mediterranean hanging light
4	7' ht. brick fascia pilaster with bullnose brick cap
5	24" round low bowl ceramic pots with ivy geraniums
6	6' brick fascia wall to match pilasters arched between pilasters, bullnose brick cap
7	Arched wooden gate finished both sides, stained with polyurethane coating (2 coats) black hardware
8	27" ht. Raised planter seat wall with stone fascia, pre-cast concrete cap
9	27" ht. Raised circular planter seat wall with stone fascia, pre-cast concrete cap
10	Playhouse staircase, redwood decking with two coats of polyurethane.
11	Playhouse mounted on top of patio cover
12	Playhouse balcony with hand rails
13	French doors to match the arched wooden gate.
14	Playhouse French doors to march the arched wooden gate
15	Bar-b-que island with double side burners, refrigerator and heated drawers and wine rack, stainless steel four burner bar-b-que
16	Belgard Dublin Cobble pavers, random pattern
17	Staircase with biblical stone rounded treads with risers, limestone Balusters, carved limestone handrail, side scalloped edging
18	Existing Ligustrum hedge
19	Zero edge collection vault with pea gravel on top
20	Colored stamped concrete patio
21	Chinese Red foot bridge with handrails both sides, (2 coats) polyurethane

Symbol	Description
22	Stream feature with rock cobble 4" to 8" to match water fall
23	Chinese Red benches to match bridges
24	Chinese Red square table to match benches
25	Water feature reservoir
26	6' ht. waterfall with stone fascia
27	Stabilized decomposed granite pathway with steel edging on both sides.
28	Spill over from fountain to stream feature
P	Planter
RP	Raised planter seat wall
T	Tree

PREFACE

Descending the Spiral Staircase is the result of visions I encountered during dreams. It is the story of how a simple construction task turns into a murder investigation, with stolen bank money, a buried storage shed, a hidden tunnel, and the reconstruction of an unused area to make it a very usable space. John and Marie are the homeowners, one of my visions, of Marie, changed the lives of many people. A grand open-house event brings concern to the family's safety. A nosy neighbor, a leak to the press about the bank reward— all these things put many agencies on full alert.

Remodeling magazine wants to film the entire event; the police and FBI scan guest photos, looking for unwanted visitors. This is not your typical construction project; there are many twists and turns to the finale. You will tear up and laugh as the characters evolve. This book is inspired by my visions and my experiences in the landscape business. I hope you enjoy reading.

CHAPTER 1

It was a bright, sunny, shining day in early spring; birds were chirping, and puffy white clouds were crossing the horizon. Breakfast was being prepared, and the aromas were so inspiring. The phone rang. *So early. Who could this be?* "Hello … yes, this is him. How may I be of service?"

"I have a residence being restored. A friend told me to call to get an estimate for the restoration, said John."

"Yes, I can help you with that. What time would you like to meet?"

How about this morning at nine o'clock?

"Today, about nine o'clock is perfect?"

What is your address? … I'll be there, and we can go over what needs to be done. Thank you for calling. I appreciate being able to serve your needs." *Wow, a referral. Those are always the best, as I don't have to go into what I have done. Patting myself on the back—that has always been hard for me to do. Thank you, God. I'll do my best to help the customer, and with your guidance, we can keep putting food on our tables.*

At nine o'clock, I arrived in front of an older mansion-type home. *Landscape is rough in appearance, some of the stonework on the entry walkway needs repair, walkway is cracked … just some little things*, I thought while walking to ring the doorbell.

A gentleman answered the door. "You must be Fred."

"Yes sir. I'm Fred, and here is my business card."

"Great. My friend gave me his, and I'll return your card to him when I see him next. So as you saw as you walked up our walkway, there is a need for some repair. The landscape is overgrown and needs to be put back to a workable condition. My wife wants to add color that will enhance the entrance and make the home welcoming to our guests and visitors. We also have work needed to be done in the backyard. Can I show you?"

"Of course, I'll follow you."

The backyard was a disaster. The perimeter shrubbery hadn't been pruned in years, the grass was almost nonexistent, and it looked as if the irrigation system had not been working in quite some time. This was going to be a lot of work. John, the homeowner, asked, "So what do you think?"

"It's a diamond in the rough. How much do you love the backyard?"

"We hate the backyard," John responded.

"Well, would you like a plan drawn to show just what your backyard could look like in the future?"

"That would be fantastic. My wife will be so thrilled."

"Is there anything that you now have that you would want to keep if I can enhance the shape and form?"

"Well, my wife likes the tree in the corner. Gives us some nice shade, but the leaf litter is too much; and when we want to sit under the tree, we have to clean the furniture since the birds like it as well. Let's take a look to see what can be done."

We walked to the tree, and I said, "Wow, this tree has not seen a pruner for a long time. There are crossed branches that need to be removed. There are branches that need to be thinned out to lift them so you don't have to duck when you want to sit under the tree for shade. I think a nice lacing of the tree that keeps its height and spread will make the tree a nice focal point for your yard."

"I'm not sure what 'lacing' means," said John.

"Here, I'll show you. I just happen to have my hand pruner on my belt." I took one low-hanging branch and pruned some of the crossing stems—lateral ones that were longer than the dominant stem. I released the branch, and it rose about ten inches higher than it was originally.

"Wow, what a difference. So you will do that to the entire tree?"

"Yes, but no more than 30 percent of the tree at one time, or I could put your tree into shock."

"Shock?"

"Yes, John. I'll give you a botanical lesson, short and sweet. The tree is under turgor pressure, which means that for the leaves to receive water, the roots imbibe the water from the soil and transfer the water to the leaf through the vascular structure. To allow the water to travel upward, the water is under pressure. God created a wonderful system. If I cut too much off the tree at one time, the vascular structure bleeds out water, and that could cause a shock to its system."

"Now you're thinking cutting leaves and stems and maybe a branch or two. That's less water the tree needs, so why the shock?"

"The tree has been providing water to the cut-off branches and stems. There is no place for the water to be used. It takes a while for the tree to adapt to its need. If it takes too long, the tree—for lack of better terminology—will panic, like when you cut yourself. You bleed, so you wash it off and put on a Band-Aid to stop the bleeding. Well, if you can't stop the bleeding, your body could go into shock—same principle. But we don't have a root structure to get more blood from the soil."

"I see what you mean."

"Pretty complex, isn't it? More to this than what meets the eye. Food and water are taken up from the roots. With the right amount of water, the leaves are really happy. The right amount of nutrients, and the leaves are sometimes bigger, giving the tree more photosynthesis, which gives us more oxygen to breathe. We're all part of the grand system created many years ago."

"How do you know all this?"

"I learned from some excellent professors, read books, and my grandmother was a horticulturist specializing in iris habitation. I work from the heart with a little help from my head. I really love what I do, and I'm blessed with the talent to aid nature to its full potential, making it not only pleasing to look at but also functional. Is either of you allergic to bees?"

"I'm not, but I'll have to ask my wife. Why do you ask?"

"If I add floral plant material. Some attracts bees, butterflies, hummingbirds, and beetles. All the critters aid the plant in pollination, which in turn creates a seed pod for future expansion of the plant."

"I should have paid more attention in science class while in college," said John.

At that time, John's wife joined us. John introduced me to his wife, Marie. "My pleasure to meet you." John told her about his botanical lesson and showed her what I had done to the tree in a few minutes. She was pleased.

John asked her if she was allergic to bees. She said, "I don't think so. Why?"

John asked me to tell her what I had told him. He thought he would leave out an important detail if he gave her the information. I told him I would, but I said that I, too, could leave something out, and he would have to fill in the blanks. John laughed and said, "Sure, like I would remember if you left something out." I told Marie what I had told John before we strolled around the backyard, ducking low-hanging branches from the unkempt hedges along the property line.

Marie asked if the hedges needed pruning. "That's the term, correct?"

"Correct, and indeed, they do need pruning if you choose to keep them. To prune and manicure a hedge and then decide to remove it is just more money for me, but more money for you to spend." I told her John and I had talked about a drawing to upgrade the existing landscape.

She looked a little puzzled. "Aren't you a gardener?"

"Well, it all depends on your definition of the word 'gardener.' I have done in the past and can currently do landscape maintenance, but I prefer doing landscape and irrigation design and building. Restoration of the existing landscape and irrigation systems gives you curb appeal and fits your lifestyle. If you're an outdoor person or just like to peer out your windows and look at the landscape from inside, those are two totally different designs. Your landscape has been neglected for many years. How long have you owned this beautiful home?"

"We bought it a few months ago," John said, "as a fixer-upper."

"I landscaped a home years ago where the homeowner bought a fixer-upper for less than half a million dollars and put in an indoor pool. He built what the city called a greenhouse—a real stretch in terms—that was attached to the house, and we landscaped the front yard and backyard and put in a lot of bells and whistles. He had it reappraised once completed. The appraisal came in at just a little over two million dollars. What impressed the appraiser the most was the main entrance into the home. We gave him a grand entrance compared with the rest of the custom-built homes. The homeowner told me that on one weekend, they had a nonstop parade of cars and pedestrians going past his home, taking pictures. I told him, 'Next weekend, set up a lemonade and pastry stand and make some money. You can also have professional photographs for them to purchase, and offer guided tours for a small nominal fee.' He liked the idea. It would give his teenage kids something to do."

John asked, "Do you do more than just landscape and irrigation?"

"Yes, I design walls, freestanding and retaining; concrete walkways and patios; wood structures; low-voltage lighting systems; drainage systems—anything except the house structure. My license does not allow me to do any work inside the structure. That keeps the roofer from doing landscape. It keeps all trades doing what they are licensed to do."

Marie said, "We have a problem on the side of the house you may want to look at. It's a mess. Let's take a peek."

Standing in front of the said part of the property, I commented, "Wow, you're right about a mess. Is this how the prior owner left it for you?"

"The house was in foreclosure, the prior owner was long gone, and the bank was holding the title on the home."

"The bank isn't responsible for cleaning up properties?"

"We don't know the legalities. We bought it as-is."

"I love that term. In homes, cars, boats, and airplanes, bank-owned, that term is used constantly. They should be held to the same standards as the rest of us. Wait a minute; let me get off my soapbox. Better not get me started on business practices. I could bore you to tears.

"Well, weeding the area first is a must. I will need to see just what needs to be corrected and provide you a separate budget for this area. By the way, I break down all facets of the project so you can pick and choose what fits your budget. There, of course, is a procedure needed to be followed. As an example, to plant the landscape before the irrigation system is running and functional is out of sequence. Putting in a patio and then installing a patio cover is out of sequence."

"How do you keep the water from coming into our home? When it rains, the water runs into the house and garage from this area."

"Removing the weeds will give me a picture of how the area is graded. From what you just told me, the grade is too high or is graded toward the home, not away from the home. This would be a prime location for a subsurface drainage system to alleviate excess water in this area."

"Sounds like you have encountered this problem before," John said.

"Yes, a few times too many, I must add."

"How long would it take for you to provide the plans?" Marie and John asked almost spontaneously.

"Wow, did you rehearse that before I arrived?"

Both laughed. "No, we think alike, and we are anxious to get started," Marie said. "We do have one other problem, but it is inside the house."

"Well, I can look at it, but my license prohibits me from doing much."

"Let's take a look. Follow us, please."

Once inside, they showed me a beautiful spiral staircase going from the foyer to the second floor. "Beautiful staircase. I love the handrails and the supports. Are they concrete or plaster? Wow, carved ... and the handrail is carved as well. What's wrong with the staircase?"

"The carpet on the steps—it's dirty, trampled, and torn. And in the center, the backing is showing through."

"Oh, now I see. I was looking too high. The handrail is breathtaking. All I would be able to do for you is remove the carpeting; a building contractor would have to complete the work. My license would not cover me being inside the structure. That would at least give you something to start from. The builder would just have his laborers remove the carpeting. You could ask him to separate his cost for removal of the carpet and compare prices. It would not bother me if I weren't successful. It's not what we excel in, and the learning curve could cause our number to be higher."

"Would you think that if we just painted the handrail, it would make it more appealing?" asked Marie.

"Anything would be an improvement, but a professional painter or craftsman could answer that question better than I can. Let's determine what you want to keep in your landscape and what needs to be removed. Also, where is the irrigation controller located?"

"In the garage," stated John. "I'll have to move some things out of the way for you to see the controller. Let me start moving some items, and you and Marie can walk the rest of the yard and determine a keep or not-to-keep list."

Marie asked me, "How long have you been doing this type of work?"

"I started yesterday."

"No, really. You seem to know so much. You really started yesterday?"

"Yes, about forty years ago yesterday."

"Oh, you shocked me. I never met anyone who just started with a company who knows as much as you do."

"Thank you for your kind words. This is a constantly changing profession—new technology versus tried and true. Sometimes it is very hard to determine if new is really better."

"I know what you mean," stated Marie.

As we walked around the property, Marie was very informative about the keep or not-to-keep list and was sure to add, "If you think it should be removed, please feel free to do what you feel is right."

I noticed that a few of the shrubs were blocking windows. The view out was next to nil, and I asked her, "Do you like the shrubs covering your windows from your view?"

"Sometimes it's nice to keep outsiders from looking into our home—not that John and I parade around without clothes or do anything that exciting for Peeping Toms to get their kicks, but sometimes sitting on the sofa and seeing the leaves move with the wind or a little bird land is nice."

"I could lower the height to the middle of the window. When you're sitting on the sofa next time, peer toward the window and see at what height the shrubs keep you out of sight from passersby. I'll make sure the shrub keeps your privacy."

"That's a great idea. I'll tell John to put a piece of tape at the level that I can see the shrub, and he can go outside and stand on the sidewalk to see what he can see at the tape mark."

"You're very clever, Marie. I was going to start pruning while having you sit on the sofa and tell me when to stop. Your idea is wonderful."

John caught up to us and told me he had moved enough for me to see the controller. We walked to the garage, and I saw the controller. The field wires were hanging down, not attached to anything. The cover was broken and barely hanging on the controller body; it was also an electrical mechanical controller, at least twenty or more years old. They didn't even make them anymore unless it was a custom order, and the manufacturer would have to dust off their manuals.

"Is it worth keeping?" John asked.

"It makes a lovely wall decoration, but as far as an irrigation controller is concerned, not so much."

Marie asked, "Are they expensive?"

"All depends on what you need it to do and how you want to operate the controller. There are some that you can adjust with your cell phone from anywhere in the world. Some are controlled by a satellite, using data over a period of five or more years. So if it rains on January 3 for five straight years, your controller would not water on that day, as an example. Some do both. Some are so sophisticated it takes a master's degree in engineering to program them. The bells and whistles will determine the cost and how many stations your system needs to water the entire property."

"Boy, there are so many things to think about. How do you remember all this stuff?"

"When you live and breathe landscape and have a burning desire to get better and better at what you like to do, most of the things just fall into place. Can I get frustrated with things as we are putting the project together? Very much so. Do I make field changes as we are installing? Yes, I can completely change based on field conditions. A product that is no longer available is a killer. Rethinking a situation during a problem can be very troublesome. Sometimes the field creates problems. Would it be okay for me to return a little later today and field-measure your property?"

"That will be fine. We will be home all day, so you're welcome to return whenever you wish."

"I appreciate it. I have another appointment, and I hate to make people wait on a gardener."

"A gardener? Yeah, right, they are in for a huge surprise."

"Thank you, John. That was very kind. It was my pleasure meeting you both, and I hope we can do some business together." I finished writing down some notes and left the job site.

I met with the other client and took notes, and they also wanted a plan with a proposal. It was not as involved as the work needed at John and Marie's mansion, but it was well worth drawing plans. I returned to John and Marie's after getting a bite to eat. I always liked having a drive-through beverage in the cup holder, unwrapping a burger or chicken sandwich, or nibbling on a french fry or my favorite tater tots. None of these was good for me, but the flavor of the tots far exceeded that of any french fry. I would quickly devour the meal and always leave a few fries or tots and beverage for the ride home—something to look forward to while stuck in traffic. I got my yellow tablet, pencil, measuring wheel, and measuring tape. My cell phone was in my pocket for photos. *Okay, I'll ring the doorbell and let them know I have returned.*

John answered the door. "Great to see you again. Feel free to measure the yard. Marie and I sat down and tried to digest what you told us and wrote down some things we would like you to incorporate into your drawings. I'll go and get the list."

"Great, I'll wait for you to return."

John gave me the list, and I put it in my binder and proceeded to measure the backyard first. I always started measuring at the entry gate and worked my way around the house, measuring the outside perimeter first, then the structure, and finally either the fence or known property line. Once in a while, the homeowner had a plot plan given to them by the escrow company; it was so nice to get one of those. The hedge was somewhat of a problem, and a couple of educated guesses got me close enough to exact. In less than an hour, the backyard was measured. I took some shots of the existing landscape, which were always good to have to see what it once looked like and how it changed when completed. Sometimes I would even forget how a plot used to look.

Off to the front yard I went. This would take some time, with there being lots of hardscape to measure. There were some steps to the front door, front porch, side yard walkway, driveway, sidewalk, and parkway. I'd always wondered how things got their name. You park in a driveway and drive in a parkway; it seemed backward. Anyway, with the sidewalk, driveway, city sidewalk, and house footprint measured, now I moved to the entryway from the driveway to the front door. This would take some time. It was meandering, with pilasters, steps, and lighting. *Finished. Well, that was fun.* Back in the truck, I took a sip of soda, which had mixed with the melted ice. The drink was getting pretty warm, but the liquid was satisfying.

CHAPTER 2

Off to the nearest traffic jam I went. I just loved bumper-to-bumper traffic. The jerk beside me would always cut me off to gain two seconds of his precocious drive home. Then I would have to keep at least four car lengths behind the car in front of me, so of course anyone near the gap could dart in, and the driver in front of me would slow down to allow more space. I also liked the drivers of cars with automatic transmissions who got me caught between gears, too fast for first gear but way too slow for second gear; I went back and forth between gears so I wouldn't lug my engine.

I really loved watching the couple in front of me having a verbal fight. I could see the male driver making hand gestures to his beloved passenger, and she, not taking his gestures lightly, made some of her own. This, of course, allowed other drivers to cut in front of them.

Would I ever get home? Sometimes I was not too sure. One day it took me almost seven hours to get from my office to my front door. The average time was a little over an hour. I had numerous stations preprogrammed in my radio, and there were days when nothing was enjoyable to listen to.

Home at last. "Hello, anybody home?" No sounds. "Oh great, a note."

Gone to visit my friend. Be home later. You can heat up leftovers from last night's meal.

She went to visit her friend. Why didn't she visit her friend while I was out meeting customers? Her friend—she didn't say which one, so maybe this one had a job. Her other friends didn't work, lucky girls. What kind of visit could this be? Both had kids, and they'd all be home from school—'Mommy' this, 'Mommy' that.

"Aren't men such jerks?" she might have said. "They work all day and expect dinner when they walk in the door. 'Here's your frozen dinner. There's the microwave. Have at it.' We're not their mothers. Oh, there's another three or four days' worth of talk just to tell you what Mommy Dearest told me about him growing up. I wish they all came with manuals."

Oh well, I was sure they were having the time of their life.

Okay, leftovers. Which container is the leftovers? Oh, maybe this one. Oh, no, not that one. It has green fuzz on top. Should I put it back or throw it out? Oh, I'll do her a favor and dispose of the culture. Maybe in this container. Oh, I remember this meal; I think it's the one we had the day we returned from our honeymoon nine years ago. This will, of course, be thrown out. I wonder what surprise I'll find in this container. Empty. She has an empty container in the refrigerator. This is not going well. I know—good old peanut butter and jelly sandwich. Now where does she keep the bread?

It was almost like being in bumper-to-bumper traffic all over again. Soon the sandwich was ready, and I poured a little milk. *Glop, glop.* "This smells really bad. No wonder—it expired the year I was born. Just what does she do all day while I'm at work? Oh yeah, the kids. Yep, the kids take up all her time." I emptied and rinsed the container and put into the trash. "Water, good old water. Can't go wrong with cool, clear water right out of the tap." *You know, if I had a dog, it would get my sandwich, and I would enjoy watching it try to get the peanut butter off the roof of its mouth. I can't remember if I had this much trouble when I was single. I always had cold pizza, cereal, or the surprise package wrapped up in tin foil, awaiting the next victim to unwrap that lovely smell with a nice tint of green fuzz. It was not much different, I suppose.*

Wait a minute, where are the kids? Her note didn't say they were with her. Do I dare text her? Yes, I had better text her. Be extremely nice with your text or you'll pay dearly later.

"Honey, the woman of my dreams, mother of my lovely children, where do they happen to be?"

"What do you mean?"

"The children—are they with you?"

"Did you check their rooms?"

"Their rooms? No, I assumed they were with you."

"Why would you assume that? Wait, Freddy, just how deep of a hole do you want to dig? Check their rooms and then respond to your blushing bride."

I shouted, "Okay, kids, Daddy's home!"

"Yeah, what's for dinner, asked Sarah?" Sarah is a fourth grader, shoulder length brown hair, dimples, brown eyes like her mother.

"You haven't had dinner, I asked?"

"No. Mom said you would make us dinner, said Rebecca." Rebecca is a second grader, brown shoulder length hair, brown eyes, just like her mother.

"Yeah, macaroni and cheese or fish sticks and tater tots, asked Sarah."

"Yeah, you can make it, right, Dad, asked Rebecca?"

"How about going out for pizza, I asked?"

"No, we had pizza a few days ago. How about—"

"I don't care. You guys pick. I'll just drive and buy, I said."

One wanted to go one place, the other another place, and the other another place. Here went the arguments between who the eldest was and who the tallest was, and I always got to pick. Too bad that the traffic jam had let up. "Make up your minds, or you'll have peanut butter and jelly sandwiches."

"Okay, we'll eat at Taco Bell."

"Great, get into my truck, and we'll go to Taco Bell."

Once in the car, I said, "All in. Everyone buckled up?"

"Yes, Dad, let's go. We're starving, said Sarah. Wait, Dad, there's Mom, she just pulled into driveway.

. Yeah, Mom came home, said Rebecca."

"Oh brother, just what I needed—Mom. Hi, dear, glad to see you came home in time for dinner."

"Just where are you all planning on going, asked Delores?"

"We're on our way to Taco Bell. Hop in, I said."

"I don't think so. We have leftovers from last night. Didn't you find the container, asked Delores?"

"I looked but did not find that one, I said."

"Men—can't live with them, and can't live without them. I'll show you the container, and I'll guess I'll have to put it in the microwave and set the table and do the dishes. So helpless, I swear."

"Mom, Dad promised that we would eat at Taco Bell. We don't want leftovers, said Sarah."

"Yeah, Dad said we could have Taco Bell, said Rebecca."

I should have continued digging the hole I started earlier. It would have been be a grave by now. All she would need to do is fill it back up. "Well, did you promise them Taco Bell, or were you just trying not to feed them a nourishing dinner?" my wife asked.

Oh no, the trap question. Either answer, you're a dead man. The kids won't bail you out of this one. Just how do women know the perfect question to ask? Well, it's the floor or couch tonight, no cuddling up. Go ahead, make a complete fool of yourself, not just now but forever too. "Remember the night you insulted my cooking?" God, help me, please. I know I got myself into this. I need to get myself out of this. "Honey, why don't we go to a place where you would like to eat?"

"What are you saying—my cooking isn't good enough for you?"

"Honey, we can have it tomorrow. You've put in a long day. I don't want to have you cook and clean up after dinner. You can just sit back and relax while others do what you would have to do. Come on, honey; you could use a break, I said."

"Yeah, Mom, you could use a break, said Sarah."

"Well, I guess you're right. Let me go in and freshen up."

Freshening up could take a little time. Be patient or your escape plan will go up in smoke. "Okay, honey, we'll wait in the truck."

"No, you all had better come back into the house. It's too cold out here."

Now you could be a smarty-pants and say, "Remember: the restaurants do have a closing time." That could give you a lifetime on the sofa. Be nice now. "Okay, honey. Kids, do as your mom says."

You know, if you keep dodging bullets, the one you don't hear will be your doom. Remember what your father told you on your wedding day: "Start each morning with 'I'm sorry, honey.' She'll ask you, 'For what?' Don't start making up stuff. Just say, 'I love you and I'm sorry; that's all.' You do that each and every day so when you do mess up, you're somewhat covered. We never really know just what we do to upset our blushing bride, but the Lord only knows. We'd better duck. Incoming."

She got ready really quickly.

"Wow, dear, you look fabulous," I said.

"Have you been drinking?"

"No, honey, you look great. Huh, kids—don't your mom look great?"

"Oh yeah, of course." A little more enthusiasm would have been well deserved. Once back in the truck, I asked, "Everyone buckled up?"

"Yep, let's go. We're starving."

"Okay, honey, where would you like to eat?"

"Let's go to the steak house. We haven't been there in a while."

"The steak house. I love steak. Let's see, four people, average of eighteen to twenty per plate, plus drinks and tip. I have no cash on me, so credit card, here we come."

The steak house had a thirty-minute waiting time. Normally I and my blushing bride would mosey up to the bar; she would have white wine, and I'd get a light beer. She would want another wine to drink with her meal, and I would get a diet soda. The kids were with us, and there was no place to sit in the lobby. *"Okay, we'll just stand and wait our turn."*

One couple was called, and two kids fought over who would sit and who would continue to stand. Everything settled back down, and another couple was called—not next to our other two kids, nope, but on the other side of the lobby. Off went the wife, Rebecca. I was standing, and more folks entered the restaurant. That party of more than twelve filled the entire waiting room. This was getting pretty awkward, with there being little to no room. Another couple was called, and of course, two of the party of twelve took those spots. The door opened, and even more people entered the lobby. Now we were packed in like sardines. Another party was called. *Wait a minute; we were there before them.* "Excuse me, I need to talk to the young lady calling out names." I went and asked, "Excuse me, my dear, but we were here before them."

"Yes, sir, you were. You have four in your party, and they had two. Please wait for your turn." What a polite way to tell customers their procedures were based on party size, not when people entered the long list. Then she called the party of twelve.

"Wait a minute; twelve is eight more than four. Now what's up? Miss, I really don't understand your method of seating customers."

"You see, sir, we can push together three tables to allow a larger party to sit. Three tables of four can give us a table for twelve. We had three four-person tables ready. That's how it all works."

"Are we next?"

"Yes, sir, you are next on the list to be seated."

Now I was getting as hungry as my starving kids. They were all playing with their cell phones, and Mama—well, if looks could kill, I was certain the hole I started to dig earlier would make a lovely place to rest my head tonight.

Finally they called our name. "Kids, let's go get some mouthwatering steak, baked potato, fresh vegetables, beverages, and dinner rolls. Put the phones away. We're going to get our table."

The waiter pulled out my blushing bride's chair, and she was glowing; he politely pushed her in the proper distance to enjoy a fabulous meal. Now I knew why she had gotten all spruced up— helping a nice college boy make enough money to go to Harvard through tips. We all got our menus; mine was the only menu with prices. The waiter told all of us at the table what the nightly specials were. As he was describing the meals, I—being the steward of the family finances—searched the price of the nightly specials; they were not listed on my menu. The kids and my blushing bride said they would like to try a couple of the specials. He had never said these meals were discounted, so I nicely asked, "How much are the nightly specials?"

"They range from twenty to twenty-five dollars per plate, not including beverage."

We were now talking eighty to one hundred dollars, including my meal. "Okay, I'll have the eight-ounce rib eye steak with baked mashed potato, sour cream, and chives, and the steamed vegetables."

"Thank you, sir. Your meal will be served shortly."

My blushing bride asked, "Eight-ounce? How come you didn't order your usual twelve ounce?"

"Not that hungry and didn't want to waste food." *Man, you're getting good in answering trap questions.*

Dinner was really good, and surprisingly, all plates were cleared of food. Starving the kids was the trick—lesson learned. All was good; the kids actually went to their rooms and to bed. Starve them and stuff them and nighty night— so that was the secret. Mama went to bed as well. Two glasses of wine, nice meal—there was her secret too. I was getting tired as well, and tomorrow I'd start drawing the plans for John and Marie.

After a great night's sleep—no getting up with worries or stress, no tossing and turning—I woke up with the alarm, which was a rare occurrence. The kids were off to school, and my dearest had a hair appointment. I was all alone. With the drawing table all set, all tools at the ready, I started drawing.

About an hour had passed when the phone rang. "Hello, it's John."

"Oh, hello, John. How can I help you this fine morning?"

"We were wondering if you could add a few more items to your drawings. We would like a new patio, a patio cover, and a barbecue island. Could you add those for us?"

"Yes, I can. I just finished your plot plan, so your timing was perfect."

"We didn't want to spring that on you after you had drawn your plan for our house."

"No, it's fine. If you want anything else, let me know as soon as possible."

"Will do. Have a great day."

"You too, and give my regards to Marie."

I needed to get my notes and add the new items so I wouldn't forget. I got another sheet and laid it over the plot plan for the construction drawing, along with a sheet each for the landscape, irrigation system, low-voltage lighting system, utilities, construction details, and landscape and irrigation specifications and legends. *Wow, lots of sheets. This will take some time.*

My blushing bride entered the front door. Her hair looked nice, and I quickly complimented her on it.

"You really like it?"

Not another trap question. The target on my back was getting bigger and bigger with each question.

"Why, yes, dear. You look beautiful."

"I know I look beautiful. What about my hair?"

"I told you it looks nice."

"I don't like it. I think she took off too much, and the color is darker than the last time."

"You look stunning. I wouldn't change a thing."

"Of course you wouldn't. You don't have to look in the mirror at this for at least three weeks."

"Honey, I have to see you all day long and look forward to seeing you in all your glory."

"Don't even try to butter me up. I'm going to my friend's house. She'll be a better judge than you. I'll be home before the kids come home from school. No going out for dinner, you hear me?"

"Yes, dear. I'm looking forward to leftovers."

All day was peace and quiet. I finished the construction and irrigation drawings and almost finished with the landscape drawing, making great progress. Things were fitting together better than planned. I forgot to eat lunch. I couldn't figure out why I was getting stomach growls when I decided I needed a break for a few minutes. Lunch would be quick and easy. *I know, peanut butter and jelly sandwich—perfect. It will fit the bill. Okay, where is the bread? No bread—kids' lunches. Okay, plan number two—bowl of cereal. Rats, no milk. I threw away the awful-smelling stuff last night. Okay, what else do we have? All the good stuff is gone or has green fuzz on top. I have to eat something … maybe celery with peanut butter in the middle. No celery either. Well, a large glass of wonderful tap water, full of governmental additives—that will work.*

My blushing bride returned from her visit and seemed a little more pleased than when she left; she came to where I was working, gave me a hug, and apologized for her behavior earlier. "Do you want some lunch?" she asked.

"That would be nice, but I don't want to trouble you."

"Well, I have to make something for me, and it's easier making for two than one. Love you, honey." She shuffled off to the kitchen.

Now where was I? I was stuck on the landscape plan. If I left some of the plant material and put in smaller stock, it could look unbalanced. If I removed everything, the home would look barren. Even with a great pruning job and after lacing out some of the shrubs, I could only prune so far. You want some foliage? Sticks would only look horrible. What to do? What to do? This was going to take some thought, and I didn't want to just sit here and stare at the drawing. *I know, I'll start the lighting plan. And while drawing that, I'll for sure come to a conclusion on my dilemma. Let's see.* I removed the tape from the corners, removed the drawing, and laid a clean sheet of vellum on top of my plot plan. When all was lined up, I taped the corners and traced the plot plan on the new sheet.

"Honey, lunch is ready. Come and get it."

Wow, such a great feeling having a loving wife. "Coming, dear. Be there in just a minute."

Into the kitchen I went, and she had moved our lunch meal to the kitchen table. "Much nicer than that steak house setup last night. Looks delicious. Great job, my love." She had made a wonderful salad.

"I'm sorry, dear; we are out of bread, so I couldn't make you a sandwich."

"This is perfect. Not too hungry, and I don't want to spoil our dinner."

"Oh, yeah, the leftovers from two nights ago, I almost forgot. I'll need to go to the grocery market after lunch and pick up a few items. Do you want to come along?"

"You know, yeah, that will help me collect my thoughts. I'm stuck on the landscape drawing and need to hash out some things in my mind to unravel my dilemma."

While shopping for groceries, I was allowed to drive the cart. *Here you are, Indy 500, leading the race by a car length, two laps to go. Steady, not too fast into the first turn. He is now trying to position himself to pass. Smooth entry into turn two. He is not on you rear tire. You have to be nearing two hundred miles per hour going down the back straightaway. He's still on your rear tire. Steady, turn three, smooth entry. He's inched up to half a car length. Turn four—*

"Honey, hello, are you okay? What do you want in the bread aisle?"

"What? I'm sorry. I was thinking about something else."

"You need to pay attention to what I'm asking you. I brought you along so you could help me with our grocery needs."

"I know. I'm truly sorry. I promise to do better."

"Here is the bread we normally purchase. How many loaves?"

"You'd better grab three. Lunches for the kids take a lot of slices."

"Three it is."

"What's next?"

"We need to head to the canned vegetable aisle."

"Okay, I'll follow you."

Turn four, Smooth, side by side, going down the front straightaway. Crowd on their feet screaming, "Go, go! Don't let him pass you!" White flag—final lap. Adrenaline is pumping into high gear. Turn one fast approaching. He's almost even with me.

"Honey, for god's sake, what is with you? Do you want corn? Green beans? What?"

"Oh my, I am so sorry. I'm still thinking about something else. How about a can of each one? Can we have some baked beans for some hot dogs and bean casserole like you make every so often? The kids and I really enjoy how you make it."

"I wasn't planning that, but okay, I'll squeeze it in this week. Grab a couple of cans and some chili for the hot dogs as well. We'll have to go back to the bread aisle and get some hot dog buns."

"Okay, dear. I'll run over to the other aisle and grab a couple of packs."

"Don't be too long. We still have more to do."

I rushed to the bread aisle. *Aha, there they are, and they're on sale. She's going to be so proud of me.* Upon returning, I asked, "Here, dear, how did I do?"

"Wonderful, dear, and in only twice the time that it would have taken me, but good job. Let's go to the dairy aisle for milk, cottage cheese, cream cheese, yogurt, coffee creamer, orange juice, juice containers for the kids' lunches, and whatever you can think of."

"Okay, I'm following you."

Through turn one, we are now even. Turn two—smooth entry, a slight slide … but controlled. Out of turn two, heading into the back straightaway. My crew chief on the radio earlier said, "You have to conserve fuel. He pitted one lap after us. He has more fuel." I want to win this race. I'm crossing my fingers and everything else on my body. We are over two hundred miles per hour. It's too fast to enter turn three. Brake hard. Downshift two gears. A little fishtail … but controlled. He's at least a tire ahead of me. Turn four fast approaching. Entering turn four, I'm slowing. My foot is to the floor. He's through the turn, heading into the front straightaway. Another car is fast approaching and passing me. I'm slowing, coming to a stop. I can see the finish line.

"Honey, are you still with me? I'm not taking you shopping next time. You're impossible. I have asked you three times about what type of milk and cottage cheese you want—no answer."

"I'm so sorry."

"Whatever is bothering you, it had better end right now. I have to get dinner ready when the kids come home from school. They will raid the refrigerator, looking for anything to snack on. Are you with me? We need to finish. Can you stay alert for at least ten minutes?"

"Yes, dear, I lost the race."

"What race are you talking about?"

"The Indy 500."

"What? You've been daydreaming about racing in the Indy 500? You haven't paid one bit of attention to me the entire time? You're impossible. We have to go to the snack aisle and get some chips. Please pay attention and try not to hit anything with the cart. You're in a grocery store, not on a racetrack. Men, I swear."

"Yes, dear, I'll do my best."

Well, shopping was done. All was bagged, carted, and paid for. We headed to the car and put the groceries in the trunk. I unloaded them into the house and helped put the food away before the kids got home. With grocery shopping all finished, Delores, headed to the bedroom to take a quick nap. "Please stay quiet so I can get a few minutes of sleep before the kids get home."

"Yes, dear, my pencil will make little to no noise, I promise." I was back to the drainage plan. *It should be a piece of cake to complete this one.*

I still had not thought about my dilemma. *Well, the drainage plan is completed. Do I start the lighting plan and then go back to the landscape, or bite the bullet and just complete the landscape plan? Decisions, decisions, decisions.* Sometimes just keeping it simple and not getting carried away while talking with customers made my life so much easier. Sometimes being too helpful could clutter my thoughts and cause me to work myself into a corner. I'd done that only a million times in my life.

I put the landscape drawing back on the board and addressed the dilemma— which I had created in my own mind, by the way; it was not a real dilemma generated by a job site situation. I decided that some of the existing plant materials were to remain and to face the consequences during the construction phase. Foundation planting at the existing size of shrubbery would balance the two-plus-story home. Too small and it would be out of balance, so to counteract the problem, I would bring the beds farther away from the home and cut down on the turf areas, giving depth to the yard as an optical illusion. I'd have to adjust the irrigation system to reflect the landscape drawing. *Whew, that was a close one. I just have to sell the design to the homeowners.* Losing some of the turf area can, at times, make the homeowner uneasy. Too much square footage of planter area would increase the maintenance cost of the landscape. More time spent weeding in lieu of pushing a lawn mower can create a daunting task.

All drawings were completed, so I went to the reprographic store and had them reproduced in two sets—one for the homeowner to approve, and one for the city and the homeowner association, if there was one for their property. Now I would complete the estimate and make the appointment to submit the proposal. One and a half weeks had passed since the first meeting. I called John and Marie to schedule another appointment. It was confirmed; in two days, they would see the plans and the proposal.

Our meeting went extremely well; the plans were beyond what they had imagined. They couldn't stop saying, "These are nice—just what we wanted. Can we go over the proposal and get back to you by tomorrow?"

"Of course. Remember: each item listed on the proposal is a standalone proposal. So if you decide not to build the barbecue island or want to make modifications to the design, it won't hurt my feelings."

"We love the design. Your proposal is in line with what we figured it might cost. One of my concerns is the property line hedge. Do we want to keep it or remove it, and if we keep it, how high do we want it to be? We don't know that neighbor, and too low of a hedge just might not grow fast enough to block their view of our home. The height of the remaining shrubs in front is still bothersome to us. We like the privacy, but we also want the opportunity to see life outside our walls. We're caught between being reclusive and being outgoing. We try to be neighborly, but we don't want to spend every waking minute talking with neighbors—at least not yet."

"I fully understand, so discuss your concerns, write down your concerns and each of your responses, and we can determine a happy solution. Give me a call tomorrow, and if you need more time, just let me know. Thank you for your time this evening, and have a great night's sleep."

Early the next morning, John called and stated that they had talked about everything last night. "It seemed like hours, and we determined that your design meets everything we wanted. If we have an option while the project is being built, can we make changes?"

"Of course. It is your home, and you'll be the ones living there. Making it enjoyable for you is my main concern."

"Great. When can you start our project?"

"To make it easy on everyone, let's start on Monday. Starting in the middle of a week can get cumbersome when doing progress payment requests. We normally start at seven o'clock, unless a later start time is more convenient for you and Marie."

"We are normally up and about at five o'clock, so that will give us plenty of time for breakfast, showers, and getting ready for our day. See you at seven."

I talked to my foreman and asked if he knew anyone who installed carpeting. "Why, yes, my cousin is a carpet installer. Are you planning on putting carpet in your home?"

"No, I just got a verbal okay to start a new project on Monday. One of the items we have to do is remove carpeting on an existing staircase, and I thought it would be a good idea to find someone with that kind of experience. Helps eliminate learning curves and making costly mistakes. Can you ask your cousin if he would be interested?"

"I'll ask him tonight when I get home."

Boy, what a lucky break. It was one part of the job I was really unsure of doing. *Now I should write down work orders for the crew.* Side yard weeding was absolutely the first thing that had to be done so I could see the scope of work. They would need to prune the existing hedge along the property line and give the guidelines to the foreman to follow. They must lace out the tree that remained for a nice canopy, cut out all cross branching, and remove the existing irrigation system—valves, heads, and controller—and turn it over to the homeowner. He did not want anything recycled. That would keep them busy for a couple of days—maybe three. All that was left for me to do was tell my blushing bride; she'd be thrilled. It would get me out of her hair for quite some time.

CHAPTER 3

O n Monday morning, the crew was all excited about starting another project; it kept food on their table as well. We pulled up to the job site and rang the bell. John answered, and I introduced Juan, my foreman, to him. All was good. We headed to the side yard and showed Juan what needed to be completed on the first day. He told his leadman to arm the crew with picks, shovels, and a couple of trash cans and clean the bed of the truck so it could hold all the debris that needed to be removed. "Let the dust start flying," I said. I did instruct Juan, "If it creates too much dust and debris, keep the area moist to lessen the airborne dust. I try to keep the job sites as clean as possible to lessen the inconvenience to our customers."

"Okay, boss, will do. If we get done early, what would be the next item?"

I liked Juan; he was always trying to stay ahead of the game. I showed him the hedges and the tree that needed lacing out and told him to call me to give him direction when he got to that point. I didn't think he knew the term 'lacing out the tree'; he looked a little puzzled when he heard that. I also wanted to be called when they were ready to start on the hedges.

"What if we run out of space in the truck? Where do you want us to put the excess pruning debris?"

"Let's stockpile it in the area you are weeding, and tomorrow we'll bring a trailer."

They had the weeding finished and loaded by their lunch break; all of them were dirtier than before they had started. Juan called me to return during his lunch break. I showed up, and Marie was standing next to Juan, looking at the progress; she was really excited. "Fred, it looks so much different … clean. I'm in shock."

I looked the area over and saw the problem that was causing the water to enter her home and garage. I showed her and Juan what needed to take place. Someone had piled soil above the finished floor elevation, and the grade from the fence to the house was higher at the fence, so all the surface water was heading to the house. I pulled out my phone and took some photos of the area and checked the weather forecast to see if any rain was scheduled in the next few days. No rain was forecast, so we were able to start pruning the hedge and then the tree.

I talked to Juan. "Hand prune only—no power bar cutter or chain saws. Nice, clean cuts." I showed him where I wanted the hedge to end up on the grass side and told him to forgo pruning the top until the sides were trimmed. He needed ladders anyway, so trimming to the right height would be difficult, if not impossible. We pruned about a five-foot length and got Marie to approve the look. She came out and said, "Is the whole hedge going to look like this?"

"I hope so, unless you want less pruned or more pruned."

"No, I love this. You gave me another three or four feet of yard space. I can't wait until John gets home to show him what our backyard will look like. I'm so pleased with what you and your crew have done!" Marie returned to the inside of the house.

I asked Juan if he had talked to his cousin. "Oh yeah, I did talk to him, and he has a couple of weeks when he has nothing for the crew to do. Can he start tomorrow?"

"Yes, he can, and I will talk with both of you about an idea that I have. Can he start at seven o'clock and ride to work with me?"

"Great idea. Of course."

"It looks like you will finish the day pruning the hedge. Remember to bring the ladders with you tomorrow. You can take the debris to the recycling center a few miles away. You know where it is, correct?"

"Yes, I know where it is. So don't prune the tree today?"

"No, just get the hedge pruned and hauled to the side yard. Try not to block the entrance to the gate, and leave John enough space to see how the side yard will look."

I returned home and had three phone calls from new and old clients. The couple I had met after meeting with John and Marie wanted to meet tomorrow and go over the contract. *Oh, this is going to be a great year for the company.* Two older clients wanted more work done on their landscapes. I returned all the calls and set appointments to meet everyone.

The next morning, I met with Juan and his cousin. John and Marie—boy, were they excited. I knew they were happy when Marie brought out a cup of coffee and a breakfast pastry for me. John said, "I was a little concerned about leaving the hedge, but I'm sure glad we followed your advice. How high are you going to leave it?"

"Maybe come down two feet or eighteen inches. Take a peek to see how it looks. Maybe we'll cut a foot, and then eighteen, and then two feet, if necessary. We will meander a border in front of the hedge to give the appearance of depth, put in floral shrubs and annual color to catch the eye from inside and encourage visitors to come outside and get a closer look. Juan brought his cousin today, and he's a carpet installer. I was looking for someone who has that experience. Can we all go inside and have him see what has to be done?"

"Of course; let's get that old carpet out of our home."

Once inside, I said, "There it is, Jose, the staircase with the carpeted steps. What do you think?"

"Pretty nice staircase. So just remove the old carpet?"

"Yes, we need to see what is underneath to determine the next phase."

"Okay, can I start now?"

"Well, John and Marie, is it okay to start today?"

"I don't see why not. Will everything be removed from inside the house?"

"Yes, and I will have them load the old carpet into the truck and the trimmings into the trailer."

"This is wonderful. Everything is falling into place, and we will be able to see what we really have. Nice meeting you, Jose. If you need anything, let us know."

"Nice meeting both of you as well, and I will get you if I find something that needs an answer."

I told Juan to have one of our laborers help carry the carpet pieces to the truck and help Jose with whatever he needed. "I have an appointment with another new client in about an hour, so I have to return home and get my proposal and plans. When you start cutting the hedge, only take about one foot off the top until I return."

"Okay, I'll tell the crew."

Jose had brought his own tools, and I told him that if he broke or damaged his tools on the job, I'd replace them.

The other meeting went wonderfully, and we picked up another project, so now I'd have to get a few more men, and Juan would have to bounce between the two projects. I was anxious to see the progress in John and Marie's home.

When I arrived back at the site, Juan met me at the truck; this was not always a great sign. "You have to see the staircase. My cousin was amazed at what he found."

Oh great, all pumped up and now deflated. "Okay, how's the hedge coming along?"

"I'll show you after the staircase."

We walked inside the house. The carpet was totally removed, and everything was cleaned up, ready for inspection. "Wow, you removed it really fast. What am I looking at? Every step is totally different—some plywood, some pieces of old furniture cut to shape, some one-inch-thick lumber, some two-inch-thick lumber. This is *horrible!* Jose, have you ever seen anything like this before?"

"No, sir, never."

"Have John and Marie seen this yet?"

Jose said, "No, they are not home—had to run an errand or something."

"This is really bizarre. Never in my life have I seen such a hodgepodge of lumber. How is everything attached, Jose?"

"Some nails, some screws, some glued."

"To what are they attached?"

"I don't know until I remove the tread, but I didn't want to remove it until someone tells me to proceed."

"And I'm sure the homeowners appreciate you waiting. Nice job on removing the carpet. Let's take a look at the hedge."

We went outside. "Wow, it looks great. I'm thinking maybe another six inches lower and it would look perfect. Can't wait for John and Marie."

Just then we heard the garage door opening. They were in for quite a surprise. John and Marie entered the house from the garage; we caught up to them just outside the kitchen, and we all gathered to look at the staircase. "Wow, what is this?" John asked.

Marie said, "How awful. It can't stay this way. Would you put the carpet back over all this mess?"

"I'm not a builder, but it needs to all come off. We don't even know how any of this is hooked together. Jose, can you remove one of the treads so we can see how this was constructed? Would that be okay with you, John?"

"Of course. Is this thing safe?"

"I won't know until we see just what was done."

Jose got a hammer and chisel from his tool belt and proceeded to remove one tread, making sure he would not damage it, since it would have to be put back on so John and Marie could use the upstairs bedrooms. Jose got the tread removed, and I could see by his expression that something was not correct. "I've never seen anything like this in my life." Between each step was concrete. It did not look finished; there was just a glob just below the bottom of the tread.

"Why would anyone mix concrete and not put a finish on it—just mix it in a wheelbarrow and dump? Very strange. How are the steps joined together, Jose?"

"I think they are just little boxes sitting on the old staircase."

"John, can we do some further investigation?"

"Yeah. Is this customary building practice?"

"No, absolutely not."

"Is this staircase even safe to use?"

"It appears that it held together for quite a few years. Did it creak or make you feel unsecure going up and down?"

"You know, I never even thought about it. I just assumed it was good."

Marie asked John if she should call the realtor who sold them this house. Her tone was unsettling, to say the least. John told her, "No, not yet. We need to take really good photos of this and make an appointment to see our attorney. Clearly someone didn't do their homework and overlooked a potential hazard."

Jose removed the entire step made of multiple types of wood to expose the glob of concrete. Each step was just sitting on the old staircase. "How is the concrete glob attached to the concrete stairwell?" I asked.

"Just sitting on top. Let me get my concrete chisel and see if I can remove some of the concrete glob."

With a concrete block chisel, a small sledgehammer, and safety glasses, he was being very careful as he tapped at the step. The concrete glob started to crack, and he gave it a harder blow and suddenly stopped.

"What? What is it, Jose?"

"I'm scared. This is not right." Jose moved back from the concrete glob in pure shock. Juan helped him down to solid ground. John and I went up to the stair Jose was working on, and there inside the cracked concrete glob was a bone fragment.

John said, "What is this? How sick is this? Call the police, honey. Get the attorney on the phone now."

"What is it, John?" she asked.

"You don't want to know. Just get the attorney on the phone."

Within a few minutes, the police arrived. One squad car with two officers came, and then another one with two more officers. Then there came a group of police cars, most of them unmarked; they blocked the cul-de-sac so no one could leave or enter. The officers had all of us step outside and started asking us questions. They took down everyone's name, address, and phone number, checked everyone's identification, and instructed all parties who didn't reside at the residence to leave the job site. The homeowner was to contact us when we could return. John and Marie were very shaken up, and so was Jose; he was trembling.

John and Marie were instructed to pack up a few items and check into a hotel for a few days while the forensic team did a thorough investigation. They could return once the home was secure and all evidence had been collected. John and Marie were allowed back into their home in two weeks and were told they could not do anything to the staircase until they were told to proceed. The investigators might have to return and search more. John asked if they could continue working on the outside of the home while waiting for approval to proceed. They could, but only John and Marie were allowed to use the staircase. The police took samples of their hair, cast prints of their shoes, and dusted for fingerprints on the handrail.

John called me that evening and said we could return to work on his home but that we could not work on the staircase or even get on it until further notice. "That's great news, John. We will return tomorrow." We worked on the tree and set up to start doing the patio and patio cover. I had Juan and a laborer remove the excess soil from along the house and taper the grade to the center. We used the excess soil to fill in holes in both the front yard and backyard, and hauled off the excess. The side yard was ready for the drainage system, but that would not be installed until later in the contractual time.

CHAPTER 4

John talked to me a few days later to keep me updated on the staircase. It was found through forensics that the bones were the great-grandmother's; she had been reported missing by the great-granddaughter quite a few years ago. "They are digging in pretty deep to gather more clues. The great-granddaughter passed away a few years ago. There is a great-grandson still alive in a nursing facility, suffering from Alzheimer's disease. Thus far, they have not gotten approval from his doctor to visit with him. The remaining family members all live out of state and have lived most of their lives away from here. We did find out that our home is the original farmhouse of many acres surrounding our home. The great-grandfather passed away when his eldest boy was in college. Two other siblings, brother and sister, left for college a few years later, never to return to the farm. The great-grandmother had no one to help with the farm, and another relative had her start selling off the acres surrounding the farmhouse to pay for maintenance of the remaining acres.

"Later, the great-grandson and great-granddaughter lived with their great-grandmother to help with maintaining the farmhouse and caring for their great-grandmother. They had an accounting firm handle the daily funding for the family. One summer day, the great-grandmother took a train to visit one of her only surviving relatives, who was ailing. This was not something the great-grandmother normally did; it was her first trip away from the farm in at least three years since her husband's death. It had to be nearly twenty years ago, based on what they have uncovered so far. The train has verification of her boarding the train and arriving at her destination. There is no one left to answer just who picked up the great-grandmother at the other end. The great-grandson helped his great-grandmother onto the train. One odd thing that was uncovered was that there is a train depot here in town, but she boarded the train about ten miles east of here. They're looking into why that happened. Something else they found out is that they don't have record of just where she got off the train after she boarded the train to return home."

"I'm glad I'm a landscaper. This is getting confusing."

"Oh, one other thing they found—the great-grandmother didn't stay the entire time as scheduled. She left about a week early. They sure hope to be able to talk with the great-grandson to straighten out some questions they have uncovered. Oh, our house may become a historical landmark. The lawyer is looking into that for us. Our realtor talked to the real estate broker, and they are returning some of our initial investment into this home because of what was discovered. Our lawyer actually used some leverage, stating he put all the evidence of the sale of the property into the press so all his future clients can decide if they have his best interest at heart."

"We're getting ready to pour your new patio in a couple of days, so you'll have less mess tracked into your home."

"Oh, that will be great. I think Marie has a party planned, and the patio will come in handy. What about the barbecue?"

"We have about another week of building and a couple of days to finish the countertop. By the way, did your order for the barbecue and accessories arrive?"

"Not until the end of the week."

"You would have thought that a large supplier would have an inventory. Well, it takes a while for that boat from China to off-load."

"No, no, these are American made."

"I know; I was just messing with you. Thanks for the update."

"What's the next piece of this project?"

"I'll help Juan to lay out the drainage system on the side yard. That's the deepest trench for that portion of the project. It is also an area that's away from the party, so no one will get hurt."

"Great idea. Can't wait to see more of your design unfold."

Juan and I went to the side yard and reviewed the scope of work. I went to my truck and retrieved my builder's level to shoot elevations. I had Juan trim back the shrubs so we could get an elevation from the back of the house. I also got a can of marking paint. I set up the builder's level, and Juan gave the shrub a light prune so I could see the rod he would be holding. Everything was ready. Juan took the rod, went to the forms we had just put in for the patio, and set the rod on top of the forms. I found him in the scope and wrote down the elevation. I asked Juan to move to the center of the yard, about ten feet closer to me. Juan set the rod on top of the turf, and I read that elevation. "Now, Juan, come another ten or fifteen feet closer." He did, and he placed the rod on the turf, and I read that elevation. We continued the same process, with Juan either coming closer or moving farther away. My final elevation reading was that of the gutter in the street.

Juan had been spraying marking paint at each elevation spot, so we ended up with a connect-the-dots landscape look. I determined that to allow the drain to work properly, we needed at least a one-inch fall per ten feet in length. We had at least a three-inch fall from the patio elevation to the gutter pan elevation. I showed Juan where we could drop the elevation from the patio at a two-inch fall, and when we reached the side yard, we could go to a three-inch fall that would allow the drain to flow quicker and help with sediment buildup in the piping. I left to go rent a trencher, and Juan continued to connect the dots so he knew where to dig. We had to get the trench dug and the pipe installed and backfilled near the patio so the party guests would not fall into the trench. The drainpipe would be on site in the morning, so trenching today would put us ahead of schedule.

I returned with the trencher, and Juan started to trench about fifteen inches deep. We had a laborer stay with Juan and clean out loose dirt falling back into the trench. When Juan reached the side yard, we lowered the trench to an eighteen-inch depth. By the time we reached the front yard, the trench would be twenty-four inches or deeper. The trenching was going wonderfully; digging in the soil was like cutting room-temperature butter with a butter knife.

Around twenty or so feet, near the center, the trencher hit something very hard, causing the boom to bounce upward. "Stop, Juan. We need to see what that is."

Juan raised the boom and backed the trencher out of the way so we could use a shovel to expose what he had hit. The utility-locating company had not flagged anything on that side of the house, so we were safe to dig. Our laborer started to dig, and Juan got a shovel and pick to help out. Upon further examination, it appeared to be a rooftop. The crew continued with a somewhat wider trench and uncovered an area nearly ten feet in length. The rooftop was shingled, so we knew it was a roof. "I have to get John. This should not be here."

John came out of the house and saw what we had found. "Should I call the police so we don't disturb evidence?"

"Good idea. We will stop until we get further instructions from them."

The detective in charge of the case returned to the home, saw what we found, and asked me, "How big do you think the structure is?"

"Do you want us to unearth the entire roof?"

"Let me call our chief and get his idea on how to proceed."

Now more officers were at the home. It was decided to expose the structure so they could determine just what this was. One officer would remain until the roof was entirely exposed, and the rest would then return. It took about two hours of hand-digging to unearth the roof. No one still had a clue about what this was used for, so the chief asked us to excavate along one side to see how deep this structure was. "This will take some time to dig by hand," the chief said. "We have an operator who can bring our excavator to unearth the side." He called his maintenance facility manager, and a small excavator and operator soon arrived.

Being very careful not to put the weight of the excavator on the rooftop, he proceeded to dig, and we got three wheelbarrows with laborers to work with the excavator to remove the soil from the area. It worked like a charm; he would get a bucketful and dump it into a wheelbarrow. The laborer would wheel it to the pile, and another wheelbarrow would be put in place and loaded by the excavator. This went on until one of the officers was allowed to get into the excavation to examine the structure. There was one window on the side that had been excavated, and the officer needed a flashlight to see if he could determine what was inside. "It looks like a storage room of some sort," said the officer. The chief told the detective to contact the office, get one of the maintenance crews to the site, and get the investigators to return with all their equipment.

Within a few minutes, the maintenance crew arrived, and the chief instructed them to remove the window. "Do not damage the structure or the window," he said. While the window was being removed, the chief told the excavator operator to remove more soil between the shed location and the house, about eight feet. "Be careful not to damage the structure or the house." Wheelbarrows lined up and were ready for hauling.

John told Marie to notify their attorney and to call her friends to call off the weekend party. John asked me, "How much is this going to cost me?"

The chief was standing near us and said that the department would cover the cost of removing and replacing the soil. "John, no need to worry about additional costs. We have it covered."

The excavator found a wall connecting the house to the shed, and Juan got a broom from our truck and swept off the brick wall. The investigator team arrived, and the window was professionally removed in pristine condition. The chief instructed the maintenance crew to give the window over to the investigating team for forensic evidence.

The investigators very carefully, with highly skilled professionalism, entered the shed. Being careful not to destroy any evidence, they found a ceiling light and pulled the chain, and the light illuminated the storage room. There was a workbench and shelving, with typical storage room stuff, including old paint cans and a box of old magazines. It looked like a very typical storage shed. "Not so fast," one investigator told the team. "We need to spray some luminol to see if there is any blood." The team stood back, and one investigator sprayed some luminol. They turned on a black light and turned off the overhead light. There were blood splatters all over where the luminol had been sprayed.

The chief was informed that this was a crime scene, and they taped off the whole area. Only the homeowners were allowed to remain on the property. It became another day of "Please leave now. Pack up the crew and tools, and without making a scene, leave." We were also instructed not to say a word to anyone about what we knew.

Upon further investigation, there was an old wooden door that led to the house. This investigating team was extremely cautious at protecting evidence; they slowly opened the door and found what appeared to be a cellar under the house. It had an earthen floor and wooden walls, and it was very narrow—about three to four feet wide. They needed help from above. Just where did this lead to in the house? There was new wood flooring in the kitchen and throughout the first-floor rooms of the home. The head inspector contacted the office to bring out equipment, such as an X-ray or infrared machine, to help locate the entry into this passageway. Within an hour, the equipment needed had arrived.

They started to try to locate an entry point. The forensic team followed the passageway to a small stairwell leading to the first floor of the home. They shone their lights upward to see if the team above could see the light. "No light, sir. Make some noise. Maybe we can hear you." They were screaming, and one of the upper members thought it was coming from underneath the spiral staircase. "Could it be that there are walls hiding the staircase? Scream again." They did. "I swear it's coming from behind this wall."

John and Marie were told that part of the kitchen would have to be torn apart. "We need to find the entry to the pathway to do forensic testing to complete our case."

"If it has to be removed, then remove it," said John.

Marie said, "This is our home. We live here. I cook in this kitchen." And she started to weep.

CHAPTER 5

They called the maintenance crew back to the home. Now the neighborhood was stirred up and wanted to know just what was going on; they seemed to think, *Such a nice couple. Just what did he do to her?* The chief knew this was going to get ugly quickly, and soon the local news stations arrived. One of the neighbors had called to report police activity. The regular officers were stationed for crowd control. Yellow tape was being strung to keep lookie-loos from entering and disturbing evidence.

The chief told John and Marie that, if necessary, he would have them in front of the television cameras so the hostile crowd would see that they were not the ones being investigated. "Some people are quick to blame and can say some pretty horrible things to both of you. We have to lessen this crowd's emotions."

The reporters were like cockroaches, running around and trying to get the best possible angles to get the best ratings. There was a lot of speculation and finger-pointing, and as always, one of the crowd put their spin on something they knew nothing about. The chief told the crowd he would have a press conference in about a half hour. "Please settle down. We're still investigating. Let us do our jobs, please."

This gave John and Marie time to regain their composure and get briefing from the professionals about what to answer and what not to answer. "We know we have a killer on the loose. We do not want anything to frighten anyone or give away what we found. Reporters are ruthless and rewrite what was said to sensationalize reality."

The news conference went very smoothly and reassured everyone that John and Marie were not involved in the investigation. Neighbors were starting to return home with nothing to spread gossip about in town or in church. "Boring. Why all this commotion? There is no doughnut store on our block," said one spectator. That did not sit well with the officers, but with all due respect, a billy club to the belly, the officer said would have make me happier.

All parties left, and reporters' heads were lowered. "This will not give us very good ratings. Who called us for this anyway?"

The wall in the kitchen was removed, and the flooring there was the same as in the kitchen. They shone a light upward toward the staircase and found another light with a pull string. The upper investigators told the forensic team to scream again, and when they did, the upper team heard them much more clearly than before. "Okay, boys, tear up the flooring."

Marie said, "Please be careful. Remember: this is our home."

The maintenance crew foreman took a small pry bar and a claw hammer from his tool bag. He then wedged the bar between the flooring planks. The first piece was removed with little or no effort. This made the next piece come out, followed by another and another until the subfloor was exposed. There was still no sign of an entry point. "Scream again," signaled the senior member of the lower team. It was heard much more clearly than before. "Do you have a board or broom handle that you could hit the floor with so we can determine just where you're located, asked the senior member of the upper team?"

"Yes, we found a broom." *Tap, tap, tap, tap.*

"Hold on; I think I found where you are." There was another small wall running perpendicular from the kitchen wall to the staircase. "They're behind this other wall. Remove the wall. Maybe there is a trapdoor behind it." Out came the other small wall, exposing more flooring. "Remove the floor." The subfloor exposed was newer than the rest of the subfloor. "Take it out. Expose the beams under this home." Heavier-duty tools were used to expose the beams, and standing at the bottom of the stairs was the forensic team member. They found the entry from the house to the shed.

The forensic team went to work scouring the walls, steps, and flooring, and they removed everything for evidence. This was not going to be easy; luminol was sprayed along the passageway, the stairwell—everywhere. Everything was documented, photographed, and fingerprinted. The shed was thoroughly investigated, and items were bagged and logged into the case record book. This took the team a few days.

Through their research of this home, it was determined that the shed stored the family's canned goods that the great-grandmother made from the garden each and every year. Being underground, the temperature of the shed remained constant; they did not have refrigeration when this home was built. They found during the investigation a rag that had bloodstains on it. They thought maybe they could get DNA from the blood. From the markings on the floor, walls, and ceiling, they came to the conclusion that some really sick person had dismembered the great-grandmother. They found some chemicals that could have been used to remove the flesh, muscle, and all remains from the bones. This was one sick person or persons. With no place to hide the bones, the killer had decided to put a false staircase on top of the existing staircase and bury the bones in fresh concrete. Then the person covered up the work with miscellaneous lumber found around the farm for the framework and treads, and had a carpet company cover up the workmanship. All was penciled out. But one main question remained: who would murder a sweet grandmother, a churchgoer who had her Bible in hand every Sunday, and who even held Bible studies in her home?

There was only one missing piece, the great-grandson, whom as of this date the doctor had not given them permission to talk with because of his illness. The chief went to the district attorney and stated their case, asking for a court order requiring the doctor to allow asking questions to the great-grandson. The judge who would issue the court order stated that the doctor and a state-provided attorney could be present at the questioning. The judge asked the prosecuting attorney if she felt that the great-grandson would be able to remember anything, since his disease might prohibit any recollection of that period. "We don't know, Your Honor, but he is the only living person we can interview."

"Good luck. Keep us informed. Be gentle and follow what the doctor feels worthy."

With court order in hand, they were off to the doctor's office to deliver it in person, find out where this person was being housed, and set an appointment with the doctor and nursing staff. All parties agreed to a date and time and which conference room would be used; no cameras from any source would be allowed. "You must maintain privacy of employees, other patients, and the facility itself. Being discreet is of foremost importance. Any mishaps, and the entire process will end."

It was horrible weather—rain, with a cold breeze. Coats were zipped up as high as they would allow. Everyone was positioned in the conference room before the great-grandson was brought in seated in a custom wheelchair designed to be inclined, if necessary, for the patient's comfort. He was very pale, almost translucent, and not very observant of his surroundings. They gave him a few minutes to adjust to the room and the people present. He looked around, but they were not certain if he knew where he was.

The doctor told Albert, "These nice people would like to ask you some questions. Would that be okay with you?" He nodded. "Please proceed with your questions slowly so he understands."

"We have records stating that you contacted the police to report the disappearance of your great-grandmother. Is this correct?"

He had a puzzled look in his eyes, trying to remember. With a slight grin, he nodded.

"How long was your great-grandmother missing before you reported this to the police?"

"This might not be able to be answered," said the doctor. "That might be too specific."

The great-grandson responded, "Week." The doctor was surprised, as was everyone else in the room.

"Was this the time your great-grandmother went to visit her relatives back east?"

The great-grandson nodded.

"Was your sister staying with you at the time?"

He nodded again.

"You were staying with your great-grandmother after your grandmother passed away, and you stayed with your grandmother after your parents were killed in an auto accident. Is this correct?"

He nodded.

"How long were you at your great-grandmother's home?"

"He probably won't be able to answer that," the doctor said. "Remember his disease, please,"

The great-grandson answered, "Years."

The attorney at this point gave the doctor a list of questions remaining. The doctor read the questions, and the attorney asked, "Do you believe he could answer any of these questions?"

The doctor responded, "It's so hard to tell. He has some moments when he could tell you what he ate for dinner fifteen years ago, with date, time, and location. But ask him if he had lunch less than five minutes ago, and he does not know. Ten years ago, lunch, everything—even the scrolling on the silverware and designs on the plates."

"Sir, do you remember the storage shed next to the house?"

He had a puzzled look again and was a little more reluctant to respond, exhibiting some twitching in his hand. Finally he nodded.

"Did you used to play in the shed?"

With another puzzled look and more twitching in his hand, he nodded.

"Did you use to play on the staircase when you were young?"

Now there was more twitching, and he turned his head toward the wall next to him. He turned back to look at the attorney with what was not a very happy face, and he nodded.

The doctor said, "How many more questions do you have?"

"I showed you the list, Doctor. These are holes in our investigation that need filling."

"Proceed. Please respect our patient."

"Are you very handy with tools, such as saws, shovels, wheelbarrows?"

This was not something that he took lightly. His facial expression was tight, there was no gleam in his eye, and he gave a cold stare at the attorney. After a long pause, they were not sure if this would be answered. He finally nodded.

"Did you help your great-grandfather on the farm?"

He shook his head.

The doctor stated, "His great-grandfather died when he was a very young boy. He was staying with the great-grandmother years after his death."

The attorney stated that they knew this but were only trying to clarify just how he had learned his mechanical skills. "Oh, I see," stated the doctor.

"Have you ever mixed concrete while working with your tools?"

This really got the gentleman unnerved. He was fussing more than ever before. The doctor called in a nurse to try to settle him down. She was his friend; if anyone could, she could. She stated, "He may have to return to his room. I have never seen him react this way before." The nurse swung his wheelchair around to leave the room.

The great-grandson was shaking and murmuring some words, and the nurse stopped pushing him and asked him, "What is it you are saying?"

"I don't like those people." It was very plain, not like his normal speaking tone.

"Why don't you like them? You were shaking and trembling when I got called into the room. Why were you so upset?"

He was rocking back and forth and said, "Concrete."

"Yes, concrete. Why did the word 'concrete' upset you?"

"I don't like concrete … too messy."

"I'm going to take you to your room now. Try to get some rest. You had a long day." The nurse returned to the conference room and told the doctor and attorneys what the patient had told her.

The doctor stated, "You must have struck a chord with the term 'concrete.' Why did you ask about concrete?"

"The great-grandmother's bones were mixed in the concrete and placed on top of the existing stair treads and surrounded by a wood frame. So the question about tools and concrete was to get a reaction from Albert. We didn't know if he would react or not. They were just questions that would help us fill in the blanks. Can we reschedule another meeting at a later date once we do more investigating?"

"That would be okay. The nurse said she would talk with him after he settles down and let everyone know what his reaction is regarding another meeting. If there is a problem, we can let you know."

"Agreed; that will save us a trip for no reason."

One of the investigators came across an article in the local newspaper from the time when the great-grandmother disappeared. The local high school had put on a a play, and one of its characters was an elderly lady. She was played by none other than the great-granddaughter. They showed her in makeup; she was stunning. She had played the part, and the cast had gotten a standing ovation from the audience for the performance. It listed the name of the makeup artist in the article, and lo and behold, she was still alive. "We're wondering if she might remember putting on the makeup of the cast." After more research, they found her in a rest home, doing fine; she was very healthy, and coherent. After a couple of calls, all seemed okay.

"She really likes company," said a nurse, to the attorney.

Back at the judge's office, they got another court order to get all doctors and opposing attorneys on board, and the rest home welcomed everyone with open arms. Maybe this would be the breakthrough everyone needed. With the date and time set in stone, all was good.

The day came, and everyone was eager to speak to the lady, and she was eager to have some company. They were in the rest home's cafeteria for the meeting, which offered the most table space in the facility. They met her, and she was glowing from ear to ear. She was such a great personality—bubbly, witty, and full of good spirit.

"First question," said the attorney. "Do you remember the high school play where you were the makeup artist?"

"Why, yes, I did all the high school and junior high school plays, you know. I loved putting on makeup and changing people's appearances. So much fun."

"Do you remember making up a young girl to make her appear as a grandmother?"

"Oh, why yes, Maybelle—such a dear and shy girl. I could make her look a hundred."

"Did you ever do makeup for Maybelle after high school was over?"

"Let me see, after high school? Hmm, yes, I remember now. It was near Halloween, and she wanted me to make her look like she did in the play years prior. She was going out of town and wanted to surprise one of her college girlfriends—to scare her, I think she said. She bought a dress from the thrift store that fit her nicely. She even had a hat and an old-time purse and found shoes that were in pretty good shape for as old as they were. Took some time. It had to be just right to surprise her friend. Why did you ask about that? Did Maybelle do something wrong? Is Maybelle still alive? I'd love to see her again."

"Were you ever at her great-grandmother's home?"

"Why are you asking me these questions?"

"We just wanted to know if you ever met her great-grandmother."

"Only once, after a high school play. She came to watch her great-granddaughter and great-grandson perform. Do you know Albert? Such a fine young man. Would do anything for you at any time. He would carry my books to class every once in a while. Asked me on a date once. My mom wouldn't let me go. 'Wrong side of the tracks,' she would tell me. They were born with a silver spoon. We were just average by those standards. They had money, you know. We were just poor folks. Do you want to know more about my makeup? I have lots of stories about lots more people."

"No, my dear, you answered what we needed to know, and we greatly appreciate your time. You're very charming. We wish more of the people we questioned were like you. We want to buy you the best lunch in the cafeteria, so if you order what you want, we will gladly pick up the tab. And if you have another patient you want to eat with, we will buy hers as well."

"Glory be. I'll go muster up my closest friend and give her the great news."

The attorney gave the cashier their credit card and said they were paying for her and her friend's meal. "Whatever they want, it's on us."

"That was well worth the trip and answered some of the most disturbing questions. So let's recap what she told us. She did make up Maybelle when high school was over for a Halloween costume, she told her she was going away to surprise an old college friend, and her brother also was in plays in high school. Very interesting. We have to find just who the great-granddaughter was meeting at the last train stop. If we can put those pieces together, along with the brother's missing persons report, we might have part of the mystery solved."

Back at the homestead, they asked the homeowners, "Remember the spiral staircase that got all this started? The police chief wanted the entire structure of the shed exposed. They had a suspicion that maybe more evidence might be located."

John and Marie said, "More evidence? Don't they have enough?"

Marie stated, "If they remove any more of my kitchen, I might want that barbecue finished yesterday." The time they had taken destroying her kitchen was a manner of minutes; remodeling was taking an eternity. "Can't put that back just yet. Still more evidence to collect, people in and out of my house daily. Can't get anything done without interruption. John's now talking of selling the house as-is and moving as far away from here as possible.

"Well, I will check with the chief to see if we can finish the patio and barbecue so at least you'll have something to enjoy. We'll complete the patio cover as well. The chief will be here in about an hour, if you would like to wait."

"Yeah, that works for me. I'll just go outside and see what else we can do while waiting for them to finish their investigation."

When he arrived, the chief stated, "The investigation is coming to a close, so you can proceed with your project, except the side yard. There're still some issues with that shed."

John told the chief, "You can have the whole shed if you want it."

"No, we need it in place to show the judge and jury the location and how it was used in the crime."

"There's going to be a tour?" asked Marie.

"Maybe. You never know just how these cases will end up."

So we started to complete what we started before the staircase issue began. The patio was poured and finished, the barbecue was finished, the patio cover was finished; they even bought some really nice patio furniture. They said it was more peaceful outside than inside their home. We completed the majority of the backyard and were getting ready to go around to the front yard when the detective in charge of the case said, "Not so fast. You have to wait until we get the all clear."

My blushing bride brought me a card from our mail. "We're invited to a party." She was so excited.

A party invite to a landscaper? This was not always top billing to impress one's friends. "This is our gardener—oh, I mean, landscaper … are your hands washed?" was the most common introduction. It was so much fun being looked on as a lower-class worker.

I was snubbed one night at a party while talking to a couple of wives regarding their landscapes. Husband number one came up, and his bride introduced me and said to her husband, "He's a landscaper."

"Well, I deal in gold and silver myself." He replied. A tone like his in a bar would get you politely floored.

"My neighbor's son deals in gold and silver; drives the top-of-the-line Mercedes. Do you deal in gold bars or bullion?"

"He deals in both."

"Sounds like a great profession."

He just walked away, all smug and uppity. Once he was beyond earshot, his wife told me he went to mortuaries and bought people's fillings and crowns. I wanted to find him and ask if his business was like pulling teeth, but I decided not to mess up his ego and decided to let him think he was above me.

While the attorneys were scheduling another meeting with Albert, sad news was given them. Albert had passed away a day before they contacted the doctor; his office gave the details. This case could go unsolved regarding who the murderer was; they knew where it had occurred but didn't know who was present or the exact time the death took place. The blood was that of the great-grandmother; they assumed she had been chemically reduced to bone and, piece by piece, entombed in the concrete of the staircase.

We started removing everything from the staircase and found the most ornate staircase I have ever seen; the workmanship was stunning. The stair treads were marble with a carved radius edge, and the sides of each step were carved with all sorts of berries, leaves, and stems. It was stunning, to say the least. We called in a professional restoration company to bring the staircase back to the glory of the initial installation. When it was finished, it could have donned any major magazine cover. There were some gold inlays that were still intact. If I hadn't known better, I would have thought this staircase was the one Led Zeppelin used to inspire their hit song "Stairway to Heaven." It was that stunning—almost breathtaking.

It was concluded that Albert and Maybelle had thought they would inherit the estate and could live high on the hog for many years, not knowing at the time that their great-grandmother had donated the entire estate to her church—lock, stock, and barrel. The church would have allowed them to stay in the home until marriage or a job offer moved them. Their plan was to dress up Maybelle and put her on a train in a town where not too many people knew their great-grandmother.

Albert would state his great-grandmother was missing, and once the property was searched and they were in the clear, he would use his skills to remodel the staircase. They added more soil on top of the shed to hide it from the inspector's view. They also covered the entry to the shed from the house. You can't inspect something if you don't know it is there. It was well planned, except they didn't do their homework. The case was closed owing to a lack of confirmed evidence.

CHAPTER 6

Since the police department excavated around the shed, leaving it exposed, that allowed us to enter the shed, as all the evidence had been gathered. Upon entering the shed from the hidden staircase and tunnel, it was determined that we would leave the shed intact. John, Marie, and I took a stroll down the stairwell, through the tunnel, and into the shed to see just how it could be used in the future. It was hard for them to imagine, since each window of the shed was looking at an earthen wall. The shed itself was in pretty good shape, well built and very usable.

"I saw what could happen if we enhanced the whole side yard using the shed as a focal point." They both turned to me as if I were entirely insane. "I saw a smaller version of the staircase inside the house—a patio with an outdoor kitchen, a seating area for parties and daily outdoor eating, a fireplace for a late-afternoon cocktail, soft stereo music playing in the background. As nighttime came, the place would light up with outdoor lighting, illuminating the seat walls and tree trunks, uplights, wall washers, and pathway lights leading guests throughout the landscaped area. We would also have a small waterfall with a seat wall so the guests could enjoy the fish and water plants. The floral canvas would be breathtaking."

After I told them all this, John and Marie wanted to go back into the house and to the side yard to see if they could see what I saw. I followed them out of the shed, through the tunnel, up the stairwell, into the kitchen, through the french doors, onto the new patio, and around the corner to the side yard. "Now," said John, "tell me again just how all this will happen."

"Okay, I need to draw you a plan so you can actually see the layout."

Marie asked, "How much would all this cost?"

"As much as you both could afford. I see how the property could be used not only to serve your needs but also to bring great value to your home. Not every vision I see becomes reality. Maybe only part of the vision is ever fulfilled. You will always know the potential. You build what is necessary now and continue as time goes by to achieve your vision."

"Wow, this all started with an ugly carpet on a staircase. Amazing," said John.

"Your home is a historical landmark. When all is completed, you can offer tours to help offset the costs. There are many ways to finance your dreams."

Marie asked, "How long will it take to complete your vision?"

"Maybe a few months. Depends on what else is buried in this landscape space. Let me show you some of the vision. You just have to follow me as I describe how it would be constructed. Your front fence between the front yard and the side yard will have to come down and be removed. We will install a chain-link fence from the property line fence to the city sidewalk, along the sidewalk to your entry sidewalk, and back to the house wall, so your home security will be our priority. We will start with the sidewalk elevation and remove the existing soil to the grade of the shed's finished floor. We will then take the existing soil from the shed's elevation to the western property line about five feet shy of the existing fence. We will remove the soil along the back fence line to the corner of the house again, about five feet, so we don't upset the existing fence. Are you following me so far?"

"Yes, we follow you."

"Once the soil is removed, providing we don't find any more buried treasures, we will start excavating the footings for the retaining walls and outdoor kitchen island. I would like to remove the roof from the shed and build a loft for the kids to play in that will allow them to come out onto a second-floor patio overlooking the adults' playground. We will put on an upgraded roof suitable to the patio cover covering the eating and seating area."

"Wait a minute; I need to catch up to you visually," said John.

Marie said, "I lost him in the front yard fencing."

"Okay, I will need to put this all in a drawing so you can visualize each piece. Getting back to the staircase, we need a way to enter the other part of your backyard. So let's go to the corner of the house for a moment."

All in position, I said, "Now you two stand here, just about five feet from the corner of the house. Now turn slightly and face directly toward the corner of the two fences, the western fence and the perpendicular fence across the two yards. Perfect. You see the fence junction?"

"Yes, we see it."

"Great, this is where you will enter into the side yard courtyard, maybe six or eight steps down with your inside staircase balusters, handrails—maybe marble stair treads, more than likely a stone step tread for safety precautions—fanning out to at least twelve feet wide at the first step, with a sweeping radius for the steps—Marie's grand entrance before the party starts. Your family and friends are waiting, soft music is playing in the background, the smell of barbecue meat is filling the air, and champagne bottles are being popped for the toast of host and hostess. Do you see the majesty of what this area could provide?"

"Wait," said Marie, "I'm still standing in all my glory at the top of the stairs. I need to catch up to your vision. What would I be wearing?"

"Oh, a beautiful outfit flowing as you gracefully step down each step, your gown slightly slipping up to expose your knee and just above. You're wearing either a pearl or diamond necklace. Your hair is up and styled just perfectly. You have a beautiful diamond bracelet and are perfumed to perfection. All hands are clapping, and John is in his barbecue chef outfit. He turns and acknowledges your entrance and holds up his glass of champagne to honor you. Your gown is your favorite color, vibrant and shimmering in the sunlight and partially shadowed by the overhanging tree branches."

"Can we do it tomorrow?" said Marie.

"Anticipation, Marie."

"John, I don't care what it costs. We need this vision to happen," said Marie.

John asked me, "What did you do before you became such a salesman?"

I just laughed. "You see, getting a vision to help others achieve something that they had no idea could be done on their behalf is the greatest gift a person can bestow. It's all part of God's plan for those to whom he has given the gift. Every one of us has a certain gift we can offer others."

"So you need to haul off a lot of soil to start off your vision?"

"No, first I have to sit down and draw the vision for you and Marie. And if we all agree on the design and we have no hiccups in the removals, then we will remove the soil and get this show on the road."

Marie was still walking down the staircase in all her grandeur. I loved to get customers into a zone where the spotlight was on only them. I finished describing my vision for John and Marie. I needed to head to my drawing board to transfer my thoughts and vision onto vellum paper.

When I got home, my lovely wife was busy doing housework; nearing the lunch hour, she asked if I would like a sandwich. "That would be very nice. I just finished meeting with John and Marie. I have to design their new side yard and scrap the prior drawings."

"Do you think what you drew before is not any good?"

"No. I had a vision of how we can take a discovery, the shed, and transform the side yard into a more usable space."

"Do you think they would want something different?"

"Yes, we all went to the side yard as I described my vision and had them act in the vision."

"Were they impressed with what you want them to do and pay?"

"I'm certain we will do some part, if not all, during this season."

"You don't think you might be wasting your time? They have gone through so much, and you have barely touched the first design."

"We would have been completed if it weren't for what we found with the staircase."

"What if you find something else buried?"

"We talked about that being a possibility. I have everything crossed that we are free of any more delays."

"Didn't you tell me the great-grandson passed away?"

"Yes, just a couple of months ago. That pretty much closed the police case. They are still getting results from the tests but gave us clear access to the shed and the tunnel from the house to the shed."

"What would you like on your sandwich?"

"Something simple and not too heavy."

"That tells me a lot."

"Whatever you feel like making, I'll feel like eating. You're it."

"I'm it?"

"Yeah, we're playing word tag. You're it."

"Go sit down, and I'll bring you some more words you can chew on."

"You're the greatest wife a man could ask for. So proud of being your better half."

"Who said you were better?"

"Oh, your crow sandwich is very good. Thank you, my love."

"Don't choke. Picking up feathers is not easy."

Lunch with the wife was wonderful. Afterward I set the plot plan on the drawing table, squared it up, and taped it down. *Wait, I want to draw at a larger scale to show more detail. Where are my measuring notes? In the file folder? In here somewhere? There they are. There's the side yard. Perfect. Fresh, clean sheet of vellum paper.* I squared it up on the drafting table, taped down the corners, and used an architectural scale to made the drawing fit between the borders. *Let's see now, 125 feet from the house corner to the western fence. I could use the quarter scale. Nope, just a few feet over. Remember: the crew uses a steel tape measure to construct. The eighth scale is a little too small, and that will cut down the detail. How much over was that quarter scale? Seven feet too long. How about the width? Ninety feet. That will fit pretty snug. Can we put half on one sheet and half on the other sheet? Let's see how that looks.*

Come on, Fred; you're wasting valuable time. You will need to draw details of all the structures. Those will be in much larger scale—maybe the one-inch-per-foot scale. That allows nice detail and gives a great picture to the customer. Okay, we'll draw the plot plan in one-eighth scale and blow up the details. I'm glad we got that all decided. On with the pencil, triangle, square, and scale.

The plot plan was soon starting to take shape. The backyard southern fence line, western fence line, front sidewalk to the entry steps, entry steps to the house, steps to the northern corner of the house, western-facing house wall, and house corner to the southern property line fence were all done. *Now let's draw in the storage shed's footprint—ten feet wide, ten feet long, eight feet from the house. Done.* Moving right along, I marked at least five feet from the property line fence and the south and western fence lines. Now I drew in the staircase leading into the courtyard; this would be a guideline to how much of and where the rest of the accessories were located. I wanted to draw a center line from the steps to the intersection of the western fence line to the house corner. I had to draw a light line; erasures always showed. It had to be a duplicable line for the field tools. I checked the arch. *Ooh, can I reference to three points? I tried that. Well, maybe that will work. Depends on the day and who measures. Where's my compass? Right where I left it last time I used it. Good thing. Last time I put it back where it belongs, it took me quite some time to find it. I love how inanimate objects can hide from an animate object like me.*

Remember the old saying "The hurrier I go, the be hinder I get," or something like that, I roughly drafted the steps. *Let's review how many feet we have from the bottom step to where the outdoor kitchen will sit. Good thing I drew the center line of the steps. I can use that line to lay out the kitchen island. How much room do I have from the kitchen island to the shed? Plenty of room for guests and kids to pass.* The retaining seat planter walls needed to be placed, and then I could draw in the barbecue island, patio cover, water feature, and decking. I also needed to tie the front yard into the side yard with an arched entry gate.

Okay, I was starting to get a good feeling for this layout; the vision would really be a nice addition to this home. The construction part of the drawing was nearing completion. I needed to review the photos of the shed; all were taken from above and at strange angles. It appeared there were windows centered on all three sides, and then there was the tunnel adjoining on the fourth side; that one would get a pair of French doors once the tunnel was widened and the second floor was in place. This would be any child's dream come true. I knew it would have been mine. *Wait, I'm dreaming this. I think that doesn't count.*

I can see Marie now coming off the staircase, the waiter handing her a glass of bubbly. She gets hugs and cheek kisses from the most prominent guests, makes it to the barbecue island, and gets her embrace from John. She turns so gracefully and thanks everyone for attending their party and tells the guests, "Please feel welcome and enjoy the party."

Just when she finishes her little speech, John's biggest surprise is about to unfold. John has hired a string quartet and a singer—and not just any singer, but Marie's favorite female singer from her favorite compact disc. Marie loves Italian love songs, and the quartet starts to play her favorite one. The singer comes from behind the crowd to serenade Marie. The guests form a circle, and Marie is nearly in tears with joy. It is such a beautiful yard, and it gets numerous compliments. "This is really amazing, so warm and comfortable." John takes off his apron and puts his arms in a position to dance with his beautiful bride; their dance so inspires the rest of the guests that the string quartet steps back with the singer to give them plenty of room to dance, and four songs later, a guest is attending the barbecue. John has almost forgotten about what he is preparing.

The party goes until twilight, and the side yard is lit up with all the outdoor lighting. The courtyard gives a new meaning to the word "wow." Even the playhouse shines with joy. In the playhouse converted to a bar, where the beverages are being served, is another surprise for the hostess—a bartender and a waitress dressed to fit the moment. She has only seen the waiter thus far and is totally shocked when the lights light up the bar and she sees the other two members of the staff.

I needed to get this drawing completed so I could join the party. The entry gate would have to be joined by a walkway that matched the existing walkway. We would refinish the existing one, and both would match. The arch would be high enough to allow for an arched gate finished on both sides, and a hanging Mediterranean-style wrought-iron lantern and two pilasters would frame the archway. There would be two matching wall lights in the same style as the hanging lantern, all amber colored to soften the entry. They would be changed in color for various holiday events. The entry wall would have pilasters every ten feet on center and custom-made pots on top, with hanging geraniums of multiple colors in each. The geraniums would fall on top of the brick wall caps, which would dip to a lower elevation in the middle of the pilasters and gradually return to the first tier of the pilaster—three tiers in all. Between each tier would be stone inlays with the bullnose brick cantilevered to give shadows during the day and under the evening lighting.

If this didn't hit the cover of the most popular magazine, I'd retire. The first party should go viral on the internet. Soft lights, great music, a fabulous singer, great food, unbelievable ambiance … in nine months, there should be living proof that this party was very successful.

The construction drawing was complete, and now came the arduous task of drawing the details of each piece. Too bad there wasn't a book that allowed designers to just cut and paste the details. What fun would that be?

"Honey, are you getting to a stopping point?"

"Almost. What's up?"

"I almost have dinner ready for you to enjoy."

"No crow?"

"No, you had that for lunch."

"Do you want to see what I have drawn?"

"Sure; I'll be right there."

"Well, what do you think?"

"Very nice. Did I get to go to the party you were talking about for the past half hour?"

"Of course, dear. You were the waitress."

"Oh, very funny. I changed my mind. Pigeon is too good for you. Crow will be served under glass. Do you want Tang with a lemon twist? I'm surprised there are no drool marks on your drawings. No, the courtyard looks spectacular. Great job, dear." I loved it when she perked up my ego.

The construction details took over a week to complete; the staircase detail was the most difficult. I had to contact the contractor who had helped restore the staircase inside the home. He said he could get it close to the appearance; no one could make an exact duplicate. The balusters were hand-carved, and the handrail had an ogee detail; he would have to have a custom diamond bit made to create a close resemblance. He would need over a month on the job site to do just the two handrails, and another month to detail the stone treads. He suggested a certain rock to use on the tread that would pose less chance of cracking and would be somewhat easier to form. He was thinking of using a modified bullnose, and the risers would be the same stone, just in a darker hue. He had a supplier that he used for such types of rocks. "You could also use biblical stones—a little pricey, but they will last forever." I told him I would get him a set of plans once the homeowners approved.

My most treasured structure was the playhouse. I spent over two days drawing the details. There would be french doors entering from the courtyard and into the tunnel. I widened the tunnel by two additional feet to allow for the french doors. The french doors leading into the courtyard would become pocket doors, so the playhouse opening was the entire side of the building. The doors would hide along both side walls. To get to the upper floor, one would have to go outside the playhouse to the stairs leading to the upper floor; a walk-around porch with handrails would allow an entry from the fabulous staircase.

A single door would allow access into the second floor. From the inside of the second floor, a pair of french doors led one out to the patio above the courtyard. I even had a fireman's pole on the opposite side toward the entry gate leading to the front yard. There was a cover to fit over the hole when not in use. I had cabinets for storing games or videos, a place for a flat-screen television or monitor, a fold-down table for eating lunch or doing homework, recessed can lighting with dimmer switch, power outlets, and a bookshelf. All was subject to change to fit the homeowners' demands. There was a lower floor and a soda fountain, or bar when adults wanted to play; a bench seat with a small folding table; some upper cabinets for storage of glassware and dishes; and a small cabinet with a countertop behind the soda fountain so banana splits could be made. There would also be a refrigerator to store beverages or whipped cream and cherries.

All was subject to modifications to fit the desires of the homeowners. I didn't like to build something that looked pretty but was never used. Fitting in the barbecue island so everything worked in harmony and allowed for flowing freely from one task to the other was time consuming. One side of the patio cover had to be placed in the raised planter, the retaining seat wall worked marvelously for additional seating, and, if necessary, the patio table could be moved to allow the seat wall occupants to place their plates and beverages on the table. There were so many things to consider while I had the mechanical pencil between my fingers. I had to consider many situations in which the homeowners could adjust to fit the scenario at hand. My brain was in high gear before I finished the construction drawings. Now I needed the plans for the landscape, irrigation system, drainage system, utilities, low-voltage lighting system, and ceiling fans under the patio cover, and then I'd sleep.

CHAPTER 7

I called John and Marie the next morning to arrange a meeting so they could see the vision on paper. It was one thing to give a voice visual; it was another to show them a drawn visual. Not everyone had the capability of hearing words being spoken and seeing what the words meant in reality. For example, I can tell you, "Look at the red rock sitting in your planter next to the lush green fern." I can see that image, and I can get you excited about what I just told you. You might be let down once you see a red rock next to the lush green fern. Sometimes I had to modify what I envisioned to fit reality. There was a "Do it and get it done" notion, and then there was "Do it perfectly." It could be as simple as turning an object to reflect a shadow. I would do this when installing boulders or a rock structure; I had to get the just-right feeling or else I would have to tear the plan up and start anew. This was very difficult to explain, but in all my prior projects, the homeowners were amazed while watching me correct visual errors or enhance the visual effect.

John answered the phone. "Hello, Fred," was his response.

"How did you know it was me?"

"My phone told me it was you."

"Smart phone. Does it know everybody?"

"Only those whom I tell it to know."

"I was calling to tell you I'm ready to show you the plans for your new side courtyard. Do you have some time this week to review the drawings?"

"Let me call Marie. I'm pretty open this week, but not sure about her schedule … Honey, it's Fred on the phone. Do you have time for him this week to show you the courtyard?"

I could hear her running toward John. "Yes, yes, oh yes, anytime. I have nothing that is as important as his plans."

John said, "Well, there you have it. Whenever you want to swing by, we are at your disposal."

"I need to get the plans copied. How about in an hour? Would that be okay?"

Marie screamed in the background, "Please hurry!"

John said, "I have never seen her this excited in my whole life. I may have to give her something to calm her down. Okay, I'll see you in about an hour."

I rolled up all the vellum and went to the reprographics store to get a copy for them. I would normally get a second copy for myself and another for the field; this time I just wanted them to have a copy until everything was approved. If there were changes, then I'd make the changes and then get plans reproduced for everyone. When the plans were all copied, I got back into the truck and drove to John and Marie's for the meeting.

I would normally stop for a coffee and doughnut—plain cake, no frills— but I knew this meeting could take some time, and I didn't want nature to call and interrupt the momentum of the meeting. I'd been at meetings where I could feel everything was going great, and then a secretary interrupted the owner or manager with a phone call. When the owner or manager returned, the momentum had shifted, and it took a while to get it back on track, if it ever did. If you can hear a pin drop, you might as well roll everything up and say good-bye.

I arrived at John and Marie's. John opened the door, and Marie almost pushed him out of the door, trying to escort me into their home. Once inside, I stopped and marveled at the beautifully restored staircase. Both John and Marie saw that I was staring at the staircase, and Marie said. "Isn't it just beautiful? You did such a great job. Everyone who sees it loves the way it turned out."

"Well, I talked with the contractor who did the refurbishing, and he thinks he can get the new one close—not exact, but very close—to matching."

"Oh, that would be so nice," said Marie.

"You may need to practice your grand entry on this one for the party."

John said, "Thanks for reminding her. She was so restless that night after you told her your vision that I thought she would never settle down and go to sleep. Crazier than a child on Christmas Eve."

"Enough chitchat. I want to see our courtyard," said Marie.

"Okay, okay, Marie. Settle down. We're on our way."

"Okay, you two, sit here, and I'll spread the plans in front of you and describe the drawings to you. You will view the courtyard from the west side of the house, just behind the shed. That's how they are drawn. Once we get started, you can turn the drawings to look down the staircase, if you desire. Everyone ready?"

"Oh, we're more than ready."

"Okay, this is the construction layout of your courtyard."

Marie almost jumped out of her chair with excitement. "Oh, John, it's just like he described. Now I can really see what he was so excited about when he described it to us."

John said, "This is so nice, and I, too, can now see what you were talking about. What is at the north entrance to the courtyard?"

"That was my surprise. I'll show you that entrance." I flipped the pages to show them the construction detail drawn with much greater detail. The drawings were opened.

John and Marie, in unison, said, "That's incredible."

"Will that really be our home?" said Marie. "John, I never dreamed that our home could look like this. Our family and friends will be amazed."

John said, "This will make the entire home feel totally different."

So I returned to the courtyard layout. Both were now a little more relaxed. It was almost as though they had just finished opening up their Christmas gifts and now it was time to play with what Santa had brought them. I went through each construction detail and saved the staircase for last. They couldn't have all the goodies up front; anticipation would stimulate the senses.

I could have just laid the cost estimate in front of them and deflated the balloon. That was construction suicide at a meeting. It was known as the Christmas tree lot scenario: You had your perfect tree in hand, but you saw another one that just might be nicer. You let go of your tree to go check out the other; while doing so, another customer grabbed your previous tree and was looking at it, ready to go purchase your tree. You now knew you made a mistake, and you would tell the other customer, "Hey, that's our tree."

"Too late, Charlie. You snooze, you lose."

You were now stuck with the other tree. But wait, where did that tree go? Another customer had seen it, and now it was gone as well. Once I showed a customer a price, I wouldn't say a word; the first one to speak would lose. That was the hardest part of any negation. I always told the customer that all the prices were standalone; if they didn't want a specific item, I would scratch it off the list of things to be done—simple.

John and Marie were becoming great customers. I told them that if they wanted to change or add anything, now was the time. "If you want to go over an item and review its details, this would be a great time."

John, being of a stable mind, spoke first. "I think this would fit our needs beyond expectations. What would cause this not to become a reality?"

"Do you mean another buried treasure like the shed?"

"Precisely. Do you think there could be something else out there?"

"As we discussed on our last visit, I have everything crossed—fingers, toes, arms, and legs—that there is nothing else. This used to be the old farmhouse, so it is possible something else is lying in wait for us to unearth. If there is something else and it is in good condition, we could incorporate it into the final product. Could be a blessing in disguise. Let's hope we find no more bones—human bones."

"I never thought about that; maybe there is a family graveyard."

Marie said, "John, you're scaring me. No more bones, please. We don't need any more bones."

They had a few questions about the remodeling of the playhouse, maybe adding some more cabinets, carpeting, and speakers—little things that could be addressed during the remodeling. They would also have to pick out colors. "Do you want window curtains and such?" John would have to price just what items he would want to enhance the barbecue island and how much more room they would take up on the patio. They also wanted some more outlets for plugging in electronics while enjoying the outdoors. There was one mention of converting the fountain into a fire pit and not putting in an outdoor fireplace—something they would want to sleep on before agreeing to construction.

It was fun watching Marie; she was so excited, and she had almost been ready to sell the property and move into a mobile home. She'd been so depressed. I asked her if she had gone gown shopping. "Oh, I want to wait until a month before my grand entrance. If I buy it now and I gain or lose a few pounds and have to have it altered, I would be so depressed."

"I will give you plenty of notice about the completion date."

John said, "Well, you know that if I tell you we need to trim the budget to make all this become reality and I see Marie look gloomy, I won't have a good night's sleep on the sofa. You two have me in a rough position."

"Well, let's take it one step at a time. We need to start removing the excess soil to unearth hopefully nothing but soil. Once we get to subgrade and start laying out the wall foundations and staircase, you'll be able to breathe easier. When we start to construct each item, we can review the costs and cut out some of the frills, but don't take away from the character of the courtyard. I have some wiggle room, and if all goes as planned, I can share that wiggle with both of you. Oh, by the way, as I was drawing your plans, I was playing in my mind your party. I didn't realize I was talking. So when I showed my wife your plans, she wanted to know if she was invited to your party. I told her, 'Of course, it was my dream. You were the waitress.'"

"I'm certain she was pleased as punch to hear that," said Marie. That broke up all tensions in the room.

I told them to keep the drawings and sit down and review them. "Test on Friday." We all stood up at the table. John and I shook hands, and he thanked me for the work I had done for them. Marie came around the table and gave me a huge hug and said I had made her dream come true. I told her my main goal was to make all aspects of our dream become reality. "I want to see you in your gown, dressed to the nines, slowly coming down your staircase in all your glory. That will be worth every penny you spend. I also want you and John to have the first dance on your new patio."

"Dance? You have us dancing in your vision?"

"Yes sir. I will share with you the party vision at a later date."

"Great, now I'll have to take dance lessons."

We all laughed.

I got back into my truck, thanked the Lord for his help, and drove back to my home. Before I went back to the reprographics, I texted John and told him to review the plans today or maybe tomorrow, no rush. If they saw something that they would like to modify, they just had to let me know so I could make the change before I reproduced my drawings for the field.

"Will do. In fact, we are going over them right now, and we may have some questions for you later today. Marie has called her mom and sister to come over to see the plans as well."

"Great, the more eyes on the prize, the better for all parties concerned."

No more than a couple of hours later, I got a text from John: "My mother-in-law asked, since the side yard looks so nice, what will you do to the rear yard to blend the two as one? She said the majority of our guests would not want to venture into the rear yard." She had a valid point; it hurt me to admit that she was right.

"John, let me give that some thought. I will unfold the original set to see just what we can modify to make it all one project. I'll get back to you in a little while. Great job, and thank your mother-in-law for me."

Okay, unroll the original construction drawings. We put in the patio as designed. We could add the fireplace off to the side of the patio. That wouldn't restrict the view from inside the house. We could put the fountain off to one side. The sound of water always attracts homebodies to venture out of doors. This will not be an easy slam dunk. I will have to rethink the entire rear yard. "Honey, can you come in here for a couple of minutes?"

"Yes, dear, what do you want?"

"I got a call from John. His mother-in-law asked, since the side courtyard is so nice, what would make a houseguest intrigued enough to want to enter the rear yard? So what she is saying is, you're over for some tea, sitting at the kitchen table, looking out the french doors at the rear yard's trimmed hedges, trimmed shade tree, and planted flowering shrubs. You see virtually the entire landscape without leaving your comfortable seat. Do you know what she is asking?"

"I think so. Your design is very nice, so she wants them to add something of interest."

"This will mean I will have to redesign this portion of the project. Do you have any ideas?"

"I'm a housewife, not a designer, you know that?"

"Yes, I know that. I want to put you in the kitchen chair. You're talking with Marie while she is getting you a cup of tea and some pastries. You're talking about girl stuff. You're gazing out of the french doors. What would make you want to get out of your chair and head to the backyard?"

"A buff gardener without his shirt on—a stud muffin."

"That would do it for you?"

"Just to get me out of my chair. But to get me to go outside, I don't know. That's a tough question."

"What would get you out of the chair?"

"That's a loaded question only a fool would answer, my dear."

"Thanks for your help. I guess I'll have to give it more thought."

"That is all you wanted me for?"

"Well, there could be more if you're in the mood."

"Dream on. I'm too busy." Response number three; she always used number one—headache. Number two was "I'm too tired," number three "I'm not in the mood." Men need to have rejection numbers; see how that feels, ladies.

Well, we have a patio. I need to connect the patio to the new staircase. I have to pretend I just walked up the staircase, following my beautiful wife. She is standing on the sidewalk, just enough room for me to stand behind her without falling backward down the beautiful staircase. What do I want her to focus on? Moving people is not an easy task. It has to be something to catch her eye.

It will have to be a fountain. The sound of moving water is always an attraction. The backyard is virtually flat, with a slight rise to the property fence—maybe a 2 percent fall. That's it … a fountain against the eastern fence with a stream moving through the yard under a bridge. The stream will be meandering, and the bridge will take the guests to a floral garden. The guests will be able to enter the bridge off the patio, so as they are drinking tea, they will see the bridge at an angle to create interest; they will not have a view from just sitting. Genius, pure genius. The bridge will be arched in the middle to give it character. To get the guests to cross the bridge, I have to have a seating area so they can view the fountain and the winding stream. Now you're talking. I have to get my darling to see if that would inspire her more than a buff gardener.

"Honey, I have an idea and would like your opinion."

"You know I'm busy. What is your wonderful idea? Another party, and I'm the waitress?"

Be careful—another loaded question. Sofa time if you respond incorrectly. "I'm thinking about putting in a small waterfall for subtle noise and a winding stream with an arched bridge from the patio to a floral island and a seating area for you to watch the fountain and the stream. Would that get you out of your chair to carry your tea out to the seating area under the shade tree to listen to the birds sing, with soothing water rushing by? Would that do it for you? Is my gardener doing any gardening? Maybe planting annual color. Can I have him earning a living or just posing for you?"

"Well, maybe he can be planting annual color until I go out and sit on your bench. Then all bets are off."

"Thanks, dear. You were a big help."

Okay, get the eraser out, etch away at the original drawing, and install the stream and waterfall. Then I'll put in the seating area, maybe two bridges to take guests back to the courtyard. I will take my two hands, angel the on top of the valium, angle them so my fingers are facing one another, maybe thirty degrees, and an earthen footpath will connect the two bridges. The floral bouquet will draw enough attention from atop the staircase to bring the guests to the fountain. The bridges will block the view of the fountain from the staircase, so you will want to see where the water noise is coming from, so you will move to the noise. You could use the bridge and go the floral route, or stay the course of the sidewalk to the patio. Then you would see the fountain and could stop and listen or go across the bridge nearest to the fountain and be seated among the floral bouquet. You know, if you were any smarter, you could retire and be a consultant.

CHAPTER 8

Ready or not, I'm calling from my office phone, about eight thirty, John and Marie, Fred thought. He dialed the number.

"Hello, Fred," said Marie.

"You knew who was calling as well."

"My phone told me who was ringing my bell."

"I think I may have a solution for your mom's question. Can we meet tomorrow and go over what I came up with to show you?"

"Of course. I have to ask John if he will be around tomorrow. Let me find him. I'll be right back. Hold on while I find him." Just a few quick minutes later, Marie was back on the line. "How about nine thirty in the morning? John has an appointment with a client at eleven o'clock. Will that work for you?"

"That is so long from now. I'll go through some withdrawals, but with the right psychologist and years of sessions, that will be perfect. See you tomorrow." With that, he ended the call.

"You have another appointment with John and Marie?"

"I'm going to show them the waterfall and stream feature, two bridges, seating area, footpath, floral garden, and your buff gardener. I'll let Marie know the buff gardener was your idea."

"How about an early dinner? Your crow is just about thawed out."

"You know, I could search the rest of my life and never find another lady that could replace you. You're so kind."

"I'd better get that crow plucked and ready for the pot. Almost time for your dinner."

"I had better start lining up the trucking equipment, Port-O-Let, and crew to get the soil removal started." I was anxious to see if there was something else buried under the soil. I hadn't found any toys or marbles yet; there was always tomorrow. *Make some phone calls. Make sure dig alert has marked everything. Definitely don't want to hit any buried utilities. That would be a costly mistake. Trucks are ready, loader and excavator is ready, the potty is lined up, crew and operator are also ready. I hope everything goes smoothly.*

My operators would have to work hand in hand to get the soil removed as quickly as possible. I would have two ground laborers so one could hold the rod while I checked the grade; the other could keep the excavator directed and make sure the operator didn't hit the shed, tunnel, or house. One false move, and there went the Christmas bonus. I'd take the revised rear yard drawings with me tomorrow while I was meeting with John and Marie. The crew could start removing the existing fence and cutting some grade so loading the trucks would be easier. *I hope everything goes as planned. I'll pray real hard tonight.*

The next morning, I had my briefcase plans, sack lunch, boots, shirt, pants, belt, hat, and vest. *What else do I need? Pen and pencil, writing tablet, camera just in case—that should be everything, except one of the most important things.* "Honey, are you in the kitchen?"

"Yes, I'm making breakfast for the kids. Why?"

"Just thought I'd give you a nice good-bye kiss. I wouldn't be so lucky. Kiss and another kiss for good luck."

"Are you finished? I don't want to burn their breakfast. You know how picky they can be."

"I know, dear. Have a great day."

"You too."

The truck was all warmed up and ready to start work. *Nice, the equipment is on site and ready to go. Operators and crew are here as well.* This was a first; usually one or the other was on time, not both. I hoped this wasn't a bad omen. I didn't think about that bringing bad luck.

"Good morning, gentlemen. Are you ready for some earthmoving and shaking today? Let's go over a quick game plan. The fence has to come down so we have access to the side yard. We need to stockpile the fence to the side, out of the way. I'll get the trailer after I meet with the owners. I will need one helper to shoot grade once we get close to subgrade. Watch for utility flags if we have any. We must dig a pothole to find the utility and protect it from damage, or no Christmas bonuses. Do you guys have any questions? Great, let's have a great day. And of course, work safe. Make sure all those working on ground wear vests and, if you have them, hard hats. Guys on the ground, make sure you are always in the view of the operators. You're very hard for them to spot. They're concentrating on their work. I'm going to meet with the owners of the house. If you need me, just ring the bell."

I walked up and pressed the doorbell. "Good morning, John. I hope we didn't wake you. We're treasure hunting this morning. They will remove the fence and start cutting down the grade, waiting for the three dump trucks scheduled to arrive in about an hour. We all hope everything is on schedule and all goes as planned. So how is your morning coming along?"

"Really well. We were so happy to see your crew and the equipment arrive. Goose bumps started when we heard the tractors being parked in front of the house."

"You'll hear them most of the day, barring any unusual discoveries that impede their progress. Let me show you what can happen in the rear yard to counterbalance the side yard courtyard. Let me first tell you how I got this vision.

"I was following my beautiful wife up your new staircase, heading into your backyard. She was standing on the new sidewalk as I approached her location. She was standing, still looking ahead, but was stopped. 'Is there something wrong, dear?' I asked.

"'No. You should see this. It's amazing.' I got around her and saw what she was looking at. There were two bridges set at an angle, a walkway heading to a patio, and I heard the sound of rushing water. 'Let's see what is over there.'

"We stayed on the sidewalk and passed the first bridge and then came to the second bridge, and there against the fence was a waterfall. 'Look, dear—a bench. Let's cross over the bridge and sit on the bench.'

"'That would be nice. And we'll watch the waterfall.' As we crossed over the bridge, there was a beautiful floral garden in full bloom—breathtaking. While we were admiring the floral show, we heard you two calling us for some tea. I went across the bridge and retrieved the tea to take to my lovely wife. While I approached, Marie handed me a cup and said she would take a cup to my wife so you and I could talk about the next little project."

John said, "This is how you visualized the rear yard? I have to see that drawing. That just might be the best way to connect the two projects."

Marie said, "Was I wearing my gown?"

"Hold on, I have to readjust my vision." I placed my right hand against my right temple and made a twisting motion. "Why, yes, you were wearing your lovely gown, and my wife also was in her best party dress. My oversight."

John said, "If all this becomes reality, I'm checking into the psychiatric ward."

Marie said, "John, we're just having fun with words and visions. You can see how this all looks after what he told us last week."

"Yes, I was following him until the teacup episode. Can we see the drawings to get a true visual?"

"Absolutely. Here is the waterfall. As you can see, it is not really high. The intent is to soften the noise to make the guest search for the soothing sound of rushing water. The water flowing over the various rocks in the stream will also add to the soothing effect. The end of the stream will have the water vanish. It will fall into a vault buried beneath the streambed, where a pump will return it to the waterfall to be recycled back to the stream and zero-elevation vault. This will be a constant run all day long. If you are to shut down the system, the vault is large enough to hold all the stream water along with the two-inch tubing connecting the vault to the waterfall. There will also be a basin at the base of the waterfall that will hold enough water to fill the stream while the water in the vault and piping fills the waterfall."

"What is the wood the bridges are made of?" asked John.

"It would be clear pine or cedar. We could go to teak, but I don't believe you want a multi-thousand-dollar bridge."

"What about that recycled wood that's on the market, very little maintenance required?"

"That would be on the deck if you chose. I'd recommend using redwood or cedar for the handrails, and they would require a resurfacing and sealing every other year. The stream and waterfall basin will be lined, and an underlayment and sealed joints will be water-tested for leaks before all the stone and sand are placed. I recommend at least a couple of hours of operation to check for leaks and adjust the amount of water and the flow. It will all be engineered to fit the field conditions."

"How will the bridges be installed?"

"If you take your hands, flat fingers pointed away from you, now turn your hands towards the center of your body at around a thirty-degree angle, that will give you the approximate angle of the bridges. I don't want right angles, since people rarely walk at a right angle unless forced to do so. I want it to be relaxing and natural, not forced. The proper low-voltage lighting will allow you to walk the path and along the stream no matter what time of day or evening. The bridges will also have an electrical outlet so you can put out holiday lights or add ambiance during parties or family get-togethers. No extension cords, batteries, or solar power to deal with, unless you choose to use them. You can also plug in a sound system to add further ambiance."

"You've done it again. I brought you a concern, and you returned with a viable, solid answer. Her mother will be impressed."

Marie said, "She might be so impressed that she'll move into our guest bedroom." The look on John's face was priceless.

"I feel your pain, John."

As we were just about ready to wrap up our meeting, my foreman ran from the side yard to meet up with us. "We have found something that you need to look at. Our worst nightmare may have just started." We all followed the foreman, and I warned both John and Marie to keep an eye on the equipment and stand clear of its operation. We turned the corner just behind Juan. The excavator was stopped, and his bucket was on the ground. They were safe to pass. The loader also had his bucket on the ground; they were safe with him as well.

"Okay, Juan, what did we hit, or what did you find?"

"Right here, we hit something solid. The last time we hit something solid, it was a buried shed. Can we get a shovel and maybe a pick from the truck?"

"Yes, they are almost here."

"Come on, guys; we need the tools," Juan said. He took the shovel and cleared some of the top for viewing. It was about three feet long so far, and about two feet wide.

"I wonder what it could be," said Marie.

John said, "Too small to be a coffin." No one laughed aloud.

It appeared to be a trunk. Juan exposed the entire top and was now digging around the sides to free it from its earthen pit. He was about halfway in depth when Marie asked us, "Can we open it?"

"Not yet. Let's get it freed and out of the way. The trucks are due to return any time for the third haul." It was soon free from all sides, and the two laborers came and put it on the mound of soil the loader had not taken. "Is it heavy, Juan?"

"Not too heavy, but not light either."

"Can the crew load it in a wheelbarrow and take it out of the way to the rear patio so we can continue to remove the soil?"

"I'll have them haul it to the back right now."

"Well, you mentioned when you walked in this morning that you were getting ready to dig for treasure. Here it is. Your treasure hunt is over, maybe." The chest was loaded into a wheelbarrow, and one of the laborers wheeled it to the patio; I could see him straining while wheeling, so it was not a light chest. There was definitely something inside.

Upon further examination, and once we used a cleaning brush to get rid of the excess soil stuck to the chest, we found some scrollwork engraved on the framework. It wasn't a cheap, run-of-the-mill trunk; nor was it a strongbox, so we were pretty certain someone hadn't robbed a stagecoach. There was a hasp with a keyhole, and the trunk was locked, or at least rusted shut. "Here's the million-dollar question. Do you want to save the chest and try to find a key that will fit the lock? Do we just break the hasp and damage the chest to find out what's inside? Do we call the police again and have them surgically open the lock and hasp? What to do? What to do?"

John opted to notify the police and have the case handler review what we unearthed, keeping the chest on site. "Have them open it here. It could be where the farmer buried his extra money, and they could just tell us it was old clothes and they threw them away." John was a great thinker. I would have just busted the hasp and open it up. A good cold chisel and a small sledgehammer would do the trick.

Marie went inside, got the detective's phone number, and called. They arrived in about ten minutes, and I continued brushing the chest to see if there was a name or some other identifiable marks on it. Two detectives arrived to look at the chest. One detective said, "We need to take this to the lab."

"We would rather the lab open the chest here first."

"Why?" asked the detective.

"Why do you want to take it to the lab?" asked John.

"To do forensic testing."

"Can't they do the testing right here?"

"I suppose they could. I'll call them."

Juan came to the patio with another discovery, this time smaller, and the crew was digging it out of the ground. *Two treasures in one day—this is not going as we planned.* The second find was a tin about twelve inches round, four inches thick, with a removable lid. "Let's just put it with the chest and wait for the forensic lab do their job."

John said, "The neighbors will think I did something to Marie this time. There will only be another unmarked vehicle, no lights or sirens required. They will all be busy watching their soap operas."

The forensics team arrived with a couple of cases to unlock the chest. The excavation came to a halt again. Juan came to us and said it was break time and the last load for the trucks today. Juan asked, "What did we find?"

"We don't know yet. The team just arrived and are preparing to unlock the chest."

After looking at the lock, one member said, "I'll bet it's a skeleton key—nothing fancy, an ordinary key." They had one in their box, and sure enough, they squirted something that looked like WD-40 into the lock and inserted the key. And yep, the lock opened. One of the forensic team started dusting the top and handles for fingerprints. They asked Juan to gather up the laborers and anyone who had touched the chest so they could have their fingerprints and handprints. They had the other team member set up a fingerprint and handprint station on the patio table. They took all prints except those of the operators who had never left their machines. They even took mine and John's, since we had both touched the chest.

They also dusted the metal tin. They found a couple of prints that were not the crew's or ours. Now drumroll, please. They started to open the chest; they first sprayed lubricant on its hinges. With latex gloves on, one member slowly started lifting the lid —very slowly in case he saw a wire that could trigger an explosive device. Boy, that would not make a happy ending to an already unplanned day. He used a steel rod with his free hand and slowly ran it from side to side to feel for any drag on the rod. "All clear, sir."

"Open it up another inch and feel it again."

"Nothing, sir."

"Another inch, try it again."

"Nothing, sir."

"Another inch."

He rodded it again.

Juan crouched down to see if he could see something inside. That did not impress the forensic team whatsoever. They both stopped and said, "Young man, please leave the area—now. If any of you want to try what he just did, you can leave now as well. We're making sure that this chest and tin are not booby-trapped. If we are interrupted and miss, we will be sitting around in heaven, talking about how stupid we were.

"If it had been booby-trapped and you busted the chest open, we would be called out to pick up your pieces. People do not think about what could happen. They think there's money or jewels or something very valuable in the chest. Don't think that people bury wealth. There are some very sick people running around. Remember that. Now where were we?"

"About three inches above close, sir?"

"Proceed up another inch and rod, please."

"Nothing, sir."

"Up another inch and rod, please."

"Still nothing, sir."

"One more inch and rod, please."

"Wait, sir, I think I feel a slight drag."

"Hold it in position. I'll shine my flashlight inside to see if there is a wire." The lid was held in position, and the other member shone his light in the chest. "Okay, will all of you please get inside the house? Detective, please call up the bomb squad. There is a small wire or string. We need their expertise."

They put a wedge between the lid and the box to hold it in place. "Sometimes you get to a certain point where, if you lower the lid, it will ignite the fuse, and boom. There are two-way switches used, and we don't know how long this chest was buried." The forensic officer explained that to us while we were shaking in our boots. He told us, "When the bomb squad gets here, you have to go to the front side of the house, and your crew will have to return to their parked trucks until an all-clear is given by the bomb squad."

Marie told John she was going to her mom's. This was too much for her to handle. The detective said he could drive her since she was so shaken. "Could you please? She lives just a few miles from here."

"Gladly, ma'am. Give me a couple of minutes, and we'll leave."

The bomb squad arrived along with three other squad cars to be used for crowd control, and they, of course, blocked off the entry into the cul-de-sac. This got all the Oprah fans now coming out of their houses. They saw Marie getting into the detective's car, and one neighbor said, "We knew it was her all the time. Why don't they have her cuffed?"

The detective was going to let her have it, but he had been down that road before and knew he would get an earful from the captain. "Don't light the fire. You're there to put out the fire," the captain always said.

The bomb squad looked at what was found and got a camera from their vehicle attached to a computer screen; they looked at the so-called wire, determined that it might just be a thread, turned the camera to examine the lid, found no wear where the string or wire was attached to the lid, and looked again at the contents.

They were talking among themselves and called over their superior. He looked at the computer screen, still being very cautious, knowing that one of the great-grandkids had dismembered their great-grandmother. Anything was possible.

They moved the lid ever so slightly and noticed that the string or wire did not move, so it might not be an activating device or trigger to an explosive. They scanned the chest again and brought in an X-ray machine; it also was attached to a computer monitor, and upon scanning the chest, it appeared to contain more bones, possibly human but maybe not. It appeared the bones were wrapped in something, but nothing else was in the chest. They opened the lid with the forensic team, and there it was, nicely wrapped in a blanket—the pet dog. They had buried their dog in a chest.

But wait, remember the metal tin? That was next. We were not out of the woods yet. The team scanned the tin with the X-ray machine; there appeared to be something inside, wrapped as well, but much smaller in size. Looking very carefully about the tin, very cautiously looking for anything out of the ordinary, and seeing nothing unusual, they used a tool to slide the lid less than an eighth of an inch and reexamined the outside for anything. Up another eighth of an inch, and they scanned the container again. Another eighth of an inch, and they scanned it again—still nothing unusual.

Now the lid was about halfway off the container; they ran another specialized tool around the edge of the lid and watched the computer screen, with the image magnified for easier viewing all the way around. It looked normal. Up another eighth of an inch, they did a reexamination, still clear. Another eighth of an inch, and after a reexamination, it was all clear. They removed the lid just to free it from the body. "Hold the camera steady to see if anything is attached to the lid." All eyes were on the screen—all clear. Nothing was attached to the lid. Taking the lid away from the body of the tin, they saw a handkerchief folded neatly around something. They did an X-ray scan.

"It appears to be a small animal skeleton, sir."

"Unfold the handkerchief slowly."

"Yes sir. Maybe a hamster or a guinea pig—some kind of pet, sir."

The detective called everyone out to examine the contents found. "The family pets were buried in the containers. How much more digging are you going to do here?"

"I'll show you the boundaries of the excavation." I took the detective to the excavation site. "We are removing the soil to utilize the area as a courtyard around the existing shed."

"How far over toward the fence lines are you going?"

"Roughly around five feet. We will stop before the fence."

"I see from your markings on the soil. No digging tomorrow. We are going to scan the entire excavation area for more buried containers. Even though those two were harmless, there could be more, possibly some that are dangerous.

Your operator will be required to unearth to just above the container, and our team will examine the container. There will be the forensic team, and the bomb squad will also be dispatched to the job site until all excavation is completed. You understand this could have been disastrous not just for you and your crew. The family that lives here and the entire cul-de-sac could be up in smoke. Under normal conditions, we would not be too excited. This is not a normal condition. We still have an open case of a horrific murder, and the killer or killers could still be at large.

"We will be here at eight in the morning. We will still block off the street to traffic and use officers to handle crowd control. This is all for public safety. You only need one operator. We will hand-shovel the soil ourselves. See you tomorrow, and let your crew know that, maybe in the afternoon or late morning, they can continue their work."

"Yes sir, I will let them know right now." I talked with the crew and told them the game plan for tomorrow. "If they want to hang out at the office until we call in the all-clear or just wait until the next day, that is understandable."

I talked with the operator and told him, "You will be very safe. They have testing equipment that will show them the size and how deep in the soil the item is located. You won't dig if they don't find anything."

The next morning, we met the forensic team and bomb squad at the house. We had to wait until the detectives in charge showed and the squad cars came to block the cul-de-sac. They arrived a few minutes after we were moving the excavator toward the excavation site.

John came outside to meet us. We talked for a few minutes, and he told us he was on his way to pick up Marie; they were to return home in the afternoon. He asked me to give him a call if we found anything so they could find a hotel to stay in for the evening. "I sure will call you. I'll keep you posted all day about what we uncover, if anything at all." As John pulled away, the detectives flagged him down and talked to him; when finished, John waved good-bye to us out of the driver's window.

The bomb squad brought out a device similar to a metal detector but much more sophisticated than anything one could purchase over the counter. Two men were sweeping the area with their machine; another man was sitting in the van, watching the computer screen. The forensic team was just standing by their vehicles, drinking their coffee. After a few minutes, one of the men sweeping stopped and went a few feet in one direction and a few feet in another. The man in the van said, "It looks like another chest."

They motioned for the excavator to head to where they were standing. One of the sweeping men marked the area to dig with orange marking paint. My operator locked his brakes, swung the bucket, and placed it on the mark. The man sweeping told him, "It's about two feet below the surface." Very slowly, the excavator removed about eighteen inches of soil in one bucket sweep; he kept his bucket full of soil off to the side of the hole so the laborers could dig down to the object.

The man sweeping rechecked the excavation and said, "Yes, about four inches below was the object." The laborers found the chest, which looked very similar to the other one; it took the laborers a few minutes to unearth it. They were very careful and made sure there were no wires or any other devices around the chest before they lifted it from the excavation. They brought a Kawasaki MULE with a pickup bed and drove the chest to the rear yard.

The sweepers continued searching more of the area. Not much later, the other sweeper stopped and swept an area. The man in the van told him to go over a foot in one direction. "Sweep there. That's it. Now mark the area; it's a little smaller than the last area."

"How deep?" asked my operator.

"About the same, maybe a few inches less."

My operator dug down on their mark and excavated about a foot in depth. They checked the excavation. "A little more to your left, same depth."

"Okay." My operator took a half-bucket width to the left away, same depth.

They rechecked the excavation, and the man in the van said, "That should be right on top of the object." Their laborers started removing some soil and felt the object. They were very careful with this hole, unlike the last one. They hit the object, stopped digging with shovels, and removed some soil with their hands. They found what looked like an old lard can or paint can. The lid was held down with metal clips; it was a five-gallon container. They were very careful and had my operator dig to the right of the can, about twelve inches deeper. They wanted a trench to free the can, and that helped them. They thought this might be a problem.

They called the forensics team to dust it for fingerprints and get the X-ray machine to scan the can. There was something different about this can that made us all nervous, the bomb squad was being awfully cautious. They freed the sides of the can and waited for the X-ray machine hooked to the computer to see just what might be inside. They were looking for any type of wire or string or pin— anything that may cause a trigger for the explosive mechanism. The man in the van asked, "Do you want the robot?"

"We don't know yet." They knew that something was very different about this container from the others. They decided to bring in the robot to lift the container from the hole. They could not check it for a triggering device. They asked the operator to dig a trench three feet wide next to the hole he had just dug so the robot could sit in the hole, grab the can, and move to the back edge. If it didn't explode, the triggering device could indeed be attached to the lid. The operator did as they directed, and they instructed him and the machine to move back to the front yard and follow the other officer's direction to get to safety. He did as he was told. There came another vehicle towing another machine. The robot would now place the container on the soil outside the hole it was sitting in, and the other machine would be used to encase the container and blow it up in a safe area.

Everything was done very slowly; everyone was safely out of the area. All the occupants of the nearby homes were moved to another area or were told to leave and advised they would be called when it was safe to return home. This was a nerve-racking process, and I was so glad I was a landscaper and not a bomb-removal person. I asked the detective, "What are the chances that there is an explosive device inside the can?"

"These are highly skilled people. When they sense something inside that could explode, this is what they do, nearly every day. They know that the killer here was a very sick person and that anything is possible. Sick minds do not care about the life and safety of others—or themselves, for that matter. We are just thankful you people called us. If anything on the property would have exploded, you, your crews, and the neighbors all could have been killed. The whole area could be flattened as a result of gas lines being ignited; the fires could be intense, and evacuation could be too late for many of the residences. Everything is done with extreme caution. Your foreman was lucky that the two objects they found did not have an explosive device attached."

After the other machine had the can and left the area, the bomb squad started searching the remainder of the excavation site. Their boss had our excavator and operator prepare to expose any more buried treasures. The two officers were moving in an organized manner, and within an hour, they had scanned the remaining area. "It appears that there are no more items buried. We're not saying the area is clear of any other dangers. Our equipment is limited to a certain depth. If you want to cut some of the grade down two feet, then we can search the next two- to three-foot depths."

"That would be great. Let me see if I can get my crew back here to work and get the trucking to return. Can your machine start in one area and just follow behind his digging?"

"It can do that, but your crew have to stay in the operator's sight range. Do you have any vests, either orange or yellow?"

"I believe we do. I'll ask and have the crew put them on for safety reasons."

I called Juan; he said the crew was at his house and could be at the job site in thirty minutes. I called the trucking company, and the three trucks could be at the job site in an hour. That was sure luck. I could not do that again. *Perfect. I will text John that the site at this time is clear of any more buried containers to three feet below the current grade elevation. We will remove that layer, and they will scan the next three-foot depth for buried treasures.*

John texted back, stating he and Marie had gone to a hotel for today and would spend the night there. "Could you keep us updated if anything is found?"

"I'll be happy to keep you informed."

By the time the crew showed up, the excavator had cleared nearly half the area to be excavated. Juan got the loader started and warmed up. He moved some of the excavated soil to a pile awaiting the trucks. The two laborers were busy shoveling soil that had fallen between the shed and the to-be-excavated area. I could now see from the shed roof to the bottoms of the windows; it looked like an island in the ocean.

The scanners did not find anything in the next layer where the excavator had been; once Juan removed the spoil, the excavator sat on the area that was graded and removed the layer where the spoils were placed. The trucks arrived, and Juan got busy loading them. The scanners were out of the way, and excavation was starting on the other half of the courtyard. Once an area was cleaned, the scanners returned from their coffee break and continued to scan the newly graded pad. The three trucks were loaded and gone, so Juan started moving the spoils so the excavator had more room to dump each bucket. The other half had been excavated and was now being scanned. If they got an all-clear, the excavator would do the same as before. With Juan running the loader, the operation would run much more smoothly. It appeared that this might be the last layer to remove, so this scan should give the site an all-clear.

The bomb squad were busy scanning the new layer provided to them from the excavator. Juan had moved all the spoils, and the excavator moved to start the final removal. The first pad was all clear—nothing detected. They took a quick break while our excavator removed the final layer. The trucks returned, and Juan got busy loading them; maybe one more round and the trucks would be finished. The term "round" suggested the haul from the job site to the disposal site and a return to the job site; when estimating work, we needed to know how long the round took. The trucks charged by the hour, and if there was a disposal fee also included in the trucking company's invoice, that could come as a real shocker if we figured only the trucking hours. A little short and I would need to open the company wallet and pay the difference. What profit?

CHAPTER 9

The bomb squad finished scanning the last pad; nothing was buried in that one either. They asked our operators to move all the equipment onto the scanned pads. They wanted to scan the front area to make sure there was nothing buried between the city sidewalk and close to where the fence divided the side yard and the front yard. They were concerned that this area was barely touched during the excavation. I mentioned to the detective that we were proposing putting in a stream feature in the rear yard. "Would you like to scan that area as well? I can mark the proposed excavation area for you to make it easier and less time-consuming."

"That would be great. Might save us on another callback."

I got the marking paint out of my toolbox and proceeded to lay out the stream feature. The front area was given an all-clear by the bomb squad, and they proceeded to the rear yard and started scanning the layout area. They said, "What about the rest of the backyard? Are you going to excavate any other areas?"

"Not back here. The stream feature would be the only excavation except for some new trees, but they are only three feet deep. Have you heard anything about the can that was unearthed and taken away?"

"Not yet. We need to open that chest in the wheelbarrow over on the patio before we pack up and leave."

"I almost forgot about the other chest. Maybe another pet dog?"

"We won't be able to answer that until we get it open, but we will use the same precautions as with the first one. We're just not convinced that whoever murdered the great-grandmother was of sane mind."

The scan of the stream feature was given the all-clear, and the bomb squad again reminded me that even though they had not detected another container, there could be something buried not using any type of metal. "Cardboard box, plastic bags or paper bags, blanket or bedding. So remain diligent in your digging. If you find anything, stop, move out of the area, and contact us to examine the article. We're going to examine the other chest, so if you would ask the forensic personnel to return to the backyard, I'd appreciate your effort."

I went out front and told the forensic personnel what the bomb squad had told me to tell them. They gathered up their gear and proceeded to the backyard. I talked to my operator and Juan about starting the footings for the retaining walls. "If you get your plans, we can get started."

I started to examine the shed. What would be needed to get that started? I noticed there was a soil line marking on the house wall above the elevation of the finished floor. I asked the laborer to get a bucket of water and a scrub brush from my truck and start removing the soil from the house. "In fact, get two brushes, and you two can get it done faster and do the same to the shed and tunnel. This way, I can get a good idea of what to save and what to demolish."

Juan returned with the plans, and we started to lay out the wall footings. I had the operator remove the larger bucket and put on the small bucket to dig the footings. The grade looked pretty good—not perfect, but close enough to get a good feeling about how the finished product would appear.

The bomb squad and forensic team entered the excavation site. They were going to take the chest off site; it was heavier than the last one. When they were opening the lid, it appeared to have a line attached to it. They had contacted the team to return with the machine to cart off the chest. They did say the metal can contained the remains of two pet cats; no explosives were in the can. "This again is only a precaution. If there is anything of value in the chest, we will contact the owner immediately. We will send you pictures of the whole operation. It all has to be documented for the files. This is still an open case because both of the great-grandchildren are dead. There may still be someone else involved."

As the footings were being excavated and the house and shed walls were being cleaned, I texted John with a current update. He and Marie were enjoying a Bloody Mary at the hotel bar when I texted. They were happy to hear that the yard was clear to continue the project. I told him that if they were going to be returning home tomorrow, I would fill in the blanks of everything that had happened while they were away.

The footing excavation was nearing completion. I contacted the rental company to pick up the equipment; getting it off rent would save both me and the homeowner. Within an hour, the rental company was there to pick up the machines. The area looked much bigger without the pieces of equipment parked on site. We would start putting in the rebar tomorrow and prepare for the footings to be poured.

The laborers exposed a small problem that I would have to talk with John and Marie about tomorrow. Juan and the operator got another bucket and two brushes from the truck to help clean the dirt off the shed. I didn't like the looks of the tunnel joining the house to the shed; it just didn't look too appealing. I'd have to rethink keeping the tunnel attached. I went to my truck and retrieved my binder, which contained a writing tablet and pencil, so I could quickly sketch another idea that just popped into my mind. All law enforcement personnel were off the job site for at least today.

CHAPTER 10

John and Marie returned the next afternoon. I had drawn a sketch of what I thought should be done to make the playhouse more attractive. The tunnel joining the house to the playhouse needed to be removed. "This will allow for more space for the soda fountain/bar, making more space for table and chairs. You won't have to move the table and chairs in and out every time you want to use the playhouse. You could also use a bigger table for playmates for the kids. You could also use it for the guys' poker table—no mess inside the house where the ladies gather while the boys lose their paychecks."

John and Marie listened to my spiel, looking a little puzzled at first until I mentioned the poker table. That got John's attention, and separating the ladies and gentlemen inspired Marie. She really wanted to go shopping for her gown; I could just tell. "The second floor would have more floor space as well. To be honest with you, the tunnel serves no purpose now, exposed. You're not planning on using it as a cold cellar since you have that marvelous double-door refrigerator–freezer combination in the kitchen. Marie, do you do any canning?"

"Nope, never have canned fruits or vegetables. Don't plan on starting now. What about the tunnel? Will we still keep the tunnel?"

"Yes, that way you can bring food from the kitchen to the courtyard without walking around the house. And if there is inclement weather, you won't have to carry an umbrella along with the food for grilling."

"Great idea. You think of everything, making our job much easier."

"Well, that's from my own outdoor cooking experience. Either something gets dropped or the rain washes off the rub you just spent time putting on the meat. Water in the potato salad is always a treat. There will be an opening between the patio cover and playhouse second-floor patio, so you might get a couple of drops, depending on how hard it's raining. You want to take a stroll in your courtyard?"

"Love to. We saw some piled dirt and wondered what that was."

"That is the spoil from the footings for your retaining seat walls."

"You dug those yesterday?"

"Yes, I had the equipment and the manpower, so I thought, 'Let's get this party started.'"

"You put a few radii in the walls?"

"I don't like the looks of a straight wall running parallel to a property line fence. As the sun moves from east to west, you will get shadowing during the day, giving a totally different look to your courtyard. You'll be amazed as you sit outside, looking at the courtyard. Picture yourselves sitting outside on the patio at the table, snacks in the center of the table—maybe a couple of friends there as well. And you're admiring the staircase, and your guests notice a hummingbird visiting one of your daylilies, which are in full bloom. As you see the hummingbird, you also notice a shadow on the retaining wall from the overhang of the cap onto the rock-faced wall. You have a lizard sitting on the wall cap doing push-ups, and everyone is in awe of nature working its charm."

"We have lizards?"

"Yes, they keep the insect population in control. Nature has its own checks and balances. There is soft, smooth jazz being played by your stereo system, which is controlled by your remote control on the table. The ceiling fans are set low just to keep the warm air circulating."

"Can we have this for tomorrow? I'm feeling a little stressed right now, and that would just make me feel like a million," said Marie.

"So once this is completed, do you two feel you'll use the courtyard a few times per week or just once in a while?"

"You know, we are mostly indoor people, but you're going to make us outdoorsmen. I'm thinking that coming home from work or a business trip, seeing my beautiful wife, sitting at the table with a cocktail, watching nature create a postcard atmosphere—nothing would be more relaxing no matter what my day was like. Of course, Marie would have dinner cooking and the candlelit dining room table all set and ready for serving. Right, dear?"

"Shh, I'm watching the hummingbird bouncing from flower to flower. What was that, dear?"

"You were going to pamper me when you get home from work."

"Why, of course, my love."

We moved along the rear yard excavation and footing and came to where the staircase would be built. John said, "I can see her now, step-by-step, heading down the staircase. Wow, so stunning and glamorous, so twinkling in the sunlight."

"John, you're going to get her all excited."

"No, he won't. I was already excited before he gave that marvelous speech."

"We have one issue we must address. Once we removed the excess soil, it exposed the house wall that had dirt piled against it. You can see the soil line, which may have to be sandblasted to remove it. You see how the builder didn't finish putting the rock fascia to the finished surface? The line is not straight and is exposing the concrete foundation. You have two options. The first option would to finish the rock fascia to the finished elevation of the new deck. Second option, build a raised planter to the bottom of the stone, waterproof and install a drain in the planter, and continue the floral bouquet against the house. Option two will, of course, soften the look between the house and the deck, giving you another seating area. Less deck space is the only drawback. I would suggest putting a ceramic pot, twenty-four-inch diameter, by the staircase entry to hide the transition of the staircase and house wall."

"What would you put in the pot?"

"I would suggest a *Cupressus sempervirens* "Tiny Tower," with ivy geranium cascading down the pot, using it for a peekaboo effect. The colors would accent Marie's gown for the perfect poster photo."

"It wouldn't take away from my entrance, would it?"

"Of course not. No one would even notice the pot. So toss it around and let me know what you would like to see for this area. I'll draw it both ways to give you a paper visual."

As we moved to the playhouse, my crew was busy scrubbing the boards to remove the soil marks. There were still some more to complete, and these too might need to be sandblasted to give us the appearance we needed. "The playhouse will need a special painter to make it all come together. I'm seeing a rustic look in lieu of something from a high-society, glitz-and-glamor look. That is all up to your likes and dislikes. Take some time to browse through magazines or online or drive around, looking at various neighbors' wood structures. Home shows can also give you some ideas. Always take photos with your phones so we will know how it fits your lifestyle. This is homework for you both to do while we construct the retaining seat wall. The playhouse will now be more of a rectangle in shape, adding a little more interest and usable space."

"I think it will be a nice piece for the courtyard," said John. "Gives us different things to do outside. I don't think we would use the barbecue as much if the only things for us to do were eat and drink."

We moved to the footing for the entry wall. "This will be an unbelievable addition to the courtyard," mentioned Marie. "Will I be entering through the gate as well?"

"You know, I was just visualizing you coming through the high-gloss-finished double-sided redwood gate, coming back from the store for your guests after the inaugural party—maybe the next day, since a couple of guests stayed the night, hungover and all. You have a nice halter top on with stylish shorts and sandals, hair still styled perfectly, and top-of-the-line sunglasses. The gate opens slowly, and you enter, telling the male guests, 'Could you gentlemen retrieve the bags from my car?' They all get up and run, trying to be the first to bring you the treasures.

"You go to the table where their wives are sitting. You say to them, 'Silly boys.' You all laugh. John is at the barbecue, cooking racks of baby back ribs and three rib eye steaks, grilled to perfection. The aroma is phenomenal. Well, that concludes our tour. Glad you could join me. Please pick up a brochure from the gate attendant on your way to the interior of the John and Marie Estate. Please stay on the walkways, and feel free to photograph the exquisite landscape."

"How much for the tour?"

"Name your price. The lines are wrapping around the cul-de-sac, and it's only been open for an hour. Your neighbors are serving coffee and cookies, taking advantage of the waiting customers. Your city councilmen are handing out their next campaign literature, and two food trucks are sitting at the entry to the cul-de-sac and doing a booming business."

"What a vivid imagination," said John.

"This all could be a reality. You can have a book for them to purchase of all that has happened at this home."

"Good idea, gift shop on the patio in the backyard or in the playhouse."

"Now you're getting the idea, John. Spare no expense, this project could be in the black before the year's end."

The crew was busy putting in the steel for the footing, tying the vertical bars for the wall. Juan was bending the L for the vertical bars while the laborers were tying the vertical bars to the horizontal ones in the footing. We were also tying a one-by-four parallel to the footing. We were making cuts to allow for the radii. I contacted the ready-mix company for the footing concrete delivery the next day. "We'll pour over nine cubic yards just for the footings."

They wanted to know what time we would need the first truck.

"Hold a minute; let me talk to my foreman. Juan, will you be ready for pour at seven o'clock tomorrow? Make it eight so that if we have some final adjustments, we can make them without delaying the truck."

"Can we have it pumped?"

"Yes, I'll have them supply the concrete pump. Hello, are you still there?"

"Yes, I heard you want the first truck at eight. Is that correct?"

"Yes, eight, and can you provide the concrete pump as well? … Great, we will more than likely need a cleanup after the first nine yards. I will call you as soon as we see just how much more we will need."

Now it was time to call the block company for delivery. Then I'd call the brick company. *Oh, wait, I have to talk to John and Marie. We may go with a precast wall cap.*

I rang the bell, and Marie answered the door. "Sorry to bother you, Marie. I have a quick question for you and John."

"I didn't order my gown yet. Maybe today."

"No, not about the gown. Did you two decide if you wanted the brick cap or the precast wall cap?"

"John, can you come here? They found another dead body!"

"What? Another dead body?"

"Boy, that got his attention. I hope he didn't hurt himself with that quick burst of speed."

Marie laughed. "Dear, do you want the brick wall cap or the precast concrete wall cap?"

"You know, I'm such an idiot. I haven't looked at the two brochures yet. Can I look at them side by side and tell you in a short while?"

"Well, I get paid by the hour, you know. Yes, that will be fine. Take your time."

Marie said, "Yeah, John, time *is* his money."

I'm glad that they are enduring this project with such lightheartedness. Feels good inside. I hope they are as joyful when they see the first bill.

The block company would deliver before noon tomorrow—perfect timing. I needed to go see my lovely bride just as soon as John let me know which wall cap he wanted. I was hoping for the brick, but either would make the walls look beautiful.

John came out about an hour later with the brochures in hand. "You know, I'm in a turmoil. They both have a unique look. I don't want to do something that I regret later. You know, this is not as easy as it looks. I don't know how you can put all these items together. Do the precast wall caps come in various colors?"

"Yes, I gave you a color chart, remember?"

"Oh brother, I have to go back and get the file folder. Right back." After a moment, John was back. "How do I know which color would work the best?"

"Let's take it over to the house and see which color offers the best contrast against the stone, since the walls will be stone-faced to match the house stone so everything blends together."

"Good idea. That was a pretty easy way not to make a horrible mistake. It appears the cream color or off-white would work."

"Be careful, John. White can stain if one of your guests knocks over a drink, or animal excretions can also discolor the cap."

"Would the beige color work?"

"Let's take the color chart and cut it into strips so it's easier to lay against the stone. I'll just cut the strips using the board for a cutting board." We made four different strips. "You can now fold each color and hold it against the stone. The stone looks grayish, but it may not be as gray as our eyes tell us."

"I'll get Marie so she can't tell me later that she wouldn't have picked that color. You know, better safe than sorry."

"Good idea. The more eyes, the better."

"What color will your gown be? We're afraid of clashing a wall cap color, so we need your assistance in selecting the perfect color."

"Men, you're all alike—can't make a decision. Don't know where to eat, what movie to see, now what color to choose. Let me see the colors. Not purple; definitely not pink or red. Here, John, put these in your pocket. See how easy this is, boys? Process of elimination. Those dark colors won't do either—they show the dirt. Hmm, five more colors that would work, but there has to be the perfect color, not the settle-for color. Here, this one will work just fine. No matter what color my gown color is, it won't distract from my grand entrance."

"The cream color, dear—are you sure? It might stain if someone knocks over a drink or animal excretions get on it."

"I'm not worried about that, John. I have you to scrub off any messes. Anything else I can help you two with? I have chores to do in the house. I don't have a maid, you know."

John said, "I've looked long and hard for that woman. Cream is the color. I think the brick cap might be too busy. The entry wall is brick. Is that correct?"

"Yes, brick faced and a brick cap due to the sweeps from pilaster to pilaster. Well, it's nearly lunch, and my little darling will be glad to see me."

"Hi, honey, I'm home!" No answer. *Is she not here? I'll check the garage for her car. Nope, no car.* "Well, hello, peanut butter and jelly on wheat bread, good old standby." I got a glass of iced tea to wash it all down. Nothing was better than a three-minute prep for lunch and five minutes to devour the culinary delight. *If I take a whole hour, I still have fifty minutes for lunch. This will be perfect. Making room for dinner makes lots of sense. She'll be pleased to see me enjoying my meal.*

I need to call the brick company for the precast wall cap and the rock to face the walls. Where's that quote? Oh, I remember. I put it in my briefcase to call them from the job site. I'll call them when I return to the job site. They will want an exact measurement for the radii.

What other trouble can I get into? Let's see if I got any email this fine day. So many people trying to get my business. I only use tried-and-true products. Cheap knockoffs are exactly that— cheap in cost and quality. I have a reputation. They need to get one. You want a cheap product? Call my competitors. Fair product for a fair competitive price—no gouging from this guy.

Maybe the mail came. Where's that mailbox key? Why, there it is. She's going to be so happy that I took time to fetch the mail. Saves her a few steps from her busy day. Now, which box is ours? Why do I always forget the box number? Maybe I should start getting the mail every day. Then I would do it automatically, no guesswork. I remember now—third box, third row. Yep. Key in the lock, and—bingo—door opens. Nothing. Are you kidding me? Nothing. I walked all this way for nothing—absolutely nothing.

Wait, my beloved is pulling around the corner. Maybe she will give me a ride back to the house. I'll just stick out my thumb. Well, that worked just perfectly. She was looking away to her left, ignoring me. Yep, she was purposely ignoring me. Garage door opening. She is pulling into the garage, and the garage door is closing. I'll just have to sneak in the house and surprise her.

"Hi, honey, I'm home!"

"Why were you sticking out your thumb?"

"You saw me?"

"Of course I saw you."

"You were looking to your left. I thought you didn't see me."

"I didn't see any good reason to give you a ride. I walk to the mailbox every day. You could use some exercise."

"Touché. I thought we could do some smooching when the garage door closed."

"Yeah, like I have time for such foolishness at this time of the day. Why are you home anyway? Is the job finished?"

"No, dear, pouring the footings for the walls tomorrow. Really just starting."

"You should leave and get back to the crew."

"I still have thirty minutes for you to entertain me."

"Well, don't most of your entertainers want dollars?"

"That was many years ago, and none of them come close to you, my dear."

"I got the mail, and it's on your drawing board."

"Yeah, I was surprised we had no mail in the box."

"Now you know why I beat you to the punch."

"Well, I have to leave and get back to the crew, like you suggested. Have a great day, my dear."

"Can you pick up a pizza on your way home? I don't feel like cooking today."

"I was dreaming about a three-course dinner, candlelight, champagne—the whole nine yards."

"Dream on. The kids like pepperoni pizza."

"Would you like some as well?"

"You keep that up and you'll need some dental work."

"Love you. See you later with the pizza."

CHAPTER 11

I got back to the job site just in time, as there was a little problem.

"We ran out of rebar. Could you get us three more sticks to finish?"

"I thought I measured correctly and gave you a couple of extra pieces. Okay, I'll be right back. Everything else doing good?"

"Yes, just like you planned. Just a little short; that's all. Happens to the best of us," said Juan.

"While I'm picking up the rebar, I'll talk with Randy, to get the wall cap and stone fascia on order ready for shipment."

Just then, my phone rang. "Hello, this is Fred. Who's calling? ... Oh hi Randy, I'm on my way to pick up some rebar. I should be there in about five minutes."

"Good afternoon, gentlemen, I need three sticks of number-four rebar, and I need to order the wall caps and stone fascia per your quote number 1536."

"What color for the wall cap?"

"The customer wants cream, and I'll need the matching color for the grout. Can I have it tomorrow?"

"Fat chance for that to happen. The wall cap is at least two weeks."

"How much stone?"

"Let's look at your quote and compare it to our stock on hand ... You'll be about two tons short. I'll put that order in today, and they have a one-week lead time."

"It is what it is. If there are any delays, please let me know. Your competitor down the street might have some in stock, lifetime warranty just like always and no restock charge in case my calculator made a mistake."

"Whatever you're smoking, you'd better ease up. It's affecting your judgment. We charge for restock on everything. That's our profit."

"Add ten bags of thin-set to that order as well. See you real soon."

Back at the job site, Juan took the rebar off the rack and started cutting and bending the Ls. "We'll be okay for tomorrows pour time?"

"We should be perfect for the pour time. I have everything ordered for the walls. The owners need to go with me to pick up the brick to face the entry wall. When you install the pilaster blocks for the gate entry, make sure you allow enough room for the brick fascia. Remember: we made that mistake on the last job and had to tear down and rebuild the pilasters. Don't want to do that again, or we didn't learn our lesson. You do have four pieces of rebar for each pilaster vertical, correct? You also tied a temporary ring around the bars to make sure they fit inside the core of the block. We missed that as well last time."

"I'll take a peek at what is completed, and if I see something else, I'll call your attention so we can make the adjustments."

"Everything looks good, and the on-center spacing is perfect. Do you have a block from another project that we can double-check to make sure each bar is in the cell?"

"Yeah, I'll have the laborer go get it out of the truck and bring it to you."

Juan called the laborer and told him to bring the block, all in Spanish. I had the laborer lift the block over the rebar, being very careful not to hit the rebar with his arm or hand. It can rip one's skin down to the bone.

"It all works very well. Excellent job, guys."

Pour days were always stressful for me; the what-ifs were numerous. What if this? What if that? Not until the truck and pumper pulled away and the pour was completed could I relax some—not much, just some. The ready-mix was right on time, and the pump was about fifteen minutes ahead of schedule. So far, so good. The crew had the tools, and we double-checked, making sure no critters disturbed our work. We were ready.

The pump operator talked with Juan in Spanish about how Juan wanted the pour to be done. "Equally informed people seldom disagree" was our motto. Everyone was ready to get the pour started. The mixer started offloading into the pump, and away we went. The mix was a little too dry for Juan, and he asked the pump operator if he could add just a little more water. The pump signaled the ready-mix operator that he had added a half a sump of water to the mix. The concrete was mixed and sent down the chute and into the pump. *Let the good times roll.* Juan signaled the operator that the mix was much better and working; the concrete was not as stiff.

When pouring with multiple trucks, you don't want the crew to kill themselves with the first load. They were absolutely wiped out before the next truck arrived. The pour was going great.

John and Marie came out with their cameras and posed. *Snap, snap, snap!* They took photos for an album they were making for the party and future reference. Both were in work clothes, and I asked if they would like to help with the pour. I asked Juan to give them an extra trowel and have them pose for a photo, looking as if they were the ones who did the footings. I had John put his finger in the wet concrete and put a couple of lines on Marie's cheeks. She was a little bit hesitant, and then I had her do it to John. They both got on their knees with trowels in hand, and Juan snapped a couple of photos of them looking as though they were putting the final finish on the footings. Those two photos were blown up to poster size for the party.

I later had them kneel down in the dirt and scoot around a little and then had them stand with arms around each other. *Snap, snap!* Those photos were made into posters as well and placed in the house entry; they had concrete on their cheeks and dirt on their knees, and Marie by accident had gotten dirt on her shirt. I told them, "Tonight go the shoe store and buy some work boots, and we will make some fantastic shots for the party."

I told Marie that a tool belt around her gown would top off her entrance. She said she would do it if I wore a maid's outfit like the Halloween costume type, including fishnet nylons and high heels. She won. No way on God's green earth would I ever do something foolish like that. I didn't need that much publicity; that would go viral. No thank you. John said, "The two of you dressed like that—I would pay lots of money even for a wallet-size photo." As if Marie needed any more encouragement; she would probably go out and buy my outfit tomorrow and hang it outside for the whole neighborhood to get a peek.

The first truck was completed, and I had called for three yards for the second truck, which arrived just minutes after the last truck left the job site. "No rest for the wicked," I told the crew. The footings were all poured just in time for the concrete blocks to arrive. The driver offloaded them by forklift, which the crew applauded with great enthusiasm. I was surprised they had the strength to applaud.

After their lunch break, Juan and the crew started setting the block along the trench to start the first course. The footing was setting up and able to support the first course's weight. By quitting time, the first course was in and setting up. The walls were looking great, and I got John and Marie outside to examine the work that they were photographed doing. Just by chance, the sun was hitting the blocks just right, and they could now see what I had told them earlier about shadows. Even one course had shadows. Tomorrow we would build the low retaining walls and then start the freestanding entry wall.

Both were just awestruck, and Marie pretended to walk through the gate opening to the courtyard, posing as if she had a champagne glass in her hand. "Wait a minute." I ran to my truck to get her a Dixie cup for her to hold while she playacted an entrance. Good times were had by all.

I told them that in two days they could sit on the seat wall to see how it felt, reminding them that there would be four inches eaten up by the deck. I had some extra pavers from another job I would place on top of the footing so they could put their feet on the pavers and then sit down on the wall. I would bring a roll of paper we used to cover flooring when we were running wheelbarrows or just construction boots over the floor. I stood back and looked at different angles of the wall from the staircase, playhouse, entry gate—every possible angle that the owners would see when they used the courtyard. There was a nice flow to the way the walls were designed. This would make the cover of some magazine.

We arrived at seven o'clock and got the second and third courses up in a very short time; by lunchtime, the majority of the retaining seat wall was nearly finished, with maybe one more full course to go. I set the pavers on top of the footing and leveled out the soil so they fit like the finished floor. By quitting time, the blocks would be set and the homeowners could sit on top of the wall. I went over to the masonry yard and purchased a precast white wall cap and brought it back to the job site to place on top of the retaining seat wall. The crew put three blocks where the pavers were placed right after lunch so they could have a little longer to set up. Even if the blocks got jarred off the wall, it was an easy repair. The retaining seat wall got its last course, and they started the entry wall's second course. It was then time to pack up and go home.

I went and got John and Marie. They were watching the walls being built from the living room window. They had set two chairs up so they could sit and watch. The sun again was doing a fantastic job showing the kinds of shadows they would see daily. I also told them, "The low-voltage lighting system will also give you the same shadows when illuminated."

I put the precast wall cap on top of the wall for them to sit on to determine if the wall was a good height for them. Marie was the shortest of us all, so we had her sit down first. "John, this is perfect for me. My feet actually touch the pavers. I won't have to have my feet swinging like on some other walls I have sat on." Marie stood up, and John sat down.

"This is really nice. I can sit here while Marie weeds and mows the grass. Can I have a hose bib here so I can get her some water when she gets thirsty?"

"We can use the Dixie cup, or would you prefer the hose?"

"Oh, the hose would be my preference."

"Why the hose, Marie?"

"He wouldn't be able to run away from his outdoor bath."

"I will have the crew waterproof the back side of the wall and fill the cells with concrete tomorrow morning. I rent a cement mixer to speed up the process. By the next day, you two can sit on the wall anytime you wish. Don't sit on the freestanding wall until we fill the cells on that wall. Once we build up to a certain elevation, we will form the arch. Then you'll see how all this will appear."

"When will we have the front gate?"

"We need to finish the area where the gate will be hung and have the gate subcontractor come out to measure the opening and build the gate and frame. The gate opening will take some time to complete; it requires lots of cuts, and it has to be perfect. He told me when I got his quote that it will take about a week to build, and he said he would talk with you when he comes out to measure about what color and finish you would like. He has photos and samples of colors and finishes. He will also show you the gate hardware at the same time."

The crew started bright and early the next morning. They started on the entry wall; they were on the second course when I arrived. I had to stop and pick up waterproofing for the retaining wall. I also had to pick up the drainage pipe for behind the wall, and the gravel would be delivered by nine o'clock. I asked Juan to allow time after lunch to start laying out the staircase. "I will pick up some quarter-inch plywood for the radius steps. I will need to shoot elevations for each step. We will set a stake on the centerline to work. It will take at least a couple of hours. Do you have a can of marking paint, or do we need more?"

"I have a partial can in the toolbox, maybe enough to mark the steps."

"We should be at the level and start the sweep to both pilasters. Do you have the Sharpie for marking the block?"

"I think mine is dried up, or there is very little left."

"I'll go get a couple of cans of marking paint and a couple of Sharpies for marking the block. We need to start filling the cells of the retaining wall. Have one laborer start waterproofing the retaining wall and filling the cells with concrete. I have ten bags of Portland cement, and the cement mixer is hooked to the truck. They will bring you gravel and sand at nine o'clock. We will hand-mix the concrete for the cells. I don't have enough for a load of concrete and a concrete pump. Once we finish the retaining wall, we can place the extra soil behind the wall, and the remaining soil we will place at the staircase. I will bring a compactor after I return the cement mixer. We may have to get another laborer to help with the different tasks ahead of us. We will mark the location of the drainage system, and the electrical and gas lines. The excess soil has to be in place, or we will be at the wrong elevation and the system won't work properly. Do you have another person who would like to be a laborer?"

"I have a neighbor who is looking for work. I can ask him if he would like to be a laborer."

"You be the judge if you think you can work with him. I'll unhook the cement mixer. The laborers can put it in the front yard and dump the sand and gravel close to where you want to set up the mixer. Do you have a blue tarp?"

"Yes, I have one."

"Place it under the cement mixer to prevent concrete splashing or errors from being put into the landscape area. I'm going back to the masonry store and getting you some rebar for the walls—horizontal inside the wall."

"Great, I only have one piece left, and we're a couple of courses from needing more."

I drove over to the building supply company and purchased the marking paint, Sharpies, rebar, two construction sponges, and two wire brushes for cleanup. It took only a few minutes, and I went to the lumber yard to purchase two sheets of quarter-inch plywood, wood stakes, string line, one-inch deck screws, and a new plywood blade to make the cuts.

I returned to the job site with all my treasures. The waterproofing was in progress, the freestanding wall had two more courses completed, and the filling of the cells was underway and about one-third completed. Life was good. Juan and Diego, my operator, had the next course of blocks set and ready to install. The mortar was mixed in the wheelbarrow, the string line was in place, and everything was nice and square—such beauty could be achieved when done correctly.

CHAPTER 12

John and Marie saw me pull up and came out to see the progress. The early morning sun was in full blaze, and various shadows were on the retaining seat wall. Marie said, "John, look at the shadows today. I love the way the yard looks, and our entrance wall now is high enough to give the appearance of entering fantasyland."

John said, "Marie, we came out to go over our homework. We have to hand it in, or we will get a failing grade. I always handed in my homework on time in school. I'm not about to make our teacher unhappy. Regarding the stonework on the house, we liked both options, and our decision was not easy. I tossed and turned all night. This was more difficult than what I face every day at my profession. I think I need to pick your brain just a little more. If we build a raised planter, what did you envision?"

"Let me go to my truck and get some wood stakes and some construction string. I'll meet you at the corner of the house." I got the stakes, string line, some marking paint, and my small sledgehammer.

I returned to John and Marie; she was practicing her entrance, her elbow bent as though she were holding the glass of champagne, with perfect posture—one foot in front of the other like a high-priced fashion model on the runway showing off the latest creation from a top-notch designer. My crew stopped what they were doing and gave her a round of applause, and she started to blush just a bit.

I put down my collection of parts and tools, pulled out my tape measure, guesstimated the end of the staircase, and put a wood stake in the approximate location. From the first stake, I measured over the twelve-foot radius and set another stake. Now seeing the width of the staircase by standing back and gazing toward the backyard, I moved toward the shed and looked in another direction at the stakes. John and Marie were watching what I was doing with a "What is this guy doing?" type of look. Before I made a complete fool of myself in front of customers, I had to convince myself that what I had told them previously was indeed a clear option and not just idle chatter.

I then measured four feet from the house next to the shed and placed a stake; from that stake, I measured five feet toward the step stake and six feet from the house and set another stake. From that stake, I split the difference from the staircase step stake and the last stake installed, measured four feet from the house, and set another stake. I picked up three more stakes and drove them in next to the house. I then got my construction string—hot pink in color—wrapped the string around the first stake by the shed along the house wall toward the staircase, and then led it to the stakes away from the house, going all the way back to the first stake, and tied the string. I had to keep it taut while fastening it to each stake. Once completed, I moved back to the retaining seat wall, looking at the staircase and raised planter layout.

John and Marie were truly puzzled now, waiting for me to tell them the next step. I moved toward the entry wall, and now the crew was watching what I was doing and saying things in Spanish—more than likely that I was loco. I moved to where the staircase angled to the corner of the yard as I had explained in an earlier meeting about how the staircase would enter into the courtyard.

"Okay, John and Marie, I think I'm ready to explain what I just did for you." I told my crew, "Please join us for a couple of minutes so you know I have not lost my mind. You all must follow me to each location of the courtyard so you, too, will be able to envision my vision. We will first look at the staircase head on. Envision where the two stakes are placed. That is the bottom of the first step leaving the courtyard. Everyone, do you see those stakes?"

"Yes, we see them."

"First view. Let's move down to the corner where the two walls intersect. Look at those two stakes again. See the stakes?"

"Yes, a little different in appearance, correct?"

"Yes, different but nicer. Let's move over to the gate location and look at those two stakes. Do you see the two stakes?"

"Yes, much different in appearance."

"Let's go over to the corner of the shed and take a final view—the same but closer view than from the gate entry, all agree?"

"Yes, that was remarkable. Why did you have us take all these different views?"

"If there is something off, I need to correct my vision, and I wanted to ensure putting a raised planter next to my focal point did not distract from the focal point. Did any of you feel the raised planter would distract from the grandeur of the staircase?"

Marie asked, "Does the string line represent the top of the seat wall?"

"Great question. I tried to string it as close as possible so that when I was viewing the area, I could see if the wall at that elevation would work. If not, then I would tell you it would be lower or higher than the string strung. Now, John and Marie, to finish your homework, I will mark on the ground the proposed footing to give you a bird's-eye view from standing on top of the staircase. So if you would, go back inside, come out the rear patio doors, walk on your proposed walkway, stop at the top of the staircase, look to the planter layout, and let me know what you think."

John and Marie arrived at the top of where the new staircase would be located. "I would like you two to scoot over about three feet more to your left ... Perfect. Now, without falling into the courtyard, can you see the outline of the planter? ... You can. Great. What do you think?"

"What would the pot look like?"

"Hold on a minute. I'll get out a push broom and a bucket ... Okay, this is going to take quite a bit of imagination. The tiny tower is an upside-down cone, so the push broom is a far cry from reality." I set it with the broom handle facing upward. I had to balance the broom on top of the bucket to give somewhat of an effect.

"Thank you. We will be right down, and we can talk about our homework."

John and Marie approached the entry gate opening. I had them stop so I could take a photo of them coming through the entrance. "Proceed slowly." Their arms were around each other, and I snapped a great photo for them. One could not have asked for a better Kodak moment. John stated that he didn't want to make a judgment call and regret it years down the road. Marie said, "I would like the raised planter, but I think it might take away from my grand entrance at the party. People could be looking at the beautiful flowers in the planter and not gazing on my beauty. Do you think the potted plant will be totally unnoticed? Lost in all the grandeur of the courtyard?"

"I think three pots in that size would balance the site and could be located at different areas when you get tired of where they are positioned. The planter is not movable. I think either option would work wonders, and I might have to move the bottom step forward of where it is now to allow shadows to fall on the raised planter."

I showed them a quick sketch of both scenarios to give them a rough visual of that area. They went over to the seat wall and laid both sketches on top of the wall, side by side. After a few minutes, John said, "Raised planter. It fills the space where I know I would put junk instead of where it is supposed to be stored. Going up and down the staircase more than a couple of times during the day, I may want to sit down and take a break. That planter should be in the shade at ten o'clock, just when the temperatures start to rise above comfortable."

"Raised planter it is. I promise not to add too much floral content to the planter."

Juan and Diego were at a point where they were getting ready to start making the angle cuts for the sweeps. I had them set blocks on top of the blocks in place. "Only one layer, gentlemen. Too much weight will push out the grout. Find the center of the wall between the pilasters. Great. Let me check on the plans. How much dip in in the center? Do we have a ten-foot or longer two-by-four? Diego, you two need to take the pilasters to the final height before we do the half-moon. I want to remove the tunnel."

I called over Manuel, who had just finished the waterproofing, to help remove the boards connecting the house and the shed. I had him go to the truck and retrieve the hammer and crowbar. When he returned, I took the crowbar and wedged it between the ends of two boards. Using the hammer handle as a lever, I got the board to free itself from the stud and followed it toward the house one stud at a time; the board came free. Since the carpenter had staggered the joints, I went to the joint and did the same process with that board, moving one stud at a time until one side was stripped from the framework. We could now get into the shed without climbing through a window opening. The other side came off even easier. Now we could walk through from one side to the other.

Manuel, being very smart, went and retrieved the ladder so I could remove the roof of the tunnel. Manuel was also staking the board against the house nails pointed downward. He gave me the ladder and returned to the truck to get two sawhorses so he could strip the boards of the nails. I freed up the roof boards after removing the shingles. I was surprised at how easy it was for the tunnel to be stripped of the fascia boards. I now had a stud frame that might take a little more effort to dismantle.

By the time Juan and Diego got the pilasters built to the proposed height, the tunnel was gone. The shed was secure, but the tunnel opening needed a tarp put over it. "I will get another sheet of plywood and make a makeshift door. I might have the gate builder build a door to match the gate, since it will be closed during the party and when no one is going from the playhouse to the house. It will have to be lockable as well."

Before I started to remove the framework, I called for Juan so we could lay out the staircase. Juan was having Diego set the last two pilaster blocks while he retrieved the building level and rod from my truck. It was hard to stay ahead of Juan; he was always planning things out in his head. Juan brought the builder's level, and I set it up to shoot grade, making sure we had not lost our original grade from our drainage plans. I set the level so I could shoot the entire excavation site and the top grade in the backyard. Juan had the sledgehammer and the wood stakes. Diego, during the removal of existing soil, had left a ramp for the staircase. He and I had talked about that, but sometimes, while so focused on the job at hand, such things can easily be missed. We would have to add more soil—but not as much as if it were all removed.

I took the plans and my tape measure and told Juan where the center of the top step should be located. "So many feet from the house and so many feet from the property line rear fence." Okay, the landing centerline stake was set. I wanted to get the elevation, but the scope was too low, so I had Juan come down the ramp and set the rod on grade until I could read the rod. He was three feet from the top before I could get the first reading—one inch. Juan could reach the house corner, so he put the rod on the subgrade, which would be the base of the bottom step. It read six feet ten inches on the builder's rod. "The deck will be four inches in height, so I will have to raise the grade two inches. The tread will be twelve inches, and the rise will be six inches. There are two steps per foot of rise. Six feet means twelve steps. That means I need at least twelve feet in distance. Juan, can you see how far back on the plans the landing is from the corner of the house?"

Juan measured and said, "It is two feet beyond the house into the courtyard."

"Line up to your centerline stake and set another stake two feet beyond the house corner" The stake was set. "Now come one foot from that stake and put in another stake ... Good. Go another foot and set a stake." We followed the process for the entire twelve steps. The ramp was a little shy of reality. We adjusted the stakes to make an arch in the staircase. It started facing west and turned to face northwest, opening onto the deck. My original two stakes were off by at least a foot from reality.

I went and got long pieces of irrigation wire from my truck. We attached a piece of it onto the end of the rebar; this would act as our compass. Juan would hold the wire at the stake referring to the centerline, and I would take the rebar and draw the arch on the ground. And to preserve the mark, I would use the marking paint to color the step location. "No paint until I like how the radius appears." The bottom step, by design, was at twelve feet; once I completed the arch, I stepped back and looked from four different locations in the courtyard. I had Juan space some stakes along the drawn line to make sure I was seeing clearly. They were about a foot apart. "Take a relook."

"Looks pretty good."

"I have to get the homeowners to verify they like or dislike the first step."

John and Marie graciously came outside to take a peek. I explained that was the layout of the last step at the landing. "The other stakes are the centerline of all the steps. Remember how we looked this morning. Follow the same principle, and let me know what you think."

They both went to all the spots, just as we had done for the raised planter. Then Marie headed through the entrance gate opening and back into the house; she reappeared, looking from the top grade stake into the courtyard. "It looks totally different from up here than down there. John, you need to see this as well."

John left us and joined his bride. "You're right, dear. It does look different. Fred, you need to see what we see."

I left Juan and told him, "You may have to tweak some of the stakes." I joined John and Marie at the step landing. I stood at the centerline stake, and my eye followed each stake's centerline. I knew what they were seeing. "You lose some of the stakes' line of vision. They almost appear as a fence if you stand in one spot. It is an optical allusion." I moved over to my left to see if that would make a difference; it helped some, but there was still a fence-like appearance. The only way I would get the true look was if I went parallel to the mid-step stake in vision and it took me to the last step centerline. I had them follow me to the mid-step stake to get a final view.

I told them, "As you descend the staircase, you will get this view of the deck."

Marie was almost giddy with joy. John was happy that she was now happy. "All looks good. Thank you for showing us the layout before it's all formed and ready for pouring, when we may not have approved."

I told them, "We are only pouring the subgrade concrete to be able to attach the stone fascia for the tread and rise."

It was now quitting time for the crew, so they finished their cleanup and packed up the truck. It had been a long day for the crew; they had worked hard and gotten quite a bit accomplished. Tomorrow would be another day.

CHAPTER 13

The next day, the entry wall was set enough that we could now stack the blocks to mark where to cut the block to form the half-moon. I brought a refrigerator box I had saved, with which we could make a pattern so all half-moons were identical. Juan and Diego were on their makeshift scaffolding, and Manuel and Jose brought them the blocks. I took a construction crayon, etched out a half-moon on the blocks, stood back with Juan, and determined that it would make a nice-looking wall. I measured up the thickness of the brick to show the actual top of the wall and relooked. To cut the cardboard to match the layout, I drew a straight line with a Sharpie on the cardboard and, from the installed block, measured from that block to the cut mark on the blocks.

When all finished marking, we cut the cardboard with a utility knife and set it against the actual markings on the block. "If I'm not perfect, I'd be lying," I told Juan.

Juan and Diego started laying the first section. *Those two are set for a few hours. I'll take the laborers over to the shed and remove the framing and the nails from the studs. That will keep them busy while I take the homeowners over to the masonry yard and select the brick for the entrance wall.* I instructed Juan, "When the laborers get finished, have them fill the two pilasters that are on each side of the gate opening. Make sure the L bolts are set up using a two-by-four drilled with a washer and nut in the countersunk hole, which will hold the bolts in place while they fill the cells."

I then rang the doorbell. Marie answered. "Will you and John accompany me to the masonry yard to select the brick for your courtyard entry wall?"

"Am I dressed okay?"

"You'll be the talk of the masonry yard for years. 'Did you guys see that beautiful lady that came in yesterday to select brick? Ooh la la.'"

"You are being awfully kind. Don't stop."

We arrived at the masonry yard, and there were bricks upon bricks upon bricks on pallets stacked higher than all of us. The salesman met us to give assistance; he was carrying two sample boards from two major suppliers. I introduced John and Marie to the salesman. I explained that the bricks were going in as a fascia to cover the concrete blocks we were now installing. I showed the salesman the construction details of the wall. "This will be a landmark structure once completed—very nice detail. The arched gate entry will be the talk of the town."

The sample boards helped John and Marie select the color of the brick. John said, "They all look red until you see them next to each other on the sample board. They're not all the same color or texture."

I asked the salesman, "Are all of them in stock?"

"Not all. Some are custom-ordered and could take three to four weeks."

"Could you tell us those since we have a party to put on and we want the day to be perfect?" John and Marie decided on a very basic red brick, fired and lightly glazed. We held it at different angles to the sun to make sure that was the look they wanted.

I asked the salesman, "Do you have a bullnose brick that matches or is not distractive?"

"The same manufacturer makes the bullnose brick in three different lengths. The concrete block is eight by eight by sixteen. The bricks are three inches, including the joint, so that adds six inches to the eight inches, so the bullnose brick with a two-inch overhang would be nineteen inches if they were double bullnose."

"That would be great for us."

The salesman said, "But that size would never be made unless reinforced by rebar. We do have an eleven-inch and an eight-inch brick. I believe they might have a twelve-inch. Will the top of the cap be seen by passersby?"

"Possibly. The wall does dip between the pilasters and sweeps to just under the bullnose cap on the pilaster."

"You can use the common brick, since they are from the same manufacturer, eight-inch bullnose, then a cut red brick, and then the other bullnose to complete the cap."

"Do you have a catalog cut sheet of the bullnose and brick for my customer, and one for me? I'll go back and do a field measure of the wall and pilaster. You want the square footage or the actual brick count?"

"The square footage is perfect. We have a brick calculator that has a 10 percent allowance."

We were all soon back in the truck with color brochure in hand, heading back to the job site. Marie said, "I only saw a couple of guys. How many does the masonry yard employ?"

"Yardmen, maybe four of five; operators, maybe three; drivers, maybe three. It all varies with the seasons. Two were enough for them to tell the others your legacy will be preserved for a long time."

I contacted the gate builder and the staircase subcontractor when I returned to the job site. The laborers had the framework completed and were filling the pilasters with concrete as directed. Juan and Diego had two sections of the wall finished with the sweeps. John and Marie were amazed that this was their home. They walked around the wall, paying attention to the shadows the wall made. Marie said, "I'm going to get my camera, not my phone, and take photos to show our guests just what makes this yard so special. We never had such a display before. We just had a mundane, cookie-cutter backyard."

"Do you think the rear yard has a chance to compete with the courtyard?" asked John.

"I'll give it my all to make sure there is enough interest for your guests and family to go exploring the entire landscape, even if I have to make signs like 'You've got to see what's over here.' Marie could always have her gown on, and I'm certain the guests will follow her. Maybe not family, but guests for sure."

I had the gate builder coming tomorrow morning and the staircase contractor coming in the afternoon. Juan and I had to get the forms set for the pour of the subgrade concrete. I had the laborers install the french drain behind the seat wall. Diego cut off the extra rebar sticking up above the seat wall, and he also took the wire brushes and removed any and all spilled concrete from the cell filling. "The french drain was finished. Start backfilling the wall, keeping it two inches from the top of the wall. Once filled and compacted, hose off the wall top and sides."

Diego was done fairly quickly; Manuel and Jose did a great job filling the cells. They were now busy removing the dropped grout from in front of both walls, so when grading started for the deck, we wouldn't have to stop and clean up the debris. The step forms went fairly nicely, and we formed the side wall, where the balusters would be placed, and the handrail above them. Manuel and Jose started filling in the subgrade under each step so we wouldn't waste concrete. Diego got the rebar bender and rebar cutter from my truck and had the laborers carry the three-eighth-inch rebar from the rack on my truck. If all went smoothly, we would pour after the subcontractor gave his blessing.

Juan and I had finished forming the steps, and he was adding more stakes for support of the forms. One thing that made any pour a nightmare was a blown-out form. That had happened to me a couple of times, and the mad scramble to repair while the cement truck kept spinning the mud, making it hotter and hotter, made finishing another nightmare.

When we finished the top step, the landing was about an inch too high. I went to my truck and got the building level and shot each step form. Sometimes the level tells you the form is level, but it may not be exact. We started shooting the elevation of the first step, compared it with the finished subgrade, put a paver on the subgrade, and checked the shot. "There is a half inch right off the bat. Great, that means the second step will have to be lowered a half inch." Juan went to the top of each form to see where there may be other errors.

Diego made a jig to make sure he had the right arch for the steps, cut the bars to the proper lengths, and used the cut pieces to tie the two bars per step together. He said, "Are you two finished? You're making me tired just watching your progress."

"Diego, I see you have been talking with my wife. That would have been one of her comments." We found the errors of our ways and made the adjustments, and all was back to normal. I asked Juan to help me get the square footage of the entrance wall. Two people holding a tape measure went a lot quicker than one. If one person is measuring and the tape comes free, it requires walking back to the start and doing it again—frustrating to say the least.

Measurement completed, I'd call the masonry yard and get the brick delivered tomorrow—or later today if all went better than planned. Juan returned to the forms and started cutting the one-by-two spreaders to keep the forms where they were supposed to be. Diego was nearly complete with the rebar for the treads; tying the steps together was a little trickier, and he needed Juan's help.

I went to the playhouse to see if I could get them something else to complete before the day ended. "We are having great weather, and no rain is forecast for the next week, so let's remove the roof off the shed. We can also remove all the benches inside the shed, and remove the one window facing the patio cover and barbecue. Oh, I need to lay out the patio cover and barbecue footings."

"Way to go, ace. Just where are your plans?"

"Of course, sitting on the front seat of the truck. You know the job so well you don't need no stinking plans. What a bonehead."

I asked Juan if he had any extra stakes. He replied, "I still have a bundle."

"How many do you need?"

"Maybe ten or so will be enough."

I went to my truck to get my can of marking paint. On my way to the truck, I checked whether I had all the right clothes on and took inventory; all checked out okay. Some days just too much went through my head that could cause a brain malfunction. I was back to the courtyard, plans in hand. *Good job, ace. Before I forget, call the masonry yard. Come on; get with the program.*

I called the salesman, and he said they could get the bricks to the job site before two in the afternoon. "You just made my day. Thank you so much."

I called Jose over to the gate entry and had him cut the grade an inch below the top of the footing using a shovel, pick, and wheelbarrow to complete the job. I told Juan, "The bricks will be here around two o'clock."

He wasn't as excited as I was but said, "Thank you."

I had a box of fasteners at the house to attach the brick to the concrete block. The fasteners would get nailed to the concrete block with concrete nails and bent perpendicular to the wall face. This was in the grout joint. This would hold the brick from falling away from the wall in due time. I'd have to go get them during the crew's lunch break.

CHAPTER 14

Back to the laying out of the footings, I needed to make a list of things to do today and attach it to my shirt with a pin. My dearest Delores would gladly pin me daily.

"Don't forget your list, dear."

"Ouch."

"Oh, did I stick you? So sorry. Here, I'll do it again."

"Have a great day, dear."

"Did you get your lunch bag? I made you your favorite sandwich—crow on rye. Can you hit another one on your way home? I'm running short."

"Let's see, ten feet from the retaining wall. Set a stake, go over to the house wall, and measure twenty-five feet to the ten-foot stake as a cross-reference—twenty-five feet six inches. Check the retaining wall from the house—thirty-six feet six inches. The plan says thirty-six feet. Well, the wall is just a little shy, but we made some field adjustments to give better shadowing. It is what it is. There is one post footing centered. Do the same for the next three posts. Two will be behind the retaining wall.

"Second stake is set. Now let's lay out the barbecue footprint. The patio post needs to be moved about three feet from where I have it staked to allow foot passage around the barbecue. Footprint first, and then move the post if necessary or move the barbecue back to allow for the clearance. The retaining wall descends in about three feet. Let's try it there, four feet from the retaining wall. Set the first stake, measure over seven feet, set the stake. The barbecue is four feet wide. Pull from the last stake, go to the first stake, pull four feet, set the stake, measure from corner to opposite corner in a diagonal line—seven feet three inches. Now do the opposite diagonal to check for square—seven feet three inches. Beautiful. Paint the footing so the crew can excavate the footings. Take a look from all angles before you waste time digging in the wrong location."

I looked in all directions, as always. I really did need to set those other two post locations behind the retaining wall. I couldn't get the right feeling. There, all stakes were set. I was going to string-wrap the barbecue just to complete the visual. *Hot pink string, such a pretty wrap. Let's take another peek.* All angles were completed. Jose was finished grading between the pilasters, Diego and Juan were nearing completion, and Manuel was finished cleaning up the mess from building the walls.

"I feel it's time for lunch." The crew was all cheerful; lunch always brought out the best in everyone. "I'll be back in a little while. I have to go get the fasteners from the house. Juan, did you bring a ladder today?"

"Yes, it's on the truck rack."

"Only one ladder?"

"Yes, only one ladder."

"I'll pick up the second ladder at the house. See you all in a few minutes. Enjoy your lunches."

"Heigh-ho, heigh-ho, off to the house I go. Worked hard all day, I'm ready to play, Heigh-ho, heigh-ho."

Hi, honey, I'm home!"

"Did you forget to take your sack lunch again?"

"No, dear, I have to pick up some items from the garage. Do you have something for me for lunch?"

"I wasn't expecting you for lunch. I can make you something really quick. What would you like?"

"You know what I would like," I said.

"Nope, none of that. Later tonight, maybe. You know that's bad for your heart, getting it all raced up. You'll get sweaty, and the crew will know you didn't have a sandwich for lunch. I'll make you bowl of soup with crackers."

"I could just change shirts and they would be none the wiser. I have multiple T-shirts, all the same color."

"So you do. It's still no."

"How about tonight?"

"You keep it up and it's couch time for you."

"Soup sounds wonderful." I just got what I needed from the garage.

CHAPTER 15

"Hi, honey. I'm back. Did you miss me?"

"With bated breath. Couldn't wait much longer without starting to become depressed and deeply saddened. Your lunch is on the table. Bon appétit. I have some chores to finish up, or I would enjoy watching you eat your sandwich. Did you want water or some apple juice in a cute little container that the kids take to school?"

"I think water would be splendid."

"Here you go. Enjoy."

"Wait, don't I get a little smooch? My other waitresses give me a smooch."

"Do you tip them?"

"Why, yes, I do give them a generous tip."

"I have one for you: don't press your luck."

Well, lunch was terrific. She was the best a man could ask for. *I'll leave her a dollar bill.*

Back at the job site, the bricks came early, and the crew was just finishing up with their lunch break. I told them I would have to run to the rental yard to pick up a brick-and-tile saw so we could start wrapping the first pilaster at the gate entry. I had the plywood to start forming the arch, and that sheet was in the back of my truck. It was tricky to get both sides out of one sheet, we couldn't make a major mistake. I had a jigsaw in my toolbox with a new blade. I wore safety glasses anytime I was cutting wood, metal, or concrete.

I took the laborers into the shed, showed them what needed to be removed from the inside, and told them to start removing the shingles from the roof once finished. Juan was with us, and if they were a little confused with what I told them in English, he backed it up with Spanish so there was no misunderstanding. I also told them to remove all the nails and put them into the five-gallon bucket.

When I turned around to leave the shed, I almost ran into Marie. "I'm sorry. I didn't see or hear you come out from the house."

"John had to go to a business meeting. I finished all my chores, and I can come outside and play until the streetlights come on," said Marie.

"Well, I hope I can keep you amused and entertained for that many hours. I have something to show you if you have time."

"Why, yes, I believe I do have some time. Let me check my calendar here on my phone. Yep, I was right. I'm free for a couple of hours," said Marie.

"You're so easy to get along with; you're spoiling me," I told her.

"Over here, madam, we have the hot pink string surrounding the footprint of your future barbecue island along with the centers of the posts for the patio cover. We will start excavating the footings as soon as the laborers remove some of the benches from the shed and the shingles off the roof. If you like the layout, then we will proceed. We will form up the arch, install the steel, and prepare to pour the arch when we pour the subbase for the steps. Once we break the forms, feel free to practice your entrance so you'll be flawless. I'll see if I can find that song they played when Bess Myerson came onto the stage for *Queen for a Day*. You know the tune: 'Here she comes, Miss America.'"

"John would just die if that was to be played. He would be laughing so hard I know I would make a mistake, causing the entire guest list to explode in laughter. I would turn beet red, which would clash with my gown. I love the step forms you installed. It's all starting to come together, one piece at a time."

"So what do you think about the barbecue and patio layout?"

"I forgot you need my approval. I got sidetracked there for a moment. Can you leave it until John gets home? He might want to change something. I'd be delighted to leave it for him to approve. I have to go back inside and do my nails before John returns from his business meeting, better known as a three-hour lunch."

"We're starting to put the brick fascia on the arch today. I have the gate contractor coming in the morning. He will need to take some measurements for the entry gate and the playhouse door. I'll have him build a door for the tunnel area as well. He will also hang a temporary door over the opening so critters won't enter the tunnel or possibly get into the house."

I went and retrieved the brick-and-tile saw and returned to the job site. The wood benches had been removed, and Manuel and Jose were removing the shingles. Juan and Diego were setting the first course of the brick fascia at the archway. Juan had already cut out the arch form; he needed some Masonite to attach to the arch for the bottom, and he would then put three one-inch-by-two-inch bands around the form to hold the bottom and give the plywood more strength. *This will be a fun pour, with the steps and the arch on the same pour. This will take lots of crossings of fingers, arms, and legs from me, Marie, and John. If one form fails, the pour could quickly become a disaster.*

I checked the step forms, and all looked ready for pouring. We just needed the subcontractor to see the setup, and we'd make adjustments if needed. His part was the most important; the final appearance would make our subgrade pour absolutely disappear.

I checked the progress of the shed demolition. The shingles were all nearly removed. Cleanup would take a little time, and it would have to be completed before the concrete pour. I'd bring the trailer tomorrow morning, and they could load the debris collected into the trailer. The roof had wood slats instead of plywood. I was not certain if plywood was available when this shed was built. The price of plywood may have been too expensive.

Manuel asked Juan if they should start removing the slatted lumber off the rafters. Juan got on one ladder and joined them on the roof to examine what they were dealing with. Juan asked Jose for the crowbar to see how hard removing a board would be. He took a claw hammer and tapped the crowbar under the first board, and it rose just a little. He moved to the next rafter and did the same; it lifted the board a little higher. Moving to the next rafter, he tapped the crowbar; now the board was free enough that the crowbar, by itself, freed the first board. It was part of the overhang, but it gave Juan the chance to pry the next board using the hammer, and it, in turn, came up and was removed fairly easily. Juan told Manuel to follow what he did, removing the boards to the top, and to call him when they reached that spot. "Be careful not to fall onto the ceiling boards inside the shed." The boards coming off the roof were nice enough that they could be used on the second-floor addition.

It was near going-home time, so the crew started the daily cleanup. They always kept job sites clean so the homeowners walking around after they left would not fall and hurt themselves. The homeowners always had friends and family visit during the construction to show off what was being constructed. Neither the homeowner nor their guests or family members needed to fall and get hurt. I was not a fan of roping off the job site from the homeowners unless I absolutely had to for their own protection.

CHAPTER 16

We had a big day set up for tomorrow, making sure the forms and all rebar for the arch were correct, installing the conduit and blocking out for the light in the arch, making sure all the drains were functioning in the pilasters before we prepared for the caps, and digging the footings for the barbecue so we could pour that concrete along with the steps and arch. Busy, busy. I wanted to get on the shed roof to examine how the rafters were fastened to the shed walls. This was an old structure, and building codes in the earlier years were nonexistent, and the farmers all helped one another; some had building experience taught to them by their father or grandfathers, who may have immigrated from Europe or another country. Most of the building materials were what was on hand; the wood sizing was true in size, not planed down to current sizes. I knew I might have to double-stud the walls to support the upper floor, and I might have to lift the shed and pour a true footing if none existed. Some builders used stacked stones for foundations, which is considered very unsafe by today's standards.

I hope I sleep well tonight. Having too much to think about causes me to toss and turn. I know my dinner will be fabulous, as usual. She's such a good cook, wife, and mother. I love her to death. Maybe I can get her to practice a grand entry, buy her a formfitting gown and sparkling zirconium diamond necklace and bracelet, and give her money to get her hair just perfect and to buy some stylish high heels and a champagne glass to pose with for the toast to the host and hostess. I'll have to bring that to her attention so she can get prepared. That will iron out the waitress comment I made by the slip of the tongue.

I walked through the front door of my mansion and was greeted by the butler and maid, who announced my arrival to my family. I strolled to where the family was gathered.

"Honey, please take out the trash."

No "How was your day?" no smooch, no hugs by the kids—just "Please take out the trash." Oh well, it could have been worse. Our male dog could have tried to hump my leg—if I owned a male dog.

When I got inside the house after doing my chores, my bride told me I had missed five phone calls from customers wanting to meet with me. "Their numbers are on your drawing board."

"Thank you, dear. I'll look at them after dinner and spend some quality time with the family."

"That reminds me, can you pick up the kids tomorrow from school? I have a hair appointment and may not be finished before the kids are let out of school."

"What time do I have to be at the school?"

"Between three and three fifteen."

"That might be tough. I have a meeting with the staircase subcontractor in the afternoon. I'll call him and have him come earlier, and if I have to leave, Juan can take notes."

"I'll give you an extra spoon of spinach for your troubles for dinner."

"That is very kind of you."

"Did you get my tip I left you for lunch?"

"Oh yes, I added another hundred dollars from your wallet last night, thinking you overlooked your generosity."

"So that's were that hundred went to—generosity. I wonder if I can write that off on my taxes this year."

Dinner was delicious as usual. I even helped load the dishwasher; that was how good dinner tasted.

I went to the drafting table and looked at the return-call papers. All five calls had come from clients for whom I had drawn plans to relandscape their yards. If these all turned into new projects, I'd have to hire more men, and Juan would have his dream come true—supervising a multitude of projects. That would turn his black hair gray overnight. I'd earned every one of mine and wore them with honor and pride. I needed my yellow pad to write down everything I needed to get accomplished tomorrow, lest I forget about something and pay dearly for the lapse of memory.

One of the calls stated they wanted to start the work as soon as possible. I pulled all five clients' file folders and put them in my briefcase so I wouldn't forget them. I also needed to pull the plans to take with me for our meeting. I'd put them into the truck so I wouldn't forget them; sure enough, I'd space that out and be caught dumbfounded.

Just then, my beautiful wife came into the office. "Did you get your messages?"

"Yes, dear, thank you for taking the phone calls."

"Honey, I'm a little tired, and I'm going to bed early. Do you want me to get you a cup of coffee?"

"No, I'm good. Since you're going to bed early, I have a dream you can dream tonight."

"Oh, you do, do you? Well, I'm listening."

"Remember the vision I had with Marie making a grand entrance?"

"Why, yes, I do. You saw me as a waitress."

"Well, I had a revised vision on the job site today. You now have a grand entrance of your own: nice formfitting gown split on the side to just above your knee, hair all styled, designer high heels—open-toed-sandal type, stylish zirconium necklace and matching bracelet, champagne glass filled with the bubbly. You come down the staircase. The guests and family have heard the announcement that the landscaper's wife, Delores, is entering the staircase. The applause drowns out the stereo system. All are standing as your heels click on the biblical stone, one foot stepping in front of the other, so glamorous, so stunning. All eyes are on your beauty. The sunlight is bouncing off the sequins on your gown. I could scoop you up and carry you to my awaiting truck and take you to our home."

"Is that the dream?"

"Yes, dear. Can you see yourself being so admired?"

"Zirconium? You only bought me zirconium? I'm dressed to the nines, and you cheapen the entire outfit with zirconium?"

"I could have seen pop beads."

"Maybe you could go to the toy store and spend maybe three bucks on the necklace, bracelet, rings, and earrings in a handy cardboard and clear plastic cover. Can they be the Disney princess collection? Please, oh please, sugar daddy."

"Are you making fun of my vision?"

"Just trying to envision trading in my waitress outfit— low cut, skirt length shameful even for a prostitute to wear—to a gown, dressed to the nines, wearing pop beads."

"Not pop beads, zirconium diamonds."

"Nice try, but I believe I will forgo that vision. Good night, dear." She gave me smooch on the cheek. "I won't wash the waitress vision from my brain just yet."

The next morning at the job site, John and Marie met me as soon as I reached the sidewalk. They almost scared me when they said "good morning." John said, "You wanted me to approve something this morning?"

"Yes, the barbecue and patio layouts. I'll show you."

Marie said, "Your wife called me before you arrived and told me of your second vision. I loved the idea, and I told her we will go together and pick out our gowns so we don't clash."

Oh, what did I do? "That sounds like you two will have a great day maxing out my credit card."

"What are pop beads?"

"They were a little before your time. You see, these were rubberized beads that young girls could fasten together to make a necklace or bracelet. They were round with a stem that would fit into the next one. Another type looked like pearls but were made in multitude of pastel colors. When you pulled them apart, they made a popping sound, hence the name 'pop beads.'"

"Do they still make them?"

"I haven't seen them in years."

John said, "Marie, I need to ask a few questions regarding the project and leave for work so we can pay for the lavish party. I'm assuming that the stringed area is the barbecue?"

"Correct."

"And the stakes are the post locations?"

"Correct. Per the drawings. Will the layout work for your needs?"

"As I'm cooking, I will be looking at the backyard fence, correct? Not the entry wall?"

"This is how the plans were drawn. If you want to look in another direction, I can make the change."

"I think I would rather look at the playhouse so I can watch the kids play. It will make me feel like part of the family, not just the hired cook."

"Let me get my tape measure and reset the stakes and let you make the call." The one corner stake would remain as designed. I measured seven feet toward the entry fence, set a stake, moved westward back by four feet, set a stake, moved back the original layout, set a stake four feet back, and set another stake. "What do you think?"

"Marie, come over here and look at what I see."

"Yes, John, I see. What do I see?"

"The L shape. The table and chairs are on the north side of the patio cover. This side will have the sunlight, so most guests will want to stand in the shade— wasted space anyway. Make it the L shape. I saw you started removing the roof from the shed. Find anything exciting?"

"Not yet, but our day has just started. I have the gate builder due to be here in about an hour. You can see we started putting on the brick fascia so the gate builder can get a true measurement. We will have the walls of the arch finished and start on the street side of the fascia so the neighbors won't have to look at gray concrete block for very long. It will completely change the appearance of your home, and with the gate and lighting installed and operating, they will set up chairs in their front yards just to watch the festival of lights each night."

"We've had a couple of neighbors walk by saying how much nicer the yard looks. I think they are trying to get a free peek. They'll just have to wait. We get to see it completed before they do. Will the gate builder put up a temporary gate over the opening?"

"I hope he can do it tomorrow or later today. That's the game plan anyway."

"Well, I have to get going to earn my keep around here. Marie will be able to answer any of your questions or at least contact me at the office."

The roof boards were completely removed, and Manuel and Jose were loading them into the trailer just to get them out of the way. We would use them on the second-floor addition.

I got on the ladder and took a peek at the framework of the roof. I noticed, when inside the shed, that the ceiling was boarded, not having an open beam or rafters. I reached down and measured from the opening to the ceiling below. "Wait a minute, that doesn't seem right." I got down and entered the shed. I measured from the floor to the ceiling—six feet six inches. I went outside and measured from the ground to the top of the wall—seven feet six inches. "That is a foot difference in height. Something is not right."

I called for Manuel and Jose to bring the hammer and crowbar with the five-gallon bucket. They did as I instructed, and I got one of the ladders and climbed up one rung. I put the crowbar between the joists of the ceiling board and pried on the board. It took a little doing, but finally the nails started pulling out of the stud. I got enough bite on the board to get better leverage, and the board finally freed itself from the joist. "There is a second ceiling," I told Manuel. "These boards need to come off. Once the first board is removed, the rest will come off easy."

I started with the second board, and I told Manuel to go get the flashlight from my toolbox. I waited for his return and freed the second board from the joist. I shone the light between the two roofs. There was something stuffed between the two ceilings, too far over for me to reach. Now I remembered what the bomb squad had told me: "Bag, sheet, bedding, or plastic bag— call us before you do something that you and the neighborhood would regret." I told Manuel and Jose we would not remove any more of the roof until we got an all-clear.

I rang the bell, and Marie answered the door. I said, "I have good news and some bad news."

"The bad news first so if I need to sit down, I won't be all excited about the good news."

"I found a bag."

"Boy, that was horrible news. A bag—I had better sit down, since finding a bag, I would think, would have been the good news."

"Under normal circumstances, I would agree with you. You have it backward, I would think. You know we have found other things buried prior."

"Yes, four or five things with pets buried in them."

"This bag is in the shed between two ceilings."

"Two ceilings? There are two ceilings in the shed?"

"Yes, I measured and found a difference of twelve inches."

"So now what do we do?"

"Call our friends and have the black-and-white parade visit us, hopefully for the last time."

"Do you think there is a bomb?"

"I don't know; nor does my crew. We don't want to be on the building crew in heaven just yet."

"I have the detective's card. I'll call him right now."

"He probably has you on his speed dial."

When I returned to the side yard, my gate builder was on the job site and was measuring the opening of the arch. "Did we set you up okay?"

"Yes, this is perfect. Thank you for putting a two-by-four on both sides of the arched entry. Saves me from drilling into the block and inserting hardware to mount the frame."

"The owner asked me this morning if you could install a temporary gate in the opening to lessen the chance of someone walking into their backyard."

"I brought a sheet of plywood and some two-by-fours and will make a temporary gate for them."

"You mentioned you have two more doors that need to match the gate."

"The shed over there, and there used to be a tunnel connecting the house to the shed. I'll show you what we need."

"When are you going to pour the steps?"

"I hope tomorrow. I'm waiting for the step subcontractor. Oh no, I forgot to call him. Excuse me for a few minutes. I need to make a call. I'll just measure the two openings for the new doors."

I called my staircase subcontractor. He told me he could come earlier; he'd had an appointment canceled on him an hour ago. He could be at the job site in twenty minutes, if that would be okay with me. "That would be perfect with me. See you in thirty minutes."

The gate builder was all finished and asked if the homeowner was home. "Follow me, and I'll introduce you to her," I said.

We walked to the house, and I rang the bell. "Hello, the contractor is on the side of the house."

Marie said, "Oh, I thought it was the police."

"That's okay. I would like to introduce you to Bruce, the fence contractor who will build the gates and doors. Bruce, this is Marie. I have to get back to the crew, if you would both excuse me."

I had Manuel and Jose start the barbecue footing. I had Juan and Diego start putting the brick on the fascia on the street side of the wall. I told them that the black-and-white parade would start in a few minutes. "What did we do now to invite the black-and-whites?"

"There is a false ceiling in the shed, and there is a bag wedged between the two ceilings."

"More fun a-coming."

The black-and-whites started arriving, and neighbors' curtains started opening in the center so they could peek out.

"Good morning, Detective," I said, "Glad to see you again."

"I heard you found another treasure. I'm getting to think that Captain Hook used to live here."

"Here, I'll show you what I found. Climb onto the ladder and shine the flashlight toward the tunnel entry. Do you see the bag?"

"Yes, what a lovely bag it is. Could you have your crew remove more boards so we can get a better look at the bag?"

"Of course; they will start immediately. We will get the rest of our people together and rendezvous in a few minutes."

"Be careful not to get too close to the bag."

I instructed Manuel and Jose to remove at least three boards so the officers could inspect the bag. The boards were removed before the rendezvous occurred. "All ready for inspection, sir."

After about ten minutes, they had the bag on the ground, and they used the X-ray machine to get a visual; it appeared to be a duffel bag. They carefully unzipped the bag, which was newer than anything else they had found previously. The bomb squad was highly skilled. The bag was opened, and the officer who was in charge of the opening stated, "Detective, you have to see this." The look on the detective's face was one of "Oh no, not again, more surprises."

The detective looked in the bag. "Well, I'd be dammed. We have been looking for that for years."

"Okay, Detective, I can't stand the suspense any longer. What was in the bag?"

"Stolen bank money. There was a bank robbery quite a few years ago. They caught one robber of the three men who robbed the bank, never found the money. The caught robber died in prison and never told anyone where the money was hidden."

"Do you mean we could have been rich if we had not called?"

"No, you would have been put in prison for spending stolen money. You did the right thing by calling. You might get your picture in the paper for solving the crime of the century. We need to do the forensics on the bag to get fingerprints and DNA. That is one reason we opened the bag by only gloving the zipper slider."

"How much money is in the bag?"

"I don't know if this is all or only part of the stolen funds. Oh, by the way, during the course of the investigation, fingerprints were taken from you and your crew and the homeowners. None of you are suspected in the murder of the great-grandmother, but we have found two other sets of prints that do not match those of the great-grandmother, great-grandfather, grandmother, grandfather, kids, or grandkids. We think there were more involved in the great-grandmother's mutilation. Please do not talk about this case with anyone, and tell your crew the same. I will tell the homeowner the same thing I told you. Do not tell anyone we found stolen money and banknotes either."

Just as the black-and-whites were leaving, my staircase contractor arrived. "So what did you do to get a police escort?"

"I stole a gumball from a nickel machine when I was eight. They got my prints off the machine and finally caught up to me. Driver's license renewal thing. Got me a couple of years back as well."

"Pretty clever answer, my friend. So you formed up the staircase in the courtyard. When are you pouring the subconcrete?"

"As soon as you give us the go-ahead, it will get poured."

"How about step lights? Were you going to light up the steps?"

"Not every one of them. I knew there was something we were forgetting."

"Every other one—was that the game plan?"

"Yes, every other one. I need to get the parts in the layout ready for you to do your magic. Let's take some measurements and check some spacing, and I'll give you a list of 'okay' or 'try again.'"

"Sounds fair."

"I'll leave you to your magic."

The barbecue footing was nearly finished. Diego went to my truck and retrieved the rebar cutter and bender. Jose grabbed five rods from the rack, ready for the steel in the footing. Juan brought two sticks of electrical conduit and dropped one at the barbecue and one at the arch. He went back to his truck and brought two buckets full of electrical parts.

I'd need to head to the masonry yard and get the gas steel sweep ninety, which was to be installed before the pour. I had to leave to get the children, and I was still in the time zone my wife had told me. I got to the school and hit the rest of the parents picking up their children—so many cars, lots of minivans and SUVs. The amazing thing was that not one was painted school-bus yellow; nor did any of the vehicles have a stop sign on the side of the car, warning drivers to stop and wait until the children were safely loaded or unloaded. "There has to be a new law made. Your vehicle must match the same laws governing school buses." The kids were loaded and ready to head home to see Mom. They were excited to see Daddy. "I don't often pick them up because of work. This is a treat for me as well."

CHAPTER 17

The next day, returning to the job site, the staircase contractor left us a list of items to correct so his finished work would match the staircase in the home. The only difference between the two would be the treads. The correctable items were not difficult but necessary.

I headed over to the electrical supplier and retrieved the necessary junction boxes and flexible conduit. I had some low-voltage cable on my truck, which I had loaded last night. I also purchased some needed electrical conduit fittings. I also got the items for the lights on the pilasters and arch. *If we get all this done before lunch, I will tell the ready-mix plant to send the concrete along with a concrete pump. I'll call the batch plant when I get into the truck to reserve the pump and mix. I just won't tell them the yardage. We will pour just what is ready to pour.*

I returned to the job site, and the barbecue footings were completed. Diego was finishing up the rebar, Juan had the trenches for the conduit, and the laborers were busy removing the lower ceiling in the shed. The episode with the black-and-whites was a small setback. I was glad there was just money or human bones in the bag. I gave Juan the box of electrical parts; everything else was in the bed of the truck. Manuel helped Juan bring everything into the courtyard. I had called the batch plant and ordered the concrete for nine o'clock, and I told them I would tell them the yardage once I saw what was ready to pour.

Juan had marked the steps where the step lights would be installed. *This will require some thought. You can't attach the junction box to the form unless you do so from the front, and you have to use screws.* We marked the holes using the junction box, drilled from the back side, and screwed them in place from the front. "Just be careful when removing the forms to remove the screws, or you will crack the concrete and loosen the junction box."

By the end of the day, the forms were corrected at the steps, the barbecue footings were ready, and the arch had everything in place and was ready for pouring. Just after lunch, I told the batch plant that eight yards would be what we needed. That was about a half yard more than what I figured. I loved to hear the drum rattle with the last little bit over when the forms were full.

John and Marie came out to see the progress. "The shed looks totally different with the second ceiling removed. Someone, years past, took some of Grandpa's paint and got creative on the ceiling."

Marie went back inside and got her camera to take a photo for the photo album they had not started. It was more than a primitive style of art, maybe that of a child of third-grade age. It looked like the poster board art I did as an elementary school student; those were the good old days. It had farm animals, a barn, a house, and, I was sure, Mom and Dad at the time. "We will preserve this artwork. It will give the playhouse character and be a great conversation piece. Nothing like nostalgia to get the vocal cords moving."

Marie just couldn't wait to practice her entrance. She told me Delores would come by sometime next week, and they would take turns perfecting their styles, go to lunch, and go gown shopping to see what was available. *What did I start?* I asked myself.

John was really impressed about how the project was shaping up. He asked, "Will your original landscape plan enhance or distract from the courtyard?"

"I'm going to have to tweak it some to enhance what we are building, but overall, the majority will be as designed. Everything is subject to availability. I have three nurseries that are putting together the quotes, and I'll have to get busy here in a couple of days to modify the plant lists."

"So your job is never just sitting back and watching the job build in front of you?" asked Marie.

"Some days are status quo, some days are a scramble, and some are horrible. I just have to take and deal with each day. That is the magnet for contractors—constant change, never a dull moment. It drives me and, I'm sure, others. Nothing is mundane."

"Are you pouring tomorrow?" asked John.

"The concrete will arrive at nine o'clock with the concrete pump, so the brick fascia will stop until the pour is finished. And after lunch, the crew can continue to face the wall with brick. Let's take a look to see how far they got today." I knew they hadn't had much time to spend on the fascia, But the first section of the wall was about half-covered.

"That really makes the wall look great," said John.

"I'm hoping that, by the end of next week, we can start putting on the wall caps. The retaining wall caps should be in by the end of next week. I need to get your rock for the retaining walls and barbecue lined up this week. I'll make a note to myself, or sure as shooting, I'll forget. Did the detective talk to you about the bag?"

"Yes, and he said we would get a reward from the bank."

"Great, I can raise my price to help you spend the reward money."

"Maybe we can get a whole orchestra to perform instead of a four-piece combo."

"Make sure you get a copy of the check to put in your album. That would just add to the excitement."

"We are hoping that if there are more people involved in the great-grandmother's death, they catch them before our party."

"Will they return the chests, round canister, and five-gallon can for you to display at the party?"

"They didn't say whether they would or not. They're concerned about the fingerprints that don't match what they have on file for the family members. They have notified the FBI with the fingerprints to see if they have any record in their files. Maybe next week, they will get confirmation on the prints they sent the FBI."

"Are you two ready for your fifteen seconds of fame? The bank will put on quite the show for the town to give you recognition. Front-page news: 'John and Marie found the lost bank money, and we hereby reward you two with fifteen million dollars. Job well done.' So, John, what do you plan to do with the reward money?"

"Disneyland with the family; that should cover the admission price. I remember when all the athletes would say that when they won the Super Bowl."

On pour day, my heart was beating out of my chest. "Here go all the what-ifs. What did we forget to install? Check the list. You have forty-five minutes to get something fixed if it needs fixing."

Juan was looking diligently at the area to be poured, Diego was making sure all the rebar was tied tightly, and the laborers had hosed out the two wheelbarrows, so they were ready for any additional concrete they could use in the wall cores not yet filled. We put plastic sheeting around the installed bricks on the archway; the concrete splatter was not easy to get off. I had the laborers make a clear pathway from the steps to the barbecue to the arch. We couldn't afford to have the hoses of the concrete pump get hung up on things lying around. We would hand-mix the footings for the patio cover. I didn't want anyone stepping into a hole while trying to complete the task at hand. I saw the concrete pump turning into the cul-de-sac—great sign. The concrete truck would be here shortly.

John and Marie came out of the house just as nervous as I was. Marie said, "This is a big day for our courtyard. So excited. Don't know how you stay so calm."

"On the outside, Marie. Inside, this is killing me."

"Where are you going to start pouring?"

"The steps are the first, then maybe the arch, and then the footings for the barbecue. All depends on how well I figured. If we are close and need a smidgen more, I'll call for a cleanup. Great, here comes the concrete mixer. The show is about to start."

Tensions mounted among the crew; all seats were filled, and the audience was getting excited. The curtains were still drawn, waiting to be opened. There was anticipation for the moment everyone had been waiting for. "Can you feel the excitement?" John said.

"Not until you started saying it. I wasn't even in the audience. I think I was out buying popcorn."

My crew was dragging in the concrete hoses and setting them where the concrete pump operator directed them. Juan and Diego had their trowels in their hip pockets and float trowels in their hands. The laborers were assisting on the hoses to help the operator do his job to perfection. Everyone had on rubber boots. Marie ran into the house, got her camera, and stood on the landing of the stairs to get a great shot of the crew doing their magic.

The pump operator was the conductor of this ensemble; he signaled the concrete mixer operator to let it flow. I could hear the concrete pump go into action, and out came the concrete from the hose. The pour started on the landing and top step, then partially fill on the next step, and so on down until we reach the last step, then back to the landing, filling the forms, top step to the bottom step. This allowed enough concrete in each step to prevent the concrete from running down and overflowing the lower step's forms. The laborers did a magnificent job at handling the hose for the pump operator. Step forms were filled. Juan and Diego were busy floating each step. Juan left Diego and had Manuel help him.

Juan had the ladders set up with a two-by-twelve-inch board between each ladder so the pump operator could fill the arch while walking on the board. Juan held the hose while the pump operator got onto the scaffolding. The arch was being filled with concrete, and Juan was beside the operator, tapping the form with a claw hammer, allowing the concrete to completely fill the arch.

I went to the concrete truck to see how much concrete was still in the mixer. "Maybe two yards," the concrete truck operator told me.

I called the batch plant and told them we might be short. "How much time would it take the second truck to arrive if I needed to add more concrete?"

"About fifteen minutes to a half hour," said the batch plant manager.

I was crossing everything now. I could not tell you what my blood pressure was registering. The arch was finished; it was now time for the barbecue footing. This was the easiest of all the things we were pouring. "Hoses in place and let her fly."

I returned to the truck to listen to the rattling of the drum; in a few minutes, the concrete truck operator took up his tool that allowed him to drag the very last bit off the chute. This was when I wanted the pump operator to shut down his pump and line up the wheelbarrows to take the final drop from the hoses. Just as I had wished for, the pump stopped. The mixer had nothing in the chute, the pump had a small amount, and the hoses were full.

The pump operator talked to Juan and headed over to the entry wall. Juan and Manuel set up the ladders and the ramp to make the scaffolding for the pump operator to fill the cells of the block. The pump restarted, pushing the final concrete into the cells. The concrete truck operator started hosing off the chute into the pump and hosed off the grate that caught anything in the concrete mix that would block the hose; the water being used would end up in the entry wall and evaporate or be absorbed by the block. The pump stopped; all was quiet. The crew started breaking apart the concrete hoses and helped the operator load them back into his truck.

My blood pressure eased back to normalcy, and the crew was now relaxed. "Break time, guys. Great job, gentlemen. The steps are starting to set up."

Diego put a nice trowel finish on the steps and used the edger to give a nice radius between the concrete and the forms. They were sitting on the seat wall, eating their lunches when Marie came out and looked at the pour. "That was fast. No problems?"

"None yet. Day is still young. You can practice tomorrow after we remove the forms." She just laughed.

I went home for a bite to eat, let my body return to normal, and said howdy to my sweetheart. "Hi, honey, I'm home to make your day complete."

"You again. Your Happy Meal at McDonald's wasn't enough to fill you up?"

"Now, dear, I just missed you, and I wanted us to sit down and enjoy each other's company."

"How sweet. You're always trying to please me. You're such a dear person. Your mother will be so proud. I can only offer you your usual. Vittles are running slim."

"Whatever you make, I'll cherish. I heard from Marie that you two are going to practice your entrances, do lunch, and then go gown shopping."

"That's correct, and if one wolf whistle is heard, you're on the couch for eternity. I really want to see the masterpiece I keep hearing about from Marie. Is she as nice as she sounds on the phone?"

"She's the real deal, complete package, just like you, my dear. She is really looking forward to meeting you and spending time together."

"Here's your sandwich, no chips or soda. Do you want some water?"

"Yeah, small glass, no ice, please."

"Did you call those clients who wanted to start their projects?"

"Yes, I have an appointment tomorrow with one of them and Monday with the other. I left messages with the others. This could end up becoming our best year in business. I may have to hire you as my private secretary. You know how to take dictation?"

"Of course I know how to take dictation. I hit the talk button on the tape recorder, hand it to the office girl, and go back to filing my nails for my manicure after my three-hour lunch. Do these dishpan hands look like I put a pen in them? If I have to work, then I want a company car, an expense account, a four-day work week, all major holidays off paid, and a three-week paid vacation."

"I have a great hire package that I offer new employees: a six-pack of doughnuts, either powdered sugar, plain, or chocolate and crumb. You can get a bus pass, no expense account, six ten-hour days paid for forty hours, paid holidays if you worked that day in the office, and a three-day vacation (Friday, Saturday, and Sunday) once per year, not on a holiday week."

"How many people jump on that bandwagon?"

"Honey, you would be the first and only specially treated employee, and you would have to sign a paper that your employment benefits would not be discussed among coworkers."

"Oh, look how your time just flew by. You get yourself back to work so you can afford to keep me. Bye, dear. Be home on time today. Your dinner gets so cold sitting on the oven."

I hope the crew is more receptive. One of a kind. It would be hard to find a replacement.

I returned to the job site, and the pour was setting up perfectly. Juan and Diego were busy putting the brick fascia on the entry wall, and Manuel and Jose were busy digging the footings for the patio cover. I looked at the planter to be installed by the staircase to see if we could start that footing. *No, maybe tomorrow. Don't want to undermine the steps and cause a failure. Let's take a peek at the plans. We have utilities, drainage system, and the irrigation system coming up next for layout, trenching, and installation. All very fun and necessary to make the final appearance sparkle. I could lay out the drainage system and trench in the morning. I have to see if the utilities will go below or above the drainage system. I need my notebook to review the elevations. It's in the truck.*

The crew was halfway completed with the front entrance wall. "Looks good, gentlemen." I got the notebook, and the drain line was figured at three feet below the original grade. That was all gone. We were nearly six feet below the existing grade and needed to reshoot the excavation to figure another course of action. *Let's look at the shed. Maybe there is something we can start on tomorrow. I need a shovel first and then see what the next step is.*

I went back to the truck, got the spade, and returned to the shed. I wanted to see what this shed was sitting on. *Great, stacked stone. Figures as much. Let's see how deep the foundation is. This ground has not been worked in years. I'll need the digger bar to get to the final depth.*

I again went back to the truck, and I got the bar. Juan saw what I was doing and had Jose start digging the hole. I returned to find Jose making good progress but straining with just the shovel. I started the digger bar about two inches deep. It was the best I could muster. We were down about twelve inches and still had not unearthed the bottom of the foundation. Down another six inches, and we finally found the existing grade, the base of the foundation. We went outside the shed and dug out the top four inches. As in the shed, we hit the foundation. We started to trench away from the shed, removing the soil from atop the foundation; it ended about a foot from the shed. It appeared to be eighteen square inches.

Manuel came over to help dig the foundation. I had them do exactly what we had done on the opposite side. "Just expose the top. I know how deep." They exposed the foundation on both sides. "I need to call an old friend who specializes in foundation repairs. I'll see if he can take a peek at this old foundation and give his recommendations. It appears that tomorrow we'll be working on the entrance wall fascia."

It was nearing quitting time, and the crew was busy cleaning up. The temporary gate and tunnel doors were closed so night critters wouldn't enter the tunnel. Time to go say hi to sugar pie.

CHAPTER 18

The next morning, I had the laborers mix the concrete for the entry wall cells; we covered the bricks on the front fascia so they would not get concrete splatter. Juan and Diego still had about 25 percent of the front face to complete. I knew that we needed to remove the forms from the steps so the homeowners could have access from the backyard to the courtyard. It made seeing the job easier for them. They spent most of their time in the rear of the house; the kitchen and home office both faced the backyard.

Juan and Diego started removing the forms from the steps. The first form came off the step, and the subconcrete looked fabulous. "Great job, gentlemen." It took about forty-five minutes to free all the forms from the steps. Once completed, I had them remove the forms from the arch. Once removed, the arch stood in all its glory—no cracks, no holes from air bubbles. Juan tapped the form just enough times and with just the right rhythm to get those bubbles freed. They could start setting some of the fascia bricks on the arch tomorrow; it still needed time to cure. I had them get the hose from the truck and spray water on all the concrete pours to allow the cure time to take a little longer; it strengthened the concrete considerably.

I turned to look at the staircase. John and Marie beat me to the punch. John said, "She tossed and turned all night long with the anticipation of walking down the steps."

"Can I walk on the steps?"

"You can, but please don't make any sudden turns on your feet. It will mar the finish. It's still very green."

"I won't sink in, will I?"

"No, it will support all our weight and then some. You'll be fine. Just be careful; here is no handrail installed."

"The concrete looks gray. Why did you say the concrete is green?" asked John.

"It's concrete terminology, so others in different trades understand the concrete is not cured and no excess equipment should be put on top of the concrete pour. We hosed off the concrete just a few moments ago, so it might be a little slick, so you both can come down and hold on to each other. Hand in hand will look nice."

Marie asked, "If I get my camera, could you take a picture of us coming down for the very first time?"

"I'd be delighted to be your photographer."

The camera must have been close to the sliding glass door; she was back in a blink of an eye. I went up the staircase and retrieved the camera from Marie. She showed me how to take the picture. I returned to the deck area, checked the angle of the shot, and determined just what step they would be standing on for the best view. I told them that I would stop them on each step and look through the viewfinder, and when the optimum shot was seen, I would have them stand still while I clicked the photo. They both agreed to wait on my command. On the fourth step from the top was perfect. *Click, click!* They came down two more steps, and I stopped them. *Click, click!* They could choose the view they liked best for their photo album.

Once on earthen ground, they both turned and looked at the stairs. "Still hard to imagine what the finished staircase will look like," said John.

"You will see the final product starting on Monday; it should be completed by the end of the following week, barring any hiccups. Without it finished, we can't start the deck. We will keep the finished staircase covered so it will stay pristine for the grand finale."

Marie turned and went back up the staircase, got onto the grass, turned around, and came back down the staircase. This time it was glamorous; she kept her hand held high as though she were holding a glass of champagne. John and the crew were applauding her entrance. I had to join in; it was absolutely priceless.

Marie asked John if it would be all right to call Delores to come over so she, too, could see how everything was coming together. "Oh no, the boss is coming? No place to hide either. I didn't even shine my boots this morning. There is no way she will decline that offer." I told the crew to look sharp. "The boss is going to come visit the job site today."

I called my friend, the foundation expert, and he said he could be there by the afternoon, after lunch or so. The gate builder called me on an update, and it would be a couple of weeks until the woodworking would be completed. He said, "The unfinished gate is stunning. Can't wait to put on the finish." He said he wanted to photograph this gate and arched entry for his brochure, if the homeowners approved.

"Hold on a minute; they are right here with me. John and Marie, the gate builder is on the phone and wants your permission to have him photograph the gate and entry to the courtyard once finished for his brochure."

"We would be excited. Will it be ready for the party?"

"Will your brochure be ready for their party? ... If he can have a week before the party, yes, it will be ready for distribution."

"Tell him we would like to have a stack set on our table for the guests to take home with them."

"Great advertisement." I told him, "You should shoot one during the daytime and one during the nighttime to show off your finish under the amber globes."

"Great idea. That would be something no competitor of mine has on their brochures. I know this house will be on a cover of some home-remodeling magazine. I'll call a friend of mine to see if they would be interested."

"You're putting a lot of pressure on me now. A cover—not just an article, but a cover. I'm shaking already."

"You'll be fine. They don't want a photo of you. The house is what they want, not a silly contractor. They have models whom they shoot and superimpose as you."

"Well, there went my fifteen seconds of fame, all in less than fifteen seconds. I'll be losing sleep the night before they arrive to be installed."

"Have a great day. Talk to you soon."

"He's going to call his friend who is an editor of a home-remodeling magazine and run your home by him, showing the remodeling. What a great feather in your hat if that becomes a reality. That would be worth a thousand or more word-of-mouth referrals. We're going to continue on putting the brick fascia on the entry wall today. I'm ordering the block for the barbecue and the small planter by the staircase in a few minutes. Feel free to stroll about your courtyard, and if you have any questions, please feel free to ask. There is no such thing as a dumb question."

My favorite response to customers was "Why do you ask?" If the customer was serious, he or she would respond with "Because I want to know, that's why." I had had one who just turned and walked away until I stopped her, telling her I was only teasing her. I didn't think she was amused.

"Oh, John, look, the arch was exposed for us to now see how the yard will appear. And look at the shadow on the ground. That's remarkable. Can we get some lawn furniture set up out here to enjoy tomorrow?" Marie asked John.

"No, dear, it's too early for that. It would just be in the crew's way, right?"

I said, "That's correct, and I would not want to cause any damage to the lawn furniture. You could put it on the patio by the sliding glass doors. You need to find the barbecue you want. It's time so we know the size to leave as an opening. Also, pick out the accessories you want to have installed to make your kitchen complete."

"I forgot all about that," stated John. "How long do we have?"

"We will start building the back wall tomorrow, so you'll see the L shape. But we can't do much with the front until we know the sizes and what you want to have installed."

"Marie, we have to do that tomorrow. No practice session permitted tomorrow."

I called the staircase subcontractor to tell him the subconcrete was ready for his magic touch. He had one project that they were finishing in two days, and he would start the very next day on the grand staircase. "Might it be sooner?"

"If it finishes ahead of schedule and is pristine, I'll call you." Two big ifs. I figured it was three days away.

Juan came over to me and reminded me that it would be nice to have the block for the wall and barbecue so they wouldn't have to sit around and wait. "Time is money."

"You're right. I'll be back in about an hour with enough block to get you going, and the rest will be delivered. How are you doing on rebar?"

"We have only a couple of sticks."

"I'll get more delivered with the block."

I left the job site to fetch the needed materials so the crew would not have to sit around and wait. I got to the masonry yard, and they loaded a pallet of block on my truck along with five sacks of mortar mix. I also got a couple of string line holders to keep each course level; they had broken the last pair. I also got a line level—easier than carrying a three-foot level. Each mason had a torpedo level to level each block. I also had the rest of the blocks set up for delivery just after lunch with the number 4 rebar and had them add on a roll of tie wire. I checked on the wall cap delivery date, and it would be next Friday.

"Do you want that delivered to the job site?"

"Absolutely. Free delivery as usual?"

"Not quite free, but very reasonable," said the manager. He did offer me a free cup of coffee and creamer or sugar, but not both. I told him I hoped they wouldn't lose any money on the free coffee.

I was all ready to return to the job site and get the ball rolling. As I pulled into the cul-de-sac, I saw a very familiar car. *Yep, it's the boss's car. This is the first time she has seen our progress. She'll be amazed, I hope.* I parked, and Manuel and Jose started unloading the block to the barbecue site. *Just in time. No break is a good thing.*

I entered through the arched entry, and my eyes were met by two glamorous ladies. Marie said, "You're back."

My dearest darling said, "So this is where you've been hanging out. I thought it was the local tavern."

"Now, dear, you know I don't drink. The bars don't pay very well either. So what do you think?"

"Well, nothing is really completed at this point. I love the staircase in the house, but you need to do more to impress me outside."

"Touché. That was better than 'What is this anyway?'"

Marie said, "I have my camera. Could you, do us the honor of a photograph, for our album?"

"I'd be delighted to photograph two gorgeous ladies."

Juan came walking up and said, "Where?"

The ladies got a chuckle from his comment. I told Juan that if I responded to his remark, I would spend many a night paying homage to the sofa. "So, Juan, what is it?"

"The foundation man came early and will come back in about an hour to meet with you."

"Perfect, I'll be ready for him."

The girls were ready to sashay down the staircase. Marie was first. It was so hard to get the right angle and lighting, but she was so photogenic that it made all photos look grand. *Click, click, click!* She landed. Now my dearest darling started down the staircase. *Click, click, click!* And she landed. The crew erupted in applause; the girls did a curtsy and started to blush just to get their cheeks rosy.

"How about you both come down together?"

"Great idea. How do you think we should come down? Hand in hand or arms around each other?"

"We can do both, or however you both feel the most comfortable. Those make the best photos. I have some Dixie cups in the truck. Wait a minute." I gave each girl a Dixie cup to hold like a champagne glass. "All ready? Let the band start. The guests are all poised, watching every move you make. Even John has his turner at the ready." *Click, click, click!* "So glamorous. You both looked fantastic. Great job, ladies." The crew applauded again. I told them, "Do not wolf-whistle, or the ladies will get very upset." The girls were off to do some shopping and, of course, lunch.

I instructed Juan that the first course around the barbecue was the only course to wrap around. "You can build the sides and taper to the first course. The back wall—take it to the finish level."

He asked, "Why?"

"The owners have not picked out which barbecue they want, and they're all different sizes, so prepare the sides to blend around to the front once we know just what is going to be installed." I got on the ladder to examine how the shed's rafters were attached. They were on the top plate, toenailed in place, almost up to today's code. These would be easy to remove after my meeting with the foundation contractor.

As I was getting down from the ladder, the foundation contractor walked through the arched opening. He said, "Nice job on the arched entry. Gives the whole project a nice flair. So you have a little concern?"

"We exposed the stacked rock foundation. Let me show you the details of the shed, which is to become the playhouse."

While the contractor, Phillip, looked at what we had exposed, I retrieved the plans from my truck. We opened the plans, and he agreed the stacked rock may not be sufficient to support the second floor. "The homeowners would have to sign a waiver to free you of any future liability. You're making this a nice place for the kids to reside. If I were younger, I'd want to play here. I'll tell you what I'd recommend. Take the shed apart, each side intact, set against the house. Remove the stone, and the eighteen-square-inch footing will be sufficient to support what you want to achieve. Pour a new footing to code and re-erect the playhouse. I could build the playhouse for you in a shorter time than you and your crew could. I have the necessary tools and expertise to complete this in about two weeks tops. Do you have any other wood structures on this project?"

"Why, yes, we have a patio cover." I showed him the details of the cover. "The rooflines are to match, and there is a storage area above the patio cover roof to hide cushions from the patio furniture and whatever the homeowners want to place above the structure."

"Great idea. Ceiling fans, electrical outlets, and speakers ... you will have a sound system?"

"There is one in the house, and the contractor that installed the system is a friend of the owner; he is scheduled to visit the job site in a couple of days."

"I could add another week to the shed and have both built for you."

"That would be fantastic. It will give me more time to build the stream feature and irrigate and landscape the rear yard, courtyard, and front yard. This could end up being the lifesaver I was dreaming about. I have two more projects on standby, and I don't want to lose them in the process. When could you start this project?"

"I'm finishing up one today. We could start in two days."

"A friend of mine is talking to a friend of his who's a publisher and managing editor of a home-remodeling magazine. If he decides to put this home in his magazine, all parties concerned in the building process will be mentioned. I'd like to add you to the list of contractors that made this happen."

"That would be fantastic—far better than a word-of-mouth referral. I'll give the homeowners a discount as long as I can have the photos taken of the playhouse and patio cover for my own brochure."

"I have a custom door that will replace the old door of the shed and the tunnel across from the shed. I also need to show you something inside the shed." I showed Phillip the artwork on the ceiling. "This needs to be protected and replaced on the new playhouse."

"That's amazing. Primitive, but it will fit the playhouse perfectly. I'm no artist, and I don't think I could do much better."

It was lunchtime for the crew. I brought my lunch and joined them on the retaining seat wall. One more day, and the staircase would become the magical showcase of the entire project. The girls sure liked coming down the stairs, and they would look beautiful on the day of the party. I had to look at the stream feature. I devoured my peanut butter and jelly sandwich; the crew called it kid food. I had a bag of chips, so it softened the chuckles from the crew. I'd have to get ready to excavate the stream, making the island, footbridges, utilities, sleeving under the stream for the irrigation system, and low-voltage lighting. *Lots of work back here—maybe three weeks of work.*

Juan caught up with me and wanted to know if the brick fascia should continue when the barbecue wall was completed. "Yes, that would be great. We need to get as much done in the courtyard as possible to get out of the way of the other contractors."

"The other contractors?" asked Juan.

"The stair contractor and the playhouse contractor will start next week, freeing us to do the stream, utilities, pathways, deck, landscape, and irrigation system, and get ready to start two more projects."

"You need to hire a couple more people. You will be jumping from here to the other projects."

"Diego will be your foreman. We will need another foreman that you can trust. I'll have to rent, lease, or buy another truck for the other foreman and Diego."

"When are the other projects going to start?"

"Maybe in two weeks, maybe sooner."

"Wow, I'm going to be running three jobs at one time?"

"Can you handle that?"

"I've only done two separate jobs at one time prior."

"New experience for you. You can handle it. I've got your back."

"My wife will be excited for me."

"You've worked hard for me, and you deserve to get rewarded with a little more responsibility. As I grow, so will you and the crew. Remember: pride in your work is the most important thing the crew and you can give to the customers."

The girls returned from their excursion. Both were carrying a catalog of fashions, leftovers from lunch, and huge smiles. It was great to see them enjoying each other's company. "Do I have any room left on my credit card?"

"I left you five dollars for your Happy Meal."

"Love you, always thinking of my best interest."

The ladies gave each other hugs. My lovely bride had to prepare her home for the arrival of the youngsters from school. I even got a kiss and a great hug; that was the best part of my day.

CHAPTER 19

There was a long, three-day wait for the staircase contractor to start doing his magic. If he could come close to matching the spiral staircase inside the home, everyone would be amazed. John and Marie were so pleased to see Stan Johnson return to their home. He and his crew were so polite and efficient and kept their home so clean as they performed a miracle on the original staircase. The repairs to the structure were unnoticed by guests and family, and the staircase shone with joy once completed. Stan was excited to show off his and the crew's expertise. No one could have completed the project with any more professionalism.

Stan had his foreman, Joseph, alongside him as we discussed the procedure they would follow. "How much space do you think you will need? I have a builder starting tomorrow on the shed, and my crew will be removing the stone foundation to allow the new foundation to be poured and the existing shed converted to a playhouse for the kids."

"We will need clear access for our work and maybe ten feet on each side just for our equipment and storage of the balusters and handrails. You know, it takes time to set and plumb each baluster to ensure the handrails fit perfectly. The homeowner knows not to use the staircase until all is in place and cured?"

"Yes, Marie and I talked about that. She, John, and the kids must stay off the staircase until they are told it is safe to use. I want to cover it to protect it from construction damage. Can that be done fairly easily?"

"We can wrap the handrails and balusters. The treads are biblical stones, which are thousands of years old, so they are used to wear and tear. The homeowner must not have the staircase become a toy for the children. Repairs can become costly and time consuming. Waiting on the biblical stones from Israel can take over a month."

"I'll let them know the importance of not playing on the staircase until the project is completed and we are all on other projects."

Stan's crew started to make some minor adjustments to the subconcrete pour, getting ready to install the first balusters. The end balusters were the most important of the staircase; once in place and cured, they could then start putting the balusters in line with the end balusters—such a tedious process. I also informed my crew not to disturb or get near the staircase until Stan said it would be secure enough for them to work around the structure. They had the end balusters in place in about two hours; they alone were making the staircase come alive.

Marie came through the arched entry with camera in hand, stopped, and turned around to look at the arch, with the brick fascia starting. She took a photo. "That is going to be so nice. I can't wait for John to see it. I'll use my phone and text a photo to him." She turned again to her staircase. *Click, click, click!* "I love it already."

The crew was starting to lay out the location for the next balusters to be placed. By lunchtime, there were eight more balusters in place, plumbed, and in line with the end balusters. Each crew member knew just what needed to be done to complete the staircase. Joseph was a master craftsman; he was so proud of the appearance and had his personal touch on each piece. Stan stood back and directed the crew like the conductor of a symphonic orchestra. I should have had Marie play some classical music on the sound system to complete the ambiance.

In the afternoon, the shed contractor showed up with his foreman to see what needed to be started the next day. I introduced Stan to Phillip, and they discussed how much room each would need. Stan informed Phillip to instruct his crew not to get near the staircase until he said it was secure. Phillip agreed and told Stan that the staircase would look fantastic. Stan asked Phillip, "Did you see the one inside the house?"

"No, I have never seen it."

"Come with me. I'll show you what inspired this staircase." They both went inside, and Marie was tickled pink to share the workmanship with a newcomer.

Phillip asked, "You built this from scratch?"

"No, we had to refurbish the old staircase. Here, I have some photos on my cell phone of what we started with so you can compare."

"This is not the same staircase. No way is this photo this staircase."

"Yes, Phillip, that is the exact same staircase," said Marie. "Can you believe this is what we purchased when we bought this home? Here is the photo of the staircase the day we saw this house. It was one of three. We had to make a decision."

"I hate to tell you, Marie, but that photo alone would have made me say 'Thanks but no thanks.' What made it so special for you to want to purchase this home?"

"Well, the other two homes had smaller yards, and one was by an elementary school, and the daily parent parade was annoying. Two hours in the morning and two hours in the afternoon was nonstop traffic. Just getting out of our driveway during those times would have been horrible."

"Well, you hired the right man to make the staircase come alive again."

"So the courtyard staircase will look similar to this one? This is Marie's dream come true. The courtyard staircase is her fantasy."

"I will see the both of you tomorrow morning, and I'm looking forward to making your playhouse comparable to the staircase. You may have two items in the courtyard that tickle your fancy. I'd love to have two or three items that draw me to the courtyard. I can't wait until evening, when it will all be lit up, adding more magic."

The barbecue back wall was nearly complete. Juan and Manuel started back on the brick fascia; the inside wall was 30 percent covered and looked like a million dollars. The staircase had four more balusters installed, and the crew was calling it quits for today—too risky to have balusters cure overnight. They now had three of the twelve steps fixed with balusters; tomorrow they would have three or four steps finished and could start fixing the handrail on the top. They would also form up the balusters' bases to give it even more detail. They were formed with Styrofoam and poured with a colored concrete that would match the baluster. The bases had an ogee-style edge that really put a sparkle on the diamond in the rough.

Marie came out and took some more photos for her album. I told her, "It will take your guests over an hour each to look at the photos. The line of your guests will be around the block. That's good for them. We can have cookies and coffee served to them—for a nominal fee, of course. So how do you like my wife?"

"She's such a doll. We had such a great time shopping and having lunch. The most fun we had was practicing coming down the staircase—our grand entrance. With each step we took, we both saw the guests with their glasses raised, the songs being played by the violins, the lady singer singing the perfect song. It almost brought us to tears with joy. We were discussing who would go down first. Could the second one down do as well?"

"You both have a unique image, both very glamorous and stylish. Your movement just flows with each step you make. I can't see how one would be better than or equal to the other. Both are very unique; your guests and family will be in awe."

"I am so glad you told us your vision. From that moment, John and I said that no matter how it turns out, we will be so thankful you're our contractor."

"I don't normally go into the detail that I went into with you and John. Something deep inside me said, 'You have to give them a glimpse of what you really are.'"

"So you don't have a set presentation that you follow at each meeting?"

"No, every client is different. Every plan has something unique. You can't have a standard when there is no standard because of variations. Remember: you can't use the staircase until Stan says it will be okay. Promise."

"I promise, and I will keep John and the kids away as well."

The next morning, bright and early, Stan's crew was busy installing the next three steps with balusters. Stan and his foreman started putting on the handrail. The very bottom balusters had the curls, so the view was almost a full-circle wraparound, and with the routed pattern, they looked unbelievable. The centers of the turns had a floral design just like the one in the house. The end wraparound would be joined by the curved handrail, heading up to the landing. The second section tied the next three balusters together, and it was fitting like a tailored glove. Stan rewarded his crew with "Perfect job, men. Everything is lining up perfectly."

I now could see how the staircase would appear while standing on the deck. They had both sides attached and were starting to pour the bases on the one that had set up the night before. The other part of the crew was setting the final set of balusters, waiting for the concrete to start to cure before they moved to the next set of eight. There were two balusters per tread, so each side would have twenty-four balusters to hold the handrail.

Marie came through the arched entry. "I'm not certain which one looks more attractive." With her gown, both would be stunning. With camera in hand, she was in awe, seeing for the first time how the staircase would appear from the deck. She aimed. *Click, click, click!* She shot three different angles of the staircase entry. "When will they start putting on the biblical stones?"

"Once the handrail is in place and cured, then there will be the arduous task of cutting the stones and making sure you see very few seams. They will also perform a round-over on the edge facing each step and then install the stone for the rise. Each one will take all the skill that the master craftsman can muster. This is all form fit—no grout lines whatsoever. It's amazing to watch. A regular mason could not do what these men can. They are highly trained."

"John and I are going to pick out the barbecue in a short while, along with all the accessories. We will bring you back the catalog and specifications so you can complete building the island. John is really excited—his toy, you know. My toy is the staircase, and the kids' will be the playhouse. The entire family will have a vested interest in the courtyard. Family affair."

"Who is going to claim the stream feature?"

"I think we will leave that to the wildlife that visits our garden. The kids are already planning of floating Popsicle sticks decorated with their own paint schemes so they will know who wins."

"Sounds like a lot of fun. I'll get my monsters to paint some as well, and they can race while the parents party. When you return, more of the handrail will be in place for you to take more pictures."

Stan's crew was making great progress. Eight more balusters were in place; only a few more and they would all be installed. Stan told me that, after lunch, they would install two more sections of the handrail and allow everything to cure overnight. He showed me the pieces that attached to the landing balusters; they looked almost like a ram's horn but were very ornate. "These are very difficult to fashion and will be the most looked at thing on the entire handrail. These are the crème de le crème of the staircase."

"Will you start the treads tomorrow?"

"Either tomorrow or the next day. The concrete is curing right on schedule, but when setting the stones, if we bump the baluster and it's not totally cured, it could make a masterpiece into a pile of rubble. Too much work to mess it up over being too quick. 'Patience, patience,' I tell myself every minute of each day. One of my very first staircases I destroyed in a matter of a few minutes. The client was not very pleased. I made it good, though I lost all sorts of money on that project, and almost gave up being a master craftsman. I did a lot of praying and asking for God's help when I got another contract. If that one had failed, you and I would not be talking right now. My confidence was in the toilet. My finances were loans—not a good position to be facing.

"I was very fortunate that my next few jobs were rewarding monetarily and built my confidence level greatly. I landed a project that opened so many doors. Word of mouth is a great sales tool. Too many contractors try the discount method: 'Buy today and get 10 percent off.' Off what, and how much did you put on the bottom line? 'I can give 20 percent off if I mark up my work 50 percent to start the negotiations.' Some people think they are getting a bargain. I couldn't sleep at night knowing I took advantage of a customer.

"I had one customer that told me, 'Whatever your actual cost plus markup comes to, put an extra ten thousand on the bottom line and put it in your pocket. I've seen your work and know your prices. You deserve more.' I thought he was joking until the final billing. He wanted to see my actual bid and quote sheets, which I gave him, and he gave me ten thousand dollars over and above my proposal. I went home that night and showed my wife the money. I thought she was going to faint.

"Well, I'd better get back to work, or my crew will fire me."

Stan and his assistant put the next two sections of handrail in place; the rest of the crew was busy cleaning up and putting things back into the truck. The job site was always in pristine condition before they hopped into their vehicles and left. They usually said good-bye to the owners if they were at home. There was nothing like getting a little praise before hitting bumper-to-bumper traffic.

The handrail was over halfway completed; tomorrow it would be completed, and the tread would start. Stan was pretty sure that the bottom two steps would be cured enough for them to start. That would make Marie so happy. *We may have to have her hold some rock to keep her grounded.* I took a few minutes just staring at the staircase; he was making our sub-concrete pour look beautiful.

Marie and John returned from the barbecue outing and were both speechless when they saw the staircase. John wanted to trade Marie the barbecue. "No way, that is not a fair trade. Yours will be a lot of work. I get plenty of that type of work daily. Mine is glamorous and stylish, fitting for a queen. That would be like me buying you a nice shiny lawn mower for your birthday. Nice gift, but it has 'work' written all over it."

"She has a point. Can't argue with a woman. Won't work ever. It's beautiful, and it's barely started. They may start putting in the biblical stone starting tomorrow. We'll see how the curing is coming along."

Stan and his crew were hard at it the next morning, putting the final pieces of the handrail on top of the balusters. Stan was correct that the final piece to the staircase was the start of the handrail from the upper landing. Once the handrail was completed, everyone got the cameras out and clicked away. Our subconcrete base was looking highly skilled, thanks to the handrail.

Stan and his foreman were checking the lower three steps to ensure the treads and risers could be installed without doing damage to the handrail. They went to the truck and retrieved enough biblical stones to lay out one step. The four-man crew quickly had the stones stacked with boards in between so as not to scuff the stones together, leaving scratch marks that would take a long time to polish out. Stan set up his worktable—not just any old table, but one designed to lock the stones in place while the router, with a diamond cutting tip, rounded the front edge of the tread. He chose a bit that would round over the edge in one pass. They hooked up an attachment that applied water to the bit to keep it from heating up and leaving a burn mark on the stone.

Joseph laid thick paper on the lower step and had a laborer help him set the first stone on the tread. They then placed another beside that stone, and then they picked up the third stone and laid it next to the second stone. I could see that there would be cuts made to the stones to fit them tightly; the laborer got two of the boards that the stones were staked on and handed them to Joseph. Joseph placed one on top of the first stone to rest the second stone. Joseph had pencil-marked the paper so they could remove the second stone and move the third one into place. They put the second board on top of the third stone. Joseph and the laborer placed the second stone on top of the boards. The cuts would be done on every stone, and before they could have the stones rounded off, the fitting cut was to be done with their special wet saw, which was being set up by Stan and the other laborer. They repeated this process with the fourth and fifth stones, leaving all in place so Stan could do his magic. These men were masters of their craft; each step was well planned and methodically carried out to perfection.

Marie and John came outside to catch a visual of just how all the pieces fit together. We all stood back and talked in low voices so as not to disturb the thought process going on between all the men. Stan went over to the laid-out stones and scribed where the cut was to be made on the first and second stones. Once those two stones were cut and fit together, they would then mark the other side of the second stone and the third. Each step could take a few hours l. The stones were picked up with great care and taken to the saw for the cuts.

Stan told everyone to stand far enough back so as not to get hit by a stone fragment; he gave us all safety glasses just in case. The stone was set and clamped to the cutting table of the saw, and Stan made the cut on the first stone. The cut was slow and precise. The crew then removed the stone and placed it on the other table for the rounding over of the edge. They put the second stone on the saw table and clamped it in place. Stan made that cut as well. The crew took the second stone and fit it next to the first one.

Stan looked at the fit and had all of us come and witness the perfection. He mentioned to us that the tread and rise process was the most tedious, nerve-racking step of the staircase, and he needed to make sure there were no mistakes. John asked Stan, "Just how long have you been doing this type of work?"

"Well, over forty years, and I could tell you in detail how much each mistake hurts. I'm just thankful that the tools I have save me from making the cuts with a hammer and chisel like they used when the two-thousand-year-old stones were crafted. You know, the craftsmen of those times could take massive blocks of stone and fit them together so tight that you, to this day, can barely fit a typical business card between them. That is a twenty-thousandth of an inch. I can guarantee you that no construction company in the world could duplicate that, even with the high-tech equipment we have today. Well, I have many more cuts to make, and the steps won't finish themselves, so if you would excuse me, my crew is getting restless."

Stan had rounded over the first stone and was halfway through the second when Marie said, "Those look beautiful. Can I take a quick photo for my album?"

"Of course, but let's keep that minimal so we don't get sidetracked," said Stan.

"Agreed," we all said in unison. This was a well-oiled machine, and each step in the process was critical.

Joseph and his assistant were laying a form beside the handrail against which the stones would be laid. It had intricate detailing on the form, so when filled with concrete, the finished product was stunning. We had other things to complete today, so standing around and watching was not on my agenda. The first three treads were cut and ready to be installed, and the fourth was cut on one end and scribed on the other, ready for the matching cut on the fifth stone. Both stones were cut and placed on the table to be routed. The sixth stone was scribed and ready for the cut; the two would be clamped to the table and returned to the step. The entire bottom step was cut and in place. *Perfect. What a difference.* They now showed the flaws of the subconcrete pour.

Marie came out to the courtyard with her camera, stopped in her tracks, and rubbed her eyes with the side of her hand like a child just getting up from a night's sleep. She said, "I'm so impressed with that look. It's nicer than the steps in the house. John needs to see this. He'll make it an early day and fly home."

Stan and the crew were busy doing the next step. They had two pieces already cut and routed, and were working on the next two stones. They now had placed terry cloth on top of the lower step so they could kneel down to set the next step. Joseph was busy mixing the cement to install the second step and the lower step, and he headed back to the office. All the cuts were completed on the second step; the cement was mixed and ready for installation. The second step was in place and laid perfectly, cementing the lower, bottom step. All cuts were impeccable; the treads on two steps were complete, ready for curing. There were ten more steps and the landing to go, and then the girls could practice on the real deal—maybe with real champagne to get the true effect.

The next morning, Stan and the crew were busy laying out the next three steps, working their way to the top landing. Joseph was setting up the risers on the bottom two steps. I gave them the covers for the step lights. We had installed the cable and curled up enough cable in each junction box. Joseph had to incorporate the cover into their cutout of the junction box. "The cover is a form fit—no screw holes to fasten the cover to the junction box. One contractor, a few years back, overcut the opening, and the cover kept falling on the step below. This did not make the customer extremely happy. The rise was a ceramic tile, so we had to remove the overcut tile and replace it with one that the cover actually fit. 'Mistakes happen' was not the right answer the homeowner wanted to hear."

Stan figured they would have the next three and possibly the fourth steps finished by quitting time. That would be the halfway point, which would put them two days ahead of schedule. That also meant that Marie could have the staircase by the upcoming Monday. Joseph had mixed and poured the first two steps' sides and would remove the forms later today to reveal the finished work. Once the treads were cut, he would form and pour the next section. I asked Stan, "Why can't he carry the side form to the top?"

"We use the side decoration to ensure the treads have no seams. It more or less helps with making sure the treads are lining up correctly. We tried to pour the side decoration as you asked. It just didn't look correct when we were finished. I have to have a certain feeling, or I feel I did the customer wrong. Too much pride and looking for perfection."

The next three steps were cut and getting ready to be cemented in place. Stan checked the time and determined that the next tread could be completed before quitting time. They got four steps completed tread-wise, and four risers were curing. This would give them a great opportunity to be three-quarters completed by tomorrow at quitting time. Stan and his crew were setting up for today's activities, and the staircase looked fabulous. They were busy covering the completed steps so they could use them for access to the upper steps. It was the same procedure as with the prior steps—paper covering, stone, board, stone, board and top stone, scribe, precision cut: step-by-step precision—an oiled machine. It was wonderful to watch, but that was not getting my job or crew motivated to keep up the pace Stan and his crew were working at.

They laid out the rest of the staircase and the landing. "If all goes as planned, the treads, risers, and landing should be completed by today. We will just have to finish the side edging tomorrow, and in two days, the staircase will be open for business."

"I will need to keep it covered until the party so the construction people and homeowners don't cause a need for additional cleanup. I may have the girls and Mom do a couple of practice entrances, but that will be the ball game."

"Just make sure it is two days after we have completed our work for cure time. I would prefer the construction employees use an alternate route—no shortcuts up the staircase to the backyard. You know what I mean?"

"Absolutely. I will also use an alternate route, not afraid of getting additional exercise. Watching my teenage figure. Well, if you have any need for me, I'll be preparing the backyard for the next phase—the stream feature. Have your crew be careful until we refill the foundation footing. We are also preparing to dig the footing for the circular planter and planter wall to the north of the tunnel door. I will keep the footings surrounded with caution tape until we get them poured."

"I will have them watch their step going in and out of the arched gateway."

Stan and his crew did another perfect job and finished the stairs and the landing. Tomorrow they would put in the side edging and wipe down the work installed; they would look for any imperfections just as a precautionary measure.

Marie came outside and shot more photos from the base to the top landing. I had no idea how many photos she took, but I would have to say she had at least two or three photo albums of the staircase alone. She was more excited than a kid in a candy store with his parent's Master Card. She was glowing from every pore of her body. I had never seen anyone with as much joy as she emitted. Stan and his crew even fit the step light grille and installed the lightbulbs and sockets. They didn't want my crew or me to take off the grille and mar the finish of the risers. I was so glad they took the time; it saved me a couple of nights of worry.

Marie asked Stan, "So is it two days from today or tomorrow until we can use the staircase?"

"Tomorrow, just to make sure everything is well secure. I don't want to see anyone get injured. The ladies I have seen are flawless, and a bruise or scuffed knee or elbow just would not be right."

"You are so sweet to say those words. I'll let the ladies know what you said. See you tomorrow. Have a great night."

"You too, Marie. Thank you for stopping by."

The next morning, Joseph was busy putting in the forms, and the leadman was busy mixing the cement; everything was curing as planned. Stan walked up one side, checking the handrail, and down the other side, looking for anything not perfect. Their work was far beyond good or great; words cannot describe the quality of workmanship that the crew produced. Everyone on the crew honored one another's work. The compliments were not just "great job," but more like "stunning and better than I have seen you do before." All crews working together to achieve excellence needed to practice what they turned out. Photos did their work little to no justice.

Stan was busy with the other laborer, tearing down their workbench and the saw table and placing it in the truck. John and Marie stopped Stan and gave him a formal invitation to the party. Marie even gave Stan a huge hug; she had tears in her eyes from all the joy he had delivered to her. "John and I will miss you and your crew; you're so talented and gifted. All of you are so well mannered, and you leave a spotless job site every day. Such a joy being your customer. Have anyone call us for a referral. Add us to your brochure if you would like for clients to call."

Stan left Joseph and the leadman on site to finish the edging and final wipe-down. Stan had another project to start. Joseph and his leadman showed up to strip the forms for the edging and do the final wipe-down and detailing. Joseph said it would take about an hour to complete the project.

Juan and I started placing stakes and caution tape around the staircase for added protection. Joseph told his leadman to get the plastic sheeting from the truck so they could cover the handrails and steps. Joseph told me that the steps were almost cured and for us to just cover them for tonight. They cut the sheeting and showed us how they needed to be covered. "It is only to protect the staircase from dew. If you cover too early, it could cause condensation, and that is just as bad as the morning dew." He would stop by in the morning and remove the sheeting, and the project would be completed. "If the ladies want to practice their entrance, have them remove their shoes for the first couple of days. The finish needs to harden."

Joseph told us, "I think the work you and your crew have accomplished will be marveled at for years to come."

"If he has a brochure for maintenance and cleaning products to use or not to use, please have him forward it to the customer or me."

"You two have a great day. It was a pleasure working with all of you."

CHAPTER 20

Phillip and his crew started on schedule. Phillip and Stan were introduced, and Stan enforced his rules of no one using the staircase until he gave the final approval. Phillip and his foreman, Raymond, went over what needed to be completed first, removing the rafters to free up the walls, and removing and protecting the artwork on the ceiling. "Number each board. Take your time while removing them. If there is a problem and removal will damage the artwork, stop and let's have everyone make the decision about how to move forward. Don't take it on yourself to make that decision. Once the walls are lifted and placed against the house, label them as well so we don't put the wrong side in the wrong location.

"The stone foundation will be dismantled by the other contractor who hired us, to be used on their water feature. Once they start removing the stones, you and the crew can start building the patio cover. Prime all lumber surfaces and use one coat of color. The final coat will be applied once it is assembled. The rough-sawn lumber for the posts and beams should be here in about two hours. Place the posts on the sawhorses and have one laborer start painting the primer coat. There are six posts and six heavy-duty column braces, and I have to purchase the galvanized bolts, nuts, and washers. There are six post caps that will hold the beams. All the wood has to be primed and painted before assembly. This is how the contractor wants it done. Pour the footings and set the base plumb to the right elevation, and the contractor's foreman will assist you. Any questions?"

"Do we get to eat lunch?"

"Only if everything is done before the lunch bell rings. Stay clear of the construction going on at the staircase. Do not bother them or get in their way, and they will do the same for our work. I have to leave to get the bolts, nuts, and washers to assemble everything. If you have the pour finished and have time, help the other laborers remove the stone and prepare the open trench for the pouring of the new foundation. The quicker we get that done, the quicker we can start building the playhouse. Here is your set of plans to follow. Build a worktable out of the lumber on the truck so we can lay out the plan set for everyone to view."

Raymond had the crew go to the truck and get the ladders and tools necessary to remove the rafters and ceiling boards. The rafters came off nice and easy. They removed all the nails and anything metal from the boards. They stacked every board in a pile, numbered each board, and listed it on the plans. Not having more roof support, with a flat top, made the shed look like a large box. Now there came the arduous task of removing the ceiling boards without doing any damage to the boards. The rafters came off with not one bit of damage, as the crew was very careful.

Ladders in place, Raymond and his leadman were on each end, and with the precision of a Swiss watch, they started slowly removing the first board with their pry bars. When the nails were out far enough, they used a claw hammer with a piece of scrap lumber under the head to take out the nails. The laborers had a bucket to gather the nails once they hit the ground. These men were well oiled like Stan's crew. The first board was freed, and sunlight shone through the opening. They could reach the second board without moving the ladder. The second board was a little tougher; some of the nails were being very stubborn. It was finally freed, and the laborers took the board outside once Raymond had marked it for reinstallation. More light shone through to the earthen floor. This process continued until the entire ceiling was removed, with lots of sunlight shining through, giving the inside of the shed light for the first time since it was built.

Raymond and the crew looked to see how the walls were joined together. It was determined they should remove the wall with the door first. So the shed did not just fall apart, Raymond and his leadman retrieved stud lumber from the truck with wood stakes. They fastened two studs with stakes to the ends of the shed not being removed first, two studs with stakes going north and south and two studs going east and west from the structure. They put blazing red flags on the supports so passersby would not trip on the angled studs. They tested it for stability before removing the end wall.

They next started removing the end wall. Nearing the final nails that held the wall together, the two laborers went outside the shed and applied pressure, pushing forward so the wall would not hit the house. The wall was now free of the nails. They had the laborers free up the pressure, and the wall moved just slightly so they knew it was absolutely free to place against the house. Raymond numbered the wall for the future. He asked Juan and Diego and the two laborers to help them place the wall against the house. Both crews lifted the wall and set it against the house. *Perfect.* The shed was now a U, no longer a square. Raymond got another stud and stakes and fastened it to the wall nearest to the staircase and red-flagged the stud just like the others.

The wall nearest the entry wall was to be removed next. They removed the studs for that side from the wall face but did not remove them from the stakes. Raymond and his leadman went back inside the shed and removed the nails holding that wall in place. The two crews worked together to slide the wall just enough for Raymond to refasten the end wall to the stake; if that wall moved inward and racked, it could cause both walls to fall, and someone could get seriously hurt. The side wall was numbered, labeled, and placed against the house ahead of the first wall.

It was time for a break for both crews. Everyone had their special block on which they sat during the break and lunch. Marie walked through the arched entryway; all eyes were on her. She greeted the crews with "Hello, gentlemen." This was the first time that Phillip's crew saw the lady of the house. With her camera, she took photos of the half shed still standing. She was very careful not to trip over the wall supports, very impressed at what she saw. She asked Phillip if he would come and get her once the shed was entirely removed so she could take some more photos. He agreed. She turned to catch a glimpse of her staircase and, of course, had to take another photo; she could not help herself. "This is a golden opportunity and can never be repeated. The different stages of construction are only there for a short time and gone forever. Kodak and I are very close—lots of pictures over the years." She then told everyone, "Great job," and she then returned inside the house.

Break time was over. "Let's take the end wall off next," said Phillip. "Could all of you stay with us, just in case both walls decide to come free at one time?" All agreed, and they unfastened the studs holding the corner of the two remaining walls and left the end studs attached. Raymond and his leadman freed the two remaining walls. Being very careful, they moved the end wall just enough to refasten the side wall with the stud. Raymond removed the stud from the end while both crews steadied the end wall. The end wall was moved to the house and leaned against the other two walls. Raymond labeled and numbered that wall as well. He then went to one end of the last wall and removed the screws holding the wall in place. Everyone was supporting the wall, and Raymond freed it from the stud supports. The crew placed the final wall panel against the other three.

"Thank you, guys. We could not have done that without your help. I'll go get Marie so she can take more photos." Raymond and Marie entered through the arched entryway. Marie was shocked at how much more room they would have without the playhouse. She took lots of photos from all sorts of angles with her camera. Then she used her cell phone to take shots to forward to John.

I thought she might want to change game plans. I was in a meeting with another client when I got her text showing the courtyard without the playhouse. *This is going to be another meeting. I can feel it.*

Marie contacted Delores to come and look at the courtyard now that the shed had been taken down. My darling bride was there in a few minutes and had to have broken every law in the time she took. Both ladies were in the courtyard and chatting before returning to the inside of the house. My crew started digging out the stones; one way or another, the stones had to be removed. Phillip's crew started putting in the post bases, and Juan helped Raymond set the grade for the bases. Phillip returned with all the goodies and saw the shed was against the house, and my crew was removing the stones so he could see the footings for the foundation start to emerge. Everything was going as he planned, and he was very pleased with Raymond and the crew. The posts were primed and drying; the beams were next on the assembly line.

Marie had now entered through the arched entryway and called to Phillip. "So what do you think of your courtyard?" asked Phillip. Marie told him that she and her husband would like to hold off on the footings until they talked with me to determine the next step. "That would be fine." I said. "He has the patio cover to construct, and that will take better than a week's time."

She was happy, and she introduced my Delores to Phillip. "My pleasure meeting you, Delores. Are you two sisters?"

"No, just friends. I'm married to Fred, the general contractor. He says I'm the boss when I stop by the projects."

"Very understandable. My wife and I are the same. She's the boss. It's a good thing as well. If I have a mistake, I have someone to blame it on."

"That would not work with me. You make the mistake. There's always a price to pay."

"You're a much harder boss than my wife. I bet you keep Fred on his toes?"

"More like on his knees."

"You look so nice and pleasant—even-keeled. I would have never guessed."

"That's what first impressions get you. Marie and I are practicing a grand entrance to the party, so the first impression we are both working on is being very persuasive."

"If I get invited, I'm bringing a Handycam to film the whole entrance of you both."

"That will be something I'll treasure for my lifetime. We, of course, would have to charge you and reserve all copies."

"That's a deal."

The footings were setting up but were still too green to install the posts. Juan told Phillip they could use stakes to hold the post plumb, and it would keep the weight supported while the concrete dried. "We have done that in the past, and everything stayed where it needed to stay."

"I'll give that some thought. We might just do that to prepare us for the beams tomorrow morning."

Most of the stones were removed, and Juan placed warning tape around the footing excavation; there was too much foot traffic. Someone could fall into the footing excavation. They had one more end to remove off the stone. They piled the little soil that was generated up out of the way.

Phillip and his crew tried Juan's idea on one post to see if they could do it for the one side on finished grade not behind the retaining seat wall. It appeared to work quite well, but he thought, *Just let them cure overnight and set the posts tomorrow.* They called it an early day and left the job site.

When I arrived, Marie and my beloved met me in the courtyard. My beloved actually gave me a kiss—better described as a peck on the lips. I thought it was a sneak attack. I waited for Marie to do the same—no chance. That alone would put me on the sofa for life.

"Well, what did I do to have the pleasure of meeting you lovely ladies this fine afternoon?"

Marie said, "I'm not sure we want the playhouse put back here in the courtyard. I like the open view and the extra space. I'm going to have to rethink the whole scheme of the courtyard if you remove the playhouse. I'm thinking you can reinstall the playhouse in the backyard, and maybe it can have a waterwheel into the stream. That would add ambience to the backyard, and the lower floor could be the waterfall and seating area. The upper could be the actual playhouse. Would that work?"

"I see you two have given this quite a bit of thought—good thought as well. You know, the waterwheel was attached to millstones to crush wheat into flour. I would have to do some research with different vendors to see if we could convert the waterwheel to power the pump to keep the stream feature flowing with water. Let me take a few minutes to visualize your vision. You two need to get a glass of wine and meet me at the seat wall."

The ladies returned with an anxious looks on both of their faces; the anticipation of "Okay, let's make the change" was apparent. "To be perfectly honest with you both, it's not a bad idea, but I'm going to have to make another drawing of both areas to determine if your idea will work. We have to worry about building codes and setbacks from the property line. By the way, I love how you both are bouncing the foot of your crossed leg; it is almost synchronized. Have you been practicing that as well?"

"Yes, we have. Do you think it will go with our entrance?"

"If you two keep working at that, no one will want to eat, drink, or dance, too busy paying attention to you, ladies. Man, I thought I could have a relaxing night off after dinner. Delores could sit on my lap in the recliner and whisper sweet nothings in my ear, just like the good old days."

"You have to be thinking of one of your past girlfriends. This girl does not have time for such foolishness. Oh, by the way, how does crow sound for dinner?"

"Pigeon is always on the Wednesday menu. You're changing for crow twice in one week?"

"It could become daily, along with the sofa," said Delores.

"Well, thank you, ladies, for making this such an enjoyable conversation I'll remember for quite some time. I need to see just what I can plan for tomorrow for all three crews."

That night, instead of watching television or goofing off, I had to unroll the plans, tape the construction drawing on the drafting board, draw everything except the playhouse, and determine just how to utilize the area. My main reason in putting the barbecue where I had drafted the location was the playhouse location. "Now that they don't want the playhouse there, I'm not partial to having a deck butting up to the house. Oh, I need another vision. It makes no sense to have a part of the patio cover located in the raised planter. The barbecue is half built, and the footings are poured for the posts. This is not going to be within reason. I liked moving the playhouse to the stream feature, and they seem all excited about moving the playhouse. When you get a block, nothing seems right. She was right about having more space, but what has been built will take away the entire atmosphere of the courtyard. I know; I'll call for my beloved darling. Honey, could you come in here for just a few minutes?"

"Yes, dear, I'm coming. What is it you need me to do—express my viewpoint?"

"I have a dilemma. I know you and Marie want to move the playhouse, and I was inclined to agree with you both. First off, I love you and admire the fact you have enough confidence to express your desires. Second, your input was top notch. My dilemma is that the barbecue and patio cover are being installed, and tearing them down and relocating them would be costly. Where they are located was in direct relation with the playhouse. It will look strange to have them where they are now located if the playhouse is missing. I'd love to dance with you in the place where the playhouse used to stand. Do you understand the dilemma?"

"So if the playhouse is removed, then you would have to relocate the patio cover and the barbecue?"

"Correct; it would take some time to replace what has been completed thus far."

"I want to call Marie and talk with her regarding what you just mentioned. Hold your thought. Don't move. I'll be right back."

About ten minutes later, my beautiful wife returned. I said, "Before you speak, I just want to tell you that you are beautiful and I'm so glad to see you at the job site; watching you have such a great time with one of my clients makes me feel proud to be your husband."

"Thank you, dear. Marie and I talked. She understands the dilemma, and she and John had a quick conversation regarding the matter at hand. They wondered what you could design knowing the playhouse will not be placed in the courtyard. How would you redesign the courtyard and bring back the ambiance it once had?"

"My dearest darling, sit here on my lap so I can further explain. Maybe you can inspire me to a different design. I've got a block, and maybe your closeness will unblock me."

"This had better not be a trick. I'll be really mad if you are trying to trick me."

"No tricks. I just need to have you close to me."

She sat down, put her arm around my shoulders, and snuggled up close. "How's this?"

"Perfect. I need to calm down and get in the right frame of mind. I've got an idea. I'll cut out the footprint of the barbecue and patio cover. Hold still, and I'll draw them on this copy paper, and you can cut them out with scissors."

"Oh, so now I get to work. This will cost you big time."

"Now I will place the cutouts on the plan, and we can determine if making a change is viable. Put the barbecue here and the patio cover here. No, it will block the entrance from the street. Here, honey, you move them around, and I'll stop you when it appears to be in the right spot and angle."

She was soon busy moving them around from one spot to another, then another, and then another. "Nothing feels right. You can't improve on your original design."

"Maybe just one more location. Nope, not there either. Why is no other location seeming right?"

"Well, I believe you have visited the job site and have seen how it all plays together, and removing one piece makes the entire design fall apart. You know, when you're putting together an outfit, pants look great, and blouse is wrong. Blouse looks great, and the pants look wrong. Finally, you go back to what you had on before you thought it all looked wrong. I've been there more than once. A few times, I just stayed home. Nothing looked right.

"Well, I'm glad we got to spend some mom-and-dad time together. Nothing got accomplished, but it was time well spent."

"Do you want to sleep on it tonight? Maybe something will come to you during the night."

"That will take some praying on my part, and I think that might be why I'm stuck. Thank you, dear, for taking some of your time to spend with me. I'll call Marie in the morning to discuss what we just did and tell her the outcome. We could make it really exciting, talk about what you desire."

"Settle down, tiger. You need to have the blood stay in your brain to fulfill your dream, remember?"

"How could I ever forget?"

Chapter 21

The next morning, my beloved was making breakfast and asked, "How did you sleep?"

"Like a fallen tree."

"You mean a log, right?"

"No, a tree—lots of branches, all dwindling and drying up."

She turned around and faced me, put her arms around me, and said, "No dream came to you?"

"No dream or vision, so maybe during my workday something will come to me."

"Marie and I talked about going to lunch again today. Will that be all right with you?"

"Can I have any leftovers?"

"Maybe, but don't hold on to your taste buds unless I'm not partial to the meal. Then I'd be happy to share them with you."

"Looks like peanut butter and jelly for lunch again. Today is tell-all and decision-making day. Phillip is going to have to know the next game plan to keep the project moving in a forward motion. I know Marie and John will want a new vision for the courtyard, and I know the answer will disappoint them. I need to sit and look at all angles to get a revelation on how to curb an issue caused by a stone foundation. The only thing that is a possibility is to mirror another raised planter next to the tunnel entry and possibly make the tunnel entry grander than it is now.

"If we were to install the playhouse in the rear yard, just where would it be placed? Could it also inhibit the view in the yard? Would it have to be a two-story structure? At what angle would the playhouse be positioned to enhance the bridges, or will I need the bridges? These are just some of the questions I need to answer to feel confident I'm doing my best for my customer. I'll have to meet with Phillip and address these issues. Maybe between us we can throw enough ideas out that one will make sense."

I had prayed last night, hoping for another vision, knowing it could just be delayed. John and Marie also might have to consider all the possibilities.

John and Marie came to the courtyard to pay me a visit. "Good morning, you two. Rough night sleeping, tossing, and turning, waiting for another vision, trying to fit the grand entrance without the playhouse," I told them.

John said, "We had the same sleep as you. We tossed and turned, got up just after one o'clock, sat in the kitchen, and had a cup of coffee. That was not the best idea. The caffeine made going back to sleep more challenging. We don't know what to do either. Their idea of making the playhouse a waterwheel is an intriguing concept. What are your feelings?"

"Well, to be perfectly honest, I was caught with my brain down or off guard. I even made paper cutouts with Delores to move the patio cover and barbecue to other locations, but none of those seemed to aid in the ambiance that the playhouse brought. I got another quick vision just a moment ago that might solve the problem. Marie, as you walked into the courtyard with the shed missing, what went through you mind?"

"I was so used to walking to my right side to avoid the playhouse and looking to see the staircase. It was nice not to have to avoid the shed," said Marie.

"Could you do me a favor and reenter the courtyard and close the gate, as if you are coming in for the first time today?"

"Okay, I can do that," said Marie.

"John, I want you to do the same after Marie. We will step aside and stand by the entry wall, looking toward the staircase. Okay, Marie, whenever you're ready, come on into the courtyard." The gate opened, and Marie entered the courtyard. "Stop right there. Close your eyes and tell me what you just saw."

"Dirt. I was looking down so I would not trip or fall on something."

"Okay, John, your turn to do as Marie, and listen for me to tell you to stop." John was outside the courtyard, and the gate was closed. "Ready—come on in." The gate opened, and John entered a few feet inside. I said, "Stop. Close your eyes. What did you see?"

"About the same as Marie, but I saw the start of the barbecue."

"I want to do as you two did. You tell me to stop when you feel I'm in the courtyard far enough." I went outside the courtyard and closed the gate.

John said, "Ready—come on in."

I opened the gate, entered the courtyard, closed the gate, and took a few steps, and they said, "Stop. What did you see?"

"I did what you two did—looked down to make sure my steps were solid. What have we just learned? No one looked at the staircase, patio cover, or retaining walls. We were worried about making solid contact with our next steps. While I digest what just occurred, could you two do me a great favor?"

"Of course, what do you need us to do?"

"Go to your kitchen and enter onto the patio from the sliding glass doors while one of you is outside; do the same for each other. Tell the one entering into the backyard to stop after a few steps."

Marie said, "I love this game. Do you play it very often?"

"No, Marie, this is my very first time playing the game. There are no rules established. Please return with your results."

They were gone for a few minutes and returned. "We both looked down at the concrete deck."

"So we have established a pattern. We really don't look at the surrounding area until we have secured in our mind that the area we just entered is safe to proceed through. Because of instinct, the shed was obstructing the view of what interested Marie. When she saw the obstruction gone, it gave her a good feeling. She didn't have to alter her course to see what intrigued her the most about the courtyard. Now, regarding guests to your home, as they enter into the courtyard through the gate, they will be looking for something totally different. It's all new to their vision. They will do as we did—look down to ensure they have safe footing. But they will be most concerned about a certain guest or you. Do you both feel that this is accurate? When you go to a party being thrown by a new friend and it's your first time in his or her home, what do you see?"

"We see the host or hostess, who takes our coats if it's cold outside and introduces us to other guests. Or, if it's a dinner party, we all converge into the kitchen or dining room or family room. We follow them."

"Do you ever stop to admire something inside?"

"No, never, not at first. We feel a little uneasy until we settle down."

"I don't want your guests to run straight to the staircase and miss the rest of the items you're putting into the courtyard. I want to slow them down and get them to take it easy and feel at home. Would that be what you two would like as well?" Why do you ask?

"So you're creating an at-ease atmosphere for our guests?" said Marie.

"Most importantly, I want you to be at ease, take it easy, enjoy the outside, see a hummingbird, butterfly, lizard, maybe a cat out on a prowl, a squirrel— anything you don't envision inside your home. Do you know what I mean? You have entered another type of world that you own but rarely venture into. I spend the majority of my days outside. I see things that bring me joy on the inside. I have seen beautiful birds, newly born grasshoppers, a baby tarantula, a hummingbird no bigger than a fly, baby mole that I held in my hand, garden snakes, and lots of lizards—babies and adults. Most people I know have never witnessed these things.

"They are inside a controlled environment. I heard years ago a radio disk jockey state, 'Life is short. Take time to smell the roses.' I had a three-hour drive to my rental home while I was going to college. During that whole drive, that phrase kept coming into my mind. I will never forget that and what it did to me. That also changed my viewpoint at the time. I'll bet you both have a favorite song you sing along when you hear it played, or a commercial that sticks in your mind."

"We thought this would be easy; should we put back the playhouse as planned?" asked Marie.

"I don't think so. You have already removed it from your minds, and putting it back would make it unusable. It will stand there all in its glory but rarely used, just something to walk around, maybe when you get a soda or a beer from the refrigerator. The kids may play on the playhouse, but if you show no interest, neither will they. This is a tough situation; I have to create a desire in you to want the playhouse to be a part of your family life. Putting it in the backyard, separating the adults from the kids, may not be the answer you were hoping to achieve."

We all sat on the retaining wall and looked toward the house. John asked if I would like a cup of coffee or water. "I'm fine. Thanks for offering."

Marie asked, "Are you going to get one?"

"I'm going in for a cup of coffee. Would you like one?"

"Yes, please, with a little milk added."

John walked through the arched gate, and Marie leaned over, kissed my cheek, and said, "I love what you bring to our family." That was so moving, and it brought me back to reality. "I didn't even think that moving the playhouse would actually separate the adults from the kids. What do you think the courtyard will look like upon completion?" asked Marie.

"I want to give it intrigue. I want you and John so stirred up inside that the courtyard brings you to nature, and that you both, with your kids, get to create your own stories about being outside. I'm tossing around in my head how now to piece this puzzle together."

John returned with the two cups of coffee. "Did you figure something out?" asked John.

"I think I might have a solution, but it's going to take a pencil and some paper and a meeting with my two favorite customers I have ever encountered. The crews should be showing up any moment, and If I don't look happy and doing something, I could get fired. By this time tomorrow, you will be sitting in the shade of the patio cover."

Phillip and crew walked through the arched entry. "Good morning, everyone," stated Phillip. "Glorious sunshiny day. Can't wait to get the posts, beams, and joists in place. Did you determine what you're going to do with the playhouse?"

"You and I need to have a meeting and kick something around. Do you have some time this morning?"

"Of course. The crew can start the posts and set the brackets for the beams while we kick it around."

John and Marie said, "Excuse us while we go back inside our house and get the monsters ready for school. Have a great day."

"So what are we kicking around?"

"I want to put the playhouse on top of the patio cover. The roof will be half one elevation and the other half the playhouse with its own roof. The shed used to be ten by ten feet. Half the patio cover makes that a perfect fit. I want to add a patio deck attached to the beams so the kids can come out and play, and definitely install a staunch handrail for protection. The patio deck will face the courtyard. Instead of a fire pole, we will install a knotted rope or a rope ladder for the kids to climb. I'm not certain if anything like that will ever be installed; just throwing mud right now.

"The door entry will be on this side, next to the entry fence. The staircase will enter from the courtyard and run parallel to the entry fence. I think you can build it off the original drawings. The soda fountain will be in the playhouse—not as large though. We will have french doors leading to the patio deck—no pocket or folding doors; those will take up too much floor space. There will be a wooden floor, plywood subfloor with a two-inch-by-three-inch-by four-feet hardwood floor for durability; threshold—the french doors; and a cedar- or redwood-surfaced four-sided deck. We may have to add two posts to support the deck. One step post will run up to the deck. I still have to pencil in the details of this process."

"So you want the shed to be placed on top of the patio cover as original?"

"As much as possible. The wood floor will be new. My trailer has the workbenches and tunnel lumber, so please use as much as possible to keep the structure appearing old. You will more than likely have to build a sill plate for structural support. You're the pro, and you know building codes. I trust you will make this the cornerstone of the courtyard.

"Oh, no pressure there, said Phillip. "We'll do a great job for your customer, and the cover of the magazine will always be treasured by our firms."

"Oh, something else: I want a roof gutter with downspouts going into the raised planter."

I left Phillip and went to see John and Marie.

John answered the door when I rang. "Do you two have a few minutes?" I asked.

"I believe we could spare you a few. Please come inside."

"Good morning again. I think I have a solution for our dilemma."

"So soon. That didn't take very long."

"Well, just talking sometimes is enough to break through the blockage and start getting the design part of my brain working again. I need your approval for my newest and greatest idea."

"We're ready to pass judgment. What do you propose?"

"I want to put the playhouse on top of the patio cover. There will be a split roof standing above the barbecue, the shed with its roof above the other half of the patio cover, two-tiered. The playhouse will be the shed, not a two-story structure. The playhouse will still have the soda fountain / bar. The stairwell will be on the north side between the patio cover and the entry fence. One of the stairwell posts will support the patio from the playhouse, all with handrails for protection of the kids. The door that led to the tunnel will be the entry door into the playhouse.

Now the kids and adults are in the same area. They will just play above you and alongside you."

"What about the noise of them playing while the adults are dining beneath their activities?"

"I know kids. They're full of energy in spurts. When they're not making noise, I get suspicious of what they are up to. We could put an insulation layer between the floor and the ceiling of the patio cover to lessen the noise level. I'm still trying to put all the details in play."

"That solves the playhouse dilemma. What about the large open space?"

"I want to put in a circular raised planter with a specimen tree, maybe a fruitless olive with a very ornate multiple trunk; a seat wall to match the retaining seat wall; and a raised planter by the staircase. I also want to add another raised planter on the north side of the tunnel door, and I want to enhance the tunnel door entry with gingerbread around the door, since now it is in plain sight and not really attractive. I want it to have some pizzazz there, but with style."

"Will the planter have lighting?"

"You'd better believe it—uplights to illuminate the trunk and branches, and wall lights to accent the seat wall. I want to put a light above the tunnel door like at the entry gate, or two wall lights on each side of the door—not sure which way yet. The raised planters will also have lighting. Pathway lights, I'm certain, would look the best. Now you have a balanced courtyard with some added ambiance and additional seating for the guests, and plenty of room for the host and hostess to dance to your favorite song played on violins. What do you think?"

"So as you walk through the courtyard gate, you'll see what?"

"You will see a glimpse of the staircase—enough for you to want to see more; circular planter seat walls; the patio cover with a playhouse on top with two different elevations of roofs—same style, same color, just split apart; the barbecue island; the retaining seat wall; and the grand staircase."

"Can you lay out the vision with stakes and your fabulous hot pink string as before?"

"It would be my pleasure. I need to see it myself. I'm still kicking around your idea of a waterwheel. That is a great idea. I have to spend some time in the backyard to absorb the vision. One vision at a time is all my brain can muster."

"How long will it take you to lay out your vision?"

"Give me at least an hour. Make it a half hour, and I'll be ready for your approval."

"You said you will use a fruitless olive. Why fruitless?"

"The mess it will make to your seat walls and deck—unless you are both huge olive eaters and know how to process the raw fruit to a jarred olive."

"Nope, just asking why," said John.

CHAPTER 22

I had everything staked and tied off when John and Marie came through the gate. I told Marie, "Every time you enter the courtyard, I hear violins playing in my head."

"What song do you hear?" asked Marie.

"It's very soft and romantic. 'Return to Me,' by Dean Martin. Well, here it is, all staked and strung."

"This will be nice," said John. "What do you think, Marie?"

"I'm still trying to hear the violins," said Marie, with shimmering eyes.

"Wait a couple of minutes until the song ends; then I will be ready," I said. "Is she easily sidetracked?"

"No," said John. "This courtyard has her mesmerized. Her parents are coming over sometime next week, she is so anxious to show them what has been completed thus far. She wants her mom, your wife, to walk down the staircase with her. I just stand back and enjoy the transformation that has occurred. She has been singing in the kitchen while making dinner. She hasn't done that in years."

"Well, Marie, are you back to Earth yet?"

"I'm ready now. What is it you want from me?"

John said to me, "Don't answer that question. She's not thinking clearly."

"Your opinion, dear. Can you live with the new layout?"

"The circular planter—is that the outside or inside circumference?"

"Outside circumference, unless you want that to be the inside."

"If it were the inside, how much wider would the planter become?"

"Add about fourteen inches for the width of the seat wall cap, twelve inches for the wall itself."

"I like it to be the inside circumference," said John. "Another foot won't take us that much room, and there is still plenty of room to move around."

"I think the seat wall will be just enough for our guests to want to see the staircase," said Marie. "Do you agree, John?"

"I believe you are correct once again, my love," said John."

"I know who has to see this to put the stamp of approval on the layout. I'll call her right now."

"Oh no, the boss again. I left her in such a dilemma. She'll think I was just keeping things from her. I didn't even have my Happy Meal this morning," I said to John and Marie.

"I'll protect you," said John. "We will tell her what we saw while talking with you earlier—tell her the game you played, have her do the same game to make sure she understands."

Phillip called over to me. "What's up?" I asked.

"The posts are all set in place, waiting for the cure to take place. They are getting ready to prime the joists and some blocking. Is the elevation on your plan the same as the patio cover, first floor to the entrance to the second floor?"

"Great question. I don't know for sure."

"How many steps do I show? Can you calculate how many steps this change will require?"

"We will have to add four four-inch posts to support the porch and patio. There may be five new posts—three on the porch and two on the patio. Okay, I'll get my drawing started tonight and get it to you in the morning. My crew can help yours lift the panels to the patio cover roof and shed floor. The final side will be an experience getting it into place. We will have to get it to the floor and position it once we have it standing on the floor. I will have to build a sill plate. The old shed has a single board. It should be double. I may also have to add a top plate as well to meet the new building code."

Within a few minutes, my dearest love arrived. I heard the girls coming; we weren't making enough noise for them to startle me. "Good morning, my dearest darling. Have you been drinking?"

"Just plain old water from the bottle."

"You'd better check the label, dearest darling."

"Yeah, right."

Marie explained the layout and told Delores to step outside the courtyard and close the gate. She did as Marie told her. "Now enter into the courtyard." She did as Marie suggested. "Stop. Close your eyes. Tell me what you saw."

"Dirt. I was looking down so I would not trip."

Marie walked over to her and hugged her. "Your husband is so smart. He had us doing that earlier this morning. We even did it leaving the kitchen, going into the backyard. The same—we looked down to where we were walking, didn't notice anything else. Are you hungry?"

"I'm getting there. Why? You want to go and get something to eat and go gown shopping?" "Do you have time?" asked Marie.

"Yes, I have my hubby bringing home the roadkill for dinner—plenty of time," said Delores.

"You two crack me up, so quick witted, unpredictable, and clever," said Marie.

"I like the new layout. It should be very nice, warm, and cozy. The extra seating will allow for more guests, meaning more applause for our grand entrance," said Delores.

"I can't wait," they both said in unison.

All the crews were watching the girls. They applauded them as they left through the arched gateway. Both ladies turned around and said, "Thank you, silly boys." And they strutted off.

Phillip measured for the stairwell; he wanted the crew to put the first beam across where the stairwell would be installed. He could go to the lumberyard and purchase the precut stringer. Since there was a subroof for the patio, the crew would need access to the upper deck, carrying materials up a ladder. It would limit how much one man could carry. He figured there would be two additional steps. "The height of the patio cover is over seven feet, or fourteen steps. The shed is a foot shorter than the patio cover. It would not be enough to add to the agreed price quoted. It's so nice to be almost correct."

In a short while, the girls graced us with their presence. It was so nice to see them both in such a great mood. "How was lunch? Any leftovers?" I asked.

"Sorry, Charlie; the lunch was too good to share. Maybe next time," said Delores.

"Delores, look at the staircase," said Marie with great enthusiasm.

"Oh, it's beautiful, I hope our gowns do it justice. When we are allowed to pose for a photo, we will have to take it to the dress shop to make sure we have selected the perfect color. We also have to make sure we don't clash standing next to each other. So much has to go into being perfect."

"We can handle it. Look what we have already accomplished. Stan, the staircase is absolutely beautiful, almost breathtaking."

"Thank you. My crew and I are very pleased with how it is turning out and hope you get many, many, many years' enjoyment from our efforts."

"You will come to the party, won't you?"

"I'll need the date and time, and I'll make every attempt to be here."

"Make sure you bring brochures to hand out to the guests and family members."

"I'll surely bring brochures. I'll have my wife carry them. It'll give her something to do to earn her keep."

"We'll keep her busy enough while you hand out the literature," said Marie.

The girls returned to the patio cover to inspect the progress being made there—one beam was up, another going up, and one waiting to be installed.

"Lots of boards laid out with fresh paint. Will all this be installed today?" asked Marie.

"We sure hope so," said Phillip. "That was my plan. Not sure if that is the crew's plan. We'll see who wins. I hate to leave you two, but my lumberyard is calling me to get on my high horse and giddyap and go."

The crew had the beams nearly all installed and were heading to their truck to retrieve their lunches. Raymond was busy marking the beams for the joist hangers, he on one side and the leadman on the other. The nail guns were all loaded; the boards were nearly dry after lunch. Once the first joist was hung, the rest would just fall into place. They would eat in the shade the following day with the rest of the crew members. They all huddled under the shade tree in the backyard, where it was pretty crowded.

The girls headed back inside to talk in private. Phillip returned with the stringers, some two-by-twelve boards, some two-by-six boards, four three-quarter-inch-by-four-by-eight-feet sanded plywood sheeting, and five sixteen-feet-by-four-by-four-inch rough-sawn cedar posts to match the newly installed six-square-inch rough-sawn cedar posts. We determined that the four-by-fours would be thirty-six inches from the beam; this would give clearance if the posts lined up. I wanted to make sure there was plenty of room for guests to walk between the posts.

Phillip laid out the footing locations and had the laborers start digging the footings. Raymond and his leadman took the joists for one section and leaned them up on one rafter. As the board was placed in the joist hanger, the other person would carry one end to the other joist hanger, set the board in the hanger, and do the next board. The leadman was putting the next hanger in place while Raymond carried the other end to his hanger; now half the patio cover had joists hung in the brackets. Both men were firing nails into the predrilled bracket holes with joist nails. Nail guns were popping off almost in unison—here a pop, there a pop, here a pop, there a pop—for a good five or so minutes.

Raymond said, "One section done. Let's move to the next section."

They repeated the same process in the section where Phillip was busy drilling holes to insert the first stringer against the beam. He was in such a hurry that a laborer stated, "Aren't you going to prime and paint the stringer?"

"You're right. Let's prime and paint one coat. I almost forgot that had to be completed before we can assemble." Phillip looked at the joist in the first section. "Great job, gentlemen. Will you be done before we head home?"

"We should be very close to finishing. This is the easy part."

"From here it looks flush. Are the joists flush with the top of the beam?"

"Yes, we made sure before we nailed."

"Do you have enough to do the blocking?"

"I believe we do, but I need to measure between the joists to make them fit," said Raymond. "I like to hang and install without stopping to make a cut on every board. Goes together really quick."

"How was the T-post cap to install?"

"Tricky but all lined up, and the beams all fit together like a charm. We still need to drill and bolt the beam to the post cap." All the lumber Phillip brought back from his lumber extravaganza was primed and painted, ready to be installed the next morning. They painted only one side of the plywood; once installed, they would prime the plywood facing the floor of the playhouse.

CHAPTER 23

Next morning, Phillip and the crew were busy installing the five posts in the brackets installed and poured the day before. They would trim off any excess post once the handrails were in place. Raymond started fastening the stretcher on the beam that Phillip had started yesterday but forgot one little detail—the paint.

All was good and perfect for today. The leadman and one laborer brought in a cutoff saw on a table for a work area. Raymond had marked the blocking on the joists, so the leadman sent the laborer with a ladder to tell him the first measurement. The leadman cut the block from the pile of painted lumber, and the laborer came and got the cut block and gave the leadman the next block measurement. The laborer taped the block in place, waiting for Raymond to screw it in place with a three-inch deck screw. Phillip and the other laborer finished drilling and installing the bolt, nut, and two washers, two per post. Everything was rolling smoothly.

Phillip got a ladder from his truck, measured from the beam to the back side of the post, and cut a forty-five on the one end of the two-by-six-inch rough-sawn cedar board. He made a pencil mark on the beam where the joist hanger would be placed with a four-foot level, and marked the post to the top of the two-by-six-inch board. The cut was made; the bracket was in place. Up went the first board into the bracket. Now Phillip drilled the post, and the first frame board was in place. He did the same on the other post before he mounted the outside board.

"We are so good," said Phillip. "The exact measurement as the other side. Can't beat perfection, gentlemen." Now he placed the outside board's forty-five cuts on both ends, drilled two holes, and put a lag bolt with a washer in the hole. He then measured from the last board installed back to the beam and took that measurement to his waiting saw.

Raymond got to a point where he could install the joists on the board that Phillip had previously installed. He had the laborer help Phillip on the posts that would hold the porch at the top of the stairs. The porch frame had to be installed before the other stretcher could be attached. There would be no place to attach the top of the stretcher without the frame.

Marie heard the saws running and knew this would be another photo opportunity. "This is going up fast. I may have to sit out here the whole day tomorrow to catch the entire phase of construction. Looks so nice. What is Raymond working on?"

"That is the frame for the patio for the playhouse."

"Are the posts going to be that tall?"

"No, we will cut them to length once we know where the handrail will be placed. We will need to have the walls in place before we put up the handrail. I will lay the deck top and the subflooring for the playhouse before we put up the rails and handrail going up the staircase. Do you want a handrail on both sides of the steps?"

"I think that would be great. It would match the staircase with its two handrails."

"Marie, I hope you know that our handrails will look nothing like Stan's—no way near in comparison. That staircase is a masterpiece. I'm in total awe of the work that crew produces. Raymond wants to be as perfect as that crew. Right, Raymond?"

"Yes, Sir Phillip, in due time. Being a master woodworker takes years to perfect. That's my goal. Choosing the right board and shaping it the way they do just don't happen. Skill—lots of skill involved."

"Most of our work is framing. The top deck is our treads, the fascia is our risers, and our balusters are all made by a computerized machine, so they are identical—not handcrafted, huge difference."

"Phillip, don't forget the 'Made in China' sticker."

"Oh yes, not even made in this country. Our paint is still made here. That's about all."

"Great job, gentlemen. I have to go pick up the children from school and start being a mommy again."

"Thank you for stopping by and chatting with us. Feel free to come by anytime. We're here to help with your questions."

They started the cleanup, put the tools back into the truck, and got ready to go back to the company yard, ending another fun-filled day. Phillip started taking notes for materials he would need for the next day. He talked with Raymond about getting my crew to help with the panels. "We could build a ramp on the opposite side to drag the panels to the top if they are too heavy to lift. We don't want anyone getting hurt. I'll bring some rope from home to help."

"Do you have a winch in the garage?" asked Raymond.

"I might have a winch. I will check the garage, said Phillip."

Phillip and the crew were on the job site, attaching the other stringer to the porch frame; they also attached the joists to the porch and were cutting the deck boards when we were asked if we could help them in an hour to lift the panels to on top of the patio cover. "We would be delighted to help you get them on the roof. Do you need any help at this time?"

"No, we're just going to cut the treads and porch deck so everyone can get to the roof without using a ladder. I will also put a temporary safety rail on the steps to prevent someone from stepping off and getting injured."

Raymond and the leadman were making the cuts for the step treads while the laborer attached a temporary staking to hold the stringer base in place. They were using three-inch deck screws to fasten the treads, drilling pilot holes to prevent splitting. Phillip was attaching a temporary center post on the stringer to hold the temporary handrail.

Phillip informed me that he was certain the homeowners would want to enter the playhouse once all the walls were in place and secured. He was going to add another top plate to the walls to ensure they were tightly secured on top and the new sill would secure the bottom of the wall. They were putting in two-by-four joists to set the new playhouse floor, with plywood sheeting on top just to put the wall in place; the plywood would be used for the roof and an underlayment, and hardwood flooring would be laid once the roof was in place.

There was a need for the homeowners to select the stain for the floor in a couple of days. Phillip had a color board in the truck he would show them. The staircase was just about finished; they were cutting the one-by-six risers while cutting the treads. Marie would be excited to see another staircase nearing completion so she could practice on that one as well.

"If you guys want to bring the panels from the house to the patio cover, that would help us when we are ready for the old heave-ho." Phillip's two laborers went to the panels, and my four crew members followed. The first panel would be the last one to be put in place. They leaned the panel against the six-by-six post and went to get the next panel. Raymond was directing them on how to lean the panels in order of installation. The panel with the door was the last panel against the house but the first one to be installed. The order was in place, and the laborers lifted the plywood sheeting to the leadman, and Raymond and Phillip had the screw gun and screws ready and placed the plywood in between the new sill plates they had just finished installing. Phillip had Raymond predrilled five-eighth-inch holes in the sill plates, spaced at sixteen inches on center and four inches from the sides. The panel was soon ready to be muscled up to the top of the patio structure.

"Is everyone ready to muscle up the panel?"

"All ready, waiting for the word, good old heave-ho."

"I'll need one person up here to help me slide it onto the floor. I have two ropes for you to attach on the panel about two feet from the end. Raymond knows how we have done it in the past. We will be able to help lift the panel once it is beyond your reach. Raymond, place two ladders so two guys can help support the panel from where the ropes are tied. Now we are ready. On three. One, two, three, lift. Perfect. Got the edge on the patio cover frame."

The panel was more than halfway up, and two laborers got on the ladder, lifted the panel nearly level, and pushed the panel to more than three-quarters onto the patio cover frame. The panel was resting nicely on the structure. Phillip's crew was on the deck, sliding the panel onto the new floor, ready to stand it up and set it in place. My crew was on standby. Phillip asked if two of my men could come up and stand on the new patio to help stand the panel on edge. The panel was now sitting on the new floor; up on edge it went, so smoothly. Everyone was in the right spot, and the crew walked it to the front porch and placed it on the new sill plate. Raymond's holes were perfect, and the bolts used to anchor the panel were being installed.

One laborer came down, moved the ladder, and handed Juan a wood stake and a screw gun to attach the stake to the side of the panel. Juan did as directed, and the laborer fastened his end to the beam. Phillip was checking for plumb while the laborer fastened the stake. The first panel was in place. Phillip checked the door to ensure it would open properly; it opened with ease and no creak. "Three more to go. Follow the same procedure as the first panel."

We took the second panel to the raised-planter side of the playhouse; the raised planter was three feet higher than from the other side. We lifted the panel to the men on the roof as it would be placed. The men on the roof would just lift it on top of the sill plate and slide it into position. Raymond drilled the holes in the existing sill plate, and we were ready to heave-ho. The lift was much easier than with the first panel; we all held the panel until the men on the roof put one end on the sill plate and scooted the panel into position. Three of my crew held the bottom of the panel flush while the bolts were being installed; another support was placed by Phillip's laborer while Phillip was plumbing the panel. They also bolted the second panel to the first one and locked it tight and plumb. The second panel was in place. "Let's get number three up and ready to install."

We lifters on the ground decided to lift the third panel from the raised planter; it was much easier, and we didn't have to extend our arms completely straight—better leverage, more stable. Raymond came down from the roof and drilled the third panel's sill plate; it was now ready to be put on the roof. He and his leadman put two more sheets of plywood on the patio cover roof so the men on the roof had a place to stand. "Don't want men trying to lift a panel while trying to get their balance walking on joists. This could get someone really hurt."

Phillip fastened the plywood down in place with wood screws so it didn't shift. The third panel was carried to the raised planter and positioned it as it was put on the roof of the patio cover; it could be slid into position without any turning necessary, and the sill plate would face the door of the playhouse. We would lift the panel's left side to the crew on the roof. Once the edge was on the patio cover, the men would work their way back to the right side of the panel and push it to the men on the roof, and they would get it into position to be installed on the new sill plate. That was the game plan anyway. We were having no issues thus far, and everything was falling into place as planned. Confidence levels were through the roof.

"Is everybody ready?" asked Phillip.

"Ready to go, Phillip. Just say 'heave-ho.'"

"On three, just like the prior two panels. Great job, guys. Keep up the good work." There were four men on the left side panel, sill plate toward the door. "Heave-ho." Up the panel went; it passed the patio cover floor, and the crew set in on the roof and worked their way back to the center. "Up and push." The panel was now under control from the roof crew. Two of our lifters ran up the stairs into the playhouse and helped the crew position the third panel in place.

"We're getting really good at this. Too bad we only have one more panel," said Phillip. That was not the consensus of the lifters of the panel. The third panel was in place and plumb. "Do you guys want to take a break or forge forward with panel four?" The crew felt a short break would help them restore some muscle endurance. The panels were not light—maybe over three hundred pounds. There was no way to weigh them, and it was a good idea not to tell the crew just how much they really weighed.

Just as the crews were sitting on the retaining wall, through the arched gateway came John and Marie. "John, look, the playhouse is almost finished," said Marie. "Can we go up the stairs and see what it looks like from up in the playhouse?" Phillip told them to follow him; he wanted to make sure there was nothing on the floor they could trip on. They followed Phillip; once in the playhouse, they both mentioned that this was a fantastic idea and that the views were stunning.

Marie asked Phillip if they could put a window on the side that faced the entry to the cul-de-sac. He replied, "We can add a window on that wall. You want to see who's coming down the street?"

"I just like the view I saw when I was standing on the porch. The mountains are on that side."

"You know, I never noticed the mountains. Not focused on views too much to think about just getting us this far. Do you two want to stay up here and watch the fourth panel being placed?"

"Will we be in your way?" asked John.

"No, you just have to stand next to the opposite wall. Do not lean on the wall until we have the fourth wall in place and anchored to the floor and other two sides," said Phillip.

"This will be a once-in-a-life-time experience for us. Love to see how this all fits together," said John.

"Gentlemen, are you ready to complete the box," asked Phillip?

Raymond was drilling the holes in the sill plate. "All ready for the old heave-ho." Raymond and the leadman positioned the two ladders to help get the panel on the deck. The panel had to be put in at an angle, and the left side lifted first. This panel had to be lifted upright, not laid on its side. "Take your time, and keep it balanced the best you can."

Phillip asked me if I could go up to the roof to help them steady the panel as it was being lifted. I told the ground crew, "You can do it. I have lots of faith in your abilities." Two of the six men got onto the ladders to aid the ground crew in lifting the panel to at least waist high. They would support the panel from wanting to lie flat.

"Heave-ho, gentlemen." The four men scooted the panel to the men on the ladders and lifted the panels with the left side toward them; they were holding it steady while the crew repositioned themselves and lifted to the level, and up it came to the floor level, resting on the floor. The floor crew held the panel, scooted it onto the sill plate, and backed up to get the panel totally on the roof. The two men ran up the stairs and helped get the panel into position on the sill plate.

Phillip was checking for plumb; he and I were on the patio deck, making sure the panel didn't lean out of plumb. The sill plate bolts were being put into place, the wall anchor bolts were now in place, and everything was getting tightened down. Juan brought us an extension ladder so we could get down off the patio. We didn't want to climb into the playhouse through the window.

John and Marie came down the steps and back onto the ground and looked up at the playhouse. "This is going to be so nice. What kinds of doors will allow passage from inside the playhouse to the patio? asked Marie.

"French doors with a light shining down on the deck, matching the one above the front door entry," said Phillip.

"There will be electrical outlets in the playhouse?" asked John.

"At least one on each wall, and a light switch to control the inside lighting and the porch lights on a separate switch," said Marie. "The porch light will be on a timer so you can walk down the steps at night by the porch light. The playhouse walls are in place. Looks really nice sitting up there."

The crew was getting the rafters from the stack of wood. Raymond was measuring the distance from the playhouse to the post and from the deck to the handrail height; he would transfer those measurements to make the handrails. He and Phillip were discussing the methods used to complete the handrails and what to do on the stairwell. Phillip asked John and Marie if they wanted the handrails painted or stained with a high-gloss varnish. "I have a sample board in the truck. I'll go get it and show you how it would look."

Marie told John, "This will be so nice for the kids. We'll have a tough time getting them to come inside to eat and sleep."

I said to them, "How about Mom and Dad? Will you have a tough time as well?"

John said, "I don't think I can get her off the staircase, and I can only cook so much food. We will get so large we will need an elevator to get into the playhouse."

"Oh, John, you know I would never allow you enough time to get fat. You'll have plenty of cleanup chores just in the courtyard, stream feature, front entry, and patio, as well as lawn mowing and weeding. I don't know when you'll have time to go to work."

"Maybe I should change my name to Cinderella."

"You may have to hire a French maid to be your assistant."

"Fat chance I'll let him have an assistant—especially a French maid. Maybe your buff gardener you told us about a few days ago. I might let him have one of those."

Phillip came back with the sample boards. They had to move from where they were sitting, as Raymond was getting ready to cut the opening for the French doors. He had set up the re-studding of the doorframe and added a two-by-twelve-inch header, double thickness, for support of the roof going in on top of the doors—no sagging allowed. Out came the panels, so now we could visualize the french doors, and the crew had access to the patio to put on the rafters. They might have the rafters and plywood in place before the day's end.

While Raymond was cutting out the French door opening, Phillip had him cut an access door from the playhouse to the other side of the patio cover. *They could store items from the yard and the playhouse under the pitched roof of the patio cover. They also would run the conduit for the electrical under the wood flooring into the walls. The junction boxes would be under the patio cover roof. The electrician mentioned that it would not be a bad idea to have an auxiliary panel in the barbecue area for easy access in case of a quick shutdown separate from the house panel. We also needed to set up the junction box for the ceiling fans, one mounted directly below the playhouse.* "*Lots to think about. Miss one detail, not pretty.*"

I was nearing my lunch break; the crew had the rafter boards set in place, ready to install. Raymond had numbered the boards when they were removed from the roof. The laborers just had to match the numbers—a no-brainer. The little time it took Raymond to mark each board saved them a huge amount of time trying to match the boards from the stack.

Marie made another call to the boss. "She's on her way," she said. It was lunchtime, you know, and there was a new staircase they could play on. Life was getting too good to be true for them.

Phillip wanted to add an overhang on all four sides of the new roof and would get the necessary materials to make that happen. He also stated the old roof had no beam joining all the rafters. The beam would have to be installed because of the building code. The roof had to support a certain load weight, or it wouldn't pass inspection. This would allow me to put an overhang on the ends and sides. It would give the structure more character.

John and Marie were going over the color boards and different finishes for the floor and french doors. That reminded me to contact the gate and door maker and tell him the door to the playhouse would come unfinished because of a contract change. Marie asked Phillip, "Can we keep these for today and give them back to you in the morning?"

"Well, I normally would say no. But since you both are wonderful people, I have to say no problem. I know where you live."

Just as I was about to go get my lunch, the entry gate opened, and in stepped my blushing bride. Marie jumped to her feet, rushed over to Delores, gave her a hug, and said, "Look what they did this morning."

Delores said, "Is that all they got done? Slackers—they are all slackers." And she started to laugh.

That took Marie by surprise. Delores was hugging her, saying, "Just giving the boys a hard time. It really looks nice, guys. Just kidding you."

Delores came over to me and said, "Let me see your hands." I showed her. "Just as I thought, clean as a whistle. Tough day watching?" That got the crew laughing.

"No, dear, I was helping with the panels. I just got the clean part of the panel."

"I see; we will have to discuss this back at the office."

She and Marie continued up the staircase to the porch, and Marie stopped and had Delores turn around and look at the mountain to the north. "They are going to put a window on this side so we can see the mountain while the boys do all the chores."

"With our wine or champagne?"

"Both. We have all day to nap it off. There is no way it will take them only a few minutes to clean up the courtyard to our standards."

"You know, the playhouse up here is not a bad idea. Look at the view from all sides. Why the hole in that panel?"

"Can you say 'french doors'?"

"Are you kidding me? French doors—whose idea was that?"

"Your hubby's idea."

"Honey, what have you been smoking?"

"What?"

"What have you been smoking? Are you deaf?" Both girls were standing on the patio now.

I told them both, "Be careful. There is no railing yet."

"You're putting french doors on the playhouse?"

"It will only be a playhouse for a few years, and then it's the adult's playhouse— bar, fold-down bed, big-screen television, stereo music, light dimmers, nice guest room for Mom when she comes a-visiting." John started to applaud with that one. "Be careful, John. Remember: no handrail."

"Now it all is making sense to me. You think Marie and I would fall for 'come on, honey, let's look at the mountain from the playhouse' line."

"Well, we would have the aroma of rib eye steaks on the grill, baked potato, fresh asparagus spears sautéed in wine and butter, dinner rolls, your wine chilled to perfection, no kids or family members visiting, low-voltage lighting. What else would you need?"

"A million dollars laid down as a tablecloth, and we will clear the table for you while you do the dishes." The crews were enjoying this back and forth, cheering on the ladies.

"Time for everyone to go back to work. We have to get the roof on before going home."

My crew headed to the backyard, and Phillip had to go get some lumber and pick out the french doors. My job was to get ready for the next project and stay ahead of this one. Marie and Delores's job was going to lunch and shopping. They had so much shopping to do; Mama was coming tomorrow to walk down the staircase in style.

Raymond and his leadman started putting in the rafters; they used a double two-by-twelve, cut to twelve feet. They marked the center and attached one side of the rafter, resting the support beam on the top plate on the door side. They made a support to fit under the beam so it was level. They went to the door side and installed the rafter, marking at sixteen inches of center; the rest of the rafters were installed like butter on a baked potato fresh from the oven. The roof support went in better than anticipated. They started installing the plywood sheeting from the patio side. The laborers brought them the sheeting so they would not have to keep getting up and down from the ladders. The first half of the sheeting was completed; now they could work from the finished side to attach the sheeting to the other side.

The laborers leaned the sheeting against the patio cover and part of the playhouse. They stayed in the raised planter and handed the sheeting up to the leadman, who lined it up on the edge of the rafters, putting it in place and fastening it with a nail gun. The plywood sheeting was completed, and Raymond started putting on the roofing paper and underlayment, readying it for shingles. They placed two tarps over the finished work and nailed the plastic sheeting so the wind would not blow the tarps from the roof. Quitting time was fast approaching; they put plastic sheeting over the french door opening in case it rained. They would start the lower roof tomorrow and tarp it if they had no shingles. The girls returned and were amazed at how quickly the playhouse become reerected.

CHAPTER 24

The next morning, Phillip returned with turned spindles for the staircase, prefabricated handrails, and a french door and casing to be installed in the opening. The electrician was due at the job site any minute. Phillip made it just in time. The electrical panel was on the opposite end of the property. It would be a long run to put a subpanel in the barbecue area as suggested. The playhouse would have at least four receptacles, two or three more were needed on the patio cover for lighting during the holiday season. The barbecue would need at least two for what John wanted to cook up, so to speak.

The electrician was on site. I talked with him while Phillip, Raymond, and the leadman were getting the French door leveled and plumbed. I suggested, "In lieu of putting the panel in the barbecue, why not put it in the tunnel? That door will be locked, and the box can be hidden from guests and fit flush into the wall."

"Can we look at the tunnel?" asked the electrician.

"Yes, it's right behind that door."

I opened the temporary door, and the electrician said, "A perfect location. How far does this tunnel go?"

"To the kitchen area, not sure of the distance. How will you get the power from the main panel to the subpanel?"

"I'm hoping we can horizontally bore from the tunnel to the panel."

"That would be ideal if it is doable."

Phillip came looking for us. "Good afternoon, everyone."

The electrician, who was Phillip's friend, said, "You never told me about the tunnel."

"I didn't think it could be used."

"I've got a friend who does horizontal boring, and this would cut quite a bit of trenching, conduit, and time from my estimate. I'm going to contact him to see if he can meet me here today or tomorrow. Now, what am I going to light up?"

"We have two main features and one minor feature for you to look at here in the courtyard. The first feature is the playhouse on top of the patio cover, the patio cover, and the barbecue."

"All three are in the same area?"

"Yes, all straight across from the tunnel."

"How do you want them wired?"

"I would like a breaker for the receptacles and lights for each entity," I told the electrician. "That would be six breakers. We could probably get by with three. I don't want them tied together. If there is a holiday party going on and all features are being used, I don't want an overload. Flickering lights have never excited me. And I want dimmer switches and a speed control for the ceiling fans."

"Can you separate the two fans?"

"I want to try to cover all the bases and allow the homeowner to adjust the lighting as they choose. I also have lights on the arched gateway and one above the tunnel entry door. I also want the capability of leaving the porch light on at the playhouse; they can remotely turn it off once down on the ground level."

"All that is very doable—some a little pricey. I understand why you want more breakers. I too hate a flickering light or lights due to lack of power. Are there any 220-volt items?"

"I think the barbecue they selected might be the only fixture. I'll get the brochure from my truck. You can verify the electrical requirements. I'm going to install a water feature in the backyard and low-voltage lighting throughout the project. I want to set those transformers, pump, and skimmer in a location near those features. I also have an irrigation controller that will need to be powered as well."

"All this will have to be ground fault circuit interrupter, correct?"

"Correct, and inspected by the city inspector."

"What is the city code for the trench depth?"

"I believe twenty-four inches unless there is a gas line, and it might go deeper. I'll check with the city and give you the information."

Marie came out for a visit. "Can I speak to you when you have a moment?"

"I have a moment right now. Excuse me, gentlemen. My, you look stunning this morning, all dressed up. What's the occasion?"

"Remember: my mom is coming for a visit."

"Is that today?"

"Yes, your lovely wife and I are picking her up at the airport, doing lunch, and then coming here to see the project. She is very excited to see how things have progressed. I only sent her a couple of photos. I want to surprise her."

"So what do you need me to have completed before you all three arrive?"

"Just make sure that there are no big messes and the area is safe for use to walk around. Can you fill in those big trenches over where the shed used to be?"

"I will get my crew moving the stream feature excavation and fill in the bulk of the trench, and we will start digging the circular planting footings, filling in the other trench as we dig. I can't say the whole foundation will be filled in, but it will be very close."

"I really appreciate that you are so flexible and willing to please John and me. You have done some amazing things for us already. I would give you a big hug, but I can't get my outfit soiled." Marie shook my hand.

Before letting go, I told her that her presence on the job site boosted the morale of all the crew and me, and that we looked forward to seeing her each and every day. "Hugs are great. All you need to do is just be you. That is more than any man could ask."

Phillip and the electrician were wrapping up the meeting; he had some tweaking in his proposal and told me he could start the work in a couple of days, if that would fit our schedule. "That would be perfect," I said. "Nice meeting you. See you in a couple of days."

Phillip's crew was busy setting up the rafters and beam for the lower roof of the patio cover. They had around 30 percent up and finished. At lunchtime, Phillip told his crew, "Great job, men. You're doing nice work."

I could now visualize how the two rooflines would appear. I stood next to the house and gazed at the silhouette of the skyline and the shadows on the patio deck. The ambiance being created by various shadows would make this area picture-postcard famous. This would be a photographer's dream come true.

By the end of the day, both roofs were erected, the roof papered, and underlayment in place and covered with blue tarps. Just before the crews were getting ready to head home, the three ladies arrived. They walked one at a time through the arched gateway. Marie was first, then her mom, and finally my blushing bride. I saw now where Marie got her looks. Mama had to have been a model in her years. "Well, Mom, what do you think of our courtyard?"

"Very nice. Makes me feel like I'm back in my hometown in Italy. Will the playhouse and patio cover have tile roofs?" asked Mama.

"I don't know. I'll ask the designer and introduce you. This is Delores's husband."

"Why hello, Delores's husband. I have heard quite a bit about you on our trip back to Marie's home. So you're the one that has my daughter all in a tizzy. She wants me to walk down some staircase, pretending I'm at a party with violins playing. And they introduce me, and the guests applaud. I'm even in an evening gown. You saw all this in a vision?"

"I did, and there is the staircase you will be blessing with your grace and beauty."

"Oh, you're a flatterer as well. Delores, you'd better keep this one very happy. You'll never find a better replacement."

"Why, thank you, Mama. I can call you Mama, can't I?"

"If you have visions like I heard, you can call me anytime."

"Okay, it's Anytime. My pleasure meeting you, Anytime."

"You're pushing your luck, young man. Be careful. I have friends in very high places. Wow, that staircase is beautiful."

"Mama, you have to see the one in the house. They match."

"Let's go, girls," said Mama. "You're getting me excited, honey. We'll see you inside, designer."

Delores came over to me, gave me a hug, and said, "Watch it. She's a very powerful woman."

The next morning, Phillip and the crew were hard at putting the final touches on the roofs—fascia boards, steel splash edging, and then the shingles selected by John and Marie. "Nice color. Looks like ceramic by a wood composite—very lightweight, and it comes with a fifty-year manufacturer warranty. Really makes the playhouse and patio cover come alive."

The access door from the lower roof to the playhouse was framed and nearly complete. Raymond was telling Phillip he should have completed the access door before they put on the plywood sheeting. It would have been much easier. Phillip had the laborers put drop cloths under the patio cover to start the final color coat. They were nearly complete in installing the tongue-and-groove cedar roof between the joists to cover the plywood sheeting. They ran the conduit into the playhouse under through the subfloor joists, through the sill plate, and up the interior wall. The walls were still bare studs. The insulation would be placed once the conduit and junction boxes were in place. There were multiple conduit runs being completed.

Phillip went to the lumberyard to pick up the hardwood flooring but probably would not start installing it until the electrician pulled the wire and did a burn test. He did not want the arduous task of removing the hardwood floor to get to some conduit. He also ran the conduit for the fans with junction boxes in place.

John, Marie, and Mama joined us right after their breakfast. They were excited to see the progress that had taken place in just a couple of hours. John said, "The roof shingles we picked out look fabulous." Mama asked if they came in terra-cotta. "No, a reddish color, but not terra-cotta. The red would not look very good in this situation."

"Well, it won't be Tuscany, but it sure looks lovely."

"Thank you, ma'am. Would you like to see the inside of the playhouse? We would love to see how it looks from the second floor. Raymond, place some plywood over the studs so our lovely guests can get a visual of your handiwork. Please be careful. The handrails are being constructed as we speak and will be installed within the hour. Put the rope back on the posts just in case, okay, Raymond?"

"Will do. Just give me a couple of minutes. It will be ready."

John asked Phillip, "When do you think it will be completely finished?"

"About two, maybe three days tops."

"Would it have taken longer if the playhouse was put back on the foundation?"

"Yes, maybe an extra week longer. Putting in the steel for the footing, the L bolts, setting a sill plate, putting back the panels, installing the pocket doors, building the cabinets—all that would have taken longer. We will start on the cabinets and soda fountain tomorrow, once the electrician has finished his work, and the interior walls will be covered."

"Still a lot of work to complete."

"The work will go quickly. I have a cabinetmaker building the boxes for the cabinets, and he will deliver and install tomorrow or the next day. It all goes pretty fast. The playhouse is level and square, so there will be very little form fitting. He has the plan for the inside of the playhouse."

Raymond said, "All ready for inspection. Welcome aboard."

They were about half done with the hand-painted ceiling, so that was an added feature that was not shared with the owners. Mama asked Marie, "When the kids are older and this turns into the adult playhouse, will you have the ceiling stripped of the primitive artwork?"

"We haven't talked about what's next yet. We're trying to keep it as close to original as possible. This might be on the cover of a home-remodeling magazine. The editor of the magazine is coming out tomorrow to take a peek at our project, review the plans, and give us his opinion. I'm a little nervous since it's not near ready for that type of inspection."

"It is a wonderful job site, has lots of character, and the design fits it like a glove. He should be impressed, as I am, Marie." Mama gave her a hug. "Not to worry; your designer has your back, and the quality of the workmanship speaks for itself."

"Let's try that staircase. Delores should be here any minute, and the three of us can practice all at once. I have some sparkling cider and champagne glasses for the practice session."

"Sparkling cider? No, dear, break out the real juice. John, you have a bottle, don't you?"

"You know, if you three just wait a few minutes, I'll run to the liquor store and buy a couple of bottles."

"You're such a good man. Marie, keep him. Don't let him out of your sight."

Delores made her grand entrance through the arched gateway, and the crews applauded her stylish moves. She made a curtsy to honor their appreciation. Even Mama gave her applause. "Simply lovely, my dear. You have that down pat."

Delores said, "I have to keep my fans happy. Oh, they are a happy bunch of workers."

Phillip said, "Happy and better be working to make up the time lost. Let's go, gentlemen. It doesn't build itself."

I reminded the ladies that they had to go to the staircase barefoot or in stocking feet—no shoes. "The finish on the biblical stone is hardening. Tomorrow you can do it in shoes, but no high heels."

The ladies went into the house and reentered the courtyard from the landing. They removed their shoes and, with the champagne glasses poised in one hand

and their right hands on the handrail, they sashayed their way step-by-step, slowly and methodically. I could see a remarkable improvement in my dearest and Marie; they descended with no hesitation, and smooth body movements. They could have kept books balanced on their heads without falling off. Even Mama was a pro, hands down; this lady had done this numerous times. They all could have hosted any awards show on television and gotten more applause than the winner of the award. The party would be talked about for years.

The gate builder was here. "Is this the scheduled day? Oh, now the ladies can enter from the arched gateway or the tunnel. So many choices and so little time for more practice." I met the builder and showed him the change for the playhouse. I asked him if they could build a surround for the new door going into the tunnel.

"I will take a photo and give it to my master woodworker to build a stunning frame."

"Can we modify the door casing as well?"

"We can make it from the same materials as the door, same finish—another work of art."

"That would be ideal, since I'm certain the door will be left open at some time or another during the party, and that would make the entire entry stunning."

"I'll have my crew install the door for the playhouse first, and then the tunnel door, and finally the arched gateway. Should be a couple of hours at the most. The new casing for the tunnel ... give me at least a week."

"That will be perfect. Oh, redo the threshold at the tunnel and take a look at the playhouse. If a new threshold is needed, figure that as well. There will be oak hardwood placed in the playhouse. That will start either tomorrow or the next day."

"I see we're having a floor show."

"Oh, yeah, there will be a ten-dollar cover charge for the show. The sign must have fallen off the gate. Oh, a two-drink minimum—water, of course. Your choice, bottled or from the garden hose. To keep cost down, it is self-service."

"Now I see how the homeowners can afford all this new construction."

The patio cover was looking beautiful; the cedar tongue-and-groove with a half-round border was perfection. When the ladies made their final runway appearance, I told them they had to see the patio cover. "You'll be amazed."

The three came through the arched gateway, the last time for the temporary plywood door. They all paid tribute to the temporary door and wished it a second hanging on another project. "Please don't cut up our door for another home."

Phillip said that if they would autograph the door, he would put it in the shop for all new customers to see. He gave them a Sharpie. "Just sign it anywhere, like a celebrity." He showed them a photo of his lobby at his business. "I'll put the door on a stand here in the corner so as a new customer walks in through the front door, they will see your signed door. If we get that on a magazine cover, I will tell the editor to photograph the door in my office." The girls were so excited; he had them practice on a piece of cardboard before making their final signatures on the plywood door. Mama was now having a great time; even John was smiling, and he told me he never had a smile when she visited until she was on the plane heading home.

Raymond had measured the opening at the end of the patio cover roof. He drew it on some paper, and he and the leadman designed a door for access into the open attic space. They would build that tomorrow and install the door when the electrician and his crew completed all the wiring. It allowed cold air inside the roof attic; once sealed, it would get really warm inside that space. The project was nearing the completion phase. Phillip told Raymond he and the leadman would be the only two working tomorrow; he and the laborers were heading to another project. The handrail for the stairs, porch, and patio were nearly finished. It was stunning how it all fit so nicely, and the stain and high-gloss finish on the handrails was brilliant.

CHAPTER 25

The next morning, Phillip stopped by to meet with the electrician. He had Raymond and his leadman assist the electrician in pulling the wiring in the playhouse so they could continue to close up the walls and start the hardwood floors. They needed to get the stain and polyurethane coat drying, for the cabinets were due to be delivered in the morning. They wanted the floor finished where the cabinets would sit. To allow for the installers not to mar the finish to set the cabinets, the boards were not stained or finished.

The electrician had his boring friend visit the job site, and all three men decided to attempt to run a conduit under the home in about two hours. "Please let the homeowners know there will be some noise generated by the boring machine. My crew was busy trenching from the tunnel to the patio cover and barbecue per the layout by the electrician."

With the wires being pulled from the receptacles to the junction boxes, it took just about an hour for that work to be completed. The electrician's crew was assembling the receptacles and light switches and installing fixtures. The porch and patio lights looked great and fit the building better than what we had imagined from the catalog picture. All the wiring was pulled to two main junction boxes located on the patio cover post. They were hidden in between the beams and joists; one really had to look for them; they were nicely installed. The trench was completed by our trenching machine run by Juan, ready for the inspector, who was due there any moment; he'd check the depth of the trench, instructing the electrician about sand bedding of the conduit and warning tape to be placed about six inches above the conduit. We were preparing the as-builts for the homeowner to keep for future reference.

The ladies were back outside, looking at what was being completed, dressed too nicely to be practicing, waiting for my blushing bride to arrive. *This is getting to be a daily thing. I hope she is doing her chores, or it's to bed with no supper—after she cooks our dinner, of course.* She showed up and wanted to enter through the gate, but it was not hung yet, so her grand entrance was stifled. She saw the ladies but couldn't cross the trench dug by our machine—not in her clothes and shoes—so she turned around and caught up to them on the landing. After lots of hugging and lady chatter, off they all went. I got waved to by the ladies before they left to do whatever they had planned.

Raymond and his leadman started putting in the insulation, and after about an hour, the leadman went to the truck and started carrying the siding boards for the inside. Phillip inspected the boards and had me see if the color was correct. The notes on the plan stated the siding was to be off-white or eggshell; these were more a cream color. "Do you have a shorter piece than these?"

"How long do you want?"

"Make a cut on one board long enough. If it looks okay, you can use the piece instead of trashing the entire board."

Phillip told his man, "Cut one piece four feet long." The piece was cut, and Phillip and I took it inside the playhouse. I had Phillip place it against the ceiling, not next to the french doors, which were now by the entry door and against the floor. Raymond had put two floorboards on the joists so we could see how all this would appear. The cream was a nice color—not quite what I had envisioned, but it would complement the playhouse.

"Go ahead and install the cream siding."

"The nails will be placed where on the siding?"

"We will predrill a small hole in the tongue and hide the nail when the groove slides over the tongue. The only nails driven into the face of the board will be hidden by the baseboard and crown molding."

"How are you going to dress around each window?"

"We will use a special molding to encase the windows, french doors, and entry door. We will use finishing nails and fill the nail holes. We have touch-up paint that matches the finish on the molding. I will have my painter work with Raymond tomorrow to do the touch-up painting. He is the one keeping me in business—highly skilled."

The arched gate was so spectacular; they finished the hardware, covering the distance between the top of the gate and the arch with the Mediterranean light fixture. I was in awe, and we hadn't seen it at nightfall. We also trenched from the main trench to the entrance wall, and we almost forgot about the lights on the entry gate and wall sconces on the outside of the gate. Wires were hanging everywhere; the electrician and the horizontal boring were nearly done. He would have the panel hooked up and powered tomorrow.

The inspector passed the trench and was waiting for the horizontal bore to reach the other side of the house and go into the predug pit. Once he saw the bit in the pit and measured to ensure the depth was per code, he would sign off the trench part of the permit; he'd be back tomorrow to inspect the panel, breaker, and wiring before they could throw the switch. Once it was approved, he would want to see and test the power to the panel and check the power to each breaker; he would watch the electrician wire the breakers and sign off the entire project. This was one inspection that I cherished.

I saw a house burn to the ground, brand-new, ready for the homeowner to move in the following weekend. The electrician crossed the common with the pilot wire, and during the night, the fire department saved the houses on both sides but not the one on fire. The firechief, almost had his fire crew die. It was an electrical fire; they could not hit it with water, or they all could have been electrocuted. They had to wait for the power company to come and kill the power to the house. That was not a couple of minutes' wait; there were too many players to make that happen in an emergency situation.

Raymond and the leadman had more than half the floor installed and about the same for the siding—a piece of cake that would be completed by tomorrow. Now that I saw the cream siding up on the walls, it was not bad, but I did not have the final say. The girls would be back shortly; once they saw the inside, that could be a whole new chapter.

The gate builder called me and said his master woodworker could complete the tunnel casing in two days. "Will that work for you? He can even mill the thresholds as we discussed. He said you should put the same wood floor in the tunnel as the playhouse. That would be a nice touch and would keep the house from having dirt tracked in from the kids playing."

"Thank you. I'll get with Phillip and have him give us a price. Thank your woodworker for getting the casing completed early and his suggestion on the flooring. I like the idea, and I'm certain the homeowner will too."

Phillip was overjoyed with the opportunity to add more work. He knew the editor coming tomorrow would have issues regarding a dirt floor in the tunnel. That alone could cause him to say, "Not this house; maybe your next project."

The ladies returned, a little tipsy, laughing until they saw the gate. There was no more idle chatter; almost all was silent at the same time. "Look at your gate, Marie," said my dearest darling. "Can we touch it?" They all looked over at me. "Well, can we?"

"How hard do you want to touch it?"

"Gently."

"That would be okay. Don't get rough with it."

"The finish is so nice. It almost is like a mirror. It fits so nicely."

"Marie, you must open the gate for the first time. Then go out to the front yard and reenter with all your grace and glamour."

Marie exited the courtyard and reentered just as my dearest darling had advised. "I think we could enter the party from either location."

"Ladies, I need you to look inside the playhouse for a minute."

"Just a minute, we are soaking in the majesty of the gate."

"Dear, I want a gate like this at our house."

"Maybe when I get finished paying off the yacht, the Ferrari, and the Rolls, we will have some extra monies for the gate. I was really trying to save up for a Happy Meal."

That got a chuckle and a not-so-nice look from my dearest darling. "The gate wouldn't cost that much. You can still have a Happy Meal."

The ladies headed up to the playhouse. "What are we supposed to look at? The walls are only half-finished. The floor is only half-finished. Are we to be impressed at work only half complete?" stated my dearest darling.

"No, the color of the siding and the floor color were the only things."

"Okay, we saw them. What do you want from us? We're confused."

"Do you like the colors?"

Marie said, "They look fine to me. When can we see it with the lights turned on?"

"I hope tomorrow we can do a burn test."

"What are you going to burn?"

"They call it burn test when you power up the fixtures and have the lights come on. If that passes, you can leave them on forever if you so desire."

"Will they do it at night?"

"No, during the day. You can see lightbulbs on during the day."

"We want to see it lit up at night."

"Just wait until dusk and flip the switch. Like magic, the lights will come on and illuminate the area."

"Will you be here?" asked Marie.

"If you want me to be here and my dearest darling is in favor, I'd be honored," said Delores.

"You and your family come over for dinner. I'll make Mama's favorite dish. You can join us for a real Italian dinner."

Before I could respond, my beloved said, "What time? We would love to have dinner with you and your family. What should we bring?"

"Yourselves. We have everything. No need to bring anything but your smile."

The crews were wrapping everything up for the day and heading back to their offices or homes. The ladies were back in the house, and my dearest darling was on her way back to our home after picking up the children from school. "See you at home, dear," said my beautiful bride, so sweetly. Once all the electrical was completed, I could lay out the drain line, finish the footing for the circular planter, cut the grade for the pavers, and put the extra soil in the circular planter.

Everyone had left the job site. I took a quick peek. "Look at some shadows. Not bad."

Bright and early, with the sun shining and birds singing, the sound of the cutoff saw cutting the siding and the nail gun putting it in place could be heard. Such a great sound. The electrician and his crew were cutting the wall of the tunnel to install the electrical panel; two men were fishing through the wires from the electrical panel to the new subpanel location. They were trying to be ready for the inspector, who was due to arrive in about an hour. The electrician was busy getting the breakers lined up in the panel: one forty-amp breaker for the barbecue, five twenty-amp breakers for the lights and receptacles. He was going to add one additional twenty-amp breaker just in case.

Phillip arrived, and we talked about putting in the flooring for the tunnel. Oak seemed to be overkill; the tunnel was rarely used at this point. It could become a factor in the future—especially for catered affairs. I asked the electrician to install at least three canister lights in the tunnel; right now, the only light was the one lighting the stairs. "You can also place lights on the walls if the ceiling would be too difficult. The walls would be easier, more like sconce lights to match the entry wall gate. That would tie the project in nicely. There is plenty of height in the tunnel so people won't bang their heads. You could also use the same bulbs as at the gate. If you make it with the same ambiance as the staircase and entry gate, the homeowner will have three choices to enter into the courtyard to please her guests. A lady with three equal choices to please her guests could be dangerous. Just what to wear, right outfit, right shoes, right champagne glass, right song—this could drive the husband insane."

"My wife has the same problem when she goes grocery shopping. 'Come on, dear, the store will close in nine hours.'"

Phillip and I decided on either cedar or redwood shiplap for the flooring sitting on two-by-six joists. We would have to give him subgrade, and we would place a two-inch layer of pea gravel, compacted, for his joists to sit on. The joists would have to be sealed and waterproofed just in case groundwater oozed up into the area. We would give John and Marie the costs for all the additions for approval. The tunnel was not part of the contract, and they needed to know and approve the work before we proceeded.

John and Marie came through the arched entry gate. "Good morning, everyone," said John. "So I hear you and your family are joining us for dinner tonight."

"That was the plan, but we need to have the electrical panel approved and the wiring completed before the inspector arrives, and he will check the work and sign it off and allow the electrician to wire up the barbecue, playhouse, and entry gate. He will return before the end of the day and witness the burn test and then sign off the electrical part of the project. We are getting the water feature ready for the inspection as well."

"Do you know what time the editor of the magazine will be here today?"

"Phillip, did he give you a time?"

"He said he would have some free time to visit after lunch. I told him the project is about 40 percent complete but the designer is on the job site and we have plans to show him what the remaining construction will look like. He is bringing his photographer with him. She is unbelievably talented. She can make a mundane remodel look like a palace. She'll take the staircases and do her magic, and you may not even think that they are the ones you use every day. This is the number-two-ranked remodeling magazine. They try harder, forcing number one to invent new tricks to stay on top. She will also talk with you two about putting you in some photos. The two will be talking among themselves during the tour. They will discuss just what needs to be shown pictorially."

Phillip asked if my Delores would be here today as well.

"I don't know her plans. Would you want her here?"

"They will love to see her make her entry through the arched gate. She may have to do it several times. The photographer will direct her."

Marie said, "What is my role?"

"Oh, Marie, you will go down the staircases in the house and in the courtyard. No one does that pose with more poise and grace. I will make sure all the ladies will be used in the photo shoot. He is one of my best friends. I have helped him, and he has really helped me and my business. My brochure is all his shots and his writer's verbiage."

"You said he will be here after lunch?"

"Yes, after lunch."

The electrician asked about the lighting in the tunnel. "Could they let me know so I can get the conduit in place with the junction boxes and replace the wallboards that we remove to snake the conduit and wire through?"

John and Marie looked at me and said, "You want to light up the tunnel?"

"The only light is at the stairs. The tunnel is dark with the door closed here. I will show you. Step inside, and I'll close the door." They did as I had directed.

John said, "You're right." He had the electrician flip on the stair light. We repeated the process, and it was agreed on to light up the tunnel. I told them that the electrician had suggested using the same lights that would be used to light up the arched gate entrance. "Great idea so they will match, giving this space more ambiance."

"We also want to put in a wooden floor, either cedar or redwood shiplap planking instead of the earthen floor now. We think it will give Marie three different entrance points to surprise your guests. The gate builder is installing a new door casing with a threshold to match the door. They are also doing a surround to enhance the door as well. The electrician will install the same light fixture above the door as the one above the playhouse door and french doors. We're going to make your home priceless—so warm and inviting no one will want to leave."

Mama joined us and said, "I can live here forever. I'll go home and pack." Marie was glowing, John not so much.

John said, "Those are both great ideas. Can I get the estimate from everyone? I do have a budget that I need to stay within."

"They will have it for you either today or tomorrow. Correct, gentlemen? Once I'm ready for the inspector, I will work on mine right here. I have crew members who can make it happen as quickly as it gets approved."

"Sounds great. I've got to scoot to make enough money to keep the boat afloat."

The inspector was a little late—maybe a half hour. He saw how the wiring was completed, checked the main panel to see how the electrician did the tie-in, and told the electrician to power up the subpanel. There was no popping of the breakers, so the panel was wired correctly. He wanted to see the subpanel shut down and used his ohm gauge to see that no power was bleeding past the main switch. "All is per code. I'll sign your permit, and I'll return about three o'clock. Have a great day getting everything ready for the burn test."

The electrician's crew started by mounting the ceiling fans under the patio cover. Another apprentice was wiring up the lights at the arched gate, and the other apprentice was wiring up the outlet for the barbecue; that was a 220V outlet and ran in a separate conduit and used a different gauge of wire. The electrician wired that circuit into the forty-amp breaker. Once wired, he put his testing tool in the receptacle and powered up the breaker. On went the green light. One breaker was completed.

The gate lights were on their own breaker, so the electrician tied in the tunnel lights with those. He put in a separate switch to turn on the light for the tunnel, and they were controlled from the stairwell. He installed the switch right next to the existing switch, and he showed Marie, once it was installed and working, how to use the switch. She came down the stairs and saw the wall lights in their full glory. She called for Mama to take a look. "Very nice, warm, and cozy. Great idea on the fixtures. Are the gate lights working as well?"

"Yes, they are on the same breaker. You want to see them?"

"Oh yes, I have waited so long."

"I can only have them on for a few minutes, or I can get in real trouble with the inspector."

Marie and Mama went outside the arched gate, stood outside, and saw the wall light and the light above the gate come on. "Oh, Mama, look how nice. This will be so inviting. I love how they tied in the gate to the tunnel—same fixtures. Great idea."

Breaker two was finished and ready for inspection. The lights on the patio cover and barbecue were completed, and the receptacles were wired and tested. Breakers three and four were completed. The playhouse lights and receptacles were wired, tested, and also finished. The electrician told his apprentice to unwire the patio and porch light from the rest of the playhouse lights. They did and asked why. "I want to use the extra breaker to power them and set up a separate switch in the tunnel to turn them off and on next to the panel. That way, at night, they can have the stairs lit up until they reach the tunnel and then shut them off. And as they enter into the kitchen, they can turn off the tunnel and stair lights." The apprentices did as the electrician told them; he had another apprentice cut the wall for the switch next to the control panel. Two apprentices went to the backyard and wired the water feature pump.

I had installed the low-voltage lighting timers and irrigation controller on the barbecue wall for the electrician to wire those as well. They also were on a separate breaker. They were finished just after the lunch break, having double-checked everything—power on, power off. The lightbulbs were all installed, and the fans were ready and working perfectly. Now the waiting game made me more nervous than the actual construction of the electrical system.

The cabinets for the playhouse arrived and were installed by the cabinetmaker. It was beautiful work. The details of the cabinets were immaculate.

CHAPTER 26

We had company. The editor and his photographer had arrived. I got Marie, my dearest darling, and Mama to introduce them to our guests. Phillip and his best friend were giving each other hugs, and Phillip also hugged the photographer. She could be a model in front of the lens, not the shutterbug. Phillip introduced the ladies to the photographer and the editor, and they all took off to see the inside staircase. I had given Phillip a complete set of plans to give to his friend. The two went to the outside table and opened up the plans. Phillip called me over to join them while the plans were being reviewed.

The editor asked, "When do you think the entire project will be completed?"

"In about two weeks. We have a drain system to install, three more raised planters, the stream feature, an irrigation system, low-voltage lighting, and the landscape."

"The front entry and front yard—the two will be upgraded?"

"Yes, the entire project gets the face-lift."

"You have made a couple of changes from the original design. Field conditions or change of mind?"

"There were a little of both. The playhouse was going to have a second level, and the original playhouse would be modified to meet current building codes. We found that the shed was built on a stone foundation. I called a friend of mine. He reviewed the plans, saw the playhouse, and recommended putting in a real foundation. Once Phillip and his crew removed the shed panels, the homeowner saw the courtyard without the playhouse and wanted it moved to the stream feature. I worked and worked on how it would all fit. The patio cover and barbecue had already been started. The courtyard would look odd where the two were sitting. Too much open space between the two, and people would wonder why someone would design such a place. I didn't want those types of questions being asked.

"I did a game with the homeowners, asking them to enter the courtyard from the arched gate. Once inside, I had them stop, close their eyes, and tell me what they saw. Both said they saw dirt—not the staircase, barbecue, or patio cover. I had them both go to the backyard and enter the yard from the kitchen.

They saw the concrete patio. I explained to them, 'Your guests will do the same. The playhouse did not obstruct your view of the staircase. It actually gave you an incentive to search farther off the courtyard.' She wanted the playhouse not reinstalled in the courtyard. That was now my huge problem.'"

"I see what you mean. You were working on the given, and now she was removing the given and did not want it returned. Why did you not put the playhouse back here?"

"It would block the view of the yard and reduce the depth. Even though she wanted a waterwheel in the stream feature, the view would be hampered. I could not envision landscaping around the shed/waterwheel feature trying to make the yard look bigger. I knew it would not be used very often, and she was going to separate the adults from the children but doing the move."

"I'm going to use your explanation in the article. Most people don't see things that way, and they should look at all aspects of how things will be used and the outcome of their decisions."

"We have started the excavation of the stream feature. I set up stakes to show the bridge location and outlined the walk path from the bridge to the seating area to the other bridge to the pathway to the staircase landing."

The editor followed the plan and asked, "If you would have put the playhouse here, just where would you have placed the playhouse?"

"I would have turned the stream feature back toward the house and set the playhouse at an angle so the waterwheel would create curiosity and move you off the patio to check out the noise and motion of the water. The seating area would be moved to this side, and possibly the other side as well. I would not add the second floor. I don't want the neighbors to think the playhouse would invite visuals of their interiors."

"I had a customer years ago who asked me if I thought her neighbor had the right to put a playhouse above the fence since they had a pool and a teenage daughter who always sunbathed in the backyard with her friends. I looked at the playhouse, and he had placed two windows on the pool side, none toward the rear yard fence, and you could see the windows on the other side in line with the windows facing her home."

"Did you ever ask the neighbor why he put that up the way he did?"

"He said it was to get the afternoon breeze through the house. At that time during the afternoon, my customer and her husband were standing on the pathway that we had just finished. We could see over the fence. We'd cut the pathway through an existing slope. There was an ocean breeze around two o'clock. While standing on the pathway, I had them turn so the breeze was hitting them in the face. They both turned toward the front of their house. So if his story was correct, the windows were on the wrong side of the playhouse. I don't believe that the wind changes from one lot to the other lot."

"I know your neighbor. I have met him and his wife a few times. He seems nice enough, but that excuse was entirely incorrect. Have him come to your house at this time, have him stand here, and ask him what I asked you. I always think things through logically. I would be very upset if one of my neighbors put up something that could look into my backyard. We try to hide windows with trees or tall hedges for additional privacy. I also had to be careful of setbacks and noise factors."

"Phillip, he states things that I know most people never think about. My writer can learn a lot from what he will tell him."

The girls joined us and wanted to show the photographer the staircase. The women were going to show the photographer my vision of them. The photographer went down the staircase very slowly, looking at the details of the handrail and the biblical stone used. "This is very nice, very close to the one inside. This one is a little nicer. Okay, show me what you've been practicing."

Marie, doing her best grand entrance moves, showed the photographer what she was going to do at the start of their party. "Did you take up modeling in high school or college?"

Mama said, "She was a little awkward in those years of her life. She has improved greatly since then."

"Thanks, Mom," said Marie.

Mama and Delores followed, each doing their best moves. "You ladies have given me lots of ideas. You're all so good. I can see why the crews stop and applaud you as you descend. This was all your husband's vision?"

"Yes, he told that to Marie and John. His dreams are far better than mine."

The playhouse was next to be explored, and the photographer went up the staircase first, opened the door, and froze. The other ladies were on various steps, and all stopped. The photographer got her camera ready and started a barrage of photos, moved inside and continued snapping photos, and moved to the patio and even took more photos. "Sorry, ladies; this place is remarkable. We don't see playhouses with this much detail. Our writer will want to come out here and write what he feels while sitting in the playhouse. This might have a separate story line all on its own. I'm going to get my editor. This is a must-see. This courtyard, your staircase, and the story from the beginning to the now ... we'll be number one for a long time."

The editor and Phillip were just getting to the staircase when his photographer called to him. "Please come see this playhouse." As they were approaching, she said, "We will make this a premier issue for at least two, maybe three months—cover and exclusive interviews."

He said, "I have never seen you like this before. What do you know that I'm not aware of?"

"The staircase you saw in the house—yes, the great-grandmother's bones were encased in concrete, and a false step was created. This shed, or playhouse now, is where she was dismembered. They had chests, a metal tin, and a five-gallon can buried here in the courtyard. There have been numerous times the police, bomb squad, and forensic teams came here, going through what was buried. They also found stolen bank money here in this playhouse. The story isn't over yet. There is still more earthmoving to do. Do you need any more reasons not to make this the biggest thing the company has ever come across?"

"Our writer needs to spend some time here interviewing the homeowners, contractors, and neighbors, and getting the police reports. If what she's telling me is true, we need to get this ready for publishing. We need to create curiosity in our readers with this month's issue. We will not disclose the actual address of the property. Even during the photo layout and story, the readers will only know the name of the city, and we may even not disclose that either. I must add that the project is cover quality, and I would be honored to be the one that brings the charm and beauty to our readers. I keep hearing about the party. How many guests are your planning to have?"

"At least one hundred, maybe more," said Marie.

"Can we come to the party, be your photographer? We will hand out our magazine and let the guests know they will be in future issues. This is going to be the event of the year. Get your mayor and city councilmen to attend. You may get the governor—huge feather in his hat attending the event of the year. We will provide the catering. I've got connections who would love to see their names plastered on the event of the year."

The girls' feet weren't even touching the floor at this point—city officials, governor, prominent socialites, all catered, and he would even get the violins and singer to perform for free. "The event of the year, can you imagine? Here? All these people coming to our home. The event of the year?"

He also asked if he could get his friend who published the gardener's magazine for a photo layout. "This needs to be seen by as many eyes as possible. I may even contact another friend who does publications for general construction to see how a shed can be converted to a fantastic playhouse. We will provide funds to you for all this exposure for our firms. This will be a very fun project for us. We're going to be dropping lots of names. All is money in everybody's pockets. You and your husband deserve a piece of the pie."

He told Delores, "Be prepared to become very sought after. This will be the project you will always remember years down the road. I'm not talking of something that you only dream about. I'm talking reality—and very soon. I have clients that I'm giving your husband's name to who are looking for talent just like his."

The inspector had returned, and the electrician and his crew were performing the burn test. The inspector was looking at everything; he plugged one of our electrical power tools into every receptacle; he also had a light gauge and was checking for any direct shorts. "Everything is checking out perfectly. I will sign you off. Great job. You have done better than most I inspect. Have a great evening. See you on the next project."

"Marie, the electrical system passed with flying colors. Enjoy your new landscape."

"Thank you for all that you did for our home. I will send an invitation to our upcoming party. Please attend. We would love to have you and your family."

"Thank you, Marie. I will keep that date open and plan on attending. If you have anything electrical come up before that call me."

Well, it was about two hours before dusk. I headed home knowing that we would be back with the kids to light up the courtyard. I was excited to see what the lighting would do for the atmosphere of the home. I got home, and everyone was enjoying a movie on television. Delores was on cloud nine and couldn't wait to sit me down and tell me what the editor had told her.

"What you're telling me is that my phone will ring off the hook, and jobs, designing, and installing will be nonstop? We won't ever have to worry about money? I'm dreaming. This isn't really going to happen. Pinch me so I know I'm not dreaming. Ouch, not so hard. I can't afford a scar." I just sat there with a stupid-looking grin on my face. I couldn't get serious about anything at this point.

Delores brought me a cup of coffee. "Caffeine? I'm already pumped up. Caffeine might take me over the edge. Thank you, dear. I'll drink it slowly. I will have to hire more people, get a real office and warehouse, get another superintendent, office manager, clerical staff, and more trucks and equipment. I hope it's not overnight. You have a business degree, right?"

"Yes, a bachelor's degree. But I have two young children to raise, gowns to model, parties to attend, luncheons with the socialites of the community, guest appearances on talk shows. Don't think I could squeeze in more on my schedule."

"Well, we'll cross that bridge when the time comes. Almost time to go see John and Marie. Are you ready to see the project at dusk and evening? It will be even better when the low-voltage lighting is installed. That's the ambiance—the character of the yard."

CHAPTER 27

We all got into our family car and drove over to John and Marie's. Delores reminded the girls to be on their best behavior, as if they were at church; they would meet two other little girls with whom they could play. "When you go outside, be really careful. There are trenches and piles of dirt. No running around. Mind your manners. Remember: 'please' and 'thank you,' no 'Give it to me.'"

"Yes, Mom, we understand. We will be really good. We'll make you very proud of us."

"We're here, girls, so be good for Daddy and me."

Marie answered the door; her girls were standing behind her, and we introduced our girls to Marie and her mama. John was running an errand and would be home in a few minutes. Marie introduced her girls to us and our girls. The four girls headed upstairs to their bedroom, where they had toys set out to play.

We followed Marie and Mama into the kitchen, which was rich with the aroma of homemade Italian food; there is no better aroma on the planet.

"I hope you like my cooking," said Marie. "These are old family recipes my mama gave me for our wedding gift. Have a seat. I'll bring you some very nice wine mama picked out when she first arrived—no screw-on cap, cork only—the real deal, made from our hometown in Italy. I gave John a list of three wineries and the vintages to purchase. We have family who work in the wineries, and they let us know the vintages to purchase. Not all years have a great harvest, so steer clear of those years. They usually are the bottles on sale."

"Marie and I want to thank both of you for all you have done for the family. My husband will join me in two days. He wants to talk to you both. My husband is a very influential man—knows lots of people, has lots of connections all over the world. He's heard from Marie, and now me, how wonderful you both are and how nice the home is turning out. He's a very successful businessman, sought after for his companies' talents. He also develops property for his clients. If he likes what he sees, he will talk with you. Please do me, Marie, and John the honor of sitting down with my husband and letting him know you from the inside, not

176

just the outside. He loves the fact that you two love each other. Family is a huge thing with my husband."

Marie told us, "He really is a great man. He was a little strict with me during my teen years—wanted to meet every boy I was going out with before the date; no meeting, no date, period. He would pull me aside in the next room and give me 'Honey, you can do much better than this guy. Tell him you can't go out, your dad said no.' One of the boys was the most popular in school. Daddy told me, 'Popularity and self-centeredness are a bad combination. You can be trapped by his wants and desires. You say no, and there goes your popularity, and talk is cheap from a lying, self-centered, popular guy or girl.'"

John returned with two bottles of vintage wine. "Good thing you gave me a few vintages, or I may still be out there searching labels."

Mama looked at the wines. "John, you did really well. You can have two pieces of cake."

Dinner was just about ready. "John, can you go up and tell the girls to wash up for dinner?"

Delores asked if she could help serve or do something; it would keep her busy. Marie said, "You can help Mama set the table and bring some food for the girls at their table. They have planned this since they got home from school. They have guests for dinner, you know. Being two girls and no yucky boys, they were all excited."

"Your girls are beautiful, just like Mama."

"So are yours. Good thing none of them resemble their fathers." That brought a laugh from all the ladies. John and I, being the only two males in the house, just grinned and bore the knife going into our backs.

"I'm glad they found humor on our behalf," said John.

The girls all had their dinners and were waiting for all of us to be served, and then Leslie asked to say grace. She said the nicest blessing I had ever heard from a young lady; it nearly brought tears to my eyes. Good thing there was the napkin to blot the tears forming.

The little girls were very quiet, too busy enjoying their meal. The food was absolutely the best Italian food I had ever tasted. "Marie, the dinner is fabulous— so tasty. I've never tasted anything like this in my entire life."

"Marie, this comes from a man who eats SpaghettiOs, thinking it's gourmet," said Delores. "Your food is the best I, too, have ever eaten. Is this one of your recipes, Mama?"

"Yes, dear. She did a great job in preparing this meal; it's nearly as good as mine."

Marie laughed. "No one cooks like Mama."

Dinner was finished, and the girls put their plates in the sink and headed back upstairs to play. I helped Delores clear the table, and it was almost showtime. "Let's get the girls back down so they can see the playhouse. Girls, come on downstairs. We are going to see the lights on the courtyard. We want to take your pictures." That was the magic word. If you tell tell little or big girls, "We're taking photos," they are there with bells on.

"We want to enter the courtyard from the tunnel. Be careful. The wood floor is not in yet, so watch your step."

The trapdoor was opened by John, and down the stairs, once the lights were on, everyone went to the tunnel. The wall lights with the amber bulbs were like a ride at Disneyland. Everyone said, "How pretty." We opened the door and turned on the switch to light up the playhouse. The little girls ran up the staircase and turned on the light switch just inside the door, and the screams of delight could be heard for miles.

"I guess they are happy," said John.

I was at the end of the line, and when I saw the inside all lit up, it was just like the movies. The light on the patio was the showstopper. With the cabinets and bench seats, the girls' smiles were ear to ear. Marie wiped some tears from her eyes. "So beautiful. I would never have imagined you transformed this from an old shed."

Mama said, "This could be a guesthouse if it had a restroom and running water."

We went downstairs to let the girls enjoy the playhouse by themselves. Down on the ground, I turned on the fans, and the lamps illuminated the area nicely, leaving no dark areas. John was impressed, since this was all his. "There will be a low-voltage light to illuminate the cooking surface that will be installed once the barbecue is installed. That should be arriving in the next couple of days. I called them this morning to verify." I showed him the conduits and the 220V receptacle that the barbecue would plug into to power the four burners.

Marie went to the staircase. "Where are my lights?"

"They will be done in a couple of days, along with some other outdoor low-voltage lighting systems. I promise your step lights and the wall lights will be the first completed before your dad arrives. We had one more item to see—the arched gateway. Always save the best for last."

I escorted the adults to the arched gateway. The little girls were all on the patio, looking down on us adults. "Hi, Mom and Dad and Grandma."

We all looked up and said "hello" in unison, as if we had practiced it over and over again. I told them we could not do that again as perfectly as we just had. "Spontaneous reaction is very difficult to reproduce."

We gazed at the lantern above the gate and saw how the sheen of the gate reflected the illumination of the amber bulbs. Out came the cell phones. *Click, click, click!* "We have to show everyone," said Marie. We opened the gate, and all stood outside the courtyard and looked at all three lights in their blaze of glory. More cell phones were out. *Click, click, click!*

John said, "This is way beyond what I had even imagined."

Mama said, "This is the ultimate in perfection."

She sent her cell phone picture to her husband and texted, "What do you think of our daughter's entry gate to the courtyard?"

He texted back, "I may come a day earlier. That is absolutely beautiful. Thank the designer for me."

Mama told me his response. "He's impressed even before seeing the entire project."

We all reentered the courtyard, and Marie told the girls, "Come on down from the playhouse. We're going inside to have cake and ice cream. Grandma made the cake just for you, girls."

"Oh, Mom, can't we play just a few minutes more?"

"You can play in the house when you get home from school. You can take some of your toys up there, and I'll get a throw rug for the floor. We ladies will go shopping for just the right rug and curtains for your windows. How about that for a playhouse warming?"

"Yeah, can our new friends come over and play after school?"

"Well, Delores, can your daughters come and play tomorrow?"

"I can't see why not. They all get along so nicely, and new friends are very important. I'm really enjoying my new friend." She gave Marie a huge hug, and she turned and gave Mama one as well. The lights were showing the glistening of tears on all three ladies.

I showed John how to turn off the fans. We all went into the tunnel, and I showed John the switch that controlled the playhouse, porch, and patio lights. The girls turned off the lights inside the playhouse, and the courtyard was ready for another night's sleep. As we climbed the stairs, I showed John the switch that turned on and off the tunnel lights; he already knew how to turn on the step lights. All was dark and resting peacefully.

The cake and ice cream were the highlight of the evening. The dinner was the best I had ever tasted, and the dessert was better than that which any five-star restaurant could serve. My wife and daughters had new friends, and John and I were innocent bystanders. We both had too much on our plates to designate a huge amount of time for social issues. The evening was the best my family had had in a long time. We thanked our host and hostess with warm hugs, and of course Mama was well rewarded. "Tomorrow's another day. Get some rest and be up bright and early."

We arrived home and put the girls to bed. We also got ready for bed; it had been a tough day, and we had more things to complete tomorrow. We both were tired and made a pact to love each other tomorrow night—no headaches, no not being in the mood—just get down to business and relieve some stress. I fell asleep fairly quickly and started to dream of what had happened over the last few days, rehashing them from beginning to end.

CHAPTER 28

The next morning, the crew was anxious to get the first course on both walls completed. Juan took Manuel and Diego took Jose to work on both walls; the race was on to see who could complete their wall. I liked it when the crew competed; it was good for all of our wallets, and the homeowner benefitted on the construction schedule. Juan had my drawing to follow; he set two blocks over the vertical uprights to see how the angle would affect each block. He marked with a carpenter's pencil, and Manuel used a rock hammer to chip away some of the edges. Manuel was a little confused, so Juan took the rock hammer and showed Manuel just how to make the edges. After one block was completed, Manuel proceeded to follow what Juan had showed him. Juan's were nearly perfect; it took a few blocks before Manuel was confident enough to match Juan's first block. Diego and Jose had a jump start, and their first course along the house was nearly finished. Jose was the block carrier and mud mixer, and Diego was the mason. When Jose got far enough ahead of Diego, he showed him how to lay block.

This was a beautiful thing to watch. Soon I would have four confident masons who in turn would teach their crews. The more skilled the crew, the more elaborate and detailed my designs could become. I had allowed one of my masons years before to have freedom to express his talents. The joy it brought him was so heartwarming, and he became the go-to guy on the crew for the younger crew members. One afternoon this mason, Ben, got confused at an inside and outside corner on a brick porch band—not an easy scenario even for a very skilled mason. He just could not see how it was possible. I used the MK wet brick and tile saw to cut out two corners, one inside and one outside, and took them to Ben, and between the two of us, we made it fit. He called over the rest of the crew and showed them what we had completed. From that day onward, Ben knew that I had his back. I took a photo with my camera and gave Ben a copy of the photo. He told me he showed his wife and kids what he had accomplished.

Marie and Mama came out for a visit; they saw that we had taken down the yellow caution tape and that the walls were becoming a reality.

"Did you sleep well, I asked?"

"Why yes, we did; we're ready to practice our grand entrance as soon as your lovely bride arrives. We're all going shopping—lunch, nails, and girly stuff today, said Marie."

"Sounds like fun for all of you and a place where being male could be damaging to one's ego, I said."

You men are all alike; we get no fun if we can't belittle you and your precious egos. May we practice on the staircase, asked Marie?"

"You may, but remember: no shoes. The sand in the soil can damage the finish on the Biblical stone. Tomorrow you can walk down with shoes. No high heels until the day after. That is the day I'm bringing my Handy cam," said Phillip.

"Do you think we can't walk in high heels asked Marie?"

"I know you can; the heels tighten your calves and bring out the best in ladies' legs," I told Marie.

"So the high heels flatter our physique?" asked Maire.

"Absolutely, from a man's point of view, I told her."

"That doesn't mean much for us damsels, you know," said Marie.

"We all have our fantasies," I told Marie.

"You can start looking for outdoor furniture if you like. I do need to know which low-voltage lighting company you would like to use. We also need to go to a couple of nurseries to tag trees and plant materials. We are getting close to needing them; this is the most fun part of the project."

Marie said, "I will have John arrange a meeting with you, I'm busy gown shopping, you know?"

"It is going to be some kind of gown for sure; I don't know how anyone could improve on your perfection."

"You are so kind; I'm telling Delores to treat you with lots of respect tonight."

Diego and Jose were now helping Juan and Manuel to finish building the circular planter. I told Juan that the other retaining seat wall needed to be started and that he should be very careful not to hit or undermine the new staircase. He was to put the excavated soil in a pile to backfill after the wall was completed. The footing layout was still marked on the ground for the crew to follow. This was the smallest planter, so the footing should take at least an hour and a half.

The ladies, now all three, were have a grand old time; they even had the real deal in the champagne glasses, which made the whole experience that much more real. After the last turn, they all put on their shoes and headed into the house, and then into the car, and away they went. The crew was now concentrating on building the walls, not watching the girls; they all appear happy. No grand entrance, they would get depressed, and worried, that the girls, would not perform for them again.

We would mix the footing by hand from our sand and gravel piles in the front yard. I would pick up the cement mixer from the rental yard. Sure would be nice to push that onto Juan; I could do more selling and designing for future work. I'd love a six-month backlog; the crews would likewise. Having the playhouse finished would give the girls a place to play; the sounds of them having fun would bring so much character to the playhouse.

Our rock fascia had just been delivered. *Beautiful—something else we can set the men working on. Tomorrow the wall caps should be delivered as scheduled. I'll call the masonry yard to see if there is any update from the manufacturer. Juan told me they need more rebar for the last wall—one piece for the footing and two for the wall itself. Can I order the concrete for the cells of the three walls? I will set that up for delivery in two days from today. If all goes as planned, we will be the only crew working on the job site in two days; we won't disrupt the other company. We will start excavating the subgrade for the pavers; that will need to be completed once the retaining walls are waterproofed and ready for backfilling. The tunnel will get a wood floor, and I will need eight inches removed from the tunnel to allow for the floor. That won't be an easy dig—all by hand, little room. The ground should not be that compacted—only foot traffic, no heavy equipment running back and forth.*

"That soil can go straight into the circular planter," I instructed Juan as we discussed the next course of action.

"When do we start the next two jobs?" asked Juan.

"Maybe next week. Have you found some more help?"

"I have two guys that are ready to come to work; should I hire them?"

"We need to get the paves going next week; bring them, and let's see what they can do for the company."

"I had a girl apply for work; her dad is a contractor. She works with him part-time. Do you want to see what she can do as well?" asked Juan.

"Are you sure you want a girl on the crew? They can be a distraction and cause conflict between crew members—jealousy. If one crew member gets romantically involved, it could cause fights."

"She appears to be all business, and she has a boyfriend," said Juan.

"Okay, we can try her out. She will have to carry her own weight; we can't afford having other laborers carry block or pavers for her."

"I think she has more muscles than our guys right now," said Juan.

"Your choice. you have to take the responsibility of getting the projects finished on time."

We went to the pallets to examine the rocks, making sure they matched the stone on the house. I didn't want to start installing and find out they did not match. The stones were a perfect match, which was lucky; this is not always possible.

"Now we must get the game plan on the right track," I told Juan. Subgrade for the pavers is foremost important; placing the stone fascia where the pavers will join is right next to the subgrade. You can put the stone on top of the pavers.

Looks odd, but companies do that and use a grinder with a cutoff blade to cut the stone to fit on top of the paver. It just doesn't look professional.

"We can start doing the subgrade right after lunch next to the retaining seat wall. Hose off the footing and wall once the subgrade has been established. Just set the subgrade two shovels' width in front of the wall, not the whole pad. We need to finish waterproofing the retaining walls to place the excavated soil. We don't want to handle the soil more than once if possible."

The crew began mixing and pouring the retaining wall footing.

"When do you and the crew want to break for lunch?" I asked Juan.

"Once the footing is poured on the last retaining seat wall. We can use the hardboard to form up the back side of the circular seat wall so we can waterproof the finished seat walls tomorrow."

I picked up a half dozen stones from the pallet and put them in the wheelbarrow, took them to the retaining seat wall, and checked how it would look on our walls.

Juan had some mortar mix in the wheelbarrow he was using. He added some thin set to the mix and brought his wheelbarrow to where I was parking the one I was using.

I got my flat shovel from the sand pile and found the top of paver mark in the seat wall. I Measured down eight inches from the top of paving for the subgrade. The grade was about three inches below the mark, so down another five was the subgrade level.

Juan brought over the hose with a pressure nozzle attached and hosed off the block. I leaned a couple of stones on top of the footing, waiting for the wall to dry from its current bath.

Juan was getting excited to see just what this rock fascia would look like.

I used the half-inch grooved trowel to spread mortar on the wall fascia. Juan used the mason's trowel to batter the back of the stone. I placed the first stone on the retaining wall surface. Juan grabbed the next stone and followed the same procedure. Then came the next stone, same procedure.

"A million more and the walls will be completed," I said.

Juan laughed. "A million stones—that would take quite some time. We would need a busload of employees to make that happen."

We started to lit the second row of stones to see how high we would have to install to get beyond the top of paving mark. It was not too bad; one and a half to two rows and we'd be able to set the paving stones.

"Remember, Juan: these two rows have to be grouted before the pavers can go next to them. Once we start the pavers, they have to have plastic sheeting placed on top and taped down to keep them clean of dropped mortar and grout. Do any of the new hires have masonry experience?"

"I think maybe one; not sure about the girl. If she has experience in masonry, that would be a blessing," said Juan.

"Do you have a baker's bag or two?"

"I have one for sure; you bought it last year," Juan replied.

"Make sure it is in good condition. How about sponges to wipe off the grout residue?"

"I have two. Do you want to use grout release on the stones?"

"Maybe. I have to see if my tank sprayer is working properly. Time for your lunch break; don't want to work the crew to exhaustion or after-lunch productivity won't be very good."

Diego and the laborers were just hosing out the wheelbarrow when Juan told them it was lunch.

I rechecked the rocks we had just placed. They made the wall look so much better. I heard the ladies coming from the house, heading to the staircase.

"You're back already?"

"Just stopped to check on you guys," said Marie.

"We see you're sitting down as we predicted," said Delores. "Leave them alone for a short time and they sit."

"Even slaves were given a lunch break—no water, just lunch," I told them. "Lucky for us there is prepackaged chicken, or we would spend the entire break catching, killing, plucking, and cooking lunch, finishing just in time to go back to work."

"We're heading for lunch right now; it's all prepared, and we don't have to do dishes, cook, or any of that stuff—just dig in and chew," said Marie.

"That's what I do when I get a Happy Meal."

"I almost remember those childhood days, going through the drive-through with Mom and Dad," said Marie. "They would say loudly, 'You'd better know what you want.'"

"Some habits are hard to break, like peanut butter and jelly—today's culinary delight."

"Later, gator; we're on a mission," said Delores.

"Practice your grand entrance while being seated; give the patrons a free side show."

"If only they would give us champagne in nice, tall glasses; we'll ask the host or hostess."

Juan asked, "Do they go to lunch every day?"

"No, it's only because Mama is in town; they rarely do this kind of stuff. My wife is always home with a bandana tied over her hair, three years' outfit, no makeup, waiting for me to walk in the door so she can expel her frustrations on me."

"That's why I want to get an office in a warehouse, away from the house. Office girls don't put bandanas on to cover their hair, wear up-to-date outfits and makeup, and bring their best personalities to the workspace."

"I worked in one office where the office girls looked like they just came off an evening out, with jewelry, styled hair, top-of-the-line clothes and shoes, perfume, and perfectly applied make-up. It was really tough going to work and concentrating on doing what the company paid me to do. There was a game the girls played with one another; whoever dressed the nicest won a free meal from the other girls. One day my superintendent, two purchasing agents, and the estimating staff paid for lunch for all the office staff; they all looked unbelievable. The guys lost that meal."

"Let's have the crew clean along the retaining wall edge, and we can start putting on some rocks."

"You need to hold the rod and set grade stakes while I run the building level. I want the tops of the pavers marked, and you can tie a string line from stake to stake while the subgrade is cut to a one-inch fall in ten feet; I hope we can get a little more."

"We'll do the city sidewalk first and then move ten feet toward the backyard, raising up one inch until we reach the retaining seat wall. Make sure you mark them with the orange marking paint so they don't get tripped over."

We continued laying out the elevations so the crew could start excavating the subgrade.

Diego had two laborers start removing the soil and backfilling the raised planters nearest to the removal. The process was well underway, so I headed off to do my chores.

I hopped into the old truck and started my rounds, going from one vendor to the next. *Pick up this, pick up that. Go over here and order this, go over there and order that. Do we have this? Do we have that? Honey, I'm home.*

"So what?" Delores would say. "Big deal."

That was my day in a nutshell, whatever that's supposed to mean. How come the stations play one good song and go to commercials for fifteen minutes then some awful song plays until the next fifteen-minute commercial break? There has to be a better way to make a living. Don't get me started about the weather report. How can they be wrong 90 percent of the time and still have a job? I have never had a weatherman apply for work in the construction field; I wonder why?

Well, I'm at my first stop. Where's my list? I may make this my one and only stop for today and then decide if the other stops were necessary. I'm sure glad I talk to myself, as no one else does. Not to themselves, but to me. Wonder what's for dinner; I'm tired of crow.

"Hi, honey, I'm home!"

No answer. Maybe in the backyard.

I opened the kitchen door.

Nope, not out there.

I turned around and walked right into my lovely bride.

"Well, I found you," I said.

"I didn't know I was missing," said Delores.

We were invited to dinner at John and Marie's. Mama had made another Italian meal, and the girls wanted to play in the playhouse with Leslie and Kim. They really liked each other; they played together very well. It sounded delightful; I couldn't wait for John to fire up his grill and burn some hot dogs. A real Italian meal—can't beat that type of eating.

CHAPTER 29

After another tossing and turning night's sleep, with bright and early getting earlier every day, I felt ready to tackle whatever obstacles this day could throw at me. My wall caps should be on the job site this morning. When I arrived at the site, Diego and Jose were busy building the next retaining seat wall. I asked Juan if they could waterproof the two other finished planters so we could have a place to put the soil.

He had plumb forgotten about the waterproofing, so the two of us started, hoping to finish before lunch.

When the waterproofing was almost done, Juan began putting perforated corrugated pipe in the circular planter.

Diego and Jose had one more course to install. I called the batch plant for the concrete and pump for filling the wall cells. They could be at the job site in two hours.

"Hold on a second, Diego; I can get the concrete for the cells in two hours—good or wait until tomorrow?"

"Tomorrow. The mortar has to set up," Diego said.

"Hello, tomorrow first thing would be fantastic, see you tomorrow. Let's check the planters, conduit stub out, irrigation stub out, drainage stub out ... all present and accounted for. Good job, gentlemen."

Marie came outside.

Delores said, "Dinner was a great idea; I am tired of preparing crow."

"Do you guys eat crow?" asked Marie.

"She makes it for me when I misspeak."

"Oh, it's a joke?" asked Marie.

"Delores is the only one laughing when she tells me I have a crow sandwich waiting for me on the table."

"I'll have to prepare some for John," said Marie,

"Delores will give you her recipe."

Marie began going up her favorite staircase, and I turned around and looked at the playhouse and patio cover, and then the arched gateway. It gave me such a nice feeling seeing it all come together.

CHAPTER 30

The next morning, the crew was all fired up, ready to start the subgrade for the pavers. Juan asked if we could rent a rototiller to loosen up the soil since there had been so much foot and equipment traffic; it would just be easier for the crew. He brought the three new employees to help with everything we needed to complete for the day. We now had Juan, Diego, Manuel, Jose, Miguel, Vincent, and last but not least, Angel. She was just as her parents had named her—our angel.

I told everyone, "Welcome aboard. We have lots of different jobs to do today, and if you're not sure how things are done, please ask for assistance. We all are here to help you. Please work safely. We don't want anyone injured. If something is too heavy, ask for help. Lift with your legs, not your backs. Juan and Diego will have you working with them to complete their tasks. I have to go get you a rototiller per Juan's request. Keep an eye open for the wall caps being delivered this morning. Juan, I need a conduit running from the staircase to the transformers once the subgrade is cut. I'll be right back with the rototiller."

I sure liked the new employees and was anxious to see how they all worked together and who would end up with whom. Starting new crews for different projects felt great. The rototiller was loaded onto the trailer, and I was soon back at the job site.

"Let's fill some planters with soil."

Juan got the rototiller, and he was having Miguel hose down the grade to keep the dust to a minimum. We had about four to six inches to bring down to get to the paver subgrade.

I called the masonry yard to see when the pavers would be delivered. "Part of your order is on the truck with the wall caps. The rest will be delivered tomorrow morning or later this afternoon." This was working all too well.

I called the sand and gravel supplier, and they, as well, were preparing to drop off half the order in about two hours and asked when I would like the remainder of the order. "Give me at least two days. I'll call you tomorrow with how everything is coming together."

As Juan was making passes with the rototiller, the crew run by Diego was loading wheelbarrows and hauling them to Juan's two guys, who were offloading the wheelbarrows into the planters, just like clockwork—two wheelbarrows being loaded, two being emptied. Marie and John were on top of the staircase, watching the crews. I went up to talk with them.

John asked, "How do you get them to work so smoothly together? I have a difficult time getting a piece of paper to move from one desk to another in a week."

"I can't take the credit for how this is being accomplished. If you show the crew how to do something, you just hope that they all jump in to get things done. Each one has a different experience level. The crew makes it all balance out. Some are strong in one operation and weak in another.

"Thank you both again for a fabulous dinner. I'm so grateful that we were invited. My girls talked the whole way home about their next playdate with your daughters. Delores is bringing them back after she picks them up from school."

"My girls have sorted out which toys get to be in the playhouse and which in their bedrooms," said Marie.

"That was so much fun to watch my girls with so much joy," John said.

"It took longer for them to go to sleep than normal, almost like Christmas Eve," said Marie.

"We're going shopping for the outdoor furniture this morning with your dearest darling to get a rug for the playhouse and, of course, curtains for the windows. Mama is very excited to make the playhouse a great place for the girls. We're all very excited to get to do our share to enhance your vision," Marie replied.

"Now you're getting into things that I am weak at. The frilly stuff is not my cup of tea. Thank goodness that is Delores's strong suit. We're getting a lot of materials delivered today. It will be pretty tight for parking, and your front yard will become a masonry yard. We will make sure we don't block the entry to your home."

"This could be a nice vision for my papa's arrival. He loves to see things in progress," said Marie.

"Since the girls are preparing to move some of their toys to the playhouse, we will make a gravel walkway from the tunnel to the playhouse and a pathway from your staircase to the playhouse and barbecue and patio cover," I told Marie. "Tracking soil or mud from the courtyard is not something you or I want to deal with. We will have some pavers in place. Not sure if we can make a walkway. We will do the best we can with the crew I have working. Oh, by the way, I want you to meet one of my newest crew members. Follow me … Angel, Miguel, and Vincent, these are the homeowners, John and Marie."

"Nice meeting you. If you have any needs while working on our home, please let me know," said Marie. "I'm home nearly all day …Wow, the planters are nearly full of soil. That was very fast."

"They all seem to work well together," said John.

"Excuse me for one moment."

"Juan, take the rototiller to the front walkway and loosen the soil from the arched entrance to the walkway. Then take it to the backyard and etch out the stream feature at least two passes. Thank you, Juan.

"Diego, once the grade is cut, get the vibratory plate from my truck, with help, and compact the area in front of the staircase, getting ready for the base layer of four inches. The base should arrive in just a few minutes. Great job, everyone. Keep up the good work. Very proud of what you're doing. Okay, where were we?"

John said, "Now I see how all this happens. If you weren't a business owner working on my home, I would have you come to my office and straighten out my desk sitters."

"You flatter me, but I'd be lost directing your office staff on how to do their jobs when I have no clue what they are supposed to be doing. My experience is doing what I know what to do, trying not to do things twice.

"I worked one day in the blazing heat, with no breeze. The crew and I were told by the foreman to drop all the soil into the driveway of the home. At two thirty, the wife of the household came out and told our foreman that her husband parked his car in the garage every night and the soil had to be moved. I looked at the foreman and said to him, 'Why did we put all the soil in the driveway?'

"He said the salesman who had designed the job wanted the soil stockpiled there. When the salesman came to the job site, he and I were doing the same job. I talked with him. We had no tools to grade the yard with. We hauled the soil three yards to a pile in the driveway.

"Now we had to load the soil into a two-and-a-half-ton truck that sat higher than the average height of the crew. It was two thirty, and the crew were not as strong as they had been at seven o'clock in the morning. The heat had taken its toll. 'What were you thinking?' I asked. I was in no mood at that time to hear some lame excuse. He told me one anyway: he had never checked with the homeowner for approval.

"'We were going to bring a smaller truck tomorrow or a trailer for them to load,' he said.

"'Why did they not have the trailer on site today?'

"'You have to ask Dave, our boss. You need to plan your jobs to save the crew's strength. You and Dave sitting at desks is far different from using a pick and shovel.'

"'Tell Dave he and I will have a chitchat soon.'"

"How did that little talk pan out?"

"I told Dave that if he ever did that to one of my projects, I would leave him holding the bag. I came from a construction company far bigger than the nursery I was employed by at the time. The nursery catered to the film industry in Hollywood—totally different styles of dealing with customers, as Dave tried to explain. As he was stepping in it deeper and deeper, I stopped him and said, 'Then these high-end customers need to have even more thought and planning than a regular construction site.' I only stayed with the company for a couple of weeks beyond that meeting.

"They transposed an address of one of my customers. I was at one end of the block, at the home to be relandscaped, and the crew was demolishing another home, which happened to be owned by a corporate lawyer. The office said the crew was on site. I told them they were not at the right house. I drove a half hour back to the office. Dave, the general manager, the owner, and the office manager were all standing in the office, pointing fingers at me. I pulled out the contract and showed them the address. Now somewhat confused, the office manager called over the dispatcher. He looked at the contract and compared it with the paper he had given the foreman. 'Oh, that is why. It's not 1321. They're at 1231 working.' The owner told the office manager and the dispatcher to meet him in his office.

"Not one of those standing around told me they were sorry about the mix-up. They tried to recapture their mistake by withholding my commission. I met the lawyer and explained the situation, and he was very understanding, to a point. 'You know, this is trespassing. Your company could all be put in jail. I'm waiting for the owner of your company.'

"I said, 'He's going to stop by sometime either today or tomorrow, and he'll pay for this. I guarantee he'll pay.'"

"Is that when you started your own business?"

"Well, sort of. My best friend talked my wife into moving to Arizona. Landscaping in Arizona is rocks and more rocks. Some throw in a few cacti just to break up the monotony. I made fifteen dollars in thirty days—not anything I would write home about when family asked, 'How is it going in Arizona?'

"My friend lived in Sedona. There you're either a millionaire or you're broke. There is no in-between.

"Fantastic, the base is here, and the sand is soon to follow. I'll lay out a pathway from the tunnel to the playhouse, and an intersection from the pathway to the barbecue and patio cover," I told John and Maire. "By the end of the day, I will connect your staircase to the barbecue pathway. You'll be walking on a base layer, better than dirt, but no bare feet unless you're really good with pain. I'll have Diego run the vibratory plate over the path; one pass will compact the base layer firm enough for foot traffic."

They had the subgrade cut. Diego had passed the vibratory plate over the grade, starting at the staircase and working his way to the gate. Juan had the crew shuttle wheelbarrows of base to start putting in the four-inch layer. They did the same routine—shovel and load, cart and dump, spread with shovels and rakes. Adding the three people today was ideal. Once the base was spread, Diego ran the vibratory plate on top of the base to compact it. Miguel applied water to the base and subgrade.

It was nearing lunch, so I had Juan blow the lunch whistle. The new hires were wiping their foreheads from the sweat. They all looked like a crew. Not one of them was as clean as when they started work. That was a great sign.

They were all sitting on the retaining seat wall in the shade of the patio cover. Marie, Delores, and Mama came down the staircase—a practice session. The crew all applauded each lady making a semi–grand entrance. They came over to Angel and asked if she would like to try. She said, "May I? That looked like so much fun." She stood up, headed to the staircase, and took off her boots.

My dearest darling introduced herself to Angel and reminded me that I was not minding my manners.

They handed her a champagne glass, and she came back down the stairs not like a construction worker—no, she did quite well, very dainty and fragile looking. All my crew stood up and applauded her. She got a standing ovation, and the other ladies made a comment.

"Silly boys, trying to make her feel special," Marie told Delores.

"Good job," said Marie. "Angel is now part of the elite club of grand entrance ladies. I'm certain that won't be her last time being invited."

My dearest darling gave her a hug, and Marie and Mama did the same. "Welcome to our membership."

"Do you mean I'm a lady now?

Marie said, "Honey, you have always been a lady; you now will be getting paid for what you do naturally."

Juan had put in the conduit and wire for the step lights; all that was needed was for me to get my knees dirty. I was to wire them into the transformer and set the time for them to come on. I tested them to make sure all were lighting up. There were a couple that were hard to see because the sun was shining directly onto the lens. Marie saw me getting my knees dirty and came over to me.

"Does this mean my steps will be lit up at dusk," she asked?

"I was trying to surprise you; now it's not a surprise anymore. Yes, they will be glowing by dusk. You're going to do a night version, aren't you?"

"In your honor, I will show my appreciation for all you have done for me," said Marie. "Maybe. I'll ask Mama and John if they want to have the girls play in the playhouse. I won't tell them that the lights are hooked up. They will go out the tunnel, and I will meet them at the staircase landing."

"Clever, very clever. Will you tell my dearest darling and have her do the same, coming through the arched gateway?"

"That is a great idea," replied Marie. "I'll ask her to bring the girls over and be here at six-thirty sharp and go through the arched gateway in style, first class. John will be pleased; Mama will be surprised. You come with them."

"You and John can talk about guy stuff. Us girls will talk girl stuff, deal?" said Marie."

"It's a deal; I get to surprise everyone but you. Do you want us to bring some dessert?"

"Cupcakes. The girls can have a chocolate cupcake party in the playhouse." Marie went and stood with my dearest darling and her mama, told them the game plan, but did not tell them the lights on the staircase were working. Their backs were turned when I lit up the steps.

"Surprise, surprise. I get my surprise after all."

My dearest darling came over to me and said, "You don't have any meetings set up tonight, right?"

"No meetings, dear. Why do you ask?"

"You're coming with me and the girls on an outing. Don't be late getting home today. Got it?"

"Yes, dear. I won't disappoint you. I promise."

Lunchtime was ending. I instructed Juan to make sure the base was spread between the paint lines I had put down while they were enjoying their lunches. "You need to connect the front walkway with the gate and the tunnel to the gate as well. Did you remove the soil from the tunnel steps to the entry?"

"We did— the same eight inches. We need to put some extra at the base of the steps."

"Phillip was to be here today. May have forgotten. I'll call him to get the schedule from him. I'll let you know. Make sure there is only a six-inch drop from the bottom step to the top of the base. You can ramp the base. Makes it easier."

The crew was bringing in base, and Diego had Manuel bring him some pavers. We still had some construction sand leftover from mixing the footings; they were starting to lay the pavers. I looked out the gate. I had forgotten that we ordered the concrete and concrete pump, and they were both coming down the street. I told Juan that the concrete and pump were here and the cells needed filling. Juan and Jose would be the ones to fill the cells. The crew would continue bringing in base and pavers as needed. The job was moving into high gear; it was so nice to witness the enthusiasm this crew was projecting.

The cells were being filled, the pavers were being placed, and Diego put up a string line to follow and keep things square. "He is going to need the tile and brick saw to fill in the area around the first step. I will have to go to the house and pull it from the garage. I will also bring some paving edges to hold what is in place in case the family decides to take a tour." I told Juan I would return with the tile and brick saw.

The truck with the sand met me at the corner. The crew would be excited to see more items arriving where we had no more room to store them. *I should remember to bring a couple of tarps and three sheets of used plywood to create a walkway if needed. So much to remember. There's the saw and the stand, and the blade is still attached.*

Great, I would not know where another one would be hiding. The plug is in the tray—so smart, something else nearly impossible to locate. Looking in a hurry, it will never happen. All is loaded, ready to for takeoff. Here we go."

The job site definitely looked like a masonry supplier's yard. Walking to the front door, one would expect a salesman to dart out from between the stacked pallets, taking at least five years off one's life. I had to get the rototiller back to the rental yard or they would charge me for another day's rent. Juan came from the courtyard. I asked him to load the rototiller on the trailer so I could return the machine. He had one of the new hires with him, so that task was easier. They also offloaded the plywood and tile saw.

I was met by Diego, who was looking for the saw; he was more than ready to see it. He had two employees with him to fetch empty pallets to make a seat for the tile-cutting person. My dearest new hire was a skilled tile cutter—no training necessary.

I told Diego, "Make sure she is skilled. Just watch her make a couple of cuts. Tell her not to panic. The owner always has everyone watched for the first couple of cuts. Safety and insurance protection are the only reasons."

The saw was set up. They had pallets for Angel to sit on, safety glasses, a tray filled with water, and a half dozen pavers marked for her to cut. Diego showed her how he marked the pavers. "If there is a squiggle line drawn, that is the spoil. The rest of the paver is the part to return to me. One of the new laborers will be the one doing the shuttling from me to you. You can ask the one shuttling what is good and what is spoil."

Diego had her turn on the saw; she knew he hadn't told her where the switch was located. She placed the paver on the sliding tray and asked Diego what piece was what he wanted and what was going to the boneyard. He showed her, and the cut was made. "Very nice," said Diego. "Two more cuts, and I will leave you alone." She cut those as well, just as he had marked them.

She asked him, "If the waste is over half, do you want me to stack them for a possible second cut?"

"That's a great idea. Set them off to the side, and I'll tell the shuttle person to bring one back when I need only a small piece."

Diego was teaching Jose how to lay the pavers after he put a layer of leveling sand on top of the base layer and used the vibratory plate to compact it.

I brought the paving edge with the nails to Diego. "When you get a stopping point, place the edging along the last course to hold everything nice and tight. Family is going to tour the area tonight and for the rest of next week. The pavers look great. Nice job. How's your cutter doing?"

"She is really good. Every cut has been perfect so far. Nice to have someone skilled working for us."

It was nearing the time to pick up the tools, drain the saw, warm up the engines, and head for home.

When I walked into the house, my two young ones were very excited. "Daddy, daddy, guess what."

"What, girls?"

"We're going to Kim and Leslie's house to play in the playhouse. Can we go now, Daddy? Please, Daddy," said Sarah.

"We have to eat first, girls. So do Kim and Leslie. We can't bother them while they're eating. Right, dear?"

"That's right, girls. You have to eat your dinner first."

"Guess what else, Daddy. Mom bought cupcakes to take with us—our favorite. And guess what else, Daddy."

"I don't know, girls. I'm about out of guesses."

"We can eat them in the playhouse, maybe on the patio too," said Sarah.

"Oh, that would be so much fun. I have never seen you two so happy. You two like Kim and Leslie?"

"Yes, Daddy."

"How long have they been your friends?"

"Just a few weeks. How come we didn't get to play with them before?" asked Sarah.

"I just finished the playhouse, and their mama and daddy thought it would be a good idea for you two to come and play with their daughters."

"Does Mommy have a friend like we do?"

"I think so. Let's ask her. Honey?"

"Yes, dear."

"The girls want to know if you have a friend like they do."

"Why, yes, girls. Marie, their mommy, is my friend. We just met a couple of weeks ago. I like Marie very much. I'm not sure if it is as much as you two like her daughters. I haven't lost my appetite, and I'm sure you both will eat a good dinner for us tonight, correct?"

"Yes, Mommy. We're hungry and excited."

My dearest told me to be ready to head out the door about six fifteen. "We can't be late, and you can't be making phone calls after dinner. Promise me. No calls or starting on plans —promise?"

"I promise. I can't concentrate right now anyway. The girls got me excited. They sure are happy."

"You keep us hidden from the outside world. We get excited when we get to go out and meet people," replied Delores.

"You all do a great job of meeting new people. I'm very proud of all of you. This is the first time I have had a customer interested in my family. It feels really good inside for me. Love to see all of you so excited. Now I know what 'Daddy' really means."

"Girls, it's about six ten. Go potty and wash up. Change your clothes if you have spilled something on them."

"Okay, Mom, we're getting ready."

"You look great yourself, dear."

"Thank you. I like going over to see Marie and her mom. They are a lot of fun to be around. Will I be able to still see them when the job is completed?"

"I would be so excited if you kept up the relationship with Marie. I like her and John not just as customers but also as friends."

"You can ask Marie. She is so upfront with people she'll tell you."

"I'm thinking she looks to you as a friend. You might just want to let her know how you feel. That would confirm your intentions and would more than likely allow her to express hers. This is girl stuff—feelings. Men play it by ear, not so much feelings. We're just put together differently. Maybe go out for coffee after her parents go back home; have some one-on-one time. You could also set up a playdate for the girls, and while they are playing, you could ask her." These are only suggestions, I want you to stay excited about life."

"How I play it is, if I get more than two excuses as to why a person can't go out or have lunch or dinner, that's my last call. I don't need to beg people to like me," said Delores. She then turned her attention to our daughters. "Girls, are you ready?"

"We're coming, Mom. We have our backpacks. You got our cupcakes?"

"No, your daddy has them."

"No, not Daddy. He'll eat them all."

"No, girls, Daddy is full from your mommy's great dinner."

We got to John and Marie's, breaking the sound barrier twice en route. "I never knew the car could go that fast, honey."

"Oh, be quiet. It was a little over the speed limit, but not much," replied Delores.

"Aren't we going to the front door?"

"No, dear, I was told they would be in the courtyard."

We walked up to the arched gateway, and the new gate was so nice. The light was shining a reflection onto the gloss finish. We could hear Kim and Leslie running from the tunnel toward the playhouse and John saying, "Marie? Where are you, Marie?"

"Here I am, John, at the top of the staircase."

"Wow, the step lights are on. Look, Mama. Look at the steps," said Marie.

That was when my dearest darling opened the archway gate.

John almost had a heart attack.

"Wow … really wow," said John.

My dearest darling entered the courtyard in the best entry I had ever seen her perform. Marie came down the staircase, ran down the gravel pathway, and gave Delores a huge hug.

My girls almost ran everyone over, screaming for Kim and Leslie, who were screaming back from their patio. "Come on up. The playhouse is so pretty now," said Leslie.

I handed John and Marie the cupcakes, and Marie told the girls to come down. "Everyone, have a couple of cupcakes." I had never seen young girls with so much energy and excitement. It was so exhilarating to see such happiness and love for one another.

Marie came over to me. "I love my staircase. I mean it. I really love the staircase. She gave me a warm and loving hug."

Mama came over toward us and said, "My husband will see this all tomorrow. I guarantee he will be in love with the entire project. I love your staircase as well. I think Marie says it all for all of us … remarkable. You all keep this up and I'll come apart emotionally."

My dearest darling asked John, "Did you like my entrance?"

John said, "If I answer that truthfully, I'm sofa bound for many years. You got my interest and admiration at the same time. At first I was surprised to see the gate opening. Then I saw you. The way you moved was more than incredible. If you do that at the party, every man in the place will stand at attention; the applause will be deafening," said John.

Marie said, "That was the best I have ever seen you do. Don't do that again. Just kidding, Delores. That was incredible to watch. Come look at the staircase. The lights are on the steps. Look how beautiful," said Marie.

"Let's do an entrance. I'll be the emcee. Attention. Attention, everyone. Now entering the courtyard, Ms. Marie." Delores started to hum a song, and we all joined in. Marie moved step-by-step by step as if she had just won an Oscar. She was so graceful, so glamorous; she needed no more practice. She had every move made perfect. She was poised from one move to another and glided down the stairs. She got to the last step, and both girls hugged—really hugged, in a loving type of hug.

I thought Delores's question was answered when John said, "If those two girls were any happier, we would all be in heaven tonight. I have never seen my wife so happy. My girls, all they talked about at dinner was your girls coming over to play in the playhouse. Their toys were selected last night. I hope it stays like this forever. Coming home from work was mundane. Now I can't get here fast enough." That was the most I had ever heard him say at one time; I wondered what was going on.

"I know Delores broke the sound barrier twice coming here. She only sped a little—'not that much,' she said. Explain that to the police officer who pulls you over next time."

John laughed. "I know how she feels. Marie, in this mood, it is really hard to say 'See you at dinner' in the morning when I leave for work. I have had to call her twice during the day. You know what? She doesn't even ask what I want now. She knows. This is how it's supposed to be."

"Do you think Marie will want to remain friends with Delores when the job is completed?"

"Delores asked me that same question a few moments ago."

"You know something—Marie asked me the same question—whether Delores would want to stay friends with her," said John.

"Should we tell them?" asked John?

"Why not?" I replied.

"Marie."

"Yes, John, what is it?"

"Remember your question to me tonight?"

"Yes, John."

"Ask Delores."

"John, that could be embarrassing. Please, John."

"Delores, remember the question you asked me tonight?"

"Yes."

"Both of you, ask that question. Please, for all our sakes."

"Marie, do you want to be my friend even after the job is finished?" asked Delores.

Marie took two steps toward Delores, put her arms around her, and said, "I'd be honored to have you as my dearest darling friend. Cupcakes, anyone?"

The little girls, in four-part harmony, said, "We do."

"If I knew life could be like this, I would never, ever, feel like dying again," I said. "Thank you, Lord."

John said, "So true, so true. How about you? Are we all going to be friends?"

"How does your wife say it? 'Silly boy.'"

"Of course," said John.

"I told Delores you have been my only customers to ever take an interest in my family. Your questions to me aren't just 'When is this mess going to be finished?' It is really nice working and being with both of you."

"We were talking with Mama last night about how glad we were to contract the work with you. With what you have had to endure while working here, we are not certain if another contractor would have tolerated so much," replied John.

"I saw the mess that was caused for you two. No way I would have just said, 'It was nice knowing you!' I couldn't do that to both of you."

Mama was up in the playhouse, playing with the girls. We could hear they were all having a great time. Marie asked the girls if they would like some ice cream. They all yelled, "Yeah! Can we eat it up in the playhouse?" One of the girls asked if she could move her bedroom into the playhouse.

"Leslie is so excited about her house. What a gift," said Marie.

All four girls and Mama were on the patio of the playhouse. Mama asked, "They want a sleepover some night. Would Mommy and Daddy object? Decision time, Mommy and Daddy. The girls have never had a sleepover. Well, Mommy and Daddy, can the girls have a sleepover? Papa would love to see these girls having fun in the playhouse."

Delores asked Marie, "Are you sure that would be okay? My girls have never done a sleepover."

"The girls will have fun—a new experience for all the girls. We can even create a video of the event. They can learn how to cook a great Italian meal. I'll send home the recipe so Mom can practice. My papa comes in tomorrow. That's Wednesday. The girls have school until Friday. Saturday would be a perfect day for the sleepover."

"You know, we all will have to put up with 'Is it Saturday yet?'" said Delores.

"I know, seventy-two-plus hours," said Marie.

The girls were so happy that we all agreed. "Okay, Saturday night, sleepover," said Marie. We all agreed, with a high five all around.

"Okay, girls, Saturday night is the plan," Marie said to them. The scream of joy was heard around the world. "We can have them over in the afternoon and teach them how to cook Papa a fantastic Italian meal. Would you like to learn how to cook?"

"Yeah, we love eating but don't know how to make food," said Sarah."

"You'll all be chefs by the time you see your mommy and daddy on Sunday," said Marie.

"Thank you, Mama," said everyone.

"Are you sure you'll be up to having four young ladies?" asked Delores.

"They're all such a joy to be around," said Mama.

Papa will be in seventh heaven. They might make him ten years younger in one visit. He loves children—likes playing games with them, taking them to the park, and watching them play. That alone to him is better than sitting in a car and showing him around the town," said Mama.

"I can't wait for Papa to see the girls," said Marie.

"That brings me great joy," said Mama.

"Let's have some cupcakes and coffee," said Delores.

"Girls, let's get some more of those cupcakes and ice cream," said Marie.

The girls ran down the staircase into the tunnel and into the kitchen. It was such a joy watching them enjoy the time they spent together. We all had to follow them or we would miss out on the goodies. We were all joined as one from this day forward; smiles and laughter were all around. All the lights were out in the courtyard for another day. "Be ready for Papa's visit tomorrow; it's the courtyard's big day, along with all of us, said Marie."

The ride home was so glorious. The girls were singing to our music. Mommy and I joined in. It was a four-part harmony; that had never happened before. So many things were changing for the better. I loved my girls, my wife, and my life. This was not a mere coincidence; this was a gift from God. Both families needed this event to occur. The vision that he gave me was for a purpose. I did not know the whys or the ifs; it was just a vision shared to explain how the design came to life. I'd never had to do that before and didn't know if it would ever happen again; it was something I would always remember and cherish. We parked the truck and the girls got ready for bed. I gave the girls hugs and kissed their foreheads. "Remember to say your prayers. Thank God for our new friends. Love you two very much. Sleep tight."

CHAPTER 31

Delores was dressed in her nightgown and sitting on the bed when I got into the room. "The girls had a great time with John and Marie's daughters. Your idea of converting the old shed to a playhouse for them was sheer genius. The staircase and arched gateway, how the place is lit at night—I don't know how you do it. Thank you. You gave them such a gift. I'm thankful for being able to share in what you strive for on each project. Thank you for Marie. I really needed a good, close friend. Did you know that as well?"

"No, honey, I didn't know you needed a good close friend. I was hoping that you two would get along. I did not know you both needed someone. Watching you two enjoying each other brings such a warm feeling inside me. Can't explain. It's just right. Are you going with Marie and Mama to pick up Papa?"

"I told Marie I would be honored to go with them, I can't wait to see the man that helped create Marie. He must be one great man," said Delores.

"Can you sleep well tonight?" I asked Delores?

"I don't know. Things are churning inside me that have never churned before. See what you have done? I love you for the feelings. Don't ever stop or feel it's unwelcome. I'm just overjoyed with emotions, and the girls are as well."

"Me too; the joy is overwhelming."

"Say your prayers tonight and every night, as the girls expressed. This just doesn't happen."

The next morning, the girls were up early. "Two more days, Daddy. Will you miss us?" asked Sarah.

"Of course I will miss you. I probably won't sleep a wink the whole night. You two and Mommy are my life. I live and breathe for you girls. I know you'll be in great hands and well protected. You'll have to do me one huge favor. Be on your best behavior. Listen to Marie, her mama and papa, and John. Will you do that for me and Mommy?"

"Yes, Daddy, we're always good girls."

"I know. That's why I love you so much. Did you have any homework yesterday?"

"No homework. I did mine in class while the other kids goofed off," said Sarah.

"I'm so proud of what you both do. I will surely miss you while you're at school."

"Mommy, can you make us pancakes this morning?"

"Let me check my menu. Yep, Thursday is pancake day. You're in luck. How many do each of you want to eat?"

"Two, Mommy," said Rebecca."

"Yeah, two, Mommy," said Sarah.

"And you, dear, how many would you like?"

"Let's see. If I eat too many, then I'll spoil my appetite for my Happy Meal. Three will hit the spot. I will miss Mommy today as well. She's going to go pick up Marie's daddy at the airport. Would you like to meet him after school?" I asked.

"Today? Can we meet him after school, Mommy?"

"I'll have to ask Marie and Mama if that would be all right. When I pick you up, I'll let you know. Is that okay with you two?" asked Delores.

"Perfectly fine with us, Mommy," said Sarah. "We can't wait. Papa and the playhouse in one day! do we have to go to school?"

"Those pancakes sure smell good, huh, girls?" I asked.

"I love Mommy's pancakes much better than IHOP's," said Rebecca.

That's because Mommy adds her love to every pancake. IHOP does not have Mommy's recipe. She does not share her secret love with them. You have to follow Mommy's way of thinking. Look how good she turned out. I always say, 'Lead by example.' And your mommy's living proof."

"Okay, family," said Delores, "say your blessings and dig in or you'll be late for work and school. I have to get myself ready to pick up Marie's daddy."

"Mommy?" said Rebecca.

"Yes, dear."

"We love you so much, said Rebecca."

"Thank you, dear. I love all of you as well."

"Thank you, dear. The breakfast was fabulous as usual. You added just enough love to hold me over until my peanut butter and jelly sandwich for lunch." I kissed her cheek and the girls', and I was out the door to earn some money.

I arrived at the job site a few minutes early. I wanted to take inventory of what was on the agenda for today. "Pavers, lots of pavers. I need to call the sand and gravel supplier and get the balance of my order delivered first thing." I looked at the retaining walls, and more rock needed to be placed so the pavers could butt up against them. Juan could use one person to get that completed, Manuel and a new hire could do the border, and Diego and the rest could get the paver field in place. "Busy day ahead of the crew. Hope all show up and no one is out sick." They all worked well together, so blessed.

Marie came out to see what I was up to. I asked her if she had a good night's sleep. "Not as good as I would have wanted. Tossed and turned more than usual—too excited about today's events."

"Me too. Lost a few minutes. I'm sure glad you and Delores will remain friends even after we finish your house. I really do enjoy both your and John's friendship. It means everything to me and my family. Thank you."

"No, thank you for bringing all this to my family. John and I talked last night for a little while. This all is because of your vision. I have not felt like this ever before. Our marriage is beyond what either of us had imagined it could be. The girls are so joyful, singing and laughing, so willing to help around the house, and their homework is being done without me pleading with them."

"Ours as well; it's almost unbelievable. Life is such a joy now."

"You know we are going to pick up Papa at the airport this morning."

"Yes, we talked about that this morning at breakfast. I'll bet you're very excited."

"I'm so jittery right now—no coffee either. John even gave me a huge hug, telling me he loves me more each day. He can't wait to see my dad. He wants to see how Dad reacts to his new daughter. Can you explain what has happened to our families?"

"No, I'm just so pleased that it has happened, and I don't want it to end."

"Neither do I. Nor do Mama or John. The girls—wow, what a difference seeing them so joyful. Makes my heart feel very warm inside."

"Mine as well. You have a safe trip today. Lots of precious cargo you're hauling around town. By the way, you look stunning; you made my day complete and it hasn't even begun. Love you."

You're going to make me cry," I said. "Be careful; I can get very emotional."

My crew pulled in, and we needed to get this ball rolling. The crew was very happy this morning. I explained to them what needed to happen today. "The rock fascia is going on the retaining walls from the pavers to just past the barbecue, halfway around the circular planter. Put in the border pavers to match the rock fascia. Lay the field to match the border and rock fascia. If we get near the total area covered, then continue with the border and walls. Lock in the field with the edging. Everyone will install the rock fascia and border pavers. Great job yesterday. Today should be a little easier—not so much hauling. If you need to cover more area with base, continue. We may fill in the entire area after lunch."

Phillip showed up to put the wood walkway in the tunnel—perfect timing. I told Phillip, "Papa is flying in today, and the walkway will be perfect."

"We will stain the lumber today, polyurethane tomorrow. We will cover it with rolled paper so they can walk on the paper to protect the stain. We should be done by lunch break," said Phillip.

The base was soon installed, ready for the decking. "Juan, have a couple of people with a wheelbarrow take out the extra base you put in yesterday for the ramp." I then told Phillip, "Give them a few minutes to remove the extra base and clear the way for you to work."

I asked Diego if he could put some pavers in front of the tunnel door so the gate builder could install the threshold and surround to the tunnel door; he'd called yesterday and said he would return today to do the install. "We will do that with the extra base that they are removing from the tunnel. Phillip will give you finished floor elevation."

"Angel, will you be making the cuts today?"

"Yes, unless Diego tells me differently."

"Diego, is Angel going to continue cutting for you and Juan?"

"Yes, she does great work, and she's fast at the cuts."

"Who will run the vibratory plate?"

"Manuel. He ran it yesterday and directed the guys dumping the base and sand, so he was key for us to keep moving forward."

"So I can go home and take a nap?"

"No. If you need something to do, we can assign you a project," said Juan.

"Very funny, Juan. We could get the stone to the wall top and start putting in the wall caps, maybe tomorrow. That would make the job look nice for the weekend. If we can get as far as we have laid out, the rest of the decking should go in rather quickly."

I had to call the sand and gravel supplier for the balance of my order. The supplier had had a cancelation and would be able to deliver it in about an hour— perfect timing. I told the supplier, "I appreciate you looking out for us. Have a great day."

I went over to the back side of the barbecue just to check the conduits leading into the low-voltage transformers. Three had conduits attached; the fourth had nothing attached. I looked at the lighting plan, and sure enough, that one powered the barbecue lights and wall washing lights. We needed to install the junction box and connect it up by Friday. *Make some note, or you'll forget. Let's check on the other planters.*

"Juan, the conduit stubbed into the circular planter and the two wall planters—which transformer runs these planters?"

"The second one from this end is set up for those planters. That's how you drew the plans for us to follow. 'When in doubt, look at the plans.' Isn't that what you preach to us daily?"

"Touché, practice what you preach. Will I ever learn?" I said to Juan. "Yes sir, I should tell myself to listen to me; can't go wrong with that approach."

Diego and the crew were making great progress almost to mid-barbecue and started back at the raised planter next to the house just a couple of rows from the circular planter. "Juan, Diego is gaining on your rocking and border pavers. Do you need one of his people to help you or have Diego put in the border pavers?"

"Have him put in the border pavers. We will be moving to the circular planter in about ten minutes," said Juan.

"Is that okay, Diego?"

"That will be fine with us. I'll have Jose start on putting them around the barbecue base."

"Just be careful of the stones," said Juan. "They are still setting up."

The girls and Papa were to be here just after lunch; they would be all excited to see how many pavers were in place. It would be fantastic if we could get the circular planter finished and get the tunnel entry to the planter installed. It might be asking too much, as they were working like a well-oiled machine. I wouldn't want to upset the momentum.

About another half hour, and then we'll break for lunch," I told Juan.

He said, "That would be perfect, since they were just about out of the thin set used to set the rocks."

I went to see how Phillip's crew was coming along. The tunnel looked great, with about three feet left to install. The boards were cut and ready. Raymond was the one installing; he had a great system. The two other men were busy putting tools and extra boards back into the truck. Only a few more boards, and they were off to lunch. Raymond said he would return tomorrow to put on the polyurethane—two coats. He would tell the homeowners when to recoat the tunnel. "Maybe in one year. Depends on the usage. It should light up the tunnel even more than before. The polyurethane will reflect the light more than the soil did," said Raymond.

He had such great pride in his workmanship and was so talented.

"The playhouse came out beautiful, and the girls love playing inside. It's their home, you know."

"They are sure fun to watch, just like little wives in learning."

"The tunnel looks great. We will see you again tomorrow."

"Can you tell Phillip that we will start the stream feature next week and he can get ready to build the bridges?"

"I sure will tell him," said Raymond. "He asked about that this morning while I was loading the truck. He said he would call you before Friday."

At lunch break, everybody was on the retaining wall. I had headed back to my truck to get my peanut butter and jelly sandwich, bag of chips, and apple. Delores had made me a thermos full of hot coffee. I'd just eat in my truck; it wouldn't take long—five minutes maybe.

"Great, the gate builder just turned the corner. The puzzle is finally getting put together, just in time for Papa's arrival. It would be great if it were all done for his debut. Can't have everything. Some mystery goes a long way."

I got out of my truck to greet the gate builder. "So glad you're here. We have put some pavers adjoining the wood flooring in the tunnel. If there is anything you need us to help you with, just let me or Juan know. If you need power, there is an outlet we installed just inside the door on your left. I'll finish my lunch snack and join you in a few minutes."

The coffee was perfect. The sandwich—well, it was edible. The chips were not my favorite but were tasty. The apple I'd save for my ride home. The sand and gravel came around the corner. "Perfect, we can get the base in so they can walk anywhere they choose." I had a little more coffee; it would help me stay awake. I'd had too much tossing and turning last night; the excitement level was above the roof.

The gate builder asked if the crew could set some pavers between the arched gate opening; he had brought the threshold for the gate as well and would install that while he was here. The base laid need to be compacted, and then a one-inch sand layer and the pavers could be installed. "They may have too much base placed. I'll get my measuring tape from the truck to double-check the depth of the base."

I got a shovel and moved the base to check the depth. It came to five inches— maybe a half inch too much. I'd just scrape some to the front walkway, get the vibratory plate, compact the base, get some sand from the pile, and set some pavers while the crew watched. I asked the gate builder, "How long before you need the arched gateway set with pavers?"

"About an hour of work here, and then I can go over and complete the threshold at the arched gateway."

"My crew is at lunch, and they will get you what you need. If I do it, I might get fired."

"You own the company, right?"

"Yes, I do, but they can fire me from the crew; it's in the employees' manual."

"Understandable. I wish my crew would fire me. Wait a minute, I am my crew. No such luck for me."

He had the surround leaned up against the house wall; that was really nice work. He was removing the old door encasement and was ready to install the new one that matched the door. It fit like a tailored glove. He did a little shimming, got it plumb, hung the door on the encasement, and opened and closed it a couple of times. The clearance was equally spaced. It was so nice to see a professional craftsman doing what he did best.

Now it was time for the surround. He asked me to help hold the surround on one side and put it into position. Part A fit part B. I could not even notice the joins, as they were so tight. He mounted it with finishing nails, used a touch of matching putty to cover the nail heads, waited for a short time, and dabbed on a little finish and color. I could not even see the nail holes.

The crew was back from lunch, and I explained to Juan what I needed at the entry gate. He decided to do the entire entry from the sidewalk. That way it wouldn't looked piecemeal. He got all hands to put that piece together in a very short time. The gate builder was eating his lunch snack while they completed the six-foot sidewalk and entry. They used all my paver edging, so now I had to head home and pick up some more. What a way to get me out of their hair. Smart.

Back to the truck and off to the house I went. I called Juan on his phone. "I forgot to ask if you need anything while I'm out and about."

"No, I think we have what we need. You're getting us more paver edging?"

"I am getting you more. We have to keep the pavers locked in place. I'll be back in a few minutes."

When I returned to the job site, the ladies were back from picking up Papa. They were showing him what had been completed, what was ongoing, and what would be in the future. I entered through the arched gateway, being careful not to cause more work for the crew. The ladies and Papa were at the staircase; he was carefully examining the details of the handrail, biblical stones, balusters, and edging. Marie and Mama were telling him all about how it was built and showing him the photo album.

As I approached, Papa stood up, and I was introduced. "Fred, this is my papa, Giorgio," said Marie.

"My pleasure meeting you, sir. You have a great family. Such a joy for me and my family. I'm honored to be their contractor."

"I have heard a lot about you. Marie and John talk highly of you, and the people you have brought to their home have all been polite, highly skilled, and professional. Marie told me you envision your projects?"

"I have been given a unique gift of being able to see things as I walk around the property while I'm meeting with the customer. When I first started doing landscape construction, I thought everyone had that gift. I just wanted to be the best and give the client the best possible landscape. Some of my first designs got me in trouble, so I now listen to the customer. If they are insiders only, there is no reason to build an outdoor kitchen, patio cover, pool, or spa. They just become a maintenance issue, deteriorate, and lose value. Marie and John showed interest in making the outdoors part of their living, I just designed what they would use."

"What I have heard and seen thus far is impressive. The girls are dying to show me their grand entrance for a lavish party you also envisioned," said Papa.

"The first vision showed me Marie coming down the staircase with glamour and style to an audience of family and guests to show off their new landscape," I said. "It just blossomed from that vision. Marie got stung by the vision and has enhanced it beyond my wildest expectations. She's one of a kind."

"I have to tell you I have never seen my daughter or my wife in such great moods. I thank you for pulling off a miracle on these ladies. I also heard your beautiful wife's entrance from your arched gateway is breathtaking."

"Did you see her doing the arched gateway entrance?"

"No, that was her and Marie showing the crews their talents. The workers were applauding them, and they liked what they heard. The workmanship is far exceeding the normal jobs I have witnessed. My granddaughters talked to me on the phone last night, and they want to show me the playhouse. I'm not to look at the playhouse without them. They are also caught up in the excitement. Your daughters are caught up as well, I heard. Whatever you have done, it is working miracles on others as well. Very impressive."

"They are, and I'm so proud of how the two families have changed for the better. God is making all this happen. I have been blessed with crews of my own and others who have pride in what they do. That pride just reflects on the workmanship of the project. Their skill levels shine. I hope you enjoy your tour. Welcome to the courtyard, and enjoy your time with your family. Mama is a marvelous lady. I'm so happy to have been able to spend some time with her; It's been such a joy for me and my family."

"They never told you her name?" asked Papa?

"No sir, just 'Mama.'"

"Her name is Sophia," Papa explained to me. "She likes 'Mama.' It's rare for a woman to like being called 'Mama' unless she is your mama. Sophia likes people to believe she is their Mama."

"I think she has it right. It puts you at ease when talking with her."

The crew was finished with the walkway into the gate, the gate builder was putting in the threshold, and Raymond was putting the final coat on the tunnel walkway. Marie told me that the patio furniture was to arrive today, and the barbecue and accessories would be here by noon. Juan and Manuel continued putting on the rock fascia, and Diego and the rest of the crew were busy putting in the border pavers and the field; it should be nearly finished by today's end, ready for the family to enjoy the entire courtyard. What a great gift for Papa's first visit.

The crew was spreading the base and sand while the paver field was gaining on them. They would soon have the pavers completed from the tunnel to the playhouse staircase for the girls; they would be overjoyed about not walking on gravel or dirt.

I need to toughen them up a little. A little tomboy in all of them won't hurt. Makes them stronger. They already are very loveable and charming—a delight to be around.

My dearest darling came over to me. "I like the pavers. Much nicer than walking on dirt. Did they finish my arched gateway?"

"Just about finished. You missed not coming in that way this afternoon?" I asked.

"I want to show Papa. He's a wonderful man. I see where Marie gets her personality. I have to go pick up the girls at school. Would you like me to stop and get you your Happy Meal?"

"Can I get the toy? I asked.

"No, no toy this time," said Delores.

"Okay, I'm trying to quit or at least cut back. Watching my teenage figure, you know."

"Watching it overlap your belt," said Delores. "I like how you're keeping it in front of you so you can keep your eyes on it."

"I love you, darling. Was the airport ride nice?"

"We all had a good time getting there and coming back with Papa. I'll never forget that experience. He treats me like he does his wife and daughter. Thank you for getting me involved. I'm so full of joy and happiness; I don't want this feeling to ever go away."

"Me too. I look forward to every day, spending time with you and the girls."

"Oh, thank you for reminding me. I have to leave right now to get there on time. See you in a few minutes. Bye." Delores scurried up the tunnel, into the house, and out the front door.

Juan asked, "Once they get the two layers along the base of the walls, where should the crew start on the retaining walls? Is there one wall more important than the others?"

"We need the barbecue rocked with the retaining wall we first put in so the wall caps can be installed. The patio furniture will arrive today, along with the barbecue and accessories, at any time now. I would like them to be able to use the barbecue and furniture for the weekend."

"We may not get the entire wall stoned, but if we start at the patio cover back toward the barbecue, that will finish where they will be spending their time outside."

"If you can get the pavers completed under the patio cover, we can set up the furniture for them. You need to start sand filling everything that's completed thus far. Maybe spread some sand on top, and Angel can broom it around while waiting on some cuts."

"She is so good at cutting, and she pulls her weight. I'm impressed with all the new hires. Good job on selecting the right people. Are they happy to work for us?"

"They all have expressed that working for us is one of the best jobs they have had."

My phone rang. "Hello, this is Fred ... Phillip, how are you? Raymond said you were going to call ... Tomorrow morning, you want to bring a contractor to the job site. Sure, that will be fine. What time? ... About nine o'clock will be perfect. You can see the job site, how far we have gotten ... The magazine editor called you, and his staff will be here tomorrow as well? I forgot all about them—too much stuff going on at one time. I'll be here all day. See you tomorrow. Thank you for calling. Have a great day."

Marie returned from picking up her girls. Papa had gone with her. The girls were so excited; they really loved their grandpa and grandma. Marie had told her girls they had to wait a few minutes; my girls, their newest best friends, were on the way. "Their mama is bringing them to our house." That really got them even more excited.

I told the crew, "The little girls are here, and they want to show their grandpa the playhouse. Make sure there is nothing lying around that they or the parents and grandparents could trip on. Diego, put paver edging on the pavers leading to the playhouse so they don't get dislodged."

I told Juan that I had two tarps in my truck that they could lay on top of the pavers while putting on the rock fascia. "Keeps the pavers cleaner." Juan was having his two guys bring in the stone from the pallets and stacking it on top of the retaining wall. There were five different sizes of stone, and they placed each size in a separate stack. That made it easy for Juan to install the rocks. The first two courses were not as difficult and were what the eye would look at above the pavers. Juan also got from my truck the wall washer lights to install as he installed the stone. They had about four feet of the wall completed from the entrance wall; they were now under the patio cover shade.

Diego's crew came in and told me that there were two delivery trucks getting ready to offload some stuff. "That's the barbecue and accessories and the patio furniture. Juan, can you and some of the crew help get those items into the courtyard? Should only take a few minutes." They picked out beautiful patio furniture, and the barbecue was very nice, made of good-quality heavy-gauge stainless steel. We would install the barbecue tomorrow with all the goodies.

All the girls were here. "Come on, Papa; we want to show you our house." Leslie and Kim led the way. My girls were holding Papa's hands, and they all made it to the stairs. Leslie and Kim told Papa that he was the first grandpa to ever see their home. "We hope you like it."

Marie, Mama, and Delores all had their cameras poised. *Click, click, click!* They took great photos for Papa and all the girls—priceless. They all climbed the stairs, and there was more clicking from cameras and cell phones.

As they opened the door and went inside, Leslie turned on the lights. Papa said, "Oh, girls, this is beautiful." He gave them all a huge hug, and of course the cameras were clicking away. Marie, Mama, and Delores were wiping their eyes—not a moment for us tough men to witness.

They had him on the patio to show him the view of the courtyard. He told all of us, "This is the most amazing place I have ever seen. I can't explain how I feel right now."

The girls asked Marie if she had any cupcakes to give to Papa for them to share. "I'll bring you all a piece of cake. I'm out of cupcakes," said Marie."

John got home from work; heard what the girls asked; headed back into the house; found the cake, paper plates, plastic forks, and serving knife; and returned to the playhouse. Marie and Delores were near the bottom of the steps, and John handed them the cake, plates, and plasticware and said he would return with the cups and fruit punch. Marie said, "John, come here." He went over to the steps, and she bent over and kissed him. "You're such a dear man. Don't you ever change."

Delores came over next to me and said the same. "Don't you dare ever change."

"Yes, dear, I promise."

The crew was starting to pick up the tools. Delores asked Angel to stick around for a few minutes. "The ladies wanted to show Papa the grand entrance, and of course, you are a part of this experience."

Angel was glowing. "But I'm all dirty."

"Even better —the real deal. He'll love it," said Marie.

Before Papa and the girls started the playhouse party, the ladies asked Papa to stand on the patio and said they had something to show him. The ladies scurried over to the staircase. John saw what they were going to do, turned around, and put on a CD of Italian music—Marie's favorite.

He turned up the stereo, and the ladies proceeded down the staircase one at a time. Papa, my crew, the gate builder, and two delivery drivers were now their audience. Angel was first; she was really getting into this now. Her entrance was model quality, each step poised and glamorous. Then my darling followed, and then Mama, and finally the first lady of the courtyard, her favorite song playing. Such glamor, poise, and grace. Everyone was applauding. Each lady was greatly appreciated by all the onlookers. There were no wolf whistles, as they all had been warned. Juan had told the new guys the dos and don'ts.

The ladies gave Angel a huge hug; she had tears in her eyes as if she had just become Miss America. She had a huge smile and was glowing with pride. Papa said, "Ladies, I'm so honored that you shared that experience with me. Come on, girls, let's have a piece of cake."

They all screamed, as little girls would, "Yeah! Cake!"

I must add that my vision had gotten better than how I saw it the first time. *Thank you, God, for bringing this all to life.* The ladies practiced one more time. It seemed the applause was addictive, but there was no way I would ever stop them from enjoying the moment. Of course, after the second passage, Marie said her famous line: "Silly boys." And she curtsied for them. It made their day as well as the ladies'.

Mama told Marie, "You need to do that every time. The men get all giddy."

I told the ladies that the people from the magazine were coming over tomorrow. "And I know they will want to see your routine. I'll call Phillip tonight and have him call his friend and have his crew bring a movie camera. If this goes on social media, it will go viral. Be prepared to be followed by the media from the time it is aired, celebrities."

I showed John his new toy. "The barbecue has arrived."

"Really? It's here?"

"We will install it for you tomorrow so you can cook and serve your first outdoor meal."

"Marie, the barbecue has arrived. You forgot to tell me," said John.

"No, honey, it's your surprise. I wanted to surprise you. You can cook for us tomorrow night. Papa likes his steak medium. Mine is medium well, in between medium and well done."

"Oh, I had better start looking up how to cook steaks the proper way," said John.

"Us girls will do some grocery shopping for your meal tomorrow," said Maire.

Now the whole family had their new toy. Marie said, "I have a great idea. The girls are spending the night on Saturday, correct? Let's check with the girls. Girls?"

"Yes, Mom."

"Are your friends still planning on spending the night on Saturday?"

"Yeah!" all the girls screamed, now all on their patio.

"Yes, Mommy," said Leslie. "Why do you ask?"

"How about if Daddy cooks hamburgers and hot dogs for everyone? Can we invite Delores and Fred?"

"Please, Mommy, that would be great—our playhouse party!"

Now all four girls were hugging and jumping up and down.

"Careful, girls. We don't want you to fall from up there. The neighbors must love us now," said Marie.

"Steaks cooked just the way you like them tomorrow night and a full-fledged cookout on Saturday?" John asked.

"Yes, dear. Can you handle it?"

"Do I get support from the main kitchen?"

Mama said, "We will make potato salad, three-bean salad, and pork and beans, all from old-school Italy."

Papa asked, "Do they weigh us before we get on the airplane?"

"No, dear, the ticket is not charged by the pound."

"Okay, bring on the calories." Papa asked the girls if he could eat with them in the playhouse.

"Yeah!" came the approval from the little girls.

Marie told the girls that they would have to be the hostesses of the party. "Would that be okay?"

"We would love to host the party," said Leslie. "Huh, girls?"

They all approved, and the excitement went through the roof.

Delores said, "Marie, we must bring stuff for this party. It's not fair for you to feed my family. We want to bring some food or desserts or something. Please give me a list to fill."

Marie gave her a huge hug. "Delores, I will give you a list. But please, you are my friend, and I think of all of you as my extended family. Have you ever tasted John's cooking?"

"No, we have never had the privilege of tasting John's cooking."

"You're in for a big surprise," said Marie.

"Is it that good?" asked Delores. "'A big surprise' doesn't say either good or 'Are you kidding me? What was it before you cooked it?'"

"You have to be your own judge. Isn't that right, John?"

"What's right?"

"Your cooking ability."

"World renowned, last I heard," said John.

"He doesn't get out much, you know," said Marie.

Delores asked, "Is his world in his own mind? It will be great just being here with you and everyone. We're used to eating crow. Anything is better than crow. Right, honey?"

"No comment, my love. That is a very leading question, with no good answer for me to give."

CHAPTER 32

"Well, we have another busy day tomorrow: guests, magazine staff, wrapping up the pavers, hooking up the barbecue and accessories, wall caps—lots of stuff. Come on, girls; we have to get you home to do homework and have dinner. Give Leslie and Kim a hug and tell them you'll see them on Saturday."

We gave hugs to everyone; even Papa got two hugs. Delores told him she was glad to meet him, as did I. All the ladies were hugging; John and I hugged as well. I called Phillip and told him to have the magazine crew bring a camera that could film the ladies doing their grand entrance practice. He agreed and thought that would be a great idea.

Early the next morning, it was Friday—payday for the employees, Big Mac day for me. I arrived at the job site and opened the arched gate. It was so nice walking on pavers and not dirt. It kept my boots cleaner. As I entered, John and Papa were sitting on two patio chairs at the newly installed patio table that my crew quickly assembled before they went home. "Good morning, gentlemen. How is everything this morning?"

"Really good. We were just looking at the tunnel door. I really like how you took an eyesore and made it a thousand times better than what it was," said John.

"Did you see the wood walkway Phillip completed yesterday?"

"No, we were just admiring the appearance from our easy chairs," said John.

"I'll open the door for you, and you can see the results from where you sit."

John said, "What a difference that makes. I'll bet that when the lights shine down at night, it's even more spectacular."

"Raymond and I talked about that very same thing yesterday while he was putting on the polyurethane coatings. Phillip and I thought this would make the house cleaner and the tunnel a place you can now use to enter into the courtyard in bad weather. Great way for the girls to get to the playhouse without going through the sliding glass doors. How are the ladies this fine morning?"

"They're up and cooking us breakfast," said John.

"You have them trained really well. Are they serving you outside?"

"I don't think they will serve us out here, but it would be really special if they surprised us," said John.

It wasn't a minute later when the tunnel door opened and out came the ladies with the men's breakfast in hand.

"Looks like you guys are getting a feast served in the great outdoors. Good morning, ladies."

"Good morning. Would you like some breakfast?"

"No, thank you. My dearest darling fed me well—even hugs and kisses as my dessert."

Marie said, "I have to remind her—don't spoil him; you'll regret it when you all retire."

Mama said no truer words had ever been spoken.

"We just have the ordinary breakfast. Hugs and kisses come after they tip us," said Marie.

"Then that depends on whether it's a hug or a kiss or both or none of the above," said Mama.

"These guys look like they're big tippers," I said.

"Do you get commission from these guys?" asked Marie.

"We never discussed money transfers," I told her.

"The girls are coming out to join us with breakfast. Will we be in your crew's way?" asked Marie.

"No, they can work on the walls on the other side. It all needs to be completed so you can have the event of the year. Did I tell you the magazine crew will be here today?"

"You mentioned that late yesterday. We will be ready," said Marie.

"Now don't quote me, but I called Phillip last night and asked the magazine to bring a camera to film your grand entrance practice session. He thought it was a great idea and said he would tell his friend. I think they might put it on their website to introduce the readers for the upcoming issues. I'm going to let you enjoy your breakfast before it gets cold. My crew just pulled up; I have to look busy or they will find a new boss to replace me."

I went over to my crew. "Good morning, rock fans. We have a slight change of plans. The homeowners are eating breakfast on the patio table, so you can rock the walls along the house and the circular planter until they finish. Everyone doing okay this fine day? Any questions or concerns regarding your job, or need of clarification regarding what I expect from each and every one of you? I just want to thank each and every one of you for doing a great job. The homeowners told me last night they are so happy to have you working on their home. Angel, you are part of the girls' grand entrance practice, which means you all will have to come to the party. The girls will help you, Angel. They are all excited about adding you to the ceremonies. I have a meeting with Phillip and another contractor this morning at nine o'clock, and a crew from the magazine will be here also. Not sure what time. They will be taking photos and could ask you some questions. I'll let them know that we have added three more people."

Diego asked, "Should we help with the walls or continue on the pavers?"

"If you have an area away from where they are eating, continue on the pavers. It won't be very long. John has to leave for work in a few minutes."

The crew started on the circular planter, putting stones in the area where Juan had stopped yesterday; the wall north of the tunnel door needed the first two rows installed as well. Diego and his crew worked the circular planter, and Juan and his crew worked the raised planter wall north of the tunnel door. The race was on to see who could complete their wall the fastest and look the best. Everything was going smoothly. Rocks were being placed at record speed; there was no actual record, but it was moving pretty quickly regardless.

We heard someone say, "Is anybody home?"

I asked John if he wanted me to answer the gate. "Go ahead. We're not buying anything—signs everywhere to stop this nonsense."

I opened the gate, and in front of me was a microphone and a handheld camera. "Hello, I'm Christal from Channel Five News."

"Good for you. What do you want?"

"Are you the homeowner?"

"No. What do you want?"

"Are they at home?"

"Look, either you answer my question or it's good-bye."

"We're here to talk with the homeowner."

"Sorry, they are not home. Call them for an appointment."

The next thing I knew, there were five more microphones stuck in my face. I closed the gate after I stepped outside to confront whatever these news stations wanted. "What is this all about? I want answers now, or I'm calling the police."

"We got a memo that the homeowners found the bank money and turned it over to the police."

"What bank money?"

"They found the money robbed from the bank many years ago."

"How do you know they found the money?"

"The memo said the bank is coming over to give them the reward."

"When is this bank coming over?"

"They should be here any minute."

"Great, wait for the bank. I need to get back to my crew."

"Who are you?"

"Me? I'm me."

"Well, me, can we talk with you regarding the bank money?"

"No. I know nothing. Have a great day, and wait for the bank. I have to call my friends at the police department."

I told the crew, "Do not open the gate or talk to the reporters."

I told Marie and John, "Someone sent the press a memo stating you are to receive a reward for turning over the bank money. Every news agency is outside your home. I'm calling the detective to get his people over here before this gets out of hand."

I pulled up the detective's card and dialed his number. "I need to talk to the detective." *Placed on hold, figures.*

"Hello, Fred, long time no hear."

"We have every news station parked on the front lawn. Can you send some people to keep some kind of civility? Someone alerted the press corps about the bank money. The bank is supposed to be here in a few minutes. They don't call the people who found the money in advance. They just send the press."

"This is very unusual. Hold the line; I've got to notify the bank." The detective returned to the line after a moment. "They supposedly called yesterday, and no one was home, so they say they attempted to make contact. And since the memo went out, they could not stop them from doing what they are legally allowed to do. I'm sending over two squad cars for crowd control. Oh, I just heard they are reporting from your street, announcing the arrival of the bank officials at any moment. Please stand by."

I talked with Marie and John. "It's official. The bank notified the news agencies and supposedly called your house yesterday and got no answer. It's legal. Do you have a lawyer you can contact? This isn't like the Publishers Clearing House money for life. I told them you were not at home. The press, they lie. So can we. See how they like it."

John said, "Do we have to talk with them?"

"I don't know. I called the detective, and he's sending a couple of squad cars for crowd control. They are airing this on television right now. This could get ugly quick."

I called Delores to ask her to turn on the television. "Don't plan on coming over until this all blows away." She turned on the regular news station, and there was my company truck right in the middle of the screen, with a reporter talking about the reward to be given to the homeowners in a short while. The breakfast club quickly got out of view from the front of the house and headed inside. The doorbell rang. John asked, "Who's there?"

"Channel Seven News. Are you the homeowner?"

John said, "No. Go away. The police are coming."

As he responded, the police arrived and began pushing the reporters from the property. "You all know this is private property. Stand in the street or on the city sidewalk. Get off the property or we will put you behind bars for trespassing."

The bank officials pulled up in a black SUV limousine; the reporters acted like cockroaches when a light is turned on, swarming the vehicle and asking all sorts of questions. The official stated he would have a news conference once he did his duty dealing with the folks who had found the stolen money. The officers were calling the precinct to send more cars for backup. There were so many cars trying to get into the cul-de-sac that it became a parking lot. One of the neighbors was talking to the reporters and told them about all the forensic and bomb squad occurrences that had been going on for many weeks. "Did he finally kill her this time?" the nosy neighbor asked the reporter.

The police officer heard her, pulled her away from the news reporter, and said, "What did I just hear you tell that reporter?" asked the detective.

"You know you guys have been at this house almost daily," said the nosy neighbor.

"Ma'am, you say another word to anyone, and I'm hauling you into jail," said the detective.

The reporter started shooting her mouth off about bombs and forensic evidence, stating that the husband was being questioned. All the agencies were trying to swarm the house. The four officers were forced to draw their guns, telling the reporters, "Stand back now." Five more squad cars arrived with officers who ran toward the press corps. Two news helicopters were hovering overhead. This was getting ugly very fast, thanks to the nosy neighbor. The detective got the police chief poised to have a press conference at the home.

The bank officials were allowed to walk onto the property with a police escort; the officer rang the doorbell, and this time, John saw it was the police and opened the door. The officer showed John his badge and told him, "These are the bank officials here to talk with you."

"Please come in. Have a seat. Marie, we have company." Marie and John introduced themselves to the bank officials.

The officials thanked them for turning over the money to authorities. They explained to John and Marie that the money recovered in the bag was nearly all the money and bank notes stolen. "Since we know neither you nor the contractor handled the money, there will be no charges brought against anyone in your household or the contractor's crew members. We are offering you a reward for being so honest. The bank is preparing the reward. They would like you two to appear with the bank ownership at the branch on Monday. There will be the press, the mayor of the city, city councilmen, one to two state representatives. and possibly the governor. They want to couple this with awarding your home designation as a historical landmark. We are very sorry about all the commotion outside. We tried to notify you yesterday but got no response. The intercompany memo got leaked to the press. This should not have happened, and we deeply apologize. Will you two be able to make the presentation?"

John asked, "Do you know how much of a reward we will receive?"

"No, not yet. We are checking past bank records to see if any of the missing money was spent. We will know by Friday."

"When was the bank robbed?"

"Over ten years ago. We think it was an inside job. Please don't quote me. This is still an open investigation."

"You will let us know the time?"

"I will contact you on Friday. You'll be home, on Friday?"

"Can you give us an approximate time—not like the cable company, which gives a four-hour window and calls fifteen minutes late to reschedule?"

"Let's say eleven o'clock. Nice meeting you both, and I will be honored to see you on Monday," said the official.

"Can we bring my parents and children?" asked Marie "Of course. We will have a limousine pick you up and bring all of you back to your home." The bank officials opened the front door, and two officers escorted them back to their waiting limousine.

The police ordered all the cars blocking the cul-de-sac to move or be towed. The street was still blocked by police cars. The chief came to address the gathering crowd. Cameras and microphones had been placed by every news agency; the press was poised to attack the chief with questions. The chief, using all his diplomacy, stated, "There is an ongoing investigation regarding a missing persons report filed over ten years ago. The current homeowners are not involved in any way. Once our investigation is completed, we will hold another police conference, and everyone will be notified."

The one reporter who got the scoop from the nosy neighbor asked, "Why did forensics and the bomb squad come to the residence?"

"Great question," the chief replied. "Can't answer anything right now. Thank you for coming out this morning. Please stay in touch. The homeowners on the block would like to have their street back."

CHAPTER 33

Phillip and his friend finally got to the house. "What was that all about? Ongoing police investigation? You know what they are investigating, don't you?" Phillip asked.

"I am not at liberty to discuss the investigation, or I'll be doing time. Are you going to introduce me to your contractor friend?"

"I'm so sorry. Going to a job site loaded with news trucks and police vehicles shakes me up. This is Brad, owner of Streams and Ponds."

"Nice meeting you, Brad. How can I help you two?"

"We came here to help you."

"You have me confused. Help me with what?"

"How many streams and ponds have you installed?"

"Maybe ten in about as many years."

"Brad is a premier stream and pond builder. He does the majority of stream features for the magazine you are going to be on the cover of. Brad will work with you, making your stream feature more than cover worthy. They can build it in probably half the time it would take your crew to build. I showed him your plans. Brad, take it from here."

"Your design is very nice. I can make it nicer and give the homeowner a highly skilled professional and a five- to ten-year warranty. If they want fish, we will make it a healthy habitat and will provide them with a monthly or weekly maintenance schedule—whatever they desire. There are some equipment changes that need to be made—better quality and locally manufactured."

"If I were to allow you to build the stream feature, how long would it take you to complete?" I asked. "Would you have your own crew, or would you need some of my crew to help? We retrieved the stones from the shed footing to be used in the stream and pond. They are part of the property and have to be incorporated into the work. They are stacked against the fence."

"To answer your questions, about a week and a half, maybe two weeks. I use my own crew. I will only need an approval to start from you. I will incorporate the stones into the water feature, making sure the homeowner knows the original and brought-in stones. We take the stream from bare soil and create a water masterpiece. I have heard stories regarding the staircases inside and outside. I want the stream feature to be a part of that story. Pride is our only name. Phillip has seen some of our work. He can vouch for our workmanship, as I can for his."

"Phillip will build the bridges as shown on the plans. He will have liberty to improve on the design to accomplish the movement of the landscape. The homeowners have become dear friends of me and my family members. I only want the best, and you will have liberty like Phillip. My talent is in design. My crew is getting much better, but they are not masters at stream building, and I can't afford any letdowns at this point. Can you start next week?"

"We can start next week. There has been some excavation on the stream—by your forces, I presume?"

"Yes, we need soil to fill raised planters in the courtyard. May my foreman, soon to be my superintendent, watch, at times, the fundamentals of building streams?"

"We will be honored to have him view the construction of the stream. He is welcome to ask questions and take written notes. The more he shows interest, the more willing we will be to share our methods."

"If you unearth anything, please stop and get me and the homeowner. Do not think it is just some trash someone dumped. Did Phillip tell you what we unearthed and what happened on the property?"

"He mentioned the staircase in the home had to be restored. It was really messed up. You found some chests and a metal can, and something in the shed," said Brad.

"You'll find out lots of details when the press is informed. There is a police investigation going on, and I'm not at liberty to say much about the investigation. At one point, the case was to be closed. A suspect died, but upon the finding of a satchel full of money—that's what the commotion you saw when you arrived was about—the case has been reopened. The chests and metal containers were removed by the bomb squad and forensic teams. As a precautionary measure, no one knew what we would encounter.

"The playhouse on top of the patio cover used to be buried in the courtyard. There have been quite a few changes on this property. The stream feature is the last major excavation. Please keep us informed, and if you find anything, stop, clear the area, and the police will come and investigate your findings. Do not totally unearth the item or items. To let you both know, there was a heinous crime committed here. Things could be booby-trapped. That is why the bomb squad and forensic people were called to the home."

Phillip said, "So that is why we were told to leave early one afternoon."

"Yes, when we unearthed a five-gallon metal can, even though this used to be the old farmhouse, and farmers are known to bury just about anything. Don't take hitting an item lightly; anything could be booby-trapped.

"I've got to get back to my crew and talk to the homeowners. Phillip, did your friend say when the magazine crew would be here?"

"He said about one o'clock."

"Thank you. Have a wonderful day, gentlemen. Nice meeting you, Brad."

Back at the courtyard, the crews were back, doing what we had talked about yesterday. Juan and his two guys had the barbecue installed, the accessories were nearly completed, and most of the stones had been put on the walls. Diego was nearly completed with laying the pavers, and lunchtime was quickly on us. "The job looks great. The homeowners will be pleased."

"Marie and John were looking for you a little while ago; they told us to have you ring the doorbell when you return."

"Thanks, Juan. I'll go see them right now."

Marie answered the door. "Please come in. Can we talk with you?"

"Of course, you can always talk with me."

"What happened today?" asked Marie.

"You mean, the reporters and all the commotion?"

"Yes, why did they do that to us?" asked Marie.

"The bank claims that they tried to contact you yesterday. You were gone all morning but were home from around two o'clock. You can't return calls or receive calls if you're not home. Why they did not have an employee or manager come by your home, I don't know. Why did an employee send a memo to all the press agencies? I don't know that either. I feel the bank owes everyone an apology. That was totally unprofessional. I wanted to punch a couple of reporters but held back."

"We have to go on Monday to receive a reward. Lots of people are going to attend. The house will be declared a historical landmark by the state. Why is so much kept secret to those involved? don't they notify people anymore?"

"I don't know what goes on in people's heads anymore; they seem to have very little respect for anyone but themselves. So many want fifteen seconds of fame and will do most anything to get the attention. I felt sorry for you two. I went out of the courtyard and faced at least a half dozen reporters sticking microphones into my face."

"We want to thank you for protecting us. You took some tongue-lashings from our media," said John.

"You know, if they had been honest with me and not tried to weasel their way into your private property, I may have been a little nicer to them. You don't demand I jump through their hoops. I don't care who they think they are or what name tag they are wearing. You don't respect me, don't expect me to respect you.

"Good news, I have a master stream builder who is going to build your water feature. He installs stream features and ponds for nearly all the magazine's clients. He wants the stream feature to be on the same level as your staircases. He seems like a very nice person. I told him that you two are not only the homeowners but also close friends to me and my family. It will keep us on schedule, and while they are building the stream with a five-year warranty on his work, he will also provide a maintenance schedule for you. We can concentrate on the irrigation, landscape, and lighting. You both seem a little down. Is it what occurred this morning?"

"Yes, do they have a right to do what they did?" asked Marie.

"No right. Trespassing and rudeness are a complete disregard to the written law. That is why I called the detective. You saw how quickly a neighbor who knows nothing can get reporters and nosy people riled up over her version of fiction."

"Why did that neighbor say such horrible things?" said Marie. "She was live on television. Lots of people saw that. Nothing she said was close to being true. She made John look like a murderer. People who saw that know who we are. They filmed the front of our home. One station took a shot of the street sign. They violated us in every which way. John had to call his office to say he would be late. His best employee acted cold to him."

"Get yourself legal counsel and sue the stations for airing such nonsense."

"Are we still safe in our own home? What about our girls? Will they get ridiculed in school over all this?" asked Marie.

"Those are questions that you need to ask the detective in charge of your case. Ask for police protection. Get that bank owner to pay for all your security costs. Demand that the employee who leaked that memo be held accountable and incarcerated, not just put on leave of absence. People need to be held accountable for their actions. I don't want to see you two sad. Remember: don't ever change, no matter what. You have to keep that feeling. You can't let reporters and neighbors take away your joy and happiness. Let's walk around the yard. The police and newspeople are gone; feel free to carry on normally."

We started in the backyard, looking at where the stream feature would be started tomorrow, using the old foundation stones along with new stones to make the water feature come to life.

John asked me why I would let another contractor build the stream feature.

"They are known in the industry, have a great reputation, and do it as their only business. It will give you a highly skilled stream. If my crew had done your staircases, they would not look like what you have. The shed would be still on the ground, sitting on old stones. I have to face reality. My vision was for you and your family. Giving you something less than the vision would not be the same. If the stream contractor can pull off a great feature, your family will enjoy the entire property. Your family and guests will talk about their experience being here. Can you imagine how you feel around my family, multiplied by all your friends and family members?

"The reward thing will blow over in less than a month. People move on to the next thing rammed down their throats by the media, looking for ratings. Your neighbor will find someone else to tell the world about as long as someone is listening to her.

"Look how unique your home has become. No one else on the block or in the neighborhood has anything close. Your photo album, displayed for the party guests to see, gets to be a part of something they may never see in their lifetime. You're going to honor them with a golden opportunity. This is your gift. God chose you to show family, friends, and guests how special you both are. Let's see how the crew is coming along, get some fresh air, stroll down the staircase, and get some of that ego fuel you so deserve.

"Marie, you have to bring yourself back to the glamour, style, and elegance of your poise on the staircase. Get applause from the crew. They love watching you. Get Angel, and call Mama and Papa out. John, your barbecue is waiting for the first cookout. Give it your all. You have the girls' playhouse party for tomorrow. Nothing has changed. We're all in this together. You both have shown my crew and the other crews working on this project that there is a reason to enjoy yourself and be free from the everyday junk thrown at us. Come on, Marie; show us your best grand entrance. You know you want the applause."

Mama and Papa joined us on the staircase landing. Marie looked at John. "Is he right?"

John told Marie, "I need you back to my Marie, and I need to get myself back to being John."

Mama said, "Marie, I'll go first to help break the ice."

"Wait, let me call Delores. Then we can all be ourselves again," said Marie.

Delores had to have broken every speed limit in town. She came into the arched gateway, and my crew all stood up and applauded her. She brought the spark that got the rest of the ladies all fired up. I asked Angel to join the ladies on the staircase landing. She ran up the stairs, and the hugs were welcome and tearful. The guys just got out of the way, joined my crew on the pavers, and enjoyed watching the ladies strut their stuff like proud peacocks. Each lady was doing her best, and the crew erupted in applause and cheers. Each time, it was more intense and louder. When all the ladies were on the pavers, we could feel the love and warmth given by all of them. Angel was now one of the ladies forever. She came over to me and thanked me. I told her the pleasure was all mine.

"You helped bring the ladies back," said Angel.

The rock fascia was moving along, the first retaining seat wall was ready for the wall caps, Juan and Manuel were laying them out and marking them to be cut, and Angel, highly skilled, showed even more talent making the cuts. The caps were being installed by Diego and Jose, and Vincent was mixing mortar for placement of the caps. Diego was giving him advice about how much water to add. The circular planter was the next to get the wall cap; the walls against the house needed a few more stones, and then they would be completed. Juan and Diego would jump over and put some stones in place while they were waiting on cuts. The wall caps once laid by Juan and Manuel were marked for the cuts; they went straight to putting on stones.

I went out front to look at our masonry yard. It was nearly gone. The crew had been cleaning up the yard as items were being used and removing the empty pallets out of the way. My vendors would haul off any empty pallet we had when they delivered. My trailer was full of overstock pavers and blocks. I told John that I would leave him a half dozen or so pavers in case any got damaged.

The family was loading up into the car to go grocery shopping and to seek lunch and relaxation. We would get to start the landscape and irrigation system on Monday, and then would come the most important thing—the accent lighting, the sparkle of the courtyard.

On Saturday morning, we could not keep the girls settled down.

"Is it time yet, Daddy? How much longer do we have to wait?" said Sarah.

"Just a few more hours. Let's go outside and do some yardwork."

"No thank you, Daddy," said Rebecca. "We can't get dirty. We have to stay clean for the party. Mom, do we have any cupcakes? We are getting hunger pains."

"Darling, could you check the snack drawer for the girls?

"I'll take a peek; if there are none, I can go to the store and buy some."

"Great, take the girls; they will help you shop. I can make myself beautiful while you are shopping."

Delores had on a bathrobe, as she had just gotten out of the shower, getting ready to transform into my angel.

The snack drawer was like Old Mother Hubbard's cabinets—bone dry. I had the girls get freshened up so we could go shopping. I went into our bedroom to give my bride some encouragement. She loved encouragement—and not just when I was willing to give her some.

"You have an errand to run and two lovely girls waiting for you. Be a good boy and bring Mommy back a treat as well," said Delores.

The girls were more than ready. "Hurry, Daddy; we don't want to be late to our first ever sleepover," said Sarah. "That would be embarrassing."

Out the front door and into the truck we all went. We got all buckled up and set the radio to the oldies station.

"Oh, goody, we have to listen to Daddy's station," Sarah told Rebecca.

"Hey, I grew up to this type of music," I told them.

"Mommy doesn't think you have grown up," said Sarah.

"Well, Mommy is not going to get a chocolate cupcake for those types of comments."

We arrived at the store, and the girls wanted to get Leslie and Kim a special gift while we were getting three boxes of cupcakes. The girls asked if we could get three more boxes for them to take to the sleepover.

Silly me, thinking only of fulfilling their hunger at the present time.

We found a goody for mommy, handpicked by her girls. She would love it; how could she refuse such an offering?

Back home, the girls got two bottles of moo juice—chocolate, of course. They took all the goodies to the kitchen table and called for their mom to join us. She had just finished with her makeup, hair, and nail painting and was still in her robe.

She joined us at the kitchen table. The girls handed her the surprise they had picked out for her. Delores was in near tears with joy.

"You both thought of me. How sweet."

Sarah said, "We wanted to make sure you had something to eat while we were gone. Daddy doesn't cook very well."

Delores gave them both a hug. She looked at me. "Well, did you get me some goodies too?"

I gave her my best loving look. "After a little while, plenty of goodies for you."

"Oh, no, I want what you were sent to the store to purchase now. What is it you bought me? The girls did very well. I don't see what you thought of me?"

I slid over a two pack of cupcakes for her to consume.

She picked up the two pack of cupcakes. "This is what you think of me?"

I stood up and went over and gave her a warm and loving hug. Later, dear. Not in front of the girls."

"Mommy, what time is it now?" asked Sarah.

"It's eleven o'clock. Let Mommy slip into some clothes, and we will head over to Leslie and Kim's house."

I was still hugging Mommy. I whispered into her ear that I could help her get dressed. My arms were around her neck and shoulders, and we were touching our bodies to one another. She nearly knocked the wind out of me when she elbowed me hard in my chest. I said to her, "I bet I get a bruise."

She said, "That is probably the most you'll get the entire weekend."

Right. Girls, tie you daddy to the chair so he doesn't bother Mommy."

We all were ready, clothed, laden with goodies, and wearing in the right places. Suitcases were in the car, with extra clothes just in case. Inventory taken, every box checked—off we went.

The girls and Delores serenaded me during the entire trip to John and Marie's. I told them they should cut a CD so I could retire in a couple of years.

When we arrived, Marie, John, Mama, Papa, and the girls had lunch ready for all of us to consume. John had made hot dogs and hamburgers for us to dine on; they had four different side dishes. Marie made margaritas for everyone, and nonalcoholic for the girls.

Let the party begin.

Wow, what a feast. They even had dessert that the girls and Mama had made just this morning.

I felt as if I needed to head home and take a nap afterward.

The hardest part of the afternoon was saying good-bye to our girls. I didn't think I could cry so much. All the way home, we both shed tears. Delores sat next to me and put her crying eyes on my shoulder. I drove the entire trip with my arm around her, and she shuddered as she wept.

The girls were so excited to spend the night that they almost forgot to say good-bye to Delores and me. Marie filled in the gap, giving us loving hugs.

CHAPTER 34

Monday morning was a fabulous day. Birds were chirping, the sun was shining, breakfast was superb as usual, and the girls were all in a great mood. You can't beat days that starting like this one. I beat the Streams and Ponds construction company to the site. I walked to the backyard to get a feel of how the first day should progress. I was joined by John, Marie, Mama, and Papa; they saw me from the kitchen window. "Good morning, everyone. Such a beautiful day. Can't ask for anything better than what we have been given."

"Is the pond contractor coming today?" asked John.

"They should be here in a few minutes."

"What will they start on this morning? asked Marie.

"I really don't know. I'm sure they will shoot grades and determine the elevation drop. The zero-collection box will be a deciding factor. I always check grades, set up falls. Water has to flow from the pond down the stream to the collection box and then recycle back to the pond. It gets a little tricky since the feature has to balance, or you'll work the pump to death. Being highly skilled, they will have that all dialed in—size of pump, distance from collection to fillers in the pond. They say to customers at the big-box stores, 'Just dig a hole, set this real nice preformed plastic shell, add water like a child's wading pool, throw in a couple of goldfish, and bingo—you have a water feature.' They forget to tell the customers you need to provide power for the pump, to fill the pond, to watch for the evaporation of the water you just put into your pond, and to watch for algae and dirt getting into the pump if you don't have a skimmer.

"You walk out of the store telling yourself, 'That landscaper wanted six or seven thousand dollars for a professional water feature. The big box store only wanted six hundred for everything.' Really? Everything? Are you sure you have everything? We deal with this regularly. Your water feature is custom built, one of a kind. They want your feature on the cover of the home-remodeling magazine. It will be spectacular. Did you call your home entertainment company about running outdoor speakers to the water feature and the courtyard?"

John said, "I did, and he was going to call me back with a time we could meet. I'll call him this morning and get something arranged."

"When you have him on the phone, ask him what size of conduit he will need to be put under the stream. I will tell Brad what he needs. It's very difficult to put it under the stream once completed. I'm putting two four-inch conduits under the stream, and I'll draw it on the plans so that if you need to cross the stream at a later date, you will have a location.

"Oh, by the way, the hamburgers and hot dogs are the best. The family loved everything served. Thank you again for having the girls over for a sleepover and the barbecue. Great times and so enjoyable."

"It was our pleasure having your family over for lunch. My parents loved being around the girls. They had a hard time going back into the house. They would have played in the playhouse all night long if we had let them. They ate their dinner in the playhouse, had snacks and dessert in the playhouse, and even had Mama and Papa over as guests.

"We weren't invited," said Marie. "'Maybe next time,' they told us. Leslie said, 'We're on a limited budget, you know, so we can't have everyone to our party.'"

"She's a smart little young lady. Should do great in life," I told them.

Brad and his crew arrived. He started by telling his leadman, Thomas, the scope of work that needed to be completed that day. My crew had rototilled the outline that I had drawn with marking paint. While Brad and Thomas were discussing the scope, I interrupted them and excused my rudeness. "But about how the layout was drawn, please feel free to enhance or put your vision on how the stream should look. I was just trying to use up rental time. They charge me for four hours, even if I use it for one hour."

Brad said, "Thank you. I was going to do some magic to the layout but would like to talk to you first."

"Feel free to express your talents. Mine more than likely would not make the cover of any magazine. If you need me, I'll be with my crew in the courtyard."

Brad had a marking paint can with him, and one other crew member had the builder's level and was setting it up. Brad and Thomas were measuring the distance I had drawn on the plan; the first minor change made through Brad's calculations was that the zero-collection box should be moved just a few feet to the west. He twisted it away from the rear fence by six or eight feet. I moved it toward the fence. Brad moved it toward the patio. That was why he was more highly skilled than I was. They spent the next hour shooting elevations; soon they had the game plan set and let the excavation begin. Picks, shovels, and wheelbarrows were in full swing in a matter of minutes.

I returned to the excavation an hour and a half from when I left Brad and Thomas. The streambed was similar, but different in many ways. I got a nice feeling from what they had accomplished thus far. I had a seating area for the guests and family to sit and watch the waterfall and fish in the pond, with the stereo playing softly in the background. This could become the go-to place for heavy thought or reading one's favorite book. I wanted to put a downlight in the tree so the area would be lit at night. Brad had bent the stream feature in that area farther from the tree, which would allow a larger bench and possibly a small table to rest wine or champagne glasses on.

"It looks really nice, Brad. I like what you have done. Makes my plan that much more accurate. I have two four-inch pipes and one two-inch pipe that need to be placed under the streambed for irrigation, low-voltage lighting, and sound system sleeves. I'll have Juan bring them to you, and we will install them for you."

"No, that is not necessary. If you give us the piping, we will make it happen. The ends of the pipe need to be taped, so if you have the tape, have him bring that as well," said Brad.

"I'll have him bring everything to you in just a few minutes."

Brad talked with me about having a pond fall into the stream, adding another water sound for the homeowners. When they put the rock cap on the wall, they wouldn't grout the joints above the stream; filling the pond to just below the rock cap would allow the water to flow over the wall into the stream. There would be two layers of rock placed for the cap so the homeowner would never see the top or sides of the block, and the valving would control the flow of water through the cap into the stream.

"Beautiful idea," Brad said. "I'm certain the homeowners will be surprised and joyous." He also mentioned that the wall would have a backlight installed to illuminate the falling water.

"I'm getting excited to see it work already," I said.

Brad laughed and replied, "In due time, in due time."

John, Marie, Mama, and Papa joined us and looked at the excavation. Marie, of course, had her camera and took a couple of photos. I said to her, "You need your parents and John to pose for a photo of the excavation. Now your photo album will be complete."

"What a great idea," said Marie. "Okay, everyone say cheese."

"Is this as deep as the stream will be?" asked John.

"No," said Brad. "We have some more to dig out, but this will be the slope for the bottom. We have a 2 percent fall into the collection box. It won't be whitewater rapids, but you can float Popsicle sticks and race them from the pond to the box. Leaves work as well as Popsicle sticks if you don't like Popsicles."

"Can you explain, in some detail, what the final pond and stream will look like?" asked Papa.

"The pond will be at least three feet deep. The stream will be over a foot deep. I don't like standing water in the stream—too much algae growth to control. The pond will be deep enough to house fish and aquatic plants. Using aquatic plants will allow fish to hide and keep the algae from growing. I'm not a fan of plastic plants or plastic fish, but if you choose to have those, then we will provide them for you.

"We offer a maintenance program to keep the aquatic garden flourishing. This is a habitat most people know nothing or very little about. This is not an aquarium, where everything is chemically balanced and the water heated. You can use koi or other carp-type fish. There are some catfish that do well outside. One problem we have encountered are seagulls feeding on the fish. That is why the aquatic plants and a hiding place for the fish is essential.

"Is your maintenance contract costly?" asked Marie.

"It's very reasonable. You can spend more per year replacing dead fish and aquatic plants than our annual maintenance fee. We have various plans for you to choose from, and if we encounter something not covered by the maintenance contract, we will provide you a detailed estimate explaining why the procedure is required. That does not occur often. Since we are the ones building your water feature, we take extra precautions during the construction to curb many of those outside-the-contract costs. Many of the additional costs we encounter in the feature are from leaking water due to inadequate construction methods. Not sealing the joints is very typical. You get what you pay for, so to speak."

"You mentioned prior you have a five-year warranty," said Papa.

"Yes, we build it right, so I can stand behind five years of warranty. We can't warranty against acts of God—earthquakes, hail, tornadoes, things like those. We just cover normal maintenance procedures and construction, said Brad."

"You changed the stream some from what Fred laid out. Is he okay with what you did?" asked Marie?

"Well, Fred, are you okay with what we did?"

"Yes, he made my design even better, and the ambiance has multiplied as well."

"I forgot you were standing there. Sorry; my mind is going a mile a minute," said Marie.

"You don't have to apologize. I forget I'm standing here as well," I said.

"You mentioned that it will take at least two weeks for the water feature to be completed?" said John."

"That would be the longest it would take. Getting the excavation correct and shaped the way we believe everyone will be happy takes most of the time. Rocking just right and in an appealing way takes the longest," said Brad.

"We don't want to keep you from your work. I will, on occasion, stop by with my camera and take photos for my photo album that will be on display during our open-house party," said Marie. "Please don't be camera shy—free advertisement."

"That is fine with me, and I might ask for a copy for my brochures, if you don't mind," said Brad.

"I'd be honored to share, though they aren't professional by any means," said Marie.

"They will be perfect for my brochure. They will show reality, not something staged or airbrushed to hide any flaws."

"I can't wait to dip my toes in the nice, cool water," said Marie.

John said, "Watch out. It may replace her staircase."

"It could," stated Marie.

"I'll do my best to make it a choice," said Brad.

Thomas asked Brad if he could shoot the elevations again so he wouldn't over excavate and throw off the fall. Brad went to the builder's level, and Thomas held the rod to check the depth. The first reading showed an inch left to remove; the second was nearly two inches too high. Thomas took a shovel, cut down the differences, and had Brad reshoot the elevations again. The first shot was perfect; the second shot was a half inch too high.

This went on for a few minutes, and finally all shots were near, if not, perfect.

The stream was now being subgraded. Two of the crew members were digging the trench for the footing for the pond. They would pour the footing and then remove the soil to subgrade and pour the pond bottom.

They asked John and Marie if they would they prefer a concrete bottom or a rubberized liner. The concrete bottom would have a drain for cleaning, and the liner would have to be cleaned with a siphon pump. "I would still put a rock bottom in, so you would never know it was sitting on concrete, stated Brad."

John and Marie asked, "Is that part of your maintenance proposal?"

"It is part of the maintenance plan," said Brad. "Maybe a cleaning in five years. They all vary. I will know by the first month's maintenance how long between cleanings. If you have fish, the water will have to be treated before the fish are returned. The pH of the water is our guideline for the cleaning. Too many nitrates in the water will kill the fish. We keep accurate records of the pH, which we test each visit."

"If we get a dog or a cat, would the pond water hurt them if they drank from the pond?" asked Papa.

"No, it will be pet safe, though maybe not as safe for the fish if you get a cat. The fish are pretty smart. They will hide from predators. They are more vulnerable during feeding time—theirs, not the cat's. We will also put in underwater lights and waterfall lights to give you a special effect during the evening hours. I heard you're having stereo sound piped into the area?"

"Yes, the sound contractor will be here tomorrow, and he will add the sound system for the water feature and the courtyard so we won't have to turn the house sound system up to hear the music outside."

"That should be extremely nice for you, your family, and guests. You could charge so much per visit. It would be a lifetime experience. Now you have my designer's instincts flowing. You're going to play the *Flipper* theme song, aren't you?" asked Brad.

"Not planning on it. Is that your favorite song?" asked Marie.

"Hardly. Heard it too much growing up. A dolphin would be too big for your pond anyway."

Papa asked, "Is it almost time to pick up my little sweethearts?"

Marie said, "Oh my gosh, I almost forgot. Please excuse us. Come on, Papa; we have to fly."

Mama said, "The girls found out yesterday while wearing their school shoes that walking on the tunnel's wood floor in their shoes makes a really nice sound. They started tapping their feet. It did sound nice, so all of us were in the tunnel, making noise. You know, it can't compete with the staircase, but clogging in a wooden tunnel that echoes the sound of hard heels tapping the floor is nice. Nothing beats the sound of hard-soled shoes tapping on wooden floorboards."

"If I didn't have on tennis shoes, I'd be tempted to give that a shot. Tomorrow I'll wear my work boots and try it then. I'll wait for the little girls, and they can show me how they do it."

"So that will be your lunch break, Brad—clogging on the wooden floor?"

"I could not clog for an hour. Maybe a few seconds tops."

"I think he's coming around to the magic of this place," said Mama.

"Maybe the girls can come to the party through the tunnel into the courtyard, clogging all the way, with the violins playing in the background," I said. "We have to have a movie camera shooting the entire event. It would go double viral in minutes. At a dollar per hit, you could bankrupt the entire world in one day."

"Now I have to get into the right mind-set or this stream feature will have flying fish or salmon and grizzly bears hunting them," said Brad.

John said, "Do we have enough room for all that? I love salmon, and my new barbecue would never shut down. Could we make the cover of *Field and Stream* as well?"

"Not unless I get really carried away," said Brad.

We heard the car doors close and the prancing of little shoes running up the driveway. Mama said, "Give them about three minutes, and they'll be running up the stairs into the playhouse. What a great idea that is—a playhouse for little girls on top of the patio cover. They will not have one ounce of fat on them until they get married. I can see them bringing their children here to play. Marie will be like me by then. I'm going to the courtyard, and maybe they will invite me up to play like they do Papa."

Brad said, "This water feature will really have to be special to be in the top three. We will pour the footing in the morning, start setting the block after lunch, and should finish by the next afternoon. We'll excavate the floor, put in the drain, sand the bottom, steel, pour, and start rocking the bottom and plastering the walls. We will plumb the feature as we build the walls, and then the rocking will take place. When we have rocked, we will fill the pond with water and check for any leakage. Usually we are the only feature of a landscape—no competition. This is going to be tough, making the cover of a magazine and still being ranked three or four for the project."

"Phillip will be here tomorrow and will start digging the footing for the bridges and setting the posts," I said. "He may have to change the locations as shown on the plans to fit the adjusted stream feature. He's quite capable of doing modifications. Well, it's just about quitting time. Gentlemen, load up the truck. We're heading back to the barn."

Mama got an invite with Papa. Maybe they'd have dinner on the patio tonight with the girls. Marie bought a small table and two chairs for the girls that folded up and were stored under the patio roof, perfect for dining with the girls under the stars.

I went to the courtyard to see if the crew finished the wall caps, grouted the stone, and cleaned up the area. The caps were completed, and the stones were mostly grouted. It would likely be finished by lunch tomorrow. The cleanup was perfect.

The girls were on their patio with Mama, and Leslie said, "Hello, sir. Are Sarah and Rebecca coming over tonight to play?"

"You know, girls, I don't really know. Can I have them call you when I get home?"

"Oh, please, will you have them call us? We would love to talk to them. We miss them so much."

"I know they miss you as well. I'll have them call as soon as I walk into the house. If I don't see you tonight, you all have a very good evening. Love you all. Good night, ladies."

As I walked into my home, Sarah, Rebecca, and Delores all said they were heading over to John and Marie's for dessert. "Your dinner is on the stove. I just put it there a few minutes ago. Should be still hot. Do you want to meet us over there when you finish eating?" asked Delores.

"You know, I will do that. The girls and Mama are in the playhouse, asking if you are coming over. See you all shortly. Love you, and please drive safely. No speeding—not even just a little bit."

I ate my dinner and returned to John and Marie's for dessert with my family. When I pulled into the cul-de-sac, I got a vision. *I will do what my dearest darling does, the arched gateway entry, not for applause but maybe laughs.* I quietly walked to the gate and heard them all talking at the patio table. *Perfect. Let's see, left hand on my hip, right arm raised, and elbow bent. Got it.*

I opened the gate slowly and appeared as Delores always did. I entered and sashayed into view. There was no applause, no laughter; no one was paying attention. *Great, all that preparation. God must have seen me make an utter fool of myself.* I heard my girls yell, "Daddy's here!" Now they all saw me; my grand entrance had been a complete flop. Oh well, I needed some practice anyway.

"Daddy," said Rebecca, "we got ice cream and our favorite—cupcakes. Grandma made them. Daddy, they are so good, and we invited her to our party. She is a great guest; she brought us flowers."

"I'll have to get myself one, cupcake. Love all of you girls, ladies, and gentlemen. Long time no see."

I decided to sit on the seat wall since all the chairs were taken. Marie got me a cupcake and ice cream and served it with one of her hugs. She said to me, "Thank you so much for being you. We really love walking through the tunnel. The girls laugh and laugh. We all are wearing hard-soled shoes to clog in the tunnel. Your girls will join us tomorrow. They have on tennis shoes. Tomorrow they will have on their hard-soled shoes as well. The sound is fantastic. We now have three ways of entering the courtyard. We may have to have dancing waiters and waitresses bring food through the tunnel during the party—very stylish and entertaining."

"Maybe your sound engineer can put microphones under the decking to amplify the sound through the sound system, like a drummer uses in today's music."

That is a great idea; I'll call him tomorrow and ask him if that is possible," said Marie.

"I suppose you ladies will have to start practicing your dance step rhythms like Gene Kelly in *Singin' in the Rain.*"

"Oh no, not more practicing," said John.

"Would you not want to hear all the ladies in step, echoing through your stereo system?" I asked John.

"Oh, sure, while I'm burning their dinners, that will make everything taste just that much better."

"John, you'll have your own cooking show in a very short time. Keep practicing."

"Oh, I will practice. I just need people brave enough to eat my jerky meat," said John. "The stream feature looks very nice. We were all looking at how the water will move through the stream, considering where we want the bench and small table for the best view."

"The bridges will start tomorrow," I informed them.

"That's what Brad mentioned. Phillip and his crew are excellent woodworkers. When finished, you will have to flip a coin to see just where you want to spend some time, I think after dinner you all could take a break at the water feature."

Marie and Mama said, "We want to be by the stream in the heat of the day and party in the courtyard under the stars and moonlight. That sounds like a great plan."

Delores said, "You'd better have two benches; I need a place to relax as well."

"That works for me. John, you'll have to hire a cook and maid and chauffeur to take up the slack."

John said, "Great idea. You forgot the butler to answer our door and run the household. John would love to work to pay others his paycheck, huh, dear, said Marie?"

"Between all the new people and the government taking their share, there are twenty-four hours in a day. That's three full-time jobs I can squeeze in. Shoot, who needs to sleep and eat? I have a staff to pay," John said with a satirical tone.

"John, you know the IRS will send you a thank-you card. You may have found a way to balance the country's budget. If only the rest of us slackers would follow your thinking, we could own the world."

Marie said, "You know, I can still take the girls to and from school, so we may not have to hire the chauffeur just yet."

"You need a designated driver to take you to lunch," I said.

Mama said, "She's always thinking of your best interest, John."

"I have to admit," said Papa, "this courtyard is sure peaceful. The lighting is perfect for the atmosphere."

Marie said, "Papa, not all the lights are in yet."

"We still have low-voltage lighting to install to boost the ambiance of the courtyard," I replied. "That will be a sight worth staying around for. I'm hoping to start the irrigation system and landscape this upcoming week, and then the lighting upon completion of the area. I hope adding the plants will breathe new life into the entire home."

"I can't wait for our first hummingbird and butterfly to visit our oasis, and the bees as well. They will be coming. Word gets out—food."

I heard a couple of grasshoppers telling a butterfly, 'Come back in two weeks; everything will be in bloom—a buffet of floral delights.'"

The girls were awfully quiet. "Girls, are you all okay?" asked Marie.

"Yes, Mommy, we're playing a board game. We're just enjoying our new playhouse. We love it so much. Thank you, Daddy; we love you," said Leslie.

"We really love our new house," said Marie. "I never imagined what that playhouse would bring to the young ladies. You know, since they started playing in the playhouse, their homework is always done, the rooms are spotless, they eat all their meals, and they never complain about helping, doing the dishes, or dusting the furniture. Being a parent is becoming boring. Shoot, John and I don't even argue. What has happened to us?"

"Love, you're experiencing what true love of family is all about," said Papa.

"You know something else?" Marie added. "No television or iPad or cell phones—nothing. They just play in the playhouse and do homework and chores, totally away from outside influences. I'm telling the school to stop having the kids use the iPad for homework. At the next PTA meeting, I'm going to tell everyone what is happening to our family—the joys we are all receiving. What if we send an article to the press?"

"It would never be printed, Marie," said John. "They would all be out of work. They live off the tabloid news they produce. Girls, you all have school tomorrow. Can you start ending your board game?"

"We're almost finished. Just a few more minutes. Please, Daddy?"

"Okay, just a few more minutes," said Mama. "You all need to get a good night's sleep."

"You'll start seeing the stream feature come alive tomorrow," I said. "I'm as excited about how it will look as all of you. Thank you for the dessert and, more importantly, your friendship and loving care for me and my family. I'm so proud of being able to bring this all to you and yours." Hugs were coming from all angles; there was so much fun and joy.

CHAPTER 35

The next morning, breakfast was fantastic. Everyone was in such good moods that it was hard to leave that atmosphere. My crew was raring to go when I got there. Diego and his crew were finishing up the grouting of the stone; Juan and his crew were ready to start the irrigation system. Brad and his crew had just arrived, and Phillip and his crew were just pulling in to start the bridges.

I asked Juan to get four sticks of three-quarter-inch pipe and eight three-quarter-inch slip-by-slip nineties from the truck. "Bring the pipe cutter also." Juan looked a little puzzled but had Angel follow him to retrieve what I asked them to bring. Phillip walked into the stream feature area first. I explained to Phillip what my intentions were. "Make a rectangle from the PVC piping and lay it across the streambed to establish the angle of the bridges. The plans are diagrammatic, and since Brad modified the stream, this will help all of us determine just where the bridges will be installed."

John and Marie came out of the house to a warm welcome from everyone. Marie stated, "I didn't even do the grand entry. This is becoming so rewarding for me."

Juan and Angel brought the pipes and fittings. Phillip and I measured where the posts would more than likely be placed—twelve feet apart. Brad was watching what we were doing with concern. I had Juan cut two twenty-foot PVC pipes to thirteen feet. The width of the bridges was five feet; two five-foot pieces would be splendid. "Connect the two thirteen-foot pieces with the two five-foot pieces and bring them to us."

Thomas said to Brad, "Just what are they doing?"

Brad said, "Not sure, but let's watch."

I was on one side of the stream, and Phillip was on the other. We laid the PVC rectangle across the stream and turned it just a smidgen. I stood up and stepped back. "Brad, join me, please." Brad was standing alongside me, and we were both looking at the rectangle. "Phillip, turn the rectangle slightly toward the tree."

Now Phillip was in a daze. "Just what are you trying to accomplish?"

Brad now understood what I was doing. "What do you think, Brad?" I moved back to the patio where the table was and sat down on a chair.

Marie asked, "Are you all right?"

"Brad, come sit down and look at the rectangle from this angle."

Brad, John, Marie, Mama, and Papa were all now at the table. "What do you think, Brad?"

"Phillip, move it back toward the staircase just a smidgen," said Brad. "What do you think, Fred?"

"I like it. John, Marie, Mama, and Papa, what do you think?"

"Not sure what we're looking at," said John.

"This is the bridge layout. You have to envision that this is where the first bridge will be placed. The ninety-degree fittings are where the posts will be installed."

The whole crew now nodded in recognition, and Raymond said, "Now we understand what you're doing."

Thomas said, "I thought you guys were going nuts. I was ready to call the funny farm."

"Now that everyone understands what the concept is, we have another bridge to lay out," I said.

Phillip and I measured for the second bridge. "Fourteen by five feet," we told Juan. He and Angel made the second rectangle, brought it over to Phillip, and laid it across the stream. Now with all the players positioned at the table, we did the rectangle dance—a little to the left, a little to the right, a little more to the right.

I got up and looked from the pond and told Thomas to follow me, which he did. "What do you think, looking at the two rectangles?"

"I have never done this before. If I screw this up, will I have to live with the results?"

"No, Brad, I and the homeowners are the deciding voice. I just wanted you to experience the moment as well. You stay here. I'm going over to the staircase landing. Marie, could you join me? Since this is your baby, I need you to stand here and look at the two rectangles. Let me know what you think."

Now I had the triangle completed. "Well, everyone, what do you think?"

Thomas said, "Looks good from where I'm at."

Marie said, "Not certain. John, can you come and help me look at the angles?"

Mama and Papa said, "We like it."

"Phillip, are we away enough for you to dig the footings at the back side of the nineties?"

"One corner is a little close, but if I move it, I will have another corner too close. We can make the bridge longer if that would help. We don't want to undermine the stream or put too much pressure on the edge. Brad stated that he needed at least six to eight inches of soil to make the stream feature watertight."

"Brad, would you and Phillip like to see the angles from where Thomas, Marie, and John are standing?"

"Good idea. We will take a peek," said Brad.

The general consensus was that it looked pretty nice. I had Thomas, Marie, and John swap positions. "Well, everyone, is this the look you like?"

"This works for all of us."

"Great, I love it as well. Good job, everyone. Phillip, you can start with the post footings."

Brad came over to me. "I'm impressed. I wasn't sure what you were trying to accomplish. Thomas and I were scratching our heads at first, and then it dawned on me it was to get the perfect angle for the bridges. Setting stakes from a plan is one thing, but getting the absolute perfect angle? How you did that was unbelievable. Thank you for sharing that technique."

"You have had to put in and tear out a prior bridge location before. I did a home years ago, and there were two to three different angles that we could have used. It was necessary to determine how the bridge would be best suited for what the homeowner wanted to achieve. I made the PVC frame, positioned it, and moved it while the homeowner directed me. Worked really well. It gave him the opportunity to envision what I saw while drawing the bridge."

Marie, John, Mama, and Papa all came over and stood by Brad and me. "That was the most remarkable thing I have ever witnessed," said Papa.

"So if you now approach the rectangle and look across the stream, this will be your view from the bridge. I have the daunting task of getting you to want to cross that bridge not just once, but daily. Then I have to have you want to venture to the seating area and the staircase."

"I'm glad I only have to deal with piles of paper," said John.

"Marie, how did you find this guy?" asked Mama.

"A friend of a friend told me about him. They didn't hire him but wished they had. They fired the one they hired after a couple of weeks, and they were embarrassed to call Fred back to fix what the other contractor had messed up. I have taken her to lunch a couple of times not to rub her nose in it but to thank her for her recommendation. They will be at the party. I'm certain they will apologize for what they caused themselves."

"I'll be kind to them," I said. "My work speaks for itself. I don't hold grudges. Business is business. Lose some and win some. No one wins every one."

Brad was busy putting in the steel for the block walls, and his crew was busy mixing the concrete. Thomas was busy putting together the copper piping for the waterfall; the other two men were getting the subgrade finished on the stream—busy, busy, and busy. Diego was finishing up the grouting of the stone, and Juan and crew were digging the trenches in the raised planters—busy and busy. Phillip, Raymond, and one laborer were getting ready to pour the footings and set the posts for the bridges. Marie and family were enjoying a cup of coffee and a breakfast roll at the patio table.

I had an appointment to meet another client in about an hour. *This will be a small project. We have a couple of months' backlog, and two other jobs starting next week. Juan and I are having another meeting about moving Manuel and Jose into a foreman's position and which projects they will run. Each will need at least two laborers. That's five new people being employed. Looks like Angel and Vincent could become the next foremen in line. More work will be required for that to occur. I may have to lease at least two or three more trucks. I have to meet with the insurance agent and dealer to make this all happen. In due time, in due time. Grow too quick, die real fast in this business. Liquidating is not profitable at all.*

The footing for the walls was completed, and the setting of the block would begin in a few short minutes. They mixed the concrete firm and used 3,200 psi concrete mix. It set up very fast. Maybe one course only before lunch would be all they could safely install. Phillip had one bridge post installed and actually installed the frame on the posts for more stability and alignment. It was nice when one had enough men to make that happen. As the concrete set up, the posts and frame were perfectly aligned. It was not recommended for an unskilled person to attempt this. The posts were staked and secured in place before the frame was put on. They had one of the three posts set and plumb, and were working on number two. Once they were all set and framed, Phillip would check to make sure everything was accurate and then leave for the day.

The homeowners would be warned not to tamper with what was installed. Tomorrow they would remove the frame to allow the stream feature underlayment and liner to be installed. They would then erect the frame and start the deck and handrails. Everything would be primed before the bridge was erected. The stream feature would have to be rocked under the bridge, so Thomas and the crew would start that first thing to allow Phillip and crew to build at least one bridge.

The homeowners had chosen Chinese red for the arched bridges. They should be stunning. Phillip was using high-gloss lacquer paint for the final coats. The sheen would be breathtaking; once dry, they would protect it with sheeting so my crew could cross from one side to the other without jumping over the stream. We would more than likely put a one-inch-thick sheet of plywood across the stream feature to allow our work to be completed without taking a chance on damaging the bridges.

I was sure the homeowners would use our makeshift bridge to keep the bridges in pristine condition; photo shoots and magazine covers had their priority. They were due back out for some more shots tomorrow. The courtyard was ready construction-wise, but the aesthetics were due to make it come alive.

When lunchtime arrived, the crews were more than ready for a break. Marie told me that my dearest darling was due to arrive for a little shopping and to pick up the girls. "We are providing the meat for John to practice cooking. I think it's hamburgers and hot dogs. He's pretty good at those."

The pond had the first course of blocks installed. After lunch, Brad said they may get two more courses installed and would stop until tomorrow on the walls.

They would install the vault and piping for the return to the fountain and pond, and maybe install the underliner and some of the liner, if time permitted. If the bridge frame was in his way, he would remove the beams that crossed the stream and reattach them for the overnight concrete cure. They were making good progress on the fountain and pond.

The lunch break was soon nearing its end. I asked Juan to meet with me once his crew was busy doing what was next for them to complete. Diego and his crew were finished with the grouting and needed someplace to start trenching. Juan would show Diego where to start away from the stream and fountain, maybe having him start in the front yard.

Just like clockwork, the arched gateway slowly opened, and in strutted my dearest darling. That got the boys all riled up; they gave lots of applause. She could do it and get applause. I would get "Oh, it's only you."

Marie saw her pull up and was at the staircase landing. She, of course, made her way down the staircase very stylishly and glamorously, glowing with confidence. She got onto the pavers, and the ladies met and hugged. The crew gave her the applause that she and my wife had grown to expect and look forward to receiving.

Delores said to Angel, "Come on; we need you to brighten up our day." Angel, too, was more than gracious, willing to please. She did just that for the boys. She had gotten really good at using the most from the staircase. If she'd had a designer gown, styled hair, and perfect makeup, she could have been a celebrity.

Mama came out, saw what was going on, and gave the best entrance I or the boys had seen her do. Papa even applauded her effort. If I had a dollar for each lady's entrance, I could retire.

Brad and his crew put on the next two courses of block and started excavating for the vault and trenching for the return pipelines. That should take them maybe over an hour, and then the underlining and liner for the stream would be placed. Once they got that completed, they would start rocking the stream from the vault to the pond. Before any rock was laid, they would water-test the stream.

Brad went to his truck to get a dirty water pump with a hose so that as they filled up the stream and it went into the vault, the pump would remove the water to the grass lawn. It was one way to water your lawn—not the cheapest way, but a way. I wanted to see how fast the water traveled from the pond to the vault; this would give them an idea on how to set up the system. His dirty water pump was stronger than the submersible pump used for the fountain and pond.

Before the ladies and Papa left to go shopping, Delores came over to me, hugged me, and said, "I missed you this morning. Just wanted to tell you I love you."

"I love you as well, and thank you for the hug. Are you bringing the girls back here or home?"

"The girls, of course, want to come here and play. Are you okay with them coming here?"

"Of course. Maybe they all can do their homework while the dinner is being prepared. They could do it on the patio at the new table and chairs. Marie bought two more chairs so all the girls can sit at the table. I should have made the patio bigger."

"See you in a little while. Do you need anything?"

"Anything?"

"Not that. Not now, silly boy." She strutted off as she had for her gate entrance.

One of Brad's employees was mixing concrete and filling the cells of the blocks. Brad didn't want the blocks to get jarred loose while digging out the base for the concrete floor. The underlining was in place, and the flow was perfect. They were installing the liner; once that was in place, then another water test would make sure they had the flow and no leaks. "It's going together very nicely, Brad."

"Usually this part is very rewarding. Getting the fountain and stream to work as one successful unit can be trying, but it feels so good when everything flows with precision."

"The homeowners will sure be happy to see this built. They wanted to tie in the backyard to the courtyard. I believe this feature will accomplish what they desire."

As quitting time neared, the crews were picking up their tools and loading the trucks. It was another day in the record books—a job well done.

The girls all arrived, and the little ones played in the tunnel for a short period, clogging with their hard-soled shoes. It sounded pretty good, actually; maybe the sound engineer could amplify that sound through the stereo system. The family was waiting on John to get the party started. The girls were up in the playhouse now, having a good time. It was nice sitting below the playhouse; the insulation Phillip had installed muffled the noise created by the girls.

My dearest darling came out with Marie, drinks in hand—not champagne this time. They both sat at the patio table, leaned back in the rocking chairs with the cushy cushions, and looked very comfortable and relaxed. Mama and Papa were invited by the girls to come sit with them in the playhouse. They loved people to come and visit them—tea party, you know. They served the best make-believe tea and cakes in town. I'd only heard about the parties, never been asked to attend—limited budget, you know. Someday, though not today, I might get invited. Delores had been asked to attend three times along with Marie. It was a girl thing; they start young.

John sneaked into the house and came out with a plateful of hamburgers and hot dogs fit for a king. "Afternoon, ladies and gentlemen. Firing up the grill should take but a few minutes. Please have our waitresses bring you our three-drink minimum during the Burning of the Burger Awards. Any allergic reaction suffered during your dining experience is, well, on you. We thank you for choosing the Burning Burger Bar and Grill this evening. Sit back, relax, and let the churning of your stomach begin."

The ladies applauded and said, "Where is our waitress? We have only one drink. We will need another before we indulge in the grilling. We need to get a little buzzed to blur our eating sensors."

"Do you need any help, John, I asked?"

"Yeah, could you keep those two entertained while I blaze their dinner?"

"Of course. Ladies, let's take a stroll to the water feature atop the staircase. Please follow me."

We arrived. It was not easy; they wanted to practice being glamorous. "Wow, they got quite a bit finished while we were gone. Just a minute, I have to get my camera," said Marie. She returned. *Click, click, click!* The shots were from different angles; she was becoming highly skilled. "How high will the waterfall become?"

"I have it on the plans as the height of the fence," I said. "Not sure how high Brad will build the fountain. I was trying for lots of noise to bring guests and family to the backyard. Brad and I will discuss a game plan tomorrow."

"I like the way the stream bends. Are you going to hide the stream some?"

"The plant materials border the stream, so you have to be on the bridges to get a full view of the stream. Interest brings the guest off the patio to explore."

Marie asked, "So your idea is to get me to go over the bridge, either go to the waterfall or go to the other bridge, cross, and head to the staircase, correct?"

"I want you to be very relaxed and take in the beauty of the floral bouquet you're envisioning. The sound of water moving is hypnotic and mesmerizing, creating interest. Your stereo music will aid in the enticement. I'm still thinking about the best way to get you to want to see the courtyard. The party will make it easy to get guests to head to the courtyard. The smells of the barbecue, music, laughter, you girls doing your grand entrance—numerous things will be happening during the party. It has to be my plantings that stir your interest. I might ask you two to list what really spikes your interest and try to incorporate that into the enticement. I can't incorporate your buff, shirtless, well-tanned gardener."

Marie said, "Well, that was the only thing that would entice me, or I'm going to the waterfall."

Delores asked, "Is the bench big enough for two?"

"You ladies are going to make this much more difficult than it should be. I have an idea on how I will get you to the staircase—maybe not daily but at least once."

John yelled, "Come and get it!"

We heard one of the little ones scream, "Yeah, Daddy, we're hungry!"

Marie and Delores went into the kitchen to get the potato salad, three-bean salad, and coleslaw, and I followed them to help carry whatever they needed me to muscle down to the patio table. They both had heels on, and they wanted to go through the tunnel, as the little girls were down from the playhouse; they wanted to make noise. They told me to go down the staircase so the little ones would join in the fun. I could hear them from the staircase; the little ones joined in the festivities. Even Mama joined in; we guys just watched and applauded their effort.

Dinner was very good. "John, your burgers are really good. Practice is going well for you. How are the hot dogs, girls?"

"Really good, Dad. He burned them just like you do."

"Did you have your cooking class and John attended? asked Delores.

"It's a fine art to burn the skin and keep the inside raw. That takes lots of practice. The food is so good; the salads perfect. If I eat any more, I'll burst."

"Bursting is okay; just don't let one fly," said Marie.

"Those weren't crow burgers, were they, John?"

"I hope not. Your wife did the grocery shopping. She wouldn't allow me to push the shopping cart. She said something about the Indianapolis 500 race. Do you know what she meant?"

"Yes, I'm the one guilty of that scenario."

"You'll have to tell me all about it sometime," said John.

The young ladies were finished with their dinner, and up the staircase they went. They came out on the patio and asked if we could let them know when the dessert would be served. Papa said, "We will bring you some when it is served." The girls all screamed with joy.

Marie, Mama, and Delores started clearing the table, taking the salads back into the kitchen through the tunnel. I saw now how much the tunnel would get used. They were clogging all the way; I could hear them laughing, having the time of their life. John said, "I used to have to clear the table after a party or outdoor barbecue. Not anymore. Thank you for making my life easier."

Spending time with family and friends was very exhilarating but tiring at the same time.

The girls laughed, giggled, and talked the whole way home. Mommy joined in, making the drive go by fast. Mommy said, "Girls, you have to get ready for bed; you have school tomorrow." The girls ran upstairs and got ready for their good-night kiss and prayers to God.

Mommy turned to me and said, "Remember earlier ... 'anything'?"

"Yes, I surely do."

"Kiss the girls, say their prayers, and you'll be rewarded when you come to bed."

I don't think my feet even touched each step. The girls had gotten into their pajamas and brushed their teeth, ready for prayers with Daddy. They said the nicest prayers I had ever heard them say. They blessed everyone and everything. I kissed their foreheads. "Nighty night, girls. Love you both so much. See you tomorrow morning."

CHAPTER 36

The next morning, my crews were digging, trenching, and getting ready for me to lay out the irrigation system. Brad and crew were putting the blocks on the lower pond wall and starting the back wall, stair stepping the blocks to almost a triangle shape. As Brad started the rock, Thomas would add more blocks to achieve the look they wanted. Thomas was busy raising the copper pipe to the elevation Brad had indicated. He also had his crews bring in some rocks of various sizes to start the streambed, where Phillip was busy priming the lumber. Brad had about an hour before Phillip started his assembly. Brad asked, "Phillip, are you going to paint the red lacquer on the underside of the bridge before you assemble?"

"We will have to, since my painter is not Michelangelo. It will be two coats, so you may have an extra two hours to rock where the first bridge will cross the stream."

Brad said to his foreman, "Start at the collection box and rock past the first bridge closest to the staircase. Use some of the stones located by the fence. We have to use them in the course of building the water feature. They belong to the house. Have one of your men scrub the stones before you install them. They were buried at one time." He instructed another laborer to fill one wheelbarrow with two-inch and smaller cobble and one with one-inch and smaller cobble. Now they had a variety of stones to work with, giving the stream a feeling of natural placement. They would also use special sand to infill the stones to hold them in place.

John and Marie joined us, and of course Marie had her camera. *Click, click, click!* Mama and Papa brought out their cups of coffee and sat on the patio to watch the installation of the water feature. "Everyone, good morning," said John. The entire crew wished them a good morning as well.

Phillip said to everyone, "We are starting to assemble the bridge this morning. Even though it looks like it is finished, we need one more day to seal the bridge and another day before you can walk across the first bridge. We will tie a sign across the entry side of the bridge to remind everyone to please wait."

Marie said, "Like my staircase during construction—look but don't touch."

"Exactly," said Phillip. "The bridge would be harder to repair—much more noticeable. You all look so nice and fresh this morning. You must have had a great night's sleep. I would cherish just one of those."

Thomas and the crew were busy installing the stones in the streambed from the zero-collection box nearly to the second bridge crossing. They dammed the upper end and let a hose run water from where they stopped to the collection box to ensure there was no standing water or pools. The flow line was absolutely perfect. Marie was busy taking photos with her camera. The entire family was standing by the stream, watching the water slowly cross over one rock to another. They did add a few larger rocks in the stream to make the water deflect from side to side.

Delores and the girls were there also; the little ones wanted to cross over the bridge that was drying. "No handrailing installed yet," I said. "Stunning piece of woodwork. Very glad my crews did not attempt this masterpiece. It is nearly flawless. It will be difficult for the magazine to cover so much quality in workmanship in just a couple of issues." I said to the girls, "This time next week, you can float Popsicle sticks down the stream. A good project for all of you would be to eat a Popsicle and let it dry, and then mommies can help each of you paint your stick just how you like it. Race your sticks to the end of the stream. Mommies can make one as well. The winner could get her own cupcake made by Mama."

"Mommy, can we have a Popsicle now?" Sarah asked.

"After dinner, Fred can go buy us a couple of boxes, huh, Fred?"

"I'd be honored to be the Popsicle stick provider. I'll even buy the first box of cupcakes for everyone's dessert for tonight."

"We have dessert made, but the cupcakes can be for tomorrow's dinner dessert," said Marie.

"I'll go in a few minutes. What flavor of Popsicle would you all prefer?"

Delores, my beloved, asked, "Do they have crow?"

"Nice one, dear. I think not. Crow is not for dessert—too many feathers."

"See if they have cherry, strawberry, or Fudgsicles. Chocolate is always a favorite among lady types. How about Dreamsicles?"

"I'll be back. Do you like white or chocolate cake for the cupcakes?"

My beloved stated, "He's a slow learner, isn't he? We just told him what ladies like. Tsk, tsk, tsk. That's why men have a hard time living without women to back them up. My mother warned me, 'Girl, there are things you have to know about your new husband.' I didn't listen. I knew it all."

Marie and Mama said, "Amen, amen."

"I'm off to see the grocer. Whatever happened to the ice-cream truck with the ding-ding-ding-ding sound coming down the block? Dig in your pocket for a dime or nickel, stand on the curb, and it would be sure delight as he reached in and pulled out your favorite flavor. Try getting a Popsicle out of your computer. Technology, who needs technology when you want a Popsicle?"

I returned with three boxes of Popsicles, one of each flavor they requested; two-dozen assorted cupcakes with sprinkles; and some fresh fruit: apples, oranges, and bananas. The girls were happy, the ladies not as much as the little ones. You can't please them all.

From my appointment two days prior, I had to leave to start drawing another project. John had a couple of hot dogs already cooked and said, "Please take at least a couple of dogs with you."

My honey came to me, wrapped her arms around me, and said, "Please drive carefully. We'll be home shortly—school tomorrow. Love you."

"I love you too. You drive safe as well. Love you all. See you tomorrow morning."

The next morning, Brad and crew were busy digging out the pond for the concrete floor to be steeled and poured. The drain was installed during the footing excavation; they filled the cells with concrete and finished plumbing the copper piping. Two men were busy adding more stone to the streambed, giving Phillip plenty of space to build the next bridge. They put the second coat of Chinese red on the first bridge and added the handrailing. The bridge was stunning; they had enhanced my drawings to perfection and beyond. A picture postcard would have done it shame. One had to see it to believe it.

The family were all on the patio, drinking their morning coffee and eating a breakfast roll. Once Phillip and crew started the second bridge, Marie quickly got her camera; and at many different angles, she clicked, clicked, and clicked. She told everyone, "Once we get the green light, I want to do an entrance across the bridge barefoot until the party."

Brad said, "I'll be lucky to be fourth or fifth in popularity at this rate. This is getting tougher by the day."

John said, "We have not seen the plants or low-voltage lighting yet."

Brad said, "I hope I beat the irrigation system." That brought the house down. Papa almost choked on his breakfast roll.

My crew was heading up the irrigation system in the courtyard, ready for planting. I talked with the family members. "Who would like to attend our nursery tour?"

All hands were raised. "We all want to see the plants up close and personal, said Marie."

"You will need to wear work boots or tennis shoes—no sandals or open-toed shoes, and no bare feet. You will get mud or at least dirt on your shoes. Even though I love ladies in high heels, the nursery is not a good place to model your firm calves."

"Can Delores come with us, asked Marie?"

"If she chooses to come, of course. Remind her what I just told everyone—no sandals or open-toed shoes, no high heels."

Marie picked up her phone, and Delores screamed with delight. "Of course I'll go. Spending time with all of you always gets a yes from me."

"I'll call the nursery and tell them to get a few golf carts charged up with their sales force ready," I said. "Brad, Phillip, do you gentlemen need my assistance today? We'll be gone for a few hours. Call my cell phone if you need anything or if something comes up unexpectedly."

Within a few minutes, the ladies had on tennis shoes. John wore work boots, and Papa had on his tennis shoes. All were shod properly; we all went into the courtyard so I could tell the crew we would be gone for at least half the workday. Diego and his crew were at another project, getting that one underway. As I finished my instructions, the arched gate slowly opened, and entering was an angel from heaven so graceful and stunning, strutting in, getting all the attention she could muster, and the crew applauded her loudly. She curtsied. "Can't say 'silly boys.' There is a mixed audience. So kind of you all." She blew them a kiss.

I've got to find a trophy to award each lady at the party. I think there is a trophy shop in a neighboring town. I can't forget the little ones either. Their feelings will be hurt.

We returned to the job site. They loved the nurseries; we could have busted my budget easily. The stream was entirely rocked, and they started putting the rocks on the outside walls. The second bridge had one coat of Chinese red but no handrail, which would be installed tomorrow; they had one coat of polyurethane on bridge one. I was now able to get the feeling of what the stream would look like. The real view would be from the bridges; those would be spectacular. Phillip knew what those views were; he had called the magazine and told them the progress. In a couple of days, they would return for more shots.

Brad told us that in two days he would fill the pond and test for leakage. If all went well, he would rock the inside of the pond. Once finished, the wall would receive its rock cap. The back wall would take a little time since this was the crème de la crème of the fountain; they needed to carry out precision mounting of just the right stone and determine how they wanted to bring magic to this area.

The day was ending for the crews. The project was coming together very nicely, and all parties were enjoying seeing the progress. The girls were off to the playhouse, and they believed it was their house; they invited family members to their home for tea and cake. It was such a great thing for the girls. The family got excited when they were asked to come visit. I asked Phillip if his electrician could come over and hook up a doorbell for them; they really wanted a doorbell. He said he would ask him.

While eating another one of John's masterpiece barbecues, everyone was gathering around the patio table, fixing their dinner plates. I asked the girls if they would like to do me a huge favor. They all said they would love to. "I have another vision. I'm not an artist by any means. Would you girls like to paint me a ceiling like the one in your playhouse?"

"Yeah, can we, Daddy, asked Sarah?"

"Maybe mommies can help you as well."

"Can you help us, Mommy, Marie, and Mama, asked Leslei?"

Delores asked, "Just where is this playhouse vision taking place?"

"Well, I see our daughters loving to play in the playhouse here. Girls, would you like to invite Leslie and Kim to your playhouse?"

"Daddy, we don't have a playhouse like Leslie and Kim's, said Sarah."

"I know. Would you like one?"

"Yeah, can we have one, Daddy, asked Rebecca?"

"Leslie and Kim, if Sarah and Rebecca have a playhouse, would you two come and visit?"

"Mommy, could we go and visit their playhouse, asked Leslie?"

Marie said, "I'd be delighted to take you to their playhouse."

"Then it's settled. I have to draw the plans; get Phillip, the gate builder, and the electrician all together and make everyone's dreams come true."

Delores asked, "I'm excited for the girls, but can we make this a reality?"

"I have a feeling that it's all coming with time. We must be patient, but I do need the ceiling painted so we keep our dream alive. I can set everything up at the house—put the ceiling together and set up chairs for everyone to sit at while creating a masterpiece. When can I have my artists over to paint?"

Marie glanced at Mama and said, "We could come over on Saturday if you would be ready."

"Honey, would Saturday work for you?"

"I'm so nervous. They are coming to my home? Oh my, I don't have anywhere for a grand entrance. It's pretty blasé; our ambiance has not arrived. Would you two mind if the house is not very exciting?"

"Of course not. Ours used to be blasé as well. It will give us a challenge to make your home come alive."

Marie asked, "Can I bring my camera?"

"I'd be honored to have a photo album like what you're making."

"Can we bring some refreshments?" asked Mama.

"Sure, I'll have coffee, tea, sodas, water—whatever you ladies and girls would like to drink. I'm so nervous right now. Thrilled but nervous. A hostess, wow. Honey, you keep putting me in situations that I have never been before. I don't want to let you down."

"That will never happen. I love to see you perform; it's exhilarating and so inspiring to me. Do I need to purchase brushes for you, ladies?"

"No, we need to go to a craft store and buy some supplies," said Marie.

"You opened up a door we have needed to enter for some time," said Delores.

"You know the girls will want this yesterday. That will just inspire me to get cracking," said Marie.

All the girls were giving one another hugs, and the ladies were doing the same. The camaraderie was oozing with love for one another.

"John's barbecue brings out the best in all of us. His burgers aren't beef jerky any longer, quite tasty and juicy now, said Marie."

The girls talked to Mom about their new house all the way home. They were so excited; even Marie's daughters were hugging and jumping up and down. The girls asked if they could have a sleep over, mommy you and daddy can pick us up and we all could go to breakfast, said Leslie What a joy it was to see. "Are you sure you want to do this? We need a place to entertain friends and family too," said Delores.

"I don't want to lose what is now our normal behavior. I have the lady of my dreams—warm, loving, caring, full of life. There is nothing worth more to me than you and the girls the way you are."

"You didn't like me the way I was?" asked Delores?

"Dear, you were fantastic before. You have just blossomed into such a loving and warm person, smiling and laughing. Don't you feel better about yourself now versus before?"

"I have a beautiful new friend, a warm and caring husband, and two beautiful, fun-loving daughters. I can't ask for more than that right now. You did a nice dodge of my question, dearest. I love me then and now. I'm just happier now. You have given me something to do with myself, not being tied to the house all day and night. I love being around Marie and her family. Seeing the girls the way they are brings me great joy. You, too, are more loving and caring, not so stressed as usual, much easier to deal with than before."

"See? We both are new and improved adult models."

Bright and early the next morning, I was going into the backyard to get a grasp on just what my crew could be doing back here, away from all the action— not much. I'd send Juan and crew to his new job today. Diego and crew were doing a wonderful job on his new project. The new hires were working out better than expected; very little training was required for any of them. I'd talk with Juan when he got here about rounding up a couple of newer hires.

Brad pulled in with Phillip right behind him. All was good. Brad and Thomas were discussing what needed to get finished today; he had another project he was going to start as soon as he completed this fountain. They set up the hose to run water from the fountain to the collection box, now using the pump to recycle the water back to the pond; it would run out onto the lawn today. This was just a test to make sure the stream was working properly.

Phillip had the handrails finished and primed, and one coat of Chinese red color had been applied. Those would be installed on the second bridge, and then the entire top surface of the bridge would get the second coat of Chinese red color; maybe by noon they could apply a coat of polyurethane. If all went as planned, they might get the second coat of polyurethane applied. If that occurred, then the homeowners would get the green light by tomorrow afternoon.

I told Phillip that I was designing another playhouse for my kids; with an L-shaped patio cover, the playhouse would be on half of the longer leg, and a barbecue under the shorter leg. I told him the plans should be ready by Monday if he would like to give me a price. "Is the playhouse the same size as the one they just finished?"

"The same. My girls love the playhouse, staircase, porch, patio, french doors—everything the same."

"Same design for the patio cover?"

"I like the valley look on the roof, access doors from the playhouse, and the end of the L for storage. I have the girls and moms all geared up on painting the ceiling boards."

"Yes, get me a set of plans, and I'll give you a good number."

Brad asked if there would be a water feature. "I'm certain that there will be in due time. I need to win the lotto to fulfill all the family's dreams."

The pond was rocked on the front fascia; the floor was excavated, steeled and poured, finished, and setting up. They would plaster the inside with white cement and get ready to rock once the back wall was rocked. The bridges were all painted and had one polyurethane coat, waiting for some dry time; then the second coat would follow to finish. They both looked stunning and should photograph very well. Marie came out with her camera and had Mama and Papa pose for her with the bridges in the background. Juan took his crew to the new project to get it going; both of the jobs were much simpler than this one.

It was Friday. Brad and Phillip were at the job site early. Phillip was putting the final coat of polyurethane on the second bridge. The green light was given for bridge number one. Marie and Mama were there at the ribbon-cutting ceremony. Both kicked off their shoes, stepped onto the bridge, and looked upstream to the fountain. Marie got her camera poised. *Click, click!* She told Mama to pose with one hand on the handrailing, looking toward the staircase. *Click, click!* "Brad, the stream is beautiful. With water flowing, this is going to be hard to beat daily. Phillip, I love the bridges. They are so nice. My girls will have a tough choice about where to play, and from the landscape design, it will only enhance what you have done. I'm so thrilled. John, you have to see the stream from the bridge. Take off your shoes and come on up on the bridge."

John said, "This is unbelievable. You got some photos, correct?"

"Yes."

"Send me one so I can show the office," said Marie. "They won't believe what I see without photos. Can you imagine what this will look like with the stream filled with water, the waterfall spilling water, the sound system playing soft music, maybe a hummingbird or a butterfly, and flowers everywhere? Why would we ever want to leave our home?"

"So you three now are starting to see the vision?" I asked.

"This is unbelievable," said John. "I don't know how the guests will respond, but we will have a hard time moving to both areas. The courtyard will draw us for fun activities and here for peace and tranquility, thinking, settling down, reflecting on the day, reading, and enjoying nature."

"When are the plants due to arrive?" asked Marie.

"Some on Monday, some on Tuesday, and some on Friday. Once the stream and waterfall are finished and operating, we will come to this side of the yard and irrigate, landscape, and do the low-voltage lighting. Once all is completed, then we will spread the mulch for the final touch. I also have to put in the natural pathway connecting the bridges and the seating area to give you the utmost from your landscape."

"I can't wait for the girls to experience this area. You said you are going to put a couple of lights in the tree to shine down so we could read a book from dusk to dawn."

"Well, you could do that, or we can set a timer to shut off lights at a given hour. And since there are four transformers controlling different areas, you can get really creative with your lighting scheme. You may just want to take a stroll through the garden and have the pathway lights illuminate your walkway; have your arms around each other, a drink in one hand; look at the stars and moon; come from your patio across the bridge; head to the waterfall, which will also be lit softly; head to the second bridge; walk down your staircase into the courtyard; visit the girls; walk to the arched gateway, out to the front of the house, and to the city sidewalk to admire what your neighbors will see each and every night; come back through the arched gateway to see the circular planter; sit on the planter and watch the girls on their patio, eating their cupcakes and ice cream; head into the tunnel; embrace with a couple of nice, loving kisses and lots of I-love-yous; head back into the kitchen area and start lap number two. It will be just like falling in love with each other every night. It will never get tiring. Remember: your sound system will be playing your favorite songs softly, romantically, easing the day's tensions. What more could you ask?"

Marie said, "Can we do that tonight?"

"Yes, you can practice tonight. And once the landscape and lighting are in, you may not make it to the tunnel before you embrace. Shoot, you may barely make it over the first bridge."

John just laughed. Marie would still want to make at least one lap to get the complete package. I couldn't have her wearing hard-soled shoes, or she would never stop clogging in the tunnel.

Early the next day, the second bridge got the green light, and the fountain and pond both passed the water test, so the final rocking was taking place. Thomas and Brad were busy doing their magic; the back wall was a masterpiece. The water would fall in numerous directions, leaving the copper tubing, leaving one stone, and falling onto another stone, changing course from the top to the pond itself. It would be amazing to watch. The pond had various sizes of stones—even a hideout for the fish. Water plant pockets were formed and would house five different species; four were flowering, and one was a reed plant, so there would be vertical beauty and horizontal beauty. The rock cap was stunning; the water would move through the cap and fall into the stream, and the backlights on the fountain and pond would be the highlight.

In the morning, Brad would fill the pond and let the stream and pond work together for the final encore performance. He told everyone that he would return at dusk to adjust the lighting for the ultimate effect. Phillip told everyone that the magazine would be out at dusk to shoot the stream, waterfall, and bridges for the cover issue. They would return once the landscape was completed and shoot the entire property. Marie, John, Mama, Papa, Delores, all the girls, and I were so excited to see the masterpiece completed; this would be a once-in-a-lifetime experience for all concerned. Marie said, "This is like Christmas Eve as a child, the anticipation. My insides are a jumbled mess right now."

She and Delores took off their shoes, holding them, and walked across the bridge, stopping to view both directions, arms around each other. They put their shoes back on to experience going from one bridge to the pond and back to the other bridge, looking the entire time at the stream and then the staircase. Then the magic happened, with each one taking her time descending the staircase—poised, glamorous, everything just so beautiful—to the courtyard. We were all on the landing, watching them perform. There was applause and cheering; the ladies responded to our appreciation. Brad said, "If they do that like that for the party guests, there had better be a professional photographer capturing every step. My wife will want to join them. I'll bet every woman invited will want a turn."

"We will see everyone tomorrow morning and at dusk. Have a great evening said Brad."

John was busy at his barbecue, and the girls were on the patio, asking, "Daddy, how much longer? We're getting hungry smelling your great barbecue, asked Sarah."

"Would you girls like to help Mommy and Grandma bring the salads and beans to the table for Daddy?"

"Can we use the tunnel?"

"Of course you can."

The girls ran to the tunnel door, and as they opened it, there were Mama, Marie, and Delores, holding bowls of food. They handed the girls their bowls so they could deliver them to the patio table. They loved to help, but they had on hard-soled shoes, so they ran back to the tunnel to do some clogging. It sounded like thunder rumbling. They also found out that, at a certain pitch, the tunnel echoed their voices; that became even more fun for them. The ladies had them take the plates, cups, plasticware, and chips to the table while they carried the beverages.

The food was nearly ready—barbecue chicken, asparagus, squash, hot dogs, and a few hamburgers. John was becoming quite gifted as the family cook. Marie was in seventh heaven; she had not had to cook dinner since the barbecue was installed and ready to burn.

The girls were able to make their plates and take them to the playhouse, where they had already set up their table. Mama brought them their beverages, napkins, plasticware, hugs, and kisses. They invited Mama and Papa to join them, and they were excited to comply. They waited for Mama and Papa, bowed their heads, and said grace. Mama and Papa told us later that they both had tears in their eyes; it was so beautiful to witness.

The dinner was fantastic. My dearest darling told John and Marie, "Tomorrow night everyone has to come to our house for dinner and dessert. We're starting to feel embarrassed. Taking advantage of your hospitality needs to be shared. Would that be okay with everyone?"

Marie got up and hugged my wife. "Of course, it is all right. We accept your invitation. Mama and Papa asked about your home a couple of days ago. They'll be excited."

John said to me, "Would you like a lesson in barbecuing? You have to burn the meat just right or the ladies feel slighted."

My dearest darling replied to John, "He has been burning our meals for years. He needs to learn how not to burn and cook the meat through and not make it jerky."

"Remember, dear, I'm a landscaper, not a chef. I can burn with the best of them."

The next morning, Brad and his crew were busy putting the final touches on the pond and fountain. They then started to fill the feature with water.

Phillip showed up unexpectedly with a surprise present for Marie and John. His master woodworker had made the bench and table for the fountain area—Chinese red to match the bridges. The armrests were modeled after the staircase entry, and the posts had been turned to match the bridges. John and Marie were nearly in tears with joy. He told them the magazine would be at their home in about an hour, and they wanted to see the bridges, bench, table, waterfall, and stream feature in operation. This was his showtime and future for his business. Brad said he should be ready and hoped there were no glitches. Thomas assured him that the checking and double-checking had proved that the system was ready.

CHAPTER 37

Everyone was now out of the house, standing, looking at the water feature. The pond was filled up not quite to the spillway; it would take maybe a few more minutes. Marie hurried in and called Delores to ask her to dress nicely and come over. The photographer from the magazine was due in about an hour. Juan and his crew showed up, and Marie took me aside. "I want Angel to participate in the photo shoot. She and I are about the same size. I have some nice clothes for her to put on. Would you mind?"

"Angel, could you come here for a minute?" Angel joined us. "Marie, go ahead and ask her."

"Angel, I would like you to join us today for the photo shoot of our landscape construction. Would you do me the honor?"

Angel looked at me and asked if that would be all right with me. I said to her, "I would be honored to have you join them."

Marie said, "Are you a size six?"

"I am a size six. Why do you ask?"

"Come with me. Mama and I will turn you from a construction worker into Cinderella."

"Are you kidding me? You would do that?"

"Trust us, dear. We can make Cinderella blush." Off they all went into the house; the ladies were on a mission to get all decked out.

Juan and a part of his crew started laying out the irrigation system. I had Juan and crew remove the soil for the pathway and steel edging to be installed. We couldn't have the bench and table sitting on the weedy soil. I took off to get the stabilized decomposed granite for the pathway. Juan was laying out the pathway for the crew to follow. I called Diego to come to the house to help Juan for about an hour. Juan marked for the sleeves under the pathway, and Vincent started to trench for them to be installed.

The pond was now spilling over into the stream. Thomas was picking up leaf litter that had fallen into the stream overnight. The water was now moving as designed to the first bridge. Brad was keeping track of how many gallons the pond, stream, and waterfall would require so his maintenance division would know how to keep it pristine. Brad told John that he would give his data to him in a formal brochure. The water was now to the second bridge, heading to the collection box. Phillip was enjoying a nice cup of coffee on the patio with Papa and John.

I took a load of material with me and had the rest of the stabilized decomposed granite loaded and following me to the job site; the masonry yard was extremely cooperative and happy to help. I told the owner that the magazine was coming to shoot the water feature, bridges, and bench, and that their material would be part of the shoot. I said I would make sure the magazine would list them as the supplier. That got the truck loaded and racing me back to the job site.

As we pulled in, Diego and crew had just arrived—perfect timing. "Get the one-inch plywood sheet and lay it across the stream to run wheelbarrows full of decomposed granite to the pathway. Juan and crew will spread and form the pathway. Be very careful not to dump the materials into the stream. Your crew just needs to haul, and Juan's crew will dump and spread. Diego, you need to help Juan make sure this gets done as quickly as possible. Juan, start at the water fountain so Phillip and Raymond can place the bench. Please compact the decomposed granite with the vibratory plate."

My dearest darling was looking fabulous. "Wow, really fabulous." She asked me where Marie and Mama were. I said to her, "They went into the house to compete with how you look. Beautiful, simply beautiful."

"Thank you. Settle down. You're working, remember?"

I didn't tell her what they were up to with Angel. I wanted it to be a surprise.

Delores called out for Marie, who told her, "We're upstairs. Come on up and join us."

As Delores reached the top of the staircase, Marie told her to close her eyes, which she did. Marie had her hand and led her into Marie's bedroom. Once inside, she had her open her eyes. Delores almost fainted; there stood Angel in one of Marie's stunning outfits. "Well, what do you think of our Angel? Angel, turn around slowly with grace and glamour."

"That outfit fits her like a tailored glove. I need to go home and find something that close to how that fits her. You're gorgeous. You can't let the crew see her like this. They won't get anything done today."

Mama walked into the room.

"Oh my, Mama, between you and Angel, I look like a ragamuffin. Beautiful outfit."

"Marie, what will you wear?"

"It's hanging on the closet door."

"Oh my, I thought I might be overdressed; now I feel underdressed."

Marie asked Delores, "What's your size?"

"I hate to say this, but maybe a tight six or seven."

"Let me see if I can help you out. Come into my closet, and we can have you try on a couple of things. How about this outfit?"

"Oh, Marie, are you sure?"

"You have to try it on and look in the full-length mirror, and you tell me what you think. Mama, can you help Angel put on a little makeup? Not much, she's got a natural look that the photographer will surely shoot."

Delores quickly removed what she was wearing and slipped into Marie's outfit. "Talk about fitting like a tailored glove. Wow ... really wow." Delores stood in front of the mirror, and Marie told her to turn around slowly.

"Honey, if that outfit was not made for you, I don't know who else it was made for," said Mama.

Delores said to Marie, "You certain you don't mind me wearing this outfit?"

Marie walked over to her and slowly put her arms around Delores. "You have become my best friend. You look stunning in the outfit. Of course I don't mind. You'll be on the cover of a national magazine with all of us. Thousands and thousands of people will see you in the most alluring, sensual outfit. They will buy it just for the cover."

The doorbell rang, and Marie, Mama, Angel, and Delores all went down the spiral staircase and met the magazine crew. As they opened the door, the crew stood there in awe. "Ladies, good morning. We're from the magazine, here to shoot the progress of your landscape remodeling." This was said very slowly, looking for the right words. I was certain they did not expect to see the ladies as they were dressed. The producer, Susanne, two cameramen, one soundman, three lighting men, we better call the caterer, said Marie.

"If you would like to follow us to the backyard, the water feature is running by now," said Marie.

"Yes, ma'am, we will follow you. May I say one thing? You all look fabulous. I don't want you to think I'm out of order. I mean it. I have never witnessed this. I'm usually met with ladies in curlers screaming at the kids to get ready for school, telling them to go this or that way. Thank you all. What a delight for me and my staff."

Once everyone was outside, the magic started to happen. The magazine crew was awestruck. The fountain was in all its glory, John had put a smooth jazz CD on the stereo to fit the perfect atmosphere, and Phillip and Raymond had placed the bench on the decomposed granite pathway, which was getting the final touch-up. The crew had removed the plywood from on top of the stream and stood in complete awe themselves, looking at the completed feature. Diego said to me, "Wow, amazing. So glad we got to help."

Juan and his crew were going to the other job so as not to bother the photographer and his staff. They saw Angel, and all of them stopped in their tracks. "Angel, is that really you?"

"Silly boys. Of course, it's me. Do you like the outfit?"

After a long pause, Juan said, "If I answered that honestly, my wife would kill me. I love how you look."

I saw my dearest darling and asked, "Is it too early for anything?"

Marie heard me and said, "Dream on, young man. Dream on."

"Silly boys, one-track minds," the ladies said in unison.

Marie's outfit was breathtaking, form-fitted—absolutely stunning. You would think *Vogue* magazine was here shooting, not a home remodeling magazine.

The stream and waterfall were spectacular. The sound of the water splashing against the rocks and falling into the stream was totally amazing. Standing on the bridges, the photographer had each lady stand and pose just the way he wanted her. I had to leave; this was killing me. I returned in about an hour and checked on the other two jobs. The ladies, still in the fabulous outfits, were talking about going to lunch at a fancy restaurant—I'm not sure which one, but definitely not a fast-food place.

"So how did the photo shoot turn out, ladies?" I asked.

"We all want to become models. Each shot was a new experience. 'Turn your head with a slight tilt, put your hand on the handrail, lightly bend you knee … just a little more. Perfect. Nice smile. Make love to the camera. The camera loves you. You have to love the camera.' Little things just like that."

"Did you show them your grand entrance and the arched gate entrance?"

"Yes, more than once. They went and got the movie camera to film from the top of the staircase to the pavers. Each of us did it at least three or four times. I did the gate entrance at least five times, stopping in a certain pose. A teasing smile is what they were looking for me to master. Here, I'll show you." Delores went out of the gate and reentered.

"I'll tell you right now, if we were alone, I could not control myself." I said. "Wow, that was fabulous, my dearest darling. Come here; I'll give you a hug." I told her tonight was going to be a great night. I said to the ladies, "You all look fantastic. There could not be a bad photo in all the shots taken. You're all model quality."

"We're going to the fancy Italian restaurant—you know, the one we go by and say, 'When we become millionaires, we will dine there every night.'"

"I know that place all too well."

"That's where we are going to lunch. Would you like anything?"

"Not that—not now, silly girl."

The ladies all laughed. My dearest darling sashayed with that form-fitting outfit, looking back over her shoulder. "Dream on, my love. Dream on."

Phillip called me on my cell phone and told me the photo shoot had gone very well. His friend said they would put the ladies on the cover in the next three issues, stating they would start stating the project was ongoing to tease the readers to keep purchasing issues. "They love the project. So many things that provide photo ops. He wants to return in two weeks. Will that give you enough time to finish, or do you need another week?"

"Make it three, and if I'm ready earlier, I will call and let them know. Thank you, Phillip. Everything you have done on this project is first cabin in quality."

CHAPTER 38

With the water feature being constructed, I took the opportunity to irrigate the courtyard to prepare for the planting. Juan and his crew started hand-trenching the raised planter behind the patio cover and playhouse. We had just backfilled the planter, so the soil was easy to dig, and it went rather quickly. Once that planter was trenched, the crew trenched the circular planter and the raised planters against the house. For those we had to use the wheelbarrows to place the trenched soil. The trenching was completed by lunchtime. Juan and I then started to layout the sprinkler heads.

Marie came to the courtyard with her camera and Mama. They wanted to see just what we were up to. I had made a swing joint assembly to show them how they help prevent breakage of the lateral line piping, keeping the repairs down to a minimum.

Angel showed the ladies how she Teflon taped all of the threaded parts so Juan could build the assemblies.

Juan showed the ladies that if the gardeners kick the riser above ground or the hit the turf head, the line pipe should never be damaged. He also showed them the difference between the PVC fitting and the Marlex fitting. The Marlex fitting is designed to break to protect the other fittings from damage. He built them an assembly on the line fitting for them to show their husbands and display at their party.

Marie asked how long he had been doing irrigation. He said it had been just about five years now, and he was still learning the trade. I couldn't wait to see all the plants installed; this place would sure be beautiful.

Just as they turned to return to the house, Delores sashayed through the arched gateway. Marie ran to her and gave her a huge hug. "How's my best friend doing this fine morning," asked Marie?

"I really can't complain; I haven't felt like this since I was in high school," said Delores.

Angel got up and went over and hugged Delores. "That looks like so much fun. I love the way you enter the courtyard. I don't want to copy your moves, but you must teach me how to get the guys to respond to your every move."

Delores said, "I'd love to teach you; a lot has to do with your desire to get attention. You just play along with their response. You know when guys are paying attention to you, right? I think so. Some turn their head if they think you caught them looking at you. Those are the ones who will applaud."

Angel said, "Talk to you later. Have a great day with Marie."

Marie and Delores continued their greetings.

"Now where were we?" asked Marie. "Oh yes, I remember. We were talking about our new way of life."

"I know what you mean. The men are in good moods, the girls—never seen them this happy. I figured this would all wear off and back to normal we would all go. I am happy that this may become our normal."

"Wouldn't that be great?" said Marie.

"If this is our normal, I'm all in, please don't change a thing. So where are we headed to this morning?"

"Breakfast. Then, of course, shopping; then lunch, more shopping, and then get the girls."

Our nursery tour lasted a good part of one day while we tagged plant materials. This was not going to a big box store and being enticed to purchase pretty flowering plants; we had a specific list of plant species we wanted to complete our landscape plans.

We were taken first to the trees—fruitless olives, Swan Hills. The salesman asked, "Standard or multis? We have both. The multi has to be a three hundred-sixty-degree tree—circular planter. The two standards should also be three hundred-sixty-degree trees as well."

We all agreed upon three of the nicest trees that we saw. It was not easy getting different personalities to come to common ground and select focal points. You can hide some deficiencies or a slight hole here or there; a tree well balanced in all angles is very tough to find. We also had a few accent shrubs which would be used to guide the eyes where we wanted them to venture to. I try not to hide an eyesore but to enhance something good about its being. Maybe a neighbor puts something up in clear view of your backyard and it's not very attractive— something you wish they would remove; you don't want that hideous item taking away from your selected beauty. I always recommend people try to enhance the item, not hide it. You may think you're hiding the item, but most of the time your guest or family member sneaks a peek at what is behind your shrub.

Regarding the windows of your home, if you can see your neighbors' windows, they can see yours as well. I have had customers want something directly in front of their windows to block the view from their neighbor. I ask the customer, "On any given day, how many times do you see your neighbor looking out their window into your window? How many times have you waved and said hello to your neighbor looking at you in your window?" Most of the time they will say it has never happened or maybe once they saw them passing by their window. If you block your window with a large shrub, you block the light, and you now can't open the window for fresh air, as the shrub blocks the airflow into your home.

I John and Marie, of a customer who always had trouble getting her two teen boys to go upstairs and do their homework. All of a sudden, she never had to tell them to go do their homework. They came home from school and ran upstairs to do their homework. Mom got suspicious of their eager attitudes. One afternoon just before the boys came home, she went upstairs to their bedrooms. The neighbor next door had just finishing building a very nice custom home. The boys' bedroom looked directly into the neighbor's master bathroom shower. The homeowner had the contractor put in mirrors set at an angle, as his girlfriend loved mirrors. The boys were not doing their homework; they were watching the girlfriend take an afternoon shower. When the boys came home, she had them sit at the kitchen table and do their homework there. They were not pleased, and they, asked their mom, "Why are you being so mean to us?" Her response was "I know what you two have been up to each day. It stops today."

That was the only time I have heard of people actually looking into a neighbor's window from theirs. Now, I know there are Peeping Toms or passersby, and you may have a fear of being seen maybe not fully clothed or in silhouette, but there are ways to block the view of your windows without putting large shrubs right next to them.

The rest of the nursery tour was enjoyable. We had to visit two other nurseries to fulfill the plant order. After three nurseries, the girls and papa were getting hungry and we found a nice quiet restaurant and had a delightful, peaceful lunch. The plants were scheduled to arrive in three days for half of the landscape, and three days after the first order, the balance would arrive.

Phillip told the ladies to get prepared to be pampered by the photographer and his staff. I just hoped they would take shots of what we had all completed, not just the female beauties that resided here. It would be difficult under normal circumstances, but with the addition of model-quality ladies, it could be very difficult to stay focused.

I reviewed what the crew had completed in the courtyard irrigation system. The piping was hooked up to the remote-control valve, all the heads were on, most of the trenches were backfilled, and the crew had just finished their lunch. Juan was flagging the front yard for the new irrigation system. I double-checked the layout and looked at the plans to verify that I had not made a mistake. It just appeared odd. I asked for a tape measure from Juan and measured from the house to the head in question. Therein lay the mistake. My plan showed eight feet from the house, and Juan was at six feet. From head to head, the number was correct. *What made the two-foot error?* I measured from the sidewalk to the head. Twelve feet—per plan. I then triangulated the head to see just what was going on. I measured from the house wall to the sidewalk. My plan showed eighteen feet, and the actual field measurement was eighteen feet. So I put a flag at the eight-foot mark and checked the alignment. The heads formed an arch from the entry sidewalk to the city sidewalk. I had Angel get about twenty feet of low-voltage wire from the truck. We wrapped three wraps on a piece of rebar and found my center point of the radius off the plans. We put a rebar stake on that point, put a few wraps of wire around the rebar stake, started at the entry sidewalk and followed it on an arch to the city sidewalk. As we scratched the ground, we found that three of the heads were slightly off the arch.

Angel said, "Wow, that was easy; what made you think something was not correct?"

"I would like to say that I'm a genius, but that would not be accurate," I said. "Since I drew the plans, there is a feeling I get when something is off just a little."

"I'll always remember how you did that; I'll always remember how nicely you made the arch. You made it look easier than it really is. You kept even tension on the wire as you made the arch. If the wire had gone slack, the arch would be off."

"I'll go home and pick up the trencher. Makes digging easier and we can get this area finished by tomorrow."

I headed home, put the trencher on the trailer, and went into the house to say good afternoon to my dearest darling.

"Ah, huh, caught you taking a quick nap," I said.

"You weren't due home for at least two more hours. While you are lying down …"

"No way, not now, I have to get ready to pick up the girls and head over to Marie's."

I returned to the job site, and the trencher was unloaded and started digging the trenches. As an area was trenched, Juan and Miguel started putting in the lateral line and line fittings for the sprinkler heads. Juan and Angel had made the assemblies before the courtyard was completed.

They counted the heads in the front yard, made the assemblies, and prepared to install them to the line fitting. As they were laying out the head locations, Juan dropped the right size of line fitting at the exact location. As Miguel and Angel laid out the piping, it became a cut-and-glue situation. Very quickly the system was ready for operation. There was a drying period for the PVC cement, we tried to allow at least one hour from application to water running through the system. If it were under pressure, we would have allowed a longer drying period. Main lines are allowed to dry overnight. If we mixed pipe schedules, such as schedule forty and schedule eighty, we followed the manufacturer's recommendation. Schedule eighty attached to schedule eighty, no matter what size, had to set undisturbed overnight. We lost considerable time on a project when we failed to follow the manufacturer's recommendation. The fittings blew apart, and we had to reglue it or cut the fitting out and replace it with a new fitting.

Schedule forty is the normal pressure line pipe. Class two hundred is the normal nonpressure line pipe. All fittings are schedule forty as normal.

Juan showed Miguel and Angel the proper way to apply cement to the pipe and fittings. If the pipe size is one and a quarter inches or larger, we first applied primer to the pipe and fitting. The primer actually cuts through the glaze of the fitting and pipe to allow the glue to weld the plastics together. Without the primer, the glue cannot cut the glaze, and the fitting joint can and will fail.

Again, our crew was taught to follow the manufacturer's recommendation. Such recommendations are provided in many languages, so if you can't read or understand English, you can tell your supervisor to provide you the language that you speak or read. The manufacturers know the field crews are changing to employees with little or no English background or schooling.

Marie and her girls came and watched the irrigation system being installed. Marie took photos for her album. Her photo album should have been published; it had more pictorial data than most textbooks. I told her to talk to the magazine and see if they could not help her get her album published and distributed.

Most of my customers worked during most of the construction; they had no idea just how things were built or the effort it takes from the crews to make it all come together. I've had projects where I have seen no one during an entire day although they were all home. If it looks like work, they get tired just watching.

By tomorrow afternoon the front yard and courtyard would be ready for the plants. The nursery called me and set up a delivery time for two days from today for half of the order. I told Juan that if we were laying out the irrigation system by the water feature, we would stop and plant the courtyard and front yard then return to the irrigation system at the water feature. If we found ourselves in need of help, I would bring Diego and his crew to this job to help.

Juan was happy to hear that; there were so many plants to install that they would have no time to work on the irrigation system. They had three days between deliveries; that would leave them no time to irrigate the rear yard. We still had the low-voltage lighting to install also.

I heard my little girls yell, "Daddy!" There is no greater sound than to hear your children call you. I gave them both big hugs. Mommy was only a few feet behind them; she got a hug as well.

They were met on the front porch by Marie, Leslie and Kim. There was so much hugging going on; what a great moment.

The crew was heading up the irrigation and nearly ready for the first valve to be tested. We had center loaded the pipe so it wouldn't leave the trench. The first valve was running, with great coverage and very little water waste. "Great job everyone." Valve two was nearly ready to be fired—a few more feet to center load. The crew was busy backfilling the first valve. Juan told the crew that valve two was going to be run, so we had to move back or get wet. Valve two began running, again with very nice coverage and again with no wasted water. We shut it off and started backfilling.

As we entered the backyard, we saw the ladies, camera in hand and shooting photos from the first bridge. Phillip had given them the green light as long as they were without shoes.

Marie said, "The view from the bridge is unbelievable; how did you know it would look like this?

My dearest darling said, "We have been together for years; when do I get this in my home?"

"Ladies, ladies, ladies, I just try to please my customers."

"Brad made it more appealing, knowing that to get you to even want to see the waterfall, he had to create a desire. Tough competition between the courtyard and the backyard. I'm starting to draw our backyard, so soon dear, to answer your question as to when."

I told Juan that he and his crew should go to the other project tomorrow. "You can help Diego get a jump start on his project," I said.

Marie asked, "When are the plants going to arrive?"

"In two days, we will get the greenery. The courtyard and front yard will be planted first; the second delivery will be for the backyard. One more week and your yard will come alive."

"When are the gowns going to be ready for pickup?" asked Delores.

"I called yesterday. They want us to come in; the final fitting is tomorrow morning. If there are not alterations required, we will have our gowns for the party, said Delores."

"Do we get a peek before the party of you in your gowns?" I asked the ladies.

"If you and John are extremely good boys, maybe," said Marie. "We still have to shop to accessorize the gowns: diamond necklace, earrings and bracelets, maybe a new wedding ring or two. We want to sparkle; shimmering light bouncing off the diamonds will top off the gown."

"I'm surprised you aren't buying a crown full of diamonds as well."

"We didn't think of a crown. Good idea—we will add that to the list, don't you think, Delores?"

"I can't see being partially bankrupt; might as well go all the way screaming to the poorhouse."

"Juan, can you hook up the valves for the front yard and the courtyard and run them automatically for the next couple of days? Repeat cycles about an hour apart to get the water to percolate deeper into the soil."

CHAPTER 39

I was flagging the plant locations in the backyard. The courtyard was flagged. *Don't want to get too far ahead of the crew. The girls are going to the gown shop, lunch, accessory shopping—all the good stuff.*

The fountain sounds really soothing, the water is passing through the rock cap as planned—looks really nice. Water is splashing into the stream from five different angles, and different amounts of water making various noises—very nice touch. The wall oozes water for three inlets, and those also are various amounts of water, making unique sound added to the fountain's stream noise—very soothing. The stream is moving at a subtle speed, no whitewater or hard splashing against rocks—lazy river. I hope the ladies return and just sit by the stream and waterfall and just listen to the music the falls and stream are making. Wait a minute; you'd better stay focused on setting up the landscape or the crew will drown you in the water feature.

The ladies finally arrived from their shopping spree.

"How did the fitting turn out?" I asked.

"We both had a smidgen to alter."

I didn't want to ask which way. Men not thinking straight would fall right into that little trap.

"I want you three to stand back and look at the fountain and stream. Just listen. Be as quiet as a church mouse."

They all three moved closer to the stream and fountain and didn't say a word, just listened to the sound of moving water.

Marie turned around after looking at the other two ladies and asked, "What are we listening for?"

"Do you like the way the water sounds falling from the fountain and into the stream from the fountain?" I asked.

'Oh, I thought there was a problem with how it sounds; now I know what to listen for," said Marie.

Marie turned back around and asked, "Will we hear that sound when music is being played by the stereo?"

"The only way to find out is turn on your stereo and pick your favorite CD."

Marie ran into the house, and we soon had soft, soothing music.

"No, it's too subtle; you can still hear some in the background said Delores."

"Come outside and sit on the bench with your favorite beverage and listen to the water moving from the waterfall to the stream. I find it soothing and relaxing."

"May not feel the same if it made me need to use the restroom," said Delores.

Now the ladies were moving their hips to the rhythm of the falling water and the music being played.

"Much better than trying on gowns," said Mama.

Delores said, "I can see myself sitting on the bench, Bloody Mary, mellow music, soft and low, gazing at the falling water, the buff gardener pulling weeds without his shirt … Yeah, I'm good with how it relaxes me. Thank you, dear, you can leave us alone now."

Mama and Marie asked, "Does he have any helpers with him?"

"Let me reset my visual dial. Yep, he has two helpers, one a little older and one the same age. Ladies, we are in business."

"Ladies," I said, "I was thinking you would be out here kicking back, relaxing."

"We are, but we need a visual stimulus. You taught me how to visualize—so glad you did."

Delores said, "How come you never taught me how to visualize like you did for Marie?"

"I was saving that for something special in the future."

"Good answer. Wrong answer, but a good answer," said Delores. "The sofa is very comfortable this time of the year, my love."

"Marie what time do you have to pick up the girls?"

"About a half hour; I'm still on the bench, watching him pull weeds. We'll have weeds, won't we?"

If not, I can get you some seeds to spread around by the bench area. Some will germinate in a week's time, so you can have weekly enjoyment."

"The bench will be big enough for two of you to sit and watch. If you came home for lunch, I've been at the bench, you will get attacked."

"That alone would be worth the price of the seeds—weeds that are hard to pull. He'll have to bend over and flex his muscles."

"Now youngsters, settle down," said Mama. "You'll end up on the diaper detail—no sleep for months or years, carting all sorts of bags, strollers, formula. You both have been through all of that joy; a little pleasure now is lots of pain later."

"If he did that to me again, I'd hire a hit man," said Marie.

Delores agreed. "Maybe we could get a discount—two for one."

"We all love our children and grandchildren and are so blessed to have them and cannot imagine life without them, but there is a price to pay," said Mama.

"I wish they came with a manual," said Delores.

"I've got power tools that come with a manual. Can't tell you if I ever read the manual; it's used mainly to cover the manufacturer from lawsuits. It puts the blame on the purchaser, operator error, I explained."

The ladies took off to get our little darlings from school.

Quiet at last. Listen to the babbling brook; that's more like what God intended. I'll just start laying out the flags for the irrigation system. The footpath and sitting area will be a nice feature as well; they tie everything together. I'll line out the pavers from the patio to the staircase and tie in the bridge to the pavers. I'm going to the truck to get my hose to layout the edge design. Uncurl the hose and lay it from the bridge to the pathway, nice radius, smooth lines fanning out in both directions so the guest or family member can take a leisurely stroll, no sharp angles, smooth and easy. Stand back and take a peek from all angles. Practice a walk from the patio to the bridge ... that is nice from the second bridge to the pathway to the staircase—nice, smooth stroll. I'll get the ladies to practice a couple of laps and take notes.

I'll lay out flags for the pathway for them to follow. I want to see what happens if I enlarge the patio with the pavers, making an arch to tie the two bridges together. You can stay on the pathway and not use the patio as a thoroughfare.

Once all of the ladies arrived, I had them return to the backyard.

"Ladies, I need your honest opinions on what I just laid out."

"This isn't a listening and learning thing again?" asked Delores.

"No, this is visual and mechanical."

"What did you do?" asked Marie.

"The flags show the outline of the pavers that connect the bridges to the staircase, so I need everyone to take a stroll and let me know if this will work for your daily needs."

"So everything between the flags will be pavers?" asked Marie.

"Yes. I'm trying not to have guests; family members have to walk through the patio to get from the bridges or staircase. I want it to be a leisurely stroll with multiple choices so the outdoor experience is rewarding. I don't want the guest to have to return to the patio to go another direction, waterfall, or staircase."

"Okay girls, let's take a leisurely stroll, see how it feels."

When they got to the first bridge, they all slipped off their shoes and carried them across bridge number one, watched the waterfall and stream, and voiced their likes about what they were viewing.

Marie crossed the first bridge, put her shoes back on, and proceeded to the waterfall. The other ladies met her there. They watched the falls and talked about how nice it felt. Then they asked where the bench would be.

"Tomorrow, ladies, tomorrow." They all turned and proceeded to the second bridge, stating how beautiful the flowers were this time of the year. "Oh look," one of them said, "a hummingbird and a butterfly."

I knew they were toying with me.

Marie removed her shoes, got up on the second bridge, and looked back at the waterfall. The other ladies joined her, and they all were looking at the stream, mesmerized by the water's movement. Then Marie said, "Let's go skinny-dipping."

That got a laugh from the ladies.

"I don't think he is looking for us to do that," said Mama.

I told them to skinny-dip, if they so desired. "Don't let me stop you," I said.

The ladies proceeded to the staircase now instead of returning to the patio. No, they decided to parade down the staircase with their elbows bent as if they were holding champagne glasses, and they sashayed down to the courtyard again, with Delores saying, "Please, you're all too gracious, silly boys; you're supposed to be working. Oh, don't stop applauding. Work can wait; you have all day."

I was now thinking I was not going to get what I had hoped to achieve. I could hear the ladies and the girls in the tunnel clogging, laughing, and having a great time. *I'll just have to use my own idea, and so be it; they had their chance.*

They all came out to the patio. "How did we do?" asked Marie.

"I'm very impressed. Great job, ladies. I wish I had a movie camera handy; the video would go viral."

Marie put her hand on my shoulder. "I love the design, and so do the girls. We were just having fun. That's what this project has done for all of us; it has brought out what we have been afraid to show in years."

Delores said, "If we didn't like it, we would definitely tell you without a doubt or hesitation."

I gave her a big hug and said to her, "That is why I married you; I would do it again in a heartbeat."

John was at the barbecue, making another culinary delight. The girls were in the playhouse and on the patio, watching John cook. Leslie asked Daddy how much longer it would be before dinner.

"Why don't you girls help Mommy bring the salads and beans to the patio table? That would be so helpful." The girls came running down the stairs into the tunnel and, of course, clogged with their hard-soled shoes into the kitchen.

They were met by mommy and the ladies; each got a bowl to take to the table and was asked to return for the plates and plasticware. They clogged through the tunnel and placed the bowls on the table, and they then hurried back to get the next load. The ladies now followed the girls into the tunnel; they all were clogging through the tunnel, having a great time, and laughing at what they had just accomplished. It is so much fun watching the joy a simple thing does to so many.

John said, "That tunnel lets me know when the girls are coming; they can't sneak up on me now."

When the girls were getting their plates ready, I asked all the females if they would like to paint a ceiling like the one in the playhouse. "Yeah, Daddy, what do we need a ceiling for? We don't have a playhouse."

"Great question, Sarah. I'm going to draw a playhouse and patio cover for our backyard. Would you all like a playhouse?" They all said yes. "And Leslie and Kim can come over to your house to play."

"Will we have a patio and porch too?" Rebecca asked. "Yes, as close as I can to what Leslie and Kim have—maybe a surprise or two for all of you to enjoy."

"When can we start painting?" asked Sarah.

"How about Saturday in our backyard? I'll get the lumber."

Marie said, "We need to go shopping at the craft store for brushes and fun paint colors."

"How about after the photo shoot tomorrow, ladies?" I asked.

"We'll be dressed too fancy for a craft store," said Delores. "No, we will make the others wish they should have dressed as we will have dressed. The sales ladies will be jumping over each other to assist us; they'll think we're rich or famous or both."

Early the next morning, I took the liberty to paint the soil where the pavers would be installed. Juan and his crew were due to arrive any minute. The stabilized decomposed granite should be here early as well.

I didn't know if Juan had paver edging. I didn't even know if we had the steel edging for the decomposed granite.

John and Marie came out the patio door. "Good morning," I said. "How are you two doing this fine morning?"

"We're doing great. I hardly slept a wink last night—so excited about the photo shoot," said Marie.

John said, "He will have to take a nap at work."

Then Marie asked me if she could have Angel for the shoot.

"It's fine with me, but you should ask her."

"I know she will be very excited; I can see her glow when we ask her to go down the staircase."

"I hope you two don't hate me for sharing my vision with you during the presentation of my plans."

Marie said, "Of course not, your presentation was so inspiring you got the attention of bother of us, which is still churning in me to this day. My mom—I've never seen her like this, and your wife has been such a blessing to me, and your girls have made my girls unbelievable."

John said, "Our life has more meaning that ever before. I'm amazed at the transformation of our yard. Everything is special. The girls can't get enough of the playhouse; they feel that it's their house, and they invited us to come and visit them. Mama and Papa get so excited to go visit with the girls. Mama always brings them flowers in a vase and some chocolate candies. The first time Mama brought them to the girls, I thought they were going to jump off the patio they were so excited."

"John and I have been invited only twice," said Marie. "They are on a limited budget, you know; they can't invite everyone every time. John thinks they want a bigger allowance."

Dinner was served. Boy, what a feast John and Marie were throwing; it was fit for a king. Delores and the girls had stopped to get cupcakes and ice cream for dessert. on their way to Marie's. The girls were ready for the goodies while we were just starting to eat. John said they must be really hungry.

"We had yucky food in the cafeteria for lunch; it tasted horrible," said Leslie.

"How was Daddy's dinner, asked Sarah?"

"It was the best, Daddy, we all ate every little bite and mopped up the juice with our buns. You don't even have to wash the dishes, they are so clean."

"If you girls would like to, go get the cupcakes, small paper plates, ice cream out of the freezer, small paper bowls on the patio, and the ice cream scoop."

They all four ran to the tunnel and, with their hard-soled shoes, clogged to the kitchen. Everyone laughed at what those girls did.

John said, "You could spend a fortune on the top-of-the-line toys; none of them would compare to the fun they have in that tunnel."

Delores asked if I could dig a tunnel in our house for the girls and ladies to play in.

"I would have to do some major alterations to our home to make that happen. We could build a covered bridge and forgo the patio cover."

"You know that would never fly with the girls; you got them to start dreaming of inviting Leslie and Kim over to their house," said Delores.

"I'm sure they will invite John and Marie as well."

"This is something I would not want to endure if you decide to alter their dream."

"I love the way they are, so happy and joyful, so willing to please—and we are to them. Marie, pinch me to make sure this just isn't a dream."

"Only if you pinch me at the same time."

"If you two wake up, don't tell us; we don't want to wake up," I told them.

The next morning, after starting the day with a fantastic breakfast, I arrived at the job site, where I was met by Phillip. He and Raymond were offloading one of the biggest surprises yet to happen. On his truck, covered, were a table and bench; both matched the bridges—Chinese Red, with two coats of polyurethane. They were breathtaking. I called Diego and had him come to this job site to install the decomposed granite pathway for the photo shoot. As the bench and table were brought to the backyard, I heard Marie call Mama, Papa, and the girls to come see what Phillip had brought us.

They all came outside, and if kudos were worth a million dollars, Phillip would have just become the world's richest man. I don't think his feet were even touching the ground. Marie gave him such a huge hug he started to blush.

Juan and Diego pulled in, and I explained to them what needed to be completed for the photo shoot. "Place the one-inch-thick sheet of plywood over the stream. Do not disturb the stream build soil on both sides. Excavate four inches deep for the decomposed granite. I'm going to pick up the steel edging and a load of decomposed granite to set the bench and table. Be right back."

I got to the masonry yard and got the steel edging and a load of stabilized decomposed granite in my truck. The manager of the store asked why I was in such a rush, and I told him that the photographers from the magazine were due at the house by nine o'clock and we needed to be ready. I mentioned that I would tell the editor the masonry yard's name to enhance their article.

He called over to the dispatcher and said, "Load up one of the trucks and have them follow me to the job site. Reschedule with the other company, letting them know that we will be a little late." The manager gave me one of his business cards to give to the magazine editor. "If they need a location to show readers where to purchase materials, use us; we'll give them free coffee and donuts."

We arrived at the job site, and the driver dumped the decomposed granite for the easiest access for the crews. Off he then went to get his next load.

As I entered the backyard, I was met by Marie and Angel. Angel asked if she could spend the day with the ladies for the photo shoot. I told her I would be honored for her to represent our firm. "I know you'll be in good hands," I said. "You two knock those photographers off their feet."

Marie's job now was to convert a construction worker into a debutant. That sounds difficult, but Angel was not your ordinary construction worker.

I told Juan and Diego that the edging and decomposed granite were in the front yard and in my pickup truck. They sent the wheelbarrow brigade to start hauling the materials. I told Juan to have the haulers stop at the plywood and return with an empty wheelbarrow. He and Diego would dump the materials where they needed them.

Brad and his crew returned to the job site to inspect how everything was working, making minor adjustments as required for the ultimate photo imagery. They turned on the pond lighting to give the best shots possible. Brad and Phillip both stood back to witness the grandeur of their work.

My dearest darling met me in the backyard, wanting to know where the other ladies were located. "Wow, baby, you look fabulous—even nicer than in your church clothes. Beautiful—simply beautiful."

She went into the house and called for Marie. Marie came out of her bedroom and met Delores as she ascended the staircase. You remember the spiral staircase; this is how the story started. As Delores reached the top, Marie had her close her eyes, and Marie guided Delores into her bedroom. With her eyes still closed,

Marie turned her and had her open her eyes. There stood Angel, completely made over to be the ultimate debutant.

Delores could not believe her eyes. "Angel, is that really you?"

"Yes, what do you think?"

"I think I'm underdressed; you look fabulous. How do you feel?"

"Like a million dollars; I have never been treated like this before."

Tears of joy were welling in all the ladies' eyes.

Marie asked Delores what size she wore.

"Sometimes a six or a seven. Depends on who makes the outfit, and if I have been good or not."

"I think I have a perfect outfit for you."

"Are you sure, Marie?" I don't want to impose.

"You're my dearest friend. It will give me great joy to make you feel like a million dollars. Mama and I are going to look like a million dollars, and you need to feel the same. Please, let me dress my dearest friend. If you like the outfit, that is all I need to hear." She handed Delores the outfit on the hangers. "Do you like the color?"

Delores held it up to herself and looked in the full-length mirror. "I love the color; I hope it fits."

Marie said, you will fill it out perfectly."

Mama said, "She will do the outfit wonders."

As Delores removed her best outfit and put on the ultimate outfit, she fought back the tears of joy. Marie was putting on her outfit. Mama went to the other bedroom and was doing the same. All of the ladies were dressed to kill. They didn't need any lights on in the room; their glow was enough to illuminate the entire house. They were the best dressed, most beautiful women I had ever seen.

The doorbell rang, and the girls all rushed down to the door. When the door was opened, there stood the photographer and his crew, in total awe. He couldn't even make understandable words come out.

He finally said, "We're from the magazine here to shoot …" He turned and asked the crew, "Why are we here? Oh, yeah, to shoot the landscape construction. Thanks, guys; I've lost all sense of reasoning right now. Ladies, I don't want you to think badly of me. I was startled by how fabulous you all look. We're used to ladies answering the door in curlers and bathrobes, telling us to go to the gate around the side of house, where the others are in the backyard, and then the door slams in our faces.

"I will do my best once I get back my composure to make this the greatest shoot ever for the magazine. I will have you all pose for me to get shots throughout the day. Remember when you are posing that the camera is a friend to both of us. I get your best image if you love my camera. This is how we make everlasting results. I have heard you all have been practicing grand entrances."

The photographer told one of his assistants to get the movie camera from the van.

Marie said, "Please come into my home."

As the photographer entered, he saw the staircase. "This is a marvelous piece; is this the staircase that started this whole scenario?"

Marie said, "Yes, this started the whole process."

"Is this where you all practice your grand entrance?"

"No, the contractor who refurbished this piece duplicated a smaller version in the courtyard; that is where I practice. Delores uses the arched gateway, and we all use the tunnel entrance into the courtyard."

The assistant returned with the movie camera and set it up for operation. "Marie, could you do me the honor of showing us how you do your grand entrance from this staircase?"

"I need to get a champagne glass from the kitchen."

The photographer told the assistant to fetch the bottle of champagne from the van.

Marie returned with champagne glasses—four of them. The assistant returned with the champagne.

"Marie, here—let's make this real." He filled her glass. "Now you can proceed."

She and the photographer's assistant ascended to the top landing. The assistant fussed with Marie's hair and fixed her outfit. They had also brought a lady stylist with them.

Marie looked even more stunning after they improved on perfection.

She started her grand entrance with the camera rolling; the photographer watched every move. She was a couple of steps from the bottom when the photographer shut off the camera and said to her, "Perfect. You were absolutely perfect: poised, glamorous, graciously statured. Ladies, you have a tough job ahead of you to beat that performance."

Marie was blushing and smiling from ear to ear. The photographer held out his hand and helped her down the last two steps.

He filmed the three other ladies doing their grand entrance routine. The photographer told all of them that his job would be easy today, as he had never had a group of ladies so poised, glamorous, and graceful as they all were.

He and his entire staff applauded the ladies. "Drink up, girls," he said, "we have more shots and more champagne; don't be shy."

They all went into the backyard. As Angel came through the sliding glass door, Juan and Diego stopped what they were doing and applauded their coworker, Juan said, "Angel, is that really you?"

She blushed and said, "Yes, I am Angel."

"Wow, you look fantastic."

All of the crews stood up and were in complete awe. The photographer asked Angel, "You're the office girl, correct?"

"No sir, I work with these men."

"I know you work with them in the office."

"No sir, right alongside with them every day."

The photographer said to his assistant, "Call to the office and get the head writer and the editor here."

The photographer, puzzled now, asked all the ladies what they did for a living.

Marie said she was a housewife, Delores said she was a housewife, Mama said she was a housewife, and Angel said, she was a construction worker.

"Have any of you ever worked as a model or been office executives, or anywhere where you were put in a position to be elegant?"

All the ladies looked at one another and shook their heads. The photographer said, "I've been photographing for over thirty years … none of you have taken schooling or been models to know how to pose in front of a camera? You're doing all of this by some practice on a staircase? How often do you practice—hours per day, every day?"

Marie said, "Maybe a couple of times per week, I'd start at the top and sashay to the bottom step. The crew would give me applause, which encouraged me to do it again." The other ladies said they didn't practice often—maybe the same as Marie.

"Can we wait a few minutes while the editor and the writer arrive? This is too good to be true. The magazine has been wanting this scenario for years. I want to take a couple of still shots of the bridges and fountain."

I asked the photographer if he could wait for a few minutes while my crew removed themselves and the tools from the area.

So Juan and Diego cleaned up the site they had cluttered and headed to the other projects.

"Thanks, guys," I said. "Great job, looks beautiful."

Now the photographer and his assistants started to do their magic.

As they were setting up for the still shots, the editor and the chief writer came through the rear yard gate. They asked the photographer what was up. They were talking away from earshot, and every once in a while the writer and editor turned and looked at the ladies.

After a few minutes, the editor came over to us and apologized about their rudeness. "We had to know why we got an urgent call from the photographer; this is not customary procedure. To make a long story short—I don't want to bore you with our professional details—I'm in agreement with our photographer to make at least three or four issues on just this location, cover to cover. He has told me that none of you ladies have had professional photography or modeling experience, correct?"

Marie said, "That is correct."

"Three of you are housewives, and one is a construction worker?"

Marie said, "Correct again."

"Will you be willing to tell my writer what you have done each and every day for as far back as you can remember?"

All of the ladies nodded.

"I heard you both have two daughters who are in school; can we bring them here in about an hour so we can have them show us their house?"

"They would be so excited to show you their house, said Marie."

"I want to remind you that you will see the entire article prior to print. If I envision what can occur, your lives could be altered from the first publication. My photographer and his assistant are highly skilled professionals and will make every effort to get the best shots possible, not only of the stunning landscape construction but of you ladies as well. I'm as shocked as the photographer that you've had no prior experience. He wants to show me your grand entrance shot he took earlier; you don't mind if I view the video?"

"No, we don't mind, said Marie."

The crew and photographer set up a monitor so all of us could watch the ladies. The photographer stated to the editor, "This is untouched—natural." He showed Marie first, and the editor and writer were in complete awe.

"Marie have you done any acting?" the photographer asked.

"No, not once have I modeled or acted."

The writer said, "We should air this prior to the release of the magazine. That would promote the first issue, creating a stir for the rest of the issues."

They continued to watch the rest of the ladies, becoming more convinced that a short preview would generate a lot of attention.

"Are there other places where you ladies enact an entrance?" the photographer asked.

"The arched gateway, the tunnel, and the other staircase leading into the courtyard," said Marie.

"While we are here, could you show us the other entries into the courtyard?"

"Yes, of course. Follow us."

The staff followed, talking among themselves and looking at the commercial aspects and funding. They arrived at the other staircase and stationed the camera crew at the base of the staircase. The female stylist was making all of the ladies look better each time she modified them ever so lightly.

Marie started the grand entrance for the editor. She put everything she had into each step, gliding down to the bottom two steps. She paused for a brief second whiffed her free hand across her brow, gave a great smile, and stepped down onto the pavers.

Each lady did better and better each time for the camera.

At the arched gateway, Delores was by far the most seductive. Her radiant smile made her the greatest teaser of all the ladies.

They all had fun in the tunnel and got the editor and writer to laugh and applaud. "I agree, we need this shot to produce a promotion for our issues. Ladies, your husbands and boyfriend are very lucky men; we will be in touch with all of you. Maybe next week the planting will be completed and we can shoot more. Are the little girls home from school, asked the producer?"

"Papa and John both went to get them; they should be here anytime, said Marie."

"If they look like their mamas, we will be in hog heaven, said the producer."

"Wait until you see them; all of them are not like regular children, said Mama."

"They're not snooty, are they, asked the producer?"

"By no means, are they anything less than charming, said Delores."

The girls arrived and came through the arched gateway, being all glamorous and flirty; it was the first time any of us saw that from them.

"This is Mr. Barns, from the magazine," said Marie. "Would like you to show him the playhouse? Would you like a few seconds to ready the playhouse for special guests??"

Yeah, Mommy, we don't have any cupcakes or ice cream to serve our guests, said Leslie."

John said, "I bought some for you, knowing you were going to have special guests. Do you want to serve on the patio downstairs or at your house?"

"Downstairs, Daddy, there are more chairs."

The four girls scurried up the stairs; we could hear them talking about having special guests and who would do what.

Mr. Barns said, "They're all adorable and so well mannered; this is a true blessing. We're all so grateful of how this all turned out. Do we wait to be called up or just head on up the stairs, asked Marie?"

"Head on up the stairs; I believe they are ready, said Mr. Barns."

Mr. Barns led the way. "This is nice work. Phillip must have done all of this, said Mr. Barns."

Leslie answered the door when Mr. Barns knocked. "Please come in, Mr. Barns and friends. welcome to our playhouse. Camera is rolling."

"Mr. Barns was nearly speechless. "Look at this place—french doors with curtains ... Look at the ceiling, painted with figures, stated Mr. Barns."

Sarah opened the french doors, allowing the cameraman to step out to shoot the view from the patio.

"Girls, this is an amazing house.," said Mr. Barns. "Can you tell me about your house, asked Mr. Barns?"

"It used to be a shed underground. We heard some bad things happened inside; Mommy and Daddy know. We just love it; don't you, asked Leslie?"

"It's the most amazing house I have ever seen, said Mr. Barns."

"Mr. Barns, my daddy makes great hot dogs; would you be out guest for lunch, asked Leslie?"

"Girls, I'd be honored to be your guest for lunch. My crew will eat with your mommy and dads; would that be all right, Leslie said of course, they need their nourishment like we do?"

"Mr. Barns, our space is limited; so is out budget. We can have one guest, but they will be our guests at a different time. We're sorry; we don't like offending anyone, said Leslie."

"We will see you in a little while, okay girls?"

"Thank all of you for stopping by, hope to see you all again."

Mr. Barns, on the pavers, walked over to Marie and Delores. Those girls are wonderful, charming, and a sheer delight. I'm their guest for lunch."

"You're a very lucky man," said Marie. "There is a waiting list which they have created. You must have made an impression on them."

"No, Marie, they made a huge impression on me and my staff. I heard John makes killer hot dogs; my staff will head to the store and buy them a truckload. They're on a limited budget, you know."

Mr. Barns sent his assistants to fetch hot dogs, potato salad, baked beans, buns, condiments, paper plates, plasticware, chips—the works. Bring two bottles of champagne, chilled, sodas and juice for the girls. "Be quick about it," he said. "The little girls are hungry."

John started the barbecue and called over to Marie; she went to him. "I'm nervous about cooking for all of these people; are my hot dogs really that good?"

"All of the girls inhale them, and they are all fairly finicky eaters. You heard what they said about the school cafeteria—how horrible the food was that they were served."

As Marie turned and started back to the table, she stopped and said, "You know, burn them like usual." The remaining crew all laughed at Marie's comment.

As everyone was getting to know one another, lots of questions came from the writer. The photographer was busy taking still shots of all of the women.

"I can't wait for the planting to be installed; this place is unbelievable and should last many years. How is it at night, asked Mr. Barns?"

"Right now it's just the fans, porch light, patio light, step lights, and lights at the arched gateway and the tunnel," John said. "The low-voltage lighting is due in next week; we can't wait to see everything lit up as envisioned."

"I have heard you mention a vision; this entire project was a vision?"

"I believe so. Delores's husband is the designer and the visionary."

"Would he be willing to share that vision with our readers?"

Delores said, "He's not one to boast and is very humble when it comes to his work. He is the first to admit that as the project develops, he will make subtle changes for the better. He takes great pride in making sure the final outcome of the construction is for the client."

Marie stated, "He has gotten us from out of our house and asked our opinion on a construction issue. John and I are not qualified to give him advice, but he insists on our opinion. We both have talked about the what-ifs: wrong decision, said yes when we should have said no, whether he really wants our opinion or is just humoring us. So far everything is turning out much better than we ever imagined. We cannot even put into words what this project has done for our family. Our friends have said, 'We feel so sorry for you going through a remodel.' Then they tell us the horror story of their remodel. On our way home, while driving, we both agree we have a true treasure, and we are so thankful he came into our lives."

The writer said, "We need to put all of that into print. I will have to tape an interview with all of you. When would you be available? Delores, would your husband mind joining us. during that interview?"

"I don't know. He's not one to hear people telling others about what he does. You would have to ask him. He would tell me no, but maybe John and Marie could ask him."

"The crew have returned; let the burning begin," said Marie.

"Oh, boy, Daddy is cooking our lunch. We are so hungry, Daddy, said Leslie."

"I'll make yours and Mr. Barns's first so you can have your luncheon. If you girls would like to fix your plates, feel free to do so."

The girls came down the stairs and greeted everyone and thanked them for joining the celebration.

Everyone thanked them for having them over.

Mr. Barns asked Marie and John if they had rehearsed all of this with the girls.

"No, this is just how they have been since the playhouse was opened to them to play. It's like they have their own apartment; it is their house."

Mama and Papa had been invited nearly daily. Mama told Mr. Barns, "When you visit them, it's like you are truly a guest in their house. That is as close as we can compare the visit to you. You may want to take notes for your readers, it is truly a remarkable experience, from such young girls, it's unheard of."

"I can't wait for the hot dogs to be ready and to walk up the stairs; the way you all explain the experience, the readers will be awestruck, as I'm sure I will be," said Mr. Barns.

John said, "Okay, girls, burnt to perfection, as you all love them." The girls lined up, and John placed two hot dogs onto their plates.

"Mr. Barns, please join us; do you want us to make you up a plate, asked Leslie?"

"No, girls I'll be right there."

"Mr. Barns, how many hot dogs would you like?" asked John.

"I'll go with what the girls chose; two will be sufficient, thank you. I always follow the hostess; can't go wrong." Mr. Barns followed the girls up the staircase and onto the porch and was escorted onto the patio to partake in the luncheon. The girls were doing their hosting to perfection, which was duly noticed by all.

Tomorrow there would be the planting by Juan and his crew, and irrigation in the backyard by Diego and his crew. Life was good.

The photo shoot continued after lunch. Hot dogs were cooked to perfection. Mr. Barns loved dining with the girls; they brought him his dessert and beverage, and told him to be sure to stop by the next time he was in town.

He told them that he would return, and that they would be interviewed about their playhouse, as the magazine would have an issue all about their playhouse. Mr. Barns and his writer left for the day, letting Marie know they would return once the landscape was planted and the lighting was ready for some night shots. He thanked all the ladies and John for having him and his crew in their home.

The ladies were now in the hands of the photographer and his staff, poised and ready to please. The photographer shot some photos of the girls and their playhouse first so he could photo the rest of the courtyard with their mamas, their grandma, Papa, and Angel.

I had to visit the other jobs to make sure all was on track.

The shoot had lasted longer than anyone expected; the ladies were getting tired physically but not mentally. Delores told me a couple of shots of her would be looked at for the cover. I told her every shot they took of her would have to be considered for the cover. "You looked fabulous," I said. "I would have a difficult time going through all the photos to determine which ones would be used for a cover to get the passersby to stop and pick up the magazine and purchase it."

Marie told Angel and Delores to wear their outfits home and bring them back next time they visited or attended their next luncheon. Delores asked if they were to be dry cleaned.

Marie said she wasn't sure. "But please don't go out of your way to have it done," she added. She had a regular company that sent a driver to pick up and return dry-cleaning. "If I do that, I'm paying you for the cleaning fee. I may need the outfit again for the next photo shoot, or we can go and buy another outfit for me. You have great taste in clothing. I want you to help me select an outfit."

Marie said, "I'm free in a couple of days; we'll do lunch. I'm so honored that you trust me that much to select an outfit for you."

Delores said, "If you had seen the look on my husband's face when he first saw me in this outfit, you would pay anything to get that look again. I wasn't even trying to get his full attention."

Marie gave her a beautiful smile. "Remember what Mama said about another little one."

CHAPTER 40

The next morning, the nursery had arrived bright and early. The shrubs were delivered first, and the trees were due in about an hour. My crane was due any minute. I had received from the nursery the depths of the boxed trees. I had all five holes marked. Juan and Diego and their crews were busy digging the plant pits when the shrubs arrived. I took two crew members and had them unload the truck with the nursery truck driver. Once everything was offloaded, I started spotting the plants where the trees would not be planted.

Marie came to the courtyard, watched me spot the shrubs, and shot some pictures with her camera. I asked her if I could take a couple of photos. She handed me her camera and showed me how it worked; we were all ready.

"Marie, do me one favor. Pose for me by the plants for a before shot."

She was a little hesitant but then decided to play along. I wanted her to look as if she were entering the garden. I told her that if she liked a certain plant, she should pose by the one she liked the best. She followed my lead; she picked a beautiful yellow rose, not without getting stuck by the thorns. I showed her how to handle the rose. "Smell the flower." She bent over slightly and sniffed.

"The rose smells good."

I showed her how to handle the flower, cupping the rose in her palm, her thumb on the petals. "Now bend and sniff. Take your time, slowly, and I will tell you when to stop and give a nice smile." She bent over slowly, cupped the rose in her hand, put on a beautiful smile, and sniffed the rose. *Click, click, click!* "That was so nicely done."

"Did I do it right?"

"Come here and take a look."

"Wow, you took a nice photo. It will look great in my album."

"I have a great subject to work with. You made the photo much better than the one pushing the button."

"Would you like to take another photo?" she asked.

"I'd love to. You pick your second favorite flower." She found a lavender flower, *Pelargonium peltatum*, or ivy geranium. She followed the same procedure as with the rose. *Click, click, click!*

"How did I do?"

"Come here and take a look."

"Not bad. You take good photos. Can I do another one?"

"Of course." She saw the sweet broom, a canary-yellow flower. She bent over and followed the same procedure as prior. *Click, click, click!*

"I'm getting pretty good at this, aren't I?"

"Marie, you are doing everything perfectly."

"One more shot, please. One more flower, and then I will let you get back to work. I like smelling the rose. Do you have another flower that smells like the yellow one?"

"I have a fragrant pink flower out front. I'll bring it into the courtyard." I went and got the pink rose, brought it into the courtyard, and put it on the circular planter wall cap. Marie got on her knees on the wall cap and bent over to smell the pink rose. I said to her, "Are you ready?"

"Just a minute." She moved at a slightly different angle. "Is that better?"

"Let me take one photo, and then you can see if that is what you like." *Click!* "What do you think?"

She looked at the photo, glanced up at me, and said, "Do you like the photo?"

I told her she was a perfect subject. "You can't improve on perfection."

"Take another one, maybe two. Ready."

Click, click, click!

"How about these shots?"

She turned and, now sitting on the wall cap, looked at all the shots. "You like these, don't you?"

"You know I do, or I would not have taken the shot."

She looked at me. "Can I ask you one serious question?"

"Do you want an honest answer?"

"I think I know the answer, but I want to make sure."

"Okay, what's your question?"

"From all the photos you took, what flower made me look the best?"

"You had me scared there for a minute."

"Why were you scared?"

"The yellow rose is my favorite shot."

"Mine too. The yellow flower makes me look nice and tanned. You didn't answer my other question. Why were you scared?"

"I can't answer that question, Marie. I could lose too much."

"Will you answer it at a later date and time?"

"I promise I'll answer your question. I have to spot more plants so the crew can start making all your dreams come true."

She turned and gave me a look over her shoulder. "Not that—not now, silly boy. You have work to do, making my dream come true."

I finished spotting the plants in the courtyard just in time. The trees and the crane arrived. The crew had one more hole to dig—the one for the circular planter. I told them to put the soil in the four wheelbarrows; there was no room to fit the tree with the plant pit spoils. Juan, Angel, and Miguel were at the first hole, awaiting the tree. I had selected an *Acer palmatum* 'Bloodgood,' standard, to be placed between the two bridges in a thirty-six-inch box. "This is a beautiful tree and will accent the bridges, said Marie."

Diego and Manuel helped the driver set the tree upright so the crane could hook to the tree to lift it over the house. I went to the sliding glass door and tapped on the glass. Mama answered the door. I told the ladies, "Please stay inside until the tree is in place."

Mama said, "Okay, we won't go outside."

The crane operator's assistant came through the gate into the backyard, where the crew and I were waiting. With his cell phone, he guided the operator directly to the plant pit. I had them spin the tree one-quarter of a turn, stood back, looked at different angles, and had them lower the tree into the pit. The operator's assistant unhooked the strap and told him he was free. Diego had one of our walkie-talkies, and I told him I needed the *Olea europaea* 'Swan Hill,' standard, next. They set up the tree, and the operator's assistant strapped onto the tree.

He returned to the backyard and met us at the next tree location. This one was close to the house wall, and I called Diego for him and Manuel to meet us in the backyard. The tree came over the house. The assistant was directing the operator, and the tree was descending slowly. We could reach the bottom of the box, where Juan tied a rope. The crew put some tension on the box as it lowered a few more feet. This procedure made sure the box didn't drift and hit the house. I had them swing the tree so the opposite side of the tree facing the stream feature. We got the tree so the bottom was at the top of the plant pit. Juan untied the rope, and Diego and Manuel were between the house and the tree box. The tree was lowered enough into the hole that the guys could move it without fear of the tree box hitting the house wall. The tree was in place. The assistant unstrapped the tree and carefully raised the crane's ball and hook above the roofline, and the operator was free to return to the nursery trailer.

There were three more trees, and two would be harder to place than the final tree. I went to the nursery delivery truck and numbered the boxes that went in each hole. I told Diego to set up tree number three, then four, and finally five. I gave Miguel and Angel the tools for breaking the steel bands holding the tree box together. They started removing the first box, and I told them to be careful of the steel. "It can and will slice your hands and arms." I gave them a claw hammer. "If you place the steel between the claws of the hammer and twist, that will also break the bands. Check the bands. Sometimes the nursery bends nails over the bands to hold them in place."

Tree three was strapped. I told the crane operator to come through the arched gateway into the courtyard. He did, and he met us at the third plant pit. Diego and Manuel followed him to help hold the rope so the tree would not swing into the balusters of the staircase. This also was an *Olea europaea*, 'Swan Hill,' standard. Here came the flying tree, straight to the plant pit. It was lowered very slowly, just to the same level so Juan could tie the rope to the bottom of the tree, and all three men pulled the rope taut. The assistant asked if they were ready. "Ready … Lower it some more," said Juan. Down the tree came to just about the height of the plant pit. This tree was perfect—no turning required. It moved slowly down a couple of feet, and now a third of the box was in the plant pit. Juan untied the rope, and the assistant lowered the tree into place.

Tree four was another *Olea europaea*, 'Swan Hill,' standard. This one was going into the raised planter about six feet west of the staircase. Diego followed the assistant to show him the next tree and returned to the next pit. The tree was raised over the pit and lowered slowly. Juan tied the rope to the box. The tree was lowered just into the hole, the rope was untied, and it was lowered the rest of the way. The tree was set and unstrapped, and we were on our way to tree five.

This tree was a multitrunked *Olea europaea*, 'Swan Hill.' This was a very special 360-degree tree. "Please take every precaution with this tree," I said. The crew had the pit all dug, ready for the focal tree. The tree was strapped with ultimate care. The operator lifted the tree off the truck bed, over the entrance wall, and over the circular planter and started lowering it slowly. The assistant directing the operator asked if we needed to use any rope tied to the box. "This one should be good—no rope required," I said. Slowly, about a third of the box was lowered into the hole.

"Is this the right angle of the tree?"

I looked from three different angles and told the assistant, "Perfect. Set it in the hole." The focal tree was in place and unstrapped. The hook and ball were raised very carefully so as not to snag a branch; he was free and clear. I went to the street and signed my life away.

The crews were removing the boxes and backfilling the trees. I went and retrieved my ladies. This time, my dearest darling was having a spot of tea with her best friend, Mama, and Papa. They all followed me to see the trees being planted. Marie brought her camera. We got to the end of the patio, and they all stopped, and Marie said, "What a difference the trees make. Can you take our photo near the staircase entrance?"

"I will do as directed. You tell me when you're ready."

The four of them headed to the staircase landing, stopped, and turned; the olive tree was in the background, with light filtering through the leaves. This shot alone could make the cover of the magazine. "We're ready if you're ready."

"I'm always ready to photograph such great subjects as yourselves." *Click, click, click, click!* "Did you see the tree in the circular planter? Wait; I need another shot. Stay where you all are. I'm going to enter through the arched gateway. It'll take me a couple of minutes." I was standing on the pavers by the staircase and had each of them descend.

Marie asked Delores to make the first entrance. She started, and I began clicking the camera. With each step, she got more seductive, poised, and glamorous. Then came Mama. If she were ten years younger, I would be in huge trouble. I was clicking with each step. Papa wanted to play around. He bent his elbow as if holding a champagne glass and descended the staircase, sashaying with each step. I was clicking as he went down the entire staircase. I told him he should practice with the ladies and get on the cover of the magazine. He laughed and said he didn't want to steal their thunder. Next was Marie, the queen of descending the staircase. Since this was a digital camera, there was no film needed. Here she came, poised, sensual, seductive, glamorous, and a little flirtatious, with a little added flair. Each step was even better than the prior. I clicked until my finger got tired.

"How did we all do? I'm glad I'm not a photographer, I ssid; I would have to excuse myself."

They all laughed and headed to the circular planter, and there she was—the focal tree.

Marie said to Delores, "Go outside and enter into the courtyard from the arched gateway." Delores did as she was told.

Marie said to me, "Take photos of her coming into the courtyard like you did for me and the flowers."

Delores entered through the gate looking so seductive, poised, glamorous, and flirtatious. Each move got more and more seductive. I almost forgot what I was doing; she really got my full attention. Marie was watching her, and when Delores stopped, she went and hugged her. She stated, "That was incredible."

Delores stated, "No one applauded me." I told her my hands had been full of camera or I would have. I went to her. While hugging her, I told her she had my full attention. "So you liked my entry?"

"Not that—not now, silly girl."

She said, "Maybe when you're not so busy, we can discuss your problem."

"Marie, what do you think of the focal tree?"

"I'm sorry; I got carried away with your wife's entrance and watching you take her photo." Everyone turned and looked at the olive tree and moved to see it from different angles. Marie went to the tunnel, opened the door, and acted as if she were coming to the courtyard from the tunnel. Delores went and stood next to her, and I took their photo. They both headed into the courtyard, moving toward the arched gateway. They stopped and looked at the tree.

Click, click, click!

Delores asked, "What are you doing?"

"I'm taking photos of you two without having either of you pose. You know, seeing you not in a posed position is very nice. It shows the real personality of both of you."

"Let us see those photos. We'll be the judge of what you just mentioned."

"Here, ladies, take a peek. You'll see you don't have to pose. You're both posed naturally."

Marie said, "You know, I think he's right. We look great together. Those should fill a couple of pages in the photo album."

"If you both had on the outfits you had on yesterday, I could send them to *Vogue* magazine."

Diego and his crew started working on the irrigation system on the island; once completed, I would set flags for the plants. Juan and his crew started planting the shrubs after they backfilled the olive tree in the circular planter. Once the tree was backfilled and watered, Marie and Delores came to the courtyard from the tunnel and sat on the circular seat wall in the shade of the tree's branches. They each had a beverage; I was certain the drinks contained a little sauce to liven their day.

I was setting plants in the two other raised planters along the house. There was something not correct. Both planters looked wonderful in bloom. I had too much bare wall from the shrub's height to the windowsills. I told the crew to hold off on planting the two raised planters along the house. "I'll be right back with some improvements." I asked the ladies if they would like to go with me to the nursery.

"We would love to go," said Delores, "but we're waiting on Mama and Papa. We are heading to the craft store; we were too busy yesterday."

"Okay, I'll see you when you return."

I hoped the nursery had something that would bring sparkle to those two fifteen-gallon planters—something showy but not overbearing. I walked with the salesman, showed him a photo of both planters, and explained I needed something that could take afternoon sun to fill the wall. We went through all their growing stock, and the ones that looked like they might work would grow too big and choke out the rest of the plants. The roses in larger can sizes were not very nice. Then we went to the vines; foliar-wise, they were nice. "That would make the planter look smaller than what it is, pushing the wall closer to the guest's vision. This is not an easy task. If I leave the planters as designed, they will become just there—'so-what' to the guest."

Then I saw what just might save my bacon. He had a pair of *Calliandra haematocephala*, pink powder puff, espaliered on wooden trellises. They were in bloom and well maintained. The salesman stopped the golf cart and called for a trailer to come pick them up.

"I need three," I said. "Do you have one more?"

"I believe so. Let me call my nursery foreman." They had one more that they were holding for a customer, but the customer had never returned for the shrub.

"Can you contact them to see if they still need one?" I asked.

"If I can get a hold of them, I'll call you right back."

He called back and stated that the customer had found a smaller version at another nursery. "They were sorry not to have called and told me what they had done," he said.

They loaded and covered them on my truck, and away I went.

Back at the job site, I had Juan and Vincent offload the *Calliandra* and spot them centered in the planters. I stood back and looked at a few angles; those balanced the walls nicely. I rearranged the plants in the planters, stepped back, and looked at the overall appearance.

The ladies had returned from the craft store. "Ladies, I need you to help me."

"Now what?" Delores asked. "You know we are both really busy. How long will this take?"

"Just a couple of minutes, tops."

They followed me to the courtyard, and I showed them the planters after they did their grand entrance through the arched gateway. "Okay, we're ready, so what do you need?"

I must have given them a look. They both said in unison, "Not that—not now, silly boy."

"You're going to say that to me, and I will make it 'That' and 'now.'"

"Dream on, dear. We're both tougher than you think."

"Look at the planter along the wall. What do you think?"

"They look really nice. You want a pat on the back?" asked Delores.

"I just need some confirmation. You know, this project has a lot riding on its appearance. I don't want to blow a chance in a lifetime."

Marie was looking all around now, since most of the planting was completed. She and Delores walked to the raised planter under the patio cover and looked at the bouquet in front of them. Marie said to her, "Stand here. I want you to watch me." Marie climbed the staircase, looked at the whole courtyard from that viewpoint, and called Delores to join her. They both were standing on the landing, looking into the courtyard, and then both started down the staircase side by side, step-by-step, keeping focused on the courtyard.

Marie stopped and said, "I love it. I'm going to get Mama and Papa and have them do what we just did."

Diego and crew were finishing up the island irrigation. I flagged the rest of the backyard, and they started trenching the shrub beds and turf areas. I had them install sleeving under the pavers to the isolated planters. We also installed two wire sleeves—one for the irrigation and one for the low-voltage lighting. I had Diego turn on the island irrigation system to check the coverage.

"Good coverage. How about the hedge line? Is that completed also?"

Diego turned on that valve as well.

"Good coverage, considering we had to work with an out-of-line hedge."

I had him change to a bigger nozzle from an eight- to a ten-foot diameter and throw on a couple of heads. "It will make a lot of difference during the summer months. Right now, not so much. We should be ready for the plants with another day's work. Once you get the irrigation completed back here, you can go to the other job if you still have hours left. How much have you completed on the other project?"

"One more day on the irrigation system, and then three days on the planting."

"Do you want Juan and his crew to help you? We can delay this project for a day."

"If I can complete the irrigation system tomorrow, we should be in good shape for planting."

"Let me know so I can inform the customer here if we have to miss a day."

I returned to the courtyard. Juan and crew were nearing a lunch break; that would give me time to spot the plants for the front yard. The courtyard was really looking great; with the lighting and mulch spread in the planters, this would be a showcase. I needed to think of some other projects that were on hold, waiting for this job to be completed. I still had a week before another one or maybe two would start.

Angel came up to me and thanked me for allowing her to model with the ladies. I said to her, "There will be more days they will want you for the photo shoot. You looked fabulous. What a difference from a construction worker to a debutant. You cleaned up really pretty."

"My dad wants to know if he could get some of the photos."

"You know, I'm sure they will give you some, but I have to ask the magazine. If they want to charge me for the photos, I will buy you a packet. I'm excited to see how all those shots turned out. I would like to have them hanging on the office wall to show new customers."

"You would hang a photo of me on your office wall?"

"Not just one. If they show our workmanship and my beautiful lady worker, that is a win-win for the company. You would be arranged with the other ladies with the homeowner's project name above all the photos. I will have all you ladies present when the wall is being put together. You can make the decision just where your photo is hung on the wall. I don't want to embarrass any of you. This is a feel-good project."

"I told my dad I love working for you. You put me at ease and are very helpful and explain just how to do things."

"With what I've seen of your work ethic and pride, I'm very lucky to have you as an employee. I want you to grow and run your own project when you're ready. We will discuss it once you have a desire to move up."

"Will I have to pose like I did here?"

"If the project is going to be in magazines and you're willing—your choice."

"I will always have whoever comes directly to you."

The ladies returned to the courtyard to take a peek. They sat down on the circular planter wall under the shade of the tree. "Ladies, glad to see you both enjoying the courtyard."

"We just wanted to see if this will have the same ambiance as the water feature," said Marie.

"Ladies, wherever you are, that's where the ambiance will be generated."

"You're talking with other people around. But if we are alone, where will we be most comfortable?"

"I would think it is going to depend on the time of the day, what's on the agenda for that day, your mood, and what's bothering you the most. Have you two sat on the bench by the waterfall?"

"We just left the bench, got a beverage, walked through the tunnel, and are sitting here, waiting for a butterfly or hummingbird."

"When you're out and about, why don't you get a hummingbird feeder? Those attract the birds more than anything."

"Where would we hang the feeder?"

"The patio cover post would be great."

Marie turned to Delores. "Let's go buy a hummingbird feeder and have your hubby install it for us."

The front yard plants were spotted, waiting for a shovel and pick. Diego and his crew joined Juan and his crew for lunch, all sitting on the raised planter wall or patio table, enjoying their lunches. I called the nursery to see if we could push up the plant delivery by one day. "That would be no problem; same time, just a different day."

"Exactly. See you tomorrow."

After the lunch break, I'd start flagging the plant locations for the backyard. The low-voltage lights should be here before two o'clock. This project may be completed by Friday, except the mulch. I'd skip that idea. We had the pavers to install. I'd talked with Juan.

"Do you want to hire a couple more people?" Angel asked me; she had a couple of friends looking for work. "Do you want to talk with them and have them meet with Juan? One is my best friend. She's a good worker—nice personality. Would it be okay to ask her?"

"You know what the work requires. If you think she can keep up and wants to learn, have her talk to Juan."

The ladies returned with the hummingbird feeder. I had some wood screws in the truck with an impact driver; it would be a couple of minutes' project. They had a lifetime supply of food for the hummingbirds. We turned on the valve to add more water to the raised planters; now we had water drops on the foliage. The ladies were in the kitchen, making the sugar water mixture for the hummingbirds. I had the bracket hung; to make sure the girls could reach the hanger, I took a tape measure and measured from the floor to where Marie could reach fairly easily, with no step stool required. The ladies made fun of what I was doing, but if I put it too high, the birds would have no food. Too low and people could bang their heads or poke an eye out.

Delores said, "Aren't you going to measure me?"

"Okay, I don't want you to feel left out." From the floor, her reach was an inch longer than Marie's.

"You're telling me that my reach is one inch longer?"

"Stand side by side." They did. "Extend your arms next to each other, straight out." They did, and they saw that Marie's reach was shorter.

Delores said, "That makes sense. I'm older by a couple of months. She's not finished growing."

"If it only worked that way. I'm pretty sure she is finished growing. I think she is over twenty-five years old."

Marie said, "Next month, I'll be over twenty-five." That brought everyone to laugh.

Mama and Papa walked into the kitchen. Mama said, "You can't be twenty-five. I'm only twenty-three."

Papa said, "I should be in jail."

"I have to hang up the hummingbird feeder. You all have fun." It was soon hung, and the girls brought out the feeder. They were still talking about the age thing.

Marie said, "The feeder is hung, and there is plenty of food. Hummingbirds, come and get it." I told her she had to learn hummingbird language to call them to dinner.

The backyard irrigation system would be completed tomorrow by Juan and company. Diego had three of the five valves completed and working. They started digging holes for Juan so the crew could concentrate on just planting. Angel was watering in all the planted shrubs while more holes were dug.

Marie and Delores were talking about getting a suntan once the crews were on other projects, looking for just the right spots to put lounge chairs for the ultimate tan. I asked if there would be any tan lines. "Yes, we won't do sunbathing in the buff. We don't need to become too famous, with spies in the sky—drones hunting for a viral photo opportunity."

"Well, let me know when," I said. "I can just drop by and say hello."

"That won't ever happen. We don't need an audience."

The ladies were getting ready to pick up the girls, this time all in one car. Mama and Papa were napping. Off they went, and the crews were packing up the tools.

"Diego," I asked, "you and your crew will be at the other project tomorrow, correct?"

"Yes."

"Can you order the plants to arrive on Thursday? They are tagged. I'll call them—delivery on Thursday morning. First drop."

It was another day in the record books.

"Angel, could you bring your friend with you tomorrow morning?" I asked.

"I'd love to bring her. Can she come to work with me?"

"Okay, one-day trial period; we will see if she can keep up with you. You can teach her some of the tasks required."

I went home to work on another drawing, knowing that the phone would ring and the girls would ask me, "Where are you?" I just wanted to get something started and try to get caught up.

In about a half hour, my dearest darling called my cell phone. "Honey, where did you go?"

"I'm at home, drawing a plot plan."

"Are you coming back for dinner?"

"Would you like me to come back for dinner?"

"Remember: not that—not now."

"Yes, dear."

"I'll see you shortly, correct?"

"The truck is warming up as we speak."

"That's a good boy. See you soon."

I was told at the dinner table—well, seat wall—that Mama and Papa would be leaving by the middle of next week. "Would they get to have the photographer and writer return from the magazine? Would the job be completed, I was thinking?"

"Can you extend it to Friday, I'll ask?"

Mama and Papa said they would call and ask if they could fly out on Friday.

I said, "I'll see if I can get the magazine to return on Thursday, or hopefully Wednesday, unless the crew would be willing to work through the weekend. I'd have to charge you for the overtime hours."

John said, "Would adding the two days make certain that they would keep their flight?"

"I'll ask the crew. We're bringing another person to start tomorrow and one more on Monday. I will give it everything I have to make it all happen."

Papa said, "We will call and ask tomorrow just in case."

John said, "I love the planting here in the courtyard."

The girls were on their patio and said, "We love it too, said Kim."

"Thank you, girls. Keep an eye out for a hummingbird."

"Daddy, are the hot dogs ready yet, asked Leslie?"

"No hot dogs today, girls. Hamburgers, steak, or pork chops on the menu tonight, said John."

"We're really starting to love the burnt hot dogs. Can you burn the hamburgers, asked Sarah?"

"I could burn the salad if Mommy would throw it on the grill. I'll give it my best shot for you, girls. You can come down and help Mommy bring out the salad, beans, chips, and sodas."

"Yeah, we're coming. We love helping. Mommies give us great, big hugs. We like hugs and making noise in the tunnel." They had that clogging down pat; it got better each time. The girls arrived in the kitchen; they knew the drill—salads, beans, garnishments, paper plates, plasticware, plastic cups, napkins, and buns. Their hands were full, and the clogging in and out was music to our ears. The girls were thinking about whom they would invite as their guest for tonight's dinner party. "Let's invite your mom and dad, Sarah and Rebecca. Would you like to ask them to join us?"

"Okay, what if they are too busy?"

"They go to the bottom of the guest list, and busy twice, they go on the no-call list."

"I'll ask them and tell them the rules."

When the ladies joined us from the kitchen, the girls asked me and Delores if we could join them for dinner.

Delores told them, "I hope I'm dressed appropriately. This is a sudden notice, but if my attire is suitable, then I would be honored."

"How about you, Daddy?"

"Well, I know my attire is less than suitable. But if you don't mind, I'd love to join you. I've only been on your patio twice since we built it."

"I believe we have cupcakes for dessert with sprinkles on top. You have to eat all your dinner, or you get no cupcakes."

"Tough rules, but I heard the ambiance is well worth following some rules."

"Dinner will be ready in a little while. Please feel free to mingle with the other guests while you wait."

The burgers were burned to perfection for the girls and their guests. "John," said Marie, you're getting so good you could become a master chef with a little more practice."

"It takes lack of patience to burn a burger on high heat. Want to make sure it's crispy top through bottom."

"Not jerky like your first barbecue meal, huh, Daddy?"

"That's right, sugar. I have practiced now on burning the meat for my little angels."

"We'll let you know, Daddy, if you cook them wrong."

"I'm sure you will. Bon appétit, my darlings."

"You know the cook very well, Leslie, said Delores."

"Yes, we go back many years. This is my favorite dining place."

"Ours too." They had their plates and told their guests not to be late. "We're starving."

Delores asked me, "Do I look nice enough to dine with our daughters and their best friends?"

"Turn around for me slowly."

She did, looking over her shoulder with a quirky smile and glow in her eyes. "Well, am I dressed to please?"

"I'd say dressed to kill me if I answer that wrong. I'm honored to be your date."

"You two had better get moving or you'll never make the list again."

"We're running now." Delores was first up the stairs, and following her was a sure delight. She looked over her shoulder a couple of times to make sure I was paying attention to her movements. She was doing my favorite song—"Wiggle When You Walk."

Delores rang their doorbell, and Sarah answered the door. "Mommy and Daddy have arrived. Thank you for coming to our dinner party. Please make yourselves welcome in our home."

"Thank you, girls, for inviting us. You do have a lovely place."

Leslie said grace as we all bowed our heads. The food was delicious, and I thanked the girls. "What a pleasure to be able to dine with all of you tonight. Give the chef my regards. Wonderful job."

Leslie called down to her dad. "Daddy, the burgers are great. Mommy, the salads are first cabin in flavor." They heard their parents tell them they were welcome. "And when finished, there are cupcakes for you and your guests."

The girls made certain all the food taken was eaten. Kim and Rebecca were asked to bring up the desserts. "Chocolate or white icing—what would you prefer?"

"White for me," I said.

"White for me as well," said Delores. All the little girls wanted chocolate.

"Four chocolates and two white icings coming up." The girls brought up the cupcakes and thanked Marie and John for a wonderful meal. "And we are to give our regards to the chef." Someday all these girls would make wonderful wives and gracious hostesses. Their gentlemen had better be top notch.

As we finished our desserts, the girls showed off their house and told a short story about it and explained how thankful they were to be able to share their blessing with invited guests. They were saddened because they would like to invite more visitors, but their budget was limited, as was the space. I learned some things from their little story; they mentioned that a second house was being planned, and future invites could be at either location. "So read your invitations very carefully."

"We hate to eat and run, but we have another party to attend downstairs. Would you like to join us? There are two very nice couples we would be honored to introduce to all of you."

"Maybe to just say hello, but we can't stay long. We have homework to finish."

"Please follow us to the other party." We all got downstairs, and we introduced the girls to the other couples. That little gesture brought so much joy to Marie, John, Mama, and Papa. They all got hugs from the little girls, and the girls then excused themselves and scurried up the stairs.

Marie said, "That almost got me to cry. We have such great children, all because we have given them an opportunity to be themselves, not just go away and play. The grown-ups are being rude to you right now in front of their friends, maybe for a laugh. I'm just amazed how a beaten-up old shed, with a little tender loving care, could bring so much joy and love to four little girls, their parents, and their grandparents."

"I am so thankful that didn't like the shed where it was originally. I thought a waterwheel and mill would look good in the backyard. I'm so glad that didn't happen. The girls would never want to play back there, being so far away from their parents. You made us really think about down the road, not just for the day."

"I have to thank the man up above for giving me visions for your home. He brought all of us together, healed vacancies in our lives, and gave me a great reason to get up each and every morning. Each day is a new day, ready to serve."

Delores said, "Marie, John, Mama, and Papa, I thank all of you for giving me the greatest opportunity of my lifetime in meeting and spending time with all of you, giving me a chance to express myself in ways I had never dreamed possible. I removed my handkerchief headwear for a glamorous, rewarding way of life I could have never dreamed of enjoying. My stomach churns each and every day with the unknown expectations of being invited over to spend time with such great, loving, and caring people."

"You two are going to make me cry. You both have done so much for John and me. We, too, are so blessed by having you and your children in our lives. We were in the same situation as both of you—lost in our own home and way of living. What if what happened here in the past hadn't been brought back to life once her bones were found? The young man who cracked open the chunk of concrete and revealed her skeleton and was shaken; he freed her soul from being encased in concrete."

"So you think that maybe her spirit and soul is working on us as a thank-you for freeing her?"

"I have no way of explaining the feelings I get around this house—especially here under the shed, in the courtyard. Your vision of me sashaying down the staircase with a champagne glass, being applauded by invited guests while violins play my favorite Italian song—I would have never done that. I'm too shy to flaunt myself in front of guests or family members. You freed me from myself. I have to watch myself out in public. If there is a staircase, I want to do a grand entrance. The magazine staff—I almost felt like stripping while descending the staircase. Good thing I had a glass in my hand, or they would have gotten a show they would have never forgotten. I would have been redder than a glass of red wine when finished. I may not have received applause either."

"Wow, Marie," said John, "I never knew you would do such a thing."

"Under normal circumstances, never would I have even thought of such a thing. It crossed my mind after the second step."

Delores said, "I hear you loud and clear. These grand entrances are compelling. I've dreamed of doing just that—entering through the arched gateway, hearing the applause. The last time, knowing my husband was shooting pictures, it almost became real. Thank goodness, you were in my vision, Marie, or off the clothes would go, arms flailing with the blouse, sliding off the britches and then the rest. I would more than likely have christened your circular planter. I'm certain my husband would have accommodated my desires."

"Ladies, you are making this rather difficult for me. I have envisioned your every word. They are truly inspiring. I hope you don't express that to the photographer or writer. This is a family magazine. Those stories would work wonders for the adult magazines. My dear, you will have to show me your dance tonight."

John told Marie, "Me too. You'll have to show me as well."

Papa told Mama, "Just whisper that into my ear."

"Well, tomorrow is a busy day," I said. "We have lots to complete, and the girls have school. My dearest darling has a job to finish. Can I borrow your camera?"

"Marie, don't you dare lend him your camera; I don't want you to see me like that."

John said, "I would like to see you like that."

Marie said, "I would make you blind if you saw her like that on my camera."

Marie and Delores gave each other hugs.

CHAPTER 41

The next morning, the plant material was waiting for us to show up at the job site. I started helping the driver to offload the plants when Juan and the rest of the crew arrived.'

Angel brought her friend Juanita, who jumped right in and started helping us offload the plants. I had Angel, Vincent, and Miguel retrieve the wheelbarrows from the backyard. "We will load the plants into the wheelbarrow and cart them into the backyard. That will work faster than carrying two five-gallon or six one-gallon shrubs."

I talked with Angel and Juanita and told them to set the plants into rows of like plants together by container sizes. "The guys will haul the plants. We have another empty wheelbarrow in the backyard to rotate to the hauler." One wheelbarrow was full, so Angel carted it to the backyard. Juanita found the empty wheelbarrow, so when Vincent brought his load, they gave him the empty one. This worked like a charm. Juan, the driver, and I loaded the wheelbarrows. Vincent and Miguel were the haulers. The girls set the plants per species and size of container in rows. I had used different-colored flags for the various species.

After the truck was unloaded, I gave Angel my list of plant species per flag color. All she and Juanita had to do was transport the right plant to the right color flag. I explained to Juan what I was having the girls do, and he thought that would work out fine. He told Vincent and Miguel to start digging the plant pits. Once that was done, the girls would start planting—production line style. After all the pits were dug, the guys would plant as well.

This was new for Juan and the crew; usually I put the plants where they belonged, and they just dug and planted as they moved through the planter. The girls were doing a wonderful job. Angel asked, "Is the flag marked in the center of each plant?"

"Yes, the flags are the center of each plant."

"That is so easy for us to follow."

To save on traffic over the bridges, Juanita would retrieve the plants per the flag colors and hand them to Angel. They created their own shuttle. Angel would tell her, "Three pink, four blue, and three white." Juanita would load them in a wheelbarrow and deliver them to Angel. That saved both girls a lot of unnecessary steps. The island was spotted, and they were working on the planter from the fountain to the gate. That went fast, and they jumped over the turf area to the planters along the house to the staircase.

By the first break, all the plants were spotted, the island was planted, and some of the pits were dug between the fountain and the gate. Marie came outside to see how the planting was doing, and of course, she brought her camera. She came over to me, embarrassed at first about what she had told all of us at dinner. I told her I was so pleased that she had been so comfortable to disclose what she was thinking while going down the staircase.

"You don't think badly of me for those thoughts?" she asked.

"If I did, then I would be a hypocrite."

"You thought about stripping while coming down the staircase?"

"No, Marie, much worse thoughts. Watching you every time coming down, thinking you were doing that for me—lustful thoughts ran through my mind."

"Really? Lustful thoughts watching me practice."

"I'm not proud of what I was thinking. I look at you now like a sister. I didn't want to disclose this to you ever. I hope I didn't lose your respect."

"No, you didn't lose my respect. Should I not do that in front of you anymore?"

"If you stopped, I'd be hurt. Don't ever stop being you. You're the one—and Delores, of course—that makes each and every day a complete joy. Please just be you. Do whatever you feel comfortable doing. It pleases me to see you so happy."

"You caused all this, you know. I'm not normally this way. You brought out all of this in me. At first my goal was to make your vision true to life. I noticed you were watching me, and that gave me a thrill—a warmness inside. I hope I didn't overdo it."

"No, Marie, you could do it all day long. It just gets better and better."

"If I get that urge again, would you stop me?"

"If it were just me and you, no; I would let you do what you wanted to do. If there were others about, yes, I would suggest that you not do that. It would not be worth what people would think, my dear friend."

"Will you tell Delores about our conversation?"

"No, Marie, this conversation never occurred. Deal?"

"Deal, we never talked—only about the landscape. Is that okay?"

"Better than okay. I love you as you are. Please feel free to talk to me about anything—I mean anything. Okay, Marie?"

"I can tell you anything?"

"Anything, anytime. I can be your sounding board, shoulder to cry on— whatever you need. I'm there for you and John—your entire family. Remember: I'm a landscaper by trade. If I can't help you with a certain problem, I will help you find someone who can professionally."

"What if I feel like doing something not appropriate in most people's eyes; would you feel badly about me?"

"I have no rules or regulations that you have to follow. If something needs to be discussed or you have an emotional need, you don't need to keep things hidden inside. They are better disclosed and dealt with to keep you as you are—no false facades."

Juan came to me and said, "There is a delivery truck that just pulled into the courtyard."

"That must be the low-voltage lighting system. We will need to get that material inside the courtyard and place the most expensive items in the tunnel. Leave enough space for the family to use the tunnel. That is the only place where we can lock the items."

Juan had Vincent and Miguel bring a wheelbarrow each to load the little boxes. Marie was very excited. "Can we have some lights put into the courtyard today?"

"I will start installing them with the help of one laborer."

"My parents will be so happy, as I am. Can I call Delores to come over and show her the yard?"

"Of course, this is your house. I want you to be as happy as possible."

CHAPTER 42

The driver gave me the shipping order, and I checked it off my purchase order, making certain we had everything. Juan asked, "Where are you going to start installing?"

"I need to light up the courtyard; make sure all the like fixtures are stacked together. I don't want to spend a lot of time searching for a certain light. I left my tracking tool at home, so once I have the lamps laid out, I'll go back home while the laborer trenches for the wire." I started laying out the pathway lights behind the retaining wall to give me time to get my tool. I laid out the raised planter next to the house and the circular planter. "There will be three uplights illuminating the multibranched olive. There are three pathway lights illuminating the circular planter."

The courtyard was laid out. I got Angel to dig the trenches. The trench was only four inches deep, and I wanted a hole dug at each fixture. I showed her what I needed. I told her I would be right back with my tool.

I arrived home, went to the garage, and found my tool. I put it in the truck and went inside the house to say hello to the missus. She was on the phone with Marie at the time. I walked over and gave her a kiss on the cheek. She told Marie that she would be at her house in less than an hour. "You sure you want me to wear shorts and a tank top?"

"We can start working on our tans."

"Okay, I'll drag out my summer clothes." She turned to me. "She wants to work on our tans today. Do you think that would be advisable with the crew?"

"The courtyard will only have Angel working. The rest of the crews will be planting the backyard. Not to risqué in the outfit, okay, dear? You know the effect they have on me. I have to head back to the job site. We're installing the lighting system in the courtyard."

"Oh, that's great news. The girls will be so excited to see the courtyard lit up from their balcony."

"Love you. Got to go now. See all of you soon."

"Settle down, tiger. I'll be fashionable, not alluring."

Back at the courtyard, I put the tester on one transformer lead-in wire to see which transformer would run which circuit. "Okay, the raised planter behind the patio cover—the one I wanted. Such luck. There are two separate wires for this transformer. The wall washers will be on one circuit, and the pathway lights on the other. The pathway and wall washers do the entire courtyard. You will be able to run one or the other or both at the same time—the marvel of LEDs. The uplights for the trees are on a separate transformer. All the trees will be hooked up to the one transformer."

I went to the backyard to see how the planting was coming along. They were nearly completed with the backyard plants. I told Juan and Diego to have the crew start removing the eight inches of soil for the pavers. "I will call for the road base to be delivered this afternoon with the sand. Do you still have the paver edging?"

"I have some in my truck. I'll lay it out and see if I need more. I'll let you know right away."

"Thanks, Juan. Great job on the planting."

Mama and Papa were out on the patio table, enjoying their morning coffee and breakfast roll. Mama said, "The plants are beautiful. Would you mind if we moved over to the bench?"

"Of course not. Feel free to enjoy the area. We're finished planning over there. When you are leaving the area, let Juan know so he can run the irrigation system."

Mama and Papa crossed the bridge and went to the bench under the shade of the tree. Marie came out in her shorts and top, crossed the bridge, and joined her parents, all with their coffee and roll, watching the fountain and stream. That shot would be worth a thousand words—all of them enjoying the outdoors. "Back to the job at hand—lighting. Stay focused, and all will work out well or as planned."

I showed Angel how to hook up the wire for the fixture. "These are wired in series, so light one ties into light two, which ties into light three, and so on and so forth. Each light gets two wire nuts." I showed her how to wire each light. "We have to connect to the wires leading to the circular planter and the other raised planters. I will find those wires while you wire up the lights in this planter. We installed conduits to each planter before the walls were constructed. We also put the wire into the conduit."

As I was locating the conduits, the arched gate opened, and in came my lovely vision dressed very fashionably with bracelets and necklace. She even had on an ankle bracelet. Angel told her she looked stunning and applauded her entrance. Delores went over and gave her a huge hug. Angel said, "I hope I didn't get dirt on you. So sorry if I did." Delores turned around so Angel could see if she had dirt on her outfit. "Nope, no dirt this time. Thank you for the hug. It made my day."

Marie was standing at the staircase landing. "My dearest friend has arrived." She sashayed down the staircase, making sure everyone was watching her every move. She got to the bottom step and opened her arms to receive Delores—another photo opportunity lost to the masses, but one that would remain in my memory for life.

I found the wire and returned to where Angel was putting the lights together. I cut into the wire she was using and spliced in the wire heading over to the circular planter. Angel only had three more lights to wire. I headed over to the raised planters against the house. I found the conduits and wires and wired them together from the circular planter—planter on the left first and then the one next to the staircase. I hooked the tester back to the transformer and tested the entire circuit. I didn't want to mix the pathway lights with the wall washers or the uplights for the tree; that would be disastrous.

Marie had gotten Delores a cup of coffee and a roll while they watched the lighting being installed. They both were sitting under the olive tree on the seat wall—another photo opportunity missed for the masses. Angel had finished the three lights in the raised planter and started wiring the lights in the circular planter. Marie gave her a hug and said, "You do that wiring so nicely. Have you done it long?"

"Less than an hour so far. Just learning how to do wiring ... a little nervous."

"You'll do fine. You have a great teacher. He won't let you fail."

She chatted with the ladies for a few minutes while wiring the lights and then moved to the planter on the left. She wired those pathway lights and moved to the staircase planter. She called me over to where she was working and said, "This is my last light. I just end the wiring cable at this light?"

"That is correct. How did you do the ends of the other planters?"

"Just like this one, but if they were wrong, I would watch you fix one and I would fix the others."

"Now I'm going to put power to the wire, and you will take a bulb and put one in each light." We went back to the first pathway light; the power was turned on, and I showed her how to remove the pathway top and install the bulb.

I asked the ladies to come and watch so if a bulb needed replacing, they would know how to fix it themselves. "Better than calling a company to run out and charge you way more than the bulb would cost—and, of course, a minimum service fee." I had Marie watch me as I removed the top with a counterclockwise twist, and I showed her how to put in the bulb. I had her do it at least five times to make sure she could do it without fear. Even my dearest darling removed and replaced bulbs. "Now remember: this is only one type of fixture. You have five different types of fixtures. Every one is a little different. You ladies are smart, so I won't test you on Friday, but I could spring a pop quiz on you at any time."

The pathway lights were near completion. We could start the wall washers now or take an early lunch. I asked Angel if she was getting hungry. "Yes, I could eat, but do the others want to stop early?"

"I'll find out. Be right back." I talked with Juan and all the crews, and they said they would be okay with an early lunch. The hard part was nearly completed.

Juan asked if I could get them a rototiller to remove the eight inches of soil. I replied, "I'll get it while everyone is at lunch. I'll bring my trailer for you to put the dirt in. I called the masonry supplier, and they are due to deliver the base and sand by one o'clock. I'll get a vibratory plate as well as the rototiller."

The ladies were getting a good dose of sun, turning a little pink. I told them the crew were preparing to take a lunch. "Just letting you know."

Marie said, "You don't like sharing us, do you?"

"Of course not. You babes are mine."

"Oh, really, we're now your babes?" said Delores.

"You have always been my babe. Marie has joined you."

"Is that all right with you, Marie? You're now one of his babes?"

"I'm flattered that he would want me to be a babe, and being one with you—that is perfect."

"Okay, we babes are going to get lunch ourselves—on your credit card, I might add. You don't want your babes to starve, do you?"

"I don't ever want to see you ladies lose your teenage figures. We'd better get ready to leave. It's getting awfully deep in the courtyard." I offered them a hand, and they stood up. "Turn around." They did.

"Why did you want us to turn around?"

"You were sitting on the wall cap. Just made sure you didn't have dirt on your shorts. You must remain perfect. You have an image to maintain."

"You didn't just want to look at our behinds in a manly way?" said Marie. "You were worried that we sat in some dirt?"

"Maybe a little of both, but you're both good to go."

Marie looked over her shoulder and said, "Not that—not now, silly boy."

I left to get my trailer and then went to the rental yard. I returned with the trailer, rototiller, and vibratory plate just in time to see the masonry truck turning the corner for the delivery. Juan forgot to tell me if he had enough paver edging; if not, I would leave to pick some up. They were almost finished with lunch, and I told Angel and Juanita that they would install the lights in the courtyard. I would show them how to wire each light. "These are more difficult than the pathway lights."

I asked Juanita if she liked doing landscaping. She said, "Yes, it's much nicer than standing at a burger place, putting in orders."

"You might be a little sore tonight and tomorrow. You're using muscles that burger employees rarely use."

She said, "My muscles need some tightening—getting a little flabby."

"Well, if you are working on something and it's too heavy, the guys will help you. Right, guys?"

"That's right. We love to help, said Manuel."

"Did she do okay this morning?" I asked.

"She did great. Never asked for help. Dug the holes, and we taught her how to plant. She did really good. She even got dirt under her fingernails, said Juan."

"Well, welcome aboard. The guys all just voted for you to become one of the team. Ask Angel how to become one of the ladies. She got invited by them a couple of weeks ago."

Angel told her, "I will introduce you to Marie and Delores. They are so much fun to be around."

I asked Juan if he had enough paver edging. "Sorry, boss; I totally forgot. I'll go right now and check my truck."

"Do you have enough nails as well?"

"I'm tying a string around my finger today to remind me to think."

The ladies took Mama and Papa to lunch with them, so it wouldn't be McDonald's drive-through; they would leave me a couple of dollars on my card. I got the parts for the wall washers and a screwdriver from my truck for the face plates. Angel had wire cutters; she'd teach Juanita how to install the fixtures. I'd ask if she had enough wire nuts as well.

I pulled out the installation instructions for the wall washers, and I had both girls read the instructions. "Look at the diagrams showing a pictorial of what it will look like once installed. I'll show you how to do one, and then you show me how to do one."

In about ten minutes, the girls were ready to learn. I located the wire to be used from the transformer to the first raised planter behind the patio cover. I found the other wire in the circular planter and tracked it back to the raised planter behind the patio cover. I tracked the wire from one side to the other side of the circular planter and found the wire in the raised planters next to the house. I had connected all the wires, so we now had a constant run from the transformer to every planter. We had to find the wire from the wall washer to the trench that connected to the transformer. Being careful not to cut the wire with a shovel, the girls dug holes behind each wall washer. The dirt was soft and easy to dig; we backfilled behind the wall but did not compact.

Once all the wiring was completed, I would have Angel flood-irrigate the trench behind the wall. I showed them one wall washer installation. The girls started on the next wall washer, and I watched them like they watched me. They did quite well and didn't cut the wire too short. The wire nuts were nice and tight, and the ground wire was in place. "Good job." I powered up the wire so that as they completed the hookup, the light was shining.

The rototiller was running and loosening up the top four inches for removal. The rototiller saved a lot of back work and allowed more soil to be removed in a shorter time frame. Vincent was hand-watering each plant installed, to ensure there were no cavities. I told Vincent to continue to water even the courtyard plants and the front yard. "Make sure all the air pockets are out from the plant pit."

I went back to the courtyard, and the family returned from their luncheon. "Did I get any leftovers?" I asked.

"Sorry, Charlie, lunch was way too good to waste it on a dirt boy."

"One can lose a title in just a few minutes around here. Thank you for thinking about me. Love you all."

Delores, Mama, and Papa went into the house via the tunnel. Marie was looking at the lighting, pathway, and wall washers as they were being installed. "This looks really nice."

"Wait until dusk. As it gets darker, you'll get the true effect of the low-voltage lighting system."

She said, "You'll be here for dinner and show us how all this works, correct?"

"I wouldn't miss a burnt offering from John's barbecue and a chance to dine with all of you."

"Can we talk when your crew leaves to head home?"

"Of course, from our conversation earlier?"

"A little and then some."

"Sure, I'd be more than happy to accommodate your wishes. I'm all yours whenever you have the urge."

As she walked away, she looked over her shoulder and smiled.

I went back to see Juan, and he said, "I have enough edging and nails." The excavation was nearly completed, and they would start putting in the base and sand layer as soon as they reached the eight inches and compacted the subgrade. The vibratory plate was humming, firming up the bottom of the excavation. The first wheelbarrow of base was dumped, and they started to spread. Here came the next wheelbarrow, dumped and spread, followed by another load. This was going quite well.

Juan put the vibratory plate atop the base and started compacting the base layer. Another wheelbarrow of base was dumped and spread, and then another and another. Manuel was directing where each wheelbarrow of base was to be dumped. It took a little over an hour for the base layer. Next would be the sand, and then the pavers—border pavers first. I said to Juan, "Make sure you do it in front of the bridges—six-inch rise only." We had moved some pavers from the front yard and courtyard while the fountain was being built. The border was connected from bridge to bridge and from the bridge to the patio. They laid some field pavers in front of the first bridge about halfway toward the patio. It was time to pack up the trucks and head home.

Marie came out and took photos of the new pavers connecting the bridges all the way to her staircase. She still had on her shorts and tank top that she had worn earlier; it was cooling down a few degrees. She did get some sun; it might sting in her shower tomorrow morning. *When I get too much sun, I get chilled easily. I'll ask her.* "You got some sun today. If you get too much, do you get the chills?"

"Oh yes, I'll put on a sweatshirt or sweater in a little while. Still fairly warm outside."

I went down the staircase to check on the lighting progress. They were on the last wall washer; I had wired the three up lights while they were installing the wall washers. Angel stated that they now had the hang of installing the wall washers. She admitted that the first two looked different from the one they were finishing now. "As long as they are lit and the face plates are attached. There's a little difference between just learning and gaining confidence; your work has to improve. I hope it doesn't digress."

The girls were putting the extra parts into a box and readying to put the box into the tunnel for the evening. I said to them, "Just leave it. I will put it away. Great job, girls. See you tomorrow morning. Have a great evening."

Marie gave me a private grand entrance once the coast was clear. "What do you think of my entrance to your courtyard?"

"Very nice. You have gotten so much better and very seductive."

"Do you want me to do it again?"

"Do you want to do it again?"

She turned around and started it again. "Is this better?"

"You're getting me pretty nervous. You keep that up, and you'll have my attention."

When she reached the bottom step, she said, "Follow me."

I followed her, and she went into the tunnel. She turned around once I was inside the tunnel. She walked up to me and planted a wonderful kiss on me. I was speechless, and she said, "You said I could tell you anything at any time."

"Yes, I did say that to you, and I still mean it now."

"I wanted to personally thank you for all you have done for me. I have never felt this way before. I don't want you to think poorly of me or think bad things about me, but you've been so good and kind. I just want you to know I'm very appreciative."

"Can I tell you something?"

"Yes, you can tell me anything at any time. Like you offered to me, I think likewise."

"I'm glad you did that. It took a lot of tension off me. I've told myself, 'You have too much to lose if you think those thoughts. She may not feel the same, and you could lose her as a friend. Both families could hate you.' So much I was thinking"

She put her arms around my neck, looked up, and said, "Your turn to return the favor." We kissed a second time.

I told her, "We have to stop this, or I won't be able to stop myself."

She kept her arms around my neck and said. "You can have *that* when you want."

"Same here, silly girl."

"Are you all right?"

"Of course not. Our lives will never be the same. We need to stay discreet and not show anything other than our normal selves. Agreed?"

"Agreed."

"Everyone should be arriving at any minute. I need to regain my composure before my dearest darling spots my appreciation."

"I did that to you?"

"That wasn't the first time."

"You should have told me earlier."

"You, your family, and my family mean too much to me to destroy them. What we have going for the families many never achieve. I don't want to bring hardships between us or them. I hope you know how much you and yours means to me. It's not just 'Hi, how are you?' but also deep, heartfelt love. If someone tried to harm any of you, it would hurt as much if someone tried to harm my family. Do you know what I mean?"

"I believe so. You have a deep love for me and my family; we are much more than just friends."

"Yes, much more than just friends."

"Did I offend you? If I did, I'm sorry."

"Do me a favor."

"What is it you want?"

"Do your grand entrance like you just did for me."

"Really? You mean it?"

"As you descend, watch me."

"I always watch you."

"No, watch me—you know."

"Oh, I get it now."

"Okay, here I go." She put so much into her grand entrance—poise, beautiful smile, grace, glamour—that it was one of the best she ever did. She got to the bottom step and whispered in my ear, "What if Delores sees you?"

"I'll tell her I saw a hummingbird."

She hugged me and said, "I'll do that for you anytime."

Dinner was delicious, and company was top notch. Mama and Papa were the invited guests. It was nearing dusk, and I had set the timers to come on in about a half hour. The girls set up some chairs on their balcony—not a patio, but a balcony. Mama and Papa brought them flowers and some candy—their favorite, of course. We were on our second beverage—mostly alcohol with some coloring mix. Delores was making her all-time favorite, margaritas with salt on the rim, with a blender, like a smoothie. Marie was in the kitchen, helping Delores; both were still in their shorts and tank tops. To my surprise, it was getting chilly, and they both had slight sunburns.

Marie told Delores that she was her best friend and loved having her and the girls over. She asked Delores if they could become sisters, closer than just friends. Delores turned, looked at Marie, and gave her a big sister a hug. "I'd love to be your sister, much closer than just friends." Marie asked her if she was getting chills. "Yes, it's starting to cool down."

"I'll be right back." She ran upstairs and brought down two sweatshirts. "Pink or yellow?"

"Yellow, unless you prefer the yellow one."

"I just grabbed two off the hangers. Let's see what color you look the best. I think the pink one makes you look hot."

"What does the yellow one does for me?"

"Not as—a little too bulky on you. Here, I'll show you how to get the most out of clothes. Put on the pink one." Marie zipped up the sweatshirt to just below the bustline, laid it open at the top, and slid it off her shoulder just a touch. She stood back and got her camera. *Click, click, click!* With each click, Delores posed a little differently, playing along. Marie then showed Delores the photos.

"Oh my, I do look hot. How are you going to wear the yellow one?"

Marie said, "Zip me up. I will tell you when." She stopped about two inches below the height Marie had zipped up Delores.

"Wow, that looks fantastic."

They took the drinks to the family sitting at the patio table—two for Mama and Papa. As the ladies came through the tunnel door, the lights all came on. "It looks so pretty. John, look at our house. I don't ever want to leave. The shadows—oh, I have to get my camera." She handed the plateful of margaritas to John, ran into the tunnel, grabbed her camera, and ran back through the tunnel. *Click, click, click, click!*

Then Delores did one of her seductive poses, and five clicks later, Marie's finger was getting tired and needed a break. The girls asked, "Everyone, come up here and see our beautiful garden."

"Very pretty. Daddy, when are we going to get ours, asked Sarah?"

Everyone was down on the pavers, and we all had glasses of margaritas; the little girls had nonalcoholic ones. Papa gave the toast. "To the new courtyard."

Everyone said, "Cheers."

There is not enough money on this planet that could compare to the event that had just happened. The ladies, little girls, and us guys were all teared up. Papa was saying to our girls, "Papa will talk to your daddy about your playhouse. You girls get that ceiling painted this weekend with Mama, your mama, and my granddaughters' mama. I want to know if I can be your grandpa too."

"Really? You want to be our grandpa too? Mommy, can Papa be our papa too, asked Sarah?"

"Well, I'd have to say yes, he can be your papa too. Is that all right with Leslie and Kim—sharing your papa and mama?"

Leslie and Kim both screamed, "Yes, that makes us sisters!"

John pulled his wallet out of his pocket, opened it up to where he kept his money, and said, "I'm going to have to get a second job—two more girls."

Marie said, "Not just two, honey. I asked Delores to be my sister just a few minutes ago."

That brought all four girls to Delores. "You're going to be our mommy too, asked Leslie?" Then they all ran over to Marie and said, "Mommy, all together."

Papa came over to me and said, "Since my daughter and your wife are now sisters, that makes you my son-in-law. You can call me Dad from now on. My wife is now your mom."

"We need another margarita, girls." I said.

"Coming right up, Dad."

Marie and Delores were walking arm in arm into the tunnel; they got to the kitchen and hugged. "This is totally unbelievable, Marie."

"You know, I could never have found anyone like you by hanging out with the girls that I used to hang out with. You're real, you're kind, you're fun to be around, you have a great personality, your girls are a godsend, and you're a godsend for me."

Delores said, "What you just said, I say double back to you. If you were my sister, I would kiss you—a sister's kiss, not like husband-and-wife kiss. Give me your lips, sister." They gave each other a kiss and started making the margaritas for the thirsty family.

"So what do you want to do tomorrow?"

"Not sure about getting more sun, but if we're so inclined, maybe an hour and then cover up and do that for a month or so, and we will have killer tans. We'll do some shopping and find out what Mama and Papa want to do. Does that sound like a well-planned day?"

"Let's play it by ear. Call me so we dress similar, like today. I thought that was so much fun how you told me what to wear. I didn't want to be in shorts and you not in shorts, and I love you in a tank top—stunning to say the least. You put me to shame. Your outfits match your personality—fit your form like they are tailor made. You just have a glow about you that I have never seen before."

"Can I be perfectly honest with you?"

"Of course, Marie. We're sisters now."

"Before we met your husband, my life was mundane—boring. I actually looked forward to taking the girls to and from school as the highlight of my day. I rarely put on makeup, styled my hair, put on nice clothes, and I never, ever made my husband the number-one priority in my life. I would yell at the girls to do their homework and clean up their room. I would buy preheat and serve meals.

That was me. Your husband awakened something in me that I never want to lose. I hated me as I used to be.

"You're seeing a woman who is a real down-to-earth woman. I love to make my husband glad to be home. I hug and kiss him every night when he walks through the door. My daughters—I have not yelled at them in two months. They do their homework and keep their rooms spotless. Have you seen the playhouse? No dust, no mess, everything is put away, not just thrown into a drawer. They have so much pride in their playhouse. A playhouse—how does a simple playhouse make all this happen? I have narrowed it down. My attitude changed, and that changed everyone else's attitudes for the better. You came along and filled a huge void that I never knew I had. I miss not seeing you each and every day. You alone have saved me tons of money on therapy. How has your life changed?"

"Pretty much the same as yours. I have a desire to please my husband and girls. They, in return, reward me tenfold for what I do for them. You, my dearest sister, friend, companion—whatever title you want—I can't tell you in words how I feel when I'm around you. You're such a special person, more than one in a million. Words just aren't enough to express the thanks my heart feels when we're together. Oh, by the way, what were we supposed to be doing?"

"Making margaritas before everyone goes to sleep. They'll appreciate them more since I'm sure their glasses are now empty."

The ladies put their arms around each other and held each other tight. They looked at each other and said, "I really, truly love you." Both had tears of joy running down their cheeks.

"Our makeup will be a mess now."

"You look beautiful without makeup anyway."

The drinks were all made, and the ladies proceeded to the courtyard. Papa raised his glass once more, stating, "To the best family a man could ask for. Thank you, God, for everyone you blessed me and Sophia with as a family." Everyone gave Papa a hug.

The girls took their drinks up to their house, came out on the balcony, and said, "Love you, Moms and Dads."

The drive home was astonishing. Delores told me what she and Marie had talked about while making the margaritas. She had tears in her eyes, saying, "She is such a great person. Now she's my sister. Doesn't get any better than that. Oh, by the way, *that* is on for tonight."

"Boy, that was the best *that* we have ever done before," I said.

She said, "*That* was wonderful. See you in the morning for a repeat."

The next morning, the crew was a little tardy but full of energy. I laid out the lighting for the girls. The pavers were being installed at a fast pace, and teamwork was in full swing. I turned on the irrigation system in the courtyard and then the front yard. We hand-watered the backyard planters so as not to wet the paving area.

I was watching the crew when I felt her hand touch my shoulder. "Good morning"

"Good morning. You ready to see some lights back here this evening?"

"Really? You're going to light up my life tonight?"

"Yes, Marie, you'll be glowing with glitz and glamour. Do you have an outfit for this occasion?"

"You're going to light up my life. That will take a special outfit. What do you think would be a perfect outfit?"

"A color that matches your eyes and smile, a little free flowing in case there is a breeze so it moves with you, a little sparkle so my lights shimmer off of you, maybe jewelry to enhance your glow. Do you have an outfit like that?"

"I will by this afternoon. I will deck out my new sister for you as well with the same specifications."

"You could have on formfitting pants and free-flowing top."

"That might be doable. I have to check with sister for her opinion, but I will surely fulfill your desires. You'd better make this place feel the same as the courtyard, or I'm going upstairs and putting on overalls and a flannel shirt."

"Oh, you make things very tough on me, but it's so worth the energy. Let's take a stroll to the bench. Ladies first, my dear. I love watching you cross the bridge. You always pause and look at the waterfall and stream. Your eyes light up in awe." I assisted her to the bench.

"Why are we here?" asked Marie. "You're not going to propose to me, are you?"

"No, I want you to enjoy this area as much as you enjoy the courtyard. Sit back and relax, watch the water splash from stone to stone, and follow the water between the stones and watch it fall into the stream and scurry past to be returned to the waterfall. If you have nice Italian music, play it softly in the background, with maybe a hummingbird or butterfly cruising by. Look up into the tree and see what the sunlight does to the leaves, shimmering and different on each leaf. Do you see what I'm trying to do for you?"

"You're getting me stirred up inside, making me feel like I did when I was showing you my grand entrance."

"Now you're getting what this entire project should do and does for you."

"So you're saying that if I come out here and relax, I will have the same feeling as I do when I perform my grand entrance?"

"You have the same results for me."

"I don't want to look, but are you telling me you're in the same mood?" The hummingbird passed by. "Should we leave or hang here for a couple of more minutes?"

"I will follow your lead. Whatever you want to do is fine with me."

"I want that hummingbird to stick around."

"Well, I have work to finish, so we can have another celebration, lighting you up with joy and happiness."

The girls were putting in the pathway lights; they should be done in another hour. I walked with Marie to the staircase, and she said, "You go down first and watch."

"Can we go to the tunnel afterward?"

"No, not today, too many people, and you need to settle down. Delores is due any minute, and I have to change into my other outfit so she and I look similar." She did and extraordinary grand entrance. "I see you really liked that one."

"You did that flawlessly."

Delores walked through the arched gateway, being so seductive. Thank goodness for that. She noticed right away the effect she was having. She walked past me, turned her head over her shoulder, and said, "Dream on, lover. Dream on." She and Marie were hugging and laughing at me, not with me this time.

"That is so good for my ego. I deserved every bit of that, I might add."

Marie was telling Delores the outfits I wanted them to be in for tonight's lighting of the backyard festivities. Delores said, "I don't have an outfit like what he described."

"Neither do I, so let's get Mama and Papa ready. We'll have breakfast and then find those two outfits."

"What do you think about formfitting pants?" I asked.

"Dream on, lover. Dream on. We'll buy what we like. He can have that fantasy on another project. We're too much of ladies to allow that to happen on our watch."

"You know him quite well, don't you?"

"You have to be on your toes all the time. He'll try to pull a fast one on you. I love him. I know he loves me, but he has these visions that he tries to make reality rather than waiting for them to actually happen on their own. You know what I mean?"

"I do know what you mean, but that is how we all got to where we are today. I don't think you would have loved the old me before the vision. I think we were pretty close to being the same. I was not a lovey-dovey wife. 'Yes, dear. Whatever you say, dear.' He ate a lot of crow and spent many a night sleeping on the couch. I loved my space. He would bother me in my space. Now I want him to bother me in my space."

"Let's find a couple of outfits that drive him crazy."

"You want to drive him crazy?"

"There's a much easier way than fulfilling his fantasy. I'll tell you about it after breakfast."

"Deal. I'm ready to learn from my sister."

The lights were nearly finished, the pavers would be completed by quitting time, all the plants were installed and watered for the second time, the controller was set and would come on in the morning, and all the lights should be completed by quitting time. All that would be left to complete was the mulch, and I wanted to do that a week before the party. We had to visit the mulch company and select one that they would like to see in the planters. Maybe Marie and John would like to take a ride tomorrow morning to visit the mulch company.

Everyone came out to take one last peek at the landscape. "We'll be back after we pick up the girls from school, said Marie."

"Have a great breakfast, lunch, and shopping spree. Love you, I said."

"Love you as well," said Delores. "See you later. Angel, who is the girl working with you?"

"I am so sorry. I was going to introduce you to Juanita yesterday, but we got so focused on finishing the lights for you to see. Delores, this is my best friend, Juanita. We have known each other since elementary school."

"Very nice meeting you, Juanita. If my husband pushes you too hard, you let me know, and he'll be a good boy from that time forward. We will have to see how you do with a grand entrance. Angel will fill you in on what is involved." Delores moved Juanita's hair up off her shoulders. "We can make you into a debutant. You have good lines. You'll do well. Angel, show her the ropes. And when we return, you can show us what you learned. Have a great day, girls. See you in a little while. Bye, boys. Don't work too hard. Looks very nice. Great job." Now she had the whole crew stirring.

We tested the lights, and they all worked perfectly. I had to position the downlight, but that one would have to wait until dusk to get the perfect angle. There were even a couple of wall lights on the retaining wall that needed lightbulbs. "Girls, you did a fantastic job with the lights. You will become our lighting specialists."

The guys were putting in the last of the pavers and setting up the paving sand on top to fill the gaps between the pavers. I took a tour of the entire project, picking up any odds and ends. I removed everything from the tunnel. The girls could clog again tonight. The job looked really good.

I called Phillip and told him, "The job is ready for another shooting. Can they return before Marie's parents leave?" I told him the date of the flight.

He said he would call his friend, the editor. "I'll let him know we are ahead of schedule and you're ready. How about your playhouse and patio cover? Are you ready to get that going forward?"

"I think in a couple of weeks or maybe next week, we can get it moving forward. What is your schedule?"

"We have a project scheduled to start in two weeks, so if we could get the bulk of the playhouse patio cover started, then Raymond and one other carpenter can put the finishing touches while the rest of the crew can start the other project."

"I'll call you tomorrow with a start time. I have to talk to Delores regarding the finances."

Everyone returned from their outing. Delores came to Angel and Juanita and asked, "Well, girls, are you ready to do the grand entrance?"

"I hope so. We practiced it at lunch break."

"I'll tell Marie and Mama to join us at the staircase landing."

Marie and Mama came out from the kitchen, and they had not met Juanita, so Angel introduced her to them. They proceeded to the staircase. They told Angel and Juanita, "Go down to the pavers and have Juanita watch what we do."

Mama went first, so graceful and poised, with flawless movements and a great smile. Juanita said, "That was really good. Angel, are these ladies professional models?"

"Nope. you'll get a lesson on being as good as they are in time."

Delores was next—so gracious, poised beyond belief, seductive in her movements, smiling like "You can't touch this, boys." Juanita said to Angel, "Will they laugh at me?"

"Nope. We all started like you will start."

Marie, oh Marie, was such a glamorous lady—styled to perfection, poised, and very seductive. With each step, she got better and better. Juanita told Angel, "I could never be as good as she is."

Angel climbed the stairs, turned, and sashayed, poised with glamorous movements. She had really improved since her first time. "Okay, Juanita, your time to shine."

She walked up the staircase and turned like Angel just had. "Wait a minute," said Delores, and she climbed up the staircase. "Marie, do you have something we can pull her hair up with?"

"I do. Let me get something, and I'll be right back. This will give me another opportunity to do a grand entrance."

Delores and Marie pulled up Juanita's hair and styled it quickly. Delores told her to unbutton her shirt's top button. Delores said, "I'll bet you have nice legs, like Angel's, from working in construction. Okay, now show us your strut."

"I'm so nervous. I want to do it like you do, but I've never done anything like this before."

"Neither did any of us, and we were just as nervous as you are now. Go ahead; you can do it. We have faith in your ability."

She started like Angel had taught her during lunch, and Angel was coaching her on every step. Juanita did very well for her first time in front of strangers. Just a few tweaks with practice, and she'd be one of the ladies. As she stepped onto the pavers, all the ladies gave her the applause she needed. They were full of compliments for her and welcomed her to their ladies' club.

Delores went to the arched gateway to show her how to enter through the gate. Delores was now a pro at this entry point. Juanita asked, "Do I have to do that entry as well?"

"Watch Delores," said Angel. "If you want to attempt her moves, let us know, and we will have you practice."

Delores came through the gate and did the best she had ever done. Juanita said, "No way could I even get close to what she just did. Can any of you do what she just did?"

Angel said, "No, she is the best we have ever seen." The other ladies all nodded in agreement.

The day had ended for the crew, and the girls were up in the playhouse. John was standing, watching over his barbecue. The ladies headed into the house to prepare the salads. Tonight they cheated some, as they had store-bought salads: macaroni salad instead of potato, ambrosia, crab salad, and three-bean salad. Of course, barbecue baked beans would make whatever meat John cooked up that much better. Delores and Marie were waiting to change just after dinner so they would not get food on their new outfits. They wanted the full effect of the surprise.

Dinner again was fabulous. I don't know how John could burn the hot dogs to perfection. The little girls were craving his hot dogs. If they kept up that craving, every man they would go out with would thank his maker. We had potato chips for a side dish, though not many were chowing down on them. The ladies had made margaritas again for everyone; a little tequila would go a long way.

Dinner was completed about a half hour before dusk. Delores and Marie excused themselves and headed upstairs to the bedroom to put on their new outfits. Marie had won the outfitting of the ladies; they had gone for the ultimate fantasy attire. The ladies removed their going-around-town outfits and put on as close as they could find to the outfit I had described to Marie. The reason Delores had agreed with Marie was that she wanted to see the look on my face as Marie came through the sliding glass door. They closed the blinds so I could not see them approaching; they had John poised to say, "Come on, Marie; it's almost dusk. What is taking you so long?" John was all for what the girls wanted him to do. He, of course, would reap the benefits of what the ladies chose to wear.

The ladies were ready. They were above stunning, and they knew they looked unbelievable. They both had champagne in glasses waiting for them by John. The stage was set. John made his entrance plea. The sliding glass door opened very slowly, and out stepped Marie. Delores was a couple of steps behind her. Both John's jaw and mine dropped in amazement. The ladies were absolutely gorgeous, stunning, and glamorous. There were not enough words to describe their outfits. "Well, what do you think of our outfits?" Marie asked.

John and I were speechless; if I said anything, it was incoherent.

They sashayed across the bridge, stopped, and showed their forms for us onlookers to admire. They continued to the bench, waiting for the light show begin.

"What if the backyard has more ambiance than the courtyard? Then what?" said Marie.

I went to the downlight using a ladder and adjusted it per the ladies' request. Their blouses were breezy enough to see more than I could bear. They both turned to me, and Delores said, "You haven't said if you like our outfits."

"They're way beyond perfect. You both look beautiful."

Marie said softly, "Did we get a hummingbird?"

Delores looked at me and whispered to Marie, "He has a flock."

Marie saw what Delores was talking about, and they both said, "We did it."

Everyone wanted to see the courtyard and the backyard from the staircase. Good thing it was getting darker; the view from the staircase into the courtyard was breathtakingly beautiful. Marie said to me, "You go down ahead of Delores and me, and we will give you our best grand entrance."

As Delores sashayed down the staircase, glamorous, seductive, and sensual, I almost lost total control. Then came Marie; with each step she took, I saw her in what she had described in her photo shoot episode. I was totally speechless by the time the two of them were on the pavers. Everyone—even the girls, from the balcony—was applauding the mommies. Delores came up to me and whispered to me, "How did we do?"

"Beyond any vision that I could ever dream of. Breathtakingly beautiful. I love you."

"Another round of margaritas for the ladies' floor show," said Mama. Both areas looked beautiful, and the ambiance could not be matched. The ladies had made this project such a joy to build, and the rewards were endless.

CHAPTER 43

After the bones were discovered in the concrete, Delores—liking to solve anything that didn't make sense—decided to go to the public library and research the family who had owned the farm. This was no daunting task; once she found a newspaper article about the family, the death of the great-grandfather opened many other articles. The great-grandfather was a very successful farmer. He was always following the commodities market and would grow crops that most farmers in the area were not growing. This kept the price of his crops profitable. From his profits, he purchased more land adjacent to the property he already owned—more acres, more crops, more money into his bank account. This went on for many years. He would purchase used equipment, avoiding the monthly draw from his accounts. He would also go to auctions and buy items the farm needed.

Great-Grandfather became ill, which caused his death. Great-Grandmother was devastated by the loss of her husband. She knew next to nothing about the farming business; she was a homemaker and very proud of it. The family went to church every Sunday and participated in all the functions—bake sales, white elephant sales, rummage sales, picnics in the park, and family reunions, where most of the church members were invited. They even had a fall harvest festival at the farm and invited the entire town for hayrides for the families and pumpkins galore at a very reasonable price. The whole town talked about the festival even during the heat of the summer, looking forward to the apple cider and homemade goodies. The ladies would bring their crafts, quilts, clothing, and artworks; many of the items were better made than store-bought items. There was something to do for the entire family. It was a weekend event, so the festival never closed.

This all came to a screeching halt when Great-Grandfather passed away. The kids and Mama had no desire to put on such an event. The farm was turning into a huge weed patch. The boys hated farming and wanted to have a job in the city; they left the farm for their dream jobs. Great-Grandfather had had to hire farmhands to replace the boys, and the daughters were all getting married and also moved away from the farm. Great-Grandfather offered all the kids a plot of land on which to build their home and raise a family. Not one of the kids took up the offer.

There was one daughter, and her husband and she were killed in an automobile accident, leaving their two children orphans. Great-Grandfather had offered his home to raise the great-grandchildren. The rest of the children raised a stink and said that would be unfair to the other grandchildren and great-grandchildren. One grandchild actually filed a lawsuit to prohibit them from having the great-grandchildren. This was putting unneeded stress on the aging couple. Great-Grandfather had stopped being involved with any of the family members; he was deeply hurt by their actions.

The newspaper article stated that this drama alone had caused Great-Grandfather to pass away. With the farm in disarray, a developer came to the house and talked Great-Grandmother into selling him part of the land that was owned by the farm. This gave Great-Grandmother enough money to keep the household running. None of the kids were aware of the fact that their mother had no source of income; nor did this much matter to them. The developer-built homes on the land he purchased were nice. Great-Grandmother could see the rooftops, but the homes were quite a distance away from the farmhouse.

As years passed, the orphaned great-grandchildren became teenagers, and their foster parents were very ill, and one was put in a nursing home. That put stress on the other parent; they asked the foster care agency to place the children into another home or give them back to the family. By this time, the family was not as involved in the farm, so the great-grandchildren moved in with Great-Grandmother. There was no fuss from the rest of the children and grandchildren, and no court orders prohibited them moving into the farmhouse. The state did pay support for the upkeep of the children until they became legal adults.

The support was nice to receive, but raising two teenagers was a burden on Great-Grandmother's bank account. The developer returned, met again with Great-Grandmother, and purchased about the same number of acres as he had purchased prior. Great-Grandmother had an attorney from church look over the paperwork to make sure everything was legal and fair. "It all appears to be fair and legal. You can sign if you want to proceed."

She now had enough money to raise the two teenagers. There were no frills, mind you; just meals, clothing, utilities, and basic living expenses were covered until they were eighteen. Great-Grandmother found it nice to have family living with her again, and it did bring family to the home for the holidays, which had not occurred since her husband's death.

Once the kids turned eighteen, they did not want to leave the nest, and Great-Grandmother was not in the greatest of health. The great-granddaughter, who was two years younger than her brother, was given the task of caring for her great-grandmother. It wasn't as bad as many others who cared for their aging parents or grandparents had it, but it did put a damper on her social life. Her brother was of no help; he worked a job, and that was plenty for him. He had no energy to give the sister a break.

The sister finally turned eighteen; all funds from the state stopped, and she, too, did not want to leave the nest. They hired a caretaker to help with their great-grandmother's care. These kids were handed everything and were never taught to be self-sufficient. This put a huge burden on Great-Grandmother's bank account.

Great-Grandmother, a couple of years prior, had met with the pastor of her church and her attorney, whom she had become friends with since her husband's death. She arranged for the remaining property and the farmhouse to be willed to the church. One clause said that the great-grandchildren could reside in the home one year after her passing. The church was well pleased with the offer. There were over forty acres of farmland remaining, plus the farmhouse, title-free. The great-grandchildren were not aware of what their great-grandmother had done.

The developer returned to Great-Grandmother and offered to purchase more acres from her. She refused his offer. "I'm selling no more land," she said. "Please stop bothering me."

The developer talked to the great-granddaughter and told her what the offer for the land would have been. This outraged the great-granddaughter; how could her great-grandmother not sell the property so she and her brother could live a life of luxury? She talked to her brother, telling him what the developer told her. He was furious. "How does she expect us to live off our wages we earn? She expects us to care for her as well. No way. Do you have that developer's business card?" She handed it to her brother. "I'll call him tomorrow, and we will get the paper rolling." Now bear in mind they had no legal right to anything; they were not even listed in the will. Even if Great-Grandmother divided up the land and the house to her own children, by the time it reached the great-grandchildren there would be next to nothing for them.

After numerous phone calls and meetings with the brother and sister, the developer asked, "Could you get your great-grandmother to sign a power of attorney for you two?" They weren't sure, but they said they would have her sign any paper he gave them.

They took the form to have their great-grandmother to sign and would meet the developer again in a couple of days; that was the plan. They concocted a story saying they needed her signature to cosign a school loan for them. She took the form and told them she would give it back to them in a couple of days. She took the form to her lawyer friend, and he explained to her that the form was not for a cosign but for power of attorney that gave her great-grandchildren access to her bank accounts and the right to sign on her behalf. "Why would they try to trick you into giving them power over your estate?"

"I don't know why they would do such a thing. I'll confront them when I get home."

When she arrived at home, the great-grandson was sitting on the sofa, watching television. She walked over to the television set and turned it off.

"Hey, what are you doing, old lady? That's my favorite program."

"I need to talk to you and your sister now."

He called for his little sister to join them.

"Sit down next to your brother."

"You seem angry, Grandma. What's the problem?"

"You two lied to me. I have to have you both leave my home by the end of the week."

"Hey, old lady, what are you talking about? Did you take your meds today?"

"I took my meds, but that has nothing to do with you lying to me."

"We still don't know what you're talking about," said the sister.

"You know very well what I'm talking about. I won't stand being lied to. Enough said. Plan on leaving my home by the end of the week. I should send you both packing now. Please leave me alone now."

They both got up off the sofa in a huff and went to their bedrooms. This was where they plotted to rid themselves of the authority blocking them from what they thought was their way to riches. They planned to dispose of the old lady once and for all. The sister had a friend who made her up at a school play to look very old, and she had similar features as her great-grandmother; she would have to talk with her friend. She'd call her in a few minutes, and the plan was for her to visit one of her great-grandmother's longtime friends back east. She would get the name and address from the files in Great-Grandmother's bedroom. She would have her friend make her up for a play, buy a train ticket to the city where the friend lived, spend a few days in the town, and return home. The brother would wait twenty-four hours and file a missing persons report. But they still needed a signature on the power of attorney form.

"Great-Grandmother always pays her bills by check, correct?" the sister asked. "Her signature is on the top check in her checkbook." She had seen a program where a forger showed the audience how to pick up the signature from the top check in someone's checkbook.

"See if that works," said the brother. "If it does, we have the signature we need."

Great-Grandma's checkbook was lying on her desk, where she did all her business. The sister took a pencil as shown on the program and lightly went across the signature line, and there was Great-Grandma's signature. Just in case, she found a letter that Great-Grandma had been writing, and her signature was on that as well, though it was not the total signature but just her first name. She took the items to the brother, and they pressed hard on a sheet of paper to transfer the signature from the check. They followed the same procedure with the paper, and bingo—there was Great-Grandma's signature.

They didn't have the form the developer had given them. They went to the stationary store and asked the clerk if they had power of attorney forms for sale. The clerk went to the forms and found what they were looking to purchase. They asked the clerk if this form was a legal document. He said to them, "Do I look like an attorney? I just work here. You have to ask an attorney, not me."

When they left the store, the sister told her brother, "We only have to convince the developer and the county clerk. I'm sure there are lots of papers required for such a transaction, and it's just a checklist for the county—you know form one, check; form two, check; form one hundred, check. As long as they have a form, it gets filed and the deed is processed. We have the check from the developer deposited. We're in the money, honey."

"How will Great-Grandma disappear?"

"Remember the old shed, buried, with access under the staircase in the kitchen?"

"Yes, I remember."

"We've been told for years not to go into the shed."

"Yes … I don't get what you're trying to say."

"You and I will trap Great-Grandma in the shed, since very few people even know it is there. We will kill Grandma in the shed … or maybe not us."

"Well, who would do such a thing?"

"I'm pretty good looking, right? Do you find me attractive?"

"Yes, so what?"

"Others will find me attractive as well."

"You're going to entice some dude to do what to you?"

"Not to me—to Grandma."

"That's crazy talk. No one is so stupid as to kill someone for one night of pleasure. You can't get someone that drunk. I don't care how pretty you are or what shape you're in. It won't happen."

"Okay then, you kill her, smarty. I will get all dolled up and get on the train, and you take care of Grandma. When do you want this to happen?"

"You tell me."

"I called my friend, and she is willing to make me up for the play. I'll go to the thrift store and buy an old lady's dress and shoes. I will get a train ticket from the next town over so no one will recognize me. Oh, by the way, I don't want to know how you plan on disposing of Grandma. I know nothing, and neither do you."

The sister took off in her car to buy the outfit in the next town's thrift store. "Too many people know her in our town."

This was how the police put this puzzle together from the forensic evidence they discovered. The brother's fingerprints and shoe prints were the only ones in the shed; there was no sign of the sister's. They had Great-Grandma and Great-Grandpa's prints and a few other relatives' prints, but interrogations of those people resulted in no conclusive evidence.

This was the only way this puzzle made sense to the investigating team. They thought the great-grandson left the door to the shed open and Great-Grandmother heard some noise coming from the shed and went down the stairs through the tunnel to investigate. That was when he killed her. The investigation found that the great-grandson had a history of mental health issues from school records and reports from two clinical psychologists. He was prescribed medication, but the prescription was never filled. One of the reports stated that the brother and sister were romantically involved, which triggered some of his issues. Their report stated that most of his issues came from being left by his parents at a very young age and tossed from one household to another, not really being a part of any family. There was one household in which he started to become a normal child, and then the illness forced them back into other homes. By the time his great-grandmother took them in, he was a mental wreck. The sister took things in stride mentally; there were no signs of mental illness in her.

Their plan worked. After they got notification that Great-Grandma could not be found and the state pronounced that she was truly missing and her whereabouts were unknown, the power of attorney was granted. The brother built wooden boxes six inches high and matched the staircase steps as best as his limited woodworking skills allowed. He then cut up his great-grandmother's body and put the bones into wet concrete on each step. The investigation report did not specify just how he removed the flesh and used only the bones in the concrete mix. They couldn't even imagine how anyone could do that to another human being. They thought he must have had a freezer of some type to perform that task. They didn't even know if he had someone to help dispose the body.

Once the boxes were built and concrete poured with the bones, he put the wood over the box frame and put carpeting on top of the wooden treads. Since there was never a death certificate, they could only guess when all this took place. They tried to determine by the train ticket the exact date and year. Since the sister had passed away and the brother had dementia, getting actuate data was near impossible. The case, at one point, was ruled closed since the brother also passed away. Then it was reopened when the bank's money was found, along with new fingerprints on the money and bag. The case was open, and officers were still working on collecting information.

This was when the developer ran into the snag. He was not a happy camper and demanded to have the check returned. The two siblings had spent a considerable amount of the money and tried to renegotiate the original deal. The developer had people who would do bodily harm to those who tried to weasel out of a deal. The sister had a job as a bank teller. The plan was that the developer would meet her and her brother at the bank on a certain day at a given time; they couldn't be late, as it was a very short window. All was planned, and it occurred as scheduled.

The robbery occurred, and out the door the developer and her brother left. To make the bank think the sister had nothing to do with the robbery, the brother knocked his sister out—a small price to pay for the robbery. When she was asked what happened, she said a customer hit her head when she turned around at the teller station while getting a form. There were cameras in the bank, but the two men never showed their faces and were disguised beyond recognition. This involved another makeup scheme that the sister got her friend to do. By the way, the girl who did the makeup for the sister, brother, and developer disappeared. She was still on the missing persons list to this day.

The money was stashed in the shed, and a false roof was installed, putting the money in a safe spot until the search cooled off. The funds for the developer were removed from the satchel to replace the amount given to the brother and sister. The plan was to spend just a little, though not in town or any neighboring town. There was no set amount or date, making tracking the expenditures difficult.

All was going great until the church told the brother and sister they had to vacate the property, showing the papers that their great-grandmother had signed. The church gave them an additional six months beyond the date of the missing persons report. This caused the brother and sister to find another place to reside. They must have forgotten about the money stashed in the shed or figured they would buy the house from the church. There was no way of knowing what occurred at that time.

The house was bought and sold at least three times before John and Marie bought the home. They had no clue about the history of this home, not having grown up in the area or having friends or family living here to inform them of what had occurred on the property. The realtor did not offer any information, if even she herself knew. The remodeling of the staircase was a real eye-opener for the new homeowners. It was bad enough having a contractor tearing up their home, but then police were called, a forensic team was brought in, and an investigation began. Personal questions regarding the purchase of the property were raised. Did they know anything about the property before the purchase? Did they have relatives living in the general area?

They questioned my whole company, not as a group but individually, looking for some differences in what was known or unknown. The finding of the shed that was buried two feet below the ground brought more forensics teams and a bomb squad in and out of the home, searching for this and that. Then, with the removal of the soil surrounding the shed and the finding of the trunks, metal canister, and metal cans, more forensics tests were performed, the bomb squad was called in again, and a nosy neighbor claimed that John had finally murdered his wife. That got the police to ask even more questions and almost got John arrested. Marie saved him from going to jail on false accusations from a neighbor they didn't even know. I was surprised that the neighbor didn't link them to a terrorist group.

To make matters worse, the bank employee notified the television stations about the bank executives preparing to make a statement to the press and give the reward money to John and Marie on local and national television. They claimed that they had tried calling the day before but there was no answer at the home. John and Marie had spent the day at the airport, picking up relatives. The nosy neighbor nearly caused a media frenzy when she again made a false statement regarding the murder of a great-grandmother. That nearly made John and Marie put a For Sale sign up on the home and leave. This was on a Friday, and the bank official told them to be at the bank on Monday morning for the presentation.

On Monday morning, at the time given to John, Marie, and the entire press corps, they had live broadcasters stationed every few feet away. To make matters worse for John and Marie, the bank had a limousine pick them up at their doorstep and deliver them to the bank. The only thing different between this and the Oscars was the red carpet. Marie told John, "I'm not getting out of the limousine. This is beyond ridiculous." The limousine pulled up to the waiting bank executives. Newspeople rushed to the open limousine doors and stuck microphones into the faces of John and Marie.

Before this meeting, the *Remodeling* magazine owner, who had some very influential friends, told the bank that no amounts would be given publicly. The governor, state senators, and city and county officials would not be received at this photo shoot for the bank. There would be an event planned for the home in a few weeks for all those people to attend. "It is known as the party of the century. Please no mention of this at this time. The date has not been confirmed, because of the course of construction. There will be numerous months of coverage in the magazine, and all parties attending this party will be given equal and ample press in the magazine." Their cooperation would be greatly appreciated. The officials' offices had been put on notice; if a person invited failed to show up to the event, it would be noted and mentioned in the magazine.

Once John and Marie were safely inside the bank, the officials of the bank presented them with the check; no amount was ever made public. The police were at the bank, making sure all went smoothly. "This is an ongoing investigation, and there are still people involved in this case at large. We are protecting the family who lives at this home. Their safety is of the utmost importance. Having their home exposed like it was really upset the investigation, stated the detective."

The nosy neighbor was actually taken down to the police station and questioned for two days. They wanted to know just what she knew, whom she knew, and how long she had known; they asked all sorts of questions over the two days. The investigators researched each and every one of her answers. She was told not to talk to anyone about the investigation or her time being interrogated, or she could do time in jail for as long as the judge determined. This was not a scare tactic; they meant that they would pursue jail time.

The festivities ended, and John and Marie were rushed back into the limousine and taken back to their home. A police escort for the limousine prohibited the news station from bird-dogging them to their home. The police chief told the news stations that if one person followed the limousine, they would be treated as conspirators and arrested.

No one knew except John, Marie, and the bank the amount of the check they were given. When they were dropped off, they entered their home and invited us all over for dinner. The girls got to play with their new friends; everyone was happy that it was over and looked forward to tomorrow.

We all talked about the upcoming party. Marie said, "You all are coming, or we will go to your home and drag you here. Come as you are. Might be a little embarrassing, since the magazine is taking photos for their issues. You might get applause depending on your attire. Your boxer shorts just might not make the cover of *Remodeling* magazine."

"Point well taken," I replied. "We will be here. Can I wear my boxer shorts on the outside?"

Marie said, "You would definitely be the only one dressed like that. Oh, by the way, it will not become a fashion statement, but nice try anyway."

"It might give him free room and board at the insane asylum, said Delores."

"Do they serve crow, asked Delores?"

"I could have them make it for specially you. I scraped one off your grill, so it's still fresh, said Delores."

"You make it sound awfully inviting, I told her."

CHAPTER 44

This all started with the spiral staircase. Remember: we were just going to remove the worn-out carpeting from the staircase so the homeowners could replace it with a new one. They were unaware what that would cause. When we removed the old carpeting and saw what it was laid on, there was no way I would recommend they lay new carpeting on the wooden boxes. We removed the tread from the first step and uncovered a clump of unfinished concrete. Why would any contractor put a blob of unfinished concrete under a less-than-professional wood box?

John and Marie asked, "Could we remove the box and blob of concrete to reveal what lies underneath?"

I reminded them, "I am only a landscaper. My license does not allow me to do anything inside the residence."

John and Marie said, "We won't tell anyone that you worked inside our home."

My foreman had his friend working with us; he was a skilled carpenter. Juan got a small sledgehammer and concrete chisel from his truck and brought them to his friend. As he was breaking up the first blob of concrete, I thought he saw a ghost. Inside the blob of concrete were human bones.

I had the homeowners notify the police, and we all stood back from a crime scene. This was how the entire project became an adventure. Day by day, something else made us call the authorities. This was not part of the original plan, one step forward and three steps backward.

I was sharing with John and Marie a revision I had drawn for the side of their home when we unearthed a shed buried two feet below the soil surface. I told Marie and John about a vision I had the night before I started drawing their side yard. I envisioned Marie with a glass of champagne coming down a staircase modeled after the one inside the house. The same contractor who refurbished the inside staircase agreed to make a duplicate one for the courtyard. While she was descending the staircase, she did it with grace, poise, glamour, and sophistication in front of waiting guests and family members. While she was descending, four violins were playing her favorite Italian song. With each step, she was poised as though she had a book on her head and was dressed in an evening gown with designer shoes, styled hair, a diamond necklace, and a bracelet. The crowd applauded her grand entrance to the party. Marie was shy and did not do well in the spotlight, but I somehow got her attention, and John said he saw a glow on her he hadn't seen in years. He forgot how she would shine when they were first dating. From that first meeting until now, she had been seeing herself making the grand entrance from the staircase.

She and my wife had envisioned being the hostesses of the event of the year. As the project progressed, Marie—with camera in hand—made a pictorial history of the remodeling. Everything done had a corresponding photo in albums to show the guests. I looked forward to her coming outside with her camera and taking photographs of the progression. Her showing that kind of interest was inspiring to me. I found out later that she was forwarding some of her photos to her parents, and they were planning on visiting but didn't want to impose on the remodeling. When she showed the side yard being converted into a courtyard, that really spiked their interest. When Marie explained the feeling she got while practicing her grand entrance, Mama came visiting first, and she, too, wanted to practice. It had now blossomed into five women going to do a grand entrance.

While we were getting ready to finish the outdoor staircase, Marie could not wait for the final piece to be installed, and she showed me and my crew her grand entrance; the applause was all she needed. That sparked a complete transformation of two families for the better. Each of the family members had his or her own toy in the courtyard—Marie, the staircase; John, the barbecue, and the girls, the playhouse. All these items would play a very important role at the party.

One very important player in the party was *Remodeling* magazine and its owner and editor. They, of course, would reap great rewards from this party but were instrumental in all the hard work involved in throwing of the event of the year. We who were building this project had some fantastic, talented craftsmen. The staircase had been crafted by masters of the trade, and the playhouse by master woodworkers. The electrician was one of the best I had ever worked with, and my crews were the glue that put all the pieces of the puzzle together and held them in place. All were very talented and gifted in their various trades— earthwork, irrigation systems, landscaping, pavers, and low-voltage lighting. The stream and waterfall had been built by a master builder and designer. All our players were working with three common goals in mind—have pride in your work, stay positive, and be happy. "Whistle while you work" was our motto.

The ladies performing daily for the crew's applause were well received. I believe that without the ladies breaking up the drudgery of the daily routine, the work atmosphere would not have been as it was. We all thank you from the bottoms of our hearts. Great job keeping morale at its highest level.

The setting up of the party was mainly done. The caterer, the violins and the singer, the sound system, the invitations, the guest list, and the bartender were taken care of by the magazine. The formal invitations to the elected officials were hand-delivered to each office with response cards attached. This was beyond the beliefs of all of us.

During the second photo shoot of the finished project, the girls were dressed and ready to pose all afternoon and into the evening so they could get the true ambiance of the entire project. The magazine also catered the photo shoot with a bartender and sound system playing in the background; it was absolutely perfect. The editor said this was their trial run for the upcoming party. They wanted to get the crew accustomed to shooting still shots and video, and to determine where to set up so they were not an obstruction yet were able to get the most from each location.

Mr. Barns, the magazine owner, was greeted by our daughters with open arms and lots of hugs. His whole crew was welcomed by the girls, and they were all taken aback by them. The lady who helped all the ladies looked and felt her best and said she had never seen young girls act the way these girls did all day long. "Such a joy being around them," she said. "They treat you better than family." She asked Delores and Marie, "How did you make them the way they are?"

"We didn't do much—just stood back and watched the miracle happen," said Delores. "Let them be them."

Marie told her, "These are the girls every parent hopes their child turns out as. Trust us; they were not always like this. The playhouse—all the credit goes to the playhouse. That's their home, you know. Not everyone is invited for dinner. They are on a limited budget, and their space is small. They tell you if you are lucky enough to be invited to their dinner party. Not everyone is invited. There is a waiting list. If you decline their offer, you may never be invited again."

"The girls tell you this?"

"Yes, always and often. They are not playing. It's for real."

"Can I get a playhouse built at my house?"

"Ask Delores's husband. He designed our project, managed it, and supervised the entire thing."

"Was it his idea to put the playhouse on top of the patio cover?"

"Yes, I wanted it in the backyard, used as a waterwheel and mill. He told me, 'You are separating the girls from the adults. It's like you're telling them they don't belong with you.'"

"Wow, that was pretty cold."

"No, it woke me up. I love my girls. Why put them in a position where they feel left out? I am so glad he was bold enough to open my eyes. I will always love him for that, and that I will always cherish."

"You're going to tell all this to our writer, correct?"

"That and as much as he wants to know. Both Delores and I are anxious to tell how all this works for our families."

"You have me sold, and I work for them. We won't be able to keep the issues on the shelves. I can see the panic in the office now. It will be counted by the minute in sales—not days or weeks. These will be our best issues ever. I have never seen Mr. Barns so excited about any project. He couldn't wait to get your call saying you were ready for the second series of photos. He watches the videos of you ladies every day, seeing how they can be improved. He has shown the videos to three major networks to be aired as a promo for the upcoming issues of our magazine. They all have signed on to promote this party and upcoming issues. You ladies will become a household name. Be prepared. You'll become famous, called on to speak at functions, go on tour, and be pampered like royalty. I have already received calls wanting to get your information. We won't do anything until the issues go flying off the shelves. You will be advised by the magazine whether you will be available or not available to specific people. Mr. Barns plays his cards very close to his chest. You'll be well guarded."

Marie and Delores were getting excited at her telling them that they would become a household name. Marie asked Delores, "Are you ready to become famous?"

"I really don't know. I'm just a housewife like you. I enjoy being around you and your girls. I would not want to lose that, would you?"

"No, we will all be together, not one going one direction and the other going in another. That won't work."

The stylist told the ladies, "When all this comes about, you have to make that part of the contract, or they will send you both in different directions. You'll have to get legal counsel before you sign your lives away. Mr. Barns and I will help you with all the ugly details. We are hoping for this to become a long-term relationship. Our readers and viewers will tell us the outcome."

The shoot progressed, lunch was delicious, and the shots were taken to enhance the landscape design. There were various angles and lighting setups to bring about the most from the ladies. Juanita was dressed in an outfit that she and Marie had picked out. She was bigger than Marie, so her outfits would not work. Marie took her to her hairstylist and gave her a new life. The ladies helped her apply makeup; she didn't even look like Juanita anymore. The crew was impressed and couldn't stop looking at her, and she started to feel embarrassed.

Marie said, "Don't be embarrassed. Enjoy the attention. Use it wisely. You don't ever want to cheapen yourself. Don't use it to steal another lady's man. There are plenty out there. You don't need the headache or the confrontation that it will cause. Oh, by the way, you're gorgeous. Never change back to the old Juanita. You leave her in the past. Go forward now."

The photographer put Juanita and Angel together on the bridges and the circular planter; both shots were poster quality. Their stylist, Susanne, always made sure the ladies were ready for each shot; the photographer would tell Susanne who would be in the next photo shoot and where the next location would be. His assistants were always at least one shot ahead of the photographer. The ladies were always given a full glass of champagne, and they could drink it or just hold the full glass. If the contents were getting flat, they would water the garden and refill the glass. Mr. Barns and the editor told the ladies, "Please don't overindulge. Even though we would like to see you flirtatious, we can't afford to have someone holding you up during the shot."

The catered dinner was better than that at a five-star restaurant—almost too good to eat. The catering was not like a box lunch; chefs were using John's barbecue and Marie's kitchen. "Please do not bother them during the preparation of the meal, said Susanne." They brought along waitresses to serve the crew and family members. "Just ask the girls, and they will bring you whatever you desire, said Susanne." Water was the most requested item.

While the ladies were getting posed and photos were being shot, the men were talking to the writer, answering all the questions and giving their life stories. Phillip, Stan, and Brad were invited to this shoot and photographed, and they told their life stories. The men were encouraged to bring their wives, and they told them to be in their finest outfits with hair styled and makeup applied by a professional. "Please give the magazine the bill, and we will reimburse the family, said Susanne." It was very important that a true picture of all the players who made this project happen was given to the reader and the viewer. Each contractor and his wife gave a presentation of their portion of the project. Every detail they could remember about what was done and why was very important.

The interviews ranged from a half hour to an hour. The writer and I spent more time than that. Mr. Barns and two other gentlemen sat in during the questioning and asked other questions that the writer jotted down. They were very interested in the vision. "Is this the case with every project? Does it happen while you're walking on the project or while you're at the drawing table? Have you forgotten where you are while you're in the vision mode? You mentioned the change that Marie wanted from your original drawing. How did that make you feel? You mentioned that you asked your wife to help you with your dilemma. Was she any help? You did something that we find utterly amazing: You put the playhouse or shed on top of the patio cover and added the circular planter in a vision while sitting on a chair in the courtyard, correct? You didn't tell John or Marie, while you were there, what you had seen in the vision? Why would you not want to let them know right then and there asked the writer?"

Mr. Barns asked, "How many projects have you envisioned that were rejected by your clients?" These types of questions went down to the interviewee's persona. They required more than a yes or no answer.

Here is how I concluded my reasoning with all in attendance: "When I get a call from a new client and meet them for the first time, I question them—not drill them, but ask a few questions that tell me the type of client they will become. If they say, 'My neighbor just put up a patio cover, and they are outside every night,' I look over the fence and see either an aluminum or plastic-covered patio cover. That tells me they are trying to avoid maintenance of the patio cover. If I see a big-box-store barbecue with a cover and there is a layer of dirt or dust on it, I know they bought it for a party or on a whim. No need to put in an outdoor kitchen.

"If they ask, 'What would a pool cost?' out of the blue, I ask, 'Do you like to swim?'

"'Our neighbor bought a pool, and when they sold their house, they got more money for their home.'

"'But do you like to swim?'

"'We want to have a magnet like they had. Their home sold fast.'

"'How many hours do you, as a family, spend outdoors?'

"'A week or month or day?'

"'You tell me how often you use the outside of your home.' If they say rarely, I know at this point that the big-box store with all the pretty flowers and items made in China is their best road to take. Custom-built landscapes are made for those who really enjoy being outside, entertaining family members or guests, or having parties for graduations, birthdays, and weddings—not those who sit in the family room and tell their company, 'See what we have—a look-at landscape.'

"I also tell my clients to maintain the property once completed and find a local gardener, not the cheapest—someone who knows the business and doesn't just give you the business. Get referrals from them and customers' addresses so you can take the time to see what they actually do for their clients. Nothing is more frustrating for me than going past a landscape that we spent hours installing to perfection and seeing that the weeds are taller than the planted plants and the grass not mowed, not being maintained.

"You want to kill your business and have that customer tell their friends you were the one who landscaped their home? I take pride in making my landscapes enjoyable to the customer. I'm not trying to please the neighborhood, just those that hire me to make their home complete inside and outside.

"I had a client years ago who wanted a raised brick planter in his front yard entry. I designed a planter on both sides of a new walkway instead of the three-foot-wide sidewalk the builder gave them. I increased the width to five feet, put in the twenty-four-inch-high planters, and put brick bands across the sidewalk to match the walls. At the end of the sidewalk before it turned toward the driveway, that became the meeting place for all the neighborhood gentlemen and their wives. Everyone came over and talked with me and my crew. You never know how your visions will actually turn out. It was not intended to be the meeting place.

"I had a customer on that block stating they wanted a meeting place for their home and asking if I would put the same design on their home. I told them I don't cookie-cutter my plans so the entire block looks the same. That's what large condominium complexes try to achieve. No one has a better landscape than their neighbors.

"In this project, I was lucky to have a customer who truly wanted to change their lifestyle from being insiders to outsiders. My goal was to give them a reason to always have that feeling—give them a good reason to enjoy the outside. Nature is a wonderful source of relaxation and inner joy. I have yet to see a cell phone or a tablet or a laptop device since I started this project. Neither the parents nor the children have their heads buried in the devices. That is so rewarding to me."

Susanne came to the table and said that the photographer wanted to see Mr. Barns when he had a moment. The interview was coming to a close, so I could continue what I did for a living. I had other projects ongoing, and they, too, needed my attention.

CHAPTER 45

The event of the year was getting ready for the first guests to arrive. *Remodeling* magazine brought their four limousines. We contacted the church that inherited the property to see if we could use their parking lot. The pastor was very gracious; the donation, of course, was well received. We used the address for all the guests to park their vehicles, and the limousines would escort them to the home. Liquor was served in the limousines, and hired models got the party started in them. Sex did sell; there was not one unhappy person who arrived to the party.

The guests had a choice to enter into the home, which we preferred, or through the arched gateway. Those guests who had been at the home on a prior date were still encouraged to enter the home to gaze at the photo albums and photos put on display by the magazine, and a home tour was given inside by a highly qualified staff. The tour guides would escort the guests through the backyard landscape and encourage them to take time to smell the flowers, strolling across the bridges, seeing the waterfall and stream, listening to the soft, serene music in the background building up the ambiance of the courtyard. We had a few folks who wanted to sit at the waterfall and take that part into perspective.

The tour guides were met by the daughters at the playhouse and tunnel. They showed the guests how they clogged down the tunnel and invited all the ladies with heels to join them. Wow, what fun all the ladies had letting down their hair, though no alcohol was served at this point.

The place was filling up. The guest of honor, the governor, was due to arrive at any minute. Two state senators were already at the party, the mayor and three city councilmen were in attendance, most of the major business owners from town were attending, three or four of the major bank owners had arrived, and a few more were on their way. All the neighbors were invited. A few showed, but not Ms. Nosy; she had put a really nice note on her invitation that Marie proudly displayed on the table next to the photo album. Most attendees just laughed at the response she had given. To put it nicely, the lady needed to be put in a nuthouse.

Once the governor arrived, had his beverage, and was stationed in the courtyard, the violins would start playing after the sound system was lowered.

Mr. Barns was the master of ceremonies for the grand entrance of the ladies and welcomed all the guests and family members.

The girls were giving tours of their playhouse to all those attending. The magazine made up a sign: "Welcome to our playhouse. We are on a limited budget, and the space is limited. Please forgive us. Only two at a time can visit our house. Love you all." All the girls had signed or printed their names on it. So many people took photos of that sign and gave the girls huge hugs when they entered the playhouse. Many of the ladies had single red roses that they gave the girls to put into the vase on the table. It looked like a flower shop in just a short time. The girls were so excited, showing off their house. Many of the guests took photos with the girls for their own photo albums. They were on cloud nine all afternoon and evening. One lucky visitor would get to see the lighting from their balcony. "That has to be someone very special. We should start a pool to see if we can guess the person or persons, I said." It would be quite the fanfare when the girls announced who their choice was.

I talked to Mr. Barns and gave him the idea; he loved the fact that he could announce their choice. I told Marie to let the girls know that they had to choose a guest or guests to attend the lighting of the low-voltage lights in the courtyard and backyard. She was thrilled almost to tears of joy when I asked her to let them know very discreetly. I also told Susanne to be aware of what was going to occur. She asked me, "Did you have a vision on this as well?"

"No, this just came from being with these girls—how important it is that they invite someone for dinner and the lighting of the courtyard."

"Can I talk with them about whom to choose?"

"If you want to spend the rest of your life watching others being invited for their dinner party and lighting festival—your choice. Personally, I would stay well away from doing that. I'm just a landscaper, not a professional event planner like yourself."

"I'd be on the never-to-invite list?"

"They have a way of making sure you learn a valuable lesson."

"Forever on the list?"

"You have to know these little girls. As soon as my daughters have the same playhouse, you would be banned from both establishments."

"I have to really sit down and talk with these young girls. I could learn from them, I'm certain."

"They have taught their moms, grandmas, and visitors some very valuable lessons. They 'take no prisoners,' so the saying goes. They don't insult you. They don't pout or make mean faces at you. They don't stop talking and showing affection to you. They just don't invite you, period."

"I have only one other question for you. Did you, your wife, or Marie teach them this behavior?"

"No one taught them this behavior. We were all just waiting our turn to dine with them. It's like being picked for a team when you were in elementary, middle, and high school—the same feeling, like being picked last. If there was anybody else to choose from, that person would be picked, and you would be left standing alone—that kind of feeling. It's not like, 'So what's so special about eating with little girls anyway?' It is special, and they make you feel special, and they are very polite, and they thank you for joining them for dinner. 'Would you like some more or another beverage?' When was the last time you had a date with someone who treated you like that?"

"Does never count?"

We received word that the governor and his party had arrived and were in the house, looking at the photo albums. The photographer was taking the family photo and welcoming them to the party. The girls heard that the governor had arrived, and they excused themselves and scurried off into the tunnel and in the home to meet him. They made such a hit with everyone nearby; the governor, his wife, and his children were nearly in tears with joy from these four little girls. The governor got down on his knee and gave them all a hug, and of course the photographer had a field day. Can you say "Four months of front cover?" I hoped they could arrange for the governor to have posters printed for his upcoming campaign.

The girls asked the governor and his wife if they could be their guests during dinner in their house. No one informed the governor about the significance of this invitation. If he declined, good-bye, governorship. He held their hands and said, "We would be honored to dine with such great young ladies. Thank you so much for thinking of us." He didn't know he had dodged a huge bullet right then and there. After that, all other opponents would be well advised not even to bother getting into the governor's race.

Susanne came over to me and said, "He's one lucky governor—very lucky. Was he informed ahead of time?"

"I don't think so. Who would have told him? A prior rejected visitor being too pompous for their own good? All of us that are waiting in line just got pushed back to another day."

"I have to tell everyone at the magazine about the talk we just had. Would you mind if I shared what you told me?"

"Not at all. Nothing prints better than the truth."

Mr. Barns took the microphone and introduced himself to the party members. "Attention, everyone. My name is Mr. Barns, owner and publisher of *Remodeling* magazine. We thank all of you for attending today's festivities and hope everyone is enjoying them. The photos posted on the easels in the main entry foyer are the proposed covers for our upcoming issues of this property. I hope you have taken time to see what has taken place at this home. The photo albums on the foyer table show the home all through the remodeling construction. This home is also going to be listed as a state historical landmarks, and the governor of our fine state will present the homeowners with the bronze plaque later on during our festivities.

"At this time, I would like to introduce you to the construction crew who put this wonderful project together. I would also like to mention that the ladies introduced—the construction company's wife, the homeowner's wife, her mother-in-law, and two construction workers—will perform their grand entrance coming down this beautiful staircase. So all of you who are in the backyard, if you would please join us at the base of the staircase. You definitely do not want to miss this performance. Also, we have four violins and three singers who will perform during the grand entrance. And if they would join us here by the barbecue, we will get the festivities started. My lovely assistant, Susanne, give them a wave. She is the one who is getting the guests of honor ready for the staircase. Are we ready, Susanne?

"We would like to introduce you to our very good friend and governor of our lovely state, Evan and Diane Bronson. Give them a warm welcome. Mayor James and Elizabeth Williams. From Stockdale Landscape Construction, Superintendent Juan and Valerie Sandoval, and Leadman Diego and Vanessa Vega. From Woods and Things, Phillip and Jennifer Alfonsi. From Just Stairs, Stan and Loriann Janssen. Owner of Stockdale Landscape Construction, Fred Stockdale. Homeowner John Albright. His father-in-law, Giorgio Canico.

"Now the ladies. We have a video of them that will be aired on PBS on Saturday at 8:00 p.m. From Stockdale Landscape Construction—yes, folks, these are construction workers, not clerical workers or office managers. These two girls get in the dirt with the men. I could not believe my eyes when I first met them. Juanita Gomez and her parents, Alberto and Oliva Gomez. Angel Vasquez and her parents, Rigo and Daniella Vasquez."

The girls gave their grand entrance with champagne glasses, decked out.

"Great job, ladies. Can you believe they are construction workers and not models? Give them another hand just for doing what they do. Now this lady I'm about to introduce, she is the mother of the homeowner—not her sister, but her mother, I kid you not. Mrs. Sophia Canico. Let's hear it for her and her grand entrance. Give her another round of applause. Wait until you see her daughter.

"Now the next lady—boy, oh boy, oh boy, we will show you her entrance from the arched gateway after the grand entrance from the staircase. Gentlemen, this lady is a housewife. Yes, you heard me correctly, a housewife married to the owner of Stockdale Landscape. Without further ado, the one and only Mrs. Delores Stockdale."

The applause was deafening. All the attendees were paying their respects.

"Can you believe your eyes? This is a housewife—no modeling experience. Let's hear it again for Delores. Now the moment I've been waiting for—and I know you have been as well. This too is a housewife—I mean, I have been around the block a few times in this industry, and you will not meet a nicer, kinder, more beautiful inside and out lady. This is one in a million, if that is really the odds. I'm certain my calcs are way off—maybe a gazillion to one. My dearest new friend, Mrs. Marie Albright. Remember, gentlemen, this is a housewife belonging to the luckiest man alive. She is a charming, gracious, glamorous lady you will want to meet. Good job, Mom and Dad.

"Now, I promised you one of the most seductive, sensual, glamorous, eloquent entrances you will ever witness. These ladies are not professional—no background in theater, dance, or drama. Could Mrs. Delores Stockdale please enter the courtyard for our guests?"

The gate opened slowly, and Delores—with everything she had —made the ultimate entrance. The crowd went wild; the louder they applauded and cheered, the more seductive she became. "As you all see, I didn't let you down. Mrs. Stockdale, wonderful job. Could we have the homeowners come forward and dance to Mrs. Albright's favorite Italian song, being sung by our singers backed up by four violins?"

They danced so gracefully, with tears coming down Marie's checks. "Can we have Mama and Papa join them, please? Fred and Delores, join them, please. All the construction crews and family, join them as well." The song ended, and the applause was enormous.

"Now, may I have the governor and his beautiful bride, along with the homeowners, join me at the base of the staircase? Here is your governor of Colorado, Evan Bronson, and his wife, Diane."

"John and Marie Albright," said the governor, "we the State of Colorado hereby submit to you this bronze plaque declaring your home as a historical state monument. Thank you both for making this farmhouse into the showplace that it has become."

Marie was messing up her makeup now, and Susanne had just fixed it a few seconds ago. Susanne ran back in where the festivities were taking place, excused herself, repaired the damage to Marie's makeup, and dashed out of camera view.

"Dinner will be served at our tables. Please eat as much as you desire. The bar is open. Please enjoy your time at the Albrights' estate."

The governor and Diane were escorted by our girls to the playhouse and thanked for joining them for dinner. "Have you had a good time at our home?" Leslie asked the governor and Diane. Their dinner was brought to them on silver-covered trays. This flipped out our daughters.

"Oh, waiter, please bring our guests whatever they need."

"I love your sign at the bottom of the stairs. I want one for my house said Diane."

"I will ask our sign company if they can make you another one, said Marie." That was how the dinner was started.

Leslie asked for Susanne to visit her. The waiter found Susanne and told her. Susanne was in shocked disbelief. "Are you sure she asked for me?"

"Quite certain, ma'am. She said 'Susanne.'"

Susanne went up the staircase and knocked at the door. Leslie answered and said, "Welcome to our home. We girls have a huge favor to ask of you. Would you do us the honor of giving this note to Mr. Barns and returning upon the announcement?"

"I'd be so honored." Susanne almost fell down the stairs, as she was so excited. The note had been signed by all the girls.

Mr. Barns received the note and thanked Susanne for delivering it. It was dusk now, and Mr. Barns got the microphone and announced, "Attention, everyone. I have a brief announcement to make. This is from Leslie and Kim Albright, and Sarah and Rebecca Stockdale. It reads, 'We are sorry, everyone, but our budget is limited, and our space is limited, so we cannot invite everyone up to our house for the lighting of the courtyard and backyard festivities. Our choice was not an easy one to make. We all voted, and many of you were on our list of guests whom we would love to join us, but the couple that we chose will be leaving us in a few days, and we wanted to thank them personally for all that they have done for us while they were visiting our home. Could Mama and Papa join us for the lighting ceremony?'"

The applause was very loud. Susanne was waiting on the porch, and the governor and Diane were descending the stairs. Mama and Papa were at the base of the staircase. Mama was crying, and so was Papa. As the governor met them on the bottom step, he and Diane hugged them and told them, "Those are the most wonderful young girls I have ever met in my life. You are so lucky to have such wonderful grandchildren. Diane wants to return and meet with them and their mothers. She can't believe this is not staged. This is real."

Mama and Papa went upstairs, and Susanne was invited to watch the turning on of the courtyard and backyard lights. Susanne was in tears of joy. The girls were giving everyone hugs.

Mr. Barns returned to the microphone and said, "The governor would like to say a few words. Governor, the crowd is all yours."

"Welcomed guests, I just had the most marvelous dinner with the crown jewels of this state. Those four young ladies should be models for the entire state's children—so gracious, courteous, loving, charming … I don't have enough vocabulary to describe the pleasure we had in meeting and dining with those four precious, beautiful young ladies. I and Diane will never forget the experience we had while with them. They did ask me to tell the singers and violins to please play 'You Light Up My Life' and for Daddy to please turn on the lights."

The violins started the prelude, and the singers sang such a beautiful rendition of the song. Tears were flowing from everyone, the governor and Diane included. Mom and Dad were total wrecks, as were Mama and Papa, Susanne, and the girls. There was not a dry eye in the house.

Diane, Marie, and Delores were all talking about having a day or two when Diane could return to spend time with moms and daughters. She and the governor were so impressed, and any and all information they could tell them so they could implement it to the schools and all agencies would be so appreciated.

The landscape was sparkling like a diamond in the sunlight, and the ambiance was twenty out of a possible ten. The girls were giving clogging lessons to more ladies in the tunnel, and they told everyone to go to their balcony and see the lights from above. The guests were scattered throughout the landscape and in the home.

Mr. Barns came up to the girls and hugged each and every one of them and thanked them for allowing him and his crew to do their jobs. "Anytime you want to visit me and my company, just give me a call," he said.

The limousines started shuttling the guests back to their cars; no one was running to the cars. Most of the guests didn't want to leave and wanted to know about the remodeling. Marie and Delores were answering question after question. They had over two hundred orders for the photos of the ladies doing the grand entrance, along with Delores's arched gateway entrance. She was asked to autograph the ones that were available at the party. She and Marie were signing like crazy.

There was a guest book for everyone to sign when they entered the home earlier, and they all noted that they wanted the magazine to send them every issue on the house's remodeling. Susanne saw the list and showed Mr. Barns; his smile was larger than ear to ear. He told John and Marie that he had figured on five months at first, but he was relooking at the five monthly issues and considering that they may not be enough.

The girls were still showing off their house, and they, too, were on cloud nine. The girls were telling one of the guests that they had felt such a warm feeling in their hearts the whole day. Delores and Marie went and visited the girls, hugging them. They could not explain the joy all of them were feeling. Both got to see the lights from the balcony for the first time. "You girls are so lucky to have such a view. This is absolutely beautiful. Thank you for making Mama and Papa so happy. We love all of you so much. You bring us so much love and joy every day."

"We're going to make you all a deal. Ready?" All of them put their right hands into the middle, on top of the others'. "Ready? On the count of three, we all state that we will never change how we treat each other like we do now. Ready? One, two, and three, said Marie."

"We'll all stay the same, and we're all sisters for life, repeat after me said Marie."

CHAPTER 46

You were introduced to the girls in prior chapters. This somewhat explains how these little girls changed the lives of their parents for the better. Growing up, the sisters were in constant competition to gain their parents' attention and be a part of their lives—not as children but as equals. They hated being directed to be placed out of their parents' sight. "Go to your room" was the same to these children as "I don't want to deal with you. You're not my equal. I have complete control over your life. Now beat it, or you're going to get a whipping." If you acted out, your parent may have spanked you before sending you to your room. Leslie and Kim Albright would talk after one or the other was punished; for these girls, punishing one was just like punishing both. Their only rebellion over their parents was to not clean up their rooms or do homework. Those were the only two options the girls had to express themselves.

That was one way they determined to get their parents' attention and have them spend time with them. They noticed that very young children, infants in particular, were getting held and talked to in very soft and soothing voices, hugged, and kissed. As they got older, all that attention stopped. Now it was "do this" or "do that," no "please" or "thank you," rarely any hugs, and never kisses to show them they were appreciated. "Nice job" didn't work. They decided this was how they did not want to live. They didn't know how to express this to their parents and feared that it would get them punished: "What do you know about life? You're still a child. You're trying to tell me how to raise you. Go to your rooms and think about what you just told your mother. Who do you think you're talking to?"

When you go to school, you get the same from the adults in charge—teachers, office staff, and principals. They all want you to act a certain way. They use threats like "We're calling your parents. We will tell them how you disrespect authority, or we will suspend you for how many days we feel is enough punishment." You haven't done anything wrong, and you haven't hurt anyone; you have just said that what they are trying to do to you is not right in your mind. You don't want a puppeteer. You want to be taught how to fit into this world and be able to converse with those you've just met or have to work with daily.

340

The golden opportunity for them to be able to show their parents, family, and guests how they wanted to be treated was owning their own space, not their bedrooms. Being sent there allowed the parents to dominate their lives. The playhouse was their house, with their rules—how they wanted to live and be treated. Their mom and dad had their toys to play with, and they had theirs. They asked people into their space only if they respected they girls for who they were, not if they viewed children as things to control. They were smart enough to know if someone was talking down to them. People who did this would not be invited for dinner or to spend time with the girls in their house. Their house was where they did their homework. The girls helped each other with their homework, making Kim just as smart as her sister. After homework, the girls talked about their day at school, who treated them kindly, and who was on the don't-need-to-talk-to-them-anymore list, including teachers.

They had worked out how not to pout or look at people with a mean expression; this only played in favor of that person trying to manipulate them. "If you give them that pleasure, then you give not only to them, but also others watching the same power. If the way they act has no apparent effect on you, then you win, not them. Their egos get boosted. Yours gets diminished. We don't give an inch of what we are or stand for to others to use against us, stated Leslie."

When the girls met Sarah and Rebecca for the first time, it took a while for Sarah and Rebecca to understand the principles of not allowing the adults in their life to control what they really desired—their love and attention. Sarah and Rebecca learned quickly how Leslie and Kim used what they had to keep peace in their family. Leslie and Kim showed them how they were treated by John and Marie. Leslie and Kim were amazed with the results.

Sarah said, "You two never get yelled at by your mom or your dad?"

"Not since we have had our own space. The playhouse is our house. We control whom we invite and how often we invite people into our world. Your mom and dad do the same thing. They invite friends and neighbors into their world. If they don't like a certain neighbor, do they ever spend time with those people? No. We have neighbors that have never been in our home or garage. Why would we want neighbors, classmates, the kids of our parents' friends in our space unless they respect us and our things? We hate it when our parents have friends over for a visit and shove their friends' kids onto us to entertain while the parents are having the time of their life. Our parents forget their friends have a certain quality that the parents can associate with. Their children may not have that quality instilled in them. We get children who truly are children—unruly, disrespectful, and wanting to dominate us and destroy our world. Our mom told us one time to show this bratty kid our room. We did, and the kid immediately started to mess with our belongings."

Leslie said, "I had two options: allow this monster to destroy my things, or punch him hard. I knew I would get punished after the guests left our house, but it was my belongings he was getting ready to destroy. The punch worked, and he went crying to his parents, saying I hit him for no reason. 'Have her get a spanking, Mommy. She's a mean person.' They made him sit with the adults instead of bother us. Your child, you raise and entertain them. Not my job.

"My mom, after they left, came to my room and asked me to explain myself to her. I told her what the boy was going to do. 'I just protected what was mine, like you and daddy do with your things.' She said she understood and would talk with my father and get back to me with the proper punishment for my actions.

"My dad walked into my room. I thought she'd sent Dad in to give me the punishment. My dad asked me to stand up. I did as he asked. He gave me a huge hug and said, 'I would have done the same as you did. I love you.' From that day forward, I knew what my parents expected of me, and I told Kim how to get the hugs she deserves."

Sarah and Rebecca heard the story told by Leslie and asked her, "Are you sure what you do works on parents?"

"I don't look at it as working to get my way. I look at it as how it's supposed to be—shared responsibility, not controlled by one side. I believe in rules, but making rules to control a lesser being to make him or her fit your mold is wrong and should be changed." Leslie told Sarah and Rebecca that she and Kim hugged each other all the time, rewarding each other for doing a good job, for helping each other do their chores or homework, or for doing whatever Mom and Dad asked them to do. "They watch how they ask or it's a no. Not to be mean or disrespectful, but it's how you ask and what you say and with what tone you say it that will get from me the response you deserve.

"As an example, say your mom asks you to help clean the house with her. That's a fair thing to ask a child. You and Mom are busy cleaning the house. Her cell phone rings. She answers the phone. It's one of her friends. While talking, she sits down in her favorite chair, crosses her legs, and puts her elbow holding the phone to her ear on the armrest, getting really comfortable. This is not a couple of minutes' call. You, on the other hand, are continuing to clean as asked—remember, to help.

"Mom sees you sitting down, waiting on her. She pulls the phone from her ear and asks you, 'What do you think you're doing, young lady? I told you to clean the house.'

"She returns her phone to her ear and says to the party on the phone, 'Kids have no respect for their parents anymore. What are they teaching my children in school?' They teach us the same thing parents just taught us—'Do as I say,' not 'Do as I do.' All this attitude has stopped in our house. We showed them that they can't come into our space if they disrespect our space and us. Do you understand?"

Sarah asked, "That really happened to you?"

"More than once. It was 'Do as I say, and do it now,' even if we were asked to help, not 'Do while I do nothing.'"

"Mom would kill us if we sat down while she was talking on the phone with someone, just like what happened to you. This is amazing. If what you say is true, we're being used, correct, asked Sarah?"

"To a degree. Using someone can only be accomplished if that someone is trained to be used."

"Then is it truly being used or played, said Leslie?"

"They are playing you, since you have been raised to be used at their free will."

Sarah said, "You're smart. How did you get to be so smart?"

"I just watched how parents and teachers used their authority. I've seen classmates being dragged into the principal's office and dragged by their parents off campus. I don't want to get dragged by anyone. Adults would not tolerate being dragged. Why do they drag a child? If children retaliate, the punishment becomes worse for them. That's put into your brain from a very young age and is amplified by other adults as you get older."

"So when you invite someone into your house for dinner, you are allowing the person into your space, correct?"

"Correct. I'm watching them from a distance. If I believe they are sincere and true to their character, Kim and I will discuss whether we feel they should be invited. If we agree, then we invite. I may think I'm seeing correctly, but Kim may see something different. We talk and decide. If we agree, then we invite. You may get a one-time shot at being invited. Your true colors may arise, and we will put you on our ignore list. Remember; you must always be polite. Don't pout or show a mean face or say bad things behind their backs or lie to them to make them feel good. None of that works. You're going to lose respect, and their bad behavior wins. All your effort was a waste of time.

"What is better for you, being yelled at or spanked, or being told they love you and given hugs, tucked in at night, and kissed on your forehead or cheek before turning out your bedroom light? They will even say prayers with you. I don't ever want hear 'I told you to go to bed now.' Do you like hearing that before bedtime?"

"No, I get mad hearing them yell that to me, said Sarah."

"How about you, Rebecca? Do you like being yelled at before bedtime?"

"No. Then I can't sleep well, said Rebecca."

"Precisely our point. We lose respect from our bad behavior. It takes work to regain that respect again, if you ever will. We have the governor's wife coming over tomorrow to visit with us. She's a nice person, and we will invite her again into our space. You girls will join us with your mother. You know what this is all about, don't you?"

"No, not really, said Leslie."

"She and the governor were impressed by the way they were treated while in our space. They thought, I believe, that we were just being cute and cuddly when

I asked them to dine with us. If they had declined our invitation, would any of you have asked them to dine again with us?"

"They seemed nice. Maybe our timing was bad, said Sarah."

"What do you feel about them since we dined with them?"

"They are very nice."

"Would you have known that by just meeting them? You see, we invited them into our space, and they responded by accepting us as we are, not as what they thought we should be. They were expecting nervousness and being looked up to because of the job title or because they are dressed in nice clothing. That is all for show. What's really inside is what we want to know. What did we know before they left our space? We could be as we are. They respected us for who we are, and we respected them for how they are.

"Now the governor's wife wants to know how we achieved our being so they can impose it on the rest of the children in schools. Schools have nothing to do with how we are. We're not puppets on their strings. We cut those strings. We aren't what they want us to become. We give respect when respect is given to us. We show respect, waiting on their response. If it's a take and not a give, that is strike one on the adult. I only give three strikes, and they're out. 'You, as an adult, look down on me because you're older, strikes two and three.' Age has no bearing on getting respect from a child unless the child has been trained regarding respecting his or her elders. Being older should not give you instant respect; nor does being young make you disrespected. Do you want to talk with the governor's wife?"

"I like her. She's kind and respectful of us. She's pretty. Most importantly, she listens to us. It should be a nice visit, said Leslie."

The next morning, the girls were getting ready for the visit of the governor's wife. Marie and Mama were getting ready also. Papa was the doorman just in case the governor's wife was running early. Delores, Sarah, and Rebecca had just arrived, and Papa let them in. Everyone hugged. Sarah and Rebecca asked if they could see Leslie and Kim and see if it was all right with them. Sarah said, "We're here for the visit. Are you awake?"

Leslie said, "Yeah, come to my room. We're in my room." Sarah and Rebecca ran up the staircase. Leslie and Kim met them on the hallway atop the stairs.

Marie came out of her room and told Delores that, if she wanted, she could come to her room while she finished getting ready. Delores, not wanting to miss an opportunity to practice, gave an Oscar-winning performance for Marie. Marie and Delores hugged in the hall and went into Marie's bedroom.

CHAPTER 47

A few minutes expired, and the doorbell rang. The little girls told Papa that a big black car was sitting out front of their house. Papa opened the door, and there stood Diane Bronson and three staff members. "Please come in. They are almost ready."

As Diane and the staff members passed Papa, the little girls were at the base of the staircase, saying, "Good morning, Mrs. Governor Bronson."

She told the staff, "These are the little darlings we told you about. Let me see, Leslie, Kim, Sarah, and Rebecca. Was I right?"

"Yes, ma'am, you are correct. We are so glad you could visit with us today. We have looked forward to your arrival. We hope your drive was as beautiful as the morning."

"Yes, the drive was very nice. Thank you."

Marie, Delores, and Mama were at the top of the stairs, and Mama told them, "I'm first." Sophia gave a stunning performance of her grand entrance; the staff had never seen this before and were in complete awe. She reached the bottom step and extended her hand to Diane. "Such a pleasure seeing you again. Thank you, and welcome to our home. Please make yourselves at home."

Delores followed and toned it down a half notch but was still seductive, sensual, poised, gracious, and glamorous. She also greeted Diane and gave her a hug. Marie—feeling very frisky, seductive, sensual, poised, glamorous, and many more adjectives—made it to the bottom step, hugged Diane, and told her she looked beautiful. "Welcome to our humble home."

Diane said to everyone, "Please come down to our living quarters each and every morning and greet me like that, and I will be on cloud nine until reelection night. You all have made not only my day but also, until this feeling wears off, maybe eternity. This is my staff. They help me stay focused and sometimes push the newspeople out of our way. This is Jeremy, Edward, and Lynda. They are everything to me and for me. The governor, at times, asks them if he could have a time and date to visit his wife. Where would you like us to sit?"

Marie said, "Forgive me for my manners. I'm in awe that we have visitors of such stature."

Diane walked over to Marie and said to her, "I want you all to think of us as family. Ignore the title. It's not forever."

Leslie asked Marie, "If Diane is now family, can she help us dust?"

Diane put her arms around Leslie and told her, "Honey, I'll do anything you and your family would like us to do. By the way, that was the job my mom had me do when I was about your age." Leslie's and the other girls' eyes lit up with joy.

They all sat at the dining room table. Mama and Delores offered everyone coffee, water, juice, tea, and a breakfast roll. The little ones brought the rolls, napkins, plasticware, glasses for the beverages, and cups for tea and coffee. Lynda pulled a notepad from her bag with a pen. She had all present put their names on the tablet so she wouldn't forget or misspell their names. Kim and Rebecca asked if they could print their names, since they hadn't been taught to sign their names. Lynda told them, "Dears, however you want me to remember you is fine with me. My signature is so bad that people ask me, 'Just what is your name?' when they see how I signed.

"This is a little embarrassing for me, but since we are all family, I know you will understand. I signed a form one afternoon, and the bank manager asked very politely and sincerely, 'Do you normally sign forms with your other hand?'

"I paused for a moment, since I had signed with my right hand, and told him, 'My left hand is hurting me today. I'm right-handed.'"

Everyone laughed. She said to the other two staff members, "If that ever gets out, I know who told everyone our secret, right family?"

Even Diane was laughing. She said, "Would you mind if I told that story at a luncheon I have to attend to next week? I promise not to use your name. That is so funny."

"It would be okay—no names. I'm still young and thinking about running for office, and that getting out could be embarrassing."

"Well, let's get down to why we wanted to talk with all of you in private. From the governor, he's sorry he could not get out of a prior engagement. He truly wanted to meet everyone again. He told me that of all the affairs, dinners, and events he has attended throughout his career, yours was his very best and will always stick in his mind. He was so taken by the whole event he is still talking about this or that to everyone who will listen to him. I've been his wife for nearly twenty years, and I have never seen him like this. He even mentioned that I have changed since being here. Again, we thank you for bringing that experience to us. We deeply appreciate everything and everyone.

"Girls, my dear, sweet darlings, we have not had a good night's sleep since we dined with all of you. The governor and I tossed and turned all evening, thinking about the joy that meal gave us. We are so impressed by all of you. This is one reason we wanted to talk to you in private. I thank you for taking time out of your busy schedule to meet me again.

"One of my concerns from that evening was that all this was planned by the magazine and they gave you a script to follow and rehearse before we arrived. The governor has, for years, been played up to because of who he is and what he can do for companies. So, Moms and Grandma, help me out here. Were these girls given scripts or paid by the magazine to be something they are not normally?"

The moms and grandma paused for a minute, looked at one another as if they were on the program *What's My Line*, then Marie said, "No script, no payment, no coaching. These girls are the real deal."

Diane asked Lynda, "Did you get that response?"

"Yes ma'am, every word."

Diane said, "Girls, can you tell me how and why you got the way you are?"

Leslie spoke up. "We all wrote you a letter explaining how and why we do what we all do. We will give that to you in a couple of minutes. Our reason is—and don't take this as offensive, please—adults, though not all adults, expect children to 'Do as you're told, not as we do' 'Mind and respect your elders,' and 'Listen to me when I talk to you'—things like that. We know you're just repeating what you've been taught when you were our ages. We know sometimes you may just be upset by something that happened—not by us but by something or someone else. This is my mom and dad's house. We live in their house. We abide by all their rules for living here in their house. We just return the favor to the adults when you visit our house.

"We respect your belongings. You need to respect ours. We abide by your rules. You need to abide by ours. I'm in Mom and Dad's space right now, and I respect being in their space. When they visit us in our space, we expect the same respect. We're not as old as all of you, but that does not mean we have to cower down and be under your control. If you and the governor had looked down on us as just children, you would not have had the privilege of dining with us. I'm sorry, but we only give three strikes to adults. Looking down on us is strike two, and ignoring us results in blacklisting for life. This is how we are. We treat everyone with respect. We are lovable. We give hugs from the heart. We just want the same in return."

Diane looked at Lynda. "I told you these girls are very special."

Lynda asked Marie and Delores, "Did either of you or your husbands teach these girls this type of manners?"

"No, we have not taught them this, and this is the first time I have heard all this. I am so overwhelmed right now. I'm holding back tears of joy."

"That was the most moving statement I have ever heard from not only a young lady but also every adult I know. Leslie, I have to ask you, have you always been like this?"

"No, ma'am, it started when we got our playhouse—or, as we call it, our house. We finally have a place that we control. We want to show the parents, guests, and family that we follow their rules. Please respect us for who we are and follow our rules.

"I watched for some time how children get punished by their parents, teachers, and principals, being dragged from one authority figure to another. And the higher up you get dragged, the harsher the punishment. Spanking physically hurts my body but also hurts my ego, spirit, and soul. If you do something bad, can I spank you? You never see a child, angry at their parents, putting them over their knee and spanking them. You never see a child waving a finger in front of their parents' faces and yelling at the top of their lungs at the parent, do you? Why is it okay for the parent to do so to the child? While you're teaching them a valuable lesson, it is not the lesson you are teaching them, is it?"

Diane and Lynda looked at each other, and Diane said, "She makes such a valid point and makes me feel like I should reconsider how I approach everything in life. Wow, I wish the governor could hear all this. It's remarkable."

Diane said to Marie and Delores, "Your darling little girls are such a treasure. I don't know how to thank you both for bringing up these girls the way they are."

Marie replied, "I used to have to yell at them to do their homework, clean up their room, and help me with housework. I have not had to raise my voice to the girls since their house was built. We, too, are on the waiting list for a dinner invitation. We have been invited just once, and we were well behaved. It's tough moving up the list. We all have benefited from the building of the courtyard, backyard, and front yard. It's an absolute miracle what all this has done for both of our families."

Delores stepped in and said, "If it wasn't for those four girls opening up our eyes, you and your staff would not be sitting here. You would be saying, 'Who are there parents? Why don't they take them upstairs and give them a well-deserved spanking?' We, as parents, get upset with their behavior at times, but are we looking at them, or are we looking in a mirror of ourselves? Do we, as adults, think about the image they are seeing in us? You know, since their house was nearly finished, the girls, Marie and I, and our husbands have not used our electronic devices. We don't keep checking emails to get alerts from whatever group wants our money and attention. We actually have family dinners. No one cares what those electronic devices tell us; we know what we need to know.

"I get more joy sitting around and talking with my girls, listening to my girls, and having fun with my girls than ever before. I think what we and our girls are experiencing is life without a twenty-four-hour, seven-day-a-week drilling from those electronic devices."

Marie said, "John asked me yesterday where his cell phone was. I told him, 'I haven't seen it lying around. Where did you use it last?' He had a strange look on his face and said, 'I don't remember the last time I even had it.' We had to call it from the home phone. The battery was nearly gone. Then I said to John,

'You'd better call mine. I can't remember where mine is either.' There was a faint buzzing from my purse. It was buried at the very bottom."

Diane said, "Girls and ladies, I have to admit I have never been so thrilled in my entire life as I am right at this moment. You have taught me so much in such a short time. I came here to find the secret of what makes you girls tick so I could pass on the message to schools to help make the classrooms more enjoyable for the kids. I was hoping for a miracle to borrow from you to tell the school districts, to teach the children step one, step two, step three, and so forth, but your little speech saying, 'You don't see the child spanking their parent for being bad,' hit home. I think what the schools really need is a good spanking from the top to the teachers—the same for all the government employees, and the same for business leaders. Just take all adults and give them one big spanking and send them to bed without supper. I'm ashamed to admit that I would be one of the first in line. We don't realize what we're really doing. Our children deserve better treatment. Everyone needs to treat each other with respect no matter what they believe, how they look, or how prominent or poor they are. None of that matters. Loving your family, friends, fellow citizens, and your God is far more important than being what you think you are or whom you aim to please.

"Girls, I have to say you're an inspiration to each and every one of us, and I am so pleased and honored to spend time with you and your moms and grandma. I will never forget this moment and surely wish the governor could have witnessed this moment with me. I know I could never give it justice by telling him, but I'm going to give it my all. We don't want to take up any more of your time, and the governor probably needs me to make him lunch."

Sarah asked Delores, "Mom, do you still have some crow for Mrs. Governor to take to Mr. Governor?"

"No, dear, Mommy's out of crow."

"What's this you eat—crow?"

"No, it's a little thing. When my husband used to say something not right and I proved him wrong, I would make him a crow sandwich."

"Wow, do you have a recipe? The governor could sure use a sandwich every once in a while." Everyone just laughed and gave each other hugs and thank-yous galore.

CHAPTER 48

You had a snippet of each of the ladies of the club. You know that *Remodeling* magazine was very impressed with all the ladies and even tested them to see if they were for real or were being coached by professionals. When the ladies were brought to a set in the studio, a host of the show started asking them how to build a patio cover, and the ladies told them, "We have no idea how the patio cover is built. We don't build anything. We're housewives. The other two ladies are part of the construction crew, not us."

Mama put it very plain and simple: "I don't drive nails into a board. I don't ever want to drive a nail into a board; nor do I care to learn how to drive a nail into a board. I'm a housewife; belong to the auxiliary club; cook breakfast, lunch, and dinner; clean the house; and take care of my husband. I don't have time to work on a construction crew."

The host acted puzzled by each of the ladies' responses. The ladies thought all this was a waste of time and were ready to ask Susanne to take them home. Just then they heard the word "cut." Mama's response was "Cut what?"

That was when Susanne came into view and told the ladies that the magazine had been filming them during the entire process. She explained, "The owner shared the video they took during the first photo shoot showing all your grand entrances, to spike their interest. It did spike their interest, and the cable companies wanted to see you in person and see how you reacted to a construction question. You ladies were marvelous. They will get back to you in a few days. They don't believe the viewers would be impressed with ladies telling the world how to build a patio cover. They are very interested in what the video does for the viewers. It airs in three days to promote the first issue of the magazine. We have some copies for you to take home and a video of what each cable company is airing. The production company was filming each of you. From what I heard and saw, they were very impressed.

"Our writer will interview each and every one of you, ladies—the two construction workers as well. I and Mr. Barns are honored to be in your presence. He loves, as do I, your daughters. They made me cry when they asked me to attend the lighting ceremony for their balcony. I was so afraid that they didn't like me and I would be blacklisted for life."

Marie said, "Yes, they will do that to adults, but you have to look down on them and show them no respect. They, in turn, will hand you a 'get out of our face' card for life. We want you to know that we did not teach them that. Their schools did not teach them that. They are not social media snobs. They are for real. They take no prisoners. Oh, and one more thing, if you tell them about political correctness, well, fair warning, they will tell you they are not politicians and neither are you. 'Here's your card.'"

Susanne said, "I love them with all my heart. I hope someday I will have a daughter who follows in their footsteps. Ladies, let's go to the limousine and get some lunch. We have reservations, and we will get you home before our little darlings get out of school."

While in the limousine, Susanne talked to the ladies about the next meeting. "This is going to be the financial meeting—how much you will make, how long you will be under contract, and what you can and cannot do while under contract. If you want to bring a lawyer with you, please do so. If you don't have legal counsel, we have an attorney on staff, and he can review the contract and give you all advice. I'm not a legal whiz kid. Couldn't tell you what's good or bad. I had a hard time understanding my hire package, let alone a contract. I hate buying cars—all that paper, party of the first part, party of the second part. I said to one dealer, 'I didn't attend any party or a second party. What is all this?' 'It's just a formality, ma'am. Just sign where we put the X.'

"My husband said, 'Wait, dear, let me take a peek at what you're signing.' He watched the dealer's eyes and decided that he wanted to read the entire form. They actually were selling me a new car in as-is condition. They told us that there was a five-year maintenance-free contract with the car. If I had signed that form, there would have been no five-year anything."

They arrived at the restaurant. They saw tablecloths, linen napkins, water with slices of lemon, and more forks and spoons than they had seen in many years. Mama asked, "Who does all these dishes?"

Susanne laughed and said, "Their staff, Mama."

"That boy must be pretty busy all day long."

"Indeed he is."

The waiter came by and told everyone that they were stunning and so beautiful. "Ladies, I'm Pierre, your waiter for today's meal. Anything you want or need, I'm here to make your lunch with us one you will remember for years."

Mama asked, "Can we get cocktails?"

"Yes, ma'am, we have a full bar and the best bartender in town. In fact, if you tell him a drink that he does not know, they will look it up and make it, and it's free."

Marie looked at the waiter with her girlie look. "What is the best drink he makes and most customers order?"

Jokingly, he said, "Bottled beer." The ladies could tell he was playing them. "Just kidding, ladies. He makes all sorts of drinks. If you would like a few minutes, I can return to take your drink order."

Susanne said she normally got white wine. "I don't drink hard liquor before dinner."

Mama said, "Susanne, we normally don't either, but I need something strong to get my head back on straight." The ladies decided on a tequila sunrise.

The waiter took the order. "Great choices, ladies. Coming right up."

They were looking at a menu with no prices. Mama asked, "How much do these dishes cost?"

Susanne said, "Mama, eat what you want. There is no cost to you or your daughters."

Marie said to Mama, "It's okay. They want you to enjoy a good meal."

Delores said, "Not like what dinner will be like—burned beyond recognition." They all laughed.

The drinks arrived, and the ladies ordered their meals and talked about life in general until the meal arrived. They shared each dish with one another. Everything they served was delicious and came with a salad—not just lettuce chunks like most restaurants. These had all sorts of lettuces, shredded carrots, beets, olives, at least three different types of shredded cheeses, cherry tomatoes, and homemade croutons—not out-of-a-box stuff. The salad alone was a meal. They got a bowl of homemade soup, nothing out of a can; a baked potato with all the goodies; real steamed vegetables; and the most delicious steaks the girls had ever had. Every one was so tender it could be eaten with a fork—no sawing through the meat with a chainsaw. They ladies were soon stuffed, with Cheshire cat smiles on all their faces.

Susanne asked if they were ready to head back to the barn. "We guess so. What time is dinner served? asked Mama.

"If you all want to stick around, we can surely buy you dinner."

Mama said, "Dear, I was just kidding. I could not eat another bite. Thank you and your company for treating us so kindly.

Marie said, "Good thing I'm wearing stretchy pants." That got all the ladies laughing.

The limousine drive back home was full of what-ifs from the ladies. Susanne answered most of their questions, and a few were beyond her knowledge of the industry. Marie said, "How can they use a video of us without our consent?"

Susanne said, "That is a great question. Let me call my boss and get you that answer." After the call, she replied, "He said, 'The legal department was supposed to send you forms. Let me get with them and get those to you right away, if they still haven't sent them.'"

He called Susanne back in less than five minutes. "The legal department is finishing them today. We will send our representative tomorrow morning if the ladies don't object."

"Will you be able to sign a consent form tomorrow morning?" Susanne asked.

"There are two girls on the construction crew still working at Marie's. It should be okay. I'll tell my husband to make sure the girls are both working on the job site, said Delores"

Susanne told her boss that it would be okay.

Marie asked, "I have a very serious question for you."

Susanne said, "I'll do my best to answer your question."

"If you had not called your boss and he hadn't verified with the legal department regarding the consent forms and they aired those videos without our consent, could your magazine have been sued?"

"I'm sure that could occur."

"Why didn't they have those forms for us to sign while we were there being filmed without our consent?"

"You know, Marie, I'm not a lawyer. I know there are procedures that they follow. I really can't legally answer that question."

"One other little issue: they are airing a video of us and marketing that video for sale to the viewers. Where is our consent for that and the contract listing how much money we receive per video?"

Susanne was squirming in her seat now. "I'll tell you what; I will call my boss right now, and you can ask him those questions. I know I could get in serious trouble answering for the company." She called her boss. "Marie has some very important questions for you, and I don't know how to answer them without getting myself into jeopardy. Here's Marie Albright."

Marie asked the exact questions to Susanne's boss. He knew it was too late to stop the videos from airing, and he legally had no right to stop them. He had given written permission on a signed form allowing them full rights to use the videos as they please. He asked Marie, "How much do you want per video? I will personally deliver you a two-year contract with the consent forms necessary to protect your image, and I'll give you full rights for all photos and videos taken of you and the rest of the ladies. Would ten o'clock be a good time to see you and the ladies?"

"That would be wonderful. See you tomorrow."

Delores asked, "What did he say to you?"

She said, "He will have the necessary forms for us to sign, and we need to come up with a cost per video we would like to receive."

Susanne said, "Marie, you asked him some very tough questions. I am so proud of you. Will you help me negotiate my next contract? You ask tougher questions than my attorney did last year. You got me to squirm in my seat. I can't imagine how much squirming my boss was doing. I hate to ask, but do you have any more questions?"

Marie had a girlie-type smile and body language. She said, "I have all night to think of others. I'm sure I can get him to squirm again."

They pulled up at Marie's house; the limousine driver opened the door and assisted all of them out of the limousine. He said it had been a pleasure being their chauffeur and he hoped he would be able to drive them every time. Susanne gave all the ladies a hug and said, "We will do this again next week. Can't wait to see everyone again. Have a great evening. Say hi to the girls for me. Tell them I love them dearly."

Delores said, "Marie, I want you to handle all our dealings. We will give you a percentage of our earnings."

Marie put her arms around Delores and looked into her eyes. "My love, I would never take money from you or any other of the ladies. I love all of you, and you give me so much of you. That is more than enough for me. Money is money. Love and friendship has no price." All three walked into the house arm in arm.

Mama said to Delores, "You just saw my little girl in action. She can be a tough cookie. She's smart and holds her ground around anyone. Papa raised all the kids in that fashion. 'Don't ever let anyone step on you,' he would tell them."

The next morning at precisely ten o'clock, the SUV pulled up to the house. Susanne; her boss, Mr. Carpenter; the company lawyer, Mr. Ruben; and his assistant, Ms. Donaldson, briefcases in hand, were all well dressed, well groomed, and smiling. Marie answered the door. "Welcome to our home. Please be seated at the dining room table. I'll get the other two ladies."

Mama and Delores were seated at the table and stood up to greet the members from the magazine. "Ladies, this is Mr. Ruben and Ms. Donaldson. We met before. I'm Mr. Carpenter."

Marie returned with Angel and Juanita, and they all stood up and shook one another's hands. Susanne said to Angel and Juanita, "Mr. Ruben and Ms. Donaldson are our corporate lawyers and have some papers for you to sign. They will explain the content of the papers and the reason why they need your signatures. Mr. Carpenter is my boss, and he will explain what the corporation will require of you once the video is aired."

Marie asked, "What day is the airing of the video?"

Mr. Carpenter stated, "In two days, the cable channels will air the video, I believe, six times throughout the day. The video is used to promote our magazine due to be on the store shelves the beginning of the next month. We brought a sample for you to look at. The entire issue is on this house, and only one piece. We shot a lot of photos and took video of the party and you ladies making your grand entrance. The cable companies received a copy of the video about three weeks ago and decided it was perfect for promoting our magazine. As part of the business deal, we have to pay for each time slot. Mr. Ruben will show you the consent form first and explain the terminology."

"Good morning, ladies. We have a consent form for you to sign. This form is allowing the magazine to utilize your photos and videos for advertisement of *Remodeling* magazine. You will be shown on three different cable television stations, as Mr. Carpenter stated, six times during the day—virtually a commercial to promote the magazine. Having been in this business for over fifteen years representing the magazine, I know we normally do not ask for consent to use photos of people since all of them are professional models working through an agency. If we need a cute couple, we call an agency and get a cute couple. If we need a female model, we call the agency, and we get a female model. In your case, none of you are models working through an agency. We have to have your consent to allow your photos and videos to be used for commercial purposes.

"You will be compensated for this activity. The compensation is based on how many photos are used and how often they are used. It is also based on where the video or photo is being marketed. As an example, we take one of your photos, and one of our sponsors sells candy bars, and your photo is on the wrapper of that candy bar. They sell over a million of your photos on the candy bar wrapper. You get compensation from the sales. We are hoping, from the sales of the magazine, your faces will be on numerous products and seen on numerous cable and noncable channels.

"Ladies, I'll be very frank with you. From what we have seen from the response of the limited view of the video, you all will become a household name. The contract we have drafted for each of you will prohibit you from entering into another deal with a competitor for one year. During the one-year restriction, if you appear by contract with another competitor, you can be sued by our company. Ladies, I want to make you understand that once you become famous, there are going to be lots of people trying to get you to sign. They want in on what you can bring to their firm. You see faces all the time for certain products and then on another product or an endorsement. The same person seems to be everywhere you turn. There are sharks in the waters out there. Hair-coloring companies will want you to say you use Clairol or whatever company. That is an endorsement. You will get paid a handsome amount. You can also get sued. Modeling agencies protect their clients from sharks. Our office can do the same for you while you are under contract. This is a major step for all of you. You will be spotted by people on the street, and they will scream your name and want an autograph. You are not used to this type of activity. We want to protect you from being harassed by people whom you could walk by today without them noticing you.

"The magazine will have all of you make public appearances. They are talking to promote sales. You may be asked to go to a store that sells the magazine and sign copies. You will get compensated for all the appearances. You will be picked up and brought back to your homes by limousines. These are the forms that need your signatures. Please take time and read the entire form before signing. Ms. Donaldson and Susanne will help you through the signing."

Marie said, "Mr. Ruben, I have one small question."

"Please, Marie, ask away."

"Will we be given ample notice for each event or showing of our video?"

"We will work around your normal schedule. If you have something planned for that date, we will either reschedule for a different date or ask one of the other ladies if they would like to take your place."

"I have one more, if you don't mind."

"Of course not. We need everything on the table."

"Will there be more than one of us per event?"

"We are hoping to have all of you at each event. It makes the lines a lot faster, and each of you have different personalities, which really helps with the question-and-answer sessions that will occur. For instance, if you get asked how many children you have, you will get that question maybe a hundred times in one session. Did the crowd hear you? Of course. They just want attention as well. Again, ladies, in each event or showing, you get compensated for your time and the number of views."

"Will you help us with endorsements?"

"Of course, we will review who they are and what they want you to endorse. We will advise you about the pros and cons of the products they want you to endorse. Years ago, Pete Rose endorsed a pitching machine and bat for kids. Some kid got injured with the toy pitching machine. Pete Rose got sued by the kid's family. Pete Rose didn't manufacture the machine. He just allowed his photo to be put on the product. We don't want to see you fall for traps like that."

All the ladies signed the consent forms and a one-year contract for the company.

Mr. Carpenter said, "Ladies, welcome aboard. We also have, working in a couple of weeks from today, a two-year contract. We will know in two days just how popular you ladies will become. We will notify you after the first airing of the response we are getting. We will definitely have you do more entrances for the item coming up on the next issue.

"In the long run, we are hoping that the construction company has many projects that we can choose from to shoot all of you for that month's issue. Marie, Delores, Mama, Angel, and Juanita, Mr. Ruben and Ms. Donaldson have never seen what we all have seen you do. Could you do us the honor and show them why you're all so special?"

Susanne said, "You are in for a real treat."

Juanita and Angel said, "We aren't dressed for this. Are you sure you want us to do the entrance as well?"

Susanne had her camera and told them, "You look great to me, and this will bring the viewers to reality." To allow the Juanita and Angel to go back to their job, Susanne asked them to go first.

Susanne led the lawyer, her boss, and the assistant through the kitchen and down the steps to the tunnel, and showed them the fun the girls and ladies had by clogging through the tunnel. She was wearing heels, and she made a beautiful sound. They all said, "They do this all the time?"

Susanne said, "Like clockwork."

Even Ms. Donaldson had on heels and joined Susanne. "This is really fun to do."

Mr. Carpenter said, "And you both look wonderful doing it."

They came out of the tunnel, Ms. Donaldson stated, "Look at this place. No wonder this is such a big deal. This is stunning."

Susanne said, "You haven't seen anything yet."

Marie gave everyone a glass of champagne to hold while walking down the staircase. The four were standing near the bottom step, and Ms. Donaldson said to everyone, "Look at this staircase. It's beautiful."

Juanita proceeded down the staircase, and Susanne said, "Bear in mind this is a construction worker." Such grace, glamour, style, and sophistication Juanita used. The construction crew was eating lunch, and all stood up and applauded her. The four people hadn't noticed them sitting under the patio cover.

Now Angel proceeded down the staircase, and she as well moved like a model down the staircase with poise, grace, glamour, and sophistication, and she posed like a model on the pavers. Susanne said, "She's a construction worker as well." The boys didn't let her down. The applause was loud and long.

Sophia was next. Susanne said, "This is Marie's mother." Her style, grace, and poised stature were amazing, and the four were in complete awe. The crew was applauding very loudly as well. She did a little curtsy at the bottom and thanked the crew and the four from the company.

Now it was Delores's turn. Susanne said, "This is a housewife, the mother of two of the sweetest girls." Oh, Delores had exactly what charged her batteries. Each step was poised, graceful, seductive, suggestive, sensual, and poised. Glamour was bouncing off her. She did a twirl on the pavers.

The crew and the four were applauding and saying, "Wow, she's not a model or professional performer?"

"Nope, just a housewife."

Mr. Ruben said, "Very lucky man."

"The last lady is the homeowner, a housewife, mother of two sweet little girls, Marie. This is what the vision was all about." Each step was so delicate, well balanced, seductive, sensual, and poised; she moved as though a book was balanced on her head. Her glass was elevated. Everything was perfectly done. We remembered she said she was tempted to remove her clothes but the glass of champagne didn't allow her. Her moves led the onlookers to believe that she was doing just that. The crew was going insane along with the four from the company. She was on the pavers and gave a curtsy, showing off her perfect form.

Ms. Donaldson stated, "I know why all this attention is given to these ladies. That was the most incredible thing I have ever witnessed."

Susanne said, "Wait a minute, Delores, could you do us the honor of entering through the arched gateway?"

Ms. Donaldson said, "There's more?"

Susanne said, "You'll see."

Delores was on the outside of the arched gate, and she opened the gate slowly and entered the courtyard very seductively, looking very sensual, very poised, and glamorous. She was walking ever so slowly, moving her hips and frame to show off her curves. The crew and the four from the magazine were spellbound until she stopped. Marie came to her, hugged her, and whispered in her ear, "I love you. That was beautiful." Now the applause was loud and long from everyone.

Ms. Donaldson and Susanne went up to Delores and said, "You have to show us how you do that. Our husbands will pay you to teach us every move. I'll make mine watch every commercial on all three channels. Then I'll tell him, 'I'm getting lessons from that lady, and you're going to pay for all the lessons. You'd better watch and learn from the commercial how your wife will receive you each and every night when you get home.'"

Delores asked, "When will I have time to teach you?"

"We will schedule your time. Marie, we will pay you for the staircase moves as well."

When they all returned to the tunnel and went back into the house, Marie said to the four, "Look at the staircase in the foyer. This is the main reason all this has come about."

"That staircase is absolutely stunning. Did you have that built as well?"

"No, it came with the house, but Delores's husband was doing us a favor by removing some worn-out carpeting covering the staircase."

"Some homeowner covered that beautiful staircase with carpeting?"

"They also built wooden boxes on top of each stem and put a blob of concrete in each step."

"Why would someone do that to such a beautiful staircase?"

"They buried their great-grandmother's bones in the concrete blob."

"They buried her bones in the concrete?"

"Yes, after they cut her body into pieces."

"They cut up her body? That is absolutely sick. You're not just telling us a story, right?"

"It's for real. The playhouse on top of the patio cover?"

"Yes. Don't tell us there's more."

"That's where they cut up her body. The tunnel we walked through used to connect to that playhouse."

Ms. Donaldson asked Mr. Carpenter, "Is that the first issue?"

"I'm not at liberty to say at this time. It will be disclosed once we get approval from the police to release the issue."

"Why?"

"Ongoing investigation. They found fingerprints that don't match any family member on a stolen money bag."

"Marie," asked Ms. Donaldson, "how do you keep from going completely nuts? I would have sold this home and gotten as far away as possible. You're calm, cool, collected, and gorgeous, and you move like an angel. This is totally unbelievable. We are so glad to meet every one of you. We will protect you. We won't allow any slanderous anything to harm your dignity—any of you. We will watch your video on the cable channels. I can't say any more without crying. I love all of you. Have a great day, and thank you for allowing us into your home."

On the second day, Marie, Mama, and Delores turned on the cable networks that were to air their video. They watched three cable programs, drank a pot of coffee, and ate two breakfast rolls. They were not hungry or thirsty, just bored with what they were watching.

Just as they were growing frustrated enough to turn off the cable channel, an announcer for the magazine came on the television. They sat and listened to the promotional sales pitch for the most interesting home the magazine had ever photographed; with so many items that had been remodeled, they were dedicating six issues with explicit details from bare ground to the finished product. It went on and on and on. "We, at this time, want to show you what is in store for you for the next six issues. We have an exclusive video for only $9.99—or, for our subscribers, the video will arrive with the next month's issue at no charge. These lovely ladies performing a grand entrance into the newly constructed courtyard are not models. They don't have any professional lessons; nor have they been in any school plays. The video was filmed on location, so without further ado, let's see Sophia, Marie, and Delores performing the grand entrance for our camera crew ... Weren't those ladies unbelievable? Remember: these are housewives. That's correct—housewives. Please call the number on the screen to get your copy of the video today."

Marie said, "Ladies, we look fabulous. I wonder how many they will sell."

Delores said, "Remodelers or house flippers will subscribe to the magazine to get a free video. Will they count?"

"I would say a few hundred, maybe a little more." Sophia said, "So we shouldn't go out and buy our mansions, book a world cruise, fly to Paris to do our clothes shopping, or book a three-month stay in Hawaii—not just yet. I was thinking about buying a Ferrari to park in my garage."

In a few minutes, Marie's phone rang; it was the magazine calling.

"Hello, this is Marie."

"This is Susanne. Are you sitting down?"

"No, I'm standing up. Why?"

"The phones at the magazine are ringing off the hook. We have surpassed all subscription sales in the past two years. We have sold—listen now, this is unbelievable—ten thousand videos after just one viewing. Many have asked, 'Do you have those ladies doing more videos?' Ladies, you are making a splash. If this continues, it could turn into a tsunami. Love all of you. I will keep you posted. Bye-bye."

Marie put her hand on one hip, gave a seductive pose and girlie smile, and said, "Ladies, we're rich. They have surpassed their last two-year subscriptions and sold ten thousand videos just from the first showing, and the phones are ringing off the hook." They stood up and gave themselves a group hug. "Let's go to our favorite eatery, buy a pick-me-up, get a sampler, and celebrate."

"We're right behind you. Buckle up."

They arrived at the restaurant where they normally had lunch. As they walked in, the bar had the cable station on the television, and the patrons were watching their video being played. Sitting at the bar would not be a good idea; they asked a waitress for a table. She said, "Follow me, ladies."

She paused just a second, looked at the television screen, and looked at the ladies. She smiled and said in sultry low voice, "You're those ladies? Come with me. You have to meet the owner of this place." She knocked on the owner's door. "Sir, I hate to bother you, but I have some ladies I would like to introduce to you."

As they all entered the owner's office, he immediately stood up and said, "I just saw your video on television. It is my pleasure meeting you. Danielle, whatever they want is on the house. I'm getting the magazine delivered. Would you all do me a favor and autograph our copy for the restaurant so we can show our customers? I would love a photo of all of you to put on our walls. Whom could I call to arrange for the photos?"

Marie said, "Call the magazine and ask for Susanne. Tell her you talked to us. Give her your story, and I'm certain she will lead you into the right direction." The ladies shook hands with the owner, and Danielle told the ladies to follow her to their table.

Marie's phone rang; it was the magazine again.

"Hello, this is Marie."

"This is Ruben. Are you at home?"

"No, we are at our favorite restaurant. Why?"

"I'm sending our publicity specialists and three security guards with them. Try to stay out of the public eye for a few days. I don't want to scare you; you ladies just need some professional guidance. What is the name of the restaurant, and what city?" Marie gave Ruben the address. "Please don't leave there until the publicity specialist arrives."

The ladies were in a booth where they had never been seated before. Delores said, "This booth is reserved for the elite clients."

A few minutes went by, and the manager of the restaurant came to their table with a chilled bottle of champagne. "Ladies, it is my pleasure to assist you. We are providing you with a bottle of our best champagne, compliments of the house. I want you to know your privacy is our utmost concern. We honor your presence at our establishment. If you require anything, please have Danielle bring it to you. We will not allow any patron to bother you. Thank you again for choosing our restaurant."

Delores, in a very low and whispery voice, said, "This is really nice."

Marie told her, "The magazine is sending three security guards and a publicity specialist to talk to us. They want to give us guidance on how to be in public."

Mama said, "Are we missing something? We're just regular ladies. What's the big deal?"

"We might have a better understanding once the publicity specialist goes over some details."

Delores said, "I'm glad I put on clean underwear this morning." The ladies all laughed.

"That was funny," said Marie.

Danielle brought them menus and said, "Please order anything you want. Our chef is standing by to cook your meal. This is not normally done, ladies. I'm not used to this. Please forgive me. I'm very nervous right now."

Marie said, "We were looking for the appetizer plate. It's too early for lunch. Can we have some rolls—simple, not extravagant? Honey, please don't be nervous around us. We are just like you. We're housewives, just like your mom. Just be yourself. Relax. We don't put on airs."

"Oh, ma'am, I got so nervous when I saw you three. My heart is pounding. I'm all jittery inside."

Delores said, "Do us a favor. We want you to go over to that doorway, turn, and walk to the table looking sassy or seductive."

Danielle turned, went to the doorway, turned back facing the table, and did as Delores asked of her. She came back to the table, and all the ladies gave her soft applause. Danielle said, "How did I do?"

Delores said, "A few more times, and you'll be one of us."

She said, "That's all you do?"

Marie asked, "How're your jitters?"

"I don't feel jittery anymore."

"Are you nervous?"

"No, not really."

"See? We are just like you."

"I'll go put in your order. Thank you. You're all so kind."

They were talking and enjoying the appetizer plate when the magazine people arrived. The manager of the restaurant came to their table and said, "We have a group of people from the magazine requesting to sit with you. Do you approve, or do you want us to send them away?"

Marie said, "No, they can come sit with us. They called me earlier. Thank you for protecting us. We greatly appreciate everything."

Walking in was a very attractive lady and three buff gentlemen. The men were all in suits, and the lady was dressed extremely well. "Hello, my name is Gisselle. I'm from *Remodeling* magazine. These are my three security guards. May I join you, ladies? Our security guards will sit at the table by the entrance. Of course, Gisselle, please join us, we'll make room, Delores scooted over allowing room, in the booth,

"Ladies, it's my pleasure to meet you. I have heard a lot about all of you for about a week now. I want you to know the magazine is busier than it has ever been. Everyone is going crazy. The response to your video is unprecedented. We have stores doubling and tripling their orders of the first issue. I'm here to give you guidance on how to appear in public."

Danielle showed everyone her new entrance and asked if anyone would like a menu or to order a beverage. The guards ordered sodas; Gisselle ordered a glass of white wine. Danielle sashayed out of the room. Gisselle asked, "Did you ladies teach her how to do that?"

Marie explained, "She was all jittery and nervous serving us. We had her go back to the doorway and enter being a little sassy and seductive. She's not nervous anymore, now relaxed and cheerful."

"Well, she sure got the security guards' attention. When you're out in public, ladies, you are going to get swarmed by the public. I was for over ten years. It can be frightful, scary, and dangerous. I had a security guard around me twenty-four seven. I still get some crazies pestering me."

Delores said, "I can see why. You're very pretty, and you carry yourself extremely well."

"Thank you. I'm just like you, ladies—a regular girl with a gift. You all have a gift, or we would not have a single call or new subscription at this time, and I would not be here talking with you. How did you get this booth?"

"We asked Danielle if we could get a table instead of sitting at the bar. As she was showing us a table, she paused and saw us on television. She took us to the owner's office, and they gave us this booth."

"I want you to call me anytime you want to head out into public. You were very lucky that Danielle took you to the owner's office first. He alerted the staff. The manager stopped us at the door and wanted to know why we were here. They are protecting you as we speak. I brought the three security guards to help usher you to your car, and we will follow you home. If we encounter someone following us, we will notify the authorities, and they will detain them. As you get more and more people recognizing you, we will provide a security team to escort all of you. Being that none of you have ever been in the public eye, you are very vulnerable. I was stalked for two years by a sick person. Finally he got arrested and put in jail." She asked if the ladies were finished.

"Yes, we are full and can't eat anymore."

Danielle returned to the room. "Would all of you like anything else?"

"No, we are nearly ready to leave. Thank you for serving us today, and we hope you will be our waitress on our next visit. Tell your owner we really appreciate the service and the care he provided. Let us know if he was not successful on getting the photos, and we will get him the copies he requires, said Marie."

Giselle said, "Ladies, that was very nice. Don't do that again. The magazine has the rights to those photos. They decide who gets or does not get photos. Can we carry on this conversation at your home?"

"Certainly. Follow us. It's not very far from the restaurant."

One security guard was in front, and the other two were following. They got to the car, and the lead security car pulled up and waited for the ladies to get inside. Giselle got into the car with the ladies, and the other two guards got into the other.

During the ride to the house, Giselle asked Marie and Mama, "Keep an eye out for cars following you. I want each of you to have a direct line to the police department. The detective handling your case needs to be on your speed dial. Ladies, this is all very important. Trust me."

They pulled into the driveway, and Giselle told Marie, "Pull into the garage and close the garage door each and every time you come home. Only get into your vehicle in the garage. Do not park your vehicle in the driveway. Your license plate can be photographed and given to numerous agencies. Remember: ladies, I was stalked for two years. There are things you have to do differently from now on. Your husbands will have to take the same precautions." The security guards pulled around the cul-de-sac, went out to the main street, didn't return for a little while, and did not pull up and park in front of the house.

Giselle said, "Beautiful home. I love your house, Marie. Can we sit at this table for our chat?"

"Please make yourself at home."

"I have been allowed to tell you all something that I'm certain you had no idea was going on. Your home has been under surveillance since the police were notified about the gruesome murder that happened in this home. When Phillip was told of what happened and how the staircase was used to hide the remains, he contacted his friend, the owner of the magazine. That spiked the interest of our staff. Then, a couple of days later, he called about them finding a buried shed. More excitement was generated in the office. Then, when the bag of money was found, that really generated a huge stir in the office. That was when I was informed that they were going to do a photo shoot, and it could be a cover issue.

"Our owner contacted our security personnel to have them put this house under constant surveillance from that day forward. He contacted the detective handling your case and alerted him of the plans. They didn't want our team brought to the attention of the neighborhood. There is one main reason for all this security. The fingerprint that was recovered from the bag of money—I'm sure you are all aware of it, correct?"

All the ladies said yes.

"Okay, you don't know whose fingerprint it was?"

"No, we were never told."

"Well, the fingerprint belongs to a well-known person in this town. He has people working for him that remove anyone who has evidence against him or is stopping him from getting what he wants. Your nosy neighbor said that there was a murder in that house when the press was here due to a bank employee alerting them of the reward money, remember?"

"Yes, that was a horrible day for us."

"Marie, it could have been a lot worse. We had two surveillance teams on your block, watching. They saw your nosy neighbor a couple of days earlier watching your home with binoculars, and not just for a few minutes. Most every day, she was watching everything going on at your home. The detectives were notified, but they had no reason to question her without giving away that we were also watching your home. Their break came when she told the press about the murder that happened in the home. They took her and her husband into the police station and questioned them for numerous hours. You see, if the person whose fingerprints were on the money bag found on your property had a neighbor paid to watch your home and she was reporting what she saw, she knows when you're at home and usually how long you're at home.

"Marie, you could have been in serious trouble every day. You are home alone most of the day. That person had no clue that the money was found. You were and are an easy target. The police disclosed to us that she is just nosy, but if she continues to watch your home, we will put her in jail. Ladies, remember, you have not heard this from me, understand?"

Marie asked, "Why don't they just arrest him?"

"How many times have you been shopping and picked up a piece of merchandise, looked at it, and decided not to buy that product?"

"We do that a lot."

"That is exactly what the attorney would argue in a court of law. They have only one video of the robbery of the bank. The only person they could identify was the sister. The actual robbers were well trained not to appear where a clear facial shot could be taken. This is how the police know this was an inside job. A regular customer in the bank has no idea where the cameras are located. The one camera that could have gotten a clear shot of the robbers had a box put in front of it—coincidence maybe, but not likely. The sister was a seasoned bank employee who knew exactly when the most opportune time was to rob the bank and when the robbers would escape without detection.

"We and the police have this person followed daily. His place of business, home, favorite eateries, entertainment, and daily routine are all monitored and observed. We are certain that he now knows that the money is no longer hidden in the shed. What your nosy neighbor disclosed was the murder on national television. If he was involved in the murder, that gives him reason to find you, considering just how much the police know. You're a very easy target. Do you understand, Marie?"

"Yes, I'm getting a pretty clear picture now."

"Ladies, the magazine is doing far more than making money on your behalf. One reason our owner wanted to film your party has nothing to do with the notoriety or a pat on the back. They shot photos of everyone in attendance and turned over all those photos to the police. They are checking FBI files and their own files to see if anyone attending was not who they said they were. They are comparing the guest book signatures to the photos. It could take a little while longer before we know if the party was crashed by one of this person's friends or associates.

"We didn't want to disclose any of this to you, ladies. But when we got such a response from your video being viewed and you were out of the house in public, that gave us great concern. You could have been in great danger. They tracked your call from the restaurant, notified the authorities, and notified the restaurant owner, who told the restaurant manager to not allow anyone near you. Do you see this just wasn't a 'Hi, how are you doing?' Mr. Ruben made that call to you to get your exact location."

Sophia asked, "Why weren't we given this information before now?"

"If we gave you this information way back when the police were first notified, what would you do every day or every time you walked out of the house? Look around to see if there were any suspicious cars or people walking around? That would have alerted anyone watching your home or you that something was not right, and your life would be in severe danger. All the players working this day were not in play at first.

"The interview of the brother was conducted to see if he would disclose the name of his accomplice. The concrete question got a response that made everyone think he was covering up that he knew how to mix concrete. Our team of experts detected a nervous twitch that he did not show on prior questions. They determined that putting the bones in concrete in the staircase and hiding it with carpet was not the brother's idea. Hiding the bag in a false ceiling was not the brother's idea. Killing the great-grandmother was not the brother's idea. You see, the brother and sister were being used. The great-grandmother was an obstacle. She was being used until she sought legal counsel. Her refusal to sell more of the farm prohibited the purchaser from securing huge financial gains. This is something that was not acceptable.

"We are trying to catch this person. You being unaware of the danger you could be in only plays into his hand. We have a device that can attach to your clothing that can alert the security team that you feel uncomfortable or when someone is putting pressure on you, maybe following you, or getting you away from the crowd." She showed the ladies what the device looked like. It was under the collar of her blouse; they could barely notice she had it on. "I go nowhere without this device on me."

Delores asked, "This might be a silly question …"

"Delores, there is no such thing as a silly question. What is it that you want to ask?"

"Are you really a publicity specialist?"

"What is in a title?"

"It's a job description, correct? Sometimes it's used to describe your position in a company, correct? You appear to be more than a publicity specialist."

"I don't want to play a cat-and-mouse scenario with you, Delores. I'm here to let you ladies know that life as you know it is not always what you think it is. I could tell you that I am something that would make you say, 'Oh, that makes sense,' and be done with the whole thing. I could leave you with any scenario that I think will satisfy your curiosity. I'm here to inform you that you are being watched, not only by us and the police but also by the one we are trying to apprehend. All of you, including Angel and Juanita, will have to wear this device. Your husbands and your daughters will have to wear it also. We will give everyone training on how to use and when to operate the device."

Marie asked, "Are our daughters being watched as well?"

"More so than you are. We're keeping a very close eye on the girls."

"So the magazine is working like undercover agents?" asked Marie.

Giselle looked at all the ladies. "Honestly, how do I explain this to you? Okay, this is not easy for me. I'm caught in a tight spot with that question. All I can say is, at this point, you have to trust us and work with us. You ladies are the sunshine on a cloudy day. We could not have asked for better people. We cherish you and your family. We don't want anyone harmed in any way."

Delores asked, "Is there really a *Remodeling* magazine? Who is Phillip?"

"You know I can't answer any of those questions, ladies. You have to believe in us. There will be another person who will be here in about fifteen minutes who will instruct you on how to work and wear this device and will introduce you to your security team. Would you have some ice tea or cold water to drink?"

Marie said, "Please excuse my rudeness. Of course, whatever you prefer."

Mama said, "Give me something with a kick."

Delores said, "Marie, I will help you."

Giselle asked Mama, "Where is the restroom?"

Mama said, "Follow me."

Delores stood beside Marie, put her arms around her, and said, "Wow, just wow."

Marie turned to Delores and said, "I had no idea that we were being watched. Did you?"

"Not one clue. I can't believe we could be a target. We know so little about all this."

While Marie and Delores were getting the refreshments, Marie's cell phone rang; it was the magazine calling. Susanne was on the line. "Great news, Marie; I hope you're sitting down. We have just surpassed the one-hundred-thousand mark for videos sold."

Marie, trying to sound excited, said, "That's fantastic. I can't wait to tell my husband."

"How was your snack at the restaurant?"

"Excellent. The service was top notch, and guess what."

"What, Marie?"

"The food and drinks were on the house. We were so lucky."

"You ladies deserve that and so much more. Love you all. I'll keep you posted. When I get the results, I will pass them on to you. Have a great day."

Delores asked, "How many millions have we earned today?"

Marie said, "More than one million; I'm certain of that."

Marie and Delores brought the beverages to the table. Mama and Giselle were still using the restroom. Marie said, "We must have said something wrong. They both are missing." Mama and Giselle came up behind Marie.

Mama said, "Did you miss us?"

Marie jumped about a foot in the air. "Mom, you scared the living daylights out of me."

Giselle continued with the question-and-answer session. "Do any of you have any more questions?"

"Do you ever think you can trap him?"

"We may not be able to trap him per se. We know we can capture one of his employees or friends that could lead to bringing him in for questioning, and then we can produce evidence to either make him confess or, upon release, get him to tell another how cruel we were to him, and 'They can't prove I was the other armed robber of the bank.' They crack at some point. Even the best at deceiving and lying have a moment. Usually, while angry, they say something that they normally would have avoided. Every day he walks around free, he becomes that much harder to convict."

"We were told the girl who did the makeup for the sister is on the missing persons list. Is that true?"

"That's true. We hope someone somewhere finds her remains. We know she is not alive. If the person we are looking to trap was involved in putting the great-grandmother's bones in the concrete mix, that girl could be buried in a construction pour. If there is a tool that can pick up bones in a concrete slab, we would buy one tomorrow and scan every building this person built from the time of her disappearance."

At that time, the doorbell rang. Giselle said, "That must be the gentleman I told you about earlier. Let me see through the peephole before you open the door … Yes, ladies, this is the gentleman. Ladies, this is Agent Freedman from the FBI, here to instruct you how to use the security device. Agent Freedman, this is Marie, the homeowner. This is Delores, the contractor's wife. This is Sophia, Marie's mother. Ladies, this is Agent Freedman."

They all shook hands, and Marie said, "Please join us at the table."

Giselle said, "I can stay for a few more minutes, but then I must leave to another appointment. Agent Freedman, can you instruct the ladies regarding the signaling device they must always wear from this day forward?"

"Certainly, Giselle. Ladies, this is a very tiny signaling device designed to alert our security staff up to a half mile in range. We do hope the security team is much closer than that to you. These devices are to be worn when you go to a public function, take your girls to school, go grocery shopping, go to the mailbox to get your mail, take your dog for a walk—anywhere you are outside the confines of your home. You may say, 'I just walked outside to get the newspaper off the driveway' or 'I just ran outside to give my kids or husband his lunch and then left on the counter.' It does not matter. If a car swings by your house, two car doors open, and two men come running after you, you have a split second to run back into the house or stand there and defend yourself. I would like to show you an example and see how you do. Please follow me."

He had a newspaper in his hand and tossed it near the end of the driveway. He asked Marie, "Could you please go get the newspaper for me?"

"Sure, that's easy."

Just as she passed him, he waved, and a car with three men came screeching to a halt. Two guys jumped out of the car, and Marie started to run to the front door. They caught her a good twenty feet from the door and dragged her back toward the car. One had his hand over her mouth. She was absolutely helpless. Agent Freedman thanked the security team, and Marie was left stunned and shaking. Agent Freedman said, "Ladies, that was ten seconds."

Marie told the ladies, "I ran as fast as I could. They are very fast."

Agent Freedman asked if Delores or Mama could get into the house and lock the door before the security men could catch them. Both ladies said, "No way, not even on a good day."

"They made enough noise for you to stop and look. You were at a complete standstill. They are trained to hit the pavement running. They were at least three to four steps closer to you before your reflexes kicked in."

"How would that little device help me?"

"You press that little device and do as you would normally do—run to the house. That ten seconds you spend gives our people ten seconds to get into place and secure the driver at gunpoint. Your abductors have no escape, and they have guns pointed at them. If they reach for a gun or try to use you as a shield, they still have no way to get away. If they try to negotiate and say they will kill you now, they all know if they pull the trigger, the first bullet will be in their head. The one who is not holding a gun is already dead on the ground. We now allow the gunman to try to say that, and those are his last words.

"Training with security forces all over the world, talking with those who see this every day, and working with special forces, we have learned that once they pull a gun, we are to kill them. If the news media tries to make you the bad guy and is screaming for an investigation, the only other eyewitness is the driver. He's in custody, and he is unable to come to a news conference at this time—or any time, for that matter. If he has talked with other inmates and wants to talk to the press about cruel and unusual punishment, he can lawyer up and spend lots of time behind bars. Your safety is all we care about. They did not pull the gun to throw it on the ground and put up their hands and surrender."

They returned to the table in the house, and Agent Freedman showed the ladies the device and how to attach it to their clothing. Giselle had hers under her blouse collar. Marie and Delores did not have blouses with collars. Agent Freedman said, "Put it near the hemline of the shirt. It will appear like a belt loop with the blouse over the top." Mama had a collar, and hers was less noticeable.

He had a monitor that was in the security vehicle and put it on the table so the ladies could test their unit. The unit was on, and he had Delores press her unit. She did, and a flashing red light signaled the security agent. He had Marie press hers, and the unit did the same. Then he had Mama press hers, and it did the same as everyone else's. "That was great, ladies, but we are very close to the unit. Marie, go to the backyard across the bridge that I see and press your unit."

Marie went to and across the bridge and pressed her unit. The red light flashed. He showed the ladies that her unit was working. He asked Delores and Mama to go to the courtyard and the bridge and try their units. Mama pressed hers first, and the red light flashed. Delores went inside the playhouse and pressed hers, and the red light flashed. "Perfect, all units are working perfectly."

Everybody was back at the table. "As you all witnessed, the units are functioning as designed. These units last over two months. We will replace the unit each month just in case. We just don't want to take any chances. You don't want to be pressing the unit, if it does not work, thinking that a security guard will protect you or rid you of someone being overly aggressive or rude, pestering you.

"Even if you are at a promotional event, you do not have to pose for a photo for anyone. You don't have to perform your grand entrance for anyone. If someone asks a question, don't feel you need to answer. And if they keep persisting you to answer, press the unit casually, not letting them or others know you are signaling security. If people attending these functions use their cell phones, trying to get a photo of you in a position not flattering to your image, press the unit, explain to the security officer, and point out the person shooting from the cell phone. The officer will escort them to a room and ask them to surrender their phone. If they refuse, they will get arrested for invasion of privacy. Ladies, what time do your daughters arrive home?"

"We pick them up around three o'clock."

"I need to meet with them today. What time do your husbands arrive home?"

Marie said, "John arrives around four or five."

Delores said, "My husband is working at our house today or at the neighbor's home."

"Can you call him and have him come here right now?"

"Of course; he listens to me or else."

"Sophia, is your husband available?"

"He's out eating breakfast or having coffee. I'll call him and have him return home."

Within fifteen minutes, both husbands were entering the house.

As I walked into the front door, I said, "Oh no, what did you ladies do now? You have a police escort."

Delores said, "You only wish we got into huge trouble so you could spend all your money bailing us out. Papa and Brainless, this is Agent Freedman. He is here to arrest you. Just kidding, gentlemen."

Agent Freedman shook both of our hands and said, "Please sit at the table." He told the ladies that they were free to roam about the yard or house while he explained to their husbands what this was all about. Agent Freedman started to explain why he was there and what they would be required to do from now on. He explained that they have been followed for their protection since the police were called about the bones found in the staircase.

Marie, Delores, and Mama went and sat at the waterfall and stream feature, discussing what they had just heard. Marie started realizing that, the entire time, her family's life was in danger, and then the what-ifs started running through her head. "If my daughters would have been abducted from school, if John would have been kidnapped and held hostage, what would have I done?" She started to cry, and then she thanked God for protecting her and her family.

Delores and Mama started to weep as well. They all said, "Look at us. Our makeup is a mess now." They all stood up and hugged one another, still weeping.

Marie's cell phone rang; it was the magazine. Susanne said, "Hello, we want to pick you up tomorrow morning for an interview for the cable network's program. You will be in our studio and sitting at a conference table, being interviewed by one of the most renowned cable news anchors. Your video has surpassed every one of their prior promotional advertisements. You all will be paid a nice sum of money, and the interview will air in the afternoon time slot. Marie, you can't imagine what it is like in our office or at the cable network's switchboard; we're getting calls from all over the United States and most of the world. We can't keep up with the orders. The video company is going to produce the video 24-7 just to fill today's orders."

Marie said, "What time are you coming to pick us up?"

"The interview is scheduled for ten o'clock. Can you have Angel and Juanita be at your home as well?"

"Yes, I will tell Delores."

"Come as you dress normally. We have a wardrobe department, makeup artist, and hairstylist here to make you all look your best. I have to tell you this is the most exciting day I have ever seen. We all thank you from the bottom of our hearts. We love you. See you tomorrow."

Delores asked, "Did we reach a million video sales?"

"No." Marie was still very shaken. "We are all going to the magazine tomorrow; we'll be interviewed by the cable networks, paid a nice income. The interview will be aired in the evening edition as a special."

Delores and Mama, still shaken about what Giselle had told them prior, were just as sad as Marie. Delores said, "I think we all should be jumping up and down about the news we just heard."

"I can't do that right now," said Marie.

Papa and I were now testing the new unit for Mr. Freedman. They were working as designed. Papa went upstairs for a short nap, and I returned to the job site. Marie, Delores, and Mama returned to the house. Mr. Freedman said, "I need to see another client. Can I return at, say, three thirty, to see the girls?"

Marie said, "That will be perfect. Thank you for showing us the units and how they function."

Marie and Delores went to pick up the girls from school; both schools were fairly close to each other, and neither pair of girls had to wait for more than a couple of minutes. Sarah and Rebecca got out at two thirty; Leslie and Kim got out at two forty-five. All the girls were very glad to see their moms. "How was school today, girls?" asked Delores.

"It was great, Mommy. We had a substitute teacher, and he was very funny. He told us stories and jokes all day long," said Sarah.

Rebecca said, "Same old boring stuff we always have. We have a show-and-tell tomorrow. Can I show them our playhouse?"

Delores said to Rebecca, "I will print out some pictures you can show your class. Can you write a story about your playhouse tonight?"

"Mommy, can you help me write a story?"

"We can work on the story together. How does that sound?"

"Great, Mommy. Right after dinner?"

"Okay. Sarah, do you want to help too?"

"Okay, we don't have show-and-tell anymore. It should be fun."

Marie pulled in to pick up Leslie and Kim, and they had just gotten to the curb. They saw Sarah and Rebecca, screamed their names, and hugged one another. Once all four were together, they didn't hear anything from the parents. Delores and Marie were talking to themselves.

They pulled into the garage, as Giselle had instructed Marie. The girls asked Marie, "Mom, why did you pull into the garage, asked Leslie?"

Marie said, "When we get into the house, we all need to sit at the dining room table and talk."

"Did we do something wrong, Mommy, asked Kim?"

"No, dears. Mommy and Delores just need to talk with you for a few minutes."

"Can we play in our house after our talk, asked Leslie?"

"Yes, dear, we just need to talk with you."

Everyone picked a chair and sat down. Marie said, "Girls, there will be a man coming to visit us in a few minutes. He will give you each a unit." She lifted her shirt and showed the girls hers.

Leslie asked, "What is that thing?"

Marie said, "Girls, if any of you have anyone bothering you or making you uncomfortable or following you or being mean to you, this unit will signal a man who is paid by the security company to come to your rescue. You will have to have it on all day long. This is not a toy. You can't just push it to see a man come running. Your friends at school can't know you're wearing this unit. They will want to play with it and get you in trouble. I will talk to the teachers and principal of your school to alert them that you must wear this at all times."

"Even in bed while we are sleeping?"

Marie said, "I don't know the answer to that question. You can ask Mr. Freedman when he arrives."

Sarah asked, "Mom, do we have to wear them as well?"

"Yes, girls, all of you have to wear them."

"Does it make any noise?"

"No noise or lights or vibration."

The doorbell rang. Marie said, "That must be Mr. Freedman." She looked through the peephole and saw that it was indeed him. Marie opened the door, and Mr. Freedman entered the home; the girls were sitting at the same table we sat at. Mr. Freedman went to the table, and Marie introduced the girls to him.

He said, "You girls are really pretty. Are any of you married?"

They all giggled and said, "No, sir, we are way too young to be married."

Sarah said, "We would have to be old like Mom." Most everyone laughed.

Delores smiled and said, "I'm not that old."

Agent Freedman showed the girls his badge and told them he worked for the FBI and that he was there to protect them from bad people. They looked at his badge and said, "Are you a policeman?"

"We are more than policemen. We help the policemen catch bad guys. Do any of you know a bad guy?"

Sarah said, "Our janitor at school. He is always yelling at us, and he hit a boy one time and got into trouble from our principal."

"Can I have one of my men talk to your janitor?"

Sarah asked, "Will you tell him I was the one who told you?"

"No, Sarah, and you can't tell that to anyone. It's our secret. Is that a deal?"

"Deal."

"Now I'll tell you why I need to see all of you. I have a unit that you have to promise me you will always have on your clothes. We have to hide it so mean kids won't push it and tease you for having it on your clothes. This is for your safety and tells us if you need help. This is not a toy. If you push it and our security man comes to help you and there is no reason for him to help, you can get into trouble. Our men are highly skilled at their job. That job is to protect you from bad people who may want to hurt you. Do you remember the story of the three little pigs and the big bad wolf?"

"Yeah," said the girls.

"Do you remember which house the big bad wolf couldn't blow down?"

"The brick house," they all said.

"Correct. This little unit is like the brick house. It protects you just like the three little pigs were protected from the big bad wolf. If you see a big bad guy trying to grab you or pull you into a car or who is mean to you, this is your brick house. Ms. Giselle, our best friend and my assistant, will tell you why you have to wear this unit, I believe, tomorrow. She is a very nice lady, just like your moms and grandma. I'm going to show you where to put your unit. Did you see your mommy's unit?"

"Mommy Marie showed us hers," said Sarah.

"Did you see Mommy Delores and Mama's units?"

"No, sir, just Mommy Marie's."

"Ladies, can you please show the girls your units?" Delores lifted her shirt and showed the girls her unit. Mama lifted her collar and showed the girls her unit. Agent Freedman asked Marie and Delores if they could assist him in putting the units on the girls.

"We would be delighted, said Marie."

Kim asked, "Agent Freedman, will these hurt us?"

"No. I'll bet that in a couple of days you won't even know that you are wearing them."

The units were shortly in place. Delores took her two girls outside to the courtyard and had them press them so Agent Freedman could show Leslie and Kim the flashing red light; they were impressed. Delores and the girls returned to the table. Marie, Leslie, and Kim went outside to the waterfall. Marie had them press their units. Sarah and Rebecca saw the red light flash. They also returned to the table.

Agent Freedman said to the girls, Marie, Delores, and Mama, "From this moment forward, only press that unit if you are in trouble. I'm sending all of your units to our security team who are monitoring them." He opened his computer, typed in a code for each unit, and sent that message to the company dispatcher. The dispatcher, in turn, sent that code to the security persons who were assigned to watch the ladies, girls, and husbands.

"Ladies and girls, I loved our time together, and I hope you never have to use your units. You all have a great evening and be safe." As they all stood up, the girls headed to their house. Delores, Marie, and Mama all shook Agent Freedman's hand and thanked him for protecting them and their families.

CHAPTER 49

One afternoon as we were wrapping up the landscape for John and Marie, Papa came to me and asked if I had a few minutes to talk. I told him I would always have time to talk with him and his whole family. "Can we sit at the patio table?" I asked. "It's in the shade."

Marie came through the tunnel, clogging all the way. She saw us heading to the patio table and asked if we would like a fresh cup of coffee and a roll. Papa and I agreed to a glass of water or iced tea. Marie said, "Coming right up." She turned and clogged up the tunnel to the kitchen.

Papa said, "She sure likes to clog in that tunnel. Great idea you had putting in the wooden floor."

I told Papa, "I was only trying to keep dirt from being tracked into the house, helping her with the housework."

"Great idea, and the girls have expanded on your idea and are enjoying every minute. The reason I wanted to talk with you this afternoon is that I really enjoy the girls. They bring so much to the table. They're honest, sincere, and fun loving, and you gave them a purpose. I don't know how you achieved what you did for those four girls, but you opened their eyes and their minds to teach everyone who crosses their paths how they want to be treated, and they show you how by treating you that way. My heart gets so warm just being around them. Mama and I both agree that the change in the girls is reflected by the playhouse—or, as they call it, their house. I love their motto: 'We can't invite everyone to our house. We're on a limited budget, and our house is small.' That is priceless, caring, heartfelt, and so sincere."

Marie brought us some iced tea. Papa asked her if she had a minute to spend with us. She said she did, but Delores was due any minute. "Can she join us?"

"Of course. We will wait for her arrival."

"Would she like a glass of iced tea? I'll go get two more glasses. Be right back."

As Marie reached the tunnel, the arched gate opened, and in came Delores. Her entrance had become her trademark. Marie stopped and ran over to Delores, gave her a hug, and said, "Please join Papa with your husband at the patio table. I'm getting us a glass of iced tea."

Delores came to our table, and we both stood up as she approached. We applauded her entrance. She actually blushed some, and she gave Papa a huge hug and told him she loved him. She thanked him for being who he was to her and her family. Marie returned with two more glasses of iced tea.

Papa said, "I was telling your husband what a great idea he had for the playhouse and, of course, the tunnel. So much joy these items have brought to my family and yours. I overheard—I apologize for overhearing—you telling your girls that they could have a playhouse as soon as you could afford the building of the playhouse and patio cover. This house above us is a godsend. My granddaughters have never been so happy, and Marie can vouch for that statement. It has changed their attitudes, given them a purpose, and given them control over their space, though not to a point of a this-is-mine-and-you-can't-tell-me-what-to-do type of attitude. If the latter were the case, we would not be sitting here talking.

"I want the same for my newest granddaughters, daughter, and son-in-law. My newest granddaughters need their own house so they can invite their newest sisters over, and vice versa. Watching those girls interact with one another is priceless. I wish that my children had been given that experience when I was a young father. I want to pay for the playhouse and patio cover to be built right away. Fred, can you burn hot dogs like John?"

"He and I could start an outdoor cooking show with fire extinguishers on hand. You know the girls have required a taste for those burnt dogs."

"I know you are talking with Phillip, telling him that as you get funds to pay him, he would have to construct the playhouse in phases. That would be a killer to my granddaughters. Build the entire structure, build the barbecue, and pave the floor. This is a gift, not a loan. I truly love being around the family, and the way they treat each other is something I have never seen before. Whatever the cost, it would not cover what those girls and all of you have done for me and Mama. Mama has changed since she first arrived. I love what this place has done to everyone.

"If you can get Phillip to start immediately, I will postpone my leaving until I can see the grand opening of playhouse two. I was not here when playhouse one opened, and I want to experience what that must have felt like for you, Marie, John, and Delores. Do we have a deal?"

I was in tears of joy. I stood up and walked over to Papa and told him, "This is the greatest thing that has happened to me and my family."

Delores was on his other side, and she said, "Papa, you are the greatest man I have had the privilege of ever meeting. I'm so blessed. We all love you more than you'll ever know."

Marie joined us and said, "Daddy, my dearest daddy, thank you. That is so kind and thoughtful. The girls will be higher than cloud nine. Could you do us one more tiny favor?"

"Of course, Marie. What is the favor you ask?"

"We want you to tell the girls so you get to see the joy of your gift. Make sure you tell them you are staying until the project is finished and you want to be the first guest in their new house."

"That, my dear, is a once-in-a-lifetime golden opportunity. Can we do it at tonight's dinner?"

"I'll make sure John burns the hot dogs to perfection."

Delores was crying with joy. "I have never ever felt this way. Thank you, Papa. Thank you."

Mama came through the tunnel, clogging all the way. She saw all of the tears and asked, "What is going on? Why are all of you crying? Papa, what did you do?"

Marie, with a broken voice, said, "Daddy just did the most wonderful thing for Fred and Delores and your newest granddaughters. He wants to pay for the second playhouse, patio cover, barbecue, and pavers for their home. He will delay going home until it's completed."

Mama looked at Papa. "That is such a great idea. You should have waited for me so I could get a few hugs and kisses." We all turned and walked over to Mama, put our arms around her, and gave her just as much affection as we gave Papa. She said, "That was very nice; there's only one problem."

"What's the problem, Mama."

"Papa didn't hug and kiss me yet."

Papa stood up and said, "Come here, woman. I'll lay one on you."

Papa asked me to call Phillip and get this project rolling. I called Phillip, and he was on a business call and said he would call me back in a few minutes. My cell phone rang, and it was Phillip. I asked him what his schedule was for this week. "My crew is wrapping up a project today, and we are to start another project in a couple of weeks."

"That is fantastic."

Phillip said, "My crew is not thinking it is so fantastic that they have to go on unemployment."

"Not so fast, Phillip. Papa has agreed to pay for the playhouse and patio cover. Can you start tomorrow?"

"You know, I'm thinking I'm dreaming and this is not happening. I'm going to hang up and call you right back." Phillip hung up, and my cell phone rang. I gave it to Papa to answer. Marie showed him how to answer, and Papa said hello. Phillip was a little puzzled, thinking he may have misdialed.

"Hello, who is this? Did I dial the wrong number?"

"This is Papa. Phillip, you need to start my playhouse tomorrow. You're not dreaming."

Phillip said, "I don't know how to thank you, Papa. I'm speechless right now."

"You can thank me by making my newest granddaughters the next-to-the-happiest girls on this planet."

"Can we be there at seven o'clock?"

"Any later and we will find another contractor. See you then."

Marie called John and told him he had only one job when he got home.

"So early, dear," he replied.

"Not that—not then, silly boy. I need you to burn the hot dogs to perfection. Can you do that for me and Papa?"

"Will that earn me *that* later?"

"There is no bargaining allowed at this time. Be prepared to make a meal only you can be proud of."

"Okay, it's a deal—burned to perfection. You drive a hard bargain, my dearest. Love you. Got to go now."

The table was set. Marie and Delores, went grocery shopping for the girls. Papa had a short walk, Mama napped, and I laid out the project for Phillip. While getting the chores finished, we waited for the guests of honor to arrive from school. The ladies headed out for lunch first and then did their chores and returned home. They always got the best jobs; that was what kept them happy, fit, and a joy to be around.

As I laid out the footing locations from the plan, set some stakes, centered the holes, stood back, and looked at many different angles, I wasn't getting the warm and fuzzy feelings I'd had with John and Marie's when faced with the plan change. I sat down on a lawn chair, staring at the flags, trying to envision how this was going to appear. The back of my house ran parallel to my property fence. *Do I want the playhouse and patio cover to run parallel between the two other structures?* I decided to lay out the patio design, and I was not impressed with that either.

I was sitting there for a few minutes, maybe five or ten, just staring at the hose laid on the ground and the stakes for the posts, my back toward the house, looking at the fence. I was not seeing what I needed to see. I got up from my chair, walked again, and looked from different angles. I went to the corner of the yard, looking back at the house. I didn't see how the layout would do anything but make the place look as if it had come from a big-box store, China made, low budget.

I heard the front door open, and in walked my dearest darling.

"Sweetheart, it's been so long," I said. "Come here, my precious gem."

"Oh no, not that—not now; maybe much later, silly boy."

"No, dear, I need you badly."

"I told you, no."

"You don't understand. I have needs too."

"Yes, I know. Your head examined would be an improvement."

"I have a dilemma."

"I fell for that trick a few weeks ago. You must think I don't remember anything."

"No, dear, I know you remember everything. Come here; I want to go over the layout with you. I don't feel the warm feeling I normally feel."

"Just for a minute. No funny stuff, or you'll wish you hadn't tried."

"I'm starting to see where the girls are getting their spunk."

"So what is bothering you?"

"The stakes are where the posts will be placed. The hose is the paver edge. Something is just not right."

"It looks like to me that everything is running in the same direction. You lost the ambiance of John and Marie's. The angle of the staircase was the focal point, as you said. The rest of the structures were to enhance the focal point, correct?"

"That's correct."

"Where is your focal point here?"

"You know, if you hadn't told me no funny stuff or I'd live to regret what I proposed to do, I'd take you upstairs right now."

"If you tried that, you would have to explain your black eye at tonight's dinner."

"Come here so I can hug you and give you a kiss."

"A hug and kiss—that's it, or you'll be sorry." I gave her a hug and a kiss and told her that I loved her.

"Back to thinking of a true focal point, what is in our backyard worth using as a focal point?" It hit me like a ton of bricks. "The playhouse will have to be the focal point—but how?"

I went to the sliding glass door, opened up the door, stood inside the living room, and looked toward the rear fence. What caught my eye first? The loose board on the rear fence, which I had been thinking about fixing for a few weeks and kept forgetting. *Can't think of chores right now. This is serious business. It has to be ready for tomorrow morning.*

I decided to make the corner of the yard the focal point. I set a stake in the corner and set another at the farthest edge of the sliding glass door—almost a perfect forty-five degrees. I measured the exact middle between the two stakes, set a stake, pulled ten feet closer to the house, set another stake, pulled ten feet from both sides of the center stakes, and put two stakes from each of the center stakes. I had now turned the patio cover to an angle that would move the patio from being directly in line with the house.

Back in the house, Delores had changed into her shorts and tank top. She stood behind me and watched me. "What are you doing, might I ask?"

"Looking, dear; just looking."

"Looking at what, might I ask?"

"I moved the stakes from where I placed them originally to a new location, giving me a focal point like you suggested. Come here; I'll show you."

She stood beside me, and I had her move directly in front of me to get the exact view. I put my hands on her shoulders and turned her slightly to line up her view with the string line. She was standing there, looking as I had been prior, and then she asked, "The playhouse will be on which side of the patio cover?"

I told her, "I'm thinking the side closest to the fence."

"So almost the same as John and Marie's?"

"You know, I'm so glad I married you."

"That was the greatest day of your life," Delores said. "I like that the playhouse is on that side, but you can't make it the same. I know the girls; they are going to think they are not special or you think lesser of them than Leslie and Kim."

"I know, I'll have Phillip make the playhouse a six-sided figure—a hexagon, not a square."

"So a hexagon on one side and a square on the other? That will make it special for the girls and give our yard some character. Since I told you no a few minutes ago, I'm a woman and prone to change my mind."

I turned her around and said, "Race you upstairs."

I had to go back to the backyard and set more stakes. "Job is finished."

Delores said, "I have to go get the girls from school. Meet you back at John and Marie's, tiger." Off she went, and I left in a few minutes.

I called Phillip and told him I had made some modifications to the original plan and would go over the changes with him. "I need a cost comparison between the two plans." He agreed to provide the difference.

When I returned to John and Marie's, John and Papa were sitting at the patio table. John was heating up the barbecue, waiting on the arrival of all the ladies and girls. I asked Papa, "You getting a little nervous?"

"Those little wonders don't make me nervous. They inspire me—fill my heart with love and joy. Did you get the layout completed for tomorrow?"

"I did, and Delores gave me a helping hand in the decision. I had a similar situation with this house. Delores reminded me that I lost the focal point of our layout. Sometimes just a simple little statement from her makes me wonder if I am the designer or her foreman."

Just at that moment, the arched gate opened, and in came the four most beautiful girls we had seen since breakfast; the girls were screaming, "Grandpa and daddies, we're home from school!" They all ran over, gave us huge hugs and kisses on the cheek, turned, and ran up to their house.

Now entering into the gate were the three most beautiful ladies in the whole wide world. Each was doing her own special entrance. We could never get over them doing that. It was worth every penny we had spent on keeping them smiling.

"Daddy, are we eating soon? We're very hungry."

"I'm putting the dogs on right now. You want to help Mom with the salads and side dishes?"

"Yeah, we're putting on our other shoes. Be right down." They came down and headed to the tunnel, which had added so much joy to those young girls. If laughter added years to life, these girls would live longer than anyone. The mommies and Grandma had taken years off their ages already.

The girls returned with four bowl of goodies, and back to the tunnel they went for their second trip, only to hear their moms and Grandma clogging all the way. The little girls got into the tunnel with the ladies, and the sound was incredible. They could probably have made an album of the different sounds they made with their footwear.

Marie and Delores had gotten phone calls earlier from the magazine, asking to meet with them sometime next week; they both agreed. They were talking about what the magazine would want to discuss with them. "John and I have a good idea what it's all about. Mr. Barns was very impressed with the floor show, videotaped the grand entrance, and has been showing the video to their clients and friends. He and I talked after we heard the news. I talked with Susanne during the party. The whole company is banking on this to lift them into the number-one spot. With more advertisers, more sales, and more guest appearances, the ladies and girls could start events in stores and businesses. If Mama is invited to come along with the ladies as an added bonus, our families will have to hire nannies for the girls. The magazine will, of course, pay for them."

John announced that the dogs were burned to perfection as ordered. The girls were very excited to get their burnt hot dogs placed on buns. They put on either mustard or ketchup; sometimes the girls put on neither and ate them plain. Kim had her mom cut up her hot dog and put baked beans on top; the other girls didn't say anything good or bad; they just watched her eat the beans over dogs. Kim gave it all she had to convince the other girls that it was really good. Mama did the same with her hot dog so Kim didn't feel like an outcast. Delores did it to one of her dogs just to hide the burnt skin; she liked helping the other ladies and girls out. None of the other girls at this time were very impressed; they just watched and smiled.

Dinner was finished except for two things: cupcakes with ice cream and Papa's announcement. The cupcakes and ice cream were asked for by the girls. They headed to the tunnel, clogged their way to the kitchen, and brought back the dessert with bowls and spoons. The ladies said had they known this was a key to household happiness, they would have given them cupcakes and ice cream for years. Marie said she was always looking in cookbooks and on the internet, trying to find desserts her girls might enjoy. They would eat nearly anything Marie made but never reacted the way they did for cupcakes and ice cream. "We're talking even plain cupcakes and vanilla ice cream—nothing fancy, basic."

Dinner was not officially finished. Papa said to the girls, "Before you go upstairs, could you sit with me at the patio table for a few minutes?"

The girls were all excited. Papa was their favorite adult. He always told them great stories. The ladies went to the kitchen to get coffee for the rest of us.

Papa said to the girls, "You know I love you very much."

"We love you too, Papa," said all the girls.

"I know that Sarah and Rebecca's mom and dad are trying their best to get money to build the second playhouse. Mama and I are going to pay for the second house."

The girls were all screaming, "We love you, Papa and Mama!" They were bouncing around with so much energy, so joyful.

"When are they going to start building?" asked Sarah.

"Do you remember Phillip?"

"Yeah, he is so nice."

"He will start tomorrow."

"Will it be done tomorrow?"

"No, it will take a little more than a week—maybe two weeks."

"Oh, Papa, how do we ever thank you? Will you stay until it's ready?"

"Yes. Mama and I will stay, but we have one request. Can we be your first guest for dinner?"

"Oh, will you? We would all love you both to join us." The girls all got up and gave Papa and Mama huge hugs and kisses, with lots of I-love-yous like a cherry on top. All four turned and ran upstairs; we heard them jumping up and down on the floor, screaming, "We love Papa and Mama!"

Marie said, "I guess they approve."

They both went over to Papa, hugged and kissed him, and said, "We love you, Papa." They also did the same to Mama.

John sneaked into the house, put on Marie's favorite CD, and came back outside when Marie's favorite Italian song was starting to play. He placed his hand on her shoulder, she turned around, and they started dancing just like at the party. I and Delores, Papa and Mama, and all the girls paired off, and we were all dancing to Marie's favorite song and the next two as well. To top off the event, the low-voltage lighting came on to add to the ambiance. Delores whispered to me, "Are you ready for a repeat performance?" I could tell by my expression that I was at her service 24-7. The song seemed longer this time than at the party.

The next morning, Phillip was at the house bright and early. Delores was getting the girls ready for school, and I went to the backyard and showed Phillip the new design on soil, not yet on paper. The roof might be a little tricky. Phillip thought that going with eight sides might make the structure more readily available, like a gazebo. "There are plenty of manufacturers who produce parts for gazebos. Not too many have parts for a hexagon." He said he'd check with his main supplier and let me know.

The post caps were his main concern; some could take weeks to get. He would also check for plans from his supplier, and resubmitting to the city was easier than creating the wheel. All was good, and Phillip was in seventh heaven with the call he had received from me yesterday. "Nothing is worse than laying off your entire crew of men, waiting for the next project to begin."

When I was ready to leave, the phone rang, and Delores answered. It was Mr. Barns; he wanted to meet with her and Marie tomorrow morning for breakfast after the girls were taken to school, maybe around nine o'clock. "I can have my limousine come and pick you both up at Marie's."

"That should be fine. What should I wear?"

"Just a nice outfit—no gowns or after-five dresses."

"See you tomorrow. Thank you for calling."

Delores was extremely excited about the call. In a couple of minutes, the phone rang again. "Marie, my dearest friend ... Yes, I just got off the phone with Mr. Barns. What are you going to wear? ... Oh really? Wow, that should look nice on you ... Breakfast in a few minutes ... You're on your way ... Of course, I'll be ready before you ring the bell."

Delores opened the door when the bell rang, and there stood Marie. Delores hung up her phone and hugged her. "You tricked me. You want to entertain my husband while I slip into something close to what you're wearing."

"Good morning, my dearest friend. How are you this fine morning?"

Marie walked over to me, hugged me, kissed my cheek, and said, "Much better now."

"So you two have a hot date tomorrow for breakfast? Not Denny's, I hope."

Marie laughed. "If so, it will be the last he sees of me."

"So what do you think he wants to see you two about?"

"I'm sure it's to push the magazine for sales, maybe more videos being taken or going to where they market their magazines or visiting some of the advertisers. He wants us to wear nice outfits, which tells me we are going to be shown off. He said we shouldn't wear anything revealing or suggestive. If he had told me that, I would have said, 'Sorry, not me. I don't want to show off my stuff to anyone but my husband.' He'd better appreciate me or else. I'm sure Delores feels the same. She might even go as far as to smack him smartly."

Delores, walking down the staircase with style and glamour, smiled at Marie, saying, "Okay, young lady, top this." She unfastened the first three buttons of her blouse, acting as if she were going to remove it. She stopped, rebuttoned up the blouse, and started laughing. "You thought I would do that?"

Marie shook her head and said, "I wasn't sure, but I love what you did. I'm sure he was hoping for more."

Delores looked at me and said, "Well?"

"Don't wake me up just yet. I'm still putting that look into my memory bank. Wow, babe, that was incredible. Now I'm worried about tomorrow."

"Nothing to worry about, my dear. I would not do anything silly or discriminatory ever. Marie and I are not that type of girl. Right, Marie?"

Marie was not expecting to be put on the spot and said, "I'm a wife, mother of two girls, have a husband who makes a great living, have some of the best friends a girl could ask for, and am a proud housewife. No man is worth giving all that up."

Delores and Marie were hugging again, saying, "Sisters forever."

"I have a couple of projects that have been screaming for my attention. You ladies have a great day." I kissed both ladies on the cheek, thanking them for taking the load off my back and the questionable thoughts from my mind.

Diego had his project just about completed, and Juan was wrapping up his project today and was ready to start another one tomorrow. I had to make a call to the city for a footing inspection for tomorrow. I talked to the city planner and explained that the plans were approved and I had made a couple of adjustments. "Will that matter?" I asked.

He said, "When the inspector arrives, tell him you're resubmitting the changes in the design tomorrow and approve the footing depth so there are no delays in construction. See me tomorrow morning at the planner's desk, and I'll review the changes."

"Perfect. See you tomorrow morning. Thank you. Have a great day."

Dig Alert was called, and they flagged all the utilities. Everything was out front, nothing in the backyard. I talked with the masonry supplier regarding the pavers, block for the barbecue, and stone fascia with the same dimensions as John and Marie's. Juan and Diego built one. Let's see how much they learned on number two. I still had to determine the gas line run and the power. I'd do that when I got home in a few minutes. This would be a great time since the ladies were out shopping and the girls were in school. It was nice and quiet. I had to make the call to the masonry supplier to see what kinds of post caps they had in stock or could order and how long it would be before shipment. They might have a steel fabricator that could make the caps with a shorter waiting period.

I came home to an empty house, nice and quiet. I went to the office, pulled out my original drawings, laid the plot plan and construction drawings out, put a clean vellum sheet on top, squared the drawings, and taped them to the table. "I know youngsters say 'AutoCAD.' Click, click, and the revision is completed in a few minutes. I know technology is a dream come true. I like to sit with my triangles, compass, pencil, and T square while I'm drawing the plot plan."

I was thinking about how I would build the project. This way I could correct any problems before it went to the field, costing me more money. My employees always asked if something didn't look right or if they needed my advice. I was still a small contractor with hands-on experience. When I got bigger, that luxury would soon be gone or given to hired help. Delegation was a great asset if I hired correctly; employment mistakes can become costly financially and time wise.

The house footprint and property fence were completed. I drew the centerline from the glass patio door to the corner to the left lightly; that would have to be erased—six-inch-square posts, ten feet apart on the line. I went to the left ten feet at a forty-five-degree angle and to the right of the line at a forty-five-degree angle, ten feet apart. I found the center of the right-side square and drew a twelve-foot-diameter circle. "Oops, too big." I reduced it to eleven feet in diameter. "Let's try that. You know, I like that size. Call the supplier. It will be six or eight posts, plus two."

I dialed the number. "Hello, this is Stockdale Landscape," I said. "I have a quick question. I'm looking for post caps for either a hexagon or an octagon patio cover. Do you have any of those caps in stock?"

"Let me check. Can you hold please?"

"Certainly, I'll hold."

"Hello, we have four of your eight post caps for the octagon, nothing for a hexagon."

"Can I pick up the four you have in stock tomorrow morning?"

"Yes, sure. I'll put your name on them."

"How long before I can pick up the other four?"

"We are ordering tomorrow. Our vendor sends our order the following week."

"Could you call your vendor and see if they have four of the caps? If they do, could you have them ship them overnight to you?"

"I'll give them a call. If not, do you want them to supply the caps and say how long before they are ready to ship?"

"That would be wonderful. Can you call me back as soon as possible? … Great, hear from you soon."

Five or so minutes later, the cell phone rang. They had only two left but would have all the caps when our order was delivered one week from today. "That's okay; better than nothing. I'll see you in the morning."

Now where was I? The eleven-foot diameter was drawn, and eight set posts set an equal distance from one another kept the posts centered on the circle. "Perfect. If I were any better, I'd be a genius. I'll just connect the posts with four-by-eight beams. Let's get the dimension onto a larger scale drawing so I can lay out the joists. This is going to be a little tricky with all the angles. The city will want to know for approval."

Bringing the playhouse to a larger scale would aid Phillip and me with the construction of the house. Phillip would enhance the design from his experience. I could also visualize the location of the front door and the french doors. I could also lay out the balcony or patio and determine the length of the posts to support the porch and patio. I was very happy with how the first playhouse was functioning—the weight the patio could support. Phillip did upgrade the two-by-fours to two-by-sixes for the frame. He said ecstatically, "The two-by-sixes are more appealing to the eye. I believe the structural strength of the two-by-sixes surpasses that of the two-by-fours."

The layout was completed for the frame. I drew in the joists, put another sheet on top, and laid out the benches and table and the access door for the girls to keep items in that were too large to carry up and down the stairs. I drew in the electrical for the lighting and receptacles and laid out the windows. So much to draw in so little time.

Just as I was getting into the groove, in came my dearest darling, looking spry and chipper. "Oh, you're home. I didn't think you would be at home. This is a pleasant surprise. How was lunch and shopping?"

"So much fun being with Marie and Mama. They make my day. Thank you for everything you have done for both families." She came over, gave me a hug, and kissed my cheek. She stood beside me for a few minutes, looking at the design.

"Do you like the playhouse?"

"No, I don't like the playhouse. I love the playhouse. The girls will go crazy for their house. You added two more sides from what you laid out in the backyard."

"The supplier didn't have the post brackets for a six-sided gazebo, only eight-sided gazebos. Delores, you smell really nice. What are you wearing?"

"A new fragrance that the store was promoting. You like it?"

"No, I don't like it. I love it."

"How much do you love it?"

"You're leading me down a path that you might not want to take me on."

"I'll take my chances."

"Okay, let's go upstairs."

Delores said, "I'll race you. Ready? Go."

When we got upstairs, I asked Delores if this counted for our bedtime. She turned and said, "Only if you're not up to it." 'That' was the best ten minutes of my day, Delores with a surprise look on her face, I said, 'That's all Folks, and left the room.

Back to the drawing board, I put in the french doors and expanded the structure for the patio. Delores came into the office, stood beside me, and said, "I have to pick up the girls. Do you want to meet us over at John and Marie's?"

"Let me smell you again."

"Not now. You just have to pretend from your past experience. I have to leave, or the parent parade will become horrible, and the girls want to see Leslie and Kim."

"Okay, I'll meet you over there just before the hot dogs are blackened. Love you. Drive safe. You have a very precious cargo. You and the girls are my life."

She kissed my cheek.

Now there was peace and quiet for a short time. "Draw like crazy so you can finish for submittal tomorrow, remember?" I said to myself. "Wives sometimes can be a distraction—a pleasant distraction. There, the french doors are drawn, the patio is drawn, and there will be four posts over twelve feet in height to support the patio and handrails. Phillip will make modifications—I'm sure of it. I really don't know what the best view from the house will be, and I don't want to upset any neighbor. All the houses have two stories, so there are windows looking in all directions. Once the structure is built and we can stand on the deck, I'll position windows where they don't line up with the neighbors'. Phillip and I will make that call. I'll just make a note on the plan set that windows will be added upon site conditions. I'll explain to the plan checker that we may have one or two windows.

"Now draw the porch and staircase from the patio door. I want to be able to see the girls going up and down the staircase from the living room sliding glass door. I know from the first house that the girls love to watch their parents busy making them dinner, and they are all very careful going up and down the staircase. There, that looks pretty nice. All is subject to change without notification.

"The biggest question that needs answering is, Is it functional? That will be answered by the girls—how they use the space. I think, though different, the floor space is just about the same, and they use all the space of the first house. Well, it's time to put the drawing on pause and head over to John and Marie's. I'll put a couple of blank sheets over the drawings so the girls are totally surprised—no peeking."

On my drive to John and Marie's, I got a vision of what I had drawn—not a great vision, but a vision. Using low-voltage lighting under the playhouse to illuminate the patio table and barbecue, downlight spotters with a dimmer switch would create ambiance and warmth. I had enough room to add a firepit or planter but was still not certain; those items would come as another plan change. I had to create another grand entrance for the ladies, or this playhouse would not be a house but just a playhouse—nothing special. I needed to create "special."

When I arrived, the girls were hanging out on their patio as I walked through the arched gateway. It was not as I would normally do, but I decided to up my entrance a few notches without being rude, just playful, as little girls were watching. "Here you go. Open the gate very slowly, create an interest." I waved a handkerchief from my pocket and waltzed into the courtyard, sashaying in ever so manly a fashion.

I heard the girls scream, "Daddy is here!" I continued to move in awkward steps toward the patio table.

Delores was watching this entrance, and she stood up and booed; yes, she actually booed me.

"You're doing it all wrong," she said. "Have you not learned anything from us ladies? We showed you over and over again the proper way, and your entrance was not even on a scale of one to ten. Leave all the theatrics to us pros. Nice try, but you need lots more practice."

John and Papa applauded my entrance. Marie was laughing hysterically. "That was so funny. I hope you were poking fun at us ladies with your entrance. You have to keep your day job," said Marie. That brought the house down; even the girls were laughing.

Delores asked, "Well, what do you have to say for yourself?"

"Friends and family, thank you for your support, and I accept this burnt hot dog as my reward. I look forward to providing further entertainment to you on a later date."

"I can't wait." Delores gave me a hug and said to me softly, "I'm glad you didn't get risqué in front of the girls. I would have killed you."

Papa asked, "Is the playhouse starting tomorrow?"

"Yes, sir. Phillip is due at the house by seven o'clock. He and I will lay out the post locations, and he will be ready for the city inspector. He'll get the posts ready to install after the inspector signs off the footings. He'll get the beams ready, and we should have a framed structure by tomorrow afternoon. He will also start putting in the joists. By Friday, I'm hoping for the deck of the house and the deck over the barbecue to be completed. Hopefully we will see some walls of the playhouse up and ready for the roof. My crew will dig the footings for the barbecue and set the steel ready for the inspector. We will also trench for the gas line and electrical service and have all that ready as well. Being that this is the second barbecue for them, there should be few or no delays. John, I hope you don't get offended, but I'm using the same barbecue as what you purchased. Is that all right with you?"

John said, "That's perfect, so either of us can burn the hot dogs at any given time."

"Yes, we can both become the guest chefs for all occasions." The girls were all in favor of the same degree of burnt offerings for their dining.

Marie and Delores said, "Maybe we can get a real chef to cook our dinners. You boys can watch a pro and learn."

John said, "That's strike two. Can't do an entrance. Can't cook. Not looking really good for us by the ladies' standards."

Rebecca yelled, "We love you, daddies! Don't change! You all promised, all the girls agreed!"

John and I told the girls, "Thank you. We love you all. Time for dinner. Come and get it." The girls got their dinners and headed back upstairs.

"John, you do make a mighty tasty hot dog, I have to admit. What is your secret?"

"I don't pay attention to what I'm cooking. I don't fuss with constant turning. Get a little black, rotate to the nonblack side until the color is perfectly matched. I don't like giving away that process, so it does not leave the courtyard."

Marie said, "If we had a dog, that would be the true test of John's cooking. If the dog sniffs and walks away from the meat, that might give all of us concern."

John said, "Or the dog gets a new home."

Sarah asked, "Daddy, are we getting a dog? We would love a dog. We can teach it many tricks."

"It's up to your mommy, girls. She is the one who brought it up in the first place."

"Mommy, can we get one tomorrow?"

If looks could kill, John would have been a dead man. Delores said, "One, two, three."

Sarah and Rebecca asked in unison, "Mommy, can we get a dog too?" Now John had both ladies giving him an evil eye. "Well, Mommy, can we get a dog?"

Marie and Delores both said, "We'll see, but not tomorrow. We're going to a meeting and won't have time."

I asked the ladies, "Aren't dogs like raising another child—feeding, bathing, cleaning up the doggie doody, housebreaking them, taking them for a walk, petting them, giving them love and affection?"

Marie said, "Not like raising children. It's more like raising husbands." The entire table started laughing. The ladies were laughing the loudest. "We'd better change this tune, or there will be a cold shoulder lying next to you tonight."

The girls were finished and ready for dessert. Marie told them where the dessert was located in the kitchen. The girls changed their shoes and clogged their way through the tunnel. It cracked me up seeing them do that each and every night. The ladies were discussing what to wear and all the what-ifs of uncertainty they could think of. The magazine did call Marie back and told her to bring along Mama; they were sorry to have omitted her on the first call. The three musketeers were back in force.

Marie asked, "What if they have built a staircase in their office and want us to perform?"

Delores said, "Marie, you're perfect at that. You put the rest of us to shame. I hope they have or take us to a location that allows you to give it your all. I'm getting a little jittery about the meeting. I loved posing for the photographer and talking to the writer and Susanne. They were so helpful and kept me at ease. What if they want us to do some type of television program?"

"We'll just have to wait and see what they want. We worry about it now, and we will look horrible for tomorrow's meeting. We have to knock them off their feet, be in a fantastic mood—be what they are looking for in talented ladies like ourselves."

The girls returned with the dessert, eating utensils, and bowls.

Dinner was fabulous, company was the greatest one could ask for, and the ride home was full of giggles and love-yous from the front seat to the backseat and back.

The girls were soon getting ready for bed with teeth brushed, pajamas on, and prayers said. They were tucked in, their foreheads kissed. Lights were out. "Good night. Love you. Sleep tight, girls. See you in the morning."

My dearest darling didn't disappointment me. She wanted me to practice my grand entry. "Put more pizzazz in your act," she said. "No, you're doing it all wrong. Here, you lie down. I'll show you, and then you show me." Well, to make a long story short, she showed me; that ended the floor show. I couldn't move the way she did; nor did I ever want to learn.

The next morning, Phillip and his crew were on site. I showed Phillip the layout, and he and Raymond proceeded to mark where the posts would be set. Since there would be six posts over twelve feet high, we decided to dig the footings eighteen inches in diameter and depth. "We'll see what the inspector says. He may want them wider."

Phillip liked the design and said, "It will look great in your backyard."

Delores poked her head out of the sliding glass door and said hello to everyone. "No grand entrance today, boys. I have to get ready for a meeting. Have a great day." She wanted to keep her supporters happy.

I had a meeting at the city for plan approval, and I told Phillip what the planner had told me to tell the inspector. Phillip was optimistic that I would return with the approved plans before they saw hide or hair of the inspector. Phillip stated, "You know how they are—punch their time clock, hop in the pickup, plan on breakfast out of sight from city hall, eat for a couple of hours, head to the first appointment, chitchat for another half hour, drive to the second appointment, chitchat for another half hour, take a break, go to a doughnut shop or 7-Eleven, drive to the third appointment, chitchat, get a two-hour lunch—you know the drill. The higher up they move on the ladder, the longer the breakfasts, breaks, lunches, and the later the quitting time, an hour after their three-hour lunch period."

"It's all good. We need their signatures to sign off on the permit. I'll return after the plan check and, of course, pay the restitution for the permit."

While the crew was digging the holes, Phillip went to the lumber yard and purchased the posts, beams, post bases, primer and color, joists and braces, and nails and screws. The hardware, bolts, nuts, and washers were for the post bases. He returned, set up some sawhorses, and had a laborer paint the posts with primer—all four sides. Once finished, he had the crew bring in the beam lumber and start painting the beams and then the joists.

By lunchtime, no inspector had shown. Phillip called the city, asking if they knew when the inspector would arrive. The clerk called the inspector, and he said they were the next stop. "Should be there in about an hour."

Phillip said, "Well, at least he will be well fed by the time he arrives." Phillip loved city inspectors with a passion. He was most impressed when they showed up belching with a toothpick hanging from their lips.

Everything was ready, and the crew even had the premixed concrete bags sitting at each hole, with four stakes to apply while the posts were plumbed. We added a piece of conduit to two post locations with sweeps for future electrical concerns, making sure they were not on the same side as the post base that didn't work really well.

Finally the inspector arrived. I gave him the revised plan that the plan checker had approved that morning. He thanked me for the updated plan, took a measuring tape from his belt, and measured each hole's diameter and depth. He asked why six holes were bigger. Phillip explained, "The posts are over twelve feet in height."

The inspector said, "Are these six-by-six posts?"

"The shorter are six-by-six. The taller posts are four-by-four."

Now the inspector was a little puzzled. "What are they supporting?"

"The patio and porch," said Phillip.

"Since there will be people weight and no wind factor will play a part, seems too big to me. But since they are dug to that dimension, proceed. Nice job on the footings."

We could now proceed to mix concrete and set all the posts. The idea was to have half of the crew mix all the concrete and stay ahead of Phillip and Raymond, who would be setting the posts. Raymond said, "When you near the last post, see where we are and set posts with us." The first posts were set and plumbed, and a laborer was cutting boards to attach to each post of the octagon being plumbed. It was great, but they also needed to stay in line, or there would be big problems in trying to set the beams tomorrow.

The girls came home from school, saw the posts being installed, and were screaming and jumping up and down with joy. Phillip and the crew all applauded the girls. Phillip got up off his knees, went over, and gave them a huge hug, telling them he missed them. They had Delores call Leslie, Kim, Marie, Mama, and Papa to come over and see their new house. Delores called, and as soon as Marie got the call, the girls were in her car, waiting. Marie said, "We'll be there in a few minutes."

Marie and family arrived, and the girls answered the door. All four of the girls were jumping up and down. "Come see, come see. Please, everyone, come see, said Sarah."

The girls opened the sliding glass door, and Phillip told everyone, "You can't touch the posts; they are not set up yet. But tomorrow you surely can touch them. Okay, girls?"

"Yes, Mr. Phillip, we won't touch them, only look at them, huh, Mom, said Sarah?"

Everyone was walking around the structure, looking at the posts and thinking about the first hot dog party. I showed them the staircase entry, and the girls were checking out the route they would have to take from the house. This would be fun. Leslie asked, "Where is their tunnel? We have to have a tunnel. We love making that noise. We're pretty good at the noise we make."

"I haven't gotten that far with the plans, Leslie. I will have to sit down and think about just where we could install a tunnel."

Phillip suggested, "How about a wooden dance floor as part of the patio? Would that work for you, girls and ladies?"

"Great idea," said Delores. "We could clog all day long, not just carry out food. The girls will love that. Benches for those who want to watch?"

"That's up to the designer. How about that, designer? Wooden dance floor and wood benches for the onlookers?"

"I have to go back to the drawing board to make that determination. I'll try to have something in a couple of days."

The following day, the ladies had a scheduled meeting, so about nine o'clock in the morning, the limousine pulled up at John and Marie's. Susanne came to the door and escorted the ladies to the limousine. The ladies were all dressed in business attire: skirts, blouses, jackets, nylons, and low high heels. With their makeup and hairstyles, they looked and smelled highly professional. Susanne stopped them on the porch, took a photo of them, and forwarded it to the office so the staff could prepare their invited guests. Susanne said, "Girls, you look beautiful—breathtakingly beautiful."

As she finished her compliments, her phone rang. "Mr. Barns, how are you? … Yes, sir, they are right here, and I sent you a photo. What do you think? … Impressive—my exact words to the ladies. We should be at the office in about a half hour … Thank you, sir. We will drive safely. Bye." She hung up. "He loves your outfits, told me to tell you good morning."

On the drive to the magazine, Susanne filled the ladies in on what today's festivities would be about. "There are three cable television executives who are going to interview you for their upcoming presentation on your home and landscape. We're planning on six issues, each highlighting a certain piece of your puzzle. The executives are aware that none of you have professional training or schooling in theater or acting. They love the idea that you are all playful in your actions, but in our video, no one has said a word. The crowd said plenty, but you ladies remained silent. I can't speak for the executives, but I'm thinking they would like you ladies to be the host of each program. Our photographer said he did not touch up any of the still shots or the video. He let the viewer see you as you are. I agree with what the photographer achieved in his pictorial display.

"Before any of this comes into play, our legal staff will talk with all of you regarding the terms and conditions the executives decide to put forth into a contract either individually or as a group. It will be decided once everyone gets an idea of how all this is to be set up. They will ask about the girls. They are thinking about having one episode just for kids. They, as well as their moms and grandma, will be under contract. There is a lot of excitement among our office and the executives from the cable networks. We have all been doing this for years, and they believe this will blossom for everyone involved. You and your families could become household names along with the magazine.

"As a highly skilled professional, I will personally protect you. Your dignity is my utmost concern. Your wardrobe and scripts will be monitored so as not to show you as something you're not. Your image is what we want to see—nothing altered. Fresh, clean—something that the world has not witnessed for years. Absolutely no facades.

"Well, we're here. Let the real party begin. Please don't be nervous or jittery. If you feel uncomfortable, please let me know." They entered the lobby of the magazine.

Mr. Barns met them at his office. "Welcome, ladies. Please come in and have a seat." He stood, gave them each a hug, and told them they looked beautiful. "So glad you agreed to meet with me today. Susanne, you briefed them on the way to the office?"

"Yes, sir. I told them of the overview we discussed prior."

"Great. Ladies, do you have any questions before we meet the cable executives?"

Marie asked, "About how long will each episode take?"

"That will vary, but usually three to four hours. We will get you home in plenty of time to pick up the girls. If not, I'm sure they would love a ride in the limousine."

Delores asked, "You mentioned scripts that we will follow. How long will we have to memorize our lines?"

"That will be determined by the writer. It's more like a question-and-answer session, not a totally scripted program. Let's see the executives, and they can explain the procedure of each shoot."

Susanne, Mr. Barns, Marie, Delores, and Sophia all entered the conference room, where the photographer, writer, and assistants were all sitting, talking to the three executives. As they entered the room, all the other parties stood up, and the introductions took place. The executives were Monica, Dominica, and Beverly, all from different cable networks. There was plenty of handshaking and hugging going on during the introduction.

Monica was the first to ask the ladies questions. "I want to say that I watched the video the magazine sent to us. I must say I was very impressed with what, I believe, you call the grand entrance. Marie, you must teach me how you do your entrance. I'd be the queen of the ball if I could master what you do. I'm at a loss for words on how I felt viewing you moving from the top to the bottom of the staircase. We are going to air that as a preview to the beginning of a six-part premiere of your home. Delores, with your gate entrance, my husband won't stop watching you. I'm almost embarrassed. He hasn't looked at me like that in years. If he is the example of what our viewers like to see, you will be on billboards, magazine covers, you name it. You'll be used to promote that product. Mama, dearest Mama, wow, we all love you, and what you bring to balance out what your daughter and her friend enlightens the audience.

"As a trio, the viewers will have all their viewing wants and desires met. We know that once these little snippets air, your phones will ring off the hook. All of what we have seen on the video, we are hoping, is the tip of the iceberg. None of you have spoken on the video. That alone is intriguing, to me at least. Your motions speak much louder than anything you could say. The cheering in the background says it all for me and our producers. If you three are in agreement and allow us to air the video we have received, we will draft up contracts for you and your girls to sign."

Dominica and Beverly both agreed with what Monica had just said; they, too, wanted to run the video as a promotion for the airing of the program. "We all understand that none of you have had professional training in acting or dance. You are all housewives—stay-at-home moms. I might add you all look stunning today and in the videos. We hope we can portray that to the audience.

"We envision all of you to be shown during the six different episodes. We are determining what item of your home will be aired first. We will have a host who will meet you in the location given to us by the magazine. Your jobs are to make that host the best host of television. You will be asked a series of questions regarding how this particular segment was built and how you feel about the construction. And of course, give it your all when asked to do the grand entrance or pose on the bridges or cook on the barbecue or dance down the tunnel and, of course, the arched gateway. Wow, that one will be impressive along with the staircase.

"Your daughters will be asked to tell everything about their playhouse—or, as they call it, their house. I have to say this right now—they are the most amazing girls I have had the privilege of viewing. In the long run, if all this works the way we believe it will, we would also like you to consider doing more for the magazine and the cable networks—a weekly program. Our writing staff is busy trying to come up with ideas. Is there anything that you ladies need to make this all happen? Do any of you have any questions?"

Marie asked, "I take my girls to school every day and pick them up in the afternoon. Will the program be shot in one day or multiple days?"

"Most of the shooting will be done in your home. We will work around the school schedule. If we run into a snag, we can have you alert the school that our limousine driver will arrive to pick up the girls. That will give the girls a thrill and become the talk of the school for a long time."

Delores asked, "How many days per week will we be required to shoot?"

"Depending on what we're shooting, it could be once per week or maybe twice per week. If all goes according to our expectations, it could become daily, with a new episode airing per day. We need you ladies to be just the way you are in the videos. When the camera is running, you are doing your thing. Your lips will start hurting after a while from all the smiling. We will provide you with a wardrobe. Susanne will keep you ready for the camera, just as she did during the photo shoot. Susanne has worked with us on numerous programs. She is flawless. We have a makeshift set in our studios that we would like to take you to in a few minutes so you can get a feel of what I've been talking to you about."

Sophia asked, "How often do we get paid?"

"Your checks will be given to you each week."

Marie asked, "Do we get a signing bonus?"

"What we have heard is that the magazine paid for the party. Is that correct?"

"Yes," said Marie.

"They were hoping the monies that they paid would be like a signing bonus, but we all want everyone to be happy, and our negotiators are quite good at smoothing out any difficulties. We are all in this to make money. You three are no exception; nor are the daughters. I believe they have a basic fee they pay and set a certain percentage of magazines sold, and we set our on-view participation. The financial part of this is handled by another department. Shall we go visit your set and see how things work out?"

They went to the studio and saw the set the cable network had built. The producer, Earl, talked to the ladies about what the scene was to portray. The idea was for them to tell the viewer of how the patio cover was built, explaining the process of putting in footings for the posts and building the frame and then the cover itself. The girls were a little taken aback since they were not in construction and had never hammered a nail into a board. Susanne quizzed Earl. "These ladies are not the two construction girls. These ladies are housewives. They could not tell your viewers how to build a patio cover. They could show them how to prepare for the party thrown under the patio cover."

Earl said, "You ladies don't help your husband build?"

Delores said, "My husband is the builder. I have never lifted a hammer, dug a hole, or planted a weed. I raise two daughters, keep the house in orderly fashion, do the laundry, cook the meals, do the shopping for the household, and chauffeur the daughters from home to school, from school to home, and to any activity that the girls have to attend. We go to church on Sunday. My week is pretty full."

"Marie, what do you do?"

"Nearly the same as Delores. I, once in a while, have a free day for myself—maybe six of those per year."

"Sophie, what do you do?"

"I make sure my husband is well taken care of. I direct the housekeeper on what needs to be completed for whatever get-together is planned, go to the ladies' club meeting once per week, put on galas for the community—little things like that. I, too, have never hammered a nail into a board; nor do I ever plan to. We are all housewives. We are the unsung heroes that are looked down on by most of you younger adults, thinking we sit on our butts and watch *Oprah*. You know something? I have never even seen her program; nor do I ever intend to spend any part of my day watching television. I don't own a computer or a cell phone. I never had one growing up and see no need to have one now. How about you, Earl? What's your day like?"

They heard a voice in the background say "cut." "Cut what?" asked Sophie.

"We were filming all of you and your answers to Earl's question."

"You were absolutely correct, Susanne. These ladies are for real—nothing held back, the real deal. We love them and are looking forward to working with them on numerous episodes. Ladies, welcome aboard. Thank you for being who you are. We will give each of you a CD of what we will air as a promotion for the magazine and our program. If your daughters are half as real as you three are, we have a gem. We love you all. Please don't ever change anything. Susanne will have our tailor measure you so your outfits will fit you like a glove." The man speaking came out from behind a hidden camera and introduced himself as Jeffery.

The ladies were in complete shock. "We were being filmed?" Marie asked Susanne.

"Yes, Marie. We needed to see the real person in you. You ladies were marvelous. I told them you all are too good to be true. You all proved me correct. I love each and every one of you—so blessed to have met you. May I take you home? The limousine is full of beverages, and we have goodies for all of you. The front office will get in touch with all of you for another meeting—a financial meeting this time. You'll have to bring your darlings. A stretch limousine will pick all of you up sometime next week. Let's get you home so you can pick up my little darlings."

On the limousine ride home, the ladies were still in shock. Marie asked, "Susanne, did they just trick us?"

Susanne said, "Marie, if they had given you a script to memorize a line, let's say ten words written by one of our writers; handed it to you; and put a camera on you with cameramen, soundmen, lighting—all the things a normal actress faces daily—it would have made you all very tense, uptight, and scared and would never bring out the real you. They wanted to make sure that what you all do is not made up by someone else or just playacting. I'm telling all of you, you all have a special gift. To walk down the staircase with the grace, glamour, and poise, staying stunning on each step, keeping everyone's eyes on you, is an astonishment to me.

"I was watching the people watching you—meaning all of you—come down that staircase. Not one person was looking at their phone or standing and talking to someone next to them. They were focused on the beautiful ladies strutting their stuff. I know for certain that all the ladies present that day were in complete awe of all of you. I'll even go so far as to say they played the same role with their husbands or boyfriends the same night. When I told the staff who were not there about that experience, they said, 'No way could that have happened.' We showed the video in slow motion, and part of the crowd was in the shot. Not one head was looking down or around—just forward the entire time.

"And another thing, it was not just Marie's performance. It was each and every one of you ladies—even the two girls in construction. No heads moved. Even our owner, the master of ceremonies, was awestruck by what he was witnessing. We will give you at least a two-day notice before the next meeting. Give my little darlings a huge hug for me. They made my day having me witness the lighting ceremony from their balcony. Such an honor. I'll never forget that experience. I was actually crying when they asked me to join them. I can't explain that feeling I had. I was somewhat in disbelief and overjoyed they picked me."

The ladies came to the backyard and saw some of the posts installed but had to go fetch the little darlings from school. "We'll be right back. We will tell you about our meeting when we return."

Phillip was finishing up the last post when they all returned. "It looks like a bunch of sticks today, but tomorrow you'll see the basic framework, ready for the top decking. If we are really lucky, I will have the staircase assembled, but please don't go up, since there will be no handrails or walls."

The ladies were nearly back to normal, and they needed some beverages—the stronger, the better. Delores and Marie were making margaritas for everyone. Phillip, Raymond, and the crew all took rain checks. They couldn't drive while under the influence. They got their rain checks with huge hugs and smiles from the ladies. Phillip said, "That might get them pulled over and tested for alcohol from their weaving in the lane. Wow, I'm going to have to take backstreets to settle down. Love you, ladies."

While everyone was at the house, it was my turn to prove John was good but I was a pro at burning dinner. I pulled my round Weber barbecue from alongside the house to the back patio area, piled in the self-starting briquettes from Kingsford, and lit them with my sick match. It was very impressive, I must say. No fancy dancy. With a gas-fed grill, I turned the knob, and *poof*, there was real fire—real heat. Nope, mine made me wait until after at least a round of drinks were consumed; that made the barbecue taste even better. When drunk, you can't tell what you are eating.

"Another margarita, please," asked the chef. My dearest darling came sashaying over to me and poured the most seductive drink I had ever had. I almost tossed the drink over my shoulder and put my little daisy on the table. Something about cooking outdoors brought out the beast in me.

The coals were turning white. I spread them out and brought on the dogs. We had the jumbo package—twenty-four or more. The burning took a little while longer than John's, and more turning was involved. I had the girls tell me when they thought the hot dogs were ready to surrender to the bun. They were starving, so I gave each of them one for a sample. I didn't think they even chewed. They were gone—totally gone. The ladies were getting jealous of my treatment of the younger girls. "Hey, what about us? We're starving too, said Marie."

"Patience, my loves. This chef serves no beef before its time."

Delores walked up to me and said, "Feed us now, or you know what you won't be doing tonight." She did have a way with words. I loved her.

The dogs were flying off the grill, burning the second round. Every dog had a new home between the buns and gone. I did see one of the ladies chew. I swear, she actually chewed the hot dog. As the second set of burnt dogs were barking, the line formed, and off the grill and onto the buns they went. Just that easy, just that quickly, batch three was on deck. They must all have had a hollow leg. I knew these dogs couldn't be that good; that would be first-page headline news in the paper tomorrow. "News flash: After many years of disappointing his family, Stockdale—yes, I said Stockdale; that is correct and very hard to believe—burned his hot dogs to perfection this evening. The family was so astonished that they had thirds. That's right, three hot dogs in one sitting. Another fact: they didn't even call the fire department to put out the barbecue fire."

"You're referring to the brush fire Stockdale started when he dumped his hot coals onto the vacant lot two doors down from his house?"

"That was so embarrassing that even our news station couldn't air that."

"I thought he got a two-year probation on barbecuing. Is he in violation of his parole?"

"Not anymore. I'm sure he will be getting a notice to appear very soon."

"Hey, Chef. Chef, hello, are you in there?" Delores said. "Not again—driving the Indy 500. Hey, Chef."

"Oh, I'm sorry, dear. I was thinking what I was going to say to the judge."

"What judge?"

"I was on probation for starting a vacant lot on fire by dumping my hot coals on dried grass, causing a three-alarm fire."

"Really? How long will you be in jail?"

"I don't know. You butted in before I saw the judge."

"I want another hot dog. You're burning these really well. Hurry, girls, while they still have one last breath in them. These are close to jerky. Great job, dear."

Marie asked Delores, "Is he all right?"

"Depends on how you define 'all right.' The grill has no more dogs to burn. Shut it down. Don't dump the coals. Let them die a slow death."

"Wait, girls," I said. "Get the bag of marshmallows from the kitchen and get some skewers. We will roast marshmallows."

Delores said, "Oh, dear God, help me. Please help me, God."

The girls returned with two bags of marshmallows and a bag of bamboo skewers. I went to the side yard and got a couple of small branches that I'd been preparing to toss on the next garbage collection day. I broke them into smaller pieces and tossed them on top of the coals. Marie watched, got up, got the garden hose with a spray nozzle, dragged it to the barbecue, gave me that girlish smile, and said, "Honey, just in case." She returned to the table.

The girls began toasting their marshmallows. Mama said to Papa, "I haven't done that in years. Let's go have some fun." They got up, the girls gave them a couple of skewers and marshmallows, and they were soon toasting with the girls.

Marie said to Delores, "Party pooper."

Delores said, "You called me a party pooper? You're not burning marshmallows, are you? No, you can't call me something while you're not doing it. That's illegal. Race you to the grill."

Now John was sitting at the table all by himself. Marie said, "Darling, if you don't play now, you won't play later either." John bounced to his feet and flew to the kettle barbecue. Now everyone was toasting marshmallows. Some got really gooey. The girls were all giggling. The ladies had marshmallow parts on their lips. Mama and Papa were having a great time. Being the chef once in a while did have its advantages.

Delores was feeding Marie one of her toasted marshmallows, and the girls asked Mom if she had graham crackers. All the ladies yelled in unison, "S'mores!"

Delores ran into the kitchen but came up empty. "Honey, could you—"

"Say no s'mores. I'm going. Chef and gofer all in the same cookout—reminds me of being the one making the beer run at parties."

I returned with two large chocolate bars and a box of graham crackers. They were all sitting at the table, stuffed. The hot dogs had finally hit their stomachs, and boom, they were all moaning and groaning. Sarah was toasting her last marshmallow. She came over to me and said, "Daddy, I love you." She gave me a hug and returned to the other girls.

Delores said, "I would give you a hug, but I can't move." They all commented on how my hot dogs were equal to John's but it took one more than John's to hit them like a rock. I blamed it on the margaritas that each of them had had at least two of, or maybe three; after one, I lost count.

The barbecue acted like a firepit for another hour, just warm enough to heat up the chill. Papa said, "This will be another fun place once it's finished." Everyone agreed; it might be tough to decide which place to dine at each night. The ladies were already saying where the lights should be placed.

"How about some speakers for that soft, seductive music? Hummingbird ... yeah, a hummingbird. Hey, buddy, you got a hummingbird, asked Delores?"

"You ladies kill me."

John, looking a little puzzled, asked Marie, "What are you two talking about?"

"I'll tell you later. Not now, silly boy."

The next morning, Phillip and his crew returned, started putting on the post caps for the patio cover, and set the beams connecting the posts. The brackets for the playhouse were four. Phillip had two left over from a prior project, and he found two more at his supplier, so he could build the playhouse frame. They started putting on the post caps and installing the first beam. Post one was connected to post two—nice fit. There was one little hiccup—the beam needed to be trimmed to match the bracket, or the next beam would not fit. They took out the beam and cut the angles on both ends. This continued until the eight sides were in position, drilled, and bolted.

Now how would they attach the beams that connected the patio cover to the octagon? Phillip took a photo of the beam leading from the corner post to the octagon and sent it to his supplier. "Is there a brace made to connect the two beams at the angle shown?"

"They make a hanger for such situations. What size is your beams?"

Phillip texted, "Six-by-eight beams, rough-sawn cedar."

The supplier texted back that he had one in stock and would call his other store. "If they have one, it could be in here in about an hour."

Phillip said, "Call them. I'm on my way to pick up the one you have."

When Phillip arrived at the supplier, the salesman told him the other bracket would be delivered to his store. He said he would call me when it arrived. Phillip headed back to the job site with the bracket.

While he was gone, Raymond and his laborers put in nearly all the joists under the playhouse. Phillip gave them the bracket, and they cut the first beam to the exact length and installed the second one. We now could see the basic shape of the patio cover. Phillip decided to begin the framing for the porch and balcony, attaching the smaller posts to the frame of the octagon. This would make it easier for the crew to climb up the stairs and onto the deck to build the second-level playhouse. Phillip had already picked up the stringer for the staircase. Raymond and his foreman put the frame on the posts and attached the posts to the beam, ready for the joists. They moved over to the balcony and followed the same procedure.

Now they were ready for the sawman to make the exact cuts to fit the joists. They would call out the exact measurement, and the saw operator would make the exact cut; they had the painter deliver the joists for Raymond and his foreman to install. The joists for the porch and balcony were ready for the decking after the main decking for the playhouse was in place.

The chore now was to install the stringers; this would take a couple of more men to hold and steady while the brackets were placed. The first stringer was soon in place; they needed the treads cut and placed to make sure the distance was correct. The bottom step was elevated to six inches from the deck. Four stakes were placed on each stringer after being driven into the ground; the top was put into the bracket and nailed. The stringers were in place; now they would put in the risers and treads and anchor the bottom step with concrete. They cut a four-by-four to the proper length, set the posts into a predug footing, and poured.

With Raymond on one side and his foreman on the other, they were calling out the cuts for the riser and treads, equipped with the right screws to be placed in countersunk drilled holes. The treads and risers began making their way up the staircase. Once the concrete footing set up, they could use the staircase to haul lumber and tools to the playhouse. Phillip's woodworking master would come with the crew tomorrow to router the step treads before the handrails were installed, making a beautiful set of steps. "This time the treads will not be painted or coated with polyurethane until the playhouse is nearly finished. Oh, the girls are going to be so excited."

The bottom post and the porch posts had been set yesterday, so Raymond and his foreman put a temporary railing between the posts to help save people from falling off the stairs. The balusters and handrailing were being machined in the shop by the woodworking master's assistants.

The supplier called Phillip to let him know the bracket had just arrived. Phillip, wasting no time, hopped into his truck, and off he went. While at the supplier, Phillip picked up a one-inch-thick piece of plywood—enough to do the playhouse floor—and three-quarter-inch plywood sheeting to go above the barbecue area. As the lumber was being delivered, the painter was busy painting the primer and one finished coat of paint. It was an ongoing job, and the paint needed to be dry before installation, or the installers got paint on their hands and then on the tools; cleanup could take its toll.

Phillip returned, and the painter was busy priming the plywood—one side this time and one side when installed. He would also get to see the view from the second floor. He used rollers on extension poles—no brushes, all rolled. The brushwork was done on the final coat. Then Phillip pulled all his painters to complete another job. The carpenter making all the cuts used to be Raymond's foreman, but that limited him to one project; Phillip might have multiple projects going on at one time, and the carpenter could now move from one to another on an as-needed basis.

Raymond controlled where he was needed the most; this was a quick project. Cuts were consistent, and the demand was quick. To keep a rhythm going, Raymond used the painter to shuttle cut lumber to the installers and vice versa. Raymond marked the ends of boards with a number so he could keep track of where each cut would be placed. It was a great system, and everyone was pleased with the progress.

Marie showed up at the house and, of course, had her camera. *Click, click, click, click!* She told Phillip they had to slow down; she was afraid she would miss part of the construction for Delores's photo album. Phillip told Marie he would buy her doughnuts if she got there at seven o'clock; when they started, she would have to wear boots and jeans with a plaid shirt and a hard hat. She looked at him and said, "Do I need a tool belt as well?"

"Oh, that might be too much for my crew to handle. Seeing you do your grand entrance wearing a tool belt will put me and them over the edge."

She laughed. "Your offer is inviting but has one slight problem. I don't eat doughnuts, only pastries, and no coffee from paper or Styrofoam cups but china— not made in China, but real china: teacups with matching saucers. I don't eat with my fingers either but on a china plate with a sterling silver fork, and a real glass of water—not tap, but filtered with a slice of lemon, no ice."

Phillip asked if he could bring his maid to serve her.

"If she is a true maid, dressed in the proper attire, 'Yes ma'am' and 'No ma'am' are the only words I want from her lips. Oh, one other thing."

"What's the one other thing?"

"She can't be prettier than me."

"Marie, I could look for over a hundred years and never find a maid that would be prettier than you or built like you. Excuse me for saying that."

"I'll excuse you this time, but watch it. Gentlemen, have a great day. The project looks beautiful. Remember my girls. Quality counts with them and me. Also remember they can't invite everyone to dinner. Their budget is limited, and their space is small."

Marie entered the house where Delores was finishing cleaning up the breakfast dishes. Marie said, "Have the maid do that for you."

"What did they put in your coffee this morning?"

"What do you mean, my dearest sister?"

"I don't have a maid or a butler or a chauffeur yet. Maybe next year, if all goes well. Cut. Play that again."

"Boy, wouldn't that be such fun having a staff take care of all your needs."

"All my needs?"

"Not that—not now, silly girl." The two gave each other a great big hug. "What to do now, my lovely sister?"

"Do you want to play house?"

"No, I do that every day. Boring. Mama and Papa are going to a movie. I have a day of freedom. Too early for lunch. What to do? What to do? I don't want to stay here and listen to a saw cut lumber all day. Let's go shopping. Let's go to a park or a lake and walk around."

"Where? A park or lake?"

"No, there has to be something better—too many bugs and mosquitoes."

"You're not being easy today. What's the problem?"

"I got so excited yesterday while they were talking with us—I mean *really* excited. I want it to start now."

"Me too. I was getting excited as well—churning inside. Not hunger or gas—a different type of churning, like I hope what we do helps others and maybe changes their lives like it has ours. You're right. I don't want to hear that saw run all day either. Let's take a drive, and where we end up is where we end up. We'll play it all day by ear. I had better change into my gown. My Cinderella outfit may turn off those around us."

"You could wear anything and turning off those around you would never happen."

"Wow, I like what they slipped into your coffee."

I arrived and saw the progress. "You guys are working fast," I said. "Phillip, do you want to see where we could install a wooden dance floor on the patio? I'm thinking of matching the playhouse so they both tie together."

"That would look great. How about putting a border along the edge? My master carpenter can rout the edge, creating a bullnose effect like he will put on the treads, porch, and balcony. Should it be one-by-one or two-by-two on the dance floor?"

"We could do a plywood base of three-quarter inch and a one-inch dance floor, oak, stained to match the treads and the playhouse floor."

"So all the items will fit together as one theme?"

"Correct, and will last for years."

"I know a perfect place to install the dance floor."

"Where, might I ask?"

"Under the playhouse. It will be protected from the sun. Your benches can be made to fit between the posts and shade the deck at the same time, and a six-inch rise from the barbecue would be very stylish and allow the floor to echo. The deck can sit on pavers to prevent rotting."

"Let me kick that around with the girls and Delores. I like the idea. I'm certain they will as well."

The next morning, bright and early, Phillip and his crew were starting to install the plywood on top of the patio cover first; those had the least number of cuts. They also wanted to stockpile the frame for the playhouse. The deck above the patio was completed in a very short time. With the joists and blocking in place, they could start putting in the shiplap while the playhouse was being built. Precision, precision, precision—it was a very well-oiled machine.

With everyone busy, Delores, the girls, and I met with Phillip regarding his idea of putting a dance floor under the playhouse. Phillip and Raymond made up a prototype for the girls and Delores to practice on. They had it set up under the playhouse. It wasn't finished or stained or coated with polyurethane but was very well built. Phillip made sure that all work above the girls' heads was stopped. "Take a break, gentlemen," Phillip told his crew. He took the girls and Delores over to the prototype.

The girls said, "Mommy, we need our hard-soled shoes." Delores and the girls went back into the house and put on hard-soled shoes. In the meantime, Phillip had the crew lay plywood sheeting from the patio door to the playhouse. The girls came from the house first, running to the playhouse. "Can we try it now?"

Phillip said, "Be my guest. Be careful not to fall."

While the girls were clogging away, Delores—not letting an audience be disappointed—did the ultimate grand entrance with high heels. The crew came apart with applause. The louder they clapped, the more seductive she became. Phillip's crew would be a wreck the rest of the day.

"Mommy," said the girls, "we love it. Please, Mommy, please say yes, said Sarah."

Delores got on the prototype and did her clogging. The echo was not as loud as in the tunnel but was quite impressive nonetheless. Phillip stretched out his hand and helped Delores to the plywood sheeting. Delores said, "I like it, and the girls love it, so this will be a fine addition to our living space." She gave Phillip a hug. "Great job."

The girls jumped back on the prototype and clogged some more. They wanted to get in extra clogs before being told it was time to get ready for school, which Delores did as soon as she turned toward the house. "Oh, Mom, can't we play just a couple of minutes more, asked Sarah?"

"As soon as I reach the sliding glass door, your time is done." The girls complied with Mama's order. Phillip told them he would keep the prototype under the playhouse for them to play on after the crew went home. That alone got those girls pumped up even more.

Phillip and I talked about the pavers under the deck. "Would that increase the echo?"

"I'll have Juan and Angel put a paver deck under your prototype to see if it adds to the echo. Can I have them do that this afternoon?"

"Once we get the deck finished for the playhouse. The crew will then be protected from anything that might fall. Just in case, have them wear hard hats."

Raymond and the crew were busy carrying the plywood sheeting for the playhouse floor to where it would be installed. They did raise the floor up six inches and then put down the plywood sheeting. The sawman was stationed on top of the patio cover, and the sill plate lumber was being put alongside his saw. They told me that if all went well, they might have half or more of the wall frames up by the end of the day.

When I went back into the house, the saw started; and according to Delores and Marie, it was running all day. Phillip took the necessary time to determine just where the windows could be placed so the neighbors' privacy would be honored. Many of the neighbors had used trees or shrubbery to hide their windows, so the playhouse windows were used for the playhouse's best view. Raymond and his foreman were installing the sill plate on the plywood sheeting. Once the angles were cut, plywood was firmly secured to the joists, and Raymond gave his rendition of clogging on the playhouse deck; only one employee applauded. The crew told him, "It's not the same. Don't give up you day job."

When Marie arrived, the crew kept her in sight so nothing could fall and hit her. She climbed the staircase and took photos of the deck and sill plate being installed. Raymond told her they would build the first wall in about a half hour and get ready to stand it up. If she would hang around for that time, she could photograph the wall being placed. "Thank you, Raymond. I will have a cup of coffee with Delores, and we both will be on the stairs to take the photo."

Raymond told the sawman to cut the two-by-six redwood to thirty-eight inches in length; they needed eight boards. The crew on the ground hurried with the two-by-six boards being cut to length. The man shuttling the boards got them to Raymond, and he installed them on the porch for Delores and Marie to stand on while taking photos. He also got a two-by-four and screwed it to the two posts as a temporary handrail. He also installed a temporary vertical two-by-four board on the four-by-eight frame and added another two-by-four connecting the temporary vertical support to the porch post. Now the porch was enclosed so the ladies should not fall off the porch. That took all of about ten minutes, tops; if one of the ladies stumbled and fell to the ground, the crew and Phillip would be devastated.

The foreman and crew were busy building the first wall to stand. Raymond checked all the dimensions, making sure it was ready. All checked out and was square. The bolts were installed in the sill plate to receive the wall; they cut stakes to hold the wall up and checked for plumb while the next panel was built. Raymond called for Delores and Marie; the wall was ready to install. The ladies gladly came from the house. It was such a joy for the crew to see these two ladies; they didn't even do a grand entrance but got a round of applause from the crew. Such influence was remarkable to witness.

The men stood the wall on the playhouse subfloor and lifted it onto the foundation bolts. Raymond checked the wall for plumb, and the washer and nuts were installed; the first wall was up and in position. Marie asked, "When will the next panel be ready to install?"

"Give us a half hour or more. This one has a window, and we have to box out for the window."

With a great smile, Marie said, "See you soon. Let us know, and we will return."

Delores asked Marie when they returned to the house, "Are we going to photograph each wall?"

"Do you not like the crew making you feel desired?"

"That is all fine and wonderful, but we need to get a life and do what we need to do. We keep getting them excited. May not turn out as well as you might think. Remember the hummingbird?"

"Oh, yeah, the hummingbird. One more photo, and then we will shoot what's up when the crew heads home."

"Perfect. I can live with that."

Raymond and the crew were able to build and install five panels from the front door to the french doors, which were secured with braces. They knew that the girls and the ladies would want to walk around on the playhouse floor. They used two-by-fours to form a temporary handrail and boarded from the last panel installed to the front door panel. The job site was secure enough to protect someone from falling from the playhouse. Raymond also installed the decking for the balcony, with the saw on the patio roof making everything much easier. They also put up a temporary handrail around the patio roof in case they wanted to stroll on that; no one did, however. Juan and Angel put a paver pad under the prototype floor for the girls to clog on. Phillip and Raymond secured the floor so it would not move.

When Delores, Marie, and the girls arrived at our home, the girls could not wait to start clogging on the floor. The echo had improved; it was not as loud as in the tunnel but loud enough to be heard from inside the house. Marie had brought high-heeled shoes with her; they stopped at her house for about an hour and sat on the bench, watching the waterfall and girl-talking. That was their walk in the park—with margaritas in hand a couple of times, we heard. Mama and Papa joined them, and they all shared the bench and sat on the waterfall wall. They all said that this was a great, relaxing idea.

I was impressed at the progress made on the playhouse, but that was Phillip— everything planned out to the minute. He left me a note that they would finish the panels tomorrow and start putting on the roof frame. "Did the girls finish painting the ceiling for the inside?" They would also start roofing the patio cover. "Can we get the electrical conduits installed first thing before we start buttoning up the walls? Did you call the doorman for the front door?" I didn't know what had gotten into me lately. I would have to say "not yet" on all those questions.

I called Juan and told him to report to my house in the morning and bring all the conduit he had to my house. He said, "I'll also bring the fixtures and electrical boxes that I have, and you can make a list before you purchase something I already have." I was at least three days behind Phillip. This was not good. I had no choice but to get focused and stay focused.

I called our doorman and told him, "We are building a second playhouse, and I need a front door. The panel is installed. If you would come to my house and measure the rough opening, Phillip is building the playhouse. If anything needs altering, let him or Raymond know. See you tomorrow. Great talking with you again."

I asked the girls and ladies if the ceiling had been painted. "Nope, not yet," said the ladies. "We just have not had time. Can we start tomorrow once you know the exact size and shape of the ceiling, said Delores?"

"That is a great idea. Thank you for putting it back on me, I told her."

"We just didn't want to have to do it twice. You made a plan change, correct, said Delores?"

"Yes, I did make a change and, I hope, for the better, I told her."

Marie came over to me, put her arms around me, and said, "The playhouse is beautiful. I can't wait to see the girls on the balcony asking you, 'Are the hot dogs done yet? We're starving.'"

The magic was continuing. We all were in complete awe. The girls were taking turns dancing on the prototype, seeing who could make the nicest noise. Mama and Papa were watching them, and Mama joined in the fun. Delores—oh, my dearest darling—she slipped on her high heels and clogged up a storm. Marie did the same. John handed me a twenty-four pack of hot dogs and five pounds of burger patties. "Here you go, champ. Burn away."

"Oh, I forgot I'm the chef. Where's my Weber? Oh, there it is, just where I left it yesterday." I loaded up the Kingsford briquettes, found my matches, and let it fire. I waited a few minutes; white hot was the best. "Marie, the chef needs a margarita to stay focused."

She walked over to me and asked, "Do you want salt on the rim of your glass, master?"

"Oh, if only I were your master."

She headed to the house, looked over her shoulder, smiled, and said, "Dream on, lover. Dream on."

"You know how one simple phrase can come back and haunt you for decades?"

John said she would have given him a verbal lesson, manners and all that speech that he had burned into his mind. "You were very lucky."

"I have one of those from Delores. I can almost say the words before she does. I'm certain I will hear those words before the night is over."

Delores brought out the margarita to me. "Drink up, dear. We put something special in yours." Then she sashayed back into the house. I asked John if he would like the first margarita.

"No, my friend. Remember: they put something special in yours. I don't want them to do that to mine."

"I'll just have to burn the food a little better tonight. Something special. Just what could they have added? I know—a loving touch and a huge smile. Fat chance of that happening."

The girls were still clogging, and they never got tired—so much energy. Finally the girls all went up the staircase, and we all reminded them to be careful. Mama and Papa joined them, and we reminded them also. Mama gave us a look only a mother could give her child. John told me, "Welcome to my world."

The girls were discussing the location of the benches and table. They walked onto the balcony, and asked, "Daddy, how much longer? We're starving, said Sarah." All that clogging had put their appetites in full gear.

The girls were telling Mama and Papa where they decided to put the benches and table and asked if they thought their ideas were correct. Mama and Papa told them, "Girls, your ideas are perfect. This house will be your home for many years. So proud of all of you." The hugs were in full swing.

The grill was in place, and the dogs were starting to sweat—not quite burned yet, but getting very close. I started turning, and by the time they were all turned, I started all over again for another burning location. We'd see how many rounds of dogs the guests would make tonight. Delores came over to me. "Are you ready for a refill? You're not feeling dizzy or anything yet, are you? Did you like our special surprise?"

"You're starting to make me think you two did do something to my margarita."

"Oh, if you only knew. But of course, you never will." She walked away and delivered the margaritas to Mama and Papa. She told John, "Marie is making you a special margarita."

John said, "I guess I'll be joining you."

I told John that I was looking forward to a romantic evening with the wife tonight.

"It may not be as romantic as you envision."

I thought a good burnt hot dog and hamburger should change the ladies' minds; all should be normal before bedtime. Of course, the margaritas would help the meal. The ladies prepared wonderful salads and side dishes and made my meat offering far more superior. The girls had their plates and buns ready for their dogs. Leslie said, "Two this time, Daddy. Three was too much for us. Two will be just right, said all the girls when the approached the grill."

"Two dogs each coming up. Bon appétit, young ladies."

Mama and Papa wanted a dog and a burger. "Dog and patty, my pleasure. Here you go. Plenty more. Don't be bashful."

Mama said, "Bashful we're not. We may return to your outdoor kitchen."

John asked for one of each; he would be back. Marie said, "One of each, please."

I shuffled through the burnt offerings. "Oh, here they are—special ones cooked just for you for being so kind as to make me a special margarita."

She gave me a look like the one her mother had given me earlier. "These better be good. I'm still making drinks."

Delores said, "You're walking on very thin ice. Do you remember she's Italian? I'll take one of each. I know mine was cooked special. They always better be cooked special if you ever want your hummingbird to return to the nest."

Being a little shaky, I asked, "How are the dogs and burgers?" I got only a hand wave; their mouths were full. Since they used all five fingers with their wave, I assumed all was well.

This time, I went to the side of the house and got more cut branches for the marshmallow toasting. I knew they had the ingredients for s'mores, as I'd bought them last night. I decided to put some food into my stomach just in case it was my last supper. John returned to the Weber and asked for another hamburger. He got the best one on the grill. Marie returned and retrieved a hot dog. Delores did too and put the dog on a fork and placed the tip between her lips. She smiled and walked away. Mama and Papa each got another hot dog. The girls headed over and started clogging again, laughing and having a great time. I was going to ask Phillip if we could keep the prototype for both houses.

The girls asked if there was any dessert. Delores said, "We have strawberry shortcake with whipped cream. I will make them, and you girls can serve our guests." Oh, were the girls happy. Cupcakes were good, but strawberry shortcake with whipped cream? They had to have seconds. I thought their little bellies had to be hurting, but nope, they were soon back to clogging. The dessert gave them a second wind.

At dusk, we started the marshmallow-roasting event. The girls were getting really good at burning them just right—not too gooey but just enough to get some stuck to their lips. John tried to kiss off some on Marie's lips and got it stuck on his; that got the ladies to laugh. All said, "Silly boy." It was another day in the record books. Beddy-bye time.

The next day, Phillip and company were there on time, and the saw started making the cuts for the next three panels. Raymond and his foreman were bolting together all the panels while they were still plumb. I talked to Phillip about making a second prototype for John and Marie's house. "Glad to make a second one. They had a good time?"

"Nonstop all the way to dark."

"We will have the roof framed today. You're going to have the conduit installed before the end of the day?"

"Yes. Juan should be here anytime now."

"We need that completed so we can button up the panels inside and outside. Insulated as well, just like the other playhouse, correct?"

"Yes, just like the other house."

Juan and Angel started drilling the holes in the sill plate for the conduit. The electrician gave them shielded flex conduit to run inside the walls with clamps. It was easier for him and the crew doing the insulation. It was also much faster for Juan and Angel. The playhouse was completed, and they moved to install the fan locations.

By lunch break, they were packing up the truck and going to another project. They would be back tomorrow to dig the footings for the barbecue. Diego would set the steel, and Juan would trench for the gas line and electrical conduit. Phillip and the crew had all the panels installed and all the roof framing completed for the playhouse and about half the roof for the patio cover. They wanted to leave room for Juan to get the conduit and junction boxes set before they blocked his access. Crawling on one's hands and knees was doable but not very cost effective. As they were wrapping up for the day, the doorman came and measured the front door opening. There was nothing to change, and he thanked Raymond for making the opening plumb.

The ladies and the girls had arrived from school and charged under the playhouse. They swapped their tennis shoes for hard-soled shoes and clogged. They always had a rotation system going so there was no pushing and shoving to get a turn. When the ladies were out shopping, Marie found a perfect CD for the girls. It was music to clog by, a must-have for all CD collectors. I had bought Marie a dozen red roses while I was out and about town. She was taking photos of the playhouse and patio cover when I approached her with the flowers hidden behind my back. "Excuse me, Marie, can we talk for just a couple of seconds?"

"Of course; what's on your mind?"

"I want to apologize for being rude yesterday. Here is a token of my appreciation for our friendship. I hope you weren't offended in any way."

She took the flowers and looked up at me with her beautiful eyes and cute smile, stating, "You survived my margarita that I made special for you. You weren't rude. A little disrespectful but not rude. Don't ever let that happen again, do you hear me?"

"I hear you loud and clear."

"Give me a hug, you fool. I wasn't mad at you. I knew you were just being you."

"I was out of line. I won't intentionally ever do that to you again."

"If you do, your hummingbird will die an agonizing slow death."

"Point well taken. I love you. Thank you for being just the way you are. Did I burn the meat just right yesterday?"

"You and John need to take a barbecue class."

"I don't think all that carbon is good for our health. What do you think of the playhouse?"

"It will be very nice once it is completed. Papa really likes the design—how the balcony wraps around four panels, and how the porch and staircase turn as well. I have to say I'm a little bit jealous. Your girls will have a nicer house than my girls."

"I'll tell you a little secret. I tried to make this house just like your house. It just didn't look right no matter what degree I turned the structure to. It looked horrible. If you did not already have a shed to convert to a playhouse, I would have done the same for you. Tearing the shed apart board by board and making all the cuts and reshaping the structure would have taken longer and cost more money."

"My girls are so excited for your girls to have their own house, and they are looking forward to spending as much time here as your girls spend in their house. They also have a courtyard and a light show every evening that they adore. You're still their number-one guy, and mine as well. Don't you dare ever change, *ever* do you hear me?"

"I hear you, and I promise not to change."

Delores said, "Hey, cheffy, those dogs won't cook themselves. Where did you get the flowers?"

"Your husband gave them to me."

"Really? Okay, buster, where are my flowers?"

"Tomorrow, dear. The flower shop only had the one dozen red roses left."

"Really? Let's head over there and make sure."

Marie told her, "We can share and split tomorrow's dozen."

"And what about the next day?" said Delores.

"Ladies, a dozen red roses per day and we will only be able to afford crow instead of hot dogs and burgers."

Delores asked Marie, "Did you forgive him for yesterday already? Oh, honey, you could have worked him for weeks. We have to talk so you can milk that cow for much more than a dozen roses. I can teach you how to make him be your pet wallet. You know something else? You reap the evening pleasures as well."

Marie said to me, "Be prepared. We talk every day, and I want to know all the details."

Delores told Marie, "You will be quite informed starting tomorrow at lunch."

I thought I'd better start burning the meat before the girls asked me, "How long, Daddy?"

Marie and Delores met up with Mama and Papa in the playhouse. They were looking out all the window openings and came out to the balcony through the installed french doors. Delores said to Marie, "I'll give you a dollar if you can knock that chef's hat off his head from here. I hope Phillip's crew didn't leave anything lying on the subfloor."

The Weber was heating up, ready to spread the coals, when a little voice was heard saying, "Daddy, we're starving. How much longer?" I thought Marie and Delores put them up to that.

"I'm putting them on right now. Give me a few minutes. I'll hurry for you." The meat was burned to perfection; the marshmallows roasted to a T.

The margaritas were the best the ladies had ever made, and the waitress delivered and then stood there until I gave her a tip. "That's a really good boy. Drink up, and I'll be back." More than one more time, and I'd have to write her an IOU.

The next morning, Juan, Angel, and Vincent returned to start the footing. Diego and Manuel came to put in the steel. I went and rented a trencher for the gas line and electrical power. When I returned with the trencher, Phillip and the crew were putting on the plywood for the roof; afterward they would put the plywood sheeting on the outside of the panels. They would have it all insulated, ready for the interior plywood.

Phillip brought us a catalog for the windows. The windows of the shed had been made in the 1930s, and the catalog had nothing close to the windows of the first playhouse. Phillip's master woodworker could duplicate the older windows, but that could take better than a week or more if all went according to plan. Delores said, "When Marie arrives, she and I will look at the catalog and determine which windows would look the best."

Marie showed up wearing a black tank top and beige shorts with sandals and an ankle bracelet. Delores had on her mommy clothes, saw Marie, and asked, "Where are we going today?"

Marie told her, "It's a surprise." She came outside with her camera poised and ready to shoot the roof being installed. One outside panel was installed, and they were fitting the second one. She walked up the staircase, stopped on the porch, took a couple of photos of the playhouse, turned, and descended the staircase in her fashion of grand entrance. That was enough to send the crew into orbit. The applause was loud and long. She gave them her normal wave with a nice over-the-shoulder smile when she reached the bottom landing.

Delores said to her, "We talked about that, remember?"

"I'm addicted; so shoot me."

Delores told her, "One day we are going to have a competition to see who gets the loudest applause and the longest. Loser gets to buy lunch."

"Deal. Tomorrow I'll call and tell you what I'm wearing. You dress similar, and we will duke it out."

"One thing—nothing racy or suggestive, okay?"

"Deal. I don't want that much attention."

I gave the girls the catalog that Phillip gave me, and they sat at our kitchen table, drinking a cup of fresh coffee that I made for them. I was such a nice man. "If either of you have any questions, please ask Phillip. I can't tell you if one is better than the other. I had to go to my masonry supplier and line up the blocks for delivery tomorrow."

I picked up the gas steel sweep ninety with a cap and a gas shutoff valve. They had the materials list from John and Marie's on the computer. "Is it the exact barbecue?"

"Exact. Not one thing will be different."

"Do you want the rock fascia at this time as well?"

"That will be fine. All the rebar as well."

"Perfect. We can have the majority of the items delivered tomorrow and the balance by the next day."

"See you tomorrow."

I returned, and the trench for the gas line was dug. Juan and Angel were digging the trench from the electrical panel to the barbecue, patio cover, and playhouse. I'd run caution tape around the trench under the patio cover so the girls wouldn't fall into the trench. They could enter to the clogging platform from under the staircase, which was better known by the ladies as staircase grand entrance number two.

Juan said he was a few feet short of three-quarter-inch conduit and gave me a list of electrical fittings he would require to complete the system. I took the list and said, "The gofer will return with the goodies."

While in my truck, I called the electrician and told him the conduit was being installed. I had a city inspector due to arrive tomorrow morning to inspect the trench depth for the electrical and gas line. I was hoping the footing would be finished so he could inspect that as well. This was moving much faster than John and Marie's; we'd had had no delays due to finding buried treasures yet.

I started laying out the paver edge on the existing turf. I was following the plan and noticed the deck would be a little smaller than what it showed on the plan because of a raised planter. I had only two feet from the planter to the post of the playhouse—a perfect place for a ceramic pot with a beautiful *Cupressus sempervirens* 'Tiny Tower,' with *Pelargonium peltatum*, pink and burgundy, as ground cover. Once they were in bloom and cascading over the top of the pot, it would be stunning. It would make a great location for the ladies to pose for a still shot.

All the trenching was son completed. Phillip and crew were putting on the last panel covering the outside of the playhouse. Tomorrow they would insulate and cover the inside and start with the siding outside and inside. Everyone was packing up for the day. Juan asked if I wanted to return the trencher. "I'll take it back in the morning. You can leave it in the backyard overnight."

The girls were racing to the prototype dance floor, and the ladies, dressed almost like twins, came in and started shooting the playhouse, patio cover, and barbecue footing with steel in place. "This is coming along really nicely," said Marie.

"The electrician will be here in two days and wire up the entire playhouse, patio cover, and barbecue."

"So the girls will have light in two days?"

"Should be lit up like Christmas."

"He'll hang the fans as well?"

"Yes, should be completed by the time he quits for the day."

"No low-voltage lighting yet, huh?" asked Delores.

"No, my dearest darling. We have to rock the barbecue and install all the fixtures, pass the gas test and electrical test, pour the barbecue countertops, finish them, excavate for the pavers, install the base and sand layer, and install the pavers. We're really just getting started with our work."

"So we cannot plan a party for the weekend?"

"No, not this weekend, unless your guests want to sit on pallets and drink Gatorade out of bottles."

"Stop it. You're getting me excited. No cups, just straight out of the bottle?"

"Not so bad. You can share with the one sitting next to you on the pallet."

"Swapping spit—how romantic."

"Oh, by the way, no party until you buy a bottle of that perfume they put on you a couple of days ago."

"That stuff is expensive, not my normal $3.99 per gallon Afternoon Delight. I wear it for those special occasions. That stuff is like smelling crankcase oil that hasn't been changed since you bought the car in 1998."

Marie said, "Delores, did you not know that was last year's fragrance? The new and improved Nooner with Bubba comes at a low new introductory price of—hold on to your bra strap—$2.75 per gallon. That's right, for one time only."

"You ladies need some burnt offerings with a side dish and salads. I'll get a-cooking, me and my Weber."

"You know he's nuts, right?"

Marie said, "You wouldn't want him any other way."

"Yeah, I guess you're right. Oh god, I'm actually used to him. Does it show?"

Marie said, "I'll make you a double, and you'll forget all about this conversation."

"So tomorrow what are you planning on wearing?" Delores asked Marie.

"I don't know just yet. I have to go through the Frederick's of Hollywood side of my walk-in closet."

"Hey, we agreed not to wear anything racy or seductive."

"You never said anything about lewd."

"Please, I can't afford to purchase an outfit to wear only one time."

"You wouldn't wear it for your husband?"

"No way, it would kill him. He would have the big one right then and there. I would have to have a series of outfits and break him in slowly."

"Take it easy. I don't have anything from Frederick's of Hollywood. Have you seen a catalog from them?"

"Is that one cup of tequila and a shooter of mix, or do I have that backward?"

"You have it backward for tonight, but there are days you forget the mix and swap spit, straight from the bottle."

The dogs were burned, the burgers getting close. The girls were getting their plates ready. Mama and Papa were enjoying their margaritas, and John was waiting for his to be delivered. The ladies were on number two or three. The service around here was not the greatest but was so much fun. No tip, no refill— that was the rule. If the barmaid was on number three, you could say you gave her a tip, and she'd say, "Oh, okay, enjoy." And she would stagger back to the bar.

We had strawberry shortcake for dessert with mounds of whipped cream for the girls. They had almost forgotten about cupcakes as their staple. Now that the roof was on it, everyone was in the playhouse, looking out the windows, or on the balcony, enjoying the glowing embers of the Weber. Adding a few sticks from my branch pile gave such an ambiance from the balcony.

Tomorrow the handrails with baluster would be installed on the staircase, porch, and balcony. The shingles would be finished in two more days, according to Phillip. The outside siding would start tomorrow and hopefully finish but might take a couple of hours the next day. The house would be a bluish color with cream-colored trim—a very nautical or Cape Cod look, like being in the Hamptons. I had the girls watch a video from that area, and they loved the blue color with the cream trim. The front door would be fire engine–red lacquer—three coats with a polyurethane top coat. There would be brass hardware, of course. It would have the same light over the girls' door and french doors as on the first house.

Phillip called the editor of the magazine and said we were doing house number two and that there should be shots of this house as well. Everyone was in total awe of how the house appeared, even in this rough stage. Delores said, "If you are a bad boy, instead of going to the couch, you can come out here."

"The girls won't mind, will you, girls?"

"Yes, Mom, we will mind. This is our house, and no one can sleep here unless we invite them for a sleepover, said Sarah."

Leslie and Kim said, "We have the same rule. Daddy doesn't plan on being a bad boy for a long, long, long time, said Leslie."

Marie said, "I think that is three days in the woman's world."

The next day, Phillip and the crew were installing the plywood sheeting and insulation in the walls. The inspector came, inspected our trenches, and was pleased. He liked the footing for the barbecue. We got an A+ on our permit card.

Juan, Vincent, and Angel were installing the conduit for the electrician. We laid the gas line along the top of the trench, waiting for the plumber to fuse the pipe and test for pressure for tomorrow's inspection. I had the warning tape that Juan laid along both trenches for the inspection.

Marie called Delores and told her what she was going to wear. "I'll bring you your outfit. We will do lunch and dazzle the restaurant employees as well." She was wearing "the outfit."

This is going to be tough to beat, thought Delores. *I'll check the credit limit on the card so I will know what I can eat.*

I rented a cement mixer for the footing. We had sand and gravel. I'd get some bags of portland cement while I was out and about. The nail guns were in high gear today, putting up the siding and installing the insulation. One gun was putting in the staples; another was putting up the siding. When they installed the shingles, that was when the installers got crazy, making up tunes with each other using the nail guns.

Phillip brought the second prototype to the house. I knew Marie would be ecstatic about the portable clogging floor. Phillip's other crew members were busy putting up the shiplap under the patio cover, and they left an opening for the ceiling fans until they knew exactly where the hole was required for the lighting. Phillip could center the fan, and the electrician could follow his lead, but it was better to have one voice. Having too many chiefs didn't win the battles.

Marie and Delores decided on a window for the playhouse. Since the house would look like a Cape Cod home, the windows would be fashioned as such. This made Phillip very happy; that was the exact window he had wanted for the house. "Great selection, ladies," he said to them. His supplier had the windows the ladies selected in stock. Phillip picked up the windows, and they were ready to install the same day. This saved Phillip many days, and they were able to put the siding exactly where it should be without guessing or having to cut it for a different-sized window.

The front door was three days early. Phillip was in paradise today. He told me if anything else went right and ahead of schedule, he was going home and sending a check directly to God. I told Phillip, "You'd better send it by FedEx. Don't use the post office; it may never arrive."

Marie showed up in "the outfit" and gave Delores "the killer outfit." These were worn for the first photo shoot. Delores told Marie, "You know, the outfit you're wearing is hands-down beautiful and fits you like a glove. You're going to make it very hard for me to win our bet."

Marie said, "I have to win. If there is a tie, neither of us wins, except how we feel from the appreciation of the boys."

"So you think we will tie?"

"You'll see. Put on the outfit. I'll help with your makeup and hair. You'll dazzle them."

The blue siding with the new windows and the cream-colored window frame and sill was absolutely beautiful. Raymond was putting on the fascia boards, also in cream. "This is going on another cover," said Phillip. I had to admit he was more than likely correct. The front door arrived and was soon being installed.

The electrician was busy hooking up all the wires for the inspector. We had added three new breakers, and all of them were installed, tested, and waiting for the inspector. The electrician's assistants were installing the wire into the conduits. The job site resembled a beehive with all the activity going on at one time.

The plumber showed and began fusing the gas line and setting up the gas steel sweep ninety. He capped the gas steel sweep ninety using a gas pressure gauge and pressured up the line from where the connection into the gas meter would occur. The gas line was pressurized, waiting for the inspector. The plumber had me verify the time he logged when the pressure test was started. The inspector for the gas line had just arrived and was checking the line and gauges. All was per plan.

Just then, the sliding glass door opened very slowly, and out came the most gorgeous lady. She was making an appearance, sashaying very seductively, and all the crew members were applauding her every step. The inspector lost track of what he was doing. He asked Phillip and the plumber, "Is this floor show for you, guys?"

"We're not certain, but wow, she is really pretty."

Then came Marie. She was doing the best moves I had ever seen her perform. Both ladies had all the production of the project at a standstill. The applause was not stopping. The ladies waved, smiled, and thanked all the guys for being so kind. They turned, reentered the house, looked over their shoulders, and smiled.

The inspector said to the plumber, "I think I'll come back in. What? Is it two or three hours per code?"

The plumber said, "Three hours."

"And you started it about a half hour ago?"

"Yes, sir."

"See you in two and a half hours. That was totally amazing."

Phillip asked the plumber, "Did you pass?"

"Everything except the test. He'll be back in two and a half hours. He might have his composure by then. They really shook him up."

Oh, the sweet sound of nail guns, drills, and wire being pulled through conduits was far better than the sound of hard-soled shoes on a wooden dance floor. The siding on the outside was nearly completed, the windows were all installed, and the front door and threshold was nearly finished. The electrician's assistants were hanging fixtures and running tests to ensure they would pass with flying colors; all the breakers were now fully operational for the test by the electrician. They would shut everything down and wait for their inspector. They decided to take an early lunch while waiting. If and we knew they would pass, the inspector would return at dusk to witness the burn test. That would take very little time, and I'd have hot dog and vittles for him and the electrician and crew. There were two new switches installed by the sliding glass door; they would control the porch light and fans.

The ladies returned to the work site to shoot some photos—no sashaying this time. They were focused on taking photos. They still received a warm welcome from all the crew. This time, the girls were blushing.

The city inspector arrived to check the electrical. He had Andy, the electrician, turn on the first breaker. He tested the terminals and asked, "What does this breaker control?"

Andy told him, "The fans and the playhouse lights."

The inspector walked over and found that the fans were lit and asked to see the fans run. Andy used the hand remote, and around and around the fans turned. "Let's check the lighting in the playhouse." The inspector turned off and on each light switch and checked the lights. The porch light was on. He went out to the balcony, and the light was on. He checked the interior lights, and the center light was on. There were two side lights so if the girls didn't want the brightness of the center, they could turn it off. Everything seemed to be in order.

Andy said, "There is one more light controlled by this switch." He opened the access door, and the light under the patio cover roof was on.

The inspector said, "Very nice touch, and very functional. Let's check the next breaker." The second breaker was for the receptacles for the playhouse and the barbecue and patio. "Turn on breaker number 2." The inspector checked the terminals. "Good job." He pulled out his plug-in tester and went to each receptacle, testing for power and any direct shorts. All receptacles were tested and passed. "Breaker number three powers what?"

"The barbecue. It is 220V. The barbecue is not installed yet. We're awaiting shipment."

"I brought a tool I have that requires 220V power, or I have a pigtail. The receptacle is installed?"

"Yes, it's already installed."

The inspector pulled out a different tester. "This is all I need." He plugged in his tester, and the green light came on. He said, "I will be back at five o'clock to witness the project all lit up. See you then."

Andy and his crew were closing up all the boxes where the wires were exposed in case there was a direct short. I had a back porch light that had come with the house. I asked Andy if they had a nautical-themed outdoor light to replace the hideous light the builder had installed. "I'll run over to my supplier and see what is available. We may have to order that fixture. I'll bring you back a catalog if that is the case." Andy left his crew to finish installing all the covers of the junction boxes.

Juan was so happy that they now had power at the barbecue. They were finishing up the countertops, ready to pour the top before they left for the day. The power put the mixer closer to the barbecue.

They started mixing the colored concrete. Angel, our dear Angel, got the job of mixing the concrete. She had concrete and color all over her. Marie could not miss this photo opportunity. She ran back inside and got her camera. Angel's hair was a mess. She had wiped her brow with the color mix, both of her cheeks had concrete and color on them, her shirt and pants had concrete on them, and her work boots had everything on them. Marie, with camera in hand, called to her. Angel turned around. *Click, click, click!* Angel said, "Wait a minute." She posed next to the mixer for a couple of shots, and she was really getting into posing. Marie took at least ten shots.

"You look adorable," Marie told Angel.

Delores joined them, and I asked all the ladies to get together for a group shot. "This will make the cover for sure." I took at least six different shots of different poses. If you put these girls in front of a camera and let it roll, they would make you millions.

Juan interrupted the shoot, saying, "Too much mixing heats up the concrete. Let us finish."

I apologized to Juan. "We're leaving."

Marie and Delores were looking at all the shots taken, saying, "Ooh, look at all of us. Great photo. We have to take these to the meeting next week. I'm sure one of these will make a cover."

Delores said, "You want to send one to *Playboy* magazine?"

"They would not ever call us. Mama and Papa would disown me in a second. John would have the big one."

"You're starting to think like your husband. Scary, huh?"

The plumbing inspector returned and looked over to the sliding glass door while heading to the gauge at the barbecue. Juan said, "You just missed the ladies."

The inspector blamed a red light. "Took too long to change." They all laughed.

The gauge held the proper amount of pressure, and the gas line passed. "Have a great day, gentlemen. I have a wife I need to visit."

Angel said, "She's going to have the time of her life. I'll bet he didn't even notice me as part of the crew."

Juan agreed, "He didn't notice that you're a lady."

Vincent said, "They all will after the magazines hit the shelf."

"We notice you every day and are proud of you," said Juan.

"You guys keep that up, and you're going to get me to cry. Back to work. Let's get these tops finished."

"Yes ma'am!"

The playhouse with the blue siding, cream trim, and red door was phenomenal. It all, by itself, was cover material. It would be even better when shingled. Phillip had another surprise up his sleeve. It was near quitting time. Everything was cleaned up, and the trucks were loaded. Crews were heading home. "Another day well done, everyone."

The ladies returned to the house with the girls. The girls ran outside and stopped in their tracks when they saw the playhouse. "Daddy, it's beautiful, said Sarah. Look, everyone; we have a front door too, said Rebecca." All four girls came over and gave me one huge loving hug. They all said, "We love you, Daddy. The house is so pretty, said Sarah.

They all ran up the staircase, opened the door, and screamed, "We love, everyone! Thank you, Papa and Mama!"

Marie, Delores, Mama, and Papa were all outside. "Do you think they like the playhouse?" asked Papa. Everyone gave Papa hugs and kisses.

"Dad, I can't thank you enough," said Delores and Marie. "You gave them all a gift of a lifetime." All the ladies were tearing up.

The girls were on the balcony, saying, "Please join us in the new house. It's not finished yet, but please join us. We love the house." And they, too, were in tears.

Marie ran into the house, got her camera, and headed up to the playhouse. The girls, Mama, Papa, and Delores were all embracing. *Click, click, click!* Sarah went over to Marie, tears running down her cheeks. Marie said, "Wait, honey." *Click, click, click!*

"I love you, Mom." They were in a great hug, and Marie started to cry along with Sarah.

The rest of the girls gave Marie a hug and kiss and said, "We love you, Mom." I'd dare Hallmark to make a card to fit that scene. This was not man-made; this was done by a much higher authority.

I dragged out good old Weber, put in the Kingsford briquettes, and fired her up. The girls and parents were busy trying out the different light switches. "Look, Mommy; this one lights the walls, and this one lights the ceiling. Look over here, everyone. This one lights the cubbyhole. This one lights up our balcony. This one lights up the front porch. Mommy, this is perfect." Sarah and Rebecca gave Papa a huge we-love-you hug. They finally got Grandpa to start crying with joy, and that brought the moms and wife to his side.

They all moved to the balcony, saw the barbecue starting up, and said to me, "We're glad to see someone doing their job." Delores and Marie took a round table and six chairs up to the playhouse so the girls could invite their first guest to join them for dinner. We had a round card table and folding chairs we used for board and card games when guests came over for a fun evening.

The girls were so excited, going up and down the staircase, getting the cups and plasticware for their first invited guests. Now came the wait to see who they wanted. They told their mommies that they needed some privacy. "We have a meeting to attend."

Marie and Delores told them they had a blender to fire up. "Love you, girls, said Marie."

I envisioned this moment as similar to when the Catholic Church elects a new pope. The world was waiting for the smoke to rise from the rooftop. The meeting ended, and the first guests to the almost finished playhouse were, as if you didn't already know, Mama and Papa. They all came down the staircase, and Leslie gave the announcement this time. "From now on, Sarah will give the announcement of the chosen guests." Leslie said, "I am speaking for all of us—for Sarah. We would like Mama and Papa to join us for dinner this evening. We are very sorry we could not have all of you as our guests. We have a limited budget and a small space. Please forgive us. We love all of you."

John said, "She's going to become a great politician. I feel it in my bones. Makes you feel special as she's pickpocketing you." We all laughed. How true was that statement.

Marie brought me a margarita. With a very sincere face, she said, "My dearest friend, I and your wife made you a very special margarita. Thank you for bringing us this day. Love you with all my heart." She gave me a hug.

"Is this the same special drink you two made me a few nights ago?"

"We could change it, if you desire."

"No, my dear, I will drink this with pride and joy. Love you as well."

Delores was delivering the margaritas to everyone else, and they made the girls a fruit drink—pineapple, strawberries, mango, and other ingredients—for the almost open-house festivities. I was so taken by the appreciation that I almost forgot I was the chef. The smell of burning dogs brought me back to reality. John said, "Once you get the adult barbecue going, we all want rib eye steaks, medium, with baked potato, sour cream, and chives; steamed vegetables; water with a lemon slice, chilled, no ice; Zinfandel wine, chilled; linen tablecloth; and linen napkins."

"I'll do my best to make that happen. Delores, did you write that down?"

"Yes, dear, so you won't forget. You're the chef, remember?"

"You're the chef's helper."

"Dream on, lover. Dream on. I'm a celebrity now, remember? We don't get dirt under our nails. Hire a maid and kitchen help to fulfill your customers' desires."

"The burnt offerings are ready to be consumed. Come and get it." The girls were already in line with their plates, and Mama and Papa were the next victims. Up the staircase they all went.

Marie and John were next. Marie said, "I hope these are special as well."

"They are my best attempt thus far. Delores, my dearest darling, you look marvelous, my dear."

She got close and said, "Smell my neck." I bent over and smelled her neck. She had a devilish smile. "For you, my dear."

I put a dog in her open bun. "After prayers?"

She just smiled and walked away with a seductive little strut.

Marie saw her action and smiled at Delores. "I know, I know," said Marie. They sat next to each other and began doing the girlie thing.

On the big day, the inside was being sided and baseboards installed. The ceiling, which the girls had finished last night on sawhorses, was being installed. Phillip brought three crews with him to finish the playhouse. One crew finished the patio roof, the other installed the finished handrailing, and another put on the Cape Cod shingles—Phillip's surprise. He'd found a company that manufactured the shingles used for the Cape Cod projects. He forwarded them a photo of the playhouse and told them it would be used in an article for *Remodeling* magazine and that they would be listed as the supplier of the shingles. The owner of the manufacturer called Phillip, and they talked; he got the shingles the next day, air-freighted to his supplier.

Phillip called his friend at the magazine; they were so excited that they were coming out tomorrow morning to shoot the second playhouse and said they would run a complete story once it was completed. Susanne called Marie and Delores and told them to get ready for a repeat performance. She was so excited. "I can't believe we get the chance to do this all over again. Love you both. See you soon."

Delores came over to me and said, "If you think last night was great, you have seen nothing yet." And she sashayed away. If she kept this up, she'd kill me.

The cabinets had arrived. Raymond had the flooring started, and he grabbed the crew putting in the shiplap and had them help him finish the floor. The sawman was going crazy now. Phillip said to all of them, "Please, this has to be done perfectly. Take your time. Please don't rush and get hurt or make a mistake."

Raymond had the flooring prestained to match the first playhouse. It would take about an hour for the polyurethane to dry, so he applied it only where the cabinets would be installed so that while the cabinets were being off-loaded and brought to the backyard and placed on two-by-fours so as not to get soiled, the polyurethane would be drying. They all took a break for fifteen minutes.

Marie and Delores came out with iced tea and lemonade for the crews—nothing fancy today. They looked like well-dressed housewives with a glow. The crews still gave them applause, and the girls said, "Thank you, silly boys." They had a way of making everyone feel special.

They also gave Angel the most loving hug I had ever seen. "Love you, my dear," the ladies told Angel. She apologized for not having concrete on her face or clothes.

They just laughed and said, "You know, you're going to be famous very shortly. Tell Juanita that the magazine will be setting up an appointment for both of you soon. Welcome to our world."

The polyurethane was dry enough for the cabinets to be installed. The crew returned to installing the shiplap. Juan and his crew were removing the soil from under the playhouse to receive the base and sand layer. They then would start putting in the pavers. It was a busy day on site. I showed Juan where the border of the pavers would be running. "So without further ado, keep digging." Diego and his crew would be joining them in about an hour. Angel was so excited. She and her friend joined together again.

Juan had Vincent backfill the gas and electrical trenches that were inside the paving layout. He also had the vibratory plate that I had picked up at the rental yard. The crew was loading my trailer with soil so I could run a load to the landfill. One of my neighbors saw what we were doing and asked if he could have the soil; he said he would pay me for it. I asked, "How much do you need?"

He said, "Let me show you what we are doing." We went to his house and looked at some raised planters that they'd had another contractor construct.

I told my neighbor, "I would not advise filling these walls at this time."

He said, "Why?" His wife was not as happy now as when we entered the backyard.

"Before I answer your question, I have one for you. When you contracted for the raised planter wall, what were you told by the contractor?"

"We were given the cost and a time schedule and what material they would use. That was about all that was mentioned."

"Did they show you a plan or provide a plan for you to see?"

His wife said, "I think he drew a sketch. Let me get our paperwork."

My neighbor said, "So what's wrong with the wall?"

"Wait until your wife returns." She came back with a sketch the contractor drew. I looked it over and said, "He made a big mistake."

"We need to know what kind of mistake he made," said the neighbor.

"You see, you have a masonry wall here in front and a wood fence behind the wall. If we fill the wall with soil, the wood fence is for security and privacy. It is not structural. The soil will push over the wood fence and start rotting the wood."

"Why would he tell us we didn't have to put up a wall against the fence?"

"Ma'am, I don't know, but I can't do something to your home that you will regret later. I'm not looking to cost you more money, making you think I'm trying to pull a fast one on you. As a contractor, I want to protect you from a much higher cost down the road. Come with me over to my house. I'll show you a real raised planter."

They followed me to the backyard, where I had installed a raised planter more than five years ago. I showed them the battered wall and our wood fence behind it. "You see, there are two walls, both structural, and the planter does not leak through the blocks."

My neighbor looked at how the planter was built. "This had to cost you a pretty penny," said the neighbor.

"It wasn't cheap, but for five years now, it hasn't cost me any more out of pocket money."

His wife said, "Doug, look at what they are building." Doug and his bride walked to the other side and looked at the playhouse, patio cover, and barbecue.

"That is really nice. Now that is costly, right?"

"You have to understand one thing. You can buy cheap big-box store, Chinese-made stuff made to deteriorate in a few years or one year and go out and buy the next latest and greatest whatever. In the long run, you will spend more and have less than if you bite the bullet and have it done professionally."

"Can we see inside your room addition?" asked the wife.

"Not today. They are putting in cabinets and finishing the interior walls. We would just get in the way. Come by tomorrow, and we will give you a tour."

"Are your parents going to live with you?" asked the wife.

"Ma'am, that is not a residence. That is our daughters' playhouse."

Doug said, "A playhouse? You built your daughters a playhouse? Costco sells playhouses for next to nothing."

"Doug, Costco sells you Chinese-made items. They may last a couple of years, they fall apart, the kids get bored, and they become yard art and deteriorate daily. You will never go out once you erect the play structure and restain and seal the structure. The bolts holding up the swings rust and eventually break, or the swing breaks. The kids get too big to go down the slide. It's all eye candy for the shopper. They put up those displays and tear them down as soon as dust appears on them. The same with all the patio furniture and patio covers with all those fancy curtains wrapped on each post. It's all about getting your attention and opening the wallet. They may have a one-year warranty with lots of fine print, which is a way for them to be not responsible for damage or deterioration. You open your wallet again for the newest and most improved patio cover. If the wind carries your patio cover next door or down the street and it's all bent and contorted, you now have to tear it apart and return to purchase another one. That is one of the sorry things that is not covered on the warranty."

Doug said, "Can you give us a price to make our planter a planter and not a look-at planter?"

"I'd be delighted to give you a price for the battered wall and to waterproof the entire planter. Can I stop by tomorrow?"

"Of course. What about the soil?"

"We will stockpile the soil and fill your planter. Do you have an irrigation system?"

"No, those are too expensive," said Doug.

"Let's talk about an irrigation system. You might be surprised. When would be a good time for me to swing by?"

Doug and his wife said, "Nine o'clock. Will that work with you?"

"That will be great. See you at nine o'clock."

Delores came out and asked, "Who were they?"

"Our neighbors just up the street a couple of doors on the left."

"They want you to do work for them?"

"They do, but I'm dealing with 'everything costs too much'—you know the type. It doesn't cost them anything to drag a hose with a sprinkler around to water the grass, and they don't water enough to keep anything alive, you know."

"I'm so happy being a housewife and not having to deal with that kind of stuff. Marie, Mama, Papa, and I are going shopping for curtains and a throw carpet for the playhouse. Should be back after lunch. Oh, after lunch, no leftovers for you. Do you want a Happy Meal from your favorite eatery?"

"Not today, dear. Thank you for asking. I'm trying to eat a little healthier."

"Healthier—hot dogs, hamburgers, and margaritas. Nice diet. Should make the bottom hundred of what not to eat."

"Love you. Have a great time."

"You're so lucky to have a wife like me. You'd better thank your Maker every day."

The cabinets were installed, and Raymond was putting the two coats of polyurethane on the oak floor. The shingles were on the patio cover, and it was time for lunch. About five minutes after the whistle blew, I called my masonry supplier to see if the barbecue had arrived. They said they were offloading it right now and should be at my house in less than an hour. Oh, this should be a great surprise for the family. I told Juan and Diego that the barbecue and fixtures were being delivered in about an hour. They were so overjoyed that they almost got up and headed home. What they needed right now was more work.

I decided that Delores was correct; a Happy Meal would hit the spot and give me a chance to get away from all the construction drama. Juan and crew were starting to bring in the base for under the playhouse, leveling it out, almost ready for Vincent to run the vibratory plate. There was something about a Happy Meal—not filling but sure tasty. I returned and left my Happy Meal bag on the kitchen table so my dearest darling knew I didn't starve. She'd be so relieved.

The crew was soon back at work. A driver arrived and met me in the backyard. "I have a new toy for you. Where would you like me to put the barbecue and fixtures?"

"Are they on pallets, and can you fit through my gate?"

"Yes and no."

"Okay, I'll get you some help. Oh, fellows, the toy has just arrived. Can I have you give the driver a hand in offloading?" Being a well-adjusted crew, everyone in the backyard stood up and applauded the driver. "Ladies and gentlemen, that is not the hand the driver was looking for. Let's try that again, shall we?"

We had thought ahead, and I had brought an empty pallet from home and picked up a pallet jack from the rental yard. They were in for a shock when they saw what was in my truck. They loaded the barbecue and fixtures onto the pallet and pulled the items into the backyard. Juan and company thanked me for thinking ahead and providing them with the proper tools. I had two purposes for giving them the proper tools: to save their backs and to save time. Both were very important factors in construction. If anyone hurt his or her back, I would lose that person for a few weeks. Everyone on the crew was very important no matter at what level he or she was at; everything counted.

As an example, I had an operator who was just operating a Dingo loader from the stockpile of pavers uphill to where the pavers were being installed. There were two men loading the loader from the pallets into his bucket, and he drove the loader uphill. When he arrived at where we were installing the pavers, he dumped his load, and there were four different sizes of pavers representing a pattern the installers were following. Now the pavers were in one pile. I stopped the operator, a foreman for the company. I was a project manager. He gave me typical body language like, "Do you know who you are talking to?"

I told him in my managerial tone of voice, "Obviously, you don't know who you're talking to."

We had two additional foremen helping install the pavers, and the crew was sitting idly at this point. I told him in a managerial tone, "You do that again, and you can go home. And on your way home, stop by the office and get your last check."

His posture was still like, "You don't know who you're talking to." He stated, "You can't fire me. You don't have the power to fire me."

I got my cell phone out of my pocket and called into the office, and our secretary, who was the personal secretary of the owner, answered. I asked her to inform our foreman that I did have authority to fire anyone in the field if I felt he or she was jeopardizing the performance of the field or being disrespectful of clients or management. She said, "Someone pushed your wrong button. Hold on a minute; I'll ask the owner."

The owner got on the phone and said, "You have all the authority to hire or fire anyone." I had the conversation on speaker so all the crew and foremen were close enough to hear. The posture of the foreman changed; he said he was sorry and should have asked before he dumped the load.

I turned and asked the crew, "Should he get another load or go home? Your choice."

They said, "Try him on another load. If he does wrong, then he can see the owner in the office."

I looked at the foreman. "You're a lucky man. Please respect the crew and anyone else in a managerial position." He became one of the best foremen the company had to this date. All the crew members on that job site that day became much better workers, not bad-mouthing any of the office personnel.

Juan and Angel started installing the barbecue accessories and storage cabinets. After those, they installed the barbecue. I had Manuel help Juan lift and install the barbecue; Angel was lying on her back and was pulling the flexible gas hose and power cord into the opening and lining up each utility. That saved

Juan lots of time since she hooked the hose from the barbecue to the gas valve and tightened the connection. This girl was far more talented than most of the members of the crew. She was not afraid of getting dirty or breaking a fingernail; she had the potential of being a girlie girl, but that was not who she really was inside. She came out of the opening, dusted herself off, and asked Juan, "What's next?"

We had the access door and one other fixture left to install. Juan told her, "The access door."

Diego and crew were busy installing the pavers under the playhouse and were nearly finished, so they continued outside the playhouse posts. Phillip saw that the pavers were installed and was smiling from ear to ear with joy. Phillip would start the dance floor tomorrow morning, make the benches for the onlookers, and let the girls rest. Phillip's master woodworker was on site today and rounded off the step edges, porch edge, and balcony edge. He would be back in two days to round off the dance floor edge and seat edges.

The staircase, porch, and balcony were finished today, and what a wonderful job the crew did. They were absolutely suitable for any of the ladies to perform a great grand entrance. Raymond and his foreman put a half-round border around the painted ceiling. What a nice touch that was. I hoped the girls would notice the details that Raymond and his crew completed. The siding in the inside looked as great as the outside. The window surrounds and the french door's front surrounds were painted in cream to match the outside. It was breathtaking. I wanted Marie to stand in the playhouse and take a photo of each person walking into the playhouse tonight. The expressions on their faces would be priceless.

The crew got from the dance floor all the way to the barbecue with pavers. Juan didn't want me to stand on base or dirt. He was such a great guy. I was so proud of him and his efforts. They were all packing up to leave when the girls came running through the house. I asked the crew to wait a minute. "Listen to the response of the girls."

They all stopped, looked at the staircase, and said, "Daddy, the stairs are beautiful, said Sarah."

They walked up the stairs, opened the front door, and all screamed, "Daddy, you have to come up and see our house!"

Rebecca and Sarah came out through the french doors and thanked everyone for such a beautiful house, with tears rolling down their faces. "Thank you, all. You have made our lives complete. Thank you so much from the bottoms of our hearts." They saw Angel and Juanita, came running down the stairs, and gave the girls one huge hug. "We love all of you." Now Angel, Juanita, Marie, Delores, Mama, Papa, and most of the crew had tears coming down their cheeks.

Marie stood back and said to everyone, "Smile." What a great photo that turned out to be. She made copies for everyone in the photo.

The crew headed to the truck. Rebecca and Sarah walked with them to the gate, opened it for them, and gave each and every one of them a huge hug with an I-love-you.

If readers and viewers of the magazine failed to witness the compassion, love, and joy those girls brought to the table, I was sorry for them. Rebecca and Sarah were too excited and crying with joy to come down to greet the crew. I stopped Marie; her makeup was a mess, and her voice was cracking. "What is it?"

I told her to go up with the girls, take some photos of the girls in their new house, and stand where she could shoot the faces of the family entering the finished playhouse for the first time. "Please, for me and for the album."

She gave me a hug. "Great idea. Love to see that myself."

I detained Mama, Papa, John, and Delores for a couple of minutes while Marie was getting photos of the girls. She came to the balcony and said, "Everyone, you have to see this playhouse." Marie was in position, and I told them okay one at a time.

Mama was in the lead and entered the playhouse, and I heard her scream, "Oh my god, this is beautiful!"

Next was Papa. I think he nearly fainted. "This is amazing."

John was next, and he screamed louder than Mama, "I love this house!"

Then came Delores. She looked down at me, wiggled her hips, and said, "Tonight." She walked in and screamed, "I love the house! Can I live here too?"

Marie came out to the balcony. "Great idea. Fantastic photos. This is a great house."

They all stayed in the house, talking and looking at all the details. Even their painted ceiling looked fantastic. They all gave high fives for how it turned out. The girls politely asked all visitors to leave; they had a meeting to attend.

John came down first and instructed me on how to burn the dogs and hamburgers. Marie was next and said, "Wait a minute, cheffy. We have a surprise. We're all getting tired of hot dogs."

Delores and Marie brought out a platter of steaks and pork chops. Delores said to John and me, "If you burn these, neither of you will get"—they set the platters down on the barbecue counter and did their girlie pose—"this. Understand?"

"Yes, dear, we understand. Perfectly clear."

"We won't tell you again. That is the one and only time you will hear that statement." They both strutted back into the house.

John said, "They mean every word."

On one platter was a meat thermometer with a little red bow and a small card with three little words: "You'd better remember." John was pulling up all sorts of barbecue tips in his cell phone while the grill was heating. He had me run into the house and get vegetable oil, a bowl, two paper towels, and salt and pepper. I got what he asked for.

The ladies said, "What is all that for?"

"I don't know. John asked me to come and get these items."

"They'd better not be preparing to pan-fry our meal," Marie laughed. "If they do, they will never see nooky again. I won't let him have a hummingbird."

John was following the barbecue king's step-by-step barbecue setup—pour the oil into the bowl, coat the grill using the paper towel folded into a workable brush, and do not catch the paper towel on fire. "Good idea. Burnt fingers never feel good."

"Hurry; the grill is getting hot."

I hurried, and the entire grill was coated.

"Salt and pepper each side of the meat. If the meat is as thick as your hand, close the grill lid. If not, leave the lid open. The meat is the thickness of our hand. Close it. Place it on the grill and cook each side for five minutes. Do not move the meat once on the grill." John set an alarm on his cell phone for five minutes. It seemed like forever.

The girls asked, "What are you cooking? It smells so good. We're very hungry, daddies. Please hurry."

The alarm went off, and we flipped the meat over. John reset his alarm. The girls brought us glass of chilled white Zinfandel and said, "This is our new margaritas. We're getting tired of those as well."

They each had a glass, and I gave a toast. "To the greatest friends I have ever had. Cheers." All glasses clinked.

The ladies yelled down, "We heard that! You guys better not be getting drunk! How much longer, boys, said Marie?"

John said, "Two more minutes."

"You guys are timing the cooking? Who taught you guys to do that, asked Marie?"

"A man called Steven Raichlen, said John."

"Who is this Steven fellow, asked Delores?"

"The barbecue king, said John?"

"So where was King Steven while you, gentlemen, were cremating our meals, asked Marie?"

John said, "He was in my cell phone."

"All this time, and now you let King Steven out to play, oh my aching stomach, said Marie?"

"How many years of driving these two before we can get a trade-in?" asked Delores.

"Let me check my cell phone. I'll ask Queen Elizabeth for what they recommend."

John's cell phone alarm went off. "Excuse us, ladies. We have cooking to do. Are the sides ready?"

"Don't get pushy, mister. We're in charge of happy hour." They both started to walk away, looked over their shoulders, smiled, turned back around, and laughed.

"I think they are making fun of us."

"You just think. I know that's what they're doing. Should we burn their steaks?"

"Remember the note?"

We tested the meat as King Steven suggested, and it was perfect. They were off the grill, onto the platters, and onto the table.

The girls came down, and Sarah gave the speech. "We are very sorry that we can't invite each and every one of you for dinner. Our budget is limited, and our space is small. Since this is our very first dinner with a completed house, we promised Mama and Papa the very first dinner. Please remember you are all our invited guests. Your turn will come shortly. Please enjoy your dinner and the festivities. Let's eat. It smells so good. Love you, Dads."

John said, "Shut down again. Not picked on the first team."

During dinner, Marie said, "Guys, these are incredible. Thank King Steven for me and my palate."

Delores said, "I can hang up my apron forever. Thanks, King Steven."

John joined in and said, "These are very tasty."

The girls said, "Dad, no more hot dogs. These are great." The girls all came down and asked for seconds. "Our budget is limited. Could you each share one and give Mama and Papa one to share?" It was on a plate, and off they went.

"Seconds? They never asked for seconds before."

Marie and Delores looked at each other and said, "Not a chance." Then they laughed. "Seconds? They barely can do firsts."

John asked, "Are they poking fun at us?"

"You'd better believe they are poking fun. It's okay; that shows us they truly love us. They are just questioning our culinary talents."

"Mommy," cried out Sarah, "what's for dessert?"

"We made something very special for your open house. Come down and meet me in the kitchen."

Down came all the girls. Each one came over and gave me a hug. "Daddy, thank you for building our new house. We all love you very much." Then they scurried off to the kitchen.

Mama made peach cobbler, and Marie bought vanilla ice cream to put on top. We could hear the girls cheering. Sarah and Leslie carried two servings, one for each of them and one for Mama and Papa. Marie put a cherry on top of all the ice creams—such a special treat for the girls. I told Marie and Delores, "Thank you for making this day so special for our little angels. They will remember this day for a long time."

Then the ladies started singing: "Memories light the corners of my minds." Barbra Streisand would have been proud of their attempt. If only I had a sound system for the backyard.

Everyone had a great time. All the girls needed to get ready for bed, as they had school tomorrow. All the girls were standing at the sliding glass door, turned, and said, "Good night, house. We love you. Sleep tight. We will see you tomorrow." They turned off the porch and balcony lights, gave one another hugs, and told one another that they loved each other. Sarah and Rebecca walked everyone to the front door. We were all giving one another hugs and kisses. "We love you" was the saying and feeling for the evening.

The girls were running up the stairs, talking about the house and which toys they would play with in it. They were so excited. They brushed their teeth, put on their pjs, got under their covers, and waited for our nightly prayers. They added, "God bless our new house. Thank you, God. We love our house you built for us."

"Good night, beautiful girls. Love you. Sleep tight. See you in the morning."

Delores was sitting in bed with the covers pulled up to her chin—not the way she usually was positioned. I sat on the edge of the bed and said, "We have the greatest friends and daughters. They make my life so enjoyable." I leaned over to kiss my beautiful bride. She had on the best perfume, and she had bought a small bottle for me. I hugged her and found out why she had the covers the way she had them pulled up.

"Surprise," she whispered to me.

The next morning, Phillip and his crew were starting the dance floor. Juan, Diego, and both crews were starting with the pavers and removing the soil in areas where they had stopped yesterday. I told them to just make a pile by the gate since the trailer was full. "I have a meeting up the street with the people who were here yesterday. I will let you know how that meeting turns out."

They all thanked me for allowing them to witness the girls' reaction to the playhouse. Angel and Juanita said they cried for over an hour and kept thinking about what the girls told them. "They are so sweet and loving," said Angel. "I want to be just like them from now on."

The girls ran out of the house and up the stairs, opened their door, and said in a loud voice, "Good morning, house! Did you sleep well? We missed you and promised we would see you today. We have to go to school now. See you when we get home from school, said Sarah."

They came down the stairs and back into the house, and they told Delores, "The house was so loving to us; it made us feel so warm inside."

Delores gave them both hugs and said, "Honeys, the house is very proud to be your best friend. I felt the same warm feeling yesterday. Marie and I are going shopping with Mama for curtains and a throw rug. They will be in place when you get home from school."

"We love you and Marie and Mama so much." They got up and gave their mom a hug she would not soon forget. Her eyes were welling up with tears; our little ones had done it to her again. They were such a great gift.

By lunchtime, the pavers were nearly completed. And on the dance floor, I swear I saw Ginger Rogers and Fred Astaire dancing their famous dance.

Doug and Silvia gave me the green light to build the battered wall, waterproof, put in a french drain, and backfill the planter with my soil. If there wasn't enough, then they would pay to have it filled. They also wanted to change the wall cap to precast concrete from the pictures I showed them of John and Marie's home. Silvia asked if Delores could take her over to Marie's sometime. She really wanted to see the entire project. I asked Delores if she would mind taking her over to see John and Marie's backyard and courtyard. "When are you starting their planter?"

"They will start with the footing tomorrow. We will start building the wall after the pavers are completed. I have two more projects starting in another week."

"Is she a nice lady or just a nosy neighbor?"

"I'll tell you what; about nine o'clock, I will take you over there, and you can meet her and make your own judgment."

"Okay, that makes sense to me."

The crews were arriving, raring to get started. I talked to Juan about sending a couple of people over to one of my neighbors to dig a footing for a battered wall. "We will go over there about nine o'clock. I also want to remove the old concrete patio we are standing on and replace it with pavers. I'll get you a compressor and jackhammer. I'll call for a Dumpster to be dropped to load the broken concrete.

Leave the broken concrete in place until the Dumpster arrives. We don't want to handle it twice. The project is looking great. The barbecue was a hit with the girls and the family."

I went to my office and called for the Dumpster. They said they could have one to me in two hours—perfect. "Honey, I have to go to the rental yard. You need me to pick up anything?"

"Not now, maybe later."

I went and picked up the compressor, jackhammer, and plenty of hose. I returned to the house, and Juan had Miguel get the jackhammer from the truck. Vincent helped hook up the hose and dragged it to the patio. "Hammer and hose are ready."

Juan asked Miguel, "Do you know how to start the compressor?"

"No, can you teach me?"

"Yes, let's go get that baby started." Juan showed him how to start and shut down the compressor. It was running, and Juan said to Miguel, "This is your lucky day. You're going to learn how to use the jackhammer." Miguel was excited to learn until he found it looked easy but there was a trick to doing it successfully. They started well away from the sliding glass door or near the house.

Juan said, "When you get to this point, stop. I will finish around the house and sliding glass door." Juan drew a line in red on the concrete where Miguel was to stop using the jackhammer. Juan used the jackhammer to show Miguel how to break up the concrete, and then he had Miguel take a turn. "Not bad, but lean into the hammer, or it will take you for a fast walk." Miguel tried again, and Juan adjusted the angle of the hammer. Miguel put his weight on the hammer and pulled the trigger; it was nearly perfect.

Juan patted him on the shoulder and said, "Just like that. Keep those safety glasses on at all times." Juan had given him ear protection prior, and he had a hard hat on his head. After a few more attempts, Miguel got the hang of running the jackhammer and got to Juan's red line in a pretty short time. He stopped and called for Juan.

Juan drew another line closer to the house and had him break to that line. When he got to the second line, Juan finished breaking out the concrete, and the patio was all broken. Juan had Miguel put the hammer back on the compressor and roll up the hose. Juan rang our doorbell, and Delores answered. He said the compressor could be returned. She said, "Thank you, Juan. I'll tell him we're finished with the compressor."

Delores came to my office doorframe very seductively and said in a soft and sexy voice, "Darling, I need you to do me a huge favor."

"Whatever you want, my darling. I'm your man."

In her mother's voice, she said, "Take back the compressor." She walked away in her old-fashioned way. She sure knew how to kill a moment.

I returned the compressor and went back to the house just in time to see the Dumpster being dropped off. I had called earlier for additional base and sand to be delivered, and they were heading down my street. This was almost too good to be true.

I went out to see how the dance floor was coming along, and the frame was finished. The joists were installed, and they had half the border boards installed. Raymond was fitting the first oak flooring pieces in marking for the cuts, and those were getting ready for installation. Raymond said they should have the floor completed, ready for polyurethane, before the day's end. Juan said to me, "Are we going over to the other house soon?"

I looked at my cell phone. "In about five minutes."

I went back inside, and Delores came down the stairs in beige shorts, a red tank top, sandals, and her famous ankle bracelet. "Well, sweetheart, how do I look?"

"Turn around for me." She did. "Let's go back upstairs?"

"Not that, and definitely not now. We have a meeting, remember?"

I called for Juan. "Bring two footing diggers with you. We will meet you out front."

Juan brought Angel and Manuel with him. When Angel saw Delores, she said, "Are you going to help us too?"

Delores went over to her and gave her a huge loving hug. "No, dear, I don't use shovels. It could break my nails."

We walked together to the house, and Silvia was expecting us. I introduced everyone to Silvia, and everyone shook hands. Delores said to Silvia, "I heard you want to see the Albright residence?"

"Silvia only knows them as John and Marie," I told Delores.

"Oh, forgive me, Silvia. May I ask why you would like a tour of their backyard and courtyard?"

"I saw the photos, and I really want something special done for this place. Doug and I have looked at every big-box store display. I want to see something built without a 'Made in China' tag."

"I have to meet Marie in a few minutes. I'll ask her if she wouldn't mind. When are you available?"

"Delores, you tell me the date and time, and I'm all yours."

"Do you have a cell phone number for me to get in touch with you?"

"Yes." She pulled her cell phone from her hip pocket. Delores had hers in her hand. They exchanged numbers.

Juan and the crew were all dialed in, and Angel and Manuel returned to the truck to get a pick and digger bar. Juan shook Silvia's hand and told her that if she needed anything, he'd be at my house all day, working. She asked him if she could come down during their lunch break and see the playhouse. Juan said, "I would be proud to escort you to the playhouse. I'll be back around eleven thirty to pick you up."

With a very appreciative smile and a gleam in her eyes, she said, "I'll see you then."

Walking back to the house, Juan said, "I'll bet she'll become another one of the ladies."

"You think she has the goods?"

"With a little practice, she'll do just fine. We'll have to have Delores show her and try her out. Maybe tomorrow they can do the tryout."

"You guys like to watch them, don't you?"

"We are all men, and no man would not appreciate what those ladies can do. The magazine is putting out a video for sale. You watch the cable channel and order from their website starting tomorrow. I'm telling everyone I know that they have to buy the video. My wife wants to learn how to do what they do. She really liked watching all of them."

"Have her call Delores. She will teach her, and if she has time, I'm sure they will ask her to join them."

Marie and Delores were in the car with Mama, getting ready to leave. I told them what Juan had just said. Delores and Marie said, "Have her come to the house tomorrow, and we will teach her on the playhouse staircase. Have her wear a nice outfit if she has one."

"I think we will ask Silvia to join us as well. Don't say anything to her. I want to talk with her first, do you understand?"

"Yes ma'am, my lips are sealed."

"Loose lips get you in huge trouble."

"I hear you loud and clear. Have a great time shopping."

The crew was removing the broken concrete and loading it into the Dumpster with a train of wheelbarrows—two loading and two hauling and dumping. They were making short order of the broken concrete. They had nearly finished placing the pavers according to the design I had laid out. They could have the entire project completed by that afternoon. That would make Delores ecstatic. The dance floor had the edges routed; the master woodworker had done his magic. Raymond and his foreman built the bench tops, and the master woodworker rounded the edges for them while he was on the job site. There would be three benches for guests to sit on to watch the ladies and girls perform.

I told Juan to run a conduit from the glass patio door to the patio cover so I could have John and Marie's sound specialist run a sound system to the patio cover and playhouse. "That will be easy for us to do. There is an electrical outlet here on the wall. Bring the conduit to this outlet. There is an outlet on the post of the patio cover. Line the conduit to tie into both outlets."

I went over to Doug and Silvia's to see how the footing was coming along. The footing was nearly completed. Angel was all sweaty, and so was Manuel. I brought them two bottles of cold water and said, "Please take a water break. Sit on the retaining wall. You both deserve a break."

Silvia came outside. She got a text from Delores saying, "We will be home in fifteen minutes. Put on something nice. We'll pick you up and take you to Marie's house." She looked fantastic.

"How do you think I look?"

"Like a million dollars."

"No, really, how do I look? Will your wife and Marie approve?"

"I have a photo to show you." I had one photo in my folder and showed it to her. The girls were in their outfits from the photo shoot. She looked at Marie and Delores.

"Maybe I should change into that type of outfit."

"No, Silvia, you look great. These were the outfits they wore for the photo shoot."

"I want to leave a good impression."

"Angel, could you please join us?"

Angel came over. "Did I do something wrong?"

"No. Silvia is going to see Marie's landscape with Delores and Marie. She is worried how she is dressed. Silvia, Angel was also in the photo shoot. What do you think about her outfit?"

"Silvia, you look stunning. The ladies will show you the nicest job I have ever seen and had the privilege of working on. Turn around for me." Silvia did. "Ma'am, you're an easy ten. Don't change. They will be very happy with you."

Silvia said, "I'm getting a little nervous."

Angel said, "You'll do just fine. Be yourself. That's all they want to see." Angel returned to the wall, finished her water, and started digging the last couple of feet of the footing.

Marie and Delores walked into the backyard, and Delores introduced Marie to Silvia. Marie gave her a hug, stood back, and looked at Silvia. "Beautiful. Great outfit, don't you think, Delores?"

Delores put both hands on her hips. "Turn around." Silvia spun around. "Beautiful. If that's not a ten, shoot me."

All three ladies headed for the car. Delores said, "Dearest darling, we will return in a short while. No Happy Meal today, understand?" She had seen the bag.

"Yes, dear, have a nice time."

In a few minutes, Angel and Manuel joined the rest of the crew, removing soil for the base and sand. Angel was working harder than most of the crew, and she had just finished digging a footing. Where did she get her energy? With the additional help, Diego and Miguel started laying the pavers to finish up where they left off. The tile saw was purring once again, and they had Juanita making the cuts, which Angel taught her. They were both the best my crew had ever had.

It was nearing lunch break, and all the crew were in dire need of a break. I called for the Dumpster to be picked up, and they said it would be retrieved just after lunch. The lady dispatcher said, "So soon. That was fast. You have a good crew working for you."

I agreed, "The best."

At Marie's house, the girls—not knowing if Silvia would be up to doing a grand entrance—slowly addressed the question to her. They were at the waterfall and had her sitting on the bench. She was in total awe at this point, saying, "How nice this project is."

Marie said, "Dear, you haven't seen the best part of the job. Let us take you to what inspired what you're looking at now." Marie extended her hand and helped Silvia up off the bench.

Delores was in the house, pouring three glasses of champagne, and Marie and Silvia joined her at the french doors. Delores handed each of them a glass and grabbed hers. Silvia, a little puzzled, asked, "What is this for?"

Marie said, "You'll see in just a minute."

They entered the tunnel, and the lights were on. Silvia said, "Wow, this is nice."

All were wearing hard-soled shoes. Delores and Marie started making noise with their shoes. Silvia said, "Can I join in?"

"We would be honored to have you join us."

They made it to the door and opened it slowly. Delores showed her how to do a grand entrance through the door onto the courtyard. Silvia said, "Do you do that all the time?"

"Every chance we get."

"Can I try?"

"Silvia, we need to be honest with you. We were hoping you would want to join us. We are in a video for a magazine, which is being aired today on three cable television stations. If you'd like to learn how we do this, we would be anxious to show you. Would you like to learn?"

"I'd love to learn. Why do you want to show me?"

"We like what we see. You have a great personality, beautiful smile. You will fit in perfectly. Marie will show you her grand entrance."

Marie got to the top landing and started doing the most premiere grand entrance that Delores had ever witnessed her doing. As Marie reached the bottom step, they said, "Silvia, show us your stuff."

Silvia drank the entire glass of champagne. "Priming my pump," said Silvia.

Delores took her glass and said, "I will meet you on the landing."

Delores went into the kitchen and poured Silvia another glass. She met Silvia on the top landing and handed her a fresh glass of champagne. She whispered to Silvia, "Give it all you've got. Don't drink from the glass until you reach the bottom step. Can you be seductive?"

Silvia turned her head toward Delores. "I'll try my best. I hope you two like what I do." She descended the staircase, reached the bottom, and downed her second glass of champagne. Both Delores and Marie were applauding her. She was glowing and glamorous.

Delores followed her. She was so poised, her hips were moving in rhythm step-by-step, and she was glamorous and gracious. She had it all. Silvia said, "You ... you are beautiful."

They showed her the grand entrance from the arched gateway, and all three gave it a shot. Then they showed her the playhouse. She was in total awe at this time. She looked at Marie and Delores and said, "I want all this—everything. Can your husband give this to me and Doug?"

They gave her a huge hug. "If you really want this, Delores's husband can make all this come alive."

Silvia said, "This isn't a sales pitch, is it?"

Marie looked at her with loving eyes and posture and said, "We aren't salespeople. We're real. What you see is what you get. We don't put on airs."

Silvia, now very relaxed, said, "I have never felt this way in my entire life."

Marie and Delores said, "It's the champagne." They all laughed as they left the playhouse. Silvia asked if she could practice coming down the stairs. "We would not expect you to do anything less. Be our guest. Enjoy. Bring it on for the boys." She got to the bottom, and the ladies applauded her again. They all joined on the pavers and hugged. "Welcome to our ladies' club."

"What if my Doug says I can't be a part of your club?"

Marie said, "You show him what you just showed us with the same zeal. He will do whatever you say. Reward him and yourself at bedtime."

"How often do you practice?"

"When we get our chores finished, or even while doing our chores."

Delores said, "Let's take her to my playhouse and have her do her entrance for the crew. She'll understand."

Marie said, "Showtime?"

The pavers were being installed, the conduit was in place, and the dance floor was nearly completed. Raymond told me he would return tomorrow and put the coats of polyurethane on. The dance floor looked unbelievable. They were putting the last bench in place when the ladies arrived with Silvia. They escorted her into the playhouse. "Oh my, this is gorgeous. Are you sure he will give me the feeling I'm getting right now—warm? So warm and loving feeling?"

"You like the playhouse?"

"No, I love the playhouse."

"Let's show you the balcony." Marie opened the french doors, and all three ladies walked out onto the balcony. They looked down at the crew putting in the pavers.

Silvia said, "You both should become salespeople. I'm sold, and Doug will be astounded." They went back inside the playhouse and exited onto the porch. Silvia mustered up enough nerve to show everyone what she had learned. As she was descending, the crew stood up and started to applaud her.

When she reached the bottom step, Angel and Juanita went to her and gave her a hug, and Angel said to her, "Welcome to the club, my dear." Delores and Marie were well accepted by the crew. They got their batteries charged.

The pavers were being installed faster than I had ever witnessed before. Once the base layer was compacted, the sand layer was placed, and the vibratory plate made a pass, the pavers were laid. They had a clear path from the sliding glass doors to the playhouse, and they were working on connecting the barbecue to the house. That was about 50 percent completed; the area behind the serving counter was totally finished and looked perfect. Juan had given Angel the chore of filling the pavers with sand to lock them in place. She was 50 percent completed with that task and was gaining on the installers.

All three ladies came out of the house, and Juan told them the pavers were safe to walk on. They all walked over to Angel, who was sweating. Delores headed back into the house and brought out water for her and the crews. "Honey, here, drink some water. Sit at the patio table. Cool down. Do you want me to turn on the fans?"

Marie said, "Yes, but keep them at slow speed. I don't want to mess up my hair." That got all the workers laughing.

The girls were checking their cell phones for the time; they couldn't be late picking up the little ones. Delores remembered something. "Oh shoot, we have to hang the curtains and lay down the throw rug before we pick up the girls."

Angel called over to Juanita. "Let's go, girl. We have a job to do for the ladies."

Delores asked, "Are you saying you want to hang the curtains?"

"We are wasting time sitting here being all feminine and all."

Delores got the bags from the house, and all five ladies headed up the stairs to the playhouse. In a very short while, they were all doing a grand entrance for the boys. The applause for each lady was loud and long. I thought it was thundering on a cloudless day. I went outside just in time to witness the newest lady perform.

"Silvia, Silvia, Silvia, you do that so well," I said.

She came over to me and said, "I love the ladies. Thank you. They have brought me out of drudgery."

"You came out of your cocoon and turned into a beautiful butterfly."

Silvia gave me a loving huge hug. "You are going to see us quite often from today forward. I want what they have. We need a drawing. Doug is going to get educated tonight."

Silvia had to say good-bye for today; she had practicing to do and needed just the right outfit for her nightly performance. Delores and Marie said, "You'll do wonderful. Great meeting you, and welcome to our world." Angel and Juanita hugged her as well. Everyone was back to doing their jobs, waiting for the little girls to show their appreciation of all their hard work.

The ladies had a few minutes to spare, so they went back to the patio table and finished their water. Delores asked Marie, "Are you ready to be Mommy again?"

Marie said, "I'm never not a mommy, and neither are you, my dearest."

The pavers were very close to being in the record books. Just a few more cuts and some sand, and the workweek was finished. All had their paychecks in hand. "Great job, everyone. Have a fantastic weekend. We'll start the battered wall on Monday and two more projects by Wednesday or Thursday."

The final paver was in place, and while the crew was putting away the tools and loading the truck, Angel was putting in the last bit of sand. When finished, she cried. "Papa, I thank you. The girls and ladies, thank you. You made everyone's life even better than it was prior. We love you with all our hearts."

CHAPTER 50

The next morning, after the girls were dropped off at school, they all had on their units for protection. Marie and Delores had the girls show them where they put on the unit, and they also showed the girls that they also had theirs on. This ensured the girls that Mommy was also doing as they were told.

The ladies were all dressed up as normal. Angel and Juanita dressed as construction workers; they had already gotten dirty from working, and they arrived as instructed. Everyone was there on time, ready for the limousine ride to the magazine's studio. Marie was telling Angel and Juanita what to expect when they arrived at the studio.

Delores and Mama were having a morning cup of coffee and a breakfast roll made yesterday by Mama and Marie. Marie, Angel, and Juanita joined them. They all took a stroll into the backyard, went across the bridge, and went to the waterfall for some peace and tranquility before the hustle and bustle of the magazine activities. Angel asked Marie, "Will we have to wear the unit you all are wearing?"

"Yes, you will get yours today. They will have you sign contracts and consent forms. Mr. Ruben will instruct you where and why you are signing the forms. Giselle will also inform you what to do and what not to do while under contract with the magazine."

"Can we ask you why we have to wear the unit?"

Marie said, "For your protection while out in the public. Giselle will explain it very thoroughly. I could just get you confused and very nervous. She is excellent at describing the reasons why."

Angel asked Marie, "Are we going to become rich?"

Marie said, "You know, I don't know for sure, but you'll have more money than you have now."

Just then, the doorbell rang. Marie said, "Ladies, before we answer the door, I just want to say that I love each and every one of you with all my heart." All the ladies gave one another huge hugs.

The chauffeur was standing at the door, the limousine was sitting out front with the doors open, and Susanne was standing by the open doors. She yelled,

"Ladies, good morning! So great seeing you this morning!" All the ladies entered the limousine. Once inside, the driver closed the door, got in behind the wheel, pulled away, and headed to the magazine's studio.

Once on the road and away from the house, Susanne said, "Ladies, ladies, ladies, the magazine had an unbelievable day yesterday. You cannot believe the chaos and commotion generated by your videos. You broke all previous records the company has ever achieved. The phones are still ringing off the hook. Some new customers said they were on hold for over fifteen minutes. We hired twenty more operators just for today, and they are interviewing at least that many more today and even more for the next day. You crashed our website three times in four hours. We had our programmers write an apology and gave them an alternate website to contact. I have been in this industry for over twenty years, and I have never witnessed what occurred yesterday in my whole career. We have offers from twelve more cable networks, and six of the regular television stations want to talk to us about having all of you shown on their standard programs. Mr. Ruben has all his staff setting up appointments for next week and the following week. Ladies, the first issue has not even hit the shelves for sale, and we have tripled our circulation numbers.

"I hope all of you are giddy inside. I could not sleep last night. My heart was racing so fast. My husband said, 'Honey, if you keep tossing and turning, I will be a wreck tomorrow. Could you please get a cup of hot chocolate and settle down?' At least he didn't tell me to go to the couch."

Marie said, "I have a question for you. Who exactly is Giselle? We know she is not a publicity specialist."

"You know, Mr. Ruben is the one to ask that question. I could answer you with 'She is the publicity specialist,' but you obviously don't believe that is her real title. I have only met her once. Yours is a special case. Mr. Ruben is taking every precaution to ensure all your safety. Ladies, you are all very special people. I have never met a group of ladies so unique as compared with the typical person we would interview or use in the magazine. Your daughters are such a reflection of all your personalities and uniqueness. The staff can't wait to be around them. I don't want to sound like I'm a spokesperson here to pump you all up or sell you on an idea that some board of directors is forcing me to tell you. I respect and love all of you too much to scam you.

"Your daughters lifted my day so high at the party that, even to this day, not only my husband but also the office staff and my family have all asked, 'What has happened to you?' I tell them, 'Four of the sweetest, most kindhearted girls I have ever met in my entire life, that is what happened to me.' I told you they made me cry with so much joy and happiness. That had never happened to me before—ever."

They arrived at the magazine's studio; Susanne had to phone to have the security guard open the studio door entrance. She told the ladies, "When you are scheduled to do a shoot, this is the door you must enter through. The front lobby usually has nonemployees and photographers lurking around."

The chauffeur opened the limousine door and assisted all the ladies from the car. Once they were all out of the limousine, the studio door opened, and two security guards came out of the building, dressed in very fancy suits. As the ladies approached the door, the security guards greeted them: "Good morning, ladies. Welcome." All the ladies said good morning to the security guards.

Susanne led the way to where the staff was waiting to make them all beautiful. They were walking down a hallway with closed doors and came to the only open one. As they neared the door and started to enter, the place erupted with numerous people clapping and cheering. There were balloons, streamers, confetti, roses, and five bunches of long-stemmed red roses with each of the ladies' names on them. They were each handed a glass of champagne in a crystal champagne glass. The ladies were shocked; all the staff were giving them huge hugs, and the lady singer and the violins started to play Marie's favorite Italian song.

Out of the crowd of people came John. He took Marie's hand, and they danced to the song. Then I came out and took Delores's hand, and we joined John and Marie. Papa came out next and took Mama's hand, and they started to dance. Angel's boyfriend came out next, and then Juanita's fiancé came out. All five couples were dancing to the song, and the four violins and the singer changed to another Italian song that was just as romantic. The ladies were all tearing up and holding their spouses very close. They had their heads on the shoulders of their mates. Cameras were rolling, and the crowd was applauding.

The cable network announcer came to the floor, took Susanne's hand, and joined in on the dance. All the ladies noticed the gentleman dancing with Susanne, and they all were amazed at how he really looked in real life. Many others in the crowd started dancing to the music, pairing off. I could see some of the girls were a little shocked when gentlemen asked them to dance. The studio turned into a ballroom; they even had a machine putting bubbles into the air.

They played one more song since nearly everyone was in a great mood. As the third song ended, all the ladies and their spouses were hugging and kissing. The magazine was getting another video to air, and the popularity of this one would more than likely surpass that of the one being aired now. Before the song ended, a beautiful lady walked out with the owner of the magazine, and they danced to the end of the song. She was having two photographers shoot them, one with a still camera and the other with a video camera.

Everyone who was dancing stopped with the end of the song and applauded the singer and the violin players and one another. Some of the girls who had been asked to dance with coworkers actually kissed the gentlemen. All the dance partners hugged each other and came up to hug the ladies as well. The owner instructed all the employees to return to their workstations, and a caterer came into the studio, handed everyone a slice of cake, and gave each person either coffee or a beverage of his or her choice. The owner of the magazine came to each and every lady, gave her a hug, and told her how pleased he was with her. "Please enjoy this day, and most importantly, have fun." He introduced the beautiful lady who was accompanying him.

Delores said to me in a whisper, "Down, boy, behave yourself."

She was a model and actress; she was very polite and gracious.

Now with everything quieting down, Susanne regained her composure after she was startled when the cable network's main gentleman grabbed her hand and escorted her to the dance floor. She was actually enjoying the dance more than a married woman should enjoy a dance with someone not her husband. "Ladies, we need to get you to makeup and get your hair styled, and then you're off to wardrobe." She told all our spouses to follow another lady to where the program would be filmed. The lady we were to follow was stunning.

Delores grabbed my ear. "Dearest darling, you behave yourself, or tonight will be couch time. Love you, my sweet."

The magazine had five makeup artists, five stylists, and five ladies in the wardrobe department. The doors the ladies passed to get to the only open door were the rooms designated for the makeup, hairstyling, and wardrobe. The ladies were treated like royalty. Each one was getting her makeup put on and then being shuttled over to the hairstylists, each time having her glass refilled with champagne or wine, whichever she desired. Angel asked for water. After her first glass of champagne, she said, "I don't drink. It makes me feel funny." Most of the ladies were done drinking after the second refill; they also chose water. The water was not the special thirty-six bottles for $3.96—no. This was the best bottled water money could buy. They had their makeup on and hair styled by professionals; it was not work that would be done for forty or fifty dollars per style. The stylists were all well known and highly sought after.

Now they were off to the wardrobe department, which had racks and racks of custom-designed outfits. The head of wardrobe looked at each lady and decided what would look the best for her. She also knew what the host was wearing and did not want to upstage the host. If he was in a tux, the ladies would be in gowns or very high-class outfits. He was in a thousand-dollar suit, so the girls would be dressed in dinner wear, not jeans and T-shirts.

Mama was the first one to be dressed with a stunning outfit. They adorned the outfit with jewelry, not Walmart-special, made-in-China costume jewelry— no, sir. It was the real deal—necklace, bracelets, and rings. Mama got to see herself in a full-length mirror, and they even put on designer high heels. Mama said, "Papa is going to be so jealous of me."

Marie was dressed in a designer outfit. She could have been on the cover of *Vogue*, as she was beyond stunning. If they had her do her grand entrance, her outfit would dwarf my greatest vision of her.

My dearest darling's her outfit was way beyond wow. It was the most stunning. She looked so good. If she did the arched gateway entrance, the video would have to be rated at least R. She had never looked this good ever.

No way was this my construction worker. This must be Angel's double. Wow, the crew would be going crazy if they saw her. Well, they would see her, and they would be going crazy for weeks. What an outfit. She was really adorable.

Juanita, oh my god, what did they do to my newest employee? No way would I allow her to dress like that in front of my crew. That would be considered cruel and unusual punishment. She was one of the greatest transformations I had ever seen, from a construction worker to a starlet. When her fiancé saw her, he would take her to the courthouse this afternoon.

The program was about to start, and the host of the show started his monologue, allowing the viewing audience in on what they were about to witness. Remember: all those were in the first studio's party and introductory and welcoming area. Yes, they were the audience. They also added a few more people to fill all the seats. They had us husbands, fiancé, and boyfriend all sitting in the front row. Mr. Ruben was sitting next to us, and the owner of the magazine and his lady friend were also in the front row.

The producer of the program told us that when the camera panned to shoot the audience, they would be shooting over our heads. He explained that they did not want our faces shown because of the nature of the ongoing investigation. We all were extremely vulnerable. All this precaution was starting to make me leery of being outside. Mr. Ruben explained, "They can only keep track of us to a point. They don't want to suggest to any people following you that you have security close by. Our security force is undercover. They blend in with what you are doing." In my case, my security persons would look like construction workers. Suits and ties would not blend well, and they would be spotted. Their vehicle was a construction truck, and they had toolboxes, pipe racks, and tools. One would never know they were security people.

Giselle talked to us while we were waiting for the girls to get ready. She told each and every one of us that they had been collecting data for the last two weeks on our daily routine to adjust the security team so they could blend in with what we did on a normal day. The young guys were amazed that they had been watched. What amazed Juanita's fiancé was that they showed him three days of his activities—what he did, whom he talked to, where he went to lunch—everything he did all day long. He said, "I never knew I was being watched."

Giselle said, "We are highly skilled and trained professionals. If you had noticed, so would those who were watching you from the bad guy's side of the equation. We have photos of anyone that was close to you for more than a normal time."

Papa said, "I go get a cup of coffee most days."

Giselle said, "We know, and we watched each and every person who got close to you or sat in the same area and left when you did. We have their photos and matched them to our computer database, checking on their identities. Gentlemen, this is very serious. You do not know how vicious this person we are trying to trap really is. We are trying to find out even more about him and whom he answers to."

The program was ready to start, and the host of the program entered onto the stage and welcomed all the viewers at home and our live audience. "We have a very special program for you today. The ladies in the video being aired for *Remodeling* magazine are here with us today. You are in for a real treat. They will do their famous grand entrance that you have seen during the promotion. Without further ado, let's have a big round of applause for a construction worker from Stockdale Landscape Construction, Ms. Juanita."

The ladies were told to do their best grand entrances. They had five steps down into the stage area. Juanita did a marvelous job. The announcer said, "I cannot believe my eyes. A construction worker. Lucky crew." The announcer took her hand and led her to her chair. The audience was giving her a round of applause.

"Our next lady is also a construction worker who is the best friend of Juanita, Ms. Angel. Please give her a warm welcome." Angel, being a little shy, did what she had done for over a month with poise, grace, glamour, and sophistication. She was stunning. The audience was applauding, and the announcer said, "The Stockdale Landscape crews are the luckiest men on the planet. Stunning, Angel. Beautiful job." He led her to her chair.

"Our next lady is the mother of the homeowner. She does not remind me of my mother. Please give a warm welcome to Mrs. Sophia." The audience was applauding, and the announcer said, "This is the mother, everyone." She had grace, style, sophistication, glamour, and poise. Each step was better than the last step. The announcer took her hand and escorted her to her chair.

"You know how I said the Stockdale Landscape Company crew were the luckiest men on the planet? Well, our next lady is the wife of the company's owner. She is the mother of two of the sweetest girls you will ever meet. That's next week by the way. Please don't miss that program. Without further ado, please give her a warm welcome. From the arched gateway to my left, Mrs. Delores Stockdale." She entered through the arched gateway with such a seductive move. It was sensual and sexy, and she poised with grace and glamour. The audience all stood on their feet, and the announcer took a handkerchief from his pocket and wiped his forehead. "Delores, if you weren't happily married, every man in this building would want to date you." He escorted her to her chair and gave her a hug.

"Wow, gentlemen, I don't know about you, but she was fantastic. Remember: she is a housewife. Our next lady is the homeowner of our project, mother of two of the sweetest girls. I'm telling you now you have to watch next week and see the four daughters. They are the most incredible young ladies you will ever meet. Without

any further ado, Mrs. Marie Albright. Please give her a very warm welcome."
Marie started down the stairs, and the whole audience were on their feet. She
was strutting down each step, looking sensual, seductive, and poised. She could
have had a book balanced on her head, and it wouldn't have fallen off. She was
sashaying more than ever before; this was one of her best grand entrances ever.
She reached the stage, and the announcer was down on one knee. He extended
his hand as he was rising, kissed her hand, and escorted her to her chair. The
announcer turned to the audience and said, "I need a cold shower now."

The announcer, waiting for the audience to settle down, said, "Ladies,
welcome to our show. I need to settle down, or I might forget what I was supposed
to ask you. Marie—wow, Marie, how long have you been doing your grand
entrance?"

"On a staircase?"

"Yes, on a staircase."

"About two months. Without the staircase, about three months."

"What got you to do the grand entrance?"

"Mr. Stockdale had a vision. As he was explaining his revised drawing to
me and my husband, he told us his vision. He said he saw me entering our new
courtyard from atop the stairs with a glass of champagne in one hand, elbow bent,
graceful, glamorous, and poised. Every move was smooth and well balanced. I
was moving to our party of guests who were applauding each and every move."

The announcer said, "You did it to me again. Cold shower, here I come. That
is amazing. Mr. Stockdale saw you in his dream. Was his wife in his dream?"

"He told her, in front of us, that she was the barmaid."

The announcer and audience laughed. He said, "I'll bet the sofa was really
comfortable that night. Ladies in the audience and at home watching, if you
did that for your significant other, your man would mow the lawn with a pair of
scissors, wash your car, do whatever you desire all day, week, and month long.
Your husband gets to see this every night?"

"And more. Yes, it keeps me in practice."

"I'd better move on or we will have to go to commercial. Mrs. Delores
Stockdale, oh my god, was what you do your husband's vision as well?"

"No, it all started by accident. I saw Marie perform her grand entrance
down the staircase. I knew I could not move the way she moves without missing
a step and falling down the rest of the stairs. Her entrance is flawless. She is only
getting better. I had to go to the store to get some groceries for our dinner that
evening. I came back, and I entered the courtyard from the front of the house.
There was a plywood gate installed by the gate manufacturer. I told myself, 'You
can dazzle them coming through the gate.' I opened the gate slowly, and with all
the seductiveness in my bones, I strutted into their vision, and then I became all
warm inside and added the sensual moves, staying poised with grace and glamour.

The construction crew all stood to their feet, applauding. And with each step, the applause got louder, which inspired me to be more seductive.

"When I reached the patio table, I said, 'Silly boys.' They all came to my care and carried in all the groceries."

"Wow, you ladies really know how to hurt us men. How long have you entertained the crew?"

"About two months."

"Your crew has to be the happiest on the planet, working next to these two gorgeous girls, having you do your entry and Marie doing hers. Do they get any work done at all?"

"My husband said the crew's morale has greatly improved with the floor shows and working with Angel and Juanita."

"All I can say is you will get thousands of applications after the videos air. I'm thinking about applying today. I make great money. I'd sacrifice all that for the floor show and working with two beautiful girls." The announcer turned to the camera. "Honey, I'm going to be a little late tonight. I have to take a cold shower before seeing you."

He turned and faced Sophia. He got down on his knees and bowed to her. "Sophia, I thank you on behalf of every man in the audience and watching the television. Thank you for giving us a beautiful daughter. As I have asked the other ladies, just how long have you been doing the grand entrance?"

Sophia looked over at Marie, turned back to the announcer, and said, "I think three weeks … maybe three and a half weeks."

"What inspired you to do the grand entrance?"

"At first I was rather embarrassed. A lady of my age doing such a thing? The walker crowd would be abashed seeing one of theirs acting in such a manner. I saw what a thrill my daughter and Delores were having, and the response from the men working on the project. Then I thought, 'What if I make a fool of myself?' All those things were rushing through my head, and Delores, sweet Delores, said, "Mama, your turn.' Being a strong-willed Italian woman, I came down the staircase from the upper platform. I heard the crew and the girls all applauding. With each step, the applause grew louder. The fancier I moved, the louder and longer the applause. When I reached the pavers, they were still applauding, and the girls all ran to me and gave me such a loving hug that my whole insides were warm. I have never felt that feeling ever."

"So naughty Delores inspired you to join her club?"

"Shame on naughty Delores, but I love you and thank you."

"Oh, by the way, she is also a grandmother. I'm in deep trouble when I get home. Angel, you are unbelievable. You have changed my entire image of construction workers. Usually they are giving wolf whistles to ladies passing by the work site. No need for your crew to act like chauvinist pigs. Have they ever made comments to you?"

"No, sir, I'd slug them if they did. The crews are so nice to me and Juanita. They are our brothers. They all treat us like their sisters. I would not have asked Juanita to apply for a job if I didn't feel respected. I have nothing but respect for the men I work with, and I know by their actions they respect me and Juanita. The little girls you all will meet next week, they taught me that all they want people to do is respect them for who they are, and they will respect you for who you are."

"People in the audience and our viewers, please look at the monitors. This is Angel during work, and this is our darling Angel today." The entire audience was standing on their feet and applauding loudly. "Angel, Angel, Angel, you look adorable in both photos and in real life. I'm so proud to have met you. You have rewritten my book on construction workers."

He turned to Juanita. "Juanita, so you are Angel's best friend?"

"Yes sir. We have known each other since grammar school. I believe it was third grade when we became friends."

"I must say you are gorgeous. Your fiancé is one very lucky man. Oh, wait a minute, I forgot to ask Angel. How long have you been doing the grand entrance?"

"Two weeks."

"I'm sorry, Juanita, I'm too flustered right now to think straight. So Angel got you a job interview? Have you ever worked in construction before?"

"No, never. I was working in a fast-food restaurant—horrible hours and no respect."

"How did it feel working for a construction company the first day?"

"I was really nervous—afraid. What if I make a mistake? I'm working with all men except my best friend, Angel. What if they say, 'Why did the owner hire someone with no experience? We have a job to finish; we can't be training.' Angel told me, 'Don't be scared. These are all very nice guys, and the owner will treat you with respect. The guys help you lift heavy items and show you how not to hurt your back.' The first day, they had me work with Angel until I got comfortable. Then Juan, our foreman, had me do something away from Angel. He told me later he wanted to see if I could work with others like I was working with Angel."

"Do you recommend other girls work in construction?"

"Work with us. I'm not sure of all companies. You can't ask to work with a better bunch of guys."

"Audience, you saw Angel as she is right now and what she looks like as a construction worker. This is Juanita now and while working." The audience went crazy; the applause was very loud and long.

The announcer said, "Juanita, what a transformation. I'm so honored to be able to host this program and meet such beautiful and charming women. When I was told I was going to host this show, my first thought was, 'Are you kidding me? Do you know who I am? You're telling me I have to interview five unknown women, not professional actresses, lawyers, doctors, housewives? And say what? Construction workers? I want triple pay.' Ladies, I want to apologize for my reaction. It was very self-centered and childish. I want to host every event you are to perform. I'll do it for free. You all taught me an unforgettable lesson. I love all of you. You're more gifted than anyone I have ever interviewed.

"Home viewers, these cameras do not do these ladies justice. They just show you the outside. Their inside is far greater than their obvious beauty, elegance, and charm. Thank you for watching today. See you on the next program."

The cameras were shut down, and the audience was standing on their feet, applauding. Their significant others came onto the stage and gave all the ladies huge hugs and kisses. The host said to the ladies, "Thank you, all. Gentlemen, you are all so lucky to have these ladies. They are such a joy for me."

The audience was all coming down to shake their hands when Susanne said, "We have a lunch set up for everyone in the other studio. Please, let's move to the larger studio, and the ladies, I'm sure, will shake your hands." The ladies and their partners were escorted to the other studio. They formed two lines to greet the audience, better known as staff. The staff entered the studio, shook the hands of the wives and partners, and told them their titles.

During the luncheon, the company owner stated, "The day-and-a-half totals are in. Subscription sales have surpassed five years of subscription sales. No matter which five years are added together, none comes close to the day-and-a-half sales. The videos have gone to nearly a quarter of a million and will reach at least a half million in the next couple of days. They are predicting well over a million videos will be sold, with the second video coming out in two more days. My dear, sweet ladies, I can't thank you enough for what you have brought to the table.

"Mr. Stockdale, I know the ladies are getting a lot of attention. Once our issues hit the stand, your vision that brought all this into the limelight will make your phone ring off the hook as well. I talked to Phillip. He wants to partner with you and build as many playhouses as you can design. Stan, who built our stage staircase and archway gate, is contracted to do at least fifteen sets for the cable companies. He is going to contact you and also partner with you on staircases. We have at least one hundred vendors who have expressed an interest in supplying your products all over the United States. We have at least fifty investors standing by to help you finance the growth of your company.

"Here is the ultimate in free offers for you to consider. There is a developer who funds most of our projects and wants to offer you an office with a warehouse for you to look into. All he wants is that your address shows the development where your company resides. They own and manage the entire business park. Plan on hiring at least a complete office staff and salespeople. You will need a designer or architectural firm to handle the workload. All business costs will be financed. Our accountant on staff will help you set up and manage the new growth. Any licensing required to do projects out of your state of residence will be handled for you. We ask only that we are allowed to photograph and write stories of projects that are similar to this one. We are hoping they'll have a lot less drama.

"As you all know, we are aiding the city police and assisting the FBI in resolving the issues that occurred with this project. Even though it is a very interesting read for our subscribers, it puts you and your family in grave danger. I want everyone to know we are very close to putting an end to this whole thing.

"Please enjoy the lunch. You all have deserved every morsel. Delores, my lady friend would love for you to teach her your entrance. If you can teach her how you achieve such greatness, I will move her from friend to 'yes, dear.' Marie, you, too, can change her life in the same fashion. I have to say she is beautiful but very shy. She is an actress and follows scripts to a T. She just needs your self-confidence to get her over her fears. We will talk after the luncheon. Angel and Juanita, you need to meet with Mr. Ruben right after lunch. He has papers for you to sign and go over.

"One last thing: We are in conference with seven major cable channels, five major networks. You ladies could have your own weekly show—with, of course, guest appearances. This is still under negotiations. We will keep you posted."

Angel and Juanita were escorted into Mr. Ruben's office to fill out the necessary paperwork. The owner and his lady friend met with Delores and Marie in the owner's office—a very plush one. Delores and Marie were shown two very plush and cushioned chairs—the type that once you sat down in, you never wanted to get back up from. The owner said to the ladies, "I'm still in shock from what happened yesterday and is still ongoing. I hope that when this momentum slows down, I don't go into withdrawals. I want to say your entrances and your responses were incredible. I don't know how you two have developed what you do, but please never change. The way you both carry yourselves is something very few women have ever been able to achieve.

"I had a well-known choreographer review your video, and I asked him, 'Have you ever seen nonprofessionals achieve these moves?' He told me he would get his most talented dancers, get the studio to bring over a prebuilt staircase, and have the girls watch your video and attempt to duplicate your moves. He allowed them a couple of hours of practice, and then they all would have to show them their moves. They were all placed in gowns, jewelry, fashion shoes, and makeup with hair styled, just like they would be dressed for a show. There were ten girls performing and filmed. These were professional dancers, hired out for very high prices per appearance. He sent me the video of all their grand entrances. Marie, none of them came close. Similar, but not close. They did the arched gateway. Delores, hands down, you made them look silly. So I ask you, would you be willing to teach Michele how you perform your moves?"

Marie said, "Mr. Barns, my moves come from my heart. The applause from the crew gets me all warm inside, and I make moves to keep the warm feeling alive. Michele, I need to know, have you ever had a warmth come over your body that you never want to leave? Oh, before you answer, it's not a sexual feeling. We all have those."

She said, "I had to play a part for a program. The director took me aside and said, 'You have to put more into the part. Reach down and give me the real you.' I stood away from the camera and crew and thought, 'How do I do that?' They were ready for a reshoot. They called me to get into position. Walking to the position, I felt a warmness. When they told me I was on, I became seductive and saucy. Each move was accented to seduce. I felt so warm inside, and I heard the director call, 'Cut.' The director came over to me right away and put his arms around me and said that was perfect. When they showed me the shot, I got embarrassed, turned at least three shades of red. I could not believe that was me. I have lived my entire life with these looks and got anything I wanted from some of the wealthiest men on the planet. They would pay anything for me to be with them."

Marie said, "Well, for you to learn how to do a grand entrance, you will have to return to your experience you achieved at that shoot."

Delores added, "I look at it as a visual tease. As Marie said, the applause, being appreciated for what you bring to those viewing you, drives me harder to please. I get in a mental zone during my entrance. Can I say what I am doing is self-gratification? No. Do I do it to get noticed or draw attention to me? No. I enjoy the applause. If someone would yell out a nasty comment, I would stop, turn around, and leave. I'm not doing it to get them aroused sexually. I'm not a stripper or exotic dancer. If they are looking for that type of show, they should go to where the girls are paid to steal their money. I look at what we do as being like watching an old-time movie starring Ginger Rogers and Fred Astaire. Her dance moves were suggestive but glamorous, and you didn't want the dance to end."

Marie added, "I feel the same way as Delores. If someone thinks I'm doing what I'm doing to arouse them, I quit and return to good old Marie."

Mr. Barns said, "Ladies, I want you to repeat this meeting with the audience on the next video. You just told me how real you two really are. The viewers will need to know what is going through your minds while you are doing the grand entrance."

Michele said, "You ladies have given me such a lift in my spirit. I know I could do what Mr. Donohue wants me to achieve. I'm going to watch your video at least a dozen times in my dance outfit. I will never be able to duplicate you exactly, but I know I can get my dearest's attention." Michele stood up and walked to an open spot in the office about twenty feet away; she had clearance. She stood there for a few seconds, getting into her actress mode. Before she started, she asked us to give her applause to see if she could feel what we were feeling.

Mr. Donohue told her to wait for a couple minutes. He talked to Susanne. "Bring in a dozen of our staff." He said, "My dearest love, I want you to bring everything to this walk. Delores will be your judge."

Susanne and twelve staff members entered the office. Marie told them, "You are going to witness Michele's debut of becoming one of the ladies."

Michele said, "You want me to join you?"

"I believe you have what it takes. This is your audition."

Mr. Donohue told the sound crew to play an Italian love song in his office. They played the song that Marie and John had started dancing to earlier. Michele got into her zone and started to move as normal, and then all of a sudden, she started to get more seductive and saucier in her moves. Without being told to do so, the staff all started to applaud her every move. As they applauded her, she got even more into every step. She turned around at the end of the twenty feet, headed in the other direction, looked over her shoulder, gave a seductive smile, and turned again to go back in the same direction. The staff was totally enjoying her. She made three passes, and the song came to the end.

Susanne rushed over to her and said, "That was unbelievable. You were gorgeous, stunning, glamorous, and graceful."

Marie and Delores stood up, went to her, and gave her a hug. Marie whispered to her, "Welcome to the ladies' club."

"Stunning. I'm in complete awe. You don't need lessons," said Delores. "You need just to be you."

Mr. Donohue thanked the staff and asked Susanne to stay and join them. Everyone was seated, and Michele said, "I feel like a million dollars. Marie and Delores, I love both of you and look forward to performing with you. I promise to get even better."

Delores said, "Careful about getting better. The only way I could compete would be to start stripping."

Mr. Donohue said, "Don't take this the wrong way, but I would pay big money to see that show."

Delores said, "Sir, save your money. It would never happen. That would just cheapen me."

Mr. Donohue asked Susanne, "Would you like to join the ladies' club?"

"Oh, sir, I can't do their moves. I could not even do Michele's moves."

Delores asked if Mr. Donohue could leave his office for a few minutes. He said, "Sure, how about five minutes?"

"Great, we really appreciate you doing that for us."

The room was soon clear of all men. Delores said to Susanne, "I need to see your body. You always have baggy clothes on—stylish but not suggestive in any fashion. Are you highly religious? Or does your religious belief prohibit you from wearing formfitting outfits?"

"I go to church with my husband and children—no restrictions on clothing."

Delores said, "I'm not trying to embarrass you. I just want to see if we can do a remake on you."

Susanne removed her loose-fitting top and baggy pants.

Marie said, "She has a nice form."

"Susanne," said Michele, "you need to show more of you."

Marie said, "Susanne, get dressed. Head over to makeup, hair, and wardrobe. Get the makeover and return to the office. When you come back to the office, get your twelve staff members together. Showtime."

As Susanne was leaving, Mr. Donohue entered though his office door. Susanne said to him, "See you in a few minutes."

Michele told her lover what was going to happen. "Please, dear, relax. Take it easy. Tell us how much money the ladies will be earning."

"Okay, ladies, what drives you—money, notoriety, celebrity status, having your every wish catered to, fancy clothes, jewelry?"

Marie and Delores both said, "Our happy family."

"What if I told you that all of you will be making over six digits before the final issue?"

Delores said, "Where's the decimal point placed?"

"At the very end of the six digits."

Marie said, "We haven't adjusted to what we have been thrown into yet. I don't know if money will make us adjust to the lifestyle. I'm afraid they will pull us apart from our girls. They are everything to me and my husband. We have established a loving relationship with Delores and her family. The girls are inseparable. I don't see how money will make that any better than what it already is for me. We look forward to spending time with one another, doing simple things. Clogging in the tunnel is such a rush for all the girls and ladies. All the other things you talked about just infringe on our freedom that we have now. We wear electronic devices, have a security team watching over our every move, can't walk down the street or go shopping at the drop of a hat, can't go out to eat at our favorite eatery, and fear being noticed and mobbed. I felt very awkward at the restaurant two days ago. I like my freedom. The money will be nice, but there is a huge price to pay."

Michele stood up, walked over to Marie, gave her a hug, and told her, "I know exactly how you feel. I want what you have. You are my hero. Teach me how to feel like you feel."

Just then the office door opened, and in came the most beautiful lady. They had done a marvelous job on Susanne. Everyone stood up and turned to gaze at the transformation. "Susanne," Michele said, "wow, I love the new you."

Mr. Donohue looked at her with adoring eyes. "My dear, you're gorgeous." The twelve staff members had just arrived, and the music started to play.

Marie said, "Show us your stuff, Susanne."

She started like Michele, a little stiff for the first few steps, and then she loosened up some and got into the song. Her movement was still a little stiff. Michele went over to her and said, "Seduce me. Get seductive. Put a little bump in your grind."

Susanne said, "I might get embarrassed."

"Embarrass me," Michele replied. "I dare you."

Susanne made the first twenty feet and started in the other direction. She took four steps, her hips now moving more freely. She looked over her shoulder with a take-me smile, and she started getting applause from the staff and the ladies. She got to the other end, made a very seductive turn, and proceeded to bring the heat to the crowd. She was in a groove. Every part of her body was flowing with her womanhood. The song came to an end, and the staff, ladies, and owner were applauding her loud and long.

Marie went to her, hugged her, and said, "That was so good. You were graceful, glamorous, sophisticated. Welcome to the ladies' club." Michele and Delores gave her hugs.

Michele said, "How do you feel?"

Susanne said, "I'm walking on a cloud. Was I that good, or were you all being just very nice?"

The staff asked Mr. Donohue, "Can you have them restart the song?"

"Sure." He called over to the sound department.

The song started, and the staff said, "All you ladies show us your moves."

One at a time, they all sashayed down the twenty-foot path. One staff member got a film crew in the room, and they began filming the events one after another. Mr. Donohue had them keep playing different songs until he told them to stop. The ladies were all in a zone, each one getting more seductive with each pass. The more seductive one lady got, the more the others tried to top the moves. They started to walk in pairs; that was something new and delightful to watch. I knew the hands of the staff had to be getting sore.

The office door opened, and even more staff members joined in on the applause. Mr. Donohue said, "Let's all move to the studio." The ladies all led the staff down the hall, and everyone was joining in on the fun. They got the husbands, boyfriend, fiancé, Angel, and Juanita, and the entire building was strutting into the studio. The ladies kept performing and getting down, so to speak. The film crew were getting the next two or three videos just in this moment.

Shy Michele lifted her skirt to a miniskirt height and showed off her legs. Delores said, "Okay, my dearest, we can all join in on that," and she moved her dress up to show off her legs. Marie, Angel, and Juanita all joined in, and so did Mama.

Michele smiled and said to Delores, "I'm not shy anymore."

Delores said, "I love you. You're doing so great."

Finally the songs ended and the skirts fell back down to how they were designed to accent the ladies' curves. All the ladies were in a group hug, and the staff and crew were all still applauding what they just witnessed. Mr. Donohue said, "Ladies, that was fantastic. As a token of my appreciation, the outfits that you are all wearing are my gift to you. No one else could ever do them justice. I love all of you. Have a wonderful day."

The men and ladies were escorted into the limousines, and Susanne joined them. Michele was also asked to join them. That was one beautiful carload of ladies. The ride to the house was fun filled; the chauffeur played music for the ladies—the types of songs that get people moving. Michele said, "He'd better be careful, or he's going to see things he shouldn't see."

Marie told Delores, "We'd better not do what I'm thinking right now."

Delores said, "If I start, there is no stopping me."

The ride time was the same, but it seemed a lot quicker. When they got to the house, all the ladies' clothes they'd had on when they arrived at the studio were all placed in the trunk of the limousine. They were on hangers and labeled with each lady's name. Attached to each hanger was an envelope; the front of the envelope showed the lady's name, and just below the name was the word "enjoy." Angel opened her envelope and screamed, "Are you kidding me?" That got all the ladies to open theirs. They all began hopping up and down.

Susanne said, "That is our thank-you, and here's mine." She hugged each lady with so much love and respect that tears of joy were messing up all the makeup.

Michele came over to Marie and Delores. She hugged both of them and said, "You two, I love you—truly love you. If you ever need anything, you call me." All three were tearing up and hugging, with true love pouring over all of them.

It was time to go get the girls. Marie and Delores played school bus and picked them up. They were all so excited to see their moms. Kim said, "Mommy, you look so pretty today. We love the way you look." They leaned over the seat and hugged both Marie and Delores around their necks.

Leslie said, "You both smell really good. Is it a new perfume?"

"We got a complete makeover from the magazine. You girls will get your turn next week, said Marie."

"We get to stay home from school for a day, asked Sarah?"

"Yes, you will get picked up in a limousine. We all will be taken to the studio, and you will get to talk to a very nice man or lady for an hour. I believe they will have a make-believe playhouse for you to call your space. We have to talk to Susanne tomorrow."

"Will we be scared, Mommy, asked Rebecca?"

"No, dears, you won't be scared. Just be yourselves. You'll do great."

"Will we get to play in the make-believe house, asked Leslie?"

"I'm sure they will let you play. I really don't know for sure. We will be there for you. We would never allow you to be afraid, huh, Marie, said Delores?"

"Yes, my dearest darlings. Mommies would never allow anyone to make you afraid."

As they pulled into the garage, the girls asked if Marie and Delores would stay in their outfits. They loved them. Marie and Delores said, "Girls, we will stay dressed as we are just for you. Grandma is dressed up as well. You have to tell her to keep her nice clothes on for you."

They ran inside the house, where Mama and Papa were having some water. They gave them both huge hugs and told Mama that she looked beautiful and to not change her clothes. "Please stay pretty for us."

Mama, tears coming down her cheeks, told the girls, "This has been a beautiful day, and they just made my day even better. I'll stay in my pretty dress for all of you, girls."

Marie and Delores came to the table. They said, "The girls talked to you?"

Mama, still in tears, said with a cracking voice, "I love those girls. They make you feel so special. Did you open the envelope?"

"Not yet, Mama. What's inside?"

"'Enjoy.'"

"What's an enjoy?"

"Open your envelopes and take a peek."

They found their clothes on the hanger, found their envelopes, and opened them. They looked at one another, and the glow was unbelievable. They both hugged each other more than ever before. While holding each other, they looked each other in the eye; both were tearing up. "Can you believe what is in the envelope?" Delores said. "Marie, enjoy." They both jumped up and down.

Marie said, "I'm enjoying right now."

Delores said, "Pinch me so I know it's not a dream."

Marie pinched her. "Your turn to pinch me. I don't believe any of this."

All pinched up, they went back to the table with Mama and Papa. They gave them huge hugs and asked Mama, "Can you believe what they did for us?"

Papa had tears of joy in his eyes as he said, "Girls, this is a dream come true. We were just talking about all this and how it all happened—a vision while sleeping. How fortunate we have become in a matter of a few weeks. This is all remarkable to us."

Mama said, "We have more money now than when we first arrived. They gave Papa an envelope as well. All the men got envelopes."

Delores looked at Marie and said, "We have two envelopes. The men know what to do to keep Mama happy."

Marie laughed. "I wonder how long before they confess to us that they are enjoying as we were supposed to be enjoying. It had better be when they walk through the door."

Delores said, "I hope they do. I won't hold how I feel right now if they don't. They have a job to do tonight."

Marie said, "They'd better not mess it up either."

Both ladies gave each other a high five.

Mama and Papa said, "Those boys have no clue what they're in for."

The girls came into the house and asked for some snacks for their house. "Our budget is so limited, you know, huh, Mommy?"

"Yes, dears, Mommy knows. What would you like? Let me guess—a cupcake?"

"Yes, and we would like a bowl of ice cream and some water."

Delores said, "I'll help Mommy so you all can go back to your house to play. Your daddies should be here any minute, and they will fire up the old barbecue and burn us some vittles."

"We really liked the steak and pork chops we had the other night. Can they cook those for us and our guests for dinner?"

"I will put the order in for the chefs. We ladies will get the side dishes ready with the salads. Here you are, girls, just as you ordered. Don't spoil your dinners, okay?"

"We won't, Mommy. We're starving." The girls gave Marie and Delores their trademark hugs, with love-you attached.

Marie and Delores returned to Mama and Papa. They said, "We challenge all parents to have better children than those four."

They were all talking about next week's appearance of the girls on television. Mama and Papa said, "The world had better pay attention to those girls. Don't know if the world is ready to get their spanking. They sure educated the governor's wife, Diane. We have to call her and let her know they will be on cable television. I'm sure she and the governor will be watching."

Delores said, "Maybe they might want to surprise the girls. Wouldn't that be thrilling to the girls and the cable viewers? Call Susanne right now."

"That is such a great idea." Marie got her cell phone and dialed Susanne direct.

Susanne said, "Marie, I love you so much and already miss you. I'm here in my boss's office. What's up?" Marie told her the idea that she and Delores had just had. "We have the cable executives here as well. I'm putting you on speaker so the entire room can hear. Go ahead, Marie. Tell them what you just told me."

"Gentlemen, Delores and I were just talking to Mama and Papa about next week, when our girls will be interviewed. We were talking about calling Diane, the governor's wife, to make sure she watches the girls. Then we thought the governor and Diane were so impressed with our daughters that Diane came to our house to talk with the girls. We thought that if you would contact the governor and Diane, they might come to the studio and surprise the girls. The girls will be so overjoyed seeing them again. You know they asked the governor and Diane to join them for dinner in the playhouse?"

Susanne said, "They handed me a note to give to the governor and invited them to dinner. Both he and his wife teared up with joy."

Susanne said, "We will call them right now. Great idea. We will let you know. Our ratings will go through the roof."

Delores asked Marie, "What did they think?"

"They are doing it right now. Please, everyone, this is a surprise for the girls. We can't let the cat out of the bag. Deal, said Marie?"

"We are all in. Lips are sealed. Can you imagine the looks on their faces when they see them again? Priceless. That video will dwarf all others, said Susanne."

Marie said, "I wish it were tomorrow." Marie's cell phone was ringing. She looked at the name—Susanne.

"Hello, I have great news. The governor and Diane are so overwhelmed with joy that they asked if you would be opposed to having the airing in two days. They can make it on the day we scheduled. They are willing to come to the airing ... not 'willing'; that is too small of a word. They are honored and greatly pleased that they were invited to be guests for dinner with the girls. Are you sitting down?"

"Hold on; I'm putting you on speaker. Go ahead, Susanne."

"There are seven major cable networks and five major networks here with me in Mr. Donohue's office. They saw the video we just shot, and they all are going to air the video and want all videos we produce. You ladies and my dearest darlings will be nationally known starting tomorrow. Welcome to becoming celebrities. Oh, the 'enjoy' envelopes are only a one-day allowance, just so you know."

Marie said, "I'm starting to cry with joy. Love you. Thank you for calling. Wait a minute, the limousine is picking us up at what time?"

"How about nine o'clock in two days? Not tomorrow, but the next day, okay?"

"Perfect. We will see you then. Love you, Susanne."

Delores, Mama, Papa, and John—who just walked in—heard the phone call. They all said, "Nationally known starting tomorrow?"

"You have to be kidding. I only have one pair of sunglasses," said Mama.

Delores pulled a notepad from her purse and started writing her name on the paper. "What do you think of that signature?"

Marie said, "It needs much more practice." She hugged Delores. "We owe all this to your husband. Where is he anyway?"

I rang the doorbell, and John answered the door. I had seven dozen long-stemmed red roses for all the ladies. John said, "What did you do? Rob a florist?"

I said, "No, John, they robbed me." I had everyone talking to me at one time after I distributed the three bundles of roses. "Hold that thought. I have some other young ladies I have to thank. Right back."

I went up the staircase and knocked on the girls' door. They answered and saw the roses. "For us? Thank you, Daddy, said Leslie." And if hugs could kill, I'd be dead.

"I love you, girls. Enjoy the flowers. Mommy has vases for them."

They all beat me back into the house. "Mommy, Mommy, Mommy, look what Daddy gave us. Daddy said you have vases for us to put them in water. They are so thirsty. Please, Mommy, please give them some water."

Marie and Delores found four vases and put them in water for the girls. "Be careful, girls. Slow down and take it easy going up your stairs."

"Do you want some help?" asked John and Papa.

"Oh please, Daddy and Papa, we would love some help getting these beautiful flowers into our house."

While they were headed to the other house, the ladies calmly informed me what had just happened. Marie walked over to me, dressed to the nines, such an alluring woman. She put her arms around my neck and looked into my eyes, giving me the womanliest look I had ever seen. "You are the most incredible man I know. I love you for what you have done for me and my family." And she hugged me. She said softly, "If you weren't married …"

Delores heard her. "Marie, you want to kiss my husband?" Marie looked over her shoulder, and Delores said, "I'll look away. Kiss him if you like."

Marie had her look again and gave me a take-me kiss. I told her, "I have to go help John, or I will have to sit down for at least an hour."

Delores said, "I hope the hummingbird stays in his nest until tonight."

"Yes, dear, come here." I hugged and kissed Delores. "I love you."

She asked, "Who kisses better?"

"Madam, I would love to answer that. It would be the last thing anyone would hear me say if I answered that question. One gorgeous lady asks that, you might survive. Two ask that, no way but the plastic bag for you, mister." The ladies both slugged me in the arm much better than a knife in my back.

John was out firing up old Betsy. "So what's cooking?" I asked.

John said, "Nothing yet. The ladies are bringing out a platter of meat. I have the cell phone ready, looking up all sorts of recipes. Did they tell you everything or just some things? We need to go over by the waterfall for a couple of minutes. Follow me." When we got there, John informed me what was going to happen in two days. "This is a complete surprise. Lips must stay sealed. Let's return to the barbecue to cook for our guests."

The ladies came out of the tunnel. John said, "If they wear those dresses every day, I'll go nuts."

"Ladies," I told them, "John and I were just discussing the benefits of how you are dressed."

Delores said, "Benefits? For whom?"

"You, my dears. You both are stunning, gorgeous—beyond beautiful."

Delores looked at Marie. "We get that from everyone who sees us."

Marie said, "Yeah, tell us something we don't already know."

John replied, "I have a stick over there in the planter you can scrape your shoes with."

"So, ladies," I said, "as my best friend just informed me, I just stepped in it big time."

They both turned, sensually walked, and looked over their shoulders. "Dream on, lover boy. Dream on."

I told John, "Good thing I'm wearing boots, or it would be all over my socks."

The girls yelled down, "Daddies, is our dinner ready yet? We're getting awfully hungry!"

"Maybe mommies need some help bringing out the side and salads. Do you want to help them?"

"Yeah, we love to help Mommy." Off came the tennis shoes and on went the hard-soled shoes. They were down the staircase, across the pavers, into the tunnel, and into the kitchen. "Mommy, guess who is here to visit you."

Marie asked Delores, "Are you expecting someone?"

"Aren't we all?"

Marie said, "Be nice, darling. Who would want to visit us old women?"

"I know," said Delores. "Two younger men."

"Mommy is being silly, huh, girls? You haven't guessed."

"I hope it's the four most beautiful, charming girls I know. Is that who?"

"Oh, Mom, you make us feel so good inside. Are the salads and sides ready to be delivered to the patio table?"

"Yes, dears, they are ready. Mama Delores will hand you the bowls."

The girls were clogging their way to the patio table. Delores said to Marie, "Are you buying me a walker? You just put twenty years onto this old frame."

Marie turned to her, put her arms around her, and said, "We will grow old together. Don't you ever forget it." She gave Delores a womanly kiss. "So, smarty, who kisses better, me or him?"

Delores looked at her and kissed her back. "You tell me."

Marie said, "If I answered that, your husband and I would be side by side six feet under."

Delores said, "My hubby is no match—not even in the same league."

Marie, turning away, looked over her shoulder and said, "I agree."

Dinner was cooked to perfection. The girls came back for seconds. "Oh, by the way, Mama and Papa are the guests of honor for this evening's dinner party."

"It's okay; we were almost picked. We know our place in society, have accepted it, and are moving forward."

The girls came onto their balcony and asked, "Do we have any dessert for tonight?"

Marie said, "Dears, we have strawberry shortcake and whipped cream. If you are all really careful, you can bring the items to us ladies, and we will serve them for you. Take your time. We need bowls and spoons for eating and serving the whipped cream, the cakes, and the strawberries. Be careful. The bowls are heavy. If you need help, call for a parent."

The girls brought everything but the strawberries. "Mommy, the bowls are too heavy for us. Could one of you much bigger persons help us?"

I said, "I would be pleased and honored to help you. Right back."

I retrieved the bowls, returned to the table, and asked the girls, "How did I do?"

Sarah said, "Your style and grace need a little more practice, your delivery time was off, and you didn't clog while in the tunnel. Other than that, Daddy, you did fine."

Delores said, "If he only asked me that question every night."

Marie asked, "He doesn't clog while in the tunnel?"

"No comment."

The ride home was quick and easy with lots of laughs. The girls were in great moods. They put on their pajamas, brushed their teeth, snuggled in bed, said their prayers, and were kissed on their foreheads. "Sleep tight, my precious angels. Lights out."

I entered our bedroom, and Delores was still in her dress and makeup with her hair still styled. "Honey, I thought you would be in your pajamas and all tucked in."

"Dearest darling, you thought wrong. You have a job to do. I did my job earlier. Should have given you an inspiration, so let's get busy, lover boy. Show me a night to remember."

The next morning, my dearest darling said, "Oh, lover boy."

"Honey, could you wait until noon? I'll be home for lunch. You get all dressed up in your dress. Put on my favorite perfume. Lover boy will make you happy."

"No, you have it wrong again. It's trash day. The cans need to go to the curb."

"I will see you for lunch."

"Can't make any promises. Dream on, lover boy. Dream on."

As I was pulling the cans to the curb, I was thinking about her last night. I almost stepped off the curb and missed the driveway approach, not thinking what I was doing. It was not a good sign. Slipping while in thought could be risky for my health. The chore was soon complete; she should be thrilled.

I went inside, and she was serving our darlings breakfast. I walked over to her, put my hands on her hips, and kissed her neck. "Chore is completed."

"Good boy. Get your bowl and fill it with cereal and eat before your truck leaves you stuck here."

"Yes, dear, I'm doing as you told."

Delores took the girls to school and returned home, and the doorbell rang. She looked through the peephole; it was Marie. Delores opened the door, and Marie walked in. "Good morning, beautiful," Delores said to Marie. Marie asked her if she had some fresh coffee. "For you, Marie, anything you wish." Delores was making a fresh pot of coffee. She went to the refrigerator, got some milk, put it on the kitchen table, got clean cups from the cupboard, and asked Marie if she would like a breakfast roll.

Marie said, "Yeah, that would be just perfect."

Delores sat down at the table, waiting for the coffee to stop perking. "So, my dearest, sister, friend, and best kisser on the planet, how are you this fine morning?"

Marie said, "I have not felt this good in such a long time."

"You must have had a night to remember."

"I think it was all the hype from the entire day yesterday. Did you have a day like I had a day?"

"Honey, we were there together all day. I don't think my feet ever touched the ground after my entrance to the sheets."

Marie said, "Mine too. I love that feeling. I don't ever want that feeling to leave me."

"You mean the warmness from the inside."

She said to Delores, "I'm sorry I kissed your husband. That was not right. I was so overwhelmed by everyone talking about how none of this would ever had happened without his vision."

Delores took her hand. "Marie, it's fine. If anyone ever kisses him, I want it to be you. I didn't mind. Honestly, Marie, I knew the emotions were running high in all of us and still are running high. You did what you needed to do. I love you for being upfront and honest; it's much better than hearing it from someone else. I'll tell you something else. This is from my heart. I love both of you. I know you would never do anything to hurt me. If you ever have that feeling and you know the feeling, you and I can talk about that feeling. Please don't do something you may regret later."

Marie said, "To be perfectly honest with you, I have had thoughts, not good thoughts, of being with your husband. I have caught myself a couple of times and smacked myself for even thinking about such a thing."

Delores asked, "Had you been drinking?"

"Some … not much."

Delores said she had had that happen to her before, and it scared her. If she'd had a drink or two more, she could not have helped what might have happened to her. Delores got the coffeepot and poured both cups. "You know, my sister, I love you. I'm always here for you. I have two shoulders for you to use at any time. If you need your spirits lifted, I can be your helper with that as well. If you need a hug, I'm there. Anything you need, you just tell me—I mean, anything."

Marie said, "Delores, I'm here for you as well. Let's finish our coffee and go shopping."

"Remember, my love: we will be recognized and maybe mobbed. We'd better wait until after tomorrow to see what we have to face. I don't want some jerk trying to grope us. I'm afraid I would put him in a hospital. Don't get me started. So what do you want to do?"

"What I want to do and what I can do are not what I normally would be doing. Let me explain. What I *want* to do is go shopping. What I *can* do is sit at home. What I normally do is houseclean—boring to say the least."

Marie and Delores talked about what their daughters might come across tomorrow; they wondered if the girls would be scared. They agreed that Susanne might be the key for them to be themselves. They both agreed that if they started worrying about the unknown, they would be mental wrecks by tomorrow's shoot.

So they started talking about curtains, throw rugs, tablecloths, and bath towels. Finally, Delores said, "Okay, let's go shopping. You have your unit on, correct?"

Marie said, "Don't leave home without it."

Off they went to their favorite stores to shop. They saw a couple of people elbow someone they were with, saying, "Aren't they the ladies on television?" Marie and Delores just ducked down another aisle and then down another one until they lost them. They ended up at their favorite restaurant.

The manager said, "Welcome back, ladies. We have your table, off in the corner booth."

Their favorite waitress waited on the table. She was still a little nervous, and Marie had to settle her down. "Remember: we are just like you. Relax. Show us how you enter a room."

Their order came, and they had their usual beverages. They were just about ready to leave when the owner came to their table. "Ladies, so glad to see you again. My manager and Danielle told me you were visiting." He put his hand on their check and said, "Ladies, I heard there is another video of you coming out tomorrow. I already ordered five copies. I sold the copies of the first video to some of my customers. I reordered twenty more. I love watching you. I'm thinking about adding a second floor to this restaurant just for a staircase, and I'll pay you a handsome sum of money to do one grand entrance. During the remodeling, I will install an arched gateway for my dearest Delores. I'm talking with the magazine staff right now to schedule an appearance for you, ladies. When you are in my restaurant, please, you and your family eat free. You make me and my staff feel special. They are sending me poster-size photos of each of you and all the ladies. I want you to call me when you are on your way, and I'll have staff protect you and escort you to your waiting table. Have a great day, ladies, and thank you for eating at my restaurant."

Marie and Delores got up to leave, and the manager and two employees walked them to their car and waited until they were in. The women then backed up and started to drive away. They watched to make sure no one was following them. They notified their detective that they were at the restaurant and had him on the line while they drove back to the house.

Susanne called and told Marie the current status of the sales of the video and the subscription count. She then told Marie that the video shot with the host had been aired and their rate had doubled. The new subscriptions were nonstop. They now offered both videos with the new subscriptions. She asked them to dress the girls as normal. They had a wardrobe set up just for them. They would do the same for the girls as they did for the women. She also said, "You, Delores, and your mom should all come as you would normally dress. And yes, dear, we will put all of you in fancy clothes." She also told her that they now sent her to makeup, styling, and wardrobe every day. "I will be with the girls on stage. They feel the girls will be more at ease with someone that was invited into their space."

Marie thanked Susanne for all she had done for her and both of our families. "Can't wait for tomorrow. Love you."

Susanne said, "I love and adore everyone in your and Delores's family. You all are such a joy to be around. I can't wait to see my little darlings."

The next morning, the girls were so nervous and excited. The doorbell rang, and in came their new sisters and Delores. The hugs were long and loving for all. Mama and Papa were having their cup of coffee and breakfast roll. Marie handed Delores a cup of coffee, and the girls got either milk or juice with their rolls. All the girls were so excited. "We're going to be on television, and they will give us a video so we can show our schools."

The schools were notified by the magazine that the girls would be absent that day. The magazine explained what was going to happen and promised to give them videos for them to show to the entire school. The girls said the principal called them into the office and gave them hugs and best wishes for going on television. He gave them cupcakes and juice and more hugs and said, "We all love you, girls." Their teachers were in the office as well. They had stationed two clerical staff to watch over the other students.

The girls were settling down, and the adults were getting nervous, though not as nervous as they had been a couple of days before. They were more restless than nervous. Everyone was not used to keeping secrets from the girls. It was getting close to time for the limousine to show up, and the ladies kept looking at the clock on the wall. John came down looking all dapper; leaned over to kiss all the girls, Marie, and Mama; shook Papa's hand, and said to everyone, "Have a great day. I wish I could go with you, but I have a client coming in from out of state for a meeting and lunch. Love all of you." As he approached Delores, he leaned over and kissed her on the cheek. "I wasn't sure if you would be receptive but told myself, 'You won't know until you try. Love you.'"

Marie told Delores, "See? I told you he likes you."

Delores said, "He could have kissed me on the lips. I don't bite." Everyone laughed.

Just then, the doorbell rang. Marie looked through the peephole and opened the door. Standing there was Susanne. "Please come on in." As Susanne entered the house, all the girls ran up to her and gave her a huge hug.

"We love you, Susanne," they all said.

She said, "There are two limousines, so we won't be crowded." The chauffeurs were out of the cars and opened the doors. Marie, Susanne, and the girls were in the first limousine. Delores, Mama, and Papa were in the second car, and they talked about all the adults being in one car while the girls were riding with Susanne. They were sure that if the girls got too nervous, it would be okay; the adults had some powerful beverages to ease their nerves.

They arrived at the studio; the drive had been perfect. They were let out of the cars, the studio door was opened, and the security personnel were standing guard. All driveways were blocked, and security guards were everywhere. The first car was emptied of the passengers and pulled up for the second car to deliver its passengers. Susanne had everyone enter the building for security reasons. They were all in the foyer and were then escorted into the studio, just as on the first day.

The girls were looking at everything. A cameraman had been filming them since the cars entered the parking lot. The girls waved at the cameraman and paid little to no attention to him after their wave. Susanne told us later she was nervous that the girls might get afraid when they saw the camera. They had discussed in the limousine that there would be a cameraman following them all day long. Marie said she was not looking her best. "Oh, dear God, we have an image to keep. Please help me," she prayed.

They walked past all the closed doors and went into the studio. Susanne stopped them for a second and said, "Are you all ready?"

"Yeah," said the girls.

Susanne said, "Let's go."

As all entered the studio, balloons, strings, and confetti were falling from the ceiling. The entire staff of the magazine were applauding; giving the girls, Marie, Delores, Mama, and Papa hugs; and saying, "We love all of you, said Susane." There were goodies for the girls and a full-on banquet for breakfast.

The violins and the lady singer were playing Marie's favorite song. Since neither husband was present, two hired escorts took Delores's and Marie's hands and danced to the song. Mama and Papa were dancing, and they had young males who danced with the girls. There were at least ten cameras filming the event. They were zooming in on the girls dancing with boy actors. So cute they all were. The two older boy actors were for Leslie and Sarah, who had seen them on television, and the girls were all nervous, but the boys put them at ease. All was perfect for the girls. Marie and Delores's escorts were actors as well; they did really well. These guys were very handsome.

When the song ended, they played a second song and asked the entire staff to join the girls in dancing. Susanne had asked the girls what they would like to have, and they said, "Everyone, dance with us." The staff all attempted to dance next to the girls and give hugs. There were enough tears being shed to fill a fire bucket. Many of the staff told the girls that they had been waiting a long time to finally meet them and started crying while giving big hugs. The girls later told Susanne this was the best birthday party a girl could have.

Susanne told them, "This is just a warm-up. Wait until it is your birthday. Wow."

Once the second song ended, Mr. Donohue got on the microphone and welcomed the girls, Marie, Delores, Mama, and Papa to the festivities. He told the girls they all looked beautiful; he went to each one and gave her a huge hug. They put the dance they just did on the big screen and showed the girls dancing. The entire staff applauded. The girls were giggling at seeing themselves on television, and their escorts were hugging them. They later were told that the younger boys were also actors; their airing would be in a couple of weeks, and these videos would help jump-start their careers.

Mr. Donohue said, "I don't want to keep talking while the food gets cold. Please, everyone, enjoy the breakfast." A crew of men started putting up tables and chairs, and the waitresses put white linen tablecloths on the tables and placed linen napkins and silverware at each chair. In a very short time, the girls and their escorts were on one side of the table. Marie and Delores with their escorts, Susanne with her escort, Mama, and Papa filled both sides of the first set of tables along the stage. The staff filled in the rest of the tables, and the waitresses asked each person what he or she would like to drink. They were not just normal breakfast beverages, but anything one wanted.

About an hour from sitting down, Susanne stood on the stage, and they began playing the videos that had been released and aired. The escorts of Marie and Delores were amazed at their videos and said to the ladies, "We want you to work with us."

Delores's escort said, "I can be the leading man, and you, my dear, will be the star."

Susanne said, "Ladies, girls, and Papa, the escorts will take you to makeup, hairstyling, and wardrobe to prepare you for the next video for the cable networks. I want to add, ladies, that the first video released was aired on three networks. This video will be aired by ten cable networks. The next video will be aired by all cable networks and seven major television stations. There are five more requesting meetings to determine the costs. Escorts, could you please take your ladies to makeup? Thank you, all, for joining the girls for breakfast."

The boys stood up, pulled the girls' chairs out for them, took their hands, had them put their hands on their bent arms, and escorted them to the makeup rooms. It was so well done. The cameras were filming the boys and girls together. The cable network executives were in Mr. Donohue's office with monitors, watching the entire filming. The ten networks were salivating over what this would do to their ratings. All the boys and moms' escorts were wearing tuxedos. The ladies knew their outfits would be showstoppers.

One by one, they were all escorted to the makeup department. Mama was escorted by Papa, who was taken to wardrobe and fitted with a tuxedo. Marie, Delores, and Susanne were treated like queens by their escorts. With their arms bent, the ladies put their hands on their escorts and proceeded to the makeup department. The entire staff had been applauding and standing since Rebecca was escorted first. All this was filmed and viewed by those proposing to air this event that evening as a special. Their network was already showing viewers this upcoming event. "Please don't miss this event," one of the first three cable networks was stating to the newcomers. "You'd better have staff manning the phones." He told them their average number of calls per minute.

Mr. Donohue stated, "Gentlemen, this is no ordinary family; wait until you see the little girls' responses to questions asked by our dearest Susanne."

One of the executives asked, "Are these girls being coached by the mothers or a professional organization?"

Mr. Donohue said, "Sir, these girls don't need coaching by anybody, professional or otherwise. They are warm, courteous, charming, and very smart. We have a special surprise for them during the shooting. We want your audience's reaction for the surprise. You will see the girls' reactions. You will be spellbound and in complete awe."

Mr. Donohue asked Michele, "My love, can you go get the latest report from our sales division and read off to these fine gentlemen what you get?"

Michele stood up, went to the sales division, and returned within a few minutes. She stood in front of all the executives and read the new subscription numbers, the total sales of the first video, the total sales of the second video, and the duration of time from the first airing until the present.

"Thank you, my love. Gentlemen, if you have any doubts that this is all staged, I'm sorry you have been airing things that your viewers think are false but entertaining. If your viewership is declining, maybe the viewers are getting sick of watching lies. This is truth, no gimmicks, no 'let's show this to trick our customers.' These people are so genuine it is almost beyond belief that they even exist."

Then one executive asked, "When can we witness these miracles?"

"In about an hour. My assistants will escort you to the larger studio and have you seated. Our audience is our staff members. We don't want just anybody seeing these at this point. Before you leave, let me tell you why security is so tight.

There is an ongoing investigation into a brutal murder and bank robbery, and everyone associated with this family is in jeopardy. One of our issues will address this once we get the FBI and local police departments to give us the approval to discuss what really went on with this house. We want each and every one of you not to disclose any information regarding these people. Is that clear? We were told that if anything happens to these people and your network is to blame, the FBI will incarcerate your entire company and affiliates. They are not just saying that, gentlemen. Your firms will make tons of money. You don't need to see everything you worked for vanish. I hope I'm making myself perfectly clear."

They were all escorted out of the room. Michele talked with Mr. Donohue. "You were very serious with those men. You meant every word."

"Dearest darling, if one of those executives thinks they can out the other with an exclusive, guess again. Every network is being monitored by the FBI. If they think they can air something that puts these people beyond normal security procedures, the station will go black. Can I tell you something? This goes no further than here, understand?"

"Yes, dear, you sure are serious today."

"They know of over three hundred people affiliated with what happened to this house. They don't know how many more beyond the three hundred. Everything is filmed, and each frame is viewed to see if any of the known three hundred were present. They even have shots of you. You are also being watched. Be really careful, my love. Do you remember dining with some of your friends a few days ago?"

"Yes, that was a very fun night."

"Do you remember going to the restroom?"

"Yes, I had to go potty pretty bad. We had been drinking."

"They photographed your every move until you reached the restroom. They photographed every lady entering the restroom until you left the restroom. They even timed how long you were in there and every lady who entered and left the restroom. They knew you had a small handbag. Fortunately for you, you left it on the table and didn't take it with you. You see, dear, until this mess is resolved, you, I, Susanne, and anyone else with information that could harm these people will be watched and monitored. I love you. I trust you. My feelings for you have nothing to do with what they are doing."

"I have been asked to join the ladies."

"Yes, I know. You will be watched, your phone monitored. Every move, everywhere you go, everyone you talk to—all of that will be notched up. Let's join the rest of the executives. Show them your stuff."

"You mean be like one of the ladies?"

"Be yourself, warm and loving, to me."

The girls and ladies were in wardrobe, getting dressed in beautiful outfits. The ladies were getting jeweled as well, and they were gorgeous. The escorts were told to take them to the back stage and sit in the front row of the audience. They took the ladies and girls into position and escorted them to their seats in front of the audience. They had been instructed not to acknowledge that they knew anyone in the audience and told why. "The viewers are told this is a live audience, not staff, FBI, security force, and local police. This is a trial run for all the law enforcement departments."

The host came to the stage—the same gentleman who had hosted the last meeting. He did his monologue, welcoming all those in the audience as the camera panned to the audience, of course not showing anyone in the front row. This was a formality, as they were spanning all the faces in the crowd, which were checked with the computer database. If someone had sneaked in, the authorities were told over earpieces who the person was and where he or she was seated. They, in turn, would rise and remove that person—and not in a discreet manner.

One of the agencies did have a person in the audience whose face was not in the computer database; they were alerted, and that person was taken into custody in a matter of a couple of seconds. They replaced that person with someone in the database. The cable network executives were shocked, as was the entire front row except Mr. Donohue. He was well informed of what was to happen. That portion of the video was not filmed; the cameramen were also alerted about what was going to occur.

All worked as planned, and the host was also informed and told not to say a word. He told the viewers that they were going to meet some of the cutest, smartest, most beautiful, most glamorous girls they would ever meet. "Before we bring them out, it's my pleasure—and I mean *pleasure*—to introduce the most beautiful, glamorous, seductive ladies you will ever meet. Would Mrs. Sophia please join me onstage?"

Sophia strutted out, displaying her moves, and met the host, who kissed her hand and escorted her to her chair. "This, ladies and gentlemen, is the mother of one of our guests and the grandmother of the girls." The audience was applauding from the time she entered the stage until she reached her chair.

"Our next guest is a mother of two of the girls, a housewife. Mrs. Delores, please join us onstage. Oh my, remember: she's a mother of two and a housewife." Delores definitely was pleasing the entire audience, and the applause was loud and long. She, too, held out her hand, and the host kissed it and escorted her to her chair. The host took a handkerchief from his pocket, wiped his brow, and said, "Delores, you just made me the luckiest man alive, ready for that cold shower I missed this morning. Wait, gentlemen of the audience and viewers, for your viewing enjoyment. This also is the mother of two of the girls, also a housewife. Guys, her husband is the luckiest man on the planet. Mrs. Marie, please join us on the stage."

The applause was loud. With each step Marie took, the applause grew louder. Her every move was filmed, and cameras zoomed in on her. She made it to the host, who was on his knees, bowing to her, kissing her extended hand. He escorted her to her chair and turned to the audience, who were still standing and applauding. He said, "I know every guy out there wishes he had my job. Trust me, gentlemen; I don't know what I ever did right to deserve this opportunity. Thank you, God."

While their moms and grandma were seated, the crew put Susanne and the girls into a playhouse that looked exactly like the first one. They had them all seated on the benches and were told, "Please stay seated. The house opens up from the middle." They showed Susanne.

"Ladies and gentlemen, it is my honor to introduce you to four of the cutest little girls on the planet. Please keep your eye on the playhouse onstage. Can we see Leslie, Sarah, Kim, Rebecca, and our cohost Susanne?"

The playhouse opened into two halves, and the audience was standing and applauding, even the ladies. The host, playing his role to the max, walked up to the playhouse, bowed down, and kissed each girl's hand. He said, "I truly honor all of you. I know the audience will see why. Love you all. Will Susanne please join me center stage?" He handed the microphone to Susanne, kissed her hand, and told her he would love to trade positions.

Susanne thanked the host and said, "I am deeply honored to be able to introduce you to four little ladies who changed my life a few weeks ago." She told the story of how they handed her a note to invite a couple to their dinner party. "I don't want to say any more. Let's go talk to my best friends."

She started with Leslie. "My dearest Leslie, tell me a little about yourself." Leslie told her how old she was and what grade she was in. She had been informed in the limousine to not disclose the name of their school or where they lived. Susanne asked her if she was married or had a boyfriend.

Leslie said, "Susanne, I am way too young to be married and way too busy to have a boyfriend. Boys are yucky."

Susanne moved over to Sarah and asked her the same questions, and then did the same for Kim and finally Rebecca. While they were answering the questions, the crew set up a round table with chairs out of the cameras' view. After Rebecca answered Susanne, she asked all the girls to join her at the table. They all took a chair. "Now, girls, the first question you all answered perfectly. We are going to roll up our sleeves and tell the world why you all captured my heart at the party. You have a fabulous house just like the one that opened up onstage. Tell me about your house—every little detail."

Leslie was given the baton by the rest of the girls. "Ms. Susanne, can I take you back to the first time we met?"

"Of course, that will be a perfect place to start."

"Mr. Stockdale had an old shed that was on the property. My mom didn't like that it blocked the view of her staircase and wanted to move the shed to the backyard. Mr. Stockdale pondered and pondered where the shed should be moved. He told my mom and dad that he didn't want to separate us girls from the parents. He decided to put the shed on top of our new patio cover, added some stairs, and changed the shed into our house."

Susanne asked the girls, "Do you live in the house?"

Leslie said, "No, ma'am, we live inside our home with Mom and Dad."

"So, girls, I'm a little confused. This is a playhouse, correct?"

"To you, Susanne, it is a playhouse. To us, it our house. In your house, you set the rules for family and guests, correct?"

"Why, yes, I do set rules."

"In our house, we set the rules. It's our space. Your house is your space. When you visit your friends and family, you enter into their space and follow their rules, correct?"

"Of course."

"We expect you to follow ours. It's the same."

"You have my curiosity stirring. This is not a little spoiled-brat game to keep parents from dictating their rule on you?"

"No, Susanne, we are not spoiled brats. We are loving, charming, and smart. If you disrespect us in any fashion, you will not be allowed in our space. If you look down on us, you will never be allowed in our space."

"So on a normal day, you get home from school. What do you girls do?"

"We do our chores that Mommy has us do. Then we go and do our homework in our house. Then we play and wait for Daddy to cook our dinner. We always have dinner guests each day. We normally invite a couple, and they eat with us, and we all talk and discuss our day, just like when someone invites you to their home and you have dinner with them—no different."

"So how is a couple invited?"

"Well, we girls have a meeting before dinner, and we vote for whom we want to spend time with. They are asked to join us."

"If they refuse your invitation?"

"They are placed on the bottom of our invite list. If they refuse a second time, they are removed from our invite list."

"I heard you can be on a never-to-invite list. Is this true?"

"As I said prior, if you look down on us or are disrespectful to any of us at any time, you will join all the others on the never-to-invite list. We are very respectful girls. We don't care what color you are, what religion you practice, what political party you are associated with—nothing that we are taught regarding how to categorize people. We look at you as who you are and how you act around younger people. If you are talking and we approach you and who you are talking with and you push us away, never will you be asked. You have to know we are just younger but have the same feelings you have. You would hate a person pushing you away or being disrespectful to you or looking down on you because you aren't doing what they think is important. We watch parents and kids. That is what we all do. We don't need your ugly side affecting us."

Susanne stood up and faced the audience. "Do you see why these girls deserve my heart?" The audience and moms all stood up and applauded. The host had tears rolling down his face. "These girls invited me for a lighting ceremony on the playhouse balcony during the party. Their grandma and grandpa were also invited to watch the outdoor lights being turned on. Ladies and gentlemen, there were well over two hundred guests at this party, and they asked me to join them and their grandparents to watch the lights. My tears of joy would not stop rolling down my cheeks. People, these are children. It was like being invited to visit the queen of England. From the day I met these girls, my life has changed for good forever. I'm so thrilled to be their friend, knowing that when I met them, I did what most adults, even those in this room, do daily—push the child away, tell them to be quiet. 'Can't you see I'm on my cell phone? Go outside and bug the dog. Get lost.' This is not how you would treat your family or friends, but you treat your children in this manner."

She returned to the girls. "Sorry, girls; I had to get that off my chest. I have a huge surprise for you. You touched our hearts beyond belief. Girls, would you like to meet your surprise?"

"Yeah, can we see it now?"

"Ladies and gentlemen, would you please do me the honor and welcome Governor Evan Bronson and his lovely wife, Diane."

All the girls stood up and ran over to the governor and Diane. The governor got on his knees and hugged the girls, and so did Diane. Tears were rolling down the governor's cheeks as well as Diane's. The makeup staff was drastically fixing all the makeup on everyone onstage; they cut for a station break.

After all the damage was repaired, Susanne handed Leslie the microphone. The girls had a quick meeting and agreed to have the governor and his wife join them at their table. When they returned, cameras were rolling. Leslie asked the governor and his wife if they would please join them at their table. The governor, voice cracking, said, "We would be honored to join you, girls. Thank you."

Leslie handed the microphone back to Susanne, whose eyes were just about filled to capacity with tears of joy. Susanne welcomed the governor and his wife to the table. "Governor, you met these girls at the event of the year. Can you tell us a little about this meeting?"

"I'd love to. I and my wife were meeting high-ranking party attendees in the foyer of the Albrights' home. We were running a little late because of traffic. I told our highway division that was not acceptable. They were very polite and waited for me to finish what I was saying. They shook my hand and introduced themselves. I told Diane I would have done what you were telling the audience about how parents and adults treat children. Leslie's eyes were filled with respect and sincerity. I knelt down and asked the girls their names, wished them well, and told them, 'I will talk with you later.'

"After about a half hour of shaking hands for reelection and camera shots—typical portrayal of what is expected—Susanne came to me. I almost pushed her away in disrespect. She handed me a note from the girls, asking for me and my wife to join them for dinner in the playhouse. I, being full of myself, put the note in my pocket. Susanne did not just walk away. She followed us through the crowd. My lovely wife took the note from my pocket, walked over to Susanne, apologized for my rudeness, and told the girls we would be pleased to join them. I have one of the smartest wives on the planet. She told me what she had done. 'You'd better behave yourself. This is important.' My thought was 'I'm the governor. I bow down to no one.'

"Dinnertime was announced by Mr. Barns. I told my wife, 'Let's go. We have dinner reservations.' She said, 'My dear, we are at a party. We just can't leave.' She took my hand and gave me a look I never want to see again, and we went upstairs to the playhouse. Diane knocked on the front door, and the girls opened the door and thanked us for wanting to eat dinner with them. Can I have my lovely wife take you through the dinner? This will make me cry."

Susanne handed the microphone to Diane. "Good morning, everyone. As the governor stated, he would get emotional from this point on because he now knows the consequences of his ignorance. When I noticed that Susanne was following us, I knew the note had to have importance. When I read the note, I had to tell Susanne that we would be honored to dine with the girls. I know Susanne returned the answer to the girls. If she hadn't returned with the answer, we would have been put on the blacklist with Susanne.

"The girls are gracious, kind, loving, charming … I could go on and on. Most importantly, they are very respectful not just because of my husband being a governor but also because he is a kind and generous man. The dinner was fabulous. The girls could never ask for better people to dine with. They were not only polite to us but also to the staff serving the meal and drinks and dessert, always saying 'please,' 'thank you,' 'how are you?' and 'are you comfortable?'

"One of the greatest things said was when Leslie had Mr. Barns hand her the microphone after we joined them for dinner. Susanne brought her the microphone from their balcony, and she announced to the partygoers, 'Attention, everyone. We girls are very sorry. Our budget is limited, and our space is small. We would have enjoyed having all of you to our house for dinner. Please enjoy our home and your dinner. Thank you.'

"At that time, I knew we were the luckiest people at that party. These sweet, charming girls took the time to invite us to their space. I started tearing up when the waiters started bringing in the meal. I used my napkin to wipe my tears.

"On our way home in the car, the governor and I talked. He was, as he is now, tearing up, thanking me for saving face. We both decided that if the girls would allow him and me an opportunity to talk with them, he would be deeply honored. A meeting date was set, and he was so anxious to meet the girls again. Unfortunately, he was unable to attend because of an emergency situation that he had to address.

"My meeting with the girls and their mothers was the greatest day of my life. I was actually very nervous. 'What if this whole thing was a put on? What if these girls were playacting? I have a staff and photographers joining me. Shame on me if I get myself embarrassed?" All this was running through my head while I was being driven to the girls' home. I even saw the headlines of the newspaper the next day: 'Governor Bronson's Wife Snubbed by Little Girls. Our Tax Dollars at Work, Folks.' Remember: my thoughts were all about me, not them.

"Within a few minutes during our meeting, all that garbage was flushed down the drain. They are not a put-on. They were not coached by anyone. They are polite, charming, and gracious. I can't praise them with words. They explained, 'We give respect. We expect respect.' Leslie asked me how often I had seen a child putting their parent over their knee and spanking them in public or seen a child waving their fingers at their parents' faces, screaming at them, and calling them names for being bad. Never. But how often do you see parents doing that to their children? She agreed that, yes, maybe the child is acting up. Maybe they deserve to be punished. Do they need to be disrespected and humiliated? What lesson have you just taught your child? You're the most respected person they know. You want them to look up to you, and you treat them like that. Why?

"How many of you out there watching can answer her questions to me? I told her that on Monday morning, I was going to spank every one of my staff with this video. I will spank every school board member with the video. If I ever see a state employee disrespecting a child or anyone, they will be either replaced or taken away from the public eye. I want to say this right now. Every department in the state has seen this video, and all know the consequences of their actions. The state senate and house of representatives are scheduled to see the video next week. I owe all that to these girls.

"When we got the call from Marie about this golden opportunity, I cried with joy. The governor could not say yes quickly enough. This is not—I repeat, this is not—a political opportunity for campaigning. These girls and their moms and grandma are real—no acting going on here. Nothing is rehearsed. We have no scripts, do we, girls and ladies?"

The governor said, "Girls, I love you, each and every one of you. You taught me a much-needed lesson. I told Diane, 'If I do anything out of hand, smack me and give me that look you gave me at the party.' I thank you for bringing so much to my life."

The entire audience and the host stood up and applauded what they had just witnessed. The cable executives were in complete awe, maybe even shocked, of the honesty of the governor and his wife. The honesty of the girls was beyond belief. Some of the cameramen were using the lens-cleaning rags to wipe tears from their eyes. Some of the staff members asked to have some tissues brought into the studio. The host, composing himself for the moment, had his microphone and said in a very crackly voice, "I am so deeply touched right now. Please give everyone onstage a huge round of applause." Then he shut down his mic and grabbed tissues from a box.

The governor and Diane stood up; went to Marie, Delores, and Mama; hugged them; and cried with them, thanking them for such beautiful girls. The Governor turned, got on their knees, hugged and kissed the girls, and said to them, "Anytime you want to come to our house, just call. You're always welcome in our home."

They got tears and huge hugs from the girls. "We love you, Governor and Diane. Thank you for being the guests at our table." The governor and Diane were crying, and the staff brought them tissues.

They announced that lunch was being served in the other studio. "Please all come eat with the girls. Their budget is on us. The space is large. Don't be shy said Mr. Barns." Susanne was an emotional wreck. There was not a dry eye in the studio. They ran out of tissues and had to bring in more.

The girls said to the governor and Diane, "Please be our guests at our table for lunch."

Diane said, "Girls, we will be honored, truly honored, to be your guests."

All the escorts, handkerchiefs out of their pockets for their companions, escorted the girls, Marie, and Delores. Mama was escorted by Papa. The entire staff and all of the executives were escorted to the other studio; a full staff of waitresses and waiters were there to assist the guests. The governor was fighting more tears while eating with the girls. Marie, Delores, Mama, Papa, Susanne, Mr. Donohue, and Michele were all wrecks at this time.

As the luncheon was winding down, the governor and Diane had to leave the event. More tears were being shed, and there were hugs of love everywhere. The governor said, "I can't wait to spend time with you again. We love all of you. Please come to our house for a visit." The governor's staff helped him and Diane back to their waiting limousine.

Everyone in the studio headed back to their jobs. The girls and Susanne were escorted to their waiting limousine, as were Marie, Delores, Mama, and Papa. Delores's escort said to her, "In my next movie, you are going to be by me to be the star. Love you and thank you for this day. You dance wonderfully." Delores gave him a huge hug and told him she'd loved having him as her escort for today.

Marie's escort said, "What he said to Delores, I say to you. Since your mother and dad are present, I'm a little nervous."

Marie put her arms around him and hugged him. "Honey, I'm over eighteen. Thank you for a great day."

By the time the limousines arrived at Marie's home, Susanne received a call from the staff. "They have broken one million video sales—not dollars, videos. Oh, by the way, keep the outfits. You all are gorgeous. Your clothes are in the limousines' trunks. Love you all. Thank you for running the company out of tissues." They all laughed and gave Susanne a huge hug. They all were tearing up again; the limo drivers had tissues for everyone.

They all got their clothes, and an envelope was attached to each hanger as prior. The girls asked, "Mommy, what's in the envelopes?"

"We'll see inside."

Susanne had to go back to work. The girls gave her a huge hug and the drivers as well, thanking them for being such good drivers and playing such good music.

The limousines pulled away, and everyone was shortly in the house. They opened the envelopes. "Mommy, what is this piece of paper?"

"Your college fund."

"College fund?" said the girls. "Don't they know we are not in college? We're too young, said Leslie."

Delores said to Marie, "We could pay off our house in cash."

Marie replied to Delores, "Or we could go and lie on one of the beaches of the world and get killer tans."

Delores said, "I will have to give that some serious thought. Come; let's let the girls play for a while. We can kick off the designer shoes and get happy."

Mama and Papa joined them at the kitchen table. Papa said, "My daughters, you both are gorgeous. The girls are pure angels. They made me cry when I listened to the governor's wife. The meeting you had here—they took a seasoned politician and his wife and turned them into mush. Her telling of that meeting brought tears to everyone in the studio. The cable executives were talking among one another, saying, 'This better not be some bullcrap this magazine is trying to shove down our throats. We'll sue the SOB.' They were all in tears before she was finished. Did you see the host? He was crying before anything was told. What a wonderful day this is." The ladies all agreed. "What would you all like to drink?"

Mama said, "Something with a kick. I'm a wreck right now. How about a Bloody Mary with Snap-E-Tom?"

Delores said, "I'll cut the celery and put in a couple of green olives." She also got a bowl with ice cubes while Marie was preparing the drinks.

Delores returned to the counter, where Marie was mixing the drinks. She put her arms around Marie's waist from behind her and whispered into her ear, "Gorgeous, you are stunning."

Marie looked over her shoulder and said, "And look who's talking."

Delores stood beside her and said, "What a wonderful day, and I got to share this with you, your mom and dad, our daughters, and two hunks."

Marie asked Delores, "Do you think, with all the millions we will be making, we can afford to keep a couple of them?"

"Hey, what about the buff gardener? What happened to him, asked Delores?"

"He's for breakfast. These boys are for dinner, said Marie."

"I completely understand, said Delores."

They heard the clogging of little feet fast approaching. "One, two, three, Mom, screamed Leslie!"

"Yes, dears, what can we do for you, said Marie?"

"We had a meeting. We want the governor and Diane to spend the night. Could you call them and tell them we want them to spend the night, said Leslie?"

Delores said, "A sleepover with the governor—that could be a very interesting read."

"Maybe Mom should call the magazine first. Like Mommy Delores just mentioned, it would make a very interesting read, said Leslie."

"You want some dessert or a snack, asked Delores?"

"What do you have, Mom, asked Sarah?"

"You name it, and we have it, said Delores."

"Do you have some Twinkies, Mom, asked Rebecca?"

"Let me see. No Twinkies. How about a chocolate cupcake with a squiggle on top, said Delores?"

"Yeah, those are really good, said Kim."

Sarah asked, "Do they have creamy centers?"

"Indeed, they do. Those are the best a girl can eat, said Delores."

Papa said, "Hey, grandpas like them too."

"Mommy, can Grandpa have one as well, asked Leslie?"

"Of course. Would you like to give him a package, said Delores?"

"Thank you, said papa."

Marie said, "Papa, I'll do some chores a little later." The girls each got a package of two, and off they went.

Marie said, "When I was delivering each of the girls, I told John, 'How could you do this to me? I thought you loved me. You just wanted to hurt me.' You know, I need to really thank him tonight. The ungodly pain then is utter joy today."

They all raised their glasses and clinked in the center of the table. "Cheers!"

After the first round, Marie freshened the drinks for those who wanted a refill. Mama and Papa said, "No more, dear. We're going upstairs and taking a nap."

Delores said, "More, please, dear, if you will join me."

Marie said, "My pleasure. Not good to drink alone."

Delores got up, got two more celery sticks and four green olives, and added them to the drink mix.

Marie asked, "How did you like today's event?"

Delores said, "If I were single, I wouldn't be sitting here. Just kidding. I loved the entire event. Very well done. Food was great. The girls were incredible. Haven't lost that many tears in years. How about you?"

"When Mrs. Governor gave her speech about what Leslie had told her at our table in the dining room, even though we were here when it occurred, it made me want to go up and hug her. When the tears rolled down my cheek, I told myself, 'That is your little girl telling a high-ranking politician what is really wrong with everything in society, not as a spokesperson's but a child's viewpoint; not written by some professional writer, rehearsed, or coached, but from the heart. I almost leaned over and hugged you."

"You thought about leaning over and hugging me? I thought the same thing as well."

"Did you think the audience would think we were lesbians?"

"Not to that extreme, but if I did approach you and you rejected me in public, that would fit to what she is saying. What lesson did I teach or learn? Public humiliation would be the worst thing one could suffer."

Marie said, "I would never humiliate you in public. I love you more than that."

Delores leaned over and gave Marie a hug. "You know, we need to talk about something else, or I'll need a box of Kleenex. Did you like the dance?"

"Yes, he was a good dancer. How about you?"

"I kept thinking, 'This is Marie's favorite song.' I don't have a favorite song. I like a lot of music, but a favorite song? Not really a favorite. What are we having for dinner?"

"I got everyone steaks. The boys seem to be getting better at cooking. I'm putting in baked potatoes in a few minutes. You can make some beans, macaroni salad, and dinner salad. The girls really like having a real dinner, not just meat and fried potatoes. We should stay dressed up. What do you think?"

Delores said, "These are killer outfits. We were driving our escorts crazy. Just think what they will do for our guys. I almost said we have to go pick up the girls from school. What do you want to do tomorrow?"

"I don't know yet. I will call you with what I'm wearing, and you can wear something similar. The boys will be home soon. We can eat another meal. It's a good thing I'm getting a regular dose of 'come here, baby,' or I would get as big as a house from all this eating."

Marie got up from the table, got potatoes from the pantry, took enough to bake, and scrubbed them in the sink. She got her aluminum foil from the drawer and asked Delores to preheat her oven so it would be ready for the potatoes. She wrapped each potato and then poked them all with a fork so the steam would be released. She started humming the song they'd played for the first dance. She had nearly all finished, and Delores started wrapping them and handing them to her for the forking and placement in the cooking pan. Delores said she usually just cooked them on the rack. Marie said, "If I'm cooking only a few, I do the same. But since there are quite a few, into the roasting pan they go."

"Do we start the macaroni salad?"

"We should. Get my five-quart pan from the cabinet next to the oven, put in water to boil, and then add the macaroni. Be quick about it, lady. We don't have all day, you know."

Delores walked up behind her and smacked her on the rump. Marie asked, "What was that for?"

"I see football players do it all the time."

"I'm not wearing a helmet or shoulder pads."

"If you were, we would have to huddle to talk about what the next play is."

The pot was full on the stove and heating up. "I have fresh green beans in the vegetable drawer in the refrigerator. Want to get me the bag and we can cut them to perfection?"

Delores got the beans from the vegetable drawer, took them to the sink, and started to rinse them. Marie heard the bell on the oven and said, "Hey, Chef, load me up." She opened the oven door and slid in the pan of wrapped potatoes. She set the timer so she would not have done all the work for no reason. It was a job well done.

She stood next to Delores, who was cutting off the ends of the beans and cutting them to an inch in length. Marie was watching her and smacked her on the bottom. Delores said, "Watch it, girl. I'm armed and very dangerous."

"We're even. You know, that was fun."

Delores said, "When I'm finished and have some free time, we will do another round. The beans are ready for some heat."

Marie said, "We'd better wait, or they will be cooked and nothing else will be cooked."

Delores took the pot of beans over to the oven and set it on one of the burners, just about ready to turn around. Smack! "Hey, it was my turn. You had two in a row."

"Not really, only one on each side."

Delores walked over to Marie, and she backed up into the cabinet so Delores couldn't give her a smack. "Nice move, lady." She put her arms around her neck and said, "If you were not so gorgeous, I would spin you around and give you a good one."

"You know, all the men tell me the same line."

"They learned it from me."

The boys came home. Mama and Papa were up from their nap, and the girls were starving. The men got their act together and started the grill. The baked potatoes had less than ten minutes to serving, the beans were in boiling water and would be ready in a couple of minutes more, and the macaroni salad was in the refrigerator, chilling. Marie, Delores, and Mama were making the dinner salad.

I went in and got the vegetable oil, paper towel, and bowl and saw my gorgeous wife at the counter, cutting up salad fixings. I went over to her, put my hand on her hip, spun her around, and kissed her. She had a nice, long blade—a very sharp knife. She said, "You are so lucky, my friend, I'm in a great mood." I kissed Marie on the cheek and gave Mama the same. *There, I just paid all the hired help.*

I ran through the tunnel, and John and I oiled the grill, put on the steaks, closed the lid, set our cell phones according to our recipe, sat on the patio chairs, and talked sports. "Tomorrow, your house?"

"Works for me. The girls will be happy to play in another one of their houses."

"Daddy, how much longer? We're starving. We're not playing with you. Our stomachs are screaming, said Leslie."

"Maybe five or eight minutes. Can you get the sides and salads?"

"We are on our way, said Leslie."

"They are all such good helpers—a little pricey, but good helpers."

John said, "I would pay them better, but then Mom would want a pay raise as well. The ladies sure look nice, don't they?"

"That's why I cherish being outside cooking and not thinking naughty thoughts when I see her."

The girls came out of the tunnel; clogged, of course; put the bowls on the table; and clogged back to the kitchen. I heard our little cloggers coming. This time they brought the plates, plasticware, plastic cups, salt, and pepper. John had flipped the steaks when the girls brought down the first load. "Girls, it'll be just about three more minutes. Tell your mommy dinner is almost ready." His back was turned to the staircase. Marie and Delores were listening to what John was saying to the girls.

Sarah said to John, "I think they know."

"Why did you say that?"

"Turn around, Daddy."

John turned around, and Marie and Delores smiled and said, "John, tell us more."

John, being quite the prankster, yelled, "Honey, the dinner's ready!"

Marie turned to Delores. "Did you hear something?"

"No," said Delores. "It must be your imagination getting the better of you."

Mama and Papa were coming down the staircase and said, "Thanks, John. We were wondering when it would be ready."

The girls said, "Guests, we have made up our minds. We want our moms to dine with us tonight."

Marie and Delores looked at each other, smiled, and went over and hugged the girls. Marie looked at the boys, and said, "Ah, too bad. You missed it by this much." They spread their arms out wide. "Close, but no cigar, as they say."

The girls told everyone, "We are deeply sorry. We would love everyone to join us, but our budget is small, and so is our space. Pease enjoy the dinner. Maybe it will be your turn tomorrow."

John was clearing off the grill, placing all the cooked steaks on the platter. He turned off the grill. The ladies very seductively and sensually placed steaks on their plates, looked over, and smiled. "Enjoy the view, boys," said Marie. They headed over to the stairs. Delores looked over her shoulder and said, "Dream on, lover boys. Dream on."

Everyone was sitting down, eating. Papa said, "John, these are really good. You're getting so much better with the cooker."

I said to Papa, "My house tomorrow."

Papa told Mama, "You'd better not have any leftovers. This meal may have to last you two days."

Mama laughed. "He's not that bad."

I said to John, "I'm bad, just not that bad, so there."

The dessert was strawberry shortcake with whipped cream, and the girls asked their daddy if there was another steak they could share. "Yes, dear, one left." He put it on a small plate, and up the stairs they went. Dessert was wonderful; all were feeling their bellies stuffed. It was so good. It was another day in the record books.

CHAPTER 51

The girls returned to school the next day. The class was told to watch the cable channel to see the girls on television. When Marie pulled in to drop off the girls, there was a mob of kids, the teacher in charge, and at least fifteen other teachers rushing toward the car, screaming as though the girls had just won an Academy Award. The teachers had to help escort the girls to class. Their teacher said, "Good morning, class. We have a new celebrity joining us today. Would Leslie Albright like to come up and tell us how it felt being on television?"

Leslie was really embarrassed by the request. *When you're in another person's space, you follow their rules.* Hesitantly, she stood in front of the class.

The teacher prodded her to tell the class what it was like. "Go ahead. We all want to know." The teacher's voice was harsh and demanding.

Leslie was not going to get humiliated in front of her classmates. She said to the class, "It was fun. I had a good time." She went back to her seat.

The teacher said, "Leslie, is that all?"

Leslie said, "Yes ma'am, that's all."

If the teacher had treated her with respect and not looked down on her, she would have explained what it meant to have the governor and his wife spend time with her and her sisters. The teacher tried again to intimidate her. "Come on, Leslie; you met the governor. What was he like? Weren't you scared? Your classmates want to know. You must tell them."

"Ma'am, with due respect to your position, I don't want to say any more about my day yesterday. Thank you."

That put the teacher in a rage. "You tell us what really happened, young lady, or you're going straight to the principal's office."

Leslie stood up, walked to the door, and headed to the principal's office. The teacher followed her. Leslie entered the office and said to the clerk, "I need to see the principal. My teacher sent me to see him."

The teacher entered the office and said in a nasty voice, "Young lady, you just can't walk out of my classroom."

The vice principal was standing next to another office staff and walked over to the teacher. "Please return to your classroom. We will handle this situation. Please leave."

Leslie was not happy at what had just occurred. The vice principal sat down beside her on a chair in front of the principal's office. "Leslie, I know you're upset. Can you tell me what just happened?"

Leslie looked at the vice principal and said, "With all due respect to you and your position, I would rather be left alone and wait for my mom to pick me up."

A couple of minutes later, the principal's office door opened. "Please come in, my dear. Have a seat. So how are you doing?"

"I'm fine."

"What brings you to see me this morning?"

"My teacher told me to come see you."

"You're a beautiful young lady and very smart. What did you do wrong? We all saw you on television yesterday. You were very charming. You made me very proud of you. Do you want to tell me why your teacher sent you to me?"

Leslie said, "Can you have someone call my mom and have her pick me up?"

"I have to have a reason why you want your mom to pick you up."

"I have been disrespected—humiliated in front of my classmates. I've been looked down on by an authority figure. Is that enough reason?"

The principal leaned back in his chair. "I am so sorry your teacher did that to you. Leslie, I don't know what to say. I have never had this type of situation occur in all my years of teaching and being a principal. I'll have the office staff call your mom to come and pick you up. Will you come to school tomorrow?"

"I don't know. I need to talk to my mom and then decide."

The principal stood up, went outside his office, and said to the office manager, "Call Leslie's mom and have her pick her up. Tell Mrs. Kingsley to report to me during the first recess. Contact a substitute teacher to report to my office to replace Mrs. Kingsley for today."

He returned to his office. "Leslie, they are calling your mom right now. I will talk to Mrs. Kingsley during the first recess. What you told me is not acceptable action from any teacher in my school. I watched your video aired on cable television. You are a remarkable young lady. I am so proud of you and deeply sorrowed right now. If you ever need to see me, my door is always open for you and your sister."

After he spoke his words, the office manager said that Kim had been sent to the office to see him. Kim entered the room, and the girls hugged. The principal walked out of his office. "You get Miss Walters and Mrs. Kingsley into my office as soon as you have two substitute teachers arrive. They both will be put on leaves of absence until the school board meeting. If any other of my teaching staff have an issue, they too will be put on leaves of absence. Do you all understand? Notify every teacher there is a meeting in the cafeteria at the last bell."

He returned to his office, and the girls were sitting in their chairs. He sat behind his desk. "Girls, please accept my deepest apology for the actions of my teaching staff. They were way out of line. They will pay a severe penalty for their actions."

In a couple of minutes, Marie entered the principal's office. Very politely, she asked, "What is going on? Why are my girls being sent to your office?"

"Mrs. Albright, I am deeply sorry for my teachers' actions against your daughters. They both will be dealt with by me and the school board. Their actions were appalling, unprofessional, and self-serving. I could add much more, but your girls have seen enough of authoritative, childish adult behavior for today."

"Thank you for your concern. May we go now?"

"Yes, please feel free."

"Come on, girls; let's go home."

In a couple of minutes after they headed home, Marie's cell phone rang; it was Delores. "Can I and my girls meet you at your house?"

"Of course; we will meet you there." Marie pulled into her driveway, and a minute later, Delores and her girls pulled in front of their house. They all entered the house. Mama and Papa were sitting at the kitchen table. Marie and Delores had the girls sit at the dining room table and asked Mama and Papa to join them.

Marie asked Leslie, "Honey, what happened to you today?"

Leslie said to her, "I was respectful to my teacher. I'm in her space right now. I respect the laws of the person in charge. She demanded me to tell the class what it was like being on television, in a mean tone. She was looking down on me and disrespecting me. I told them it was fun and returned to my seat. The teacher was not happy with what I said and had to question me more. She became more and more mean sounding with every question and told me that if I didn't answer, I would be sent to the principal's office. She tried to scare me into answering her questions. I got up and left the classroom and walked to the principal's office. My teacher left her classroom and followed me to the principal's office. Then, in the office, she humiliated me in front of the office staff."

Everyone at the table was in tears. "How could anyone do that to a child?" asked Papa.

Marie said, "People who are arrogant, pompous, self-centered, and set on an agenda of their beliefs, trying to force their ideals and undermine anything not in line with theirs—that's who." Marie telephoned Susanne and told her she wanted to talk to Mr. Ruben now.

Susanne said, "Marie, what's wrong? Mr. Ruben is in a meeting with a couple of clients."

"Please, Susanne, tell him this is very important. He knows the consequences of his actions if he rejects me. Susanne, please."

"Marie, hold the line."

Marie entered the meeting that was being held. "I'm deeply sorry about interrupting your meeting. Mr. Ruben. Marie Albright is holding on the line. Needs to talk to you now. She said you know the consequences if you reject her."

Mr. Ruben apologized to the members seated in his office and told Susanne to get them whatever they wanted. "Gentlemen, this must be very important."

Mr. Ruben picked up the line and told all those within earshot to leave their desks until he returned. "Good morning, Marie. What can I do for you?" She told Mr. Ruben what had just occurred to all the girls at school. Mr. Ruben said, "Marie, this is very serious. I have a meeting to finish. In maybe an hour, I will come to your home with a couple of my staff and Susanne. We will file action against the school and the school board. We will notify the governor right now. Tell the girls we all love them and greatly appreciate them. See you in a couple of hours."

Marie told everyone what Mr. Ruben told her and asked the girls if they would like something to eat or drink. They requested juice and asked whether they could go to their house with it. "Of course, girls. Go to your house and relax. We will come and get you when Mr. Ruben, Susanne, and the staff arrive."

It wasn't fifteen minutes later when Marie's cell phone rang. A secretary from the governor's office asked her to please stand by. "The governor wants to talk to you."

She held for less than a minute before the governor said, "Marie, this is Governor Bronson and my wife, Diane. I will put you on speakerphone. What happened?" As Marie was explaining what occurred, the governor interrupted her. "Marie, please wait. I'll have my legal staff enter my office in a couple of minutes." Then the governor told Marie that they were being joined by his legal staff. "Please continue. I briefed them up to where I rudely interrupted you, and I'm deeply sorry for doing that."

Marie continued explaining what happened to Leslie. Once she finished, the governor said, "This is such atrocious behavior for an educator."

The legal staff, comprised of four attorneys and two assistants, stated that, "We need to have a deposition from all the girls. Can we visit you tomorrow morning at your home?"

"Yes, of course, said Marie."

The governor and Diane stated, "We will join them. Please accept all our apologies. This is absolutely horrendous. Please don't talk to any member of the press or schools until we resolve this matter."

Delores's cell phone rang; it was the principal of her girls' school. "We want you to bring back your girls. The teachers have agreed to apologize to them."

"All due respect to you and your title, no thank you. Too little, too late. Have a nice day."

A few minutes after Marie hung up her phone, Susanne called. "Marie, we were contacted by the governor's office. They want us to be there tomorrow morning, not to visit you today. Will that be okay with you?"

"Yes, that will be fine. Thank you for calling."

Delores said, "The gall of that principal, thinking that an apology from two teachers would iron out this whole ordeal. How stupid do they think we are anyway?"

Marie told her what the governor and his legal staff had told her. "Do not talk to the press or the school or school boards, period."

Papa said, "There are going to be lots of heads rolling from this issue. This won't just be on local television. This is major. The governor's legal staff? This will get the attention of the bureaucracy. Like Diane said, she was going to her office on Monday and giving all her staff a spanking. I hope they have her holding up a swat board like the one they used on us in school for acting up."

Delores said, "With the holes drilled in the wide part of the board so there is less wind resistance. I almost enjoyed that after the first few I received."

They were all having a second cup of coffee and a breakfast roll. The girls came in from the tunnel, clogging all the way. "We're starving, Mommy. Is it too early for lunch?"

"Yes, dears. How about a snack?"

"Can we have a glass of chocolate milk to go with our snack?"

"Let's see what we can muster up for our precious daughters."

Delores said, "I make a killer chocolate shake."

Marie said, "The blender is in the corner on the countertop."

"I see it. Girls, get me some ice cream from the freezer, some chocolate syrup from the cupboard, and some milk from the refrigerator." The girls were so happy to help retrieve what their mommies wanted.

Mama said she had made a sweet roll for tomorrow's breakfast and told them they could have that. "We are having company tomorrow, and I'll make three more for them. Girls, would you like to help Grandma?"

"Yeah, we love to help you bake. We get to lick the bowl."

Delores poured in some milk, added the vanilla ice cream, added the chocolate syrup, and hit the switch; the pitcher was frosting up on the outside. Delores asked Marie, "Do you have any long-handled teaspoons?"

Marie asked Leslie, "Can you get all of them from the silverware drawer?" Marie had gotten the perfect glass from her cabinet that she used for sundaes, and she also got from the refrigerator a jar of maraschino cherries. She also had some whipped cream to top off the shakes.

Delores poured and filled two glasses and started making more. There were some starving girls here, and they needed something to fill their bellies now. Delores made four batches for starters and was ready to make a backup if necessary. The girls joined Papa at the kitchen table. Mama, Marie, and Delores went to the dining room table. Delores said, "We need to put on our fabulous dresses we got yesterday and see if they still fit after eating these."

Marie asked, "Delores, could you help me zip up the dress?"

"You have any pliers?"

Mama said, "We could always exercise."

"You do that," said Delores. "I'll pull up a chair, watch, and cheer you on."

Marie said, "These are so good and so sinful."

The girls asked if they could have just a little bit more. "We really like these."

Delores got up, made another quick batch, and refilled all the girls' glasses. "Thank you, Mom," all the girls replied. "We love you."

After the snacks, Papa said, "Time for a nap. Come on, Mama; let's take a nap."

She said, "Papa, a nap only—nothing more." She gave us a smile, and a twinkle in her eye said it all.

The girls clogged their way through the tunnel and back to their house. Marie and Delores went to the bench to watch the waterfall, stream, and nature. Marie turned on some stereo music before they went to the bench. While they sat on the bench under the shade tree, the sunlight was filtering through the leaves. Birds were singing with the music playing, and then they saw a hummingbird hovering around the flowers in bloom. They looked at each other and said, "It got out of its nest."

Delores said, "I'll kill him."

Marie just laughed. "It must have been important, don't you think?"

"I hope he had fun. Coming back to the nest will be a learning experience for him."

"What do you think will come out of all of what happened today?" asked Marie.

"Your dad was correct. Heads will roll. Will it make a difference? I hope. Maybe all the parents will get up in arms and protest each school board meeting, and if the teachers start picketing or create a walkout, the governor should do what Ronald Reagan did to the air traffic controllers—fire them all."

Marie said, "I wanted to take Leslie's teacher out of the classroom and beat her. Maybe they will allow Leslie to give her swats with all the media around. All news stations around the globe will show what bad behavior looks like."

"Leslie is too sweet of a girl and would get a few seconds of fame, and then the ones benefiting from all this would take it out on her."

Marie said, "I would be honored to give that teacher the swats. The headline on the next day's paper would be 'This Is What It Is Like Hitting the Broad Side of the Barn.'"

Delores said, "I love that. Talk about humiliation. Then put all the girls' teachers in stocks, with all school board members shackled together in a circle with their backs toward the teachers in stocks. Call all the news stations to film their pride and joy. Then have all the senators and Congresspersons get the same treatment. We need to tell that to the governor tomorrow morning. They also need to play it the entire month or two during the elections—especially when they preach about everything they did during their term in office. You know, we could start a movement—cleaning out the swamp. Have baseball caps with 'COTS' written across the front."

"Let's go inside and write all this down and draw some pictures for the visual." They went back inside. Marie got some construction paper out of the cabinet and some writing utensils, and they recreated what they had just talked about.

Delores said, "This would be greater for the good than a stupid court case and allowing those special interest groups to profit from donations. 'Save our teachers. We don't want them fired.' They would profit from a GoFundMe account. No way. Humiliate them. Take that to the bank. I have a whole big bag of humiliation to deposit."

"I hope the governor finds this informative and pursues it. It's the only way to stop all this chaos." They finished drawing their vision. They held it up and looked at their creation. They gave each other a high five and, of course, hugs and love-yous.

The ladies lay back in their chairs. Marie said, "You know, life is like a bed of roses. They are beautiful, you handle them with tender loving care, and all is well. If you don't handle them with care, love, appreciation, and respect, they can cut you."

Delores said, "You know, they were just jealous of our girls. They wanted to create a scene to cause damage to our girls' image—turn the spotlight off the girls and onto themselves. They're teachers, you know. Do you remember the sad story near Election Day where a teacher was asking for more money? She and her husband couldn't afford to buy a house near where she teaches school. Please pass whatever bill was attached to her sad story. I just have to say, 'Too bad you chose your profession. You knew the amount of money you would be paid. We can't afford the house we would like to buy either. Give me back some of the tax dollars your organization has sucked out of us so we can buy what we would like. You know, Marie, we aren't finished."

Marie said, "Do you think we are bitter about what happened to our daughters?"

"I'm not bitter. I'm furious at what happened to our daughters. There was absolutely no call for their actions. I might say that if one of our girls had a misbehaving teacher, she might just have been having a bad day. But four teachers with attitudes? No, absolutely not."

The girls all came in and sat at the table with their moms. "Mommies, why did our teachers do what they did to us? Don't they like us anymore?"

"You know, girls, this is hurting your mommies as much as it is hurting you. We have asked ourselves the same thing. We don't know the whys. The governor is coming to our house tomorrow. Let's ask him why. He's the one in charge of every department of the state government. They are the teachers' bosses. They are responsible for the actions of their employees. He'd better have the answer for the why. I'm almost ready to cry. You girls mean so much to us. None of this makes any sense. Are you getting hungry for some lunch?"

"What were you drawing and writing?"

"Here, we will show you. This is a stock. In the time of the pilgrims, if you did something bad, they put you in a stock, and the people of the town would walk by you and shame you with their words. So we will ask the governor to put your teachers in stocks. The people around the teachers will be handcuffed together with their backs to the teachers in a circle, with signs telling all who walk by what they did. See, girls, your teachers humiliated you in front of your classmates, telling them that it's okay to make fun of you and that they won't get into trouble for doing so. If that action started, you girls would be the laughingstock of the school. The teacher would become praised for bad action. But they took away from you what they could never have done."

"So our teachers purposely tried to hurt us?"

"We don't know if it was on purpose. We believe that was what they may have talked about in the teachers' lounge—not allowing you to become the school heroes."

"We don't want to be heroes, Mom. We like who we are—loving, charming, respectable, polite, and willing to help anyone if we can."

"We know, dears. That is what scares your teachers. They can't let you have that power. Being unlike them, in their minds, is not correct behavior."

"Mommy, can we all give you big hugs?"

"Well, I can't see any reason why not. Oh, before you start, it has to be the biggest hug we have ever received."

About a half hour later, Marie's cell phone rang; it was the governor. He introduced himself and asked if he could speak to the girls. "My wife is in my office. I will put the phone on speaker. Would that be okay?"

Marie said, "I'll call the girls. Delores is right here. I'll get the girls. Be right back."

Delores spoke with the governor and Diane, and they all heard the girls coming in the house, saying, "Hello, Governor and Diane. We love you both."

The governor said, "We just finished crying together over what happened to you girls at school. Tomorrow morning, I'm bringing a legal staff from my office to talk to you. We will get to the bottom of what occurred today. We are so sorry that this happened. You are our favorite girls. You all are so special to us. We watched the video last night and cried. We went through a whole box of tissues. I promise to all of you I will do everything to stop this madness."

Diane said, "Girls, I'm coming with the governor tomorrow morning. Remember when I said I was going to my office and giving all my staff a spanking?"

"Yes, Diane, we remember."

"Well, they are all crying today."

"I can't wait to see all of you. You all mean so much to me and Diane, beyond words can express. I just wanted to say let us take care of this issue. It is the least Diane and I could do for you. I have already put a hush, a legal hush, on all school board members throughout the state. All schools have been notified with warrants that if any member of any school has a press conference from now until they get an all-clear order from my desk, that member will lose his or her job and be put in jail. One more thing: if they have legal counsel try to bypass the order given, they will be immediately disbarred. This is not going to be used for political gain. I won't have it—not one minute of any of it. They are trying to hurt my sweetest, charming, polite, beautiful girls and my best friends' lives. We both love and adore all of you. Please have a great evening. We have this. Don't worry about anything, okay?"

"Thank you, Governor and Diane. We all love you. You have a great evening as well," said Marie.

Mama and Papa came downstairs. "Was that who we think it was?"

"Yes, Dad, it was the governor. He said I wouldn't want to have a school superintendent, one of those teachers, or any government official come tomorrow. They have already put out a court order to every school district and school. This is serious business, everyone. I guarantee there will be no book deals coming very soon."

Papa just said, "All this mess for what? They showed no professionalism. What are they teaching our children? Girls, we all love you, and that should be enough for you. Learn from how adults never grow up. This just sickens me. Trying to hurt my granddaughters ... I won't have it—not one minute of it."

Marie and Delores made everyone lunch: sandwiches with three different luncheon meats, three different sliced cheeses, french rolls, lettuce, tomatoes, and Italian yellow peppers—not hot but with lots of flavor—with beverages and chips. The girls put on mustard or mayonnaise or vinegar and oil. Each day, Marie and Delores made sandwiches better than any sandwich shop could equal. Marie and Delores gave each other high fives and hugs for their achievements. Marie and Delores asked the girls if they wanted to eat lunch at the patio table. "Please, that would be so wonderful."

"Could you help take the food to the table?"

"That will be fun for us. Come on, Papa and Mama, you can sit outside with all of us too."

Mama and Papa were seated, and the girls played waitress. "Thank you, ma'am."

"Can I have your order, sir?" They all ran into the house and told the chef what their customer wanted.

Delores and Marie loved this game the girls played. They filled the order and put it on a dinner plate. One of the girls got the napkins and silverware, one carried the beverages, and two carried the plates. Then either Marie or Delores would be the next customer. The girls would take their order, and all the girls would deliver the food. Delores went first. Marie made her plate, tried to remember what she put on her plate, and gave the girls her order. They came into the kitchen, got Marie's order, and delivered. They came back into the kitchen and got their plates, and up the stairs they went to their house, and they ate lunch there.

When all were finished, the girls would come down from upstairs, take their plates to the kitchen, and then proceed to clear the table of the adults. Then they would ask what they wanted for dessert. They had chocolate cupcakes, snowballs, Twinkies, and doughnuts. The dessert order was taken, and the girls would deliver the orders on a dessert plate. The majority of the time, someone would leave them a tip. The girls would thank them for coming to their restaurant. "Hope you enjoyed your meal. Please come again real soon." They would run upstairs, and we could hear them say, "They were such good customers."

Marie said, "I have to unbutton my pants after that lunch."

Papa said, "Hey, that's a man's line to get his date to feel sorry for him."

"That's where I heard the line from—a date while in high school. I'm certain he is out of the hospital by now." Everyone was laughing. Boy it felt good to have a great laugh.

The boys were home and started the ritual of barbecue, belching, and man talk. After dinner, we headed home, and we talked about what might happen tomorrow. I said to my dearest darling, "You have it under control, but if you need me, just call me. I have to see how the wall is going at Silvia and Doug's house."

That was when Delores said to me, "You know they aren't married any longer, correct?"

"What are you talking about?"

"They are no longer married from the time they threw a party. He just pays her rent. She's nearly ready to tell him to move somewhere else. If she can get a contract from the magazine, he's gone. She asked me to design a dream job for her."

"She said you two talked, and you said I could make her dream come true. She wants what John and Marie has—a playhouse, an outdoor kitchen, and a bar."

"Do you know she used to be a bartender?"

"She makes great drinks."

"Marie and I went and saw her a couple of days ago. I told her I would talk to Susanne—see if we could add her to our ladies' club."

"You like her that much?"

"Marie and I had her do a grand entrance and arched gateway entrance. She is really gifted. Her moves, with a little practice, might put our moves to shame. Her arched gateway entrance—you would be amazed. Hear me loud and clear: you'd better never touch. Look all you want. If you touch, you won't be happy for very long."

The next morning, breakfast was delicious. She was such a great cook. I had a couple of appointments, and then I was over to Silvia's and then to one other appointment. Delores and the girls were getting ready to meet the governor. I thought that if I didn't have so much work to complete, I would love to see the governor again. I heard on the radio on my way to see Juan and crew that the governor's polling numbers had more than doubled since the airing of the video of him and the girls on cable television. They were poking fun of the poll. "If you call the same phone numbers over and over and over again, you too could double your poll numbers." I changed the radio channel. I was tired of listening to the same old garbage.

Delores arrived with the girls, with lots of hugging and giggling from the girls. The ladies were all dressed up and looking great. Papa said, "I guess I'd better not answer the door in my boxer shorts."

"Why, Papa?" said Delores. "They want full disclosure from all parties."

Mama said, "Newsprint headline: 'Old Geezer Answers Door for the Governor and Diane in His Boxer Shorts and Striped T-shirt with a Can of Beer.' 'Way to go, Gramps. Now that's class,' said the cohost. Scrap our contracts, coat hanger checks, beautiful dresses, and jewelry. Thanks, Gramps."

The ladies went into the kitchen, and the girls went to their house. Delores's cell phone was ringing. "Hello ... Who? ... Oh, yeah, good morning ... No, they won't be in school today ... What? You want a what? Doctors' excuse for both girls before they can reenter their class? I'll see what I can do to assist your wishes. Can you quote me the district's rule number for future reference?" The secretary hung up without answering.

A couple of minutes later, Marie's cell phone rang. The girls' school was calling. "Mrs. Albright?"

"Yes, this is Mrs. Albright."

"Will your daughters be attending school today?"

"I'm afraid not. They are staying home today."

"You know that the school has a policy that requires a doctor's excuse before we can accept them back into school?"

"Do you have that policy number?"

"Ma'am, we don't give out that number. You got a packet when you enrolled the girls in school."

"That was over four years ago. I'm certain the policy in my enrollment package has been changed in four years, correct?"

"I can't answer that question. I will tell the principal that the girls won't be coming to school today."

Marie said politely, "You do that."

Less than a half hour later, the front doorbell rang. Marie went to the door, and we all followed her. She looked through the peephole and saw Susanne. "Come on in, Susanne. Would you like a cup of fresh coffee?"

"I would love a cup of fresh coffee."

Papa, being quick witted, said, "Me too. Here's five dollars. I take mine with cream."

Susanne said, "He's joking, right?"

Marie said, "Don't pay any attention to him. He wanted to answer the door in boxer shorts and a striped T-shirt, holding a beer."

Susanne said, "That would be special for the governor. Me, not so special. Mr. Ruben and staff are a few minutes behind me. It would be great if Mr. Ruben and the governor's legal team arrived at the same time. Legal briefs would be flying out of the briefcases faster than speeding bullets. I have great news for all of you. Everything is flying off the shelf, and orders galore are still coming in at a record pace. The girls' video has sold nearly as many copies as the other two combined. The governor's approval rating has doubled overnight."

Marie handed Susanne a cup of fresh coffee. Then the doorbell rang again. Marie, following exactly what Gisselle taught her, looked at who was on the porch and opened the door for Mr. Ruben and staff. All were soon inside with their cups of coffee and sweet rolls.

After a couple of minutes of chitchat, the doorbell rang again. Marie asked Delores to please get the girls. Marie and Susanne went to the door, and standing there were the girls' favorite man and his wife. "Governor, Diane, please come on in, and welcome to my home." The governor gave her and Susanne a hug, and Diane followed. "My legal staff should be here in a couple of minutes."

As they all turned and headed for the kitchen, the sound of little feet were heard, and then came the scream the governor had paid big money to hear. "Governor Bronson and Diane, how are you? We love you both." There were hugs and more hugs for both the governor and Diane.

Diane was tearing up. "I love you, girls."

Delores brought the governor and Diane fresh cups of coffee. Diane said, "Thank you. I really needed a cup of coffee."

The doorbell rang again, and the governor said, "Excuse me, Marie; I will check to see if that is my legal staff. You wouldn't know them … Yes, that is the legal staff."

Marie opened the door, and the legal staff, comprising of four attorneys and two assistants said, "Governor, you beat us here."

"Come on in. Please make yourselves at home, and Delores, my maid, will serve you coffee."

Delores said to Marie, "I got promoted? Wow, two more dollars a day. You're so generous."

They had just turned around when the doorbell rang again. Marie looked through the peephole, and she didn't know who these people were. Susanne ran to the door and looked through the peephole. "It's about time." She opened the door; it was the caterer with a trunkful of food and supplies. She had them go through the arched gate and bring everything into the courtyard. Another truck pulled in behind the first truck, and out came tables, chairs, a hot serving table, and two chefs. A limousine showed up with the staff of waitresses, waiters, and serving staff.

"This is starting to look like the twelve days of Christmas: one governor, two chefs, three waitresses, and so on, said Delores." That got everyone laughing.

Everyone had coffee and a sweet roll; a full breakfast was being set up. There were plenty of chairs and tables to accommodate the entire party. Delores entered the courtyard where everything was being set up and said to Marie, "Miss Marie, can I have the day off? It's my time of the month."

The governor and Diane looked very confused. "Marie, does she really work for you?"

"No, she's just playing along with a comment I made earlier."

"Governor, I'm not from this state. I emigrated from the West Coast. I'm sorry; I crossed the border at night so no one would see me."

The governor said to Delores, "You and Marie missed your calling. You should be a comedy team."

"We need to get this party rolling. We need the girls to meet us in the courtyard."

The girls were in their house, and Marie called for them. They came onto the balcony. "Yes, Mom?"

"Can you come down and sit with the governor and Diane? Some men would like to talk with you."

The girls came down, gave the governor and Diane a big hug, and sat down. The legal team from the state, Mr. Ruben, and his staff sat down. The catering crew arranged the tables in a square so everyone could hear. They had a sound system with headsets for everyone so they could hear what was being said without the neighbor listening in. The governor told the girls he wished this had not happened to them and that he was deeply disturbed when he heard the news. "It's not right, and it is being corrected as we speak."

He introduced Mr. Herbert. "He will ask you the questions after you girls tell us what exactly happened to you yesterday. Okay, girls? Leslie, could you tell Mr.

Herbert what happened?" Leslie told Mr. Herbert the details of exactly what had happened to her from the time she stepped into the classroom.

About halfway through, Marie got up and asked the catering crew if they had tissues; they had brought bring a couple of cases. "Could you distribute those to the guests?"

When she finished, Mr. Herbert turned to the governor. "Do you want to kill that teacher, or can I?" Mr. Herbert said to Kim, "Please tell me what happened yesterday."

Kim gave an accounting of what her teacher had done to her. She hadn't willingly left her room. Her teacher dragged her to the principal's office and, in a very mean voice, when she walked into the office, said, "This brat needs to be sent home and suspended." That response got the governor and Mr. Herbert really upset. Firing would be too nice for her.

They went to Sarah and asked her what had happened to her. Her account was as bad as Kim's. Delores said, "I'm going to kill that witch."

The governor said, "You won't have a chance. I'll beat you to her."

Then Mr. Herbert asked Rebecca, "What happened to you yesterday?"

Rebecca started to give a detailed accounting but then started to cry very hard. That got every tissue box emptied. For the next three or four minutes, she was crying more and more. Mr. Herbert motioned for one of his aides to get the paperwork started. "Go to the courthouse and get these four teachers arrested."

The governor asked Mr. Herbert, "Are you sure? Could this blow up out of proportion?"

"Let it. Their actions are criminal. They will be put away for a long time. I want the legal battle from the teacher's union. I want to expose all this nonsense. These are little girls. They are adults, for one, but also authority figures, and the students can't defend themselves against severe punishment. I'm tired of hearing all the garbage being told to protect them!"

Rebecca said, "There is more."

The governor said, "I'm sorry, Rebecca. Please continue."

"She dragged me from my desk, and one of our boys opened the door and dragged me to the principal's office and called me bad words all the way to the office. She told the office staff, 'This brat, get her out of my sight!' Mommy came to pick us up in a few minutes. The principal gave me a lecture like the one he gave Sarah."

"Put out a warrant of arrest for the principal and any office staff who interfere."

One of the assistants came into the meeting; they had been watching all news channels for any reporting. "Two stations are reporting the incident."

"Call the station to stop airing, or we will pull their plug for life."

They called the channel, and the news anchor refused to stop talking about the incident. "Send the cars now."

There were soon numerous FBI and local and state officers raiding both television stations, arresting all personnel. The cameras were still rolling, but no one was onstage. One employee was saying, "This is in violation of our First Amendment."

An officer said, "You have the right to remain silent." The employee said something to the officers, and he was taken in a van away from the scene and read the remainder of his Miranda rights one fist at a time.

Mr. Herbert said, "I'm busting three hundred people involved in the scandal. I got proof yesterday enough to put our developer away for life."

The governor said, "Are you sure it will stick this time?"

"I'm talking life and possibly the death penalty."

The two news station employees were being processed, and the jails were overrun with employees from other news stations. There were two other police units from neighboring cities coming to their aid, and they formed a barricade at the police stations holding the news teams. The governor said, "Call in the national guard. Shoot to kill. This has gone on far enough."

The governor got a phone call from his state office. People were starting to picket, carrying signs bearing slogans about police brutality. "Get security on the line and local police forces and stop this from getting worse. Marie and Delores, we will have armed guards surrounding your home twenty-four hours a day, beginning in a matter of a few minutes."

Mr. Herbert called his office and said, "Enforce all the warrants now. The roundup begins." He said to Marie and Delores, "The roaches won't have a hole to hide in. The border crossings are all roadblocked. None of the three hundred suspects will escape. My and local forces are a stone's throw from all of them."

Warrants were issued, and all four teachers and one principal were cuffed and taken into custody. The governor went to the city hall in the next city in case any roach might do something to harm the ladies. He called the local press, more roaches, and said to them, "The massive manhunt is underway, and four teachers and a principal have been arrested. I will give an address at five o'clock. Any more outbreaks, and the national guard will be dispatched."

Mr. Herbert and his team headed to the jails where the news teams were being held. When he arrived, the state police made plenty of room for him to enter the building. He got inside and asked who the manager of the station was. "All managerial employees into that conference room now. Keep them cuffed, and shackle their feet. Sit down, all of you. I'm going to make this loud and clear. You're all accessories to murder. You all had better hope we round up all three hundred people under investigation. You're all idiots—stupid fools. You put two families in harm's way right now. What in god's name were any of you thinking? You will not be released on bond. You won't be released until all three hundred people are in custody. We don't care who you are. If I get one call about any of those fine people being harmed, you will all get the death penalty."

The owner of the station said, "We have our rights. We get to talk to an attorney."

"You gave up your rights, when you violated the warrant you received yesterday. I suppose you must have failed to read the warrant. Too bad for you and your staff. I'm sick of looking at you people. Get them out of my sight."

They went to the second station, and there were not as many reporters outside. Of course, they were facing officers in riot gear, and they were not messing around. Mr. Herbert entered the station house and asked for all managerial personnel to move into the conference room. "Shackle their feet. Leave them cuffed. Sit down now." He told them exactly what he had told the first station house. "Absolutely no calls until the final minute allowed by law, and not until we say it is all clear."

He got back to his vehicle and headed for the courthouse. The governor and Diane arrived in the state capitol. Picketers were blocking the driveway entrances. The governor had a police escort, and the crowd opened up a pathway for the vehicles to pass. The security around the governor's entrance was very tight. They entered the capitol.

The staff were eager for him to address the state with an announcement as promised. Diane was escorted to their personal residence to freshen up. They would film in his office. The staff had prepared a speech for the governor to tell the state's people. He looked at what was written, thanked the staff, and asked to be left alone so he could ready himself for the speech. The film crews were ready, the producer of the program was in place, and the spokesperson for the governor was ready. All systems were ready.

"Five, four, three, two, one, the director, was counting off with his fingers."

"Good evening. Live from the capitol, this is Amy Clark, the governor's press secretary. Here is Governor Bronson, live from his office."

"Good evening. Today has been a horrible day for the state. As you were told, some teachers were removed from their classrooms and replaced with substitute teachers. The teachers' unions were up in arms, saying, 'This is against state policy. How dare the state remove these fine, upstanding teachers?' On and on and on.

"Yesterday every news station was put under a warrant. All school districts and schools were under warrant so as not to bring this to your homes. This is not to hide anything from you. This was to protect two families from certain death if this was broadcast statewide and nationwide. If you are unaware of the fact, we shut down two news stations for violating that warrant.

"Without getting into details, there was a horrific murder that took place in the home of one of the families years ago. We have over three hundred people under surveillance for this and a few more crimes. We were waiting for some more evidence to come forward before we would arrest all those under surveillance. These two rogue news channels forced us to start taking these three-hundred-plus individuals into custody. They are now charged as conspirators to murder. They won't be coming home very soon.

"We will release a video tomorrow of why the teachers were replaced. They were also arrested for their actions, which were of a criminal nature. I am saying this to all educators: you are not above the law. Please allow our officers to do their jobs in protecting families and all of you from heinous crimes. Tomorrow we will post the photos of all the remaining criminals still at large. They will be running all day until each and every one is in custody. If you know the whereabouts of anyone in the photos shown, you will be rewarded for their capture. This is serious. They are all dangerous and could be armed. Do not try to apprehend these individuals. Thank you for taking your time this evening. Have a pleasant evening. Good night."

The regular programs returned as scheduled. There were officials from all the departments in the governor's office after his speech. The head staff official asked the governor, "Why didn't you read what we put together?"

"These two families are our friends. I'm not taking this time for political gamesmanship. I care too deeply for the well-being of these families and your family and their family. I couldn't care less about gaining votes. Your writings were political in nature. This is a very serious, extremely dangerous situation. These families were put into danger by two arrogant news stations. Excuse me, everyone. I have an important call to make ... Hello, this is Governor Bronson. I need to speak to the detective in charge of the Albright case now."

"Hold, please."

"Hello, Governor. How may I be of help?"

"The neighbor lady and her husband who live next to the Albrights."

"Yes sir, we have talked with them before."

"Arrest them now. Hold them in custody until all the three-hundred-plus people are in custody."

"Do you think they may have a connection?"

"I don't really care if they do or not. I'm trying to protect that family. Let my office know when you have them in custody."

"I will dispatch a unit to arrest them right now. Have a good evening, Governor."

He called the magazine. "Let me talk to Mr. Ruben or Susanne."

Susanne answered the phone. "Governor, what a pleasant surprise. I saw your speech. I loved it. How may I be of help?"

"I'm concerned. All the video you shot at the Albrights' party—have you found anyone that was not accounted for?"

"You know, you'll have to talk with Gisselle. I really don't know, and Mr. Ruben is in a meeting."

"Get him for me, please."

Susanne went and said, "I'm sorry, Mr. Ruben. The governor is on the phone and needs to talk with you right now."

"I know the drill."

Mr. Ruben picked up the phone. "Good evening, Governor. How may I be of help?"

"I'm trying to touch all bases as they run through my head. The Albrights' party—you videotaped everyone at the party, correct?"

"Correct, video and still shots."

"Have you identified everyone at the party, matched to the guest book?"

"I believe everyone has been accounted for. I'll get Gisselle on her cell phone and have her call you direct."

"Thank you, Mr. Ruben. This is very important."

The governor then got a phone call from the detective. "The neighbor and her husband are in custody."

"Thank you. Great job." The governor started writing down what he knew and didn't know regarding the Albrights on a yellow pad. He decided to call John and Marie. "Marie, this is Governor Bronson. Has anyone talked to you and Delores about staying in the house for the next few days until we have all in custody?"

"No, Governor, there was such a wild dash of everyone earlier. No one said much of anything."

"You must stay inside the house. Lock up the arched gate, the playhouse, the tunnel. Set your house alarm. Have one of the officers watching your home put an officer in the backyard and courtyard. Tomorrow morning, set your outdoor lighting to run from dusk to dawn. This is very serious, Marie. If they enter your home, you're perfect hostages. Do you understand?"

"Yes sir, we will keep everyone inside the house."

"Love all of you. I'm praying for you. Have a great evening. Call me in the morning."

The governor called Delores and told her the same thing. "Tell the officers to put one man in the backyard and any other place where the house is vulnerable."

"Governor, Gisselle is on the line. Do you want to talk with her?"

"Please put her through … Gisselle, how are you tonight?"

"Fine, Governor. What can I do for you?"

"The video and still shots of the Albrights' party—were all the guests identified, and did they sign the guest book?"

"We have all but three identified. We have five names in the guest book with no photos that match. That's not uncommon. We may have a photo on file that was shot years ago."

"I hate to bother you. I need those names and photos released by tomorrow morning. We have around 175 suspects still at large. We're running all photos on all networks and cable networks tomorrow morning, and yours will be added. I will have them forwarded to you by six o'clock in the morning. Can you text me the photos and names and then submit them to my staff at six?"

"Of course, Governor. I have them on my computer, and it will take me a few minutes. Your number? … Great, got it. Thank you." The Governor stated, he will let them know when they arrive on his computer.

Gisselle forwarded the photos and the names to the governor. He called in his head of security, and they transferred the data to their computer files. They started searching the three photos in their database to find a match. Two of the photos came up in a few minutes, and there was still one that was unidentified. The names listed in the guest book were matched with photos of each person, and they were all known businesspeople in the community. Security told the governor they should have the identity of the person in the third photo in a short time. They transferred the photo to the FBI for identification.

Since I had a job with Silvia and Doug, they ran them through the database to make sure they were not tied to this or any other case. They got a hit on Doug; he had been arrested a few years ago for possession and drug trafficking. The governor said, "Pick him up. Hold him until all this blows over."

Silvia checked out, except the surveillance tapes showed that she had visitors numerous times per day—male only. She was either selling drugs or selling herself. They would bring her in for questioning in the morning. The governor told security, "Plainclothes officers, unmarked car. Make it appear they are just friends coming over for a visit. Male and female officers dressed in normal street clothes. Make it appear that they are all going out for breakfast or coffee."

They asked the governor, "Why?"

"If she is tied to this case, she is more than likely being watched. This could trigger someone we don't know to go after the families."

The next morning, there were more protests from the teacher's union, stating how unfair it was to arrest the teachers and a principal over four students not behaving properly. Some of the teachers were saying that if the arrested teachers were not released, they would walk out in support.

Amy had a press conference to refute what was being stated. "The teachers broke the law and violated professional standards. It was not the children. If this continues as planned by the unions, and walkouts are performed, the governor will take disciplinary actions against those who walk out. That is a violation of state and federal laws. Until the investigation is complete, you all are advised to stop this nonsense. You're all professionals. Start acting like it"

There were a number of teachers in a picket line, voicing their opinions, standing in unity with those put in jail. One hour after the airing, they too were arrested as coconspirators to murder.

The two news stations that had been raided the day before were showing reruns of sitcoms. They made a plea. "Please free our staff to the public." There was a lot of political chatter going on, with all sorts of know-it-alls trying to get airtime.

The governor issued another warning to cable and regular television networks, radio stations, and internet providers. "You all will be shut down if you continue to hinder an ongoing investigation. We are very serious. We will tolerate no more. The president of the United States warned the communication mega-giants that until all associates involved in the ongoing investigation are in custody, you are advised to stop and stop now."

There were a few reporters with their vehicles in front of John and Marie's home setting up, and they were all arrested with their vehicles impounded. Mr. Herbert was amazed at the arrogance of the media. They were having meetings regarding pulling the plug on every one of the stations airing any information to the public. They received word from all local police and FBI that there were still over one hundred on the list still at large. They told the state offices to have all stations air the photos of the suspects still at large. The cable networks under contract with the families were showing the suspects every hour, on the hour. The two stations with their crews in jail said they would show those photos only if their crews were released. Mr. Herbert said, "There are no negotiations. You chose to violate the warrant." Mr. Herbert ordered that the news crews be separated and placed in different jails around the state. "Do not disclose their whereabouts to anyone." He even did the same to the teachers and principal.

Finally, after midday, nearly all the suspects were in custody. There were very few left. They then got the major breakthrough they had been hoping for. One of the suspects started talking about what he knew. He had been a concrete foreman during the time that the girl who did the makeup for the bank robbers mentioned that the house they were pouring the floors in had been excavated over one foot deep. The normal house pad was four inches with a foundation that was poured on a prior date. He found that odd. "Why would they overpour a certain house and not others?" He gave the police the location. The concrete mix had been too wet, but they were told by their superintendent to pour and stop complaining. While on their lunch break, a van with three or four guys put something into the concrete. The van blocked their view of what they were doing. He had been on three of those pours.

When they took him to the home in a police vehicle, he mentioned that after the third pour, he was replaced with another foreman because he was asking too many questions. "Just do your job, or you'll be fired." The state contacted the homeowners and told them to work with them; they would purchase a new residence in the same area for them to move into. All three homeowners agreed to move once they found out what might be in their floors.

The first house was demolished, and the concrete slab was carefully cut and loaded on a flatbed truck, covered with tarps, and hauled to a forensic lab. They found the remains of the girl who had done the makeup. The police had a list of all missing persons from the time of the great-grandmother's murder to the present. With the girl's remains were two other missing persons' remains.

The second house was demolished, and the concrete slab was also cut, loaded onto a flatbed truck, and hauled to the forensic lab. More remains were in the concrete slab. They were working hard to put all the pieces together: who filed the missing persons report, whether that person was on the list of more than three hundred suspects, and whether there were more than three hundred suspects.

Finally, once the third house was demolished and remains were found in that concrete pour as well, they helped in solving the connections. There were two suspects who were not on the list. These even shocked the governor. One was a retired state senator who had passed away a year prior. A large celebration had been thrown in his honor. The other was the retired president of the bank that had been robbed, who had passed away six months before. They found the missing link; this would put the majority of the three hundred into prison for many years.

They arrested the man who had been the concrete company's superintendent at the time of the houses' construction; he was now old and frail. They told him that he would serve the rest of his life in prison if he did not cooperate with the investigation. He gave a few more homes for which he had been told to dig the pads deeper than normal. They put information provided by the two—the superintendent and the foreman—together to find the exact locations of those pours. Both men were emotional wrecks; they did not know what was being put into the concrete pours.

The investigators continued to question all those who were in custody. The developer would not talk and wanted legal representation, and he would not be strong-armed by the police or FBI. Unfortunately for him, those who were semi-involved would talk.

The final nail in the developer's case was a personal secretary and an office manager. They turned over a storage unit with files, bank records, and contracts that they had stored in their own units. The developer was shocked to hear that the records he had told them to destroy were actually stored. The personal secretary said he made too many passes at her and demanded that if she would not comply with his wishes, he would do to her as he had had done to others. She refused his advances and never returned to work. The office manager and she were good friends. The office manager helped her get the files out of the office and stored.

With evidence piling up, the developer decided to try for a plea bargain. "Nothing doing," said Mr. Herbert. They had uncovered ten of the missing persons on their list. More bones were still being investigated.

The governor called Marie and talked with her for at least a half hour, mostly about the girls. They were now being professionally tutored in their home, along with Sarah and Rebecca. There was no need to put the girls under pressure.

The four teachers were fired, spent sixty days in jail, and were found guilty by juries. There were more cases being filed by parents against other teachers and school board members for almost the same charges. Everything was calming down. Still, they were investigating the other missing persons whose bones had been found in seven different concrete pours. The news station crews were released, and the station had to pay very stiff fines and money for each employee in custody. They also had a two-year probationary period. If they broke any law, back into jail they would go.

The magazine was getting new subscriptions, and the ladies were touring, performing at various events. They added Silvia, Susanne, and every once in a while, Michele. The girls had their own cable television program, and *The Playhouse* became a huge success for not only the magazine but also all the cable television stations. Every video of the ladies sold millions. Silvia's video, not R rated, sold hundreds of thousands. Susanne's sold about the same. Silvia's R-rated videos, borderline X rated, sold nearly one hundred thousand copies. Silvia was the very naughty lady of the bunch. The ladies were thinking of not having her as a part of their performances and allowing her to perform by herself at different locations.

The girls gave a school assembly, but not at their original school. They performed in the arena where the pro basketball and hockey teams played. All the schools in the state were issued a video of the girls with the governor so they could show them in school auditoriums. Diane would make a guest appearance when the special program was to be shown.

CHAPTER 52

The ladies' club became very successful. Once the videos launched, there was such a demand for them to appear at all sorts of functions. The ladies were happy to add new ladies to the club. Susanne loved to perform with the girls; she was their best adult friend. She was not comfortable sashaying her body in front of others. She was very attractive and had an altercation with one promoter who caused her to decline going out regularly. She appeared numerous times on the girls' program *The Playhouse*. If the event was done in a large venue, Susanne would perform. The magazine always had the makeup, hairstyling, and wardrobe departments at every event for the ladies.

Silvia became a regular with the ladies. After she had her interview with the police and FBI to determine just how she was living with no signs of an employer disclosed, no one ever believed her story of her so-called husband telling his friends he would share his wife. They did find out his friends were actually his deliverymen for distributing illegal drugs. Silvia and Doug had met at a party; he enticed her the first night of their meeting with illegal drugs. After she threw Doug out of the house, her wages did not cover her expenses. Doug needed a place to stay and agreed to pay her rent money. The facade of their being married played well with the neighborhood.

After the interrogation, Silvia was given a real job at a company owned by one of the officers' friends. When she performed for the magazine and cable companies, they had her sign a contract and consent forms. She made enough money doing the ladies' performances that she quit the job she had started.

Silvia got her dream backyard; it took a little time, but her yard had as much ambience as John and Marie's. She didn't have room for a courtyard or staircase. She talked about putting a second floor onto her house; she really wanted a staircase. She got an arched gateway, water feature, raised planters, low-voltage lighting, an outdoor kitchen, and a bar. She had no lawn to worry about maintaining. Since she did not have two-story homes in her area and had a large enough patio for lounge chairs, Marie and Delores would go to her house and work on their tans.

Silvia wanted a playhouse but did not have any children of her own who were still young. Most of her immediate family's children were as old as or older than Silvia's. There was talk about putting a second floor on top of the patio cover that could be used as a bar. She was still considering that idea. One drawback of the bar on top of the patio cover was that it would cut down on the sunbathing area—more shade, less sun.

The bar would be fashioned after our playhouse—a double octagon. The two panels that would normally enclose the structure would be left out. The roofs would be tied together, so one would enter the side with the tables and benches, and the actual bar would be on the other side.

Silvia would be with Marie and Delores for most of the events. She would do one event, and Mama would do another. It mostly depended on the nature of the event. Silvia would do the party girl's events, and Mama would do the crocheting ones. They all performed for holiday events; even Susanne would join them. At Christmas events, the girls would join them.

The girls always had a playhouse in which they entertained their guests. At one event, they had Silvia and Susanne as guests. They asked Silvia, "Could you dress like Susanne? We are a children-based program, and some of your outfits may send the wrong message to our fans." Silvia then wore a dress that hung past her knees when she sat down. Her dress was buttoned up to her neck; it was loose fitting to an extent, not baggy but well tailored. She wore a string of pearls around her neck, and her hair was up and styled. She wasn't dressed like an old-time schoolteacher, but her look was very conservative. Susanne had helped with her outfit. Susanne's outfit was a little shorter on the skirt and formfitting. She looked like a high-end business executive.

All the ladies and girls had fan clubs with followings. The girls chatted with Susanne and Silvia, and then they had lunch served by guest students the girls' ages. They had weekly contests, with the students telling the girls why they would like to meet them and spend a day with them. They sent photos with their letters, which the girls never saw; those went to the cable company staff to review. The girls would announce the guest students at the end of each program. They had the students stand with them at the end of the program, and they gave one another hugs. It was very well done. The cable company gave the students items to take to their schools.

Marie and Delores were the girls' guests a few times. Those were the most requested shows on video. They showed the audience how they all played off each other. One time their dads joined Marie and Delores. John had a barbecue set up in the studio and burned enough hot dogs to feed the entire staff, the ladies, the girls, and the students. Mama and Papa showed up with restaurant pans full of baked beans, potato salad, green salad, and chips. That was the most requested program.

A few months later, all the guests were there, and Susanne and Silvia joined in on all the fun. This was the summer vacation scene. The ladies were in shorts and tank tops, and the girls were dressed in shorts and tops. That program surpassed sales of all the videos produced. The water balloon fight between everyone, from two years prior, was still requested. They were also using squirt guns, so if they ran out of balloons, they could grab a squirt gun that the staff kept loaded.

One of the girls sneaked up behind the staff member filling up the squirt gun and unloaded hers on the staff member. The young staff member tried to return fire, but Leslie grabbed the gun she had just filled and returned fire. While the staff member was chasing Leslie, Sarah filled up two guns, started shooting the staff member, and gave Leslie the other gun. She now had two girls shooting her. They interviewed the staff member, dripping wet, and asked her how she felt. "Wonderful. It was really a lot of fun. The girls won hands down. Looking forward for a rematch."

They interviewed Sarah and Leslie, and they told everyone, "We will give her a rematch anytime. We did feel bad about getting her outfit soaked. Ours were bathing suits made to get wet. She will have to wear a bathing suit next match."

The staff member came over, hugged both of the girls, and said to them, "You're on."

After the water fight, they took an hour break and restored the cast to a filming look that was familiar to the viewers. They were all eating lunch as the cameras ran again. They were talking about how much fun the water fight had become. They were challenging each other to get even for what one or another had done to them. Of course, hot dogs burned to perfection was the meat course. The catering chef would not prepare the hot dogs in a burnt-skin fashion, so John took on the challenge. This got the whole staff wanting to share in the burnt hot dog event. The girls were all excited. "Daddy's cooking, yeah!"

The newest addition to the ladies was touring to different locations; only Marie, Delores, and Mama did this. A few times, there was one event going on in one city and another event in another only a few miles away. This was when they scheduled each event at different times so all five ladies could perform for both venues. The people attending the venue were in complete shock when they got to see all three ladies. At some of those events, the videos surpassed the normal sales to more than double.

All these appearances caused Stockdale Landscape Construction enormous growth—office and warehouse, multiple trucks, and crews. All the original employees were now foremen or forewomen and supervisors. Everyone was growing within the company. Angel and Juanita were guest ladies for events. Angel would wear a special tool belt for her appearances. She would come onstage with a fabulous outfit, get to her chair, put on the tool belt, and model the outfit as how she would wear it working on the job site. She was actually helping with designs and no longer was going out and getting her hands dirty.

Susanne became such a utility lady. She could wear gowns, executive attire, and conservative outfits for meeting with the girls, while still putting in time with the magazine. She hosted the program showing the latest designs from the construction side, gave tours for the viewers, and talked with homeowners and construction employees. She understood that if one showed respect to everybody, one would be respected by them. When she heard what the girls told Diane, the governor's wife, about their philosophy on how you get invited for dinner or put on the maybe-later list or forget-it list, she started applying some of that to her way of thinking. She found that some of her so-called friends were not really friends, so they went on her maybe list; she had a never-call list as well. She found that she had more time for those whom she really liked being around her; those friends even became closer to her.

A couple of shows after the water fight, the girls invited the staff member who had challenged them to another one for lunch along with another girl staff member who treated them with respect and dignity. Both guests were asked to wear a bathing suit with a pair of gym shorts on top. "Please, a one-piece suit. Children are watching." All seven ladies were also going to be there, as well as their dads and grandpa. The studio was set up as a beach scene, like one from the sixties movie *Beach Blanket Bingo*.

John was the griller of the dogs. One producer of the program wanted his recipe. John just laughed. "Burnt offerings are ready. Come and get them while they are hot." He also put another batch on the grill so no one went away hungry.

Marie, Delores, and Mama made up plates for the cameramen and brought them to them. Marie had on a jet-black suit with a three-color band going from her left shoulder to her right hip. Delores had the same, just with the band going in the opposite direction. Marie and Delores did that fairly often while shopping— purchasing similar outfits with just enough difference to make them not exact.

Lunch was coming to an end, and the staff members were getting the water balloons and water guns prepared for the rematch. There were buckets and tubs full of water balloons and numerous water guns full and ready. The two staff girls asked to join in on the water battle were wrapping up the talk with the girls. They all gave one another hugs and wished one another the best of luck on the rematch. All was so warm and sincere. Then the shields came off, and every girl was for herself.

Actually, the older girls—in their early twenties—took the four younger girls under their wings and opened the door for them to attack the adults. Water balloons were being tossed, and many were direct hits. Delores had Silvia in the crosshairs, and *boom*, she was hit from the blind side, now severely drenched by at least four balloons. Delores was laughing very hard at what had just occurred and was the next one to get hit from many angles at one time. She, too, was severely drenched, and some of the adults were taking the same approach of teaming up. Many balloons were thrown at one time.

There was one person who was still dry—but not for long. Susanne received an onslaught of balloons from the girls, the staff girls, Marie, and Delores all at once. There may have been a couple of balloons that were off target. Susanne pulled a white handkerchief from her bathing suit and waved it in the air.

John entered the game from cooking the hot dogs. He was pretty quick and knocked a few balloons away before they hit him. He was using a kung fu move. More than one was tossed, and he went for one and got hit by three—and not in a place where one would like to be hit. He had concentrated on the wrong balloon. Marie took credit for the one that did the most damage to his dry clothes.

The girls got the two staff girls cornered and were pelting them one after the other; they too pulled out white handkerchiefs. If a person was being hit so often that he or she couldn't take any more, that person surrendered. The girls and the staff girls were all hugging when they were being water-gunned by all the ladies; one gun after another was emptied on the six girls.

The best attack was that of the dads on the moms. They took no hostages. There was not one part of their body that was not dripping wet. The makeup was gone, and their hair was hanging in strings, wet. Delores said, "You may have won the water gun battle, but the day is still young."

All the staff, ladies, husbands, and girls had a one-hour break to dry off, get a new makeover, get into different clothes, and prepare to end the program. The girls and the ladies never had a script to follow. "Be yourselves, have fun, and act like this day is greater than yesterday, and tomorrow will be even better, said Susanne." The ladies' outfits were gorgeous, and the girls were dressed really cutely. The guys—well, they looked like dads in business casual, so they looked as if they were taking their brides out for the evening. What makeup, hairstylists, and wardrobe did for the cast was beyond a miracle—soaking wet to red-carpet gorgeous. While the cameras were off, the stagehands did another marvelous job of cleaning up the studio. One would never know that a water fight had just ended.

The men were seated, the ladies did a grand entrance, and the girls entered their stage playhouse. When everything was ready, the girls and Susanne—seated on the benches—got a standing ovation from the staff watching the episode. Susanne, being the host of the program, stood up, came to center stage, and called the girls over to her—two girls on one side, two girls on the other. She gave a very moving dialogue, telling everyone how much these little sweethearts meant to her. She started welling up while expressing her love and appreciation. Getting drenched by them, watching them giggle, and enjoying themselves in the process were Susanne's way of thanking them for what they had done for her. They all had a group hug.

Susanne stated, "Please tune in tomorrow for a special program that, we're sure, everyone will enjoy." She gave the time that the program would air. "Love you and God bless all."

The special that aired the next day was a thank-you for all those who had supported the ladies and the girls. Most of all, the cable networks and the magazine were becoming more successful every day.

The special program had interviews with all the ladies and the girls; they showed video clips from the construction stages, the event of the year, and other projects that all the girls or ladies promoted. They shot the place where Phillip and his crew put another playhouse on top of a patio cover. The girls met the children of the new house and showed them how they played in theirs. The boy and girl were so excited to have movie stars—that was what they told the girls—playing in their house. The boy and girl were younger than Rebecca, so the girls felt as if they were adults. The playhouse was almost exactly like Sarah and Rebecca's house. They were missing two windows; the neighbors' second-floor bedrooms were in view of theirs. The parents were too afraid of the girls seeing into their bedrooms; no one was home during the daytime. All three families met when the floor was put on top of the patio and looked where a window might be placed. The girls' parents had a flat-screen television installed on one panel and a floor-to-ceiling bookcase where the other window would have been installed.

The program had Susanne as the hostess, and they had a catered lunch, played some games, and talked about how to use the playhouse. The girls showed the children how to be a gracious host and hostess. When the program was coming to a close, Leslie asked Susanne, "Do we get dessert?"

Susanne said, "Listen; someone is coming up the stairs."

Knock, knock, knock! The little girl opened the front door, and a man in a chef's hat brought in a dozen cupcakes and a half gallon of vanilla ice cream.

That was the first half hour; during the second one, the ladies were interviewed. They all, of course, did their signature moves, grand entrance, and arched gateway entrance before being seated and interviewed. Susanne was not the interviewer; she was now a performer and being interviewed. The original host who first introduced the ladies got the call to interview the ladies. He told the audience that he now knew what heaven would be like for him.

He interviewed Susanne first and asked her what she felt like while doing the entrances. Remember: Susanne was reserved. She said she got a very warm feeling inside her. "You want to do your best. You do start liking the applause from those who are watching you. It's not easy being yourself and making up moves at a snap of your fingers. Marie and Delores helped me get over thinking that I was not going to be accepted as being a nice girl. How you move in front of a job site crew or a camera should be the same. The only difference is you know most of the crews. You don't know who's watching the programs. After the butterflies leave you, you settle down and just try to do your best. My husband has really enjoyed watching me practice."

The host said, "He's a very lucky man. Seeing you do that every night is one of my favorite dreams,"

The host now turned his attention to Silvia. "Dearest Silvia." The host kissed her hand.

Silvia said, "Please, don't stop."

The host mentioned that she was one of two girls not spoken for. "Does that make you feel uncomfortable?"

"Only a couple of times did I ever feel uncomfortable. One time all the ladies had their spouse, boyfriend, and fiancé at a dinner party. I could have asked the magazine to provide a male escort. I really want to meet the escorts before I spend a whole evening with them. I've had a couple of escorts, no connection whatsoever—different backgrounds, different likes and dislikes. One liked the mirror more than any man I have ever been around or dated. I think the mirror was his best friend. That was more annoying than the one guy who must have taken a hundred selfies in the time we were together."

"So as I asked Susanne, how do you feel while you're doing the grand entrance or arched gateway entrance?"

"I think the entrance, for me, is when I can tease the viewer. I try to show ladies viewing that you want your man to pay attention to you. You're the most beautiful person in the room, and she belongs to you. Eat your heart out, everyone. You may think, you would like to be with her, tonight. Dream on, young man. She's mine, keep dreaming."

"Have you received letters after you perform an entrance?"

"Letters, all social media outlets, phone numbers on napkins given to me by a waiter or waitress—you name it. I have received some very complimentary, some naughty, some vulgar."

"What does performing the entrance do for you?"

"I get very loving inside and stay that way until I get up the next morning. The more I perform, the longer I stay loving. I love how my dress reflects my inner feelings."

"Has being one of the ladies increased your loving feelings, or were they always there and you now can bring them to the surface?"

"It's a great release for me, not all bottled up inside. Like Mama used to tell me, 'Be a good girl, Silvia.' It's hard being good when you're thinking bad thoughts."

"What is your dream come true?"

"Bringing warm and loving feelings back into relationships. We are losing how to love one another. We are losing the one-on-one contacts we used to have. Sitting down and having a lunch or a snack with a good friend is being replaced with drive-through fast-food restaurants, hurry here, hurry there, pick up kids from school, one thing after another; it's driving all of us apart."

"What do you think is the major cause of all this?"

"I can't speak for everyone. For me it seems that the electronic world wants your full attention; it wants you lost in that world so nothing else matters. 'Don't call me. Text me. I'll get back to you sometime.' You do that to me too often, and I won't bother you ever again. If you pull out your cell phone to check whether someone else is trying to get your attention, I'm gone. Rude appears to be the new normal."

"Silvia, thank you. You're a great talent. You look marvelous, my dear."

The host moved to Juanita. "Well, one of our tool-belt ladies. You certainly don't look like any construction worker I've ever been around. How did you choose to don the tool belt?"

"My best friend ever, Angel, asked me if I would like to work with her at her new job. I told her I had never done that kind of work before. She assured me that the men were very kind to her, the boss was very helpful, and she had never worked anywhere else like this company."

"So you get your hands dirty, your clothes get dirty, and you're outdoors all day long in the heat or cold. Most ladies would not think that would be a dream job. Do you really like what you do?"

"I love what I do. You work not only with your hands but your mind as well. Each day is a new experience. You're constantly learning how to do something and finding out ways to do it easier or in less time. Like your job, what keeps it from being mundane is you interview different people. If you had the same person day in and day out, you would get bored, correct?"

"Dearest, boredom I could endure. The network would be closed due to lack of viewers. I'd get a cardboard sign for my street corner. Aren't you afraid of getting too muscular and less feminine?"

"The job involves some lifting but not enough to build bulky muscles. It really keeps my body firm and fit through exercise. People pay lots of money to go to the gym. I get paid for staying fit—no gym fees."

"So how has being a lady changed your life?"

"It has made me more self-confident. All the ladies help me improve, my boyfriend became my fiancé, and we're getting married in a few months. He's very supportive and loves watching me perform onstage and while practicing. He gave me a male perspective, which really made me feel better."

"How did his perspective make you feel better?"

"Well, at first I thought what I was doing was lewd, enticing men to applaud, trying to get me to do something not nice, demeaning me. He told me it's an art form. Very few people can pull that off and enjoy what they are doing. It gives me a warm feeling inside I never knew I had. The hugs and approval from the other ladies are far greater than the applause."

"Angel, another construction worker. I'm thinking about changing my profession. It's so hard to believe that you are a construction worker. So how long have you been doing construction?"

"My sophomore year of high school, my dad would take me to the job sites during my summer vacation. He would have me do cleanups, mostly, at first, and then he taught me to swing a hammer. When my dad started slowing down his business, we talked about me finding another company to work for. He felt bad laying off one of his original crew members to allow me to continue to work."

"What is the hardest thing you ever had to do in construction?"

"Marie and Delores wanted me to do the grand entrance on the staircase. I was so nervous. I had seen them do it quite a few times, and I knew I was nowhere near as good as they were. They encouraged me to at least try. The other crew members were so nice to me. 'Go ahead, Angel. You can do it. We have seen you dance. You're a good dancer.' Dancing at a club or a wedding is one thing. You're among a crowd of people. When you are the one that everyone is watching, that is totally scary."

"So doing the grand entrance was more difficult than any other thing you are required to do daily?"

"When you work on a crew, everyone respects your capabilities. They aren't there to embarrass you. Juan, Diego, and the rest of the crew are so helpful, always telling you 'Good job.' If you get stuck on something they asked you to do, they encourage you to ask them for assistance.

"One time the owner of the company asked me to learn how to wire low-voltage lighting fixtures. I knew nothing about wiring lighting fixtures. He took time to show me how and watched me do what he had just taught me. I wired maybe four lights, and he checked what I did. A couple were loose, and he tightened the wire nuts. I told him I was afraid of breaking the wire off. He said, 'Let's say you were Wonder Woman and twisted the wire nut so tight you broke the wire off. You have a pair of wire cutters. Strip off more insulation. Twist on the wire nut. You just fixed the broken wire.'"

"So do you only do low-voltage wiring systems?"

"No, I do everything that the company provides our customers. Some days I just get dirty. Some days I have glue on my hands from putting pipe together. It all varies. That is why I love working for Stockdale Landscape Construction. I also enjoy having my best friend in the whole wide world working beside me."

"I've seen you while working in photos. Seeing you now, what an amazing transformation. Do you enjoy dressing up?"

"It is totally different from what I do daily. At first I felt a little embarrassed until the crew saw me dressed for the photo shoot. They were so nice to me. Compliments galore made me feel good inside and very appreciated. That means everything to me."

"You are the other single lady of the bunch. How does that make you feel?"

"My boyfriend and I have talked about marriage. He has to finish college. I may go back and get my degree for construction management."

"Is he in construction?"

"No sir, he wants to be a doctor of medicine."

"How much longer does he have before graduation?"

"We hope three, maybe four years. He's a very smart man. I'm so thankful he chose me to be his girlfriend."

"I would say he's lucky that you allow him to be your boyfriend."

He turned to Mama. "Mama Mia, you look marvelous, as always. I want to thank you for having a beautiful family. None of this would be real without your daughter. So how did she get her dear, sweet mother to sashay down a staircase and through an arched gateway, and clog through a tunnel?"

"That's what great Italian cooking can do for your children. I'm just so happy for her. She can come and go out of her shell. My granddaughters—wow. They all mean so much to the entire family. I thank God every day, sometimes twice, for blessing me and Papa with their family."

"Had you ever done the grand entrance before doing it at your daughter's home?"

"No, Marie and I share the same ideals. We turn it on and off quickly. I was a very shy young girl and young adult. I could get embarrassed at the drop of a hat. Papa made me feel wonderful, even to this day. The girls and Marie have inspired me to be more than just a watcher. I really enjoy clogging with my daughter and granddaughters. Makes me laugh inside and out."

"How long do you want to do the grand entrance, arched gateway entry, and the tunnel entrance?"

"As long as the girls want me. Getting invited to dinner with my granddaughters is such a blessing. It keeps me in good shape and always wanting more."

"My sweet Delores, how do I love thee? Let me count the ways. Every time I see you do the arched gateway entrance, I know you're entering just for me. Every man in the room is thinking the same thing. Now tell me, my dear, am I correct in my thinking?"

"All I can tell you is dream on, lover. Dream on."

"What does doing the arched gateway entry do for you?"

"The very first time I did the entry, Marie had just finished her grand entrance, and three different crews were applauding very loudly. It gave me goose bumps. I told myself, 'How can I compete with her?' I was standing just inside the arched gate, and I went back through the gate, closed the gate, and reopened it slowly. I was hoping someone would notice me. I reentered the courtyard in a sultry, seductive way. Now I had to move in the same fashion that I had entered in. I accentuated each step, making it more alluring, sultrier, and more seductive than the last step. The crew started applauding. With each move, it got more aggressive. That triggered something inside me to show more and more and more.

"When I got nearer to my husband, Marie came running to me and almost knocked us both off our feet. She gave me a hug I'll never forget. We hugged the longest she and I have ever hugged. Until you step out of your comfort zone and get appreciated for doing so, you can never understand how someone feels. I love that feeling. In each arched gateway entry, I try to get that feeling to return."

"How do the girls feel about seeing Mom on television?"

"They get excited seeing all of us perform, as we do them. We all really like performing at the same place at the same time. The best comes out in all of us."

"Have you and your husband been invited to the girls' house?"

"We have been invited by them, and it is a treat how all the girls interact. They just make us feel special. We almost forget they're our daughters. When we got the first invitation, we both teared up from joy."

"What would be the worst thing that could happen while you are performing?"

"The audience thinking, 'Ho-hum, this is boring,' and not showing appreciation for the hard work we all put into entertaining them."

"I almost forgot." He picked up Delores's hand and kissed the back of it. He went back over to Mama and Angel and did the same for them as well. "I'm such a dummy. Sorry, ladies, for my ignorance. What does your husband say when you do your entrance?"

"He's the one that had the vision, just not my exact entrance. He always applauds all of us. He applauds from his heart, not because he thinks he has to applaud."

"We have heard that, at one time, you were thinking of disrobing in front of your husband while he was shooting photos of you doing your entrance."

"That crossed my mind. It was just him, Marie, and me. I chickened out."

"Have you had similar thoughts since that time?"

"No, it was just a one-time thing. Thank god for that."

"Marie, Marie, our dearest Marie." The host was on his knee and kissed her hand. "You know none of this would be possible without you. Tell us, my dear, what inspired you to do what you do?"

"It all started during our walk around the backyard and side yard, discussing the changes from our original drawings. The crew was trenching for the irrigation system and hit something under the ground. They exposed the roof of something. They dug down one side of whatever they had hit and discovered it was a buried structure. They called the police back to our home and then unearthed the shed. They removed one of the windows to enter it. Forensics stopped everyone from going in and found blood splatters everywhere.

"Anyway, our beloved landscaper had a vision and put it in his drawings. To describe his drawings, he shared his vision with me and my husband. While they were talking, I kept going back to his vision. His vision was me, dressed in a formfitting gown glistening from the sun's reflection, with diamond necklace, diamond bracelet, perfect makeup, perfect hairstyle, a glass of champagne in one hand, elbow bent to show the glass of bubbly, coming down a staircase to the courtyard with numerous guests, family, and friends, with soft music playing. All eyes were on me as I took one step at a time, making the most of every move. Everyone was applauding me. As I got these warm feelings in me, I enhanced each step and made more seductive moves, looking sensual, poised, glamorous, stunning. I could not get that out of my mind.

"The men were walking to the front yard, and I called out to them. 'Like this?' I asked. I started to move on flat ground—no stairs. They watched me for about ten steps. My husband told me to turn around and do that again, so I did. I proceeded to move again. My husband said, 'Honey, move your body; display your body. Try it again.' So I did. This time they both started to applaud. That applause got me stirred up inside. I walked the entire distance to the guys, and my husband hugged me. I was hooked and said to both of them, 'I want it. I want it now.'"

"Wow, I can see you were very excited about getting your staircase."

"Every day I make it happen. I go down the staircase. I wait for Delores, and we both do the grand entrance, and Delores has to do the arched gateway entrance. We try to improve our moves every time. We ask each other, 'What about this move?' or 'What about that move, hand position, facial expression, upper or lower body movement?' We try to help each other perfect our routines. We don't use professional teachers. We don't want to look like everyone else. In fact, neither one of us ever watched video, television—nothing that could influence another's moves."

"Do you get excited every time you perform?"

"I love the applause. I love looking at those who are looking at me. What excites me is the warm feelings I get in pleasing others. Once the grand entrance is completed, I go back to my real self very quickly. That's my safeguard so I don't get into trouble."

"During your grand entrance, if someone were to disrupt you, what would happen to you?"

"Let's say that as I'm descending the staircase, my husband is behind me, and I don't know he's there, and he touches me. I would immediately go into my 'me' mode, and all excitement would end."

"After our station break, ladies, we have a surprise for you. Be right back after these brief messages."

While they were on station break, the ladies were escorted to get touched up or whatever they needed to do for five minutes. While they were gone, the stagehands pushed in the playhouse with the girls and Susanne. They were behind the curtain in front of which the ladies were sitting in chairs. They rearranged the chairs to a V formation in lieu of a straight line. Marie and Delores would be in the two center chairs, and the rest of the ladies would be placed beside them. The girls were told to be very quiet so they could surprise their moms.

The host returned to the stage and reintroduced the ladies one by one, taking them from the escort and seating them in the proper chairs. He said, "I love my job," as he escorted the ladies.

Silvia said, "I could make you love it even more."

That brought the audience to their feet, saying, "Go for it, Silvia."

The host, when he sat her down in her chair, leaned over, kissed her on the lips, and said, "Maybe later, my dear." As he walked to escort the next lady, he was waving his hand like, "She's hot." That got the audience applauding, hooting, and hollering.

He kissed Delores's hand and seated her in her chair. She said, "I'm married, remember? Only Silvia." The host snapped his fingers and moved his hand like, "I tried. She's tough."

Marie was the last to be escorted to her chair by the host. She also said, "I'm happily married, but if I weren't, it might cross my mind."

"Welcome back, ladies. As I mentioned before our short station break, we have a pleasant surprise for you. As you know, you all have performed for our cable network and the magazine for nearly a year. We thought we would surprise you with male strippers as a thank-you, but being that this is a family show, frankly, we couldn't get enough one-dollar bills from the staff. We did the next best thing. All the way from the studio next door, here are your daughters."

The staff audience stood up, applauded, and cheered as the playhouse opened, and the four girls and Susanne were seated on their benches. The playhouse came to a stop, and the girls jumped off and gave the ladies a huge hug, saying "I love you" to everyone.

The host said that the other studio was set up for a gala event, live music, food galore, balloons, and confetti. "Please make yourselves at home. Open bar. Everything is on the house as a thank-you gift." Everyone was having a great time.

After the meal was served, the tables were cleared and the guests were encouraged to dance. There were escorts for the girls, Silvia, and whoever else needed one. Papa, John, Juanita's fiancé, and Angel's boyfriend were all picked up in the limousine and brought to the studio. They were watching the entire performance backstage. The cable station had escorts for all the women lined up but not facing the ladies. They had the ladies tap the escorts' shoulders to ask them to dance. The ladies were all in a line, and they all walked up to the escorts in front of them. "One, two, three, tap their shoulders, said Susanne." The husbands, boyfriend, and fiancé all turned around together. The ladies screamed when they saw their mates. Silvia got the leading man on her favorite soap opera.

The band stopped playing. Four violins and a lady singer played Marie's favorite song. Everyone was dancing with her and John onstage with a spotlight on them. It was so romantic and was being broadcast live for the viewing audience.

Delores and Marie toasted to their new success with their fourth glass of champagne. All the ladies, the girls, and the men posed for photos and thanked everyone for all they he or she had done for them. Everyone had a glass of champagne; they all raised their glasses for a toast presented by the host.

It would be back to work for the staff, the ladies, the girls, the men, and all the viewers who worked for a living tomorrow. The band played on with a list of requests.

Author's Note

I want to thank each and every one of you for taking time out of your busy life to share this story. I hope you gained some insight on how a simple vision blossomed into reality. I'll be saddened by not having my characters with me each and every day, but they were shared among you. I felt that the characters were family. That might seem odd, but I had never felt this way before; this is something that I cannot explain. I was glad you got to see them as I saw them. I can't tell you that the Stockdale's became rich and famous. I can't tell you whether the girls married and had successful lives. I can't tell you whether John and Marie sold the home and became highly successful. It is up to you to believe how they moved through their life's challenges.

I can tell you that this story was inspired by a higher power. The girls' story tells us to look at what we are told to do and how we are supposed to model our children—those who are friends and family. I know this is not what you see on social or news media; this was inspired by a higher power. I am not a pastor or a highly educated biblical scholar. I read scriptures regularly. I learned from TBN pastors daily to further my understanding of God's Word, applying what I learned to my lifestyle. Prayers each and every night help me correct errors I made or am due to make.

The landscape contractor in the story is, by and large, how I functioned while visiting customers, dealing with the crew, and facing some of the challenges that life threw on me while I was trying to be a good father and grandfather. Unfortunately, I erred on the husband side of the equation. The latter part of the story reflects that had I only practiced what I preached, maybe my husband side of the equation would have made my life easier.

Delores, Fred's dearest darling, is a combination of my experiences with the opposite sex. I tried to portray the back-and-forth that one encounters with a spouse. I like the latter part of the story—the change from a back-and-forth to being as one. Delores makes Fred's life much easier, and he makes her life easier as well. They owe all this to the behavior of the girls; the interaction between the family members changed, all for the better. They are all ready to give it their all to make one another as happy and joyful as possible.

The one thing that inspires Delores is being Marie's best friend—something both ladies were previously missing in their lives. One can be a soccer mom for only so long. One really does need a close friend. Removing the facade, which we all have, and showing a true friend the real you is not an easy task. I tried to display how one may have feelings toward someone who may have the same feelings toward you; neither one wanted to disclose what she really thought in fear of being rejected. The husbands talked and disclosed that both ladies were thinking about the same thing, so the husbands forced the issue to the ladies. Once it was out in the open, both ladies became close friends. I enjoyed showing the joy Delores felt after getting applause from those who watched her do her arched gateway entrance. The entrance shows just what an uplift someone receives when others show gratitude and appreciation.

John is your typical neighbor. You can talk about anything with him at any time. He loves cooking outside and burns just about everything that hits his grill. He just enjoys having people eat what he considers hot-off-the-grill delightful food. Marie is happy to have him do the cooking outside, as it means less cleanup and dishes for her. She can spend more time making salads and side dishes, and making sure family, friends, and guests are being well taken care of. This frees up her oven and stove, so she makes wonderful side dishes to enhance John's burnt offerings. He becomes much better with practice, and the girls are crazy about his burnt hot dogs.

Thank you again for reading *Descending the Spiral Staircase*.